Praise for Hannah Fielding

'An epic romance like Hollyv.

Peterborough Evening Telegraph

'*Burning Embers* is a romantic delight and an absolute must-read for anyone looking to escape to a world of colour, beauty, passion and love.. For those who can't go to Kenya in reality, this has got to be the next best thing.' Amazon.co.uk review

'A good-old fashioned love story ... A heroine who's young, naïve and has a lot to learn. A hero who's alpha and hot, has a past and a string of women. A different time, world, and class. The kind of romance that involves picnics in abandoned valleys and hot-air balloon rides and swimming in isolated lakes. Heavenly.' Amazon.co.uk review

'The story hooked me from the start. I want to be Coral, living in a more innocent time in a beautiful, hot location, falling for a rich, attractive, broody man. Can't wait for Hannah Fielding's next book.' Amazon.co.uk review

Praise for *The Echoes of Love* (winner of the Gold Medal for Romance at the 2014 Independent Publisher Book Awards):

'One of the most romantic works of fiction ever written ... an epic love story beautifully told.' *The Sun*

'Fans of romance will devour it in one sitting.' *The Lady*

'All the elements of a rollicking good piece of indulgent romantic fiction.' *BM Magazine*

'This book will make you wish you lived in Italy.' *Fabulous* magazine

'The book is the perfect read for anyone with a passion for love, life and travel.'   *Love it!* magazine

'Romance and suspense, with a heavy dose of Italian culture.'
                                                                    Press Association

'A plot-twisting story of drama, love and tragedy.' *Italia!* magazine

'There are many beautifully crafted passages, in particular those relating to the scenery and architecture of Tuscany and Venice ... It was easy to visualise oneself in these magical locations.'
                                                                    Julian Froment blog

'Fielding encapsulates the overwhelming experience of falling deeply, completely, utterly in love, beautifully.'   *Books with Bunny*

Praise for *Indiscretion* (winner of Gold Medal for romance at the IBPA Benjamin Franklin Awards and Best Romance at the USA Best Book Awards):

'A captivating tale of love, jealousy and scandal.'   *The Lady*

'*Indiscretion* grips from the first. Alexandra is a beguiling heroine, and Salvador a compelling, charismatic hero ... the shimmering attraction between them is always as taut as a thread. A powerful and romantic story, one to savour and enjoy.'
                                    Lindsay Townsend – historical romance author

'Rich description, a beautiful setting, wonderful detail, passionate romance and that timeless, classic feel that provides sheer, indulgent escapism. Bliss!'
                                                                    Amazon.co.uk review

'I thought Ms. Fielding had outdone herself with her second novel but she's done it again with this third one. The love story took my breath away … I could hardly swallow until I reached the end.'

Amazon.com review

Praise for *Masquerade* (winner of Silver Medal for romance at the IBPA Benjamin Franklin Awards):

'Secrets and surprises … Set in Spain in the 1970s, you'll be enveloped in this atmospheric story of love and deception.'

My Weekly

'Hannah Fielding writes of love, sexual tension and longing with an amazing delicacy and lushness, almost luxury. Suffused with the legends and lore of the gypsies and the beliefs of Spain, there is so much in this novel. Horse fairs, sensual dreams, bull running, bull fighters, moonlight swims, the heat and flowers and colours and costumes of the country. A superb read.'   Amazon.co.uk review

'This was honestly one of the most aesthetically pleasing and sensual books I've read in a long time.'   Amazon.co.uk review

'*Masquerade* contains the kind of romance that makes your heart beat faster and your knees tremble. This was a mesmerising and drama-filled read that left me with a dreamy feeling.'

Amazon.co.uk review

'This engrossing, gorgeous romantic tale was one of my favorite reads in recent memory. This book had intrigue, mystery, revenge, passion and tantalizing love scenes that held captive the reader and didn't allow a moment's rest through all of the twists and turns … wonderful from start to finish.'   Goodreads.com review

'When I started reading *Masquerade* I was soon completely pulled into the romantic and poetic way Hannah Fielding writes her stories. I honestly couldn't put *Masquerade* down. Her books are beautiful and just so romantic, you'll never want them to end!'

Goodreads.com review

Praise for *Legacy* (final book in the Andalucían Nights Trilogy):

'*Legacy* is filled to the brim with family scandal, frustrated love and hidden secrets. Fast-paced and addictive, it will keep you hooked from start to finish.'   *The Lady*

'Beautifully written, and oozing romance and intrigue, *Legacy* is the much anticipated new novel from award-winning author Hannah Fielding that brings to life the allure of a summer in Cádiz.'

Take a Break

'In the vein of *Gone With The Wind*, this particular book is just as epic and timeless. Written with lively detail, you are IN Spain. You are engulfed in the sights, sounds and smells of this beautiful country. Great characters … and a plot with just enough twists to keep it moving along … Start with book one and each one gets better and better. I applaud Ms. Fielding's story telling skills.'

Amazon.com review

'Flawless writing and impeccable character building. *Legacy* takes the readers on a journey through the passions and desires that are aroused from romantic Spanish culture.'   Goodreads.com review

Praise for *Aphrodite's Tears* (winner of Best Romance award at the International Book Awards, National Indie Excellence Awards, American Fiction Awards and New York City Big Book Awards):

'For lovers of romance, lock the doors, curl up, and enjoy.'

Breakaway

'With romantic settings, wonderful characters and thrilling plots, Hannah Fielding's books are a joy to read.'   *My Weekly*

'The storyline is mesmerising.'   Amazon.co.uk review

'An intriguing mix of Greek mythology, archaeology, mystery and suspense, all served up in a superbly crafted, epic love story.'

Amazon.co.uk review

Also by Hannah Fielding

Burning Embers
The Echoes of Love
Aphrodite's Tears

The Andalucían Nights Trilogy:

Indiscretion
Masquerade
Legacy

Concerto

Hannah Fielding

LONDON
WALL
PUBLISHING

First published in hardback and paperback in the UK in 2019 by
London Wall Publishing Ltd (LWP)

First published in eBook edition in the UK in 2019 by
London Wall Publishing Ltd (LWP)

All rights reserved. No part of this publication may be reproduced, stored
in a database or retrieval system, or transmitted, in any form or by any
means, without the prior permission in writing of the publisher, nor
be otherwise circulated in any form of binding or cover other than that
in which it is published and without a similar condition including this
condition being imposed on the subsequent purchaser.

Copyright © Hannah Fielding 2019

The moral right of the author has been asserted.

A CIP catalogue record for this book is available from the British Library.

All characters and events in this publication, other than those clearly in
the public domain, are fictitious and any resemblance to any real person,
living or dead, is purely coincidental and not intended by the author.

Every effort has been made to obtain the necessary permission with
reference to copyright material. We apologize for any omissions in the
respect and will be pleased to make the appropriate acknowledgements
in any future editions.

HB ISBN 978-1-9164895-0-9
PB ISBN 978-1-9164895-1-6
EB ISBN 978-1-9164895-2-3

10 9 8 7 6 5 4 3 2 1

Print and production managed by
Jellyfish Solutions Ltd

London Wall Publishing Ltd (LWP)
24 Chiswell Street, London EC1Y 4YX

Harmony is pure love, for love is a concerto.

Lope de Vega

*You know my faithfulness to you, never can another
own my heart, never – never!*

Ludwig van Beethoven

PROLOGUE

When she woke up that morning to the dazzling blue sky of Nice, Catriona Drouot had no idea that the past was about to catch up with her. No premonition, no sense of something momentous waiting to happen. As far as she was concerned, this was simply another routine day. She certainly had no inkling that the meeting fated to take place in the next hour would set in motion a train of events that was to change her life irrevocably for the second time in ten years.

She hurried down the hill of Vieux Nice, the old town of the Riviera's capital where she lived with her mother and her nine-year-old son in a beautiful house at the foot of Castle Hill, and from where there were breathtaking panoramic views. She had overslept, after poring over some paperwork into the small hours, and was late for her first appointment at the clinic. L'Esperance Drouot was a small, though highly acclaimed, psychology practice, set up four years earlier with her business partner and best friend, Marie-Jeanne Berger. Now the clinic was rapidly establishing itself as one of the most respected of its kind in Nice. Catriona specialized in a variety of psychological disciplines but, above all else, it was music therapy that fascinated her most and was closest to her heart; somehow using music to alleviate other people's suffering eased the pain of the frustrated musician within her.

Ten years before, at eighteen, she'd had much grander ambitions – those of becoming an international opera singer – but life had other plans for her. Then, because she could not live without music, she had decided to divert her passion in another positive direction. She had become an authority in the field of music therapy, with respected research papers and books to her name. As a result, her clients came from all corners of the globe to seek her help and advice.

Catriona pulled the scarf up higher under her chin. It was a spring morning, with more than a touch of mistral, despite the bright sunshine. She made her way through the maze of narrow cobbled streets bordered with tall pastel buildings, their faded blue shutters shut tight against the fierce gusts. Catriona had always thought those streets, which daylight scarcely penetrated, felt much more Italian than French – and not surprisingly, given that Nice was reunited with France only in 1860; Garibaldi had been born here and Catriona's mother Marguerite had often enjoyed pointing out that the great general had been baptized in the parish church of Saint Martin-Saint-Augustin, where Catriona herself had been christened.

Although the wind had died down a little, the newly washed linen, threaded from balcony to balcony high above her head, flapped in the breeze so loudly that one could only just discern the shrill *patois* of the chattering women as they gossiped in front of their doors, an occasional sleeping dog at their feet, or the similar babble of another group as they queued outside the bakery for warm croissants. She loved the hustle and bustle of this typical Provençal city with its colourful markets of flower, vegetable and fish stalls from which the local people bought their produce.

As Catriona entered the clinic, Nicole, the young receptionist, came quickly over to her, seeming slightly flustered.

'*Bonjour, Docteur* Drouot. There's a lady in the waiting room. She's been here since the clinic opened this morning and ...'

'*Bonjour*, Nicole, I know I'm late.' Catriona gave her a brisk smile. 'No need for coffee today,' she added. 'If you could just bring in my first patient, I'll get started.'

'That is what I was about to say ... *le petit* Jean's mother called to let you know that he's sick and won't be able to keep his appointment.'

'Oh, so who were you talking about?'

'An elderly lady sitting in the waiting room. Not one of our clients, I think. A foreigner, Italian maybe. When I told her this week's appointments were all booked – that was before *le petit* Jean cancelled – she said she would stay here until you saw her.'

Catriona raised an eyebrow. 'I see, a determined lady ... Well, in that case, she's in luck. Has she filled out a form?'

'She refused, saying you would understand once she had spoken to you.'

Catriona sighed. 'Okay, just give me a few minutes to open my mail, then send her in. And I will have that cup of coffee, please. The lady can be filling out the form in the meantime.'

Nicole nodded. 'By the way, Marie-Jeanne is back. She cut her holiday short ... was bored, she says ... couldn't stay away, apparently.'

Catriona smiled. 'Ah! That's good news. It's been so hectic this past week without her. Thanks, Nicole,' and with her light but energetic step, she hastened down the corridor and spiralled up the staircase to the first floor, where she had her office.

Catriona was tall, her body slender and supple, innately graceful. Her features had a delicacy that was faintly deceptive: she was not quite as vulnerable as she seemed, yet her hazel-brown eyes, a little too big for her face, had an occasional sadness, as if something haunted her, added to which her long, delicate throat made her seem fragile. Still, the feature that turned heads whenever she went by was the colour of her long, abundant silken hair. It was a rich dark brown, close to the colour of polished chestnut, and when she wasn't wearing it in a neat bun at work, it fell in loose waves down her back. Even during clinic hours, in her elegant suit with her hair tied back, there was a natural warmth about her, and her charm was purely feminine.

Although the pale yellow room Catriona had chosen for her office was not the largest in the clinic, it was the most cheerful. South-facing, the sunshine streamed in through the wide bay window when the striped silk voile curtains were pulled back, and you could see beyond the small garden all the way to the Mediterranean. There was nothing clinical or austere about the room, nothing to remind the patient that he or she needed treatment. The walls were adorned with photographs of renowned concert maestros and conductors, and Catriona had endeavoured to render a feeling of comfort and warmth, with tan vintage bijou armchairs positioned opposite her desk. A compact library cabinet on the right-hand wall held biographies of her favourite composers and a collection of antique leather-bound music folios, which she bought at auction whenever she had the opportunity. On a low table to the left was a variety of small musical instruments – a violin, guitar, glockenspiel and assorted woodwind instruments – that she sometimes used with children to break the ice during the first interview.

Catriona sat down at her walnut desk and began flipping through the small pile of mail. A moment later, Nicole brought in her cup of coffee, then it was Marie-Jeanne's turn to pop her head round the door.

'I'm back, like a bad penny,' she announced breezily. 'A holiday from hell, which started off when I lost my luggage! But I'll tell you all about it over lunch.'

'You're never very good at holidays.' Catriona grinned up at the other woman. 'In any case, it's good to see you. I can't say that I'm not relieved to have you back. We've been so hectic and I don't think it'll slow down for a while. We're in for a busy period.'

'Excellent! I need to get my teeth into something after lolling about with nothing to do on the Seychelles beaches. Anyway, I'll let you get on.'

'I'll see you later.'

Catriona gulped down her coffee. No time today to savour every sip; nevertheless, she was glad to feel the welcome effects of the caffeine. She went back to the small stack of letters. A large yellow courier envelope caught her attention. Frowning slightly, she slit it open with an antique silver penknife and extracted the contents – a much smaller, handwritten off-white envelope. A spasm of shock made her stomach muscles clench as she recognized the address and the crest that adorned the upper left corner: a black-and-white coat of arms depicting a crowned golden eagle owl holding a key in one talon and a sword in the other, belonging to the Rolando Monteverdi family. Echoes of a voice deeply seductive, intriguingly foreign, floated hauntingly across the mists of time, seeping into Catriona's memory. With trembling hands, she opened the letter, her eyes darting to the signature: Calandra Rolando Monteverdi, a famous name in the world of opera though she had long retired from the stage.

Catriona had never had the privilege of hearing the diva sing live but she owned many recordings of Calandra's glowing performances. Before her marriage to Viscount Vittorio Rolando Monteverdi, the young soprano had been Isabella Lombardi, yet her rapid rise to stardom soon left that name behind. Because of her beautiful voice, the press, and very soon everybody else, nicknamed her 'La Calandra' – 'lark' in Italian – and thereafter the prima donna was known only by that sobriquet. Yet Calandra herself was not the reason why Catriona paled at the sight of the illustrious name; just seeing 'Monteverdi' on the page conjured up painful memories, the scars of which would haunt her, she thought, for the rest of her life.

She was just about to begin reading the letter when there was a knock at the door. Catriona swore under her breath – this must be Nicole with the determined foreigner who wouldn't fill out any forms. Damn it! Now she would have to wait until the end of this meeting to know what the disturbing missive disclosed.

'Come in.'

The new patient walked in and Catriona sucked in a breath. The woman was tall and straight, still beautiful for her age, Catriona thought as she met the emerald-green eyes that surveyed her expectantly.

'I wrote you a letter.' The older woman's gaze flicked to the paper still clutched in Catriona's hand. 'I see you've received it. I am Calandra Rolando Monteverdi.'

Catriona quickly got to her feet and shook the woman's hand, which was covered by a black kid glove. 'Yes, I know who you are. Please have a seat.' She tried to keep her voice even as she struggled to recover from her second shock that morning. Keeping her gaze level, Catriona sat down, leaning back in her chair to give a semblance of composure.

The elegant woman slid into one of the armchairs opposite and peeled off her gloves. 'I must apologize for turning up without an appointment but I thought it would be quicker this way.' She smiled that coaxing diva smile that was once part of her charm in the days of her prime. 'And honestly, I didn't think I would be able to wait for your answer. You see, this is quite a pressing case. I've waited too long already, and he's not getting any better …' She was agitated, talking all at once so that Catriona couldn't get a word in edgeways. 'He's already tried to commit suicide, you see …'

Catriona's mind stumbled to keep up. 'Suicide? Who are you referring to?'

Calandra tossed her head irritably. 'My son, of course. Umberto Rolando Monteverdi, the great concert pianist and composer.'

Her glittering eyes narrowed almost accusingly as they fixed on the young woman in front of her.

A cold hand gripped Catriona's heart. *No, it couldn't be … Fate couldn't do this to her!*

'You must have heard of him, even though he hasn't given a concert for four years since he became blind,' Calandra stated imperiously.

Catriona had read about the accident that had robbed the virtuoso of his sight, but nothing about a suicide attempt – the family must have kept that from the press. The gossip columns had long ceased to detail the many women who passed through the life of the young composer – evidently his womanizing days had been curtailed by this sudden blindness – and yet if the press had found out that Umberto Rolando Monteverdi had tried to kill himself, he would have instantly been front-page news again. 'Yes, I heard of that terrible tragedy,' she said quietly.

The diva, barely listening, went on relentlessly. 'You must save him. I've read all about you, I know you are the one person who can help. A doctorate in music *and* one of the best music therapists in Europe. Not only do you have experience with patients suffering from depression but you also work with blind children, I'm told. You even know how to teach Braille so they can read an orchestral score. Am I right?'

Catriona tried to control the trembling in her voice. 'I see you've done your homework on me, *signora.*'

Calandra gave a brusque nod. 'Of course. An old singing friend of mine had heard of your work, which led me to research your qualifications. Which are, I may say, impeccable. It seems you are uniquely placed to help my son.' Calandra's alert eyes continued to study Catriona, who could detect a thread of anxiety lacing the diva's confident stare.

Catriona paused before continuing. 'Yes, music therapy can have a significant effect on depression. In some cases, it has been remarkably successful, but nothing is guaranteed. My technique does try to strengthen the mind and even heal the body. It is all about unlocking the creative spirit in the patient.'

'Umberto is a musician. I'm sure that, above all people, you can do something to help him.'

For a moment a vision swam into Catriona's mind of the old house, Les Platanes, where she had first heard those exquisite strains of piano music floating in through her bedroom window late at night.

She cleared her throat before she answered. 'Where is he living now?'

'He's at our home in Torno, on Lake Como. At first, when we thought he might get his sight back, his spirits revived. He had even started to write a new concerto. Then we found out that he would be blind for life, and he's been slowly deteriorating once more. You are our last hope.'

'So, will you be moving to Nice?'

Calandra looked perplexed, a frown creasing her haughty demeanour. 'Nice? His home is in Torno, I tell you. You can't possibly expect him to move to Nice. Umberto left Nice a long time ago.'

Now it was Catriona's turn to look confused. 'But my clinic is here.'

'Be that as it may,' Calandra waved the thought away with a graceful hand. 'I have come to ask you to move to Torno.'

Catriona tried to keep outwardly cool despite the turbulence going on inside her. 'But …'

'You will be handsomely remunerated.'

'It's not a question of money. My business … my family … You're asking the impossible.'

'Nothing is impossible, *Dottoressa*. I am aware that you have a son and a mother in your charge. We can relocate all of you without any difficulty.'

Catriona's eyes now rounded in disbelief. 'You can't expect me to disrupt my whole life for just one case.'

Reaching into her bag, Calandra took out her purse. Her long fingers dipped deep inside it and she produced a small photograph that she laid on Catriona's desk.

The young woman took the picture and, almost fearfully, looked down at the image. Her hand began to shake. It was a photograph of Umberto and herself, taken ten years ago. She could hardly bear to see how young and radiant she looked, how happy and alive, and in a fleeting instant she was there at Le Beaumont Club restaurant in Saint Paul de Vence; she could sense him, feel him next to her and even catch hints of his aftershave, Armani's City Glam, which still had the power to conjure up painful memories whenever someone wearing it passed her in the street.

'It's you, isn't it? You were very young then,' the diva murmured, invading Catriona's cherished but sad reflection.

'Yes. Where did you find this?'

'When I went to pack up Umberto's house in Villefranche, after he'd decided to sell it following the accident, I found it in a stack of other photographs. It struck me because you looked so young and innocent ... and you both seemed so happy.'

Catriona's usually golden complexion was now creamy white, her lips trembling slightly as her eyes finally tore themselves from the photograph and met the now softened gaze of Calandra.

'As I said, your qualifications are only part of what convinced me that you are the right person to help my son.'

It took a lot to shake Catriona's customary composure but this situation had certainly succeeded in doing so. With an acute effort she regained her equilibrium and gave a small nod. 'I see,' she whispered, emotion still choking her.

'You knew Umberto, although I don't know to what extent. Intimately, no doubt, judging by this photograph.' Calandra searched Catriona's stunned face as she spoke. 'So, when I began looking into your work and saw your picture in a newspaper article about your clinic, I remembered the snapshot I had seen at the house. You've hardly changed despite the years.' A small smile curved her lips.

'I thought that maybe you could be the one to cure his depression. He's already tried to take his life once, and now seeing him becoming more and more self-destructive ...' A haunted look crossed her face. 'That's why I decided to come here myself to meet you in person and try to convince you to take on his case. Or at least to give it a try for a few weeks.'

Catriona's head was throbbing suddenly. For a moment she looked away from Calandra's pleading expression and stared silently at the trees outside the window. Across the sweeping lawn a stand of tall birches shivered and bowed restlessly under the onslaught of the wind. Catriona could see the Mediterranean glinting in the distance, its usually serene surface agitated and troubled – a reflection, it seemed to her, of her own mood. Little whitecaps contrasted sharply with water that was even bluer than the Côte d'Azur sky but, for once, the breathtaking beauty of the scene failed to soothe her.

Aware that the woman in front of her was waiting on tenterhooks for an answer, Catriona shifted in her chair. Finally, she looked up at the mother of the man she had once loved ... the man she still loved but could not bring herself to forgive. She heaved a deep sigh and rubbed her forehead in a weary, resigned gesture. 'I honestly don't know, I have responsibilities ...'

'You are widowed or divorced presumably, you have no husband?'

Catriona shot her an uneasy glance. 'Yes, I'm a widow, but I have other obligations. My son's at school, I simply can't uproot him. I've got a business to run too.'

Those bright green eyes looked at her levelly. 'As you said, I've done my homework, *Dottoressa*. You've left your son with your mother before so that you can pursue your studies. You still do on occasion, so you can attend conferences. Regarding your business, I have no doubt that the sum I will pay you for, let's say, three months, you would have difficulty earning in one year.'

Catriona was fighting for self-control, her hands clasped tensely together. 'I have clients who need me and a partner who works with me on several projects.'

'No one is indispensable, *Dottoressa*. From what I hear, your partner is perfectly capable of holding the fort and keeping your clients happy while you're away. Anyway, you will have the funds to employ a temporary replacement. All I am asking for is three months of your life to save that of a virtuoso, who still has so much to offer to the world and who dearly needs your help. In this particular instance you *are* indispensable.'

Viscountess Calandra Rolando Monteverdi rose and held out her hand. 'I will not take up any more of your time, *Dottoressa*. I leave you to your conscience. You will find my contact details in the letter I sent you. *Buona giornata,* good day.' With that, she turned on her heel and left the room.

With a sinking feeling, Catriona stared at the grains of sand filtering slowly down through the hourglass on the desk in front of her. She was faced with a choice that would finally decide her fate, a choice that pitted her heart against her conscience. As if overwhelmed by an invisible outside force, her pale cheeks suddenly burned, her light-brown eyes blazing almost black.

There was unfinished business between Umberto Rolando Monteverdi and herself. Over the past ten years she had tried to exorcise him from her body and soul through rigid self-control; she felt as though her whole being had been in one position for so long that her body was cramped, her blood supply almost cut off, making her numb inside. Now destiny, uninvited, had come knocking on her door. The diva's visit had set the blood coursing through her body and the pain and elation of it was terrifying.

Chapter 1

Ten years previously – Nice, 2002

Les Platanes had been sold. It had been empty ever since Catriona de Vere and her mother had moved to Nice when she was eleven and moved into Les Charmilles, the house next door. Up until then Catriona had spent her childhood growing up in the wilds of Norfolk, with its chalk downs and still waters, a remote location where few of her friends were within easy distance. When Sir William de Vere, Catriona's English father, had died in the spring of 1997, her mother Marguerite, who had never taken to the English weather, decided to leave Norfolk and move to Nice, her native home.

Les Platanes had from the very first day attracted Catriona's curiosity. It was a handsome, two-storey belle-époque house, built of pinkish-red brick, with white shutters and completely surrounded by terraces. A high wall enclosed the grounds, encompassing a large square garden at the back, kept in pristine condition season after season by a couple of gardeners whom Catriona glimpsed from time to time, even as the house itself remained unoccupied. Old plane trees, their wide spreading branches laden with dark palmate lobed leaves, cast their welcoming shade in the summer; in winter they were pruned back to tall and contorted bare stumps, which in the moonlight resembled eccentric-looking giants.

She remembered when she'd first found out more about the house. It was one morning, after they'd been living at Les Charmilles for a few years. Catriona, by then a teenager, was passing by the gated entrance of Les Platanes on her way to a singing lesson when she saw one of the gardeners coming out of the property and locking the gate. On impulse she stopped and smiled.

'*Bonjour, Monsieur.*'

Turning, the old man lifted his cap and smiled back at her. '*Bonjour, Mademoiselle. Que puis-je faire pour vous?* Good morning, Miss, what can I do for you?'

'I'm curious. Why is this beautiful house always closed?'

'It is still for sale, *Mademoiselle.*'

'For sale? Who owns it? And why hasn't it sold? It's so beautiful.'

The gardener pocketed his keys and slung his bag of tools over one shoulder. 'It belongs to Ronald Heiss. You know, the famous American actor found dead on his yacht last year. It's been on the market ever since. People are afraid to buy it now.'

Catriona's perfectly arched eyebrows drew together. 'Surely people aren't so stupid? Such a magnificent house …'

It appeared that the gardener was all for a bit of juicy gossip. He came closer and lowered his voice. 'It's believed the house is cursed.'

'Cursed? What do you mean? Why?'

The old man came closer still, so much so that Catriona could smell the garlic on his warm breath. 'The number of owners, or members of their families, who've died shortly after buying this building is suspicious, to say the least. Shocking, in fact.'

Catriona's eyes widened.

'Yes, *Mademoiselle*, it's true. The first to die was the infant son of the first owner, the great Italian architect Giovanni Morelli. In the fifties … meningitis, it was. That was followed by the suicide of his wife, Claudia. A couple of years later, the Spanish bullfighter Manuel de la Cueva was found dead in his bath, murdered. Then the beautiful actress Maria Pia Gasman died in a car accident. A sad and terrible history this place has – and now that nasty business of the American found dead too.'

Catriona shivered and gazed up at the mellow brick and closed pale shutters of Les Platanes. It was as if the villa was asleep. 'It looks such a peaceful house.'

The old man glanced at her with amusement before turning to lock the gate. '*Ah, Mademoiselle, il ne faut pas se fier aux apparences*, do not be fooled by appearances.'

'Thank you. Er, I'm sorry, I don't know your name.'

The gardener smiled. 'Jeannot, *Mademoiselle*. Jeannot Bonnet.'

'*Au revoir*, Jeannot, *et à bientôt*.'

'*Au revoir, Mademoiselle* …?'

'Catriona.'

'*Au revoir, Mademoiselle* Catriona.'

Thereafter, although Catriona had regarded the house with a mixture of fear and respect, its gruesome background neither lessened her awe of its beauty nor her interest in it; in fact, her fertile teenage imagination conjured all sorts of images of the past lives led behind its elegant walls. On long summer evenings, she often sat on the veranda outside her bedroom and contemplated the fine proportions of the house next door – its mien changing with every shift of light and shadow – and wondered who the next occupants might be.

While smaller, it was true that Catriona's house was just as grand and beautiful in style as Les Platanes. It was one of a cluster of smart villas built on the flank of the mount, a prestigious residential area of Nice known as Mont Boron. From there they could see down to the Port of Nice and beyond to the whole of Villefranche. In the distance you could just make out Monte Carlo and Bordighera on the Italian coast. The luscious green of the fifty-seven hectares of forest acted as a separating wall between Cap de Nice on the western tip of the peninsula and Villefranche-sur-Mer, the small town to the east, and the rich parkland gave this sought-after quarter a rural feel while being not too far from the centre of the town and the sea.

Les Charmilles had been the Drouots' holiday home when Marguerite was a child. The greyish-blue villa with its turquoise shutters and wrought-iron balconies was surrounded by a handsome garden, with beech trees and graceful *pins parasol* that were indigenous to the area. The garden was a profusion of beautiful roses and oleander bushes, centred by a fountain where birds came to drink. Catriona had always loved it, but now its charms seemed to pale in comparison with those of the house next door. Les Platanes was intriguing – her dream, her secret … a strange, wild, contradictory place. One day perhaps she would own it, she told herself.

Catriona had taken to her new life in Nice like a duck to water. Enrolled at Le Collège Privé Sainte-Marie-de-Chavagnes, the teenager soon left her mark in the subjects of music and languages, taking up Italian since she was already fluent in English and French. But it was through music that Catriona's creative imagination really took flight. From an early age in England she had learned the piano and violin and quickly progressed with these in her new school in Nice. However, Catriona's teachers, having soon noticed her unusually beautiful voice, had suggested to Marguerite that she send her daughter to a singing teacher to develop her voice. Everyone agreed that this was where her true gift lay, and that way the young girl had the opportunity to embrace a career in opera if she wanted to take her talent further.

By the time Catriona reached sixteen, she had joined Le Conservatoire à Rayonnement Régional de Nice, the regional music and dance conservatory. Singing now her principal study, she was preparing for a competition that would grant her entrance to the Conservatoire National Supérieur de Musique et de Danse in Paris. So far, Catriona had won every level of the competition.

Now, there were only two finalists competing for the prize of a place and she was working long hours to ensure her victory – admission to the coveted conservatory that would, hopefully, launch her career in the world of opera.

So, on this spring night of 2002, having practised her singing for a couple of hours before dinner, Catriona went to bed early, too exhausted to even pick up the book on her bedside table. She was in the habit of reading a few pages to unwind and make her drowsy before turning off the light, but tonight she could scarcely keep her eyes open.

She was woken out of a sound sleep by the insistent blare of wild music. It was usually so quiet in this part of Nice, with only the roar of the surf against the rocks and muffled traffic noises drifting occasionally from the road a quarter of a mile away to break the stillness. The sudden, unexpected intrusion into the quiet night made her sit bolt upright in bed, her heart pounding, her mind disorientated. She looked around the shadowy room. Had she left the radio on inadvertently? She would never have put on music like that: a strident, pounding rock beat that hurt her musical sensibilities as much as her ears. She listened carefully. The sound seemed to be coming from outside.

Catriona jumped out of bed and went to one of the three windows, peering out at the night-cloaked municipal tennis courts to the left of the house, thinking that the music might be coming from midnight hooligans with a loud CD player. This had happened occasionally in the past – once her mother had had to call out the police – but tonight the terracotta-coloured expanse was deserted.

She then went to another window, pushed open the long shutters and stepped on to the veranda. There it was: Les Platanes was ablaze with light. Dressed only in thin cotton pyjamas, shivering in the cool night air, she hugged herself tightly and stared at the house. The curtains had been pulled open and she could see several people milling about inside and out on one of the wide terraces.

Suddenly the music stopped and she could hear loud voices raised in laughter and shouted conversations. It must be a party, she thought, now completely awake and fascinated to see who could be occupying the house that had been empty for so long. She gazed out into the darkness, trying to get a better look at the people, but the house was too far away and all she could make out were dim, moving shapes. There did seem to be a lot of them, though.

Then some music began again but it was different this time. Someone was playing the piano: Beethoven's 'Moonlight Sonata'. It had once been likened by the German poet Ludwig Rellstab to the effect of moonlight shining on Lake Lucerne, and to Catriona tonight it suggested the silvery orb shining on the Mediterranean. Entranced, the eighteen-year-old musician listened with a beating heart to the liquid notes that floated to her through the night, a mesmerizing melody that held her in its charm long after it had ceased to play. Although she was cold, Catriona waited a little longer on the balcony in the hope that the pianist would grace his or her audience with another piece but instead it was the rock music of before that blasted through the open windows again. Heaving a disappointed sigh, she went inside and returned to bed. Soon after, the noise ceased as abruptly as it had started.

The next morning when she passed by the house on her way to the Conservatoire she gazed up with an even greater interest. However, it was exactly the same as it had always been: shutters closed, utterly silent, seemingly uninhabited. There was no sign that the night before it had been animated by a crowd of people and that haunting piano playing. Had she dreamt it all? No, she remembered it quite clearly. It had been real enough.

For the rest of that day Catriona was distracted, unable to chase from her mind the plaintive sounds of the 'Moonlight Sonata', so masterly executed. She was impatient to return home.

Curiosity and her vivid imagination had already painted pictures of the occupants of the house and, more specifically, of the pianist with magic fingers.

The sun was setting when the bus dropped Catriona at the Mont Boron stop, a five-minute walk to her home. Although she had a driving licence and an old Deux Chevaux car her mother had given her for her eighteenth birthday, most days she preferred taking the bus even though it was an almost forty-minute ride to the Conservatoire. The traffic during rush hour in and out of the Provençal capital was quite heavy and it meant she could enjoy the view or read a book during the journey.

As she reached Les Platanes Catriona noticed that the gates were ajar. She walked slowly towards them, closer than ever before, and stood for a long time staring up at the stunning edifice in the setting sun. There was absolutely no sign of life. She sighed somewhat impatiently at the realization she would probably never know what this house was like inside. But why shouldn't she? she asked herself defensively. After all, the gates were open, weren't they? They had never been left open before. What if someone had broken in? She was still wondering whether she should go in to investigate when suddenly she heard the sound of music. That decided her, and curiosity won over prudence. She went in, letting the slow, delicate and plaintive piano strains guide her steps.

The music was clearly audible now. Although it bore shades of Chopin, it was not a piece Catriona recognized. A few seconds later it stopped abruptly, the discordant sound of someone bringing their hands down hard on the keys ending the strangely poignant melody. Catriona was surprised, as much by the angry disruption of the piece as its sudden cessation. Cautiously, she mounted the steps to the terrace and tiptoed round the curve of the building. She was just about to peep around the side of an open French window when she almost bumped into the man who was coming out of it.

'What on earth do you think you're doing? Who are you?'

Caught unawares, Catriona was almost scared out of her wits by the angry voice that accosted her. She looked up to face her interrogator.

In the silence of that moment her impression was that a foreign sculptor had made this man and then stood him in the wind and the sun, allowing them to weather his face into a dangerous attraction. He was perhaps in his mid-twenties and very tall, his lean frame making his height not apparent at first glance. His dark hair was windblown into a fashionably wild look. The very bright emerald-coloured eyes staring down at her were glittering with anger but riveting in his bronzed face, the contrast somehow increasing the threat he emanated as he towered over her.

Catriona swallowed hard, not sure how to handle this, but she knew instinctively that, in the blink of an eye, her pleasant, peaceful existence had been shattered. Still, the man's strong, chiselled face with high cheekbones and aristocratic mien, was familiar. It wasn't a face one forgot … where had she seen him? Recognition lurked at the edges of her brain, but how could she possibly think straight with him looming over her like that?

'I was walking,' she offered hurriedly. 'I heard music … the house has been closed for years …'

'So, you came to spy on me.' He spoke with a strong Italian accent.

'No. Why would I want to do that?'

'What else would you call it?'

'I was curious, that's all,' she exclaimed, recovering a little from her fright. 'I'm sorry, I thought the house was unoccupied.'

'Well, it's not. I live here now,' he declared flatly.

Catriona let out a breath with a gulp. 'Well, now I know.'

'What is your name?' he asked casually.

'Catriona … Catriona de Vere.'

'Sounds like a stage name.'

Was that amusement in his voice?

'Well, it isn't,' she said.

'Do you live around here?'

'Yes.'

'Where?'

'There.' Catriona pointed to the grey-blue house with its turquoise shutters.

'So, we're neighbours, *eh*?'

'Yes.'

He glanced at her again. 'Girl of few words, aren't you?'

She flushed, her creamy skin colouring slightly. 'Yes.'

'I see.'

She was about to turn to leave when the man caught her arm, his eyes narrowing with a sudden gleam. 'So, what d'you do with yourself in Mont Boron, Caterina de Vere?'

Her cheeks blazed as she pulled away from him. 'Nothing that would be of any interest to you.'

He laughed, his green eyes dancing. 'Try me.'

She turned and he caught hold of her arm again.

'Not so fast! You can't run away like this.'

This time she tried to wrench her arm from his grip. 'I really have to go.'

His dark brows arched mockingly. 'Why so nervous?'

'I'm not nervous,' she snapped, struggling to get free of him.

'I'm not about to make a pass,' he drawled. 'No need for your pulses to flutter.'

Catriona stared back at him, her face icy, though an unnerving heat passed through her skin where he was touching her. He was far too handsome for his own good, and too confident into the bargain. 'My pulses would never flutter for you,' she said scornfully. 'You're not my type.'

His bright mocking gaze held hers intently. 'Famous last words,' he said with a sudden grin and let go of her arm.

Catriona took a step back. 'My God,' she sighed, rolling her eyes, 'you ought to buy a suitcase to carry your ego around, the weight must be killing you!'

His laughter rose again, untouched by her sarcasm, but Catriona had already turned away and she hurried down the steps, moving with a natural agility across the garden and out of the gate, pursued by the memory of the stunning-looking but obnoxious stranger and his disarming emerald eyes.

Then just as she was reaching her doorstep she remembered where she had seen him. Only that morning his photograph had been plastered on posters all over the walls of the Conservatoire, announcing his upcoming piano concert. She had read about him in gossip magazines and broadsheet newspapers but had never heard him play. Until now she hadn't given him any thought at all, preoccupied as she was with her own life and dreams. His name was Umberto Rolando Monteverdi, a rising star in the world of classical music and the son of the famous opera diva, Calandra. With a name like that, no wonder the man had such an inflated ego.

To say that Catriona lived in a world of her own would not have been quite correct. Yet, growing up over-protected in many ways, the young girl had got used to withdrawing into a world where she found her freedom – a world of music, from which she came back refreshed, enlivened and somehow fulfilled. It hadn't actually been her intention, but Marguerite de Vere had made sure that her daughter was so shielded from the realities of life that at the age of eighteen Catriona was still innocent, unaware of the pitfalls of love, ignorant of the harsher aspects of life. Because of this, among her feelings of indignation and scorn at the arrogance of Umberto Rolando Monteverdi there lurked the undercurrent of something thrilling and novel that spoke to her wilder side and pushed away all coherent thought.

As Catriona ran up the steps that led to her front door her pulse, contrary to what she would have liked to admit, *was* racing. With trembling hands, she put her key in the lock. A wave of irritation swept over her as her mother called out predictably, 'Is that you, Catriona? You're rather later than usual, I was worried.' Now all she wanted was to get to her computer to look up the new virtuoso.

'Yes, it's me, *Maman*,' she answered, rushing up the wrought-iron staircase that led to the first floor and her bedroom.

As she slid into a pair of jeans and a smooth, winter-white cashmere sweater her gaze moved to the open window and fell on the dark shape of Les Platanes that loomed in the gathering shadows of nightfall. The brick walls that usually appeared so softly charming seemed massively defiant this evening. The light was on in the room facing the terrace where she and the pianist had had their argument, a pool of ghostly radiance in the dusky twilight, and suddenly she wished that this first encounter with the budding composer had not turned out the way it had.

She had been trespassing, he was quite right to be angry. She had heard about stars hounded by fans and the paparazzi. Of course, that's what he'd meant when he said: 'You came here to spy on me' – he'd taken her for a journalist.

'Catriona, dinner's ready,' her mother called out.

'Coming!'

It was Sidonie the cook-housekeeper's night off, so Marguerite and her daughter were having their meal in the warm Provençal kitchen that formed the heart of the house. The room had a homely, rustic feel that Catriona loved, its baked-earth colours highlighted in the warm terracotta marbled worktops and stone floors. When her mother was away on business Catriona always ate with Sidonie, sitting at the chunky beechwood table on folding French chairs whose simple beige-and-cream-coloured seat covers made the room feel even more relaxed. Close to the large central island were high dressers, hand-carved in solid oak and painted in matt cream, displaying china on their shelves, where a number of cookery books were also stacked.

Catriona loved cooking. When she was younger she often spent her afternoons baking or concocting savoury dishes while listening to Sidonie's merry chatter – she would either gossip or recount legends from her native Corsica. Now, unfortunately, with the long hours needed to practise her singing for the upcoming competition, Catriona didn't have much time to pursue such hobbies.

'You came in later than usual, *ma chérie*,' her mother said as she ladled soup into the bowl Catriona was holding out to her. 'I was rather worried. There was a bus accident the other day on the airport road.'

'Yes, I was delayed at the Conservatoire,' she lied. She doubted Marguerite would approve of her sneaking over to the house next door uninvited, and getting caught red-handed by the new owner. Particularly when that owner was Umberto Monteverdi. An image of the dark and dangerous-looking musician swam into Catriona's vision; she placed her steaming bowl on the table and stared down into it as though the contents held something entirely fascinating – anything to avoid her mother's gaze.

Although Catriona and her widowed mother were close, and an easy-going and charming relationship existed between the two of them, Catriona, being an only child, was very private. Discussing matters of the heart was something that she and her mother seldom did and, anyway, Catriona had neither the time nor the opportunity to discover the opposite sex. This was uncharted territory for her and the exploration of such a mysterious landscape was an adventure yet to be embarked upon for the teenager; and one which her mother would have delayed as long as possible if it were within her power.

Marguerite de Vere, perhaps as a result of being an only child whose parents were emotionally absent from her life, was an odd combination of self-sufficient career woman, who wanted the same independence for her daughter, and over-protective mother who couldn't quite let go. Her own mother and father had died shortly after she had married Sir William and she was a wealthy woman in her own right. Having no siblings, she had inherited everything from her parents, who were from the rich *haute bourgeoisie*. Both had been wrapped up in their careers – her father a renowned cardiologist and her mother a talented cellist who had played professionally for the French National Orchestra and was often away on tour. The young Marguerite had seen little of them while growing up.

At twenty-four, the intelligent and deceptively energetic Marguerite had been physically similar to Catriona, delicately pretty with a slight figure. However, the dark-haired, brown-eyed young lawyer had not inherited her mother's gift for music. Marguerite had ideas of her own. Very down-to-earth, she had studied international law and had met her future husband while on secondment at the commercial section of the French Embassy in London.

Sir William was considerably older than Marguerite and they had married within a year. His young bride had immediately become pregnant but returned to work at her English law firm quickly after Catriona's birth, pursuing her career with characteristic zeal and efficiency until her husband's death, the summer before Catriona was due to go to boarding school. Faced with such a momentous upheaval, with typical decisiveness Marguerite decided to pack their things and leave England. She had never had the heart to put her daughter through the English public school system and, taking a two-year sabbatical, devoted her time to Catriona while they settled into their new life in France.

Despite having money, bringing up her child single-handed was a lonely business. Yet Marguerite was no stranger to loneliness and if she cocooned Catriona a little more than she intended while she was growing up, it was no doubt due to her determination not to echo her own mother's apparent indifference. Like many fragile-looking women, Marguerite had a strain of toughness that disagreeably surprised anyone who challenged her most treasured convictions, the strongest of these being that her one child was distinctly more remarkable than anyone else's.

Now, mother and daughter were sitting at the table with their soup, talking about their respective days, Marguerite cutting into the warmed baguette bought by Sidonie that morning. The local *boulangerie* was owned by the housekeeper's cousin, which meant that the kitchen of Les Charmilles had no shortage of fresh bread and pastries, most of which Sidonie managed to consume herself quite happily.

'I think Les Platanes has finally been sold,' Marguerite remarked as they started on their main course.

Catriona felt her cheeks sting with bright pink as she feigned surprise. 'Les Platanes? *Mon Dieu!* I thought the old place would fall down before someone actually bought it.'

Marguerite buttered them both some bread. 'It's in quite good repair, I think. The garden has always been attended to meticulously. One of the gardeners came to borrow some of our topsoil this morning.'

Catriona kept her eyes fixed on her *cassoulet*, the rich, slow-cooked casserole they always had on Sidonie's night off, the recipe for which had been handed down through generations of Marguerite's family. It was made with meat, pork skin and white beans in a thick tomato sauce and was a speciality of the South of France.

'Oddly enough, it's a musician who's bought it,' Marguerite went on.

Catriona felt her cheeks deepening to an even brighter pink. 'Yes?' she managed to say.

'He's well known … a promising new composer. Italian, I can't remember the name now. I thought we might invite him to our next drinks party … a fresh face.'

'Your *cassoulet* tonight is the best you've ever made, *Maman*,' Catriona declared, trying to change the subject.

Her mother gave her a pleased smile. 'Have some more.'

'No, thank you, I've already had two helpings.' She stood up to clear the plates away.

'To come back to our new neighbour. On second thoughts, it might not be such a good idea to invite him after all. The gardener said that he had a party last night. A wild bunch, by all accounts. Apparently, they threw their cigarette butts in the garden. The place was a real rubbish tip when he arrived this morning.'

'How disgusting and rude! Good idea, let's keep away,' Catriona agreed quickly.

'You surprise me. I would have thought you'd be excited about having a fellow musician as a neighbour.'

'Not if he's throwing wild parties and keeping people awake.'

Marguerite's brown eyes were darker than her daughter's but no less penetrating. 'Were you disturbed by their party then? I must admit that I was so exhausted last night, it would have taken a crashing thunderstorm to wake me.'

Catriona turned to put the dishes in the sink. 'I … What I meant was, he must be a rather inconsiderate type, judging by what you said.' Inconsiderate was one word to describe him, she thought to herself. Add to that arrogant, presumptuous, overbearing, too tall, smugly handsome …

'Well, perhaps it was a one-off.' Marguerite took a final sip of her red wine. 'If he's some kind of star then I suppose the odd party now and then is to be expected. I do wish I could remember his name. Anyway, it's a marvellous coincidence to have another up-and-coming musician living next door.'

Catriona laughed. '*Maman*, really, what do you mean? I'm hardly in the same league. You said he's a well known composer, I'm still a student.'

'Be that as it may, *ma chérie, Madame* Haussmann has great hopes for you.'

'I know, *Maman*, and that is very encouraging. But like my friend Sophie says, it's not all slog and brilliance. There are so many other factors at play. You have to be in the right place at the right time, with the right people around.'

'And that's exactly what I meant, *ma chérie*. Maybe we should pay a courtesy visit to our musical neighbour.'

'That is not what *I* meant, *Maman chérie*. It'll do my self-respect much more good if I succeed on my own. Don't fret, *Maman*.'

Catriona was grateful that her mother always supported her musical aspirations, wanting her to pursue her studies and have a glittering career. Yet she was also aware that for all of Marguerite's determination in her own life to be self-sufficient, she appeared to have a blind spot where Catriona was concerned.

Marguerite smiled at her daughter's earnest expression. 'Well, *peut-être* you're right. After all, there is something about you. And you may still be only a student, but when you sing, you have a quality that …' Her eyes filled with pride, '… carries your audience away. Something one can't teach, I'm sure. It's a special aura that transports the listener into another world.'

Catriona went up to her mother and gave her a big hug. 'I love you, *Maman*. You've always been my backbone. Honestly, without your encouragement, I don't think I would have come this far.'

They had some fruit and a cup of coffee, did the dishes together and then Catriona was able to retire to her room at last. Her eyes went straight to the open window and to Les Platanes. The lights were off, the shutters closed. The house lay as seemingly deserted in the night as it had always been – until yesterday – and if it wasn't for the conversation she'd just had with her mother at dinner, she would have thought the whole appearance of a raucous party at Les Platanes had been a figment of her imagination. Still, there was also the fact that she had now met the new occupant of the house, and she couldn't get her disturbingly attractive neighbour out of her mind.

Although Catriona wanted to see what she could find out about the composer on the internet, it was quite late and she needed to get up early in the morning so she climbed into bed. It took her a long time to get to sleep and even when she eventually dozed off, she was troubled by bizarre dreams infused with intangible images and a strange feeling of malaise.

Her first thought when she woke the next morning was of Les Platanes and her pianist neighbour. She looked out of her bedroom window but the house presented the same lonely and uninhabited aspect that it had all these years. On her way to the Conservatoire, she turned to the gates in the hope of glimpsing the old gardener but there was no one around.

At the Conservatoire, she headed straight for one of the posters advertising the young composer's concert and breathed a sigh of relief when she saw it was to take place the following week. She hadn't missed it.

On her way home that afternoon she went by L'Opéra Nice Côte d'Azur, the city's opera house, to buy two tickets for the event. She would invite her student friend Sophie, who also had a passion for music though she wanted to teach rather than perform.

Acquiring tickets for Umberto's concert was almost impossible, the man at the box office informed her. 'Everyone wants to hear the new maestro play, they don't care what they pay. I'm not sure there's any left.' He peered at his screen, then raised an eyebrow. 'Seems like you're the lucky one today, *Mademoiselle*.'

A cancellation had just occurred and Catriona was able to secure two excellent seats. She thanked the man and, as she did so, spied the shelf at the back of the booth. It was stacked with CDs of the young composer's music that had just come out. The box office man winked. 'I guess you'll be wanting one of these too? It's his first. I've had a lot of young ladies buying these. Not just the young ones either.'

Catriona gave a deliberately casual pause. 'Yes, I think I will.' He had played Beethoven's 'Moonlight Sonata' so beautifully and the fluid notes of that other unknown piece she had heard him play as she was creeping on to the veranda had also caught at her heartstrings. The man grinned at her conspiratorially as he put a CD in a paper bag and handed it over. Catriona shot him a haughty look and hurried away, irritated by his assumption that she was one of the crowd of fawning girls – that wasn't it at all, she was simply interested in his music.

It was a balmy late afternoon and Catriona decided she'd window-shop for a while; the spring sales were on and she wanted to buy a new dress for the concert. She rang her mother to tell her she would be late.

She visited Rue Paradis in the Carré d'Or quarter – a real paradise for designer junkies. The fashionable Masséna *zone pietonne* was a popular walkway, not only renowned for its exclusive shops selling haute couture but also for its exquisite boutiques, where creation and elegance were expressed at a more reasonable price. Its nightlife also made it a key destination, with lively entertainment in the outdoor cafés, bars and restaurants, as well as strolling musicians and pavement artists adding colour to the festival atmosphere.

Here, almost immediately, Catriona found the dress she was looking for. It was a Paul Jordan tiered mini dress and the opulent red-and-green floral print on a black ground epitomized the acclaimed new designer's romantic aesthetic, so the boutique's attentive assistant informed her. Youthful yet sophisticated, the Italian-made design was cut to a loose fit from thin silk and its flirty, multi-layered skirt gave Catriona a flattering drop-waist silhouette that was sexy and feminine. She realized that she had just the right coral earrings, pendant and charm bracelet to match it.

'You should try these sandals with it,' the shop assistant told her. 'They're just made for that dress.'

Catriona had to agree with her. The high heels were crafted from black leather and satin embroidered with roses in red and green. Black adjustable ankle straps kept the shoes perfectly in place.

Delighted with her purchases, Catriona decided to call it a day and go home, although it was not yet seven o'clock and the shops would be open well into the evening. Just as she was approaching the bus stop she saw a blond and wiry figure she recognized. Jean-Jacques, a friend of hers she'd met through Sophie, was coming out of the *boulangerie*. Though nice enough, he had always shown an interest that Catriona wasn't entirely comfortable with.

'Ah, Catriona … *ça va?*'

'*Oui, oui, et toi … en forme?*'

'*Oui*. It's been a long time, where have you been hiding?'

'I'm preparing for the entrance competition for a place at the Paris Conservatoire.'

The young man whistled admiringly. 'That's sounds hard.'

'Hard, but worth it. What about you?'

'I'm coming to the end of my articles with Emile Salomon et Frères. Hopefully, they'll offer me a place.' He stared at her speculatively. 'We should get together one evening.'

'Yes, of course.'

He laughed. 'You always say that and then you disappear for months! I'm putting you on the spot. Let's fix a date now.'

She smiled politely. 'I promise that I'll ring you once I've had a look at my diary.'

Jean-Jacques didn't press her further and he walked away with studied nonchalance after they had said their goodbyes. A moment later, Catriona turned to see if her bus had arrived and she swore under her breath. The No.14 was across the road, its doors about to close, the last passenger having just stepped aboard.

'Oh, I'll miss it!' she groaned. The next bus was at seven-thirty. Without a second thought, she leapt out into the road, her arm raised to attract the attention of the bus driver.

There was a grinding of brakes and a sleek red sports car swerved violently to avoid her. She jumped back on to the pavement, the colour draining instantly from her face. The driver of the Maserati stopped dead, backed his car a few metres and climbed out to confront her.

Heart beating and trembling, despite the shock of the moment she recognized the man who had been on her mind the whole day. His angry expression shifted only slightly as he saw her. 'Aaah! Little Miss Curious … we meet again, *eh*? Do you realize I nearly killed you? You stepped off the pavement without looking, almost under my wheels. If I wasn't a damned good driver, I'd have left you in a dozen bits!'

Catriona's feeling of guilty self-reproach dissolved under this tongue-lashing. She felt her spine bristle with antagonism. Admittedly she was at fault but he had no right to shout at her in the street like that, and with such insufferable arrogance.

Her golden-brown eyes were stormy as she glared back at him. 'You were driving too fast, we don't expect lunatics to come down the road at eighty miles an hour. You're not on a motorway here, you know. Don't you realize you're in the centre of town?'

'I was barely doing thirty,' he said through gritted teeth. 'Have you ever driven a car, *Mademoiselle*? If you have, you should know that drivers depend on people doing the sensible thing, like looking before they step into the road!'

She glanced down the road to see the bus receding into the distance. 'Now I've missed it!' she said furiously. 'I'll have to wait another half hour for the next one.'

'At least you'll get there in one piece,' he observed disagreeably.

Catriona turned away, her head held high, and began to walk down the road. She cursed under her breath, feeling the weight of her shopping bag on her arm, and her spirits sagged at the thought of this unpleasant second encounter with Umberto Rolando Monteverdi.

Just then she felt a hand on her arm. Turning, bristling and ready for a further argument, she was surprised to see her adversary smile. 'I'll drive you home. Come on, why don't you get in the car?' He cocked an eyebrow. 'After all, we're heading in the same direction, aren't we?'

Catriona almost refused, her mood defiant, but then she spotted the figure of Jean-Jacques walking back up the street. He'd clearly witnessed the whole episode and must be thinking this was the perfect opportunity to speak to her again. She cursed inwardly.

'Fine. You can drive me home, thank you,' she said curtly.

Umberto opened the door of his car and gestured for her to get in. He climbed into the driver's seat, immediately buckling the seat belt. He glanced at Catriona. 'It would be a good idea to do your belt up,' he suggested, indulgent amusement dancing in his eyes. 'My being a lunatic, as you pointed out.'

'You don't need to tell me, I was going to do it,' she answered defensively, ignoring his quip. Yet she had to admit she would have forgotten to do so entirely, so disturbed was she by the aura of the man sitting beside her.

She watched appreciatively as he drove, unable to avoid admiring the way his long, capable fingers that knew so well how to coax music from the piano were equally adept at handling the wheel. Suddenly she was shocked to realise she was imagining what else those hands were skilled at.

They drove out of the city centre in silence, neither of them speaking during the first mile or two. Catriona sat motionless in her seat, intensely aware of the silent, authoritative figure beside her. To the unworldly eighteen-year-old he seemed so much older than her, a man not a boy, and the thrill of that realization made her feel suddenly grown up. Slowly, they climbed the long, gently sloping carriageway, pines, cypresses and ilex growing on the wooded slopes on either side. There was not much traffic. They began to eat up the distance, very soon passing the bus that had left her behind. The car moved like the wind but was luxurious and smooth in its speed. Catriona had never ridden in one of these low sport cars and always thought they looked so uncomfortable – she was used to her mother's spacious BMW or her own small Citroën.

Umberto gave her an arrogant quirk of a smile. 'You'll be home before the bus at least.'

They were now facing glorious views: on one side the whole of Nice stretched out below them; on the other, beyond the city, low rolling hills undulated in the distance, dim in the twilight of the setting sun. Stone walls separated villas and open spaces from the road as the car wound its way up and down the terraced landscape towards Mont Boron. They passed large gardens big enough to accommodate private orchards. Here, lemons hung pale and innumerable in the thick groves, their branches so close to each other that it seemed as though they were embracing. Even the trees, like the Mediterranean people themselves, seemed happiest when clustered together jovially, Catriona thought, smiling to herself. Women, vague outlines in the orchards' under-shadow, were still picking the bright fruit, moving about slowly as if under the sea. There were heaps of lemons stacked in wicker baskets under the trees, glowing like primrose-yellow smouldering fires. Catriona had never really noticed their beauty before.

Umberto had brought down the car's soft top and a fragrant breeze played through Catriona's hair, mingling the sweet scent of mimosa and jasmine from the gardens with the sharper zest of the lemon groves. It was getting dark now; on the steep terraces high up above the sea the cliff houses seemed to be nearly on top of each other in places. The evening shadows sloping down from tall gates and garden trees – olives and medlars, mulberries and almonds – accentuated the feeling. The car glided through the dusk; over the brow, down the cobblestone streets between the houses, and across the side of the naked hill they went.

To their right, Umberto pointed to the horizon above La Baie des Anges, where a red sunset mingled with curdling dark clouds and some gold. 'Look at that! A concerto of colours, *vero*?'

Catriona nodded, unable to speak as emotion welled up in her, a lump forming in her throat. Everything looked so much more beautiful this evening and she knew it had much to do with the presence of the man sitting so close, making her heart pound so alarmingly.

'The Bay of Angels,' he mused in a low voice, as if talking to himself. 'A beautiful name. *La mer de Nice est la mer azure des dieux, faite pour porter les Vénus et les Amphitrites*, the sea of Nice is the blue sea of gods, made to carry the Venuses and the Amphitrites.' He turned to Catriona, his green eyes sparkling like the distant waters. 'Théodore de Banville wrote that. Do you know the legend attached to it?'

She cleared her throat. 'No, I don't.'

'Well, there's actually more than one legend.'

'Will you tell me one?'

'*Cela me fera grand plaisir*, that will give great pleasure. It is said that after Adam and Eve were kicked out of Paradise and they were standing outside the locked gates, looking at their new hostile surroundings with nowhere to go, they heard the sound of rustling wings. They glanced up and a band of angels were flying overhead, motioning to them. They watched the angels, who flew across the waters and then began to hover over a glorious bay, in front of an expanse of land as lush and beautiful as the forbidden

Eden they were no longer allowed to enter so they stopped and made their life in this magical place. That is how the magnificent bay down there was named La Baie des Anges.'

Catriona glanced sideways at the finely chiselled profile, the sleek angle of cheekbone, the jut of the strong chin. Was he himself angel or devil? Or perhaps some magnificent combination of both? He was certainly a man one would find hard to forget.

She tore her eyes away and swallowed hard. 'That's a lovely story.'

He glanced at her and grinned. 'So, are you going to tell me what you do with yourself in Nice, Caterina de Vere? That is, when you are not trespassing or stepping under cars?'

He had remembered her name, she noted with a skittering of her pulse, though he had translated it to Italian and made it his own. 'I'm a student at the Conservatoire.'

'A fellow musician, *eh*?' he said, his Italian accent strong and lilting. For a split second he took his eyes off the road to glance at her again and the intensity of his emerald green irises made Catriona think that she had never seen anything like it before.

She looked away shyly. 'You're very kind, but I'm hardly a fellow musician. I know who you are.'

'So, you *were* coming to spy on me yesterday?'

She tried to remain calm. 'No. I'll admit that I was curious to know who our new neighbours were because ever since we moved here the house has been empty. But when I saw you I knew your face was familiar, and it's only when I left that I realized who you were.'

'So, what do you think of my music?'

She hadn't had the opportunity to listen to his music yet, but Catriona was not about to admit that. 'I've bought your first CD. Does that answer your question?'

Umberto raised his dark eyebrows and gave her a disarming grin. 'Umm, not sure, actually. It seems to me a little evasive, but

I won't dig.' That made them both laugh. 'So, what instrument do you play?'

'The piano and the violin, but I'm majoring in singing. I'm hoping to become an opera singer.'

He gave her a sidelong look. 'An opera singer? That's quite ambitious. You'll have to sing for me one day. Are you any good?'

The directness of his question threw her. 'I … I've been told that I've got potential,' she said, embarrassed in case he thought her conceited. 'I mean, I'm not afraid of hard work. I know it's not easy and I realize that even talent and hard work often aren't enough to make a career of it.' She knew she was gabbling now but Umberto unnerved her so much she couldn't help herself. 'Hopefully, I'll be lucky. That's an essential ingredient of success, isn't it?'

He let out a bark of laughter. 'So, I've just been lucky, is that it?'

Catriona's face reddened. 'Oh no, that's not what I meant …'

Umberto threw her a glittering look. 'Maybe you could become my muse. What d'you say?'

Was he mocking her? Catriona smiled demurely and quickly changed the subject. 'I loved the way you played the "Moonlight Sonata" the other night.'

'Is that a subtle way of telling me it kept you awake?'

She coloured a little and laughed. 'No, no! It's just at night it's so calm that the breeze carries any noise.'

'That's not good. I'll make sure the windows are closed next time when I'm practising, I would hate to wake the whole neighbourhood.'

'Oh no, please don't!' Catriona exclaimed with such fervour that he turned and looked at her in that strange, intense way he had, which had made her stomach flutter more than once on their journey.

'You are very beautiful,' he said suddenly. 'The sweetness of your soul shines through your face … your voice, too, Caterina de

Vere, the opera singer.' He laughed softly and, unexpectedly taking her hand, placed it under his on the wheel so that she felt the warm, strong clasp of his fingers. A delicious dizziness engulfed her whole body, a tingling she had never experienced before. Her eyelids lowered and for a few moments in the velvety smothering darkness she gave herself up to her rioting senses.

There was a bend at the corner of the road and then the car slowed to a crawl. 'We're here,' Umberto murmured, releasing her hand. He drew up outside her house, then turned to stare at her lazily.

'As we're neighbours, you must come in and have a glass of wine. It's from our family vineyard outside Milan.'

Confused and more than a little alarmed at the effect he was having on her, Catriona tried to react naturally, giving him a pale smile. 'Thank you, I'd love to, really I would, but my mother will be waiting and I wouldn't like to worry her.'

'Yes, of course, you mustn't do that. Quite right, another time.'

'Yes, well … I'd better be off,' she repeated unnecessarily.

Catriona reached for the door handle. She fumbled with it a moment and Umberto bent across to help her, his lean face inches from hers, his elbow brushing against her knees as he opened the door. Catriona told herself it was the chilliness of the air that explained the shiver now feathering along her spine.

'Goodnight,' she murmured, turning to face him, hoping he couldn't hear the acceleration of her heartbeat. 'Thank you for the ride.'

Umberto inclined his head in a silent acknowledgement.

'I— you're not cross with me, are you? I mean, for not … for not coming in for a drink.'

Umberto smiled once more, a slow, enigmatic smile. 'Goodnight, Caterina. Go on in, don't catch cold.'

The darkness in which she had been lost seemed to be in his eyes now, in those dilated black pupils and in those shining green irises fixed so brightly on her that she could see her own reflection in soft focus, cloudy and shimmering. In that one second, as Catriona stepped out into the night, the woman latent in the still-unscribed page of her young heart awoke, and she knew she would be in thrall to this man forever.

CHAPTER 2

In the week that followed, Catriona could barely contain herself, so great was her anticipation of the concert. She hadn't seen Umberto since the evening he had dropped her off in front of her house. Since then Les Platanes' shutters had remained firmly closed and the house looked as secretive as ever.

Throughout the days and nights leading up to the date of the performance Catriona thought of nothing but the pianist and her new-found passion. She went about feeling morose, bored and irritable. She was so distracted during her singing lessons that *Madame* Haussmann kept her back one afternoon after class, a worried furrow on her brow, asking if she was feeling ill or if anything was wrong at home. Was she tired? Had she been working too hard? This was not the time to slow down, she admonished the somewhat dazed-looking Catriona. Slackening now could cost her the much-coveted place she had been working so arduously to secure. Yet even while being chastised, Catriona could not stop the exhilarating feeling flooding over her at the mere thought of Umberto Rolando Monteverdi. He was handsome and charismatic, talented and sophisticated … dangerous and intriguing. For the first time, she felt that life had scooped her up in its arms and made her heart thump with dizzying excitement. *He* was life, and she yearned for more of this thrilling sensation.

In the mornings, when Catriona woke up, Umberto was her first thought. Before anything else, she'd rush to the window to see if there was any sign of life in the house next door. In the evenings, too, he was her one preoccupation and she would hurry home from the Conservatoire in the hope that he would be back, practising his piano. The tension that swept over her during that week spread like wildfire through her blood as she spent her time constantly looking out for him.

After dinner, on the pretext that she needed to get some exercise, she would run down to the street to see if any lights were on in the rooms that were not visible from the windows of her house. She felt faintly self-conscious, something of a voyeur, as she performed this nightly ritual, acting like one of those star-struck teenagers for whom she had always held a certain contempt. *Still, why shouldn't I be here?* she asked herself defensively. *Or anywhere else I choose to go?* Somehow she managed to convince herself that she was just having a walk in the neighbourhood to unwind before going to bed.

But Catriona's jumpy and evasive behaviour was not lost on Marguerite. Busy with work, Catriona's mother had not been home for dinner as often as usual but that didn't stop her being alert to her daughter's odd change of mood. After her sabbatical Marguerite had thrown herself back into her career and had set up her own shipping law firm when Catriona was thirteen, her own way of rising to the challenge of being a single parent. Since then she had proved amply that she could combine the roles of devoted mother and accomplished professional and, despite those years re-establishing her career, her awareness of her daughter never waned.

Now she was quick to see that something was up with Catriona but although Marguerite interrogated her numerous times, her daughter hugged her secret passion closely to her heart, jealous of sharing it with anyone else. Instead, she fobbed off her mother with the explanation that she was getting more anxious as the time of the competition approached.

The night before the pianist's big concert Catriona hardly slept. She was beside herself with excitement at the thought of the next day's event and at eleven o'clock she was still sitting on the veranda, ignoring the chill air and admiring the spectacular view of the moon playing on the sea. But this was not the only cause of her sleeplessness. As she gazed dreamily out at the ocean, inhaling deeply the tangy, fragranced air, it finally happened: she saw the red Maserati glide elegantly down the road, enter the gates of Les Platanes and pull up in front of the steps leading up to the house.

Suddenly she no longer felt the cool of the night as heat shot through her. A large tree blocked her view so she hadn't been able to see him but, minutes later, the lights went on in that same room she had heard him playing in before. The room that she had never set eyes on but which had become part of the world of her imagination. Holding her breath, she waited for the music to start.

A few minutes more and there came to her strains of a melody she didn't recognize, music unlike anything she had ever heard before. At first, it was so quiet that it might have been merely a sigh of the breeze or the far-off lapping of the sea on the shore. Then, without warning, it began to hum and swell like the ocean waves, growing louder, then louder still, until the notes seemed to leap across the garden, heading directly towards her. Catriona closed her eyes and now it was everywhere, falling out of the sky, surrounding her, embracing her in its powerful arms, clasping her against its throbbing heart. Then, as the music built and surged, she could almost imagine that the gates of Paradise had opened, giving passage to a chorus of angels like the very ones guiding Adam and Eve that Umberto had told her about, their moving limpid voices flooding the night with a melody that was sweet and sad, yet at the same time brave and bold. Oh, and beautiful, so beautiful! It filled her ears, her head, and touched the deepest recesses of her soul, filling her with such emotion that tears welled up in her eyes and rolled down her cheeks in an endless stream.

There was one last mighty thunder of sound that shook Catriona to the core, and then it stopped. In a split second it had gone; the music had ceased, taking with it all the enchantment, the elation and the jumble of glorious feelings that had flooded her, leaving in its wake the most dreadful and desolate gulf Catriona had ever known.

She sat there straining her ears, hoping the magic would start again, but soon the lights went off in the room and Les Platanes returned to its muted melancholy in the dark night.

The next day went by on leaden legs until at last Catriona was dressing for the impatiently awaited occasion, gathering her excited thoughts. She would wait for Umberto at the end of the performance to ask for his autograph, determined to see him, to speak to him once more. There was nothing forward or sensual in her mind – somehow she had an overwhelming presentiment that she needed this last meeting as if she would be confronting her fate.

Just as Catriona was slipping into her new pair of unusual high-heeled sandals, Marguerite came in. She smiled at her daughter ruefully. 'You've become a beautiful young woman, *ma chérie*. I can hardly believe my eyes. *Hier encore tu n'était qu'une enfant en Bermudas et de longues tresses,* yesterday you were just a child in Bermuda shorts and long braids. I'm so proud of you.'

Catriona went over to her mother and hugged her. *'Je t'aime, Maman,'* she said simply.

Marguerite stepped back to look at her with a more speculative gaze. 'Is this a new dress? I've never seen you wear it. The cut is exquisite and that V-neck is really quite alluring. It's very striking, not the sort you usually wear … it makes you look much older than your age.'

That was exactly Catriona's secret hope and she gave a self-conscious smile. 'I fell in love with it. Don't you think the coral jewellery you gave me for my birthday matches it perfectly?'

'Yes, it's as if it were made for it.' Marguerite looked at her daughter quizzically. 'Are you meeting other friends at the opera apart from Sophie?'

Catriona coloured slightly. 'No, just Sophie.'

Marguerite paused as though she was deliberating on asking another question but had thought better of it. 'Well, you look lovely, *ma chérie*, and I hope you have a wonderful time.'

Catriona grabbed her black Dior cashmere cloak, which she had bought half price at last year's Grande Braderie de Saint Tropez, and her black leather clutch. Then, after a peck on her mother's cheek, she hurried down the stairs and out of the house.

She drove through Nice in a state of elation. Her eyes were shining and she was trembling, praying that she would have a few minutes to talk to Umberto alone. What would she say to him? She hadn't the faintest idea but she would find something … surely she would find something?

She parked at the Cours Saleya car park, a short walk from the opera house. Sophie was waiting for her at the entrance.

Catriona's friend was tall, with jet-black hair that she had cut in a trendy bob, accentuating her modish style. Full of joie de vivre, she was a good friend to Catriona, who secretly admired her for her confidence and easy humour, not to mention her consummate skill at flirting with boys. As one of three children of divorced parents, it was Sophie's good fortune to enjoy far more liberty than Catriona, which she exercised as frequently as possible. This also meant she'd had the opportunity to lose her virginity by the time she was seventeen, another thing that made Sophie more grown up in Catriona's eyes.

'Oh, you look fabulous,' her young friend exclaimed, kissing Catriona on both cheeks. '*Ta robe est superbe*, your dress is beautiful.'

Catriona beamed. She hoped that Umberto would notice it, too. 'Thank you. You look lovely yourself, I love that pendant you're wearing. The green is so brilliant.'

Sophie glanced down at it. 'It's an emerald. My grandmother left it to me when she died.'

Emeralds ... the colour of Umberto's eyes, Catriona thought as she reached out to touch the jewel lightly with her fingers. 'An amazing colour,' she whispered dreamily.

Sophie linked arms with her. 'Come on, let's go inside. We don't have long before the performance starts.'

The opera house of Nice had an old grandeur that Catriona loved and she went to as many concerts and operas here as she could. The imposing nineteenth-century building was one of the most beautiful opera houses in France, a listed building with curved pediments and a glass and ornate wrought-iron awning covering the entrance, itself topped by six marble columns that framed the granulated stained-glass mullion windows.

Looking up from the entrance, one could admire the top of the sumptuous north façade with its colonnade consisting of five bays topped by two pavilions, between which stood Raimondi's statues of four of the Muses: Euterpe for music, Melpomene for tragedy, Thalia for comedy and Terpsichore for dance. Everything about its neoclassical style reflected both architectural and cultural prestige, so it was no wonder that the opera house attracted a cosmopolitan audience.

Catriona and Sophie went straight to their places in the stalls. Catriona wanted to be as close as possible to Umberto and so it was lucky that the two cancelled tickets had been for seats in the middle of the first row, with an excellent view of the stage.

Arranged in a horseshoe, the auditorium was a sumptuous assault on the senses. Fitted out in typical Italian style, the vibrant red and gold of its classic baroque decor was warm and plush, if slightly over the top. The upper galleries consisted of three entire rows of gilded boxes, giving the impression of a honeycomb, separated by pillars and decorated with composite capitals and medallions representing Shakespeare, Goldoni, Corneille, Beaumarchais and Schiller. Catriona always thought how intimate the boxes looked, each one its own little lounge furnished with draped red curtains, but as they were oriented towards the room rather than the stage she and Marguerite never bought seats anywhere but the stalls.

Catriona looked around her, feeling her excitement rising. The theatre was packed. Hundreds of beautifully gowned women and tuxedoed men sat awaiting the entrance of the virtuoso. The atmosphere was saturated with wealth and opulence. Under the monumental crystal chandelier of six hundred lights, the *parures* of the bejewelled ladies shone with the brightest lustre. The women, Catriona realized, by far outnumbered the men in the auditorium, such was the lure of the handsome and gifted maestro they had heard so much about.

The light in the main theatre dimmed, the heavy red curtains rose and a figure stepped on to the stage amid thundering applause. The beam from the spotlight held him in its harsh brilliance. There he was finally, the handsome tuxedo-clad pianist who had held her mind captive these past days and nights. Catriona could see Umberto clearly: that perfect profile and the long agile fingers of his elegant hands which moved so quickly over the keys they were almost invisible. He sat at the magnificent ebonized grand piano, a Lilliputian figure in the middle of the huge illuminated platform, and it struck her that a setting like this would surely intimidate all but the most outstanding of musicians. But Umberto seemed totally at ease.

The first haunting, sensual notes began and Catriona recognized it at once: the piece she had heard the night before. The man with the magic hands soon had his audience captivated and Catriona felt as if she were floating, once more lulled into a distant world by the rhythmic melody. Her heart was like a trembling leaf carried by the wind. The world around her might just as well not have existed, so urgent and all-absorbing was the music.

Catriona watched Umberto, never taking her eyes off him, seeking, sensing, clinging to him with all her being.

The music was rising tempestuously around her as he plunged and swooped up every scale with the power of an eagle, catching the octave leaps like easy prey; Catriona's longing followed him, passionate, helplessly in thrall to the man and his music. She had to exert all her self-control to force herself to sit there, so powerful was her urge to run up to the stage and put her arms around him. Her feelings were a mad chaos of awe and frustration. There were only a few metres separating her from the stage, yet it was impossible to reach him. Catriona drew a long breath; she was only a fan, he was a big star … but she was here at least. That was all that counted.

The huge auditorium was hushed and still as the plaintive melody drew to its final crescendo. At the staggering last cadence, the notes hanging in the air for mere seconds, Catriona felt as if every bone in her body had turned into water. Amid thunderous applause, Umberto leapt from his chair and went to the front of the stage. He smiled that incredible smile. '*Merci, grazie,* thank you,' he called out, bowing low. He looked more attractive than ever and Catriona felt the sheer longing of the hundreds of women who were packed into the opera house, caught helplessly in the snare of the musician's charisma. The applause continued, louder and louder, extending to a standing ovation. '*Encore! Encore!*' they shouted, whistling and stamping their feet as single red carnations flew through the air and on to the stage.

Bowing to the request of his audience, Umberto sat down once more at the keyboard of the grand piano and, as the languorous opening strains of the next piece floated gently into the room, Catriona recognized Beethoven's 'Moonlight Sonata'. Her heart gave a skip. Was it possible that he'd chosen this for his encore because he knew she'd heard him play it? She blinked away these foolish thoughts. Of course it was a coincidence. But whatever the truth of it, the rest of the auditorium was as seduced by his talent as Catriona, and Umberto's audience listened enthralled until the moment the last notes died away. Then the applause erupted louder than ever. '*Bravo! Bravo!*'

The performance was finally over.

'That was fabulous,' Sophie breathed as the lights went on. 'He's very charismatic, don't you think?'

Catriona nodded, almost too dazed to speak at first. 'Yes … very.'

Sophie lowered her voice. 'The woman next to me was fidgeting in her seat. Her eyes were riveted on him.' As they both got to their feet, she added: 'I'm starving. Shall we have dinner somewhere?'

Catriona hesitated just for an instant. She had already rehearsed her reply in her head. 'I wish I could but I promised *Maman* that I would be back immediately after the concert. You know how she worries, especially at night.'

Of course this was a little white lie: Catriona had other plans. She intended to go to Umberto's dressing room to ask for an autograph and didn't particularly want her friend to know about it.

'That's a shame but, yes, you ought to get back in that case. Where are you parked?'

'At the Cours Saleya car park.'

Sophie raised her eyebrows. 'So far away? I came early and got a place at the Conservatoire.'

Catriona had guessed Sophie would choose to park closer to the opera house and was relieved that this would mean they would have to go in separate directions when they parted.

Sophie grabbed Catriona's hand and began gently jostling them through the sea of people heading into the foyer. 'I've parked quite close to the exit so, if I hurry, with any luck I'll be able to get out before the crowds.'

They separated at the theatre's front door and, after kissing her friend goodbye, Catriona dived inside again, pushing back through the throng. She knew where the artists' dressing rooms were and, as she hurried to the first-floor landing, in her longing and desperation to get there she felt like one of the ill-fated Greek lovers in the murals gracing the walls of the foyer. Thisbe choosing death rather than life without Pyramus, the fruit of the mulberry tree stained forever to honour their forbidden love. Wasn't it a force as powerful as that gripping her now? Somehow Umberto had cast a spell that was transforming her, body and soul, her innocence craving a knowledge only he could provide. She reached the top of the stairs, her emotions gathering into the steady excitement of anticipation, like the intense notes of the music she had just heard.

At the door of Umberto's dressing room a queue of fans waited, eager to see the maestro, to touch him and talk to him as she was intending to do. A wave of disappointment flooded over her. She chided herself for her naïvety. After all, Umberto was a star, it was natural that he would have a following. She was better off waiting for him outside the theatre, where she would have a greater chance of catching him alone.

So, as the evening air suddenly cooled to a fresh breeze, Catriona stood outside the theatre in the shadows, waiting for Umberto to appear. Everyone else had left and by now the lights were being turned off. It must have been almost an hour later that she heard steps … *at last*! They came closer and closer. Shaking, she leaned further back into the shadows against the wall. Was it Umberto? Then she heard more steps, the rustle of silk dresses and laughter. Yes, it was him, but he was not alone: a noisy group surrounded him.

'The audience was in the palm of your hand. You've demolished your public here, Umberto. Now, it's New York!'

Umberto laughed. 'Not so quickly, Jean-Michel. Let's read the reviews tomorrow. Some of these critics are merciless.'

'I wouldn't worry,' said a sophisticated-looking redhead as she took the pianist's arm and sidled up to him. 'You were sublime. I've never heard you play so well.'

Catriona could only see the woman from the back but she looked near to Umberto's age and was dressed exquisitely in a shimmering, figure-hugging gown and fur stole.

'You've always been too indulgent, *ma chérie.*'

'*L'amour est aveugle*, love is blind, the saying goes, *n'est-ce pas, mon amour*? Isn't that so, my love?'

'*Oh là là, tout de suite les grandes declarations*, suddenly the great declarations,' the man called Jean-Michel mocked.

They were too far now for Catriona to hear Umberto's answer.

She was numb with disillusionment, so numb her mind had almost stopped functioning as if there were a void in her brain. She walked like an automaton for an hour along the Promenade des Anglais, facing the sea. Overhead were countless great stars, their light so active it was as though they were alive in the sky. One in particular blazed above the open sea, giving Catriona a dejected pang in her heart because she was used to seeing it hang just above the roof at Les Platanes so close to the moon. That same star had kept her company all through those long nights, when she had sat on her veranda in the hope of seeing Umberto – and to that star she had entrusted the secret of her longing.

Swish went the sea beneath the promenade as she walked briskly, holding her cape tightly around herself as the mounting mistral whistled mournfully in reply. The air felt colder now that the wind had whipped up. The seagulls that wheeled above the eddying tide during the day had now returned to their nests. Near a bench, a ragged beggar girl was nursing her baby and tending to a grimy, fat infant boy. She stood a yard away and gazed at Catriona with her big, dark eyes. Catriona went up to her and gave her a couple of euros. '*Merci, mademoiselle. Que le bon Dieu vous protège*,' came her grateful blessing.

Far along the coast the feeble flash of a lighthouse appeared at intervals. Out from the ridges of sand in the less deep waters at the entry of the port, in the momentary gurgling of the waves one could hear the eerie almost-human sob of a bell-buoy as it rang and whistled, rising, rolling and sinking in the waves. Catriona might have continued to walk aimlessly if the strident sound of her mobile hadn't brought her back to reality. It was Marguerite.

'It's past midnight, *ma chérie*. The concert finished at ten, I was worried.'

Catriona sighed quietly. 'I'm on my way, *Maman*. I stopped to have something to eat. I'll be home in the next half hour.'

Most of the time Catriona was perfectly content with the love and care lavished on her by her mother. Yet sometimes, like tonight, the over-protectiveness of Marguerite irritated her. The golden cage Catriona had lived in since birth, and especially after her father died, was beginning to suffocate her.

She was eighteen. Other girls of her age came and went freely, she thought testily. Most of them had even had their first sexual experience and were no longer virgins. When they told her she didn't know what she was missing, Catriona just shrugged: her music was her world, her passion, and as long as she could play the piano and sing, she was happy. Yet now, suddenly, another passion had muscled in to her dreams, intruding into her world. A strange sort of overwhelming feeling which, although exulting, was frightening because it was so alien to everything she had known.

All the lights were on at Les Platanes when Catriona arrived home and music was blasting out of the windows. The house that was normally mute was tonight singing at the top of its voice, celebrating Umberto's success. She looked away from the lit-up windows and shadowy figures inside, trying to block out the sound. Her hand was not entirely steady as she entered the key into the lock of her front door.

'Catriona?' her mother called out from the living room as the door banged behind her.

'*Oui, Maman.*'

Marguerite's face blazed with relief and delight as Catriona stepped into the room. 'Did you have a nice time, *ma chérie*?'

'Yes, the concert was wonderful … a great success.'

'They're really celebrating next door.'

Catriona forced a smile. 'I noticed as I came in. Very jolly indeed.'

'It's a good thing they're not often here. I couldn't live with this noise going on every night.'

Catriona nodded sagely but she wasn't in the mood to make conversation tonight; besides, she already felt guilty about the lies she had told so glibly. Innocent white lies, perhaps, that didn't harm anyone. Still, she had never lied to her mother and she was afraid to stay in Marguerite's company any longer in case she ended up spinning herself into a web of more untruths.

Marguerite frowned. 'Is everything all right, *ma chérie*?'

It was clear to Catriona that she was probing, knowing with a mother's instinct that something unusual had happened in her daughter's life.

'I'm fine, *Maman*. It's been a long day and I'm just a little tired.'

Her mother's dark, intelligent eyes, which habitually saw through the various characters that stood before her in the witness box, flickered over her daughter. Marguerite shook her head. 'Why do I have this distinct feeling you're keeping something from me – for all the wrong reasons?'

Catriona was saved from answering as Sidonie barged into the room. 'Ah, Catriona! Home at last!' she exclaimed. 'Would you like something to eat? I've made a delicious *soupe au pistou*.'

Catriona knew that even if she was hungry, she couldn't be seen to be eating if she'd apparently already done so. She smiled weakly. 'Thank you, Sidonie, but I've already had dinner. Keep me some and I'll have it tomorrow.'

The housekeeper shrugged. 'I'll make you some fresh tomorrow,' she offered and then sailed out again.

'*Are* you keeping something from me?' Marguerite persisted.

Catriona sighed. '*Non, Maman.*'

'Then what's wrong with you? You don't look happy, it's not like you.'

Catriona rolled her eyes upwards. 'Nothing. I'm just very tired, I didn't sleep well last night.' She went up to her mother and put her arms around her. 'If you don't mind, I'll go up to my room now and I'll tell you all about the concert tomorrow.'

'*Avec ce vacarme et ce boukan je doute que tu trouveras le sommeil, ma fille,* with this din and racket going on, I doubt you will get any sleep.' Marguerite stood up. 'I'll get you some earplugs. I have so many of them. At least long-haul flights have one advantage.'

'I don't need them, *Maman*, thank you. I'm sure I'll sleep as soon as my head hits the pillow.'

'As you wish, *chérie*. You sleep well.' Mother and daughter hugged and kissed and, finally, Catriona was able to run away to the sanctuary of her bedroom.

There, she immediately crossed to the window and opened the shutters. She stepped outside and took a deep breath. With her delicate hands pressed to her heart, as if their ineffectual touch could still that heavy beating in her chest, she stood looking into the darkness at the floodlit house. There were people milling in the garden, shadowy figures of men and women, some holding hands, others locked in an embrace. Lovers – oh, how she envied them! Where was Umberto? Was he one half of one of those amorous couples silhouetted in the shadows under a tree? His loving arms intertwined, perhaps, with those of the gorgeous redhead?

From time to time when the music stopped she'd hear peals of laughter in the distance. Oh, she could very well imagine him moving around – tall, confident, charismatic – amid all that laughter and talking, the king of the evening!

The party was still going strong when fatigue finally caught up with her an hour later and she collapsed into bed.

That night, Catriona dreamt that she had gatecrashed the party and that she was joining in with the alcoholic merriment. She'd fallen into a fit of hectic gaiety – drinking and drinking, singing over-emotional songs with the other guests, totally giving in to an urge to dance and rejoice without restraint – so completely unlike herself in reality. Then suddenly she felt as if something either cold or blazing hot had been laid on her heart. She stopped short: he was there. Umberto was there, standing in the alcove of the window from which he had appeared to her not so long ago, gazing admiringly at her with an expression of desire, sending her entire body into a state of turmoil. At last, she thought, he was looking at her with all the unconsciously passionate force of his being, and she trembled so much that the glass she held in her hand and was raising to him fell to the ground with a shattering crash.

She woke up, sitting bolt upright on her bed with a throbbing headache, panting and wet through with perspiration. Still dazed by the power of her dream, she sank back against the pillows and didn't move for a couple of minutes. Then, taking stock of her surroundings, her eyes drifted straight to the open window and met with the stark darkness of the night.

Slowly, she slid out of bed and went out on to the veranda. Les Platanes was shrouded in shadows, mute and forbidden once more … as inaccessible to her as the bright star that shone above it. Still disorientated, she returned to bed and went back to sleep.

Catriona awoke to bright slats of watery sunshine illuminating the bed through the half-drawn *persiennes*. To her relief, the throbbing ache that had plagued her in the middle of the night had gone and she sprang out of bed and opened the shutters wide. It was a beautiful morning. The birds were singing with what seemed to her an almost Eden-like rapture. In the distance the sea was as calm and smooth as an ornamental lake, glittering under a limitless azure vault. Although the sun was shining from a cloudless sky, the air was still bracing at this hour.

Catriona noticed immediately that there was life at the house next door. Windows on the ground floor were open and staff were sweeping the terraces, vacuuming carpets and moving furniture around. Outside, gardeners were tending the grass and generally tidying up the place.

She did not linger any longer at the window. Gone was her gloomy mood of the previous night, which had been replaced by a vigorous optimism, and she was washed and dressed in no time. Today was another day. Besides, ignorance was bliss, she reasoned. Perhaps Umberto hadn't been one of those amorous couples in the garden last night. It was perfectly possible, especially if he was having to play host at his own party. He might even be unattached and, if she never tried to find out, she'd never know. What had she to lose?

Marguerite was already sipping her coffee and reading a copy of *Le Monde* when Catriona burst into the kitchen, beaming and full of energy.

Her mother lifted her head and smiled. '*Bonjour, ma chérie.* Did you sleep well?'

'Like a log, thank you, *Maman. Bonjour*, Sidonie,' she said, helping herself to a warm croissant the housekeeper had brought in fresh from the *boulangerie* on her way to work.

'*Bonjour, Mademoiselle* Catriona. Will it be coffee or hot chocolate this morning?'

Catriona's crystalline laugh filled the kitchen. 'Definitely hot chocolate today.'

Marguerite eyed her daughter over the newspaper with a wry smile. 'I prefer to see you in this mood than in the state of mind you were in last night.'

'You worry too much, *ma p'tite Maman chérie*.'

Marguerite glanced at her watch and sprang up. 'I must be off. Are you driving or taking the bus today?'

'I'll take the bus.'

'I'll see you tonight. Try to be home on time for dinner, and then you must practise your singing. I've noticed you've been neglecting it of late and the competition is round the corner. You've only got two weeks.'

'Yes, all right, *Maman*, but don't stress. I promise to practise seriously from now on. I've been tired lately ... it must the change of weather,' she added lamely, not knowing how else to explain her distraction.

No sooner was her mother out the door than Catriona picked up her briefcase. She was excited as she'd decided to stop at Les Platanes and have a chat with the old gardener. She hadn't spoken to him since the house had been bought. Maybe she'd learn something about Umberto or get a glimpse of him. Maybe, if she was lucky, he'd come out while she was there and they would talk, or he'd give her lift like the other day ... so many possibilities!

'I must be off too,' she said as she placed a kiss on the housekeeper's chubby red cheeks.

Sidonie's eyes went to the clock on the kitchen wall. 'A little early, aren't you? It's twenty minutes till your bus.'

'Yes, but it's such a beautiful morning. I'll take my time instead of rushing to the bus stop,' Catriona answered quickly, avoiding her gaze. She wasn't in the habit of being deceitful and this new evasiveness she was practising at home made her uncomfortable. But she couldn't help it – her preoccupation with the young maestro was all encompassing and much stronger than any other feeling.

An unbridled elation swept through Catriona as she left the house. She was indeed in luck. The gates of Les Platanes were open and a small garbage truck piled high with large black sacks was parked in front of the house. The gardener was just coming out as she passed the gates.

'*Bonjour, Mademoiselle.*'

Catriona offered him a friendly smile. '*Bonjour, Monsieur.* You seem very busy this morning.'

'Yes. The new owner keeps us on our toes.'

'I take it there was a big party last night.'

The old man shook his head disapprovingly. 'A wild lot, they are. The house and garden were a real tip when they'd finished with it.'

'Who's the owner?' Catriona asked innocently.

The gardener made a vague gesture with his hand. 'Oh, some foreign rising star with a long, unpronounceable name. The son of that singer, Calandra.'

'Oh yes, I remember now, my mother told me … a well known pianist, I think.'

He raised his eyebrows in sudden recollection. 'Yes, that's it.'

'Lives alone?'

'He doesn't live here. Uses the house for parties.'

Catriona frowned. 'Strange … are you sure? So, where does he live?'

'They say he has a small house on the sea in Villefranche. That's where he actually lives when he's in France. Les Platanes is only for giving these big parties. It makes sense, I suppose. I wouldn't want that sort of guest at my home. But I think – that is, from what I've understood – his real home is somewhere on the Italian lakes.'

'Does he have a family?'

The old gardener shook his head. 'Don't know. Doesn't seem like it. No one's mentioned a wife … probably leaves her behind in Italy.' He laughed. 'Don't blame him, with the goings-on that happen at these raves.' He took off his cap and scratched his head.

'I'll tell you something though, he's not short of female company so either he's not married or he's one of those misbehaving types,' he added with a conspiratorial wink.

Catriona glanced at her watch. 'I must go,' she said reluctantly, 'or I'll miss my bus.'

'It was nice talking to you again, *Mademoiselle* Catriona.'

'You too. *Au revoir*, Jeannot.'

Catriona hurried away but by the time she got to the bus stop she'd missed her bus and had to wait half an hour for the next one, which made her late for her piano lesson.

It was not a happy *Madame* Haussmann who greeted her when she arrived at the Conservatoire. Her singing teacher was a tall, thin woman in her mid-seventies with a sturdy posture, short white hair, gnarled hands and pointed features. Her small, sharp, grey eyes now fixed on Catriona with frustrated concern.

'I don't know what's going on with you, Catriona,' she said, shaking her head. 'I thought you were serious about this competition. What's come over you? The way you're carrying on, Françoise will win the place in Paris. You don't realize how lucky you are to have been chosen in the first place. You've done well to have come so far in the competition. So many young people are just as gifted as you are – some even more so – and would give anything for this opportunity. You've worked so hard up until now, I really don't understand.'

Madame Haussmann's disappointment was palpable. She had immediately seen her student's potential, which is why she had decided to enter her for the Saint Cecilia contest. Catriona was instantly contrite. At once she knew that something infinitely precious was slipping away from her with tragic speed.

'I'm sorry, *Madame*. I missed my bus – it won't happen again, I promise.'

Yet her tutor was not to be distracted from her full rebuke. 'It doesn't pay to be over-confident in this game. If you continue with this laid-back attitude you've had of late, that place might just be snatched away from under your nose.'

'I will work doubly hard until the contest.'

'I'm pleased to hear it,' *Madame* Haussmann replied dryly and then she handed her some paperwork.

'Here are some forms and all the details about the contest. The Conservatoire requires you to fill these in,' she said, pointing to the various documents.

Catriona examined the papers thoughtfully and then, without raising her head, she asked in a low voice: 'What are my chances? Have I blown it by relaxing a little these last weeks?'

'Two weeks ago, I would have said the odds were on your side. Just now, I wouldn't like to hazard a guess. Of course, there are many factors involved …'

'Such as?'

'For one thing, we don't yet know who the judges will be. Distinguished in their own field, *bien sur*. Some will be the Conservatoire's own teachers, but not all. I've always found that different people are looking for different qualities.' She bit her lip, her brow furrowed.

'*Honnêttement*, to be honest, the margin between Françoise and yourself was quite wide a few weeks ago, but I heard her yesterday. She sang the *Marriage of Figaro* "Voi Che Sapete" aria brilliantly. I would say that she's almost caught up with you. Still, *you* sing with emotion. With Françoise, it's all about technique.'

Catriona glanced up nervously. 'And what do the judges prefer?'

'The singing specialists on the panel are, quite legitimately, looking for technical excellence. The other professional musicians, those brought in from outside, may look for something more original … something musically arresting. At the end of the day you can never tell because each of them is entitled to his or her own tastes.'

Catriona let out a pensive sigh and then caught sight of the details about the competition day. '*Guest appearance by Silvana Esposito to introduce the competition*,' she read out. Her eyes widened. 'I think I read about her in *Classica* magazine.'

Madame Haussmann nodded. 'Ah yes, very talented! Silvana Esposito is the up-and-coming protégée of the great Calandra. I've never heard her sing but if Calandra has taught her, she must be good. We shall see.' She shuffled some music sheets.

'Now, let's begin. Start your warm-up exercises while I find the piece I want us to work on, something with plenty of coloratura. All that idling means we'll need to concentrate on rebuilding vocal agility. Let's not waste any more time.'

*   *   *

During the following weeks Catriona strove to concentrate on her singing. Her chosen piece was a classic from the soprano repertoire, the 'Un Bel di Vedremo' aria from *Madam Butterfly*, the heartbreaking melody perfect for her expressive voice. She had been practising with the help of recordings and now, every evening after dinner, she went through the aria again and again, trying to perfect every phrase. She was so tired and so worried that she had jeopardized her chances by neglecting to practise that she dismissed from her head all thoughts of Umberto and her infatuation. It helped that Les Platanes' shutters remained determinedly closed. She took it as a sign that he must have left Nice and that most probably their paths would never cross again.

As Catriona went through a veritable hell of conflicting hopes and fears *Madame* Haussmann didn't make it any easier, demanding a rigour that was unrelenting and accepting nothing but excellence in her student's performance. A good many tears were shed in the privacy of Catriona's bedroom when she suddenly felt overwhelmed by the task at hand. Bitterly she remonstrated with herself for her previous lack of discipline. How could she have allowed her foolish daydreams over Umberto to distract her, particularly when now he was nowhere to be seen? Thinking of the impending performance she had to give, her confidence began to desert her and Catriona thought she would never win.

'There's no need to panic at this stage,' the old professor told her in a disagreeable but oddly bracing way whenever she sensed that her pupil was wilting. 'People who succumb to nerves during this final phase seldom reach the top. Endurance is an essential part of becoming an artist. You have that quality, if you put your mind to it.' This acted as a spur for Catriona to take up the challenge. She practised the *Madam Butterfly* aria with renewed determination and most of the time she remained cheerful.

Everyone at home as well as at the Conservatoire spoke of little but the upcoming contest. Catriona was interviewed by *Le Journal des Arts* and the TV channel *ARTE*; her fellow students flocked around her excitedly, generous in their good wishes. Marguerite was more supportive than ever, although Catriona could see how nervous her mother was, and Sidonie made sure she cooked all her favourite dishes to make sure *Mademoiselle* Catriona was well fed and in the right frame of mind while she was practising.

A week before the competition Marguerite announced that she had to go away for a few days to deal with a shipping incident in Guadeloupe. She often took on arbitration cases, some of which demanded she fly to the other side of the globe. She tried to control her travelling so as not to be away from her daughter for long periods; however, once she committed to a case, her schedule was driven by arbitration hearing dates and Marguerite's time was not her own.

'It shouldn't take long,' she reassured Catriona. 'Don't worry, I'll be back for the performance and in the meantime Sidonie will take care of you.'

But the night before the great day her mother rang from Guadeloupe to explain that the case was much more serious than she had at first thought and she wouldn't be able to attend the contest after all. Catriona could hear the uncharacteristic anxiety in her mother's voice: she was mortified at letting her daughter down, but this was a difficult litigation with millions of euros at stake for one of her best clients.

Catriona tried to hide her disappointment. She knew that her mother would have done her best to be there for her if she could and that this was a case of *force majeur*. Instead of a warm hug from Marguerite before bed to quieten her nerves, she received a bracing call from *Madame* Haussmann, who rang to make sure her student was having an early night and to tell her that she had nothing to worry about.

'Don't forget to stay away from chocolate, peanut butter, milk or any sort of dairy product. That is just about the worst thing you can eat before performing,' she warned, before wishing her good night.

Catriona was touched by the call and it did manage to calm her nerves. She was in a better frame of mind after that and so she had an early dinner and made sure she did a few scales before she went to bed.

*   *   *

When she awoke next morning, Catriona was immediately aware of the most frightful sinking of the heart. Any confidence she'd ever possessed seemed to have drained away, leaving her to wonder what insane impulse had prompted her to engage in this appalling gamble. Wouldn't she have been better off waiting another year and then going through the official examination, like most students of her age? She would have had more time to work on her technique and would have been mature enough to handle it.

At the morning rehearsal, *Madame* Haussmann was complimentary about her singing. No doubt her teacher knew from experience that it would be fruitless to change a thing now, on the day of the competition, and to make any new suggestions would likely have a detrimental effect. Once or twice she stopped her student, made her try a phrase or two again, but Catriona could see that the usually demanding old tutor was happy.

As Catriona was leaving, *Madame* Haussmann placed an arm around her shoulders.

'Catriona, I seldom offer praise until a performance is safely over but, because this is a competition that's so important to you, I'm going to tell you that in my judgement – which is a very good one – you are well suited to the role of Madam Butterfly.' She nodded to herself as if deciding to impart a secret piece of information. 'In fact, of all my students, you are the only one who could do the role full justice.'

Catriona was almost incredulous. 'But how? I'm totally inexperienced and sick with nerves.'

Madame Haussmann released her with pat of the hand. 'You're right to be nervous, you wouldn't be an artist if you were not. But your very inexperience is one of your advantages in this role. You're portraying a young woman who is naïve, unknowing, bewildered. This alone of course would not be sufficient if you didn't also possess a unique sense of musical expression and impeccable vocal technique.'

Catriona gave a shaky little laugh. Unconsciously, she squared her shoulders. 'You mean that? You really think I could win against Françoise?'

'If I had thought otherwise, dear child, I would not have encouraged you to enter,' *Madame* Haussmann replied drily.

Catriona took a deep breath and smiled at her tutor. 'I will succeed,' she declared resolutely.

After that she felt almost tranquil for the rest of the day and when it was time to go to L'Ecole de Musique de Saint Cecilia for the competition, she was fired up and ready to take on the challenge that lay before her.

In the afternoon, Marguerite called to wish her good luck and to tell her that although she knew that Catriona would win, it wasn't the end of the world if she didn't. The most important thing was that she'd done her best, her mother told her. 'Just think yourself into the part, *ma chérie*. Tonight, you will not be Catriona but Madam Butterfly.'

A few hours later, with just minutes to go before she went off to the concert hall, Catriona was in her room, zipping up her dress. When she surveyed herself in the long cheval mirror she was amazed at her own transformation. Her gown was a warm yellow, cut in simple and subtle lines from cascading chiffon that she and Marguerite had bought after she'd been chosen as one of the two finalists. Its sunny colour reflected its golden tones on her already tanned skin. The long, elegant dress was of Grecian inspiration, crafted with a wrap-effect front and nipped in at the waist. The fluid design had a full skirt that moved gracefully when Catriona walked and the deep V neckline revealed just enough cleavage to be seductive without being too provocative.

For the occasion Marguerite had lent her daughter a simple, classic Zolotas necklace in hammered twenty-two-carat yellow gold with matching earrings, which added the last glamorous touch to Catriona's outfit. Slipping into delicate gold stiletto sandals, she glanced once more at her reflection in the mirror for reassurance. The alarm clock on her bedside table showed 6.50pm: still five minutes left before the taxi arrived. Taking a deep, steadying breath, Catriona left her room.

Sidonie went into raptures when she came down the stairs.

'Ah, *Mademoiselle* Catriona, your mother would be so proud of you! A young lady. One day, not too far away, you'll be wearing a wedding dress when you come down these stairs,' she said, her voice choking with emotion. She went to give Catriona a hug but stopped herself in time. Not wanting to put a hair out of place, the old housekeeper merely rubbed Catriona's arms warmly and touched her cheek.

Catriona laughed. 'I'm only eighteen, Sidonie! Much too young to be married.'

Sidonie squeezed her hand. 'Ah! *Amour, amour, quand tu nous tiens …* When love gets hold of you, when it knocks at your door, age is not important. Nothing else matters then!'

Love? For a few seconds Catriona's thoughts flew back to Umberto: where was he? Would she ever see him again? She wished he could see her in this beautiful gown. Still, she quickly chastized herself, now was not the time for such flippant thoughts. She was so near to her goal yet anything could go wrong so she must not get distracted. With the end in sight, her whole being needed to be concentrating on her performance.

She gave Sidonie a big hug, causing the housekeeper to chuckle with delight, before setting off to meet her fate.

*   *   *

Backstage in the hall was crowded and the atmosphere tense. Technicians were holding microphones, trailing wires. As Catriona entered, she saw *Monsieur* Lasalle, Françoise's teacher, standing with his pupil off to one side, obviously giving her a pep talk. Françoise, who looked very striking in a red *tape à l'oeil* gown, turned and caught Catriona's eye and they both exchanged sickly smiles, trying not to hate each other.

Catriona moved on, peering at the various people huddled around as she looked for her own teacher. She made her way quickly through the musicians tuning up and chatting, some of whom smiled at her encouragingly. Then, just as she had paused beside one of the violinists, thanking him for wishing her good luck, her arm grazed a figure moving quickly in the opposite direction.

'I'm sorry, I didn't mean to—' But all Catriona caught in response was a pair of grey eyes flashing in irritation, a long mane of red hair and the sweep of red silk as a stunning figure flounced past, barely sparing her a second glance before she headed towards the door leading to the stage.

As Catriona stared after her, realization dawned as to who the young woman was. A hand grasped her arm and *Madame* Haussman's voice confirmed it: 'Silvana Esposito. She's about to do her opening appearance.' The teacher was dressed in a beautiful long pale-grey organza gown and her grey eyes twinkled with an excitement that Catriona had never witnessed before. Clearly the old tutor was in her element amid the pre-performance frisson of anticipation. 'The hall is filling up splendidly,' she told Catriona. 'Come and see for yourself. There's a convenient peephole at the side of the stage.'

But Catriona shook her head. 'It'll only make me more nervous.'

'Quite the reverse, actually. Somehow it's better to receive the impact of the scene before you make your entrance then you don't have the shock when you start singing of perhaps finding that it's different from what you've visualized. Besides, you'll be able to see the panel of judges. They're a good mix and all excellent within their professions … opera singer, composer, professor and conductor. I'm very much reassured.'

Suddenly curious to see the people who held her fate in their hands, Catriona followed *Madame* Haussmann and positioned her eye at the peephole. For a minute it was difficult to focus. Then the complete scene came into view and as she saw the judges sitting in a row, notebooks in front of them, she let out an audible gasp.

CHAPTER 3

U mberto Monteverdi was among the panel of four judges. *Oh, it can't be!* Catriona exclaimed to herself.

For a few moments she remained perfectly still, as though continuing to examine the hall. Then, when she thought that her expression had become neutral, she turned to *Madame* Haussman. 'You're right. That was a good idea. There won't be any surprises now when I go onstage. Thank you for thinking of it.'

Catriona went to her dressing room and sat down, trying to relax. Her heart was racing so fast that she thought it might pop out of her mouth and her hands were clammy and icy cold. There was no time to think of Umberto, no time to think of anything but her singing. *I'm not going to let this shake me*, she told herself, clenching her hands until the knuckles went white with the effort of controlling her panic. *On the contrary, I'll show him what I am capable of.*

Of the two finalists, Catriona was to sing first, after Silvana Esposito's appearance. The walls were thin in her dressing room, enough for her to hear Françoise practising in the room next door. She listened to her rival appreciatively, unafraid, and after a while, spreading her hands out in front of her, she saw to her astonishment that they displayed not the slightest tremor. When Marguerite rang to wish her good luck and to tell her once more how sorry she was not to be able to be there on such an important day in her daughter's life, Catriona was happy that she could speak to her mother with genuine self-confidence.

When she was finally summoned to take her place in the wings, Catriona took a seat next to the side curtain. She had a view of the front of the stage but the judges were just hidden from sight, much to her relief this time. The music college was not particularly large and yet the anticipatory murmur of the audience hummed loudly through the concert hall. Then Catriona heard applause break out. Silvana Esposito had come on from the opposite side and was crossing the stage to take her place at the front of the orchestra.

As the dramatic trembling strings began their opening, Catriona recognized 'The Queen of the Night' aria from *The Magic Flute*, one of the most technically brilliant coloratura solos a soprano can sing. Silvana's voice resonated, bright and clear, as she leapt acrobatically from note to note with an impressive ease. Catriona listened with admiration, her eyes transfixed on the singer, whose red hair shimmered with every intense gesture of her outstretched arms. The bewitching performer was every inch the image of Mozart's fierce queen asserting her power. This was a diva-in-waiting if ever there was one.

As the song echoed through the hall, Catriona's mind drifted back to the sound of the laughing woman outside the Nice opera house, and Umberto arm in arm with a gorgeous redhead. The soaring flight of notes pressed on urgently, whirling Catriona up with it. She had only seen the woman's back but her figure, and that gleaming red hair, meant it had to be her.

The final notes sounded and the audience burst into applause as Silvana Esposito smiled and walked to the front of stage, taking her bow. From her vantage point Catriona watched as a tall male figure approached the stage from the opposite side and the soprano went to meet him. She swallowed against the slick of numbness creeping up her throat. It was Umberto, holding a large bouquet of yellow roses that he presented to the singer, kissing her on both cheeks. Together, they left the stage.

Catriona could feel her chest tightening uncomfortably. Silvana Esposito was undoubtedly the beautiful woman he'd been with on the night of his concert. Were they lovers? Was that why the soprano had opened the competition? Because Umberto was one of the judges? Of course. Why hadn't she realized before? Silvana Esposito was the protégée of his mother, Calandra, so she and Umberto must know each other. She wondered what had been going through his mind as he'd kissed the glamorous redhead on stage but it had been impossible to read him. Something inside her had kindled once more when she'd seen Umberto, and now she suppressed the pangs of longing, need and jealousy that fluttered around inside her like frenzied birds.

Then a quiet voice at the back of her mind pierced the turmoil of anxiety: *You've waited a long time for this. Don't throw it all away now.* Catriona closed her eyes for a moment. On opening them again, she was resolved. As she prepared to make her own entrance to the stage an almost frozen composure possessed her, although beneath that calm there was an uneasy feeling. What if she should forget her lines? What if her voice froze? *Stop that nonsense immediately, girl, and brace yourself,* she told herself.

As she walked on to the stage, erect and graceful in her beautiful Grecian dress, she saw Umberto sitting with the other judges in the front row. She watched his striking green eyes fasten on hers. They were glittering and intense, and she thought she saw the shadow of an encouraging smile lurking in them.

She went over to the small podium, her gaze skittering away from him. There was complete silence as the conductor waited patiently for her sign to begin, yet Catriona's gaze was still dropped to the floor. A quiet filled the hall and the audience seemed on the edge of their seats with tense expectation, as if wondering whether or not she was going to sing at all.

Then she lifted her head and finally nodded to the conductor. She stood there, calm and self-possessed, while the orchestra played the introduction to the poignant 'Un Bel di Vedremo' aria from Puccini's *Madam Butterfly*. Catriona cleared the huskiness from her throat and then softly took the opening phrases like the most consummate professional, rivalling even the talent of Silvana Esposito.

There was anguished pleading and tones of hope in Catriona's beautiful, well schooled voice as she moved through the dreamlike melancholy of the opening phrases, but there was also an irresistible strength of purpose in the melody's rhythmic simplicity, representing Butterfly's steadfast and urgent longing for Lieutenant Pinkerton, her love. There was such poignancy and innocent clarity in Catriona's tone that she held her audience utterly captive as she sang about faithfully awaiting her beloved's return. As she came to the words '*Vedi? È venuto!* Do you see it? He is coming!' Catriona's gaze found Umberto's once more and it was as though she sang only for him.

During the whole performance, Umberto's eyes did not leave Catriona's, gazing at her with the same expression of desire she had seen in her dream. His looks became increasingly ardent as the aria progressed, immersing her entirely in fire. Catriona could feel her cheeks burning and her whole body come to life, vibrating with a passion unknown to her until then; and more than ever she sang as though she truly was Madam Butterfly, awaiting the return of her beloved husband, whom people were saying had deserted her. Melodically, this aria was one of Puccini's most beautiful inspirations, the reason why Catriona had chosen it over other, easier-to-perform solos. Emotionally, it could tremble on the edge of lush sentiment unless sung impeccably, *Madame* Haussmann had warned.

Still, this evening, under Umberto's intense, fixed gaze, she could not put a foot wrong. Faultlessly, she trod the golden tightrope between sentiment and true pathos, her voice soaring with devastating power alongside the shimmering accompaniment of the orchestra, again and again *fortissimo*, and finally rising to her highest note in the aria on the word '*aspetto*', I wait.

There was a moment of stunned silence at the end of the aria and then the applause broke out into a roar of clapping and cheering that went on and on. The display of enthusiasm in the shouts and whistles almost rocked the hall and showed very clearly who the favourite was going to be. Most of the audience was standing, including Umberto, who was looking at her as though utterly fascinated. Catriona took a quick deep breath, still caught in the dream of her singing, and had to tear her gaze away from him. Her eyes now travelled across the audience and she was able to pick out some familiar figures who had come to wish her good luck. She raised her hand and waved at the upper reaches of the hall from which came ecstatic cries of '*Brava*, Catriona! Well done, Catriona!' Then she stepped forward and, totally composed, bowed and gave a smile while she expressed her thanks to the audience.

As she left the stage and resumed her place in the wings, Catriona barely registered Françoise entering the stage from the opposite side, or the orchestra when it led her rival into her aria from *The Marriage of Figaro*. All she could think about was Umberto and the way he had looked at her.

He had been moved by her singing, that was clear – the emotion he felt clearly reflected in his eyes all through her performance. If she had felt uncertain about his feelings before, then Catriona had no doubt what they were when she had finished singing.

It seemed only moments later that the director of the Paris Conservatoire took to the stage to announce the winner. 'Catriona de Vere!' she heard through the fog of her tumultuous feelings, followed by a thunderous burst of applause.

Half-stunned, Catriona walked on to the stage once more, her mind awhirl. *You've done it … you've actually done it!* Elated and breathless, she stood in front of the cheering, shouting audience as single blooms were thrown on to the stage. Her eyes went immediately to the front row, where Umberto was beaming and applauding as heartily as the rest. It was only then that Catriona noticed the cool figure of Silvana Esposito sitting behind him at the end of the row; she too was applauding but the smile she wore was decidedly fixed and, from time to time, she threw Umberto edgy glances.

Catriona's hand flew to her chest as she looked round the auditorium with incredulous thanks. When her eyes returned to Umberto's seat, however, she saw that it was empty. Where had he gone? Glancing to the side of the hall, she caught sight of him following Silvana Esposito out. She saw him pause at the side door to look back – *was it at her?* – but he was too far away for her to read his expression.

She swallowed her feelings of confusion while she continued to bow and smile at the audience. Once again, the virtuoso had disappeared and a cloud floated over her happiness. Why was he leaving so soon? Had she misread him during the performance? Wasn't it the height of rudeness to disappear before she had even left the stage? Perhaps there was something between him and Silvana Esposito after all. Still, she had to see this through to the end and, deep in her heart, Catriona clung to the certainty that she had secured his admiration, if nothing else.

Backstage, photographers and journalists crowded round wanting to interview her, while the judges wished to offer their congratulations; but Umberto was still elusive. Everywhere now there was a confused whirl of excitement. She was relieved when *Madame* Haussmann pushed her way through to stand beside her.

The teacher hugged her fondly, tears in her eyes. 'All the judges without exception were blown away. You were magnificent, *ma petite*. You must ring your mother immediately.'

Catriona was taken aback by the pride shining in her tutor's features. '*Merci, Madame*. It was wonderful … I've never experienced anything like it. I was completely lost in it,' she said truthfully, then gave a wistful smile. 'I wish *Maman* could have been here.'

Madame Haussman pressed one of her papery hands to Catriona's cheek. 'She rang just after your performance. She saw you performing. There was a broadcast of the competition on ARTE and she watched it on satellite from her hotel room. Go and ring her now and I will see you in a bit for the celebration reception.'

Somewhat dazed, Catriona escaped to her dressing room to ring her mother and tidy herself up before the party. Already there were baskets of flowers waiting for her, one from each judge, and the largest – a huge bouquet of red roses – had a small envelope pressed between the stems. She quickly tore it open, her pulse skipping. Sure enough, it was from Umberto: '*To Caterina de Vere, the opera singer. Perhaps I really have found my muse,*' she read. Smiling to herself, she tucked the note into the side pocket of her bag so that she could take it out and look at it again later. Then she changed out of her Grecian gown and put on the new Paul Jordan dress that she'd worn to Umberto's concert a few weeks previously.

She rang her mother from her mobile. Marguerite was beside herself with joy. 'You were wonderful, *ma chérie*. I never had any doubt that you'd win the competition after that performance. I've never heard you sing so beautifully. Whenever the camera moved to the judges, I could see they were enraptured.'

Catriona, who had been pacing the room unable to contain her energy, now flung herself down into a chair with a joyful sigh.

'Oh, *Maman*, I'm so happy! I can't believe my dream has come true. Now I have a real chance of becoming an opera singer.'

'Yes, *ma chérie*, you do. I've always said so,' came Marguerite's emotional voice. 'I'll be back at the end of next week. I'm so sorry, this case is turning out to be a nightmare. Don't worry, I'll make it up to you. We'll go on holiday to the Maldives, if you like.'

'Thank you, *Maman*. I'm so glad you were able to watch me.'

'Me too. You were marvellous. I am so proud of you. But I have to go now. I'll ring you next week to give you the exact date of my return.'

*   *   *

The reception was well under way when Catriona made her entrance. The high-ceilinged room, in an older part of the college, was packed with people and the reflection of the guests in the mirror running the full length of it made it seem even more so.

Catriona was immediately surrounded by her friends from college and various members of the orchestra, who came up to congratulate her. Even Françoise, gracious in defeat, complimented her on her rendition of the *Madam Butterfly* aria, while *Monsieur* Lasalle, her rival's teacher, shook Catriona's hand with an earnest nod and a murmured, '*Vraiment merveilleux.*'

Madame Haussmann made her way over, glass in hand, and lightly took her student's arm. 'Here, drink this water before you touch any champagne,' she advised kindly, handing a glass to Catriona as a waiter approached with a tray of fluted glasses.

'Thank you. I'm dying of thirst now,' smiled Catriona, almost draining the glass before she swapped it for some sparkling champagne.

A photographer stopped to ask them to pose for a photograph and then *Madame* Haussmann steered Catriona into the crowd.

'Come, *ma petite*, there are so many people wanting to meet you before the speeches begin.'

Catriona was on a high, talking to everyone who came by to shake her hand warmly and marvel at her performance, though her thoughts often flitted to Umberto. From her position on the edge of the room, she could see a long line of people reflected in the wall mirror, chatting and drinking, and she couldn't help her restless gaze travelling over the crowd again and again. Eventually she had to concede that he must have left for good, squiring Silvana to some restaurant or other or taking her back to his house in Villefranche – who knew? She quashed a pang of disappointment. Surely he should have stayed for the reception?

Suddenly she felt sapped of energy now that the adrenaline had left her body and she fixed her gaze on the mouth of the lady judge, who was speaking in the group of which she was part, without listening to the words. When she next looked up, a movement caught her eye in the reflection of the mirror. A tall male figure over by the window on the opposite side of the room had detached slightly from his group and was looking at her.

Umberto. Catriona's stomach turned a full somersault as she saw him in the glass, his intense green eyes shining like bright jewels. Their gazes locked, the look on his face one of almost humble adoration. It took Catriona's breath away and she gazed back at him, longing in that moment to speak to him, but he was surrounded by what looked like a cluster of fans, while she too was hemmed in by well-wishers. He seemed to silently acknowledge their mutual dilemma, the edge of his mouth quirking in a smile, then someone spoke to him and he looked away.

Where was Silvana Esposito now? Catriona half glanced around the room to try to spot her but it was impossible to tell if the soprano was here or not, the place was so crowded. Perhaps she was waiting for Umberto somewhere else, somewhere he would disappear to again later. Catriona frowned. She needed to master these confusing emotions somehow. She was the focus of everyone's attention this evening and must rise to the occasion.

Although Catriona was having a good time, praised and admired by students as well as by teachers, she was disturbingly aware of Umberto's keen emerald gaze as it followed her around the room. Although they didn't actually speak, all through the evening he was talking to her mutely, sending silent messages filled with frisson, and every particle in her body was responding to his silent adulation.

At some point in the evening, after the speeches and toasts, when a few of the guests had started to leave, Catriona moved to a table in the corner, looking for somewhere to put down her glass that was now sensibly filled with fruit juice. There were fewer people here and, thankfully, no one stopped to engage her in more conversation. She put down her glass and, beginning to feel peckish, surveyed the table, hoping to find something to nibble. There were only olives and she ate one, savouring its sharp tang.

'Not a fellow musician, *eh*?' The strongly accented voice came from behind her. She spun around and met Umberto's intense gaze.

Catriona stared at him, confusion dulling her thoughts.

'Last time we met, you were far too modest about your abilities, it seems.'

He paused, momentarily tongue-tied, his eyes fixed on her as if he couldn't tear them away. 'Well, congratulations on your triumph. You were magnificent, Caterina.'

As he said her name Catriona's heart beat a frenzied tattoo in her chest and she blushed. He was here, inches away from her; she could reach out and touch him.

Umberto smiled wryly when he saw the expression on her face. 'I really thought the skies had opened and an angel was singing.'

His deep accented drawl and the sight of his thick dark hair, tousled slightly so that she itched to touch, it made her feel slightly light-headed. 'Thank you,' she whispered, her eyes, if he could read them, telling him that she had sung for him. 'Your flowers were beautiful.' She laughed nervously. 'I really don't know how I'll get all those baskets home.'

'I'm sure the college will arrange that for you,' he said, still staring at her intently.

The room seemed suddenly devoid of the hubbub around them so that all she could hear was the sound of her own thundering heartbeat.

'Your note was very flattering.'

'And thoroughly deserved.'

'But, honestly, I think I have a long way to go before I deserve the title of "opera singer".'

'Not so very long.' His expression remained sincere.

Catriona blushed, her pulse still refusing to slow. 'Nowhere near the level of someone like Silvana Esposito,' she found herself saying. 'Her "Queen of the Night" was amazing. That coloratura's fiendish!'

He nodded and helped himself to an olive. 'Silvana is technically very accomplished, it's true. Raw talent like yours is rare to find, however. The Conservatoire will be lucky to have you.' He licked his finger and Catriona's eyes lingered on his mouth, which curved into a knowing smile.

She cleared her throat. Now that they were on the subject she was unable to resist probing him about the beautiful soprano. 'You know her well, don't you? I mean, if she's Calandra's protégée ...'

Umberto raised his eyebrows and now amusement sparkled in his gaze. 'Are you sure you're not spying on me, Caterina? You seem to be pretty well informed.'

Catriona's cheeks coloured. 'It's only what my tutor told me about her,' she explained hastily. 'Your mother is such a famous singer, after all. I just ... well, I wondered if you'd studied together.' It was partly true; the thought had crossed her mind.

'No, we didn't.' Umberto paused, as though reluctant to go on. 'We're childhood friends. Silvana is my godmother's daughter. She has been taught by my mother, as you say.'

Catriona's awe was unashamedly apparent. 'What an incredible opportunity for a singer! I've never seen your mother perform live on stage but I've watched her on television and I'm a great fan. Her *bel canto* technique is an inspiration.' She spoke breathlessly, the words almost tumbling over each other. 'I can't get over her range, you know. Sometimes I try pinpoint staccatos like hers and can't get anywhere near the precision. I saw her version of Bellini's *Norma* and she was stunning. Anyone taught by her is supremely lucky.'

'*Sì, davvero*, yes, indeed.' He appeared to watch her effusive reaction with fascination, the corner of his mouth curving in a sensual way.

Catriona pressed on. 'And your mother didn't come to hear Silvana sing?'

'My mother's health isn't what it was.'

'Oh, I'm so sorry to hear that.'

He nodded. 'I almost had to order her to rest. She's a stubborn woman.' A flash of something like frustration crossed his face. 'She tasked me with mentoring Silvana and so, when I was asked to be one of the judges on the panel, I arranged for her to sing tonight.'

'Has she been staying at Les Platanes too?' Catriona tried to make her question sound casual as she refilled her glass with orange juice.

'Yes.' He fixed her with an amused, quizzical look. 'I've put her up, along with some of our mutual friends, while I've been performing here.'

'Les Platanes has certainly looked … lively recently,' she observed.

He laughed and it was a deep seductive rumble, like velvet brandy that warmed Catriona from head to toe. 'I'm sorry if my parties have kept you awake. *Have* I kept you awake at night, Caterina?' He regarded her with a devilish smile, one eyebrow raised, which did nothing to help her equilibrium.

She took a sip of juice to cool her throat, trying to think of an answer. Yes, of course he had kept her awake. Frequently. Oh, why did she have to feel like a blushing schoolgirl when she was in his presence, so out of her depth? How was she to think of a sophisticated, witty retort when he looked so intensely attractive and drove all rational thought from her head? 'You're laughing at me, aren't you?'

His smile became softly contrite. 'I'm just teasing you, Caterina.'

She raised her chin. If he was going to make her feel uncomfortable, two could play at that game. 'So why isn't Silvana at the reception? I saw you leave the concert hall with her.'

There, it was out.

'She had to return immediately to Italy for another recital tomorrow. I escorted her out the back, in case there were any photographers lurking by the entrance.'

'It must be hard for you. I mean, being followed around by the press all the time.'

He popped another olive in his mouth. 'It goes with the territory, I suppose. My mother is the great Calandra, after all.'

Catriona looked him directly in the eye. 'Though you do seem to rival opera tenors in your reputation with women. Are you really the womanizer the gossip columns say you are?'

He laughed loudly again. 'Oh, opera tenors are much worse than me,' he grinned. 'So, do you have any more?'

Her brow furrowed. 'More what?'

'Impertinent questions.'

Catriona's eyes widened. Perhaps she had overstepped the mark. 'I'm sorry, that was rude of me.' She dropped her gaze sheepishly as she took another sip of her drink. 'You must find me terribly gauche.'

'On the contrary, I find your natural lack of artifice refreshing and … captivating.'

Her gaze flew up to his face. His smile was a quirk of the lip but his eyes were serious.

Again, she was lost for a response. The attraction was mutual, that much she was sure of. Yet was all this just mere flirtation? She wished she was experienced enough to know. He continued to stare and she looked into his emerald eyes, trying to read their enigmatic expression.

'Catriona, there you are! I've been wondering where you … Ah, *Monsieur* Monteverdi, I'm glad you haven't left without saying goodbye.' *Madame* Haussmann had appeared, her face glowing with pleasure as she caught sight of Umberto, making her look ten years younger as she smiled graciously at him.

'*Madame*, having had such a fascinating conversation with you earlier tonight, I could never do such a thing.' Umberto gave her a rakish grin, clearly enjoying the older woman's blushes. 'I should congratulate you again on your excellent teaching. I was just saying to Caterina here how captivating she was.'

His eyes sparkled with controlled humour as he glanced at Catriona, whose cheeks pinkened.

Madame Haussmann nodded, pleased with his charming compliments. 'I'm very proud of her.'

'Your pride is well deserved. Hers was easily the best performance of the evening.'

Catriona raised her eyebrows. 'Now you're just flattering me, *Monsieur*. You're forgetting Silvana Esposito.'

Umberto looked at her meaningfully. 'No, I'm not.'

'Yes, a beautiful girl, Silvana, and such stage presence,' interjected *Madame* Haussmann. Then her thin lips curved in a knowing smile at Umberto. 'But I'm inclined to agree. Well, I must be going. I'm not as young as I was and I need my sleep.' She turned to Catriona, assuming the habit of teacher once more.

'My dear, I promised your mother I'd make sure you got home safely, so will you get a taxi soon?'

Catriona hesitated. She was sorely tempted to stay longer and see where the evening went with Umberto, and yet the sensible voice inside her said she should leave.

'Don't worry,' Umberto's smile was all charm, 'Caterina and I are neighbours, didn't she tell you? I'll make sure she gets home.'

Did she detect a teasing note in his words? Catriona's stomach gave a nervous flutter at the idea of leaving with him. 'I'm sure I can get a taxi. I wouldn't want you to leave on my account,' she said quickly.

'And I wouldn't want you going home on your own,' Umberto replied decisively.

Madame Haussmann smiled at him. 'Thank you, *Monsieur*.' She turned to Catriona. 'I will see you on Monday, *ma petite*. Make sure you get plenty of sleep over the weekend.'

'I'll do nothing but sleep, I'm sure,' replied Catriona as the old teacher kissed her on both cheeks and made her farewells.

After *Madame* Haussmann had gone, Umberto said: 'Shall I wait for you downstairs, Caterina?'

She was keenly aware that the frisson between them had immediately returned. 'Yes, please. I must fetch my bag from my dressing room and say goodbye to everyone,' she murmured, not daring to meet his gaze. As she walked away, she could feel Umberto's eyes following her.

*   *   *

He was waiting for her outside the back entrance to the college. His dark, broad-shouldered figure was instantly recognizable leaning against the wall, and Catriona's pulse gave a reflexive skip. As she appeared, he gestured to the taxi stand on the other side of the road.

'It's been empty since I got here, so you're stuck with me now.'

She couldn't help laughing. 'My fate is sealed.'

He looked at her for a long moment, studying her face intently. 'How old exactly are you, Caterina? Eighteen? Nineteen?'

She lifted her chin. 'I'm nearly nineteen. Why?'

His gaze stayed on her, seeming to deliberate. 'Have you ever been taken out to dinner?'

'Well, yes, of course.'

An amused smile spread across his face. 'I mean, by a man.'

Somehow the sound of those words in his mouth sent a rush of heat down through her body. Her face coloured furiously and inside she was kicking herself for her naïvety. 'No … no, I haven't …' she said in a quiet voice.

'In that case, it's about time that was remedied. This is your night, you should be celebrating.'

'But …'

'Is anybody waiting for you?'

She hesitated. *Maman* was away. She could ring Sidonie and tell her that she was having dinner with a friend. This was her opportunity. He was right – this was her night, wasn't it? Still, she shouldn't be doing this …

'Your mother is away, isn't she?'

Catriona looked at Umberto and swallowed hard. That piece of information from *Madame* Haussmann had evidently not passed him by. Oh, indeed, tonight it was the devil not the angel who stood there watching her. 'Yes, she's away.'

'So, you're free to do as you please.'

Still she hesitated. 'I don't know … I …'

'Come on,' he said, his voice low and enticing.

Oh, how beautiful he is, she thought, with his strong jaw and full sensual lips that were curving now in a coaxing smile. Those shockingly green eyes held laughter but also a hint of something strangely vulnerable as she gazed into them, intrigued. She had daydreamed of something like this. To be alone with him, to talk to him, learn about him. She wanted to know everything about him.

'We'll have dinner at a small restaurant in Saint Paul de Vence. Its *Boeuf en Daube* is one of the best in the region.'

She didn't answer ... she *couldn't* answer.

'And then I'll take you home ...'

Still she hesitated. She'd have to lie to Sidonie, who would never condone this.

He looked at her with smiling eyes, his head tilted to one side. 'Not hungry? You don't want to at least join me in a glass of champagne to celebrate your success?'

Catriona smiled back at him, secretly flattered by his persistence. She really shouldn't. She could sense danger hovering in the air around her, yet she heard herself reply with her crystal laugh: 'To tell the truth, I'm starving and I can't think of anything better than joining you in a glass of champagne.'

'That's the spirit, *cara*! So then, let's go.'

The evening was mild with a full moon beaming down on them.

'Don't you have a coat?'

'This shawl is fine.'

They made their way to the car and Umberto pulled back the soft top, then took off his jacket and wrapped it around Catriona's shoulders.

'These nights are deceptive this early in spring. I wouldn't want you to catch cold.'

'But *you're* going to catch cold.'

He smiled broadly at her, showing perfect white teeth. 'I'm used to sleeping almost naked under the stars.' He turned on the ignition and away they went.

Naked under the stars? She felt an unfamiliar stir in her loins. Swamped in his large jacket, cocooning her against the fresh breeze coming in through the window, Catriona revelled in the warmth and male scent of him. The adrenaline that she was still feeling from her winning performance tonight was now transforming into a new kind of excitement that thrummed through her blood, making her want to burst free, like some creature emerging from a chrysalis.

'I need to ring Sidonie, our cook. She is probably waiting up to give me supper,' Catriona said quickly, taking out her mobile and calling the old housekeeper.

She answered immediately. There was a flurry of excited chatter as Sidonie, who'd heard the news already, gave her congratulations. Catriona turned away from Umberto, embarrassed that she was about to be selective with the truth. 'Don't wait up for me, I'll probably be late. Everybody's celebrating at the Conservatoire. Don't worry, you go home. I'll get a lift back ... I've got my keys.'

'Are you with friends?'

'Yes.'

There was a sense of liberation and risk in what she was doing. She was floating on a cloud, feeling the sweetness of truancy; weightless and carefree. For a split second Catriona wondered guiltily what Marguerite would say if she knew what her daughter was up to, but she quickly put her qualms aside; after all, she was nearly nineteen and she was living her dream.

It was a clear night. The world was enveloped by a lustrous light as tender and lovely as that reflected from mother-of-pearl, and the air was full of warm, sweet scents. The Maserati sped along a white road, smoothly winding and unwinding into the hills. Vines hung festooned with their full ripening clusters while the giant crags that rose in front of them were wreathed with wisps of diaphanous mist and cut with deep purple shadows. Far behind them lay the Mediterranean, with Cap d'Antibes extending into the deep's rippling, iridescent glow, which by day looked more like a giant finger gloved in green, jutting out into the blueness of the sea.

'Do you know Saint Paul de Vence?' asked Umberto.

'Yes, I love the old square. Its plane trees are like the ones you have in your garden. They're wonderful, so elegant.'

'The Tree of Hippocrates.'

'The Tree of Hippocrates?'

'That's what the Greeks used to call them, didn't you know?' Umberto began. 'Legend has it that Hippocrates of Kos, who is considered the father of medicine, taught his pupils while sitting under a plane tree. And because seeds from that tree were spread all over the world, it's believed all planes are descendants of that one ancient tree.'

'You seem fond of legends.'

He glanced at her with a smile. 'Because my mother was a famous prima donna, travelling to the four corners of the earth – and my father died when I was a baby – I was brought up by Adelina, my nanny. It was she who used to tell me such wonderful legends. I was never one to watch television – cartoons and children's films bored me.'

'How long did she stay with you?'

'Oh, Adelina never left. She still lives at our family home in Torno. It's about an hour from Milan,' Umberto added in response to Catriona's inquisitive look. 'She's retired now and uses one of the cottages on our estate. She still insists on coming over to help when we have big parties or guests, and makes a point of feeding me when I'm home. She's a marvellous cook, so I don't object,' he grinned.

'*We*? Do you have brothers and sisters?'

'Yes, well, not quite. I'm an only child but the others use it as a base. Silvana and my cousin Giacomo come and go.'

At the mention of Silvana, Catriona's eyes lingered on his face but his expression betrayed nothing. Not wanting to appear intrusive again, she asked no more questions about the soprano; besides, she was here with Umberto and that was all that mattered.

Umberto slowed to take a sharp bend as the car climbed higher through the wooded hills. 'My mother, now that she's retired, is there full time now as well.'

'It's such a shame she doesn't perform any more.'

'But she still has a sublime voice. She preferred to quit while she was at the top of her career. "That way people will always remember me as *la grande* Calandra," is the way she put it.' He smiled tenderly.

From Umberto's tone, Catriona gathered that he was enormously fond of his mother. A boy brought up by two doting females ... no wonder he had such confidence and a relaxed way around women. Strange that his upbringing was not that removed from hers, cocooned as she was by the loving ministrations of Marguerite and Sidonie.

'There it is,' Catriona exclaimed, pointing to the radiant mass of the old town as it came into view in the distance, the golden glow of its lights outlined against the night sky.

The medieval town of Saint Paul de Vence stood perched high up at the very heart of a vortex of hills. During the day one could see it for miles at the top of a fertile sun-kissed plateau, jutting out between two valleys with the ground falling sharply away from it on every side but one. There, a narrow passage not more than eight feet wide with three archways, each protected by a massive iron-studded portcullis, was the one point of entry. An ancient bishopric, the fortified walled citadel was famous as a haven for artists who loved to paint the town's narrow twisting streets – so winding that one could lose one's sense of direction – as much as they did the surrounding fields of roses and grassy slopes studded with violets and primroses.

Soon the town's great grey battlements rose up before them. The outlines of the walls, up to twenty-five-feet thick, seemed even more forbidding in the shadows of the moonlit night.

'We'll have to leave the car here and walk up,' Umberto said as they drove closer. 'The restaurant is at the top but it'll be an enjoyable walk. It's such a beautiful night. The moon's shining so brightly, it's almost as clear as daylight.'

'That sounds wonderful.'

They left the car in a grassy square near La Colombe d'Or, a fashionable haunt of the rich and famous, where Marguerite and Catriona usually lunched when they visited the town.

Catriona shrugged out of the Umberto's jacket and held it out to him. 'Thank you. I would have been cold without it but I'll be fine now.'

'Sure?'

She smiled up at him. 'Sure.'

He took the jacket from her. 'Umm,' he murmured as he slipped it on, 'nice and warm for me … and now it has your fragrance on it. Like orange blossom.'

'It's Guerlain's Aqua Allegoria Mandarine Basilic,' she said, her breath coming out in a half laugh. 'Not a particularly romantic name.'

He took a step closer and ran a finger along her hairline, tucking a stray lock of hair behind her ear. 'It's the woman that makes the fragrance romantic, *carissima*, not the other way round, and *you* make it sexy and alluring.'

His words sent her into chaos. The sound of his deepened voice and the promise in the emerald eyes that met hers made her ache for so much more.

Catriona swallowed. Why was she hesitating? Every nerve, every pulse in her body was telling her that she wanted him. Still, not like this – a casual encounter prompted by a brief, transitory desire on his side and an indefinable feeling on hers. But maybe this was all there was for her. She might want more, but she was still sane enough to recognize that she could be crying for the moon.

'Caterina …' he whispered again, taking her chin between his thumb and forefinger and tilting her face up towards him.

She was trembling as if in frost, as if in a fever, unable to control her own racing blood. 'Umberto …' she said huskily.

He reached out and lifted the heavy fall of hair, letting his hand stroke her neck and round to her throat, caressing the delicate line of her jaw with his thumb, making her shudder as her legs almost curled under her.

Umberto bent his head towards her, touching her mouth with his in a kiss as light as a drifting feather, and Catriona learned that the lips she had thought sensuous were everything that she had never allowed herself to imagine.

Umberto's hand moved again under her hair, clasping the nape of her neck, pulling her towards him as his kiss deepened, lengthened and possessed. Letting his hands slide the length of her body to her hips, he moulded her against him in a slow sweet fusion that made her thrillingly aware of his desire for her.

'See the effect you have on me,' he whispered as they pulled apart, his eyes glittering with almost stunned surprise as though searching hers for an answer she did not possess.

'I'm sorry, I've never …' her voice trailed off, too embarrassed to admit that no man had kissed her before, let alone a kiss that left her whole world reeling.

Catriona blushed once more, hiding her face against him, but he slipped a hand under her chin, forcing it up so that she had to look at him. 'Don't worry, *cara*, you've nothing to apologize for. I couldn't help myself,' he said, his voice husky. His expression now became fathomless. 'Come, let's walk up.'

As they walked together closely up the hill, Catriona turned her head away, unable to meet his gaze, but she knew that he glanced at her frequently. The silence swirled around them like the mist around the tower; his arm had slipped around her so that now she could feel his hand gently in the small of her back.

They entered the town through the sturdy old gateway and climbed the steep cobbles, winding their way from street to narrow street through ancient arches. The surroundings were so medieval it was as though the present had been banished altogether.

They passed by beetling walls, pierced with tiny unglazed windows, their original worm-eaten shutters closed to the night air. Some of the old dwellings had been turned into shops, their narrow doors reached by worn steps. With the merest flight of fancy one could picture a peasant in his tattered greatcoat and old-fashioned breeches climbing the slope that led to the top or some old-time priest wending his way with swinging cassock, dreaming of ecclesiastical matters as his fingers moved along a rosary.

Finally, they came to a high brick wall right at the top of the hill, a little out of the way. 'We're here,' Umberto announced, the first to break the silence they seemed to have tacitly kept as they worked their way up the hillside.

'I always thought this was a private house,' Catriona said with surprise, recognizing the black gate in the wall.

'Patience, Caterina *cara*,' he grinned as he rang the intercom and gave his name.

They walked through a narrow, arched avenue lined with plane trees, at the end of which stood a building on a large plateau above. To Catriona it didn't look like a restaurant, its deep buttresses surmounted by pinnacles and vast windows patterned with bar tracery. 'It looks like a church.'

'It was once a church,' Umberto told her, 'but it was almost destroyed in the nineteenth century. Then it was bought in the 1920s and turned into a private members' club with a restaurant and a handful of bedrooms.'

'Have you been here often?'

'Before I bought the house it was handy. Being only twenty minutes from Nice, it was a good place to stay between long-haul flights. Besides, the restaurant has three Michelin stars and the service is *ecclente*. I do have a weakness for good food,' he said, smiling.

Catriona looked up at the impressive building. How much more sophisticated a life Umberto had led than her own, she thought, feeling suddenly provincial and inexperienced.

Umberto carried on. 'The place never changes. Peaceful and yet exciting … Like true love, which shares those very qualities and retains them forever.'

True love? Catriona felt a startled little leap of her pulses that he should say and think such a thing. She stole a furtive glance but he was strolling along nonchalantly, hands in pockets, the merest smile touching his lips.

'Even before I bought my house in Villefranche I came here when I gave concerts in Antibes and Cannes. As I said, it's handy.'

They rounded the edifice, the front of which faced the hills, the back looking south towards the sea. The lower walls were pierced by small windows with a distinctive curved triangle shape. Despite its decoration, the exterior was relatively simple and austere, giving little hint of the richness Umberto assured her lay within.

They were greeted by two waiters at the door.

'Ah, *signor* Monteverdi. How wonderful to see you again! It has been a long time,' exclaimed the older of the two men. 'We thought you would be visiting us a few weeks ago when you gave your concert in Nice.'

The composer smiled. '*L'homme propose et Dieu dispose*, man proposes and God disposes … I intended to come, but then something came up and I couldn't.'

'Your usual table, *signore,* next to the window? It is free tonight.'

'Yes, please.'

'*Incroyable*,' Catriona murmured as she gazed out into the dark night through the great arched Gothic windows. It was all so romantic …

The night was of the softest blue as wisps of cloud moved slowly across a pale full moon, while below the walls cultivated land spread in ordered, terraced symmetry either side of steeply tumbling paths. In the distance the sea seemed to have withdrawn into remoteness, the ocean waves suddenly frozen under Cap d'Antibes' flashing lighthouse beam. For Catriona tonight, there was no grander or more exhilarating view in the whole world.

Although the room was of average size with lovely ornate gilt pillars, the vaulted ceiling was very high. The walls were richly decorated and many of the windows bore images of saints and rosettes in stained glass. A large rose window with flamboyant tracery dominated the western wall, while the quatrefoils of the dado arcade, inset with painted and gilded glass, displayed scenes of saints and martyrs. Umberto and Catriona climbed the few steps to a raised dais where the tables were small and intimate, and from where one could easily look out of the windows while dining. Below them were a few refectory tables with benches, which were used for banquets when the room was rented to a club member for the night, Umberto explained as they took their seats.

'It's a stunning room, larger than many a chapel, and these beautiful old paintings and statues are wonderful, don't you think?'

'Yes, this place is amazing,' Catriona sighed, still surveying her surroundings in awe. 'And the scenery outside seems so unreal,' she added, looking through the window. As she felt Umberto's emerald eyes on her and knew that he was studying her, she could hardly believe what was happening. Romance had played an elusive role in her life but now she was actually on a date with the man of her dreams.

She turned and glanced up at him. A smile was playing around his lips and his gaze slowly roamed over her features until they settled on her eyes. 'I wonder ... what are you thinking as you look at me with such innocent eyes? You, *carissima*, are like a pool that hides things beneath a limpid surface.'

'You make me sound secretive,' she murmured. She thanked the heavens that he seemed unaware of her feelings and it was something she wanted to keep that way.

'Not secretive, just a little remote. Has anybody told you how beautiful those golden eyes are?'

Catriona shrugged. 'They're too big for my face.'

He tilted his head to one side, still studying her features as though weighing up her claim. 'Ah, but that irregularity is exactly what gives your face piquancy and charm. If I were an artist I'd want to capture that inspirational uniqueness somehow and immortalize it in a portrait or a sculpture.'

She shook her head, embarrassed by such words, and changed the subject in earnest. 'This place is so beautiful, I wonder if I'm dreaming.'

The waiter brought the menus and asked if they would like an aperitif before their meal.

'I think it's time for that celebratory glass of champagne, don't you think?'

Catriona laughed. 'Yes, why not? I've already had one this evening but another can't hurt,' she said enthusiastically.

'*Perfetto.*' He turned to the waiter. 'Unfortunately, I'm driving so we won't have a bottle. Just two glasses of Moët, please.'

The waiter nodded courteously and after he was gone Umberto picked up the elegantly printed card in front of him. 'Shall we look at the menu?'

'Yes, I'm starving.'

He grinned. 'Good! I like a woman who enjoys her food. Women nowadays are always thinking about their weight and I find it totally spoils the pleasure of eating out. I'm glad you're not obsessional around food and don't suppress your appetite.'

Was it her imagination or did he seem to focus on her more intently as he spoke? Catriona felt herself blush under the ardent stare of his disturbing eyes, which now moved from her face, lingering only a second on her throat then travelling lower, before once again holding her gaze. All sorts of strange sensations were assailing her at the thought of which appetite he was referring to.

'I just generally try to be healthy, I suppose,' she replied awkwardly and lowered her eyes quickly to concentrate on the menu.

The waiter came back with two sparkling flutes and Umberto clinked his glass against hers. 'To Caterina, the opera singer.'

Catriona smiled shyly and took a sip of the pale bubbles. A feeling of warmth invaded her ... magic was stealing over the night. She took another sip and returned to the menu.

'So difficult to choose,' Catriona said eventually.

'I would recommend *Manureva d'Oursins* to start with. It's a very colourful dish made of sea urchins and crème fraîche. A speciality of the house and a favourite of the Surrealist painter Chagall, who lived in Saint Paul de Vence and was a regular at this club.'

'Strangely enough, I've never been tempted to taste sea urchins.'

The smile Umberto gave her was loaded with mischief. 'There's a first time for everything, *cara*. Trust me, you'll like them. They are *molto appetitosi*, very moreish.'

'So be it,' Catriona smiled.

'In Italy, sea urchins are regarded as hearts of petrified children or stones fallen from the sky. Superstition has it that if one places them on the roof of the house it makes for a happy home. They are also, of course, regarded as an aphrodisiac. In some remote fishing villages, they are still a traditional part of a newlywed couple's dinner ...'

Catriona smiled again, with a demureness that hid any recognition of the allusions he was making. Did he realize what he was doing to her?

'And I also recommend their *Ragout de Chevreau*.'

This time she laughed openly. 'I've never tasted goat. *Maman* has always been afraid of Mediterranean fever, which these animals carry apparently.'

Umberto winked. 'Maybe we can make an exception tonight and not obey *Maman* to the letter.'

Catriona inclined her head; she was well beyond that already. 'I submit without a murmur, *signore*,' she said, inwardly chiding herself for mentioning her mother. How young and immature she'd sounded. She wished she was as worldly and alluring as the women with whom he was used to dining. They, undoubtedly, would know how to join in his flirtatious banter.

The waiter came along to take their order. Umberto had chosen for himself the same dishes as he had recommended to Catriona and, as he ordered, she looked out of the window and gave herself up to the almost eerie beauty of the night.

'You look miles away, Caterina. And so serious. What are you thinking?' he said once the waiter had gone.

Catriona's brow wrinkled. 'You must think me very unsophisticated.'

He smiled. 'Not at all, *carissima*. You simply have that uncomplicated freshness about you that is very rare these days ... *come posso spiegarlo*, how can I explain it, pure and unadulterated,' he added, his voice quieter and more thoughtful.

'I went to a convent back in England and I've always been closely chaperoned and guarded. You see, I'm an only child and my mother was widowed when I was quite young,' she explained.

Umberto said nothing and just nodded. 'As you know, I'm an only child too, although my experience was very different. It probably helped that I was a boy.' He gave a quiet chuckle. 'I was left to run wild in the grounds of our big house on Lake Como while my mother was away, which she invariably was. Adelina, bless her, didn't believe in overprotecting me. "I *ragazzi devono crescere per diventare uomini*, boys must grow up to be men," she would say.'

'And yet she told you legends.'

'Ah, but that, *cara*, was when I was very young. From the age of eleven I was left pretty much to my own devices. I was precocious … *very* precocious,' he murmured, smiling to himself as if caught up in a private joke.

Catriona wished she could read his thoughts and the feeling that she was out of her depth returned. She took a fortifying sip of champagne and, not knowing how to respond, persevered with her questioning.

'You said your cousin – what was his name…?'

Umberto's smile faded. 'Giacomo.'

'Giacomo … you said he lives at the house with you. Did you grow up with him?'

'I did.'

'It must have been a bit like having a brother.'

'Giacomo?' He gave a slight laugh, adding enigmatically, 'No, Giacomo was nothing like a brother. We didn't spend much time together.'

She put her glass down and fiddled with the stem. 'And Silvana grew up with you too?'

'Later on, when we were teenagers. When her mother died, Calandra took Silvana in. There was room for all of us in such a large house.' He levelled his gaze at her. 'Did you find it lonely, growing up on your own?'

Catriona noticed how adept he was at changing the subject and his stare succeeded in distracting her. She shrugged. 'Sometimes. But I had school friends, and *Maman* and I are very close.'

Just then the waiter came with the first course and placed Catriona's napkin on her lap with a flourish. 'Oh! This looks delicious, and so pretty,' she exclaimed, looking down at the three urchins set upon a small bed of saffron rice on a blue plate. 'What wonderful colours! It's like the golden tones of Provence with the blue of the Mediterranean.'

'A beautiful painting. It's like our eyes eat first, *eh*?'

They ate in silence for a while, which was broken when a photographer approached the table. '*Buona sera, signore*. Good to see you again. May I take a photograph of you with the charming *signorina*?'

'Of course,' Umberto grinned, his eyes twinkling at Catriona. 'As Cesare Pavese quite rightly said: "We don't remember days, we remember moments."'

He reached out, covering her hand with his, and an exhilarating current slipped through Catriona's whole body. Her eyes caught a glimpse of the underside of his wrist, where a dark red birthmark, shaped peculiarly like a crescent, stained the skin. It made her want to trace it slowly with her fingers, so much so she felt herself blush. His gaze held hers for a moment.

'That is, if you don't mind?' She swallowed and nodded. They both smiled up at the camera.

There was a flash, then the photographer gave a little bow. '*Prego, signore*,' he said as Umberto nodded his thanks. 'I'll leave the photograph with Batiste. Enjoy your meal, *signorina*,' he added, before moving away to offer his services at another table.

Umberto was still holding on to Catriona's hand. He turned it over tenderly, brushing his thumb across the delicate skin.

'Like a lotus, curled and a delicate pink,' he murmured. 'Did you know the Ancient Greeks made wine from the fruit of the lotus and it was thought to produce contentment …?' He released her hand and sat back in his chair, biting into a piece of bread, watching her with his piercing green eyes. Against the medieval background of the room he seemed entirely at home, his dark angular features as dramatic as those of a magnificent angel in human form.

Catriona tried to ignore the way her skin felt as if he'd left a searing trail of fire where he held it. Somehow she found her voice. 'I'm afraid I haven't read as much mythology as I'd like to, I've mostly concentrated on my music.'

'There are so many myths in music. Most operas are taken from legends.'

Naturally, she knew that. Why hadn't she mentioned that herself? 'Yes, of course.' She blushed, kicking herself for her youth and inadequacy as a conversationalist. 'That champagne must be fuddling my brain.'

'I'll get some water.' Umberto snapped his fingers and a waiter rushed to the table. *'Une bouteille d'eau minerale, s'il vous plait.'*

She thanked him as he poured some water into a glass before adding, 'Your mother appeared as Eurydice in Rossi's *Orfeo*, didn't she?'

'Yes, she did. One of many tales of the bewitching nature of music. So, you know the legend?'

She sipped at her water. 'Yes, of course. Orpheus makes the gods jealous because his music is so wonderful. It was said that nothing could resist the sound of his lyre, even the trees and rocks were entranced by it.'

The way you and your music entrance me, Umberto.

Unaware of her thoughts, he took up the story. 'Then his beloved wife and muse, Eurydice, is bitten by a viper and dies, and the grieving Orpheus travels into the underworld to get her back. He plays his lyre with such grace and skill that the sound of it sends Cerberus, the three-headed guard dog of Hades, to sleep. Finally, he's granted Eurydice, but on one condition: that he shouldn't look at her until he gets to the surface. He can hear her footsteps behind him as he walks towards the gates of Hades and, just as he's nearly there, he turns, unable to resist.'

Catriona found herself watching Umberto's mouth as he spoke, the same mouth that less than an hour ago had kissed her so sensuously. 'He sees her like a ghostly mist and she fades to nothing, returning to her place among the dead.'

A shiver slipped down Catriona's spine. 'Such a lovely story, and so very sad.'

'Yes, indeed, *cara*. In his grief, Orpheus wants only death but Jupiter tells him that he and his beloved, along with his lyre, will be transformed into constellations.'

'Immortal. Like the power of music.'

'And yet both of them die in the end.'

'That's a pessimistic interpretation.'

His eyes twinkled with amusement. 'Is there not a pessimistic streak in many musicians? Tragedy has always inspired great music, after all.'

Catriona returned to her champagne, tasting a little thoughtfully. She could well believe that this man sitting before her had a dark and passionate side. How else could he produce such sublime compositions?

'When did you know that you wanted to be a composer?'

He shrugged. 'As long as I can remember I was surrounded by music. It never occurred to me that I would be anything but a composer, and I loved the sound of the piano … I was fascinated by the black and white notes.'

'You play divinely, but I suppose you know that.'

'It is always flattering to hear it from the lips of a beautiful and talented *signorina* like you, Caterina.' Oh, the way he said her name! It sounded like music in his mouth. She glanced at him shyly, feeling the tingling relaxation induced by the champagne. 'You're very gifted yourself. Have you always wanted to be an opera singer?'

'Yes, I suppose I have. I guess music runs in my blood. My grandmother on my mother's side was a cellist in the French National Orchestra in Paris.'

'You have a most unusual and beautiful voice, almost unique in its individuality.' His face suddenly became serious. 'Tell me, do you want to sing more than anything else in the world?'

Catriona nodded wordlessly.

'Well, your future depends primarily on you yourself, and your capacity to work. I saw how single-minded my mother was.

Nothing else must get in the way if you want to make it to the top. Nothing.'

Nothing else did get in the way until you came along, Catriona told him silently, but aloud she said: 'I'm very well aware of the dedication it will demand of me.'

He rubbed his chin pensively, his green eyes appraising her. 'Yes, I think you probably are.'

'And you,' she said, emboldened by the champagne, 'your star is rising. You allow nothing to interfere with your ambitions?'

His eyes were alight with amusement but he answered without prevarication. 'Of course not. It's a sacrifice we musicians must make.'

The next hour went by easily and Catriona was glad that her initial nerves had relaxed, though the awareness between them remained heightened. They spoke of music, art and of the world of theatre in general. Umberto asked her many questions about herself casually, throwing them out lightly into the conversation. He was a brilliant raconteur but also a good listener.

When the meal came to an end, Umberto called the waiter to order some coffee.

'One espresso for me and one Café Diablo for *Mademoiselle*, please.'

Catriona looked puzzled. 'Café Diablo? It sounds rather naughty.'

He held up his hand, gesturing with his thumb and forefinger. '*Solo un po*', only a little bit,' he replied with twinkling eyes. 'If I were spending the night here, I would have asked for a Café Diablo. It's a great treat and, in my opinion, the best way to drink coffee – especially when the cognac is as good as the one they serve here. You don't have to drink it all, but it's definitely worth tasting.'

When the coffee came, Umberto took it from the waiter and passed it over to Catriona. The flame licked blue across the surface of the coffee cup in his hand, and it seemed to her that a similar flame crept and curled in the depths of his eyes.

Catriona smiled and drank her coffee slowly. The warm brew was not only delicious but the pleasurable heat invaded every part of her body. Was it so enjoyable because Umberto was sitting opposite her?

When they had finished, Umberto paid the bill and once more they were out in the night air. He offered her his jacket but again she declined. The hot coffee had done a good job. The full moon was now high in the vaulted velvet sky, flooding their path with its brightness as they walked towards the gates.

'That was wonderful,' she murmured as they left the grounds of the restaurant. 'Thank you.'

Umberto put his arm around her. 'It's for me to thank you, Caterina, for your most refreshing company.'

The scent of lemons wafted through the air. It was dark in the tangled narrow streets, a kind of muffled darkness that made it hard to avoid the loose stones of every size and shape on the path as they made their way down. A sudden languor had swept over Catriona, and she realized that the champagne and brandy-infused coffee had affected her more than she'd expected. She felt so good clasped next to Umberto. All she could do was let him guide her steps, trusting that he would prevent her from slipping on some fragments of rock beneath her feet. There were only a few lights in the houses they passed, shining brightly through high windows. Nothing stirred in the warm night, everything appeared stilled for all eternity in a strange and haunting tableau before their eyes. It was as if a spell had been laid on the sleeping town, as well as on them, as if they had been carried away and deposited in some unknown land. No sound broke the frozen hush except their steps on the crisp surface of the stones.

Catriona's cheeks burned and her heart was racing. As she leaned in a little closer and Umberto's arm tightened around her, she felt agitated and alive. In the silence they walked on down the cobbled way that led to their parked car. *What a lovely night of danger was this!* Catriona exclaimed to herself as she tried to marshal her startled thoughts, but she was dizzy and overcome by an overpowering torpor. She sighed and her eyes closed just as they were going down the steps at the great gateway of the ancient citadel.

Suddenly Catriona's cry tore the silence of the night as she slipped down the last few steps, landing on her side. In no time Umberto was beside her, helping her up.

'Have you hurt yourself?' he asked in a worried voice.

'Not seriously,' she said. 'I must have tripped over. I didn't see the steps.'

Her dress was ripped, from the waist all the way down one side, as were her tights. Her leg was badly scratched and smeared with mud and blood.

Before she could protest, he had picked her up, locking her against his body, and was striding quickly towards the car. The heat of him and the feeling of his hard chest against the side of her breast made her feel doubly light-headed, all at once glad she no longer needed the use of her legs.

'I'll take you to hospital,' he said.

'No, no, please. It's only a few scratches, really. I'll go home, have a bath and I'll be as good as new.'

'I can't let you go home like this in a torn dress. What will they say?'

'There's no one at home. I told Sidonie to go home.'

'Do you have any disinfectant … plasters?'

'Must have. Not exactly sure where she keeps them but I'm sure I'll find something in the bathroom …'

He frowned. 'Not good enough. Your leg needs cleaning properly.' He paused, weighing the options. 'There's nothing at Les Platanes. I'd better take you to my house in Villefranche.

I have some Betadine and a proper first aid kit there. You don't want to get an infection.'

He was taking her to his other house, alone.

The thought wavered across her mind that Umberto was straight out of Stendhal with his brooding power, his pagan face and his insistence that she obey him. Her fingers clasped the warmth of his neck nervously and, through the flickering of her lashes, she saw his face bent to hers – close enough for his breath to stir across her eyelids. A dangerous flare of need lit in her mind and her anxiety took on an edge of excitement at the forbidden adventure of it all. She went limp, curving closer to the warm male scent of him.

They had reached the car now and Umberto settled Catriona comfortably before slipping into the driver's seat.

The Maserati glided through the night, bound for Villefranche, as the countryside rolled by under the full moon. Umberto was driving silently and quickly, a dark frown on his face. Catriona could make out his powerful profile and his hard, sensual mouth defined in the penumbra of the car. What was he thinking? Was he annoyed? She'd been clumsy. What a disappointing end to a perfect evening – and it was all her fault. He was probably irritated with her, and with good reason. Dejected, she stared ahead at the countryside as the car pressed on.

'Look across there!' Umberto pointed suddenly to the way they had driven earlier. The whole coast was like a strip of twinkling stars. 'We could be on an island, cut off from the world.' At his words Catriona relaxed – he wasn't cross with her after all.

Soon they were running along the seafront corniche and it wasn't long before they had reached Col de Villefranche. The view of the village harbour on one hand and Nice, Antibes and the Estérels on the other was breathtaking.

The moon was shining her silver beams over the ocean and when they had reached the extreme point of the promontory Catriona couldn't help but exclaim: *'Oh, que c'est beau!'*

Umberto nodded, still looking ahead. '*Sì, davvero magnifico!*'

A truly magnificent sight burst into view on the east side. It embraced the promontory of Saint Jean and Cap Ferrat, with the lighthouse standing out in the sea, and the deep gulf of Villefranche encompassing the indented coastline of the Mediterranean as far as Bordighera, with the little town of Èze standing on the top of a high mountain, overlooking the deep glittering waters.

The road wound round the point and they began their descent down the hill on the west side of the bay of Villefranche, passing along the very edge of precipitous cliffs. By now the night breeze had sobered Catriona up and she was wide awake, although still thinking herself caught up in a dream from which she did not want to be roused.

The little town of Villefranche was a quaint Moorish-looking place, with steep narrow streets and most luxuriant vegetation, situated at the head of the bay nestling at the foot of the lofty Maritime Alps. Umberto smiled and turned his face to her for the first time since they had left Saint Paul de Vence. 'It won't be long now,' he said. 'I'll be able to look at those nasty grazes and there's plenty of hot water for a shower.'

'Thank you,' she whispered. 'You've been very kind, worrying about me like this. I hope I haven't spoiled your evening with my clumsiness.'

'Not at all, *carissima*. It just means I'll have more time in your company which, believe me, I've found delightful.'

I've nothing to wear, she thought, wondering what she would change into once she had cleaned up.

As if he had read her mind, Umberto said: 'Don't worry about clothes. Guests come and go at Villa Rossini. There's always a supply of spare clothes of all shapes and sizes.' He gave her a sidelong glance and grinned mischievously. 'I'm sure you won't pose a problem.'

Catriona gazed at his gorgeous smile. Why was he so incredibly attractive? She smiled back awkwardly, her heart beating a little faster, and let out the breath that she had been holding.

The Maserati twisted and turned down the tortuous streets – past villas surrounded by high walls and gardens with ancient cypresses, *pins parasols* and native beech trees – until they were almost at sea level. They continued a while along the asphalted corniche before Umberto drove through a set of tall, wrought-iron gates that opened by remote control.

'*Eccoci*, we're here,' he said, pulling up at the back of the house. 'Don't move.' He slid out of his seat and a few strides brought him round to her side. A small gasp escaped Catriona's lips as his strong arms picked her up and carried her towards the front of the house.

Chapter 4

The Villa Rossini stood facing the sea above a private sandy and rocky beach that was reached by a spiral staircase. The house was much smaller than Catriona had expected; a low-lying round building, all on one floor, with arched windows and doors that overlooked the whole of the bay across to the Italian Riviera.

The garden at the back of the house was floodlit, illuminating a leafed pergola and a frescoed fountain, with a beautiful view of the moonlit forest and the whole glory of the Alps, which gave the garden setting a lingering quality of enchantment.

Umberto carried Catriona through the pergola to the magnificent, raised, stone-flagged terrace that encircled the house. It was almost as large as the villa itself and paved with colourful *Pierre de Bourgogne*. Bounded by a low wall, it was set with statues and ancient Provençal urns planted with dwarf orange and lemon trees, laden with fruit. The air was filled with their heady fragrance, which mingled with the smell of iodine and salt coming from the sea.

Catriona was immediately caught up in the bewitching feel of the place. Yet what enthralled her most of all were Umberto's arms enveloping her and the feel of those strong, confident hands holding her. It was as though she was being carried through a romantic dream.

'It's magic,' she whispered as they rounded the villa.

Umberto placed her down gently and searched in his pocket for the key. 'It's not very large, but it's large enough for me,' he said with a smile, unlocking the front door. 'Are you okay to walk?' he asked solicitously, and Catriona replied that she was, before stepping a little gingerly over the threshold.

She was immediately in a central *salone*, a wide room bathed in moonlight, and even before Umberto had turned on the light, Catriona noticed that it was bare, save for a black baby grand piano and a stool. Painted white, the room had large picture windows and doors on to the terrace that framed the breathtaking scenery outside, a beautiful oak parquet floor laid out in geometric squares, and a huge stone fireplace on the back wall. The very starkness of the place gave it a sense of grandeur.

'It's lovely,' Catriona said and stepped inside, mesmerized by the view through the window opposite.

'The house was originally divided into smaller rooms but I knocked down the walls. Now, I have only this room and a kind of compact library, as well as the bedroom, bathroom and kitchen.'

Catriona glanced back at him, thinking what a perfect haven for two this was. How many other women had he brought here?

As if guessing her thoughts, he added: 'I live alone here. I like the solitude.'

Umberto's eyes twinkled. He took a step towards her and she caught her breath as he scooped her up again and carried her into the bedroom, turned on the bedside lamp and laid her on the large four-poster bed covered in beautiful dark-green brocade.

This room was quite different to the stark *salone*, where the piano was king. It was painted a very pale green and had a white ceiling scattered with branches of old coloured stucco, in a design as gentle and tangible as a piece of music by Mozart. Two great glass-panelled doors, which Umberto opened, gave on to the terrace overlooking the sea. The room was a dream!

'What's more relaxing than sitting in a field of flowers looking out over the sea, *eh*?' Umberto said, enjoying her dazed reaction.

He walked over to a door in the opposite wall, opened it and switched on the light. 'The bathroom is here. Feel free to use the clothes and clean towels in the cupboard. In the cabinet above the washbasins you'll find all the disinfectant and plasters you need. There's plenty of hot water.'

Catriona smiled gratefully. 'Thank you.'

'*Di nulla è nemmeno parlarne*, don't even mention it.'

The bathroom was as luxurious as the bedroom but minimalistic and very masculine. The stone walls and floor were of rough green onyx – rugged but beautiful. There was a mirror down one side, next to which a floor-to-ceiling window looked out on to the terrace, with a roll-down blind for privacy. There was a bath, a walk-in open shower and two sinks under which were cupboards. Catriona opened one and found towels and a variety of toiletries – men's and women's – stored in neat rows. The perfect love nest, she thought, her heart giving an uncomfortable little squeeze … but tonight she wouldn't dwell on such things.

Catriona took off her lovely dress, now torn and soiled, and stepped into the shower. She stood under the warm water for a long while, enjoying the heat seeping into her bones.

Half an hour later she was clean and dressed in a tan kaftan she'd found hanging in one of the cupboards. Her hair, washed and dried, shone like chestnut silk hanging down her back. She glanced at herself in the mirror and, for the first time in her life, she was aware of her looks. *I'm actually quite pretty*, she told herself. But was she pretty enough to compete with all the elegant and beautiful women who surely paraded through the virtuoso's life?

Back in Umberto's bedroom, Catriona turned off the light and sat on the bed in the dark. The windows were open, as he had left them. Through them, a few miles out over the moving waters, she could see the beam flashing from the lighthouse on the rock. Further up the coast, another light winked and beyond that yet another – a long way off, small but bright. The sound of the ocean filled the room … it was warm and fitful gusts of sea air caressed her cheeks. Catriona could hear the waves breaking below, though she could see only a vague white line of breakers stretching away unevenly on the beach. The cadence of waves hitting the rocks was a lovely but lonely sound, very much the keynote of this place. *Was Umberto ever lonely?* she wondered.

A knock at the door interrupted her reverie.

'Are you all right, Caterina?'

'Yes, yes! I'm fine, thank you,' she said, getting up. Ignoring her leg's slight ache, she hurried to the door and opened it.

Umberto was standing on the threshold with a glass of what looked like whisky or cognac in his hand. He had changed into comfortable trousers and a linen shirt.

'Why in the dark, *cara*?'

'I was listening to the waves. It's so quiet here.'

'Ah, the waves. Strange and wonderful music. I listen to them in bed at night and the sound lulls me to sleep. Usually, next day when I wake up, the first notes of a melody have taken shape in my mind. Did you find the antiseptic and plasters?'

'Oh, I showered but didn't get round to it.'

He frowned and put his glass down on the chest of drawers opposite the bed. 'You need to clean those scratches properly.'

'I'm sure I can manage,' she called out as he disappeared into the bathroom but, as he reappeared with a first-aid kit, she met a look in his eyes that told her he would brook no argument.

He motioned to the bed. 'Please, sit.' She did as she was told and perched on the end of it, pulling the kaftan up to her knee. Umberto inspected the graze gently. Catriona sucked in a quiet breath as she felt his hand slip behind her leg to keep her steady as he dabbed some antiseptic on the side of her slim calf, where the cuts were still red. Even though her leg was sore, the feeling of his long, capable fingers on her skin was heavenly. The atmosphere between them thickened, making them keenly aware of each other.

'Am I hurting you?'

'No ... not at all.' Mesmerized, she looked at his face so close to hers but he did not look up at her.

He unpeeled a plaster and pressed it gingerly to her leg. '*Ecco fatto*, there,' he said softly. 'That should do it.' He stood up and their gazes locked, emerald on golden brown, and a deep sigh escaped his lips as he picked up his glass.

They walked into the *salone*, which was lit with tall, two-arm wall lamps in the shape of pineapples. The golden light they diffused was mellow and gave the room a romantic, muted atmosphere.

'Will you join me in a drink?'

Catriona had already drunk two glasses of champagne and she wasn't used to alcohol. Although a little voice at the back of her mind advised caution, she liked the state of hazy euphoria it created in her. 'Maybe something light?'

'A small glass of grappa, perhaps?'

'Ah, yes! All I know about grappa is that it's almost Italy's national drink, but I've never tasted it.' As she said the words she winced at how unsophisticated she must sound to this worldly man.

'You're right, it's my country's most popular drink, so you should try some.'

Umberto went into what Catriona guessed was his library and came back with a decanter and a small glass. He took her hand and poured a couple of drops of grappa on the back of it. 'Rub it in with your other hand, *cara*, and then breathe in the aroma.'

Catriona looked puzzled, but did as she was told.

'The friction helps some of the alcohol to evaporate and makes the grappa's natural scents more apparent. Now, sip it slowly, *cara* … it is quite a potent drink,' he added as he poured one finger of the pale tan liquid into the glass and handed it to her. Catriona met the emerald eyes that held hers for a moment and she felt them heat her blood in a sudden leap of desire. He had kissed her once before, would he do so again? Hoping, fearing he would, she moved away towards the piano.

His eyes followed her intently. 'You're a very beautiful woman, Caterina, but I suppose men have told you that already.'

Catriona felt herself blush. 'Will you play something … maybe your new concerto?'

'Perhaps another piece.' His gaze seemed to refocus on her in a different way. 'There's a refrain taking shape in my mind right now as I look at you, *tesoro*,' he murmured, putting down his glass and the decanter of grappa on the top of the baby grand. He took his place on the stool and smiled up at her, then began to play a sweet, uplifting melody with one hand.

'Something about you, makes me think of a mysterious pool, showing glimpses of delight beneath its surface and yet hiding something tantalizing … out of reach.'

He then began to play in earnest as Catriona stood beside the piano, sipping her drink while she listened and watched Umberto's long, slender fingers move gracefully up and down the keyboard. He was wonderful, his fingers were sure, strong and dextrous. The music filled the room as passionately as moonlight filled the darkness. There was something sensual about his hands touching the ivory keys, something exciting, something erotic. She tried to dismiss such thoughts but it was hard for her to separate his touch from the music that enveloped her, holding her captive.

Umberto watched her face with a dreamy quality in his eyes as the music swelled and grew under his touch, a wild wind moving about restlessly. He had shifted into another key and now his playing took off, moving them both into another world with his fingertips as surely as if he had transported them physically to a land of magic. It was a world they shared, one they both knew by heart. United by their love of music, wordlessly they spoke the same language.

Soon the music had changed from the lovely uplifting melody to a more urgent, harsh tempo, contemporary and new. Catriona felt her heart begin to soar. There was power in this and she found herself reacting time after time to the dramatic swings in mood. Putting her glass down, she leaned unselfconsciously with both elbows on the shiny ebony surface. Her long hair fell over her shoulders and she was so caught up in the music that she was oblivious to her own radiant reflection in the highly polished wood, while Umberto's gaze kept moving back and forth from her face to the keyboard, the expression in his glittering emerald irises as mesmerizing as his music.

The notes began to pound harder and harder, an imperious, majestic sound with rolling chords that gathered momentum as the melody surged over the top like a passionate blaze of fire. Umberto was lost in his music, his dark head bent over the keyboard, his eyes following the difficult patterns his hands had mastered as the composition softened to a complicated and repetitive movement. When he finally looked up again, his eyes crinkled around the edges as the mood of the music changed to a capricious, whimsical note. The music rose to a crescendo, the lovely and uplifting main theme he had played at the beginning reaching its climax in a sudden burst of energy, the sound of the final chord melting into the quiet swish of the sea beyond.

They were both silent for a while, his fingers still on the keyboard. 'Songe d'une Nuit d'Amour,' he murmured.

'Oh, Umberto, that was truly magnificent …' She was lost for anything else to say.

Catriona looked up at those emerald green eyes and saw the fire in them and knew they reflected that in her own. He was excited. The electric thrill emanating from him was utterly infectious.

'It's you that created it, Caterina. You are an infinitely powerful muse. It's not your beauty, you see, but your natural lack of artifice that inspires me.' He stood up, poured himself another drink and, walking to the French windows that were flung wide open, stepped on to the terrace.

'Come …' he commanded, his eyes still smouldering, 'enjoy the beauty of the bay with me.' There was passion in his voice, but also pride.

Catriona followed him wordlessly. She caught her breath at the utter splendour of the view that met her gaze. Below the house lay the darkly shimmering and moving sea and she could see the masts and ropes of the fishing boats in the little harbour of Villefranche, frosted by the orb of night. The bay was hung with a necklace of houses enveloped in shrouds of night mist. Above them, the full moon smiled its crooked smile and stars burned away in pale gold fire that flamed like little jewelled pinheads, filling the sky with their unusual brightness. The tree-lined cliffs flanking the bay seemed to imprison the coastal town and its waters in their shadowed arms.

Standing barely an inch from Umberto now, Catriona was conscious of the warmth of his body and the masculine scents that she was coming to recognize – shaving soap and amber – filled her nostrils for one heady moment. They stood silently watching nature's grandeur in all its magnificent force.

'Utterly spectacular,' she looked up at him with glowing eyes. 'You must love this place with every beat of your heart.'

'You're right. This place is very dear to me,' he replied distractedly. 'It's different from the other towns of France. It has a totally unique atmosphere, maybe because it was once part of Italy.'

'Yes, it does have a spirit all of its own.'

'Everything here speaks of the sea. The bars are crowded with fishermen and sailors and there's always a carefree air of mariners on shore leave, with accordions playing dance tunes. I often go walking on the docks and all through the day there's the sound of hammering and scraping of boats. This place has a music of its own.' He took a sip of brandy.

'Fishing nets are spread for repairs in front of the chandlers' shops and in the early morning I frequently stop to talk to the fishermen and buy a fish that is still alive and wriggling in its bucket.' Umberto's nostrils flared a little. 'It's utterly captivating. You see,' he laughed, making a helpless gesture with his hands, '*mi sono innamorato* … I'm in love …'

Catriona felt a startled little leap of her pulses at his words. True, he was speaking about Villefranche but still, the reserved English part of her was disconcerted by the Latin tendency to say outright what sprang into the mind.

He gulped down his drink in one go. 'Come, let's go for a walk on the beach.'

She looked up at him and smiled hesitantly. What was she doing here in this house? What was she waiting for? She couldn't think straight. Her eyes locked with his and once more she put any thought of caution to the back of her mind. She knew now there was no way he would be able to drive her home and at this hour she would never get a taxi. All she could do now was accept his hospitality with the best possible grace.

Umberto held out his hand. She put hers in the strong palm, a thrill of pleasure running through her as they walked down on to the beach. Glancing down at her hand in his, Catriona knew then, all warnings aside, that she had met a man to whom she could lose her heart … forever.

The silence of the night was stupefying. No sound broke the frozen hush except the soft crunch of their steps and the waves whispering gently as they slid up on to the sand. The sky was a deep, unclouded mirror above the moonlit ocean. Catriona's feet were cold but she felt nothing now except the exhilaration of being alone with the virtuoso in this magical setting. There was a curious calm within her and she felt as though she was entering some enchanted enclosure where Umberto was the nucleus. Yes, the earth here was too beautiful indeed for anyone but lovers, she found herself thinking, its wanton loveliness by rights for them alone. She belonged in this fairy-tale setting with Umberto Rolando Monteverdi; it was a love story she was living.

They walked in silence at the edge of the shore, where the wavelets died in small bubbles of sea-foam, until they reached the end of the private beach. Here, large rocks and boulders were enthroned in the dark and deep-looking waters.

Umberto turned towards Catriona and was the first to speak. 'This is the boundary of my place,' he told her. 'I often come here for a swim when there's plenty of moonlight. The water is deep but warm because of the rocks. They form a sort of basin that attracts the hot rays of the sun during the day. It's also protected from the stronger current further out. It's a lovely spot.'

Umberto's eyes met Catriona's, deepening to forest green, an unspoken question glittering in their depths. Had it been there all along? Afraid of what she read in them, Catriona turned her head slightly away from him but, waiting, her heart beat expectantly. Umberto reached out his hand and stroked her soft, chestnut hair before pushing back a stray tendril. Touching her chin with his thumb and forefinger, he lifted her face to his and leaned forward. His mouth brushed hers tentatively at first, the pressure becoming more insistent until she yielded to its claim without any restraint or resistance.

The music he had played for her had been an intimate bond and now, as she parted her lips for his tongue, it was as if all the tension and excitement it had created had drained away, leaving them with what had been there between them from the very beginning. An unfamiliar ache of longing was intensifying, drowning out any rational thought as Umberto held her hard against him, their embrace becoming charged with a current of emotion, making Catriona's body tremble with a passion that she hadn't known existed.

Umberto groaned, pulling his mouth away from hers and uttered an oath. 'I need to cool down …' he mumbled, as though to himself, without looking at her. Without further ado, he stripped off his clothes and stood poised at the edge of the rock, gloriously and unselfconsciously naked. Catriona had never seen a naked man in real life but even she could tell that Umberto was well endowed. The urge to touch him was so great that she sat down on a rock, feeling her legs might give way otherwise. Wide-eyed, she watched Umberto as he dived in, coming up again within seconds and letting the water slick back his hair.

He gestured to her. '*Vieni anche tu, l'acqua e' meravigliosa*, join me, the water is wonderful.'

Catriona hesitated. 'But I'm not wearing a bathing suit.'

Umberto laughed, his eyes glittering with mischief. 'Neither am I.'

She shrugged and gave a little demure laugh. 'But I could never do such a thing.'

'Are you not wearing any underwear?'

She looked shocked. 'Of course I'm wearing underwear.'

'*Allora non fa differenza*, then there's no difference. It's the same as wearing a bikini.'

This was madness, she told herself.

'Can you swim?'

'Of course I can swim.'

'*Dai!* So, come on!' he cajoled. 'You don't know what you're missing … it's the most delicious sensation to feel water against one's naked skin.'

The intensity of his concentrated gaze under the moonlight made her tremble. Catriona was tempted. The dull ache low down inside her was refusing to subside, as though she had no control over it; she could feel her gaze drawn to where his body was hidden beneath the water. With a sudden impulse she tore off her kaftan and in her flesh-coloured lace underwear, plunged head-first into the dark water.

She surfaced in front of him, panting a little. The sea was fresh and a shiver ran through her, sobering her up.

Umberto cocked an eyebrow at the strip of cloth that covered her breasts. 'You look almost bare, so why not just be as nature intended? There's truly nothing like being totally naked in the water …' He was merely inches away and looked at her with all sorts of little lights dancing in his jewel-like irises.

'You have the body of a goddess, Caterina, so why suppress its freedom? Why not reward it and pleasure it?'

Catriona closed her eyes briefly to shut out the intoxication of seeing Umberto trembling for the want of touching her. Embarrassed, she sank back down in the water, letting it cover her to her chin, and swam away from him. Still, the physical ache of her own longing was seducing her even without him touching her. She could feel the whisper of the water over her legs, a stirring, swelling press of excitement that communicated itself to her almost by osmosis.

Suddenly, Umberto was behind her. Catriona sucked in her breath as she felt his hands on her back and she turned to face him. Before she knew what he was doing, he had deftly pulled the lacy bra down, freeing her breasts to the gentle sway of the water. His hands were poised to cup the richness he'd revealed but he watched her face. '*Solo se anche tu lo vuoi. Sei tu che decidi*, only if you say so. You make the rules.'

He looked directly into her eyes and she was captured by the vulnerability she saw there. The mute longing she read in them was the final straw to her resistance. Catriona's hands found Umberto's in the water. She brought them up slowly until her fullness pressed into them and she gasped, almost climaxing at his touch.

'*Come sei bella, mia colomba sensuale,* how beautiful you are, my sensual dove.'

'Umberto, I've never …'

'Tell me what you want.'

She shook her head, uncertain. 'I don't know. I want … you.' The words were out and that seemed all that she needed to say.

'Then do what comes naturally, *mia cara*. Listen to your body, that magnificent body that has been driving me crazy all evening. Let it sing, *carissima*, and guide you.' Umberto's voice was as liquid as the water around them and he let a hand drift down to her panties, relieving Catriona of their constriction. His arms came round, curving her intimately into his body.

'Oh, Umberto …' she whispered as she felt an almost unbearable pulsing need between her thighs and the most delicious languor sweep over her. 'Umberto …'

'Shush! I will make each atom in your body sing until they meet in a magnificent chorus. Just relax and let me show you how.'

The warmth of his mouth against hers silenced her and Catriona gave herself to his kiss with a new fervour, holding nothing back. His skilled hands were soon playing her like a cherished instrument, coaxing her body to abandon itself completely to him. As they began to move with exquisite power over breasts, belly, hips – finding all the hidden sensitive places and bringing them to flower – Catriona's eyes drifted shut, an overpowering pleasure beginning to build in her, dragging a low moan from her throat that echoed above the sigh of the sea.

His voice was a low rumble. '*Incredibile*, so responsive!'

Her breathing came in short, shallow gasps. The delicious warmth soon built relentlessly, the molten core expanding; he was pushing her further and further towards the precipice and when her climax came, it burst within her with a rending force and she clung to him, her nails digging into his shoulders, inundated by an overriding relief. If this was what Paradise was about, Catriona thought as she came back down to earth, then she wanted to die now.

Umberto kissed her forehead almost reverently and pushed back the wet hair plastered over her cheeks that, despite the cold, were burning with a mixture of passion and embarrassment.

He smiled wryly. 'I can tell that no man has done that to you before …'

She nodded mutely.

'Truly an innocent,' he murmured hoarsely, seemingly to himself, as he carried her out of the water. 'The rarest of flowers.'

Catriona wrapped her arms around Umberto's neck and buried her face in the hollow of his shoulder. She was shivering now and he held her tight against his muscular body. 'I'll make you a hot drink when we get back to the villa. It'll warm you up … All you need now is a good night's sleep.'

She wasn't really listening, her body lying inert and satiated in his powerful arms, her eyes closed.

Once back on dry land Umberto gave her a rub down with his shirt and wrapped her in the cast-off kaftan that was lying in a heap on the rocks before pulling on his trousers.

A curtain of cloud had now appeared in the sky, spreading across the moon. Through each fleecy wrinkle, small stars peeped out and twinkled like fishes in a net. The night had become inky and a small wind was starting up, rippling the surface of the now jet-black sea.

'I can walk back, thank you,' Catriona said as Umberto went to pick her up again.

'No, *cara*, you're tired, the sand is cold and the moon seems to be sulking up there. It's dark and you've already fallen over once this evening. You could cut yourself on a shell or twist your ankle in one of the many crab holes on the beach.'

Umberto reached out, hauling her up into his powerful arms once more, and this time Catriona didn't resist, sliding hers about his neck, only too happy to slip back into his embrace. His shoulders felt hard and strong, his straight back only adding to his height. He walked quickly with long strides; so assured, so commanding. Her face was inches away from his and his particular male scent came to her, mingling with the pungent salted iodine fragrances of the sea, tantalizing her already tormented and excited senses. Catriona had been given a taste of what pleasure could be in Umberto's arms and her sensitized body was clamouring for more. There was a stirring inside her, a whisper in her heart, something infinitely special and rare. The perfection of the moment was such that she closed her eyes to savour it, memorize the smells, the sounds and the touches.

Back at the Villa Rossini, he took her straight to the bedroom and set her down on the four-poster bed. 'I will leave you to shower, or maybe you would prefer a hot bath? I'll go and make you some hot milk. Afterwards you'll sleep *come un bambino*, like a baby.'

She looked puzzled. 'But …'

'You will sleep in this bed. I'll use the sofa in the library.'

Was she disappointed? Had she hoped they would be sharing a bed? Hoped for a repeat of those lustful games of which he had given her a brief taste? Still, she smiled at him. 'Thank you, Umberto, that's very sweet of you.'

He stared down at her. There was an unfathomable look in those mesmerizing eyes, as though he was sending her some sort of encrypted message. '*Non c'e' di che*, don't mention it,' he said, a softly mocking note in his voice.

An impulse she wasn't sure she wanted to investigate made her add rose-scented bath oil to the water. Voluptuously, she gave herself up to the soothing heat, letting the tension seep out of her body. She rubbed herself down vigorously with the rough loofah sponge, turning her skin to a warm pink, and washed the salt from her hair.

Twenty minutes later she was out and wrapped in a huge warm towel when Umberto knocked at the door.

'Come in,' she said, hugging the towel around her.

'Your milk, *signorina*.'

Catriona smiled tremulously at him. He was barefoot, wearing a silk robe that exposed the crisp, damp hair curling on his chest.

'There are nightclothes in that cupboard,' he said, signalling the wardrobe with his head, 'and extra blankets too, if you're cold. The weather is changing. Looks like there'll be a storm tonight.'

'Thank you … thank you for everything. It's been a wonderful evening,' she murmured, a little disappointed at seeing him move towards the door.

Umberto stopped and stood at the threshold, watching her for a brief moment, a tense unreadable expression on his face. He was slightly flushed, his eyes very dark, almost black. He seemed unable to tear his attention away from her. Catriona's throat suddenly went dry. Could he … did he …? But then abruptly he looked away.

'*Buonanotte*, Caterina,' he said in a thick voice and was gone, shutting the door quietly behind him. Had the tension she thought she had read in the line of Umberto's body been desire or regret at what he had done to her out there in the sea? Perhaps he thought her too naïve and inexperienced to venture any further.

Catriona went to the cupboard and chose a nightdress in primrose-coloured silk that fitted her beautifully. It was trimmed with lace and she loved the way its soft material brushed sensually against her body. She wasn't accustomed to luxury nightclothes like these; hers were usually plain cotton and purely functional. Certainly nothing so obviously feminine. Again she felt a pang of discomfort, wondering who might have worn the delicate nightdress before her. How many women had Umberto brought here? No doubt they were used to wearing such things – oh, this was all so new to her!

She crept into bed, slightly shell-shocked by what had happened between them, the way she had been a slave to Umberto's touch. Her whole body had hummed with pleasure and yet he had not sought his own. She cursed her innocence, disliking the thought of other women who undoubtedly drove *him* over the edge. Still, if she were to believe her friends' experiences, this selflessness was not the norm among men, the majority of whom, she'd been told, used women solely in pursuit of their own gratification. Maybe he wasn't overly attracted to her … she was not sexy enough, perhaps. Thinking back to the beautiful redheaded Silvana Esposito, her heart gave a sad little squeeze – true, she was in no way as sophisticated and alluring as the soprano.

While these tormenting thoughts milled around in her hazy brain, Catriona was beginning to feel drowsy. The exciting events of the day were catching up with her and soon she slipped into what felt more like a coma than sleep.

*   *   *

She woke to the sound of the wind roaring with a riot, as if Orion had struck the earth. The woodlands at the back of the house were being battered by it, sounding as though panting and crying into the dark, throbbing at each mad bluster from above.

Catriona leapt out of bed and ran to the window. Day was almost breaking and the stars were fading in the morning pallor. Angry thunderclouds rolled their rainy pillows in fantastic forms, continually torn, scattered and reunited by the driving wind. She watched them march across the firmament like an avenging army. The battle opened. Thunder rumbled and crashed in the distance before a zigzag of vivid lightning turned the wan sky into a riotous jazz that mocked the solitude of the endless sea and pried into the secret places of the earth. Catriona had always loved a storm. As a child she had been fascinated by the story of Noah's Ark; as she grew older this fascination had turned into exhilaration and tonight, more than ever, she was bewitched by this unleashing of nature.

Without thinking, she ran out of the bedroom and into the *salone*. The lights were off but a warm glow came from a log fire burning in the chimney, its purple and orange flames leaping and dancing to its crackling song. She saw him immediately. He stood leaning against the open French windows to the terrace, his back to her. Umberto stirred and turned as she came in and Catriona almost gasped, realizing that he was only wearing black briefs.

'I'm sorry,' she mumbled, stopping dead in her tracks. 'I …'

He stood utterly motionless for a few seconds as though he himself had been struck by lightning, and then he smiled. 'Afraid, *cara*?'

Her eyes went wide at the question, meeting his intent gaze. Was he referring to the storm or something else? She swallowed. 'No, no … I'm not. I'm sorry if I've disturbed your privacy.'

'*Non mi disturbi affatto*, you haven't disturbed me at all. Doesn't the thunder and lightning bother you?'

She stared back at him. 'No, I love storms. They excite me.'

At her words, his look was as turbulent as the clouds in the distance. 'Then come and watch with me. Nature's orchestra is playing Wagner's "Ride of the Valkyries" for us.' He stretched out his arm in invitation.

A loud crack of thunder tore the air, followed by a bright flash of lightning as she hesitantly went to him. His sculptured features were taut. His eyes smouldered and travelled up her body with dark intent before they fixed on her cleavage. Emotion surged through her, fierce and unexpected, as she read in them his need for her, making her blood leap in response. She wanted Umberto, she wanted him utterly, completely.

Her gaze, flooded with desire, lifted to his. 'Umberto,' she breathed, the plea in her voice unmistakable.

'*Sì?*' Green emerald eyes glittered down into hers, boring into her soul – no doubt a man with his experience was reading her like an open book. And in the unreal chromatic light that inundated the room, he seemed more like a dream than a man. A wild and dangerous dream.

Catriona's heart thundered uncontrollably in her chest, making her mute, the aching need for him writhing within her like a snake. She placed her hands on his stomach and slowly slid them up his bare chest.

She felt him tense, every muscle rigid as though turning to steel. 'You play with fire, *mia cara* – there's a limit a man can take before the beast within him slips the leash.' The air around them felt heavy and dense, just like nature before a storm, and yet around them the storm had already begun.

Warmth was flooding her loins, the ache driving her crazy. Her mind was begging him to touch her, take her, fill her. Driven by demons that had never visited her before, Catriona recklessly pushed up on tiptoes to brush her mouth lightly against his, offering herself, maintaining eye contact as if willing him to surrender to his feelings. 'Teach me … take me …'

'*Che Dio ci aiuti,* God help us both,' he groaned almost savagely as he pulled her into his embrace, his arms dropping around her lower back and arching her soft shape against his, letting that tender curve at the apex of her thighs feel the blatant demand of his body that she provoked within him.

Catriona's legs quivered as Umberto gently pushed her away from him. He looked down into her eyes once more as though asking her if she realized what she was doing. She knew he wanted that validation and she nodded, her will to resist gone. Whatever he desired she would grant. No conditions. No strings. He could be leading her to hell and she would follow.

Umberto pushed the straps of her nightgown aside, allowing them to slip down her arms. His breath sucked in on a hiss as the material fell from the crest of her breasts and his pupils ignited feverishly. He made them slide further until the silken garment had dropped to the floor and Catriona stood naked in front of him.

Instinctively, she wrapped her arms around herself but Umberto reached out and pulled them gently away.

The flaming gates of morning were opening on the horizon. A shudder moved the east; the stars were burning low above the crystal cradle of a day that was newly born. For several breaths he just stood there, staring at her body, which had taken a golden hue under the vermillion light illuminating the sky.

Transfixed, Umberto gazed mutely at her. 'I've been dreaming of you like this all evening. *Sei l'incarnazione di Eve ... quasi troppo bella da toccare*, you are the personification of Eve, almost too beautiful to touch.'

Long fingers slid up her arm to her shoulder, then to the back of her neck as he lowered his dark head, his hot mouth opening on hers, taking her willing lips. It was not a gentle kiss but one of branding. Spellbound, she followed his lead, her heart pounding, every bone in her body melting at the exquisite tugging sensation that connected directly with a pulse that throbbed between her legs. She wanted to learn all the forbidden secrets of this rough magic that people called sex.

As the first glow of honeysuckle dawn gradually burned the heel of night and spilled its radiance over the countryside, Umberto picked Catriona up and carried her across the room, where he laid her reverently on the thick rug in front of the fire.

'Your skin is like the petals of a rose.' He paused. 'A rosebud, like you ... closed, yet full of the promise of beauty to come.'

Catriona looked up at him standing there, her eyes swimming with desire as they dropped to the bulge pushing against the black material of his briefs. She lifted herself on one elbow, reaching out to touch him, but then withdrew, confused by conflicting instincts. One part of her said touch him, love him, the other said, don't, stop now while there's still time.

'Why are you looking at me like that?' Umberto asked, still standing over her.

His question caught her off guard and she answered it honestly. 'Because I want to touch you and yet part of me says I mustn't.'

'Ignore it,' he breathed, pulling off the barrier that was shielding his hard masculinity from her eyes … and from her touch. Umberto lowered himself to his knees beside her and his breath fanned her skin. 'Touch me, *amore mio*,' he murmured as he bent over her, tracing the line of her jaw with tiny teasing kisses. His emerald irises grew darker and his pupils dilated, making her aware of the tide of emotion possessing him.

Still propped on her elbow, her mouth opened eagerly and hungrily beneath the onslaught of his; the other questing hand slid around his waist and moved down between his legs, gently squeezing his well endowed manhood, drawing a hoarse groan from deep in his throat.

'Is this how you want me to touch you?' Catriona asked between kisses, as she felt him growing still harder under her fingers.

'*Sì, sì, amore mio* … ' He closed his eyes. Yes, she could read the pleasure in his face as his cheeks became flushed and he bit his lower lip. She liked it, she liked being in control.

Umberto took the hand that was caressing him and turned it over, pressing his burning lips to the centre of her palm. 'I love what you do to me, *mio cucciolo*. You enflame my senses. When you touch me it's …' he closed his eyes ' … *indescrivibile*. But we're just starting. We have to be sensible so that the pleasure lasts a long time. Trust me. Now that I know how it feels to be touched by you, the waiting, the wanting, will only make it better in the end.'

As he spoke, he was pushing her back gently as he lowered himself down over her, inch by inch, with the slow carnal expertise of a male who liked to tempt and excite. 'Relax, think pleasure beyond your wildest fantasies,' he whispered hoarsely, his feverish gaze welded to hers as he pushed her arms over her head, charging her quivering length with the most intense anticipation.

His warm hand slid under her hair, fingers closing around her nape as his thumb lightly caressed the base of her skull. He brushed his other thumb over her lower lip. Catriona's vision blurred, her insides melting, her lips throbbing with expectation.

The kiss that followed was a promise in itself – voracious, domineering, all-consuming – and Catriona gave herself up to it in unadulterated surrender. Their lips and tongues played an almost primitive dance, desire rushing through them in a wild fire that nothing but total fulfilment would have any hope of extinguishing.

The warm velvety smoothness of Umberto's flesh made Catriona's hands tingle with the desperate need to touch him, but he held her wrists together with one hand as his hot lips began exploring her skin in ways she never knew existed, each skilled, slow, caressing slide of his wet tongue a tantalizing pledge of things to come. There was no limit to the intimacy of his caresses, no spot on her body too private, provoking an unrestrained reaction from her with every brush of his fingertips, with every stroke and teasing probe of his tongue.

Catriona's heart hammered wildly. She moaned uninhibitedly, her body writhing as she abandoned herself to the sensations that this man, this stranger, was creating in each secret place of her tormented body. Somewhere in the back of her mind she registered how out of character this was for her, how shameless, how reckless. Still, as long as Umberto kept touching her the way he was, she didn't care how heedless or utterly outrageous she was.

His mouth slid around to her ear, his teeth nipping then sucking suggestively at the tender lobe. 'You like the things I do to you, *Caterina, mio uragano bello e passionale,* my beautiful and passionate hurricane, *eh?*' His hand moved to shape her breast, cupping the swollen weight, his thumb stroking the already stiff peak that longed to be taken in his mouth. Still playing with her nipple, Umberto kissed his way across Catriona's chest to whisper hotly against her other ear.

'For instance, I know when I'm playing with this responsive little spot here, you are thinking of the other one, the secret place that gave you so much pleasure when I touched it earlier. You want me to go there, *vero?*'

'Yes,' she breathed.

'The throbbing down there is tormenting you, *e' cosi?*'

'Yes,' she panted, her breasts heaving against Umberto's bare chest. She wriggled helplessly and instinctively, her thighs dropped apart, inviting his touch, something deep and powerful and primitive within her wanting him to possess her entirely.

Umberto's hand tightened on her breast. His emerald passion-filled eyes devoured each part of her; then, releasing her wrists, he began a new painstakingly erotic journey down her aching body with both hands and mouth. With each sweep of his hand, the soft pressure of his strong fingers, the scorching heat that shimmered in waves off Umberto's skin sent electric tingles up and down Catriona's back as her aching breasts were crushed against the hard muscles of his chest and the soft curve of her stomach pressed against his.

She pressed closer into him, shuddering in delight as his arm encircled her waist, pulling her on to her side, drawing her against the lean strength of his body and the hard warmth of his virility. Her curves slotted into his angles as if they were made to complement each other. Catriona drove her hands into his midnight-black hair, clutching him more tightly to her as she lifted her top knee and her hips ground against his potent need for her.

And so, dipping her hand between their bodies, she let her fingers slide down to Umberto's belly and, lower still, to his groin and the hard, silken length of him. She relished the tremor that ran through him at her touch and heard him groan with pleasure. His stiff arousal bucked in her hand and Catriona felt as though he was about to pull away but, not knowing exactly what she was doing, she strengthened the stroke of her hand, drawing to the silken tip, before sliding back to its base, encircling it like a cuff. Her other hand joined the first and she began to massage him, her palms roaming over the soft sacks, exploring his hard maleness, moving up and down in an instinctive rhythm, relishing the sensations she felt quiver through him as she maintained her slow, steady pace.

Suddenly it wasn't enough; she wanted more. Releasing him for a moment, she slid down the length of his body. And then, dipping her head and parting her lips, she took the whole of him into her mouth, sucking and licking, revelling in the velvet steel of his manhood, in his powerful virility, wanting to be part of it … part of him.

She felt Umberto's whole body shudder as though he had been struck by lightning. Then he cried out her name in a hoarse voice. He began to tremble at her assault, his hips pressing and straining against her head, as if to amplify her action. He was growing harder, the groans louder. And then suddenly, a deep unarticulated sound ripped from his throat as he pulled away from Catriona's head.

'*No, amore mio, no … non ancora*, not yet,' and he looked down at her and stared, his crazed eyes turning molten, sparking with green fire as he quickly flipped her over on to her back, his face sliding down her body, pulling her thighs apart almost violently and burying his face in the soft moist warmth of her desire, his tongue seeking and finding her essence.

Catriona's focus blurred, her senses in shock. Her lips parted on a deep moan as the hot contact of his tongue met her wet heat. Panting, she half closed her eyes as the urge for release clawed at her relentlessly; she gripped Umberto's hair tightly with both hands, pressing his head deeper against her pulsing need. She came apart instantly, her body arching and shuddering, her cries resonating in the silence of the room as ripple after ripple of ecstatic pleasure rolled over her, the warm juices of rapture running down her thighs.

Still Umberto hadn't finished with her. Lifting himself up, his gaze was piercingly bright; he looked as though in a fever. 'Now you're ready for me, *amore mio*. I can see … Still swollen and moist, my insatiable Caterina, but I must make sure before you open up to me. Like the rose opens to the sun …'

Swept away on the storm of emotions, not knowing what to expect but craving his possession of her, Catriona seemed incapable of anything more than a single gasp. 'Please …'

'Open your legs again and relax,' he said hoarsely, his eyes turning a beautiful, mysterious deep green. 'Trust me, *dolcezza, mio tesoro, mio angelo*, I will be very gentle,' he whispered as he lowered himself on top of her, helping her to do as he asked, pressing her bent knees gently further apart.

Catriona waited, breathless, rising anticipation exciting her while Umberto ran his hand up and down the inside of her thigh. Almost spellbound, he was gazing at her aroused womanhood, which only enflamed her more. She licked her dry lips, feeling herself grow wet again as waves of longing flooded her, and dropped her knees even wider for him.

'I want you. Take me … please, Umberto,' she pleaded, her yearning to feel his touch making her breathless. Still watching her, he slid his silky tip along her moisture, making her shudder and arch her hips. 'Just tell me when you want me to stop.' He slipped one strong finger into the hot secret part of her, and then two, and Catriona's hips bucked as he stretched her body slowly. Then, lifting his hand to his mouth, he slowly licked her dew from his fingers.

'You taste of honey and spice,' he murmured. His eyes clouded. 'I've never deflowered a virgin before ... do you trust me, *mio tesoro*?'

'Oh yes, *yes*, my love,' she groaned. 'I want you to be the first.'

He lowered himself and settled between her thighs, replacing his exploring fingers with the tip of his hard length. 'I'll try not to hurt you,' he whispered. 'Do you want me inside you, *angelo mio*?'

'Please, yes, I need you ...'

Inch by inch, he found his way into her, withdrawing slightly with each push to give her time to get used to the feel of him. There was a slight burning sensation but the more she moved against his hips, the more it gave way to a yearning need to have still more of him deep inside.

'Now?'

'Yes, now ...' she breathed against his ear.

He ran his fingers down her cheek and followed them with kisses, capturing on his lips her sharp gasp of pain as he finally thrust to the hilt.

Tears rolled down Catriona's cheeks, the unmistakable light of shock shining in her eyes, and Umberto kissed her tenderly, murmuring words of endearment as he patiently waited for her body to accept him.

She responded with eager desire for him, her flesh and nerves quivering to the potent feel of him. She was his and he was hers.

Even the pain was welcome because he caused it and when it subsided, then came the pleasure, throbbing and streaming through her body to its utmost reaches, and she was allowing him to move deeply and smoothly within her. She sucked in a breath, a breath of awareness and of sheer pleasure.

'Yes, oh yes, Umberto,' she sighed, her hips rolling against his. The sensations were becoming sweeter with every second; her eyes flickered with renewed desire, her sinuous movements an unmistakable invitation.

And so Umberto rose up on his hands above her and rode her repeatedly, tirelessly, with slow, tender care. They danced to the erotic rhythm and sensual music of their mutual desire, all thoughts dissolved, great currents of emotion rolling up from the depths of their hearts. Their movements were sweet, hot and silken; his breath mingled with hers in kisses that were tempestuous.

They were lovers in the true sense of the word, engulfed in all-consuming flames that sang a rapturous melody, melting their control away again and again as they tipped over cliffs of great height and soared together. Their bodies, which had no secrets from one another now, were consumed by insatiable desire that engulfed them in a dizzying world where passion and rapacious hunger knew no bounds.

When it was over they collapsed in each other's arms, staring in mystical silence into each other's eyes, overcome by the passion they had shared. Finally, they drifted off to sleep, satiated, their exhausted bodies still entwined.

Outside, everything that had been grey was suddenly bright. The dawning sun flushed the singing waters of the sea, which had sparkled like silver under the moon. Now that the white foaming waves were dressed in sunshine, each rock looked as if it were veiled with rainbow light and, in the garden, a lark hailed the morning with all his might, thrilling the countryside with his song.

*   *   *

Some hours later, Catriona was dragged from the depths of sleep by a strange banging noise. Blinking her eyes open, her vision met the afternoon light dappling the ceiling. As she heard the hiss and sigh of the waves below the house, she thought she'd been dreaming. She turned to see the line of Umberto's tawny shoulder rising over her, his arm still lying loosely across her waist, an anchoring warmth. He too stirred, his eyes at first focusing sleepily on her as he pulled her closer.

Then the noise came again, more insistent this time; someone was hammering on the door. There was a man's muffled shout: 'Umberto! Umberto, *ci sei*, are you in there?'

Catriona's eyes widened and she pulled away from him and sat upright, drawing the sheet up to her neck. 'Who's that?' she whispered. Her blurry thoughts immediately registered that she was naked and in Umberto's bed.

More banging. 'Umberto, *è* Mirko! *Sono bisogno di parlarti urgentemente*, I need to talk to you urgently.'

Umberto swore in a gutteral tone and swung his legs over the side of the bed. He ran a hand roughly through his hair. 'That's my agent … What time is it?'

Catriona glanced at the bedside clock: 'One o'clock. We've slept half the day away. Were you expecting him?' Suddenly she felt mortified that she might be caught in such a position by a complete stranger.

He threw her an apologetic smile. 'I'm sorry, Caterina. No, I wasn't expecting him.' He frowned. 'It must be important for him to drive out here when he couldn't get hold of me on my mobile.' Umberto stood up in all his naked glory and moved quickly over the cupboard to grab some clothes, pulling on jeans and a T-shirt.

'Don't worry, *cara*. I'll get rid of Mirko and be back in a minute.' He grinned wolfishly. 'Stay where you are.'

Catriona heard him answer the door and then there were murmured voices in the other room. Deciding that she felt too vulnerable lying in bed naked, she fumbled with her clothes, dressing as quickly as possible. She barely had time to absorb the strangeness of her feelings: being in Umberto's house after they had shared such intimacy the night before; how she had offered her virginity to him so willingly and hungrily; and how he had taken her somewhere she had never dreamed existed.

He had transported her to a place of passion and unfathomable pleasure, a world painted with a thousand colours like a wonderful kaleidoscope, where her mind had vibrated with the same ecstasy that had overcome her body. Her friends had been right; now she did indeed know what she had been missing. A secret smile stole across her lips. The twinges in the sensitive parts of her body were reminders that Umberto had made her a woman last night.

A few minutes later, Umberto returned, looking dazed. He came towards her with a strange look in his eyes. Catriona had turned towards him and was brushing her fingers through her hair in an attempt to return some neatness to her dishevelled locks. 'Has he gone?'

He nodded. 'Yes. He's had some incredible news. We've been waiting for confirmation of a US tour for over a year now and, finally, it's come. It's a complete surprise. I hadn't expected it.' His face was incredulous and he ruffled both hands through his hair as if to make the news sink into his brain more thoroughly. '*Dios mio*, it's finally happened!'

Catriona gazed up at him, smiling. 'Umberto, that's wonderful! Congratulations.' Her mind then caught up with the meaning of what he was saying. 'When does the tour start?'

His eyes clouded as he refocused on her intently. 'I leave for New York tomorrow.'

Catriona froze. *Tomorrow?* But they had only just …

'This trip … it's come almost out of the blue,' he went on, 'and it's something I've been wanting for a very long time.'

Still stunned, she tried to keep her voice steady. 'When will I see you again? How long will you be gone?'

'I don't know. Months … more than a year. Maybe even longer. It's impossible to say.' Umberto reached out his hand and stroked the side of her cheek. He looked bewildered and she would have almost felt sorry for him if she hadn't been numb with shock herself.

'I'm sorry, *cara*. You're an incredible young woman and what we shared last night was special, *fantastico*. I was hoping we'd spend the weekend together and then maybe …' Something changed in Umberto's expression, as though he was overwhelmed by too many thoughts crowding his mind. His fingers ceased their caress and he dropped his hand.

'This is a golden opportunity. I understand, Umberto,' Catriona whispered.

Part of that was true. She did understand. Another part of her was dying inside.

His emerald gaze searched her face. 'My life is now so fly-by-night, Caterina, such a whirlwind. I'm never in one country for more than a couple of days, it seems, before I'm flying somewhere else.' The shadow of a smile hovered on the beautiful mouth that had loved her with such passion only hours before.

'It's not fair to ask you to wait. I respect you too much to be anything but honest with you. You're young, you've got your life, your studies, your glittering career that you've worked so hard for ahead of you. When I come back to Nice again, then who knows? I'll know where to find you. But for now, let's just keep this as a perfect memory. It's better that way, trust me.' The tone of regret in his voice was unmistakable but Catriona could not look in his eyes to see if that same sentiment was reflected there.

She turned away, her throat painfully tight. 'I need to gather my things together.'

'Yes, of course,' came his voice behind her. 'I'll wait outside and then drive you back home.'

'Thank you,' she said, so that he would not see the tears threatening to come, but he was already walking out of the room.

They drove back in silence. Umberto was far away and Catriona could see he had undergone a transformation. He was distracted, distant, and it was as though a sheet of glass lay between them. The die had been cast and there was nothing she could do. Devastated, she stared out of the window, enduring the rest of the interminably long drive back to Nice.

When they arrived in the street where Les Platanes and Les Charmilles nestled close to each other, Catriona glanced up at the two houses. Their proximity seemed to mock her now – just a heartless reminder of all her broken dreams and foolishness.

Umberto walked her to the gate at the front of her house. '*Au revoir*, Caterina. Remember, the future is yours to make as you wish.'

He leaned forward and kissed her gently on the cheek. His lips felt almost cruelly warm and soft on her skin but there was none of the passion they had held before.

As she closed the gates behind her she saw Umberto's tall, imposing figure stride back to his house. Catriona willed him to look back at her just once, but he did not. The journey to America was his present – his future – and she was already in the past, one adventure in an ever-continuing chain. She stared after him, yearning and misery crashing together inside her as she realized that she would never see him again.

CHAPTER 5

Nice, 2012

'And that is the pitiful story of my one and only whirlwind night of love,' Catriona ended. She was sitting at a small table with Marie-Jeanne, staring down into her hot chocolate as she stirred it.

After work they had ended up, as they often did, at Chez Madeleine, an art-nouveau *salon de thé* on the Promenade des Anglais, sitting at a table near the window facing the scintillating sea. The mistral had died down and the sun was shining. Everybody and their dogs seemed to be out on the pavements at this hour, enjoying the temperate early spring afternoon. The passing crowd seemed to comprise every nationality and multiple languages could be heard as the pedestrians bustled along the seafront.

Catriona gave Marie-Jeanne a weak smile. She had never related the full details of those past events to anyone, not even her mother. Now it seemed her past was bidding to catch up with her and she sorely needed to confide in someone.

Two years older than Catriona, Marie-Jeanne had become like a sister. Ever since the two had met at university, her friend had been generous and understanding – and today she was no different. Marie-Jeanne had been popular at college, a honey pot surrounded by bees. Tall, slim, dark and vivacious, she was a girl who had cut her way through the world by dint of her own talents, and having her as clinic partner was the best thing Catriona could have wished for. Although her friend had married early, settling down as a happy wife and mother, she was still very ambitious in her career.

After Viscountess Calandra Rolando Monteverdi had swept out of the office of L'Esperance Drouot that morning, Marie-Jeanne had clearly witnessed how shaken Catriona had appeared and wasted no time in suggesting a trip to Chez Madeleine that afternoon. Now, Catriona found herself unburdening everything to her friend inside the small but elegant *salon de thé*, where wide, gilded mirrors reflected back the cosy, ornate surroundings and chattering patrons. She shared everything about that secret night of passion with Umberto ten years before, a night that had tormented Catriona ever since.

Catriona took a sip of her hot chocolate. 'I tried to get on with my life in those first weeks but, naïvely, I hoped that he would change his mind and come back to Nice to look for me. That never happened, of course.'

Silently, eyebrows drawn into a deep frown, Marie-Jeanne laid her hand on Catriona's. '*Ma chérie*,' she sighed sadly.

A sorrowful shadow darkened Catriona's face. 'I won't bother to describe to you the hellish torment of waiting against all hope … and then the despair when I finally found out that I was pregnant, along with the realization that he had obviously forgotten me.'

'You were very young,' said Marie-Jeanne, her lopsided smile full of understanding. 'Naïve maybe, but wasn't it really just youthful innocence?'

Catriona looked rueful. 'Not so young at eighteen. Girls of my age had already had at least one affair.'

'If it's any consolation to you, I hadn't.'

'But you married young.'

'I was lucky. Jean-Paul and I grew up together, we were friends. I didn't experience a *grande passion* like yours. I've never known that elation – that fire you talk about – if only for one night. But I'm grateful. Jean-Paul is kind and loves me, and that's worth a lot. But don't forget that you've had something special, something not many women will ever know.'

'Maybe, but the consequences were hard. Oh, don't get me wrong, I love Michael and I don't regret having him, even though I had to give up a future in singing.' Catriona shrugged and smiled wistfully.

'I guess it all turned out for the best. I love my job and wouldn't have it otherwise. In many ways it's a much more fulfilling career. Healing people, helping them through music – something I'm truly passionate about. What more could I ask? But it was tough at the time.'

'You're a strong woman, *ma chère*.'

'I wasn't then, trust me. When I found out I was pregnant, I really hit rock bottom,' Catriona murmured. 'I tried to hide it but Sidonie guessed immediately … my morning sickness gave me away. It was horrendous. *Maman* was away at the time.'

'How did you tell your mother? Knowing Marguerite as I do, it must have been a terrible shock to her – you, her innocent little girl whom she had tried so hard to protect.'

'Believe it or not, she was wonderful. At first, she wanted to know if this had happened with my consent. Then she asked who it was, thinking, I suppose, that the boy could be encouraged to make an honest woman of me. When I told her that the person was a tourist and that it had been a one-night stand, I think that shocked her more than the fact that I'd had sex and was pregnant.'

Marie-Jeanne's eyes widened in surprise. 'You've never told your mother the identity of your son's father?'

Catriona heaved a sigh. 'No. Otherwise, she would certainly have tried to get in touch with him. She's a lawyer and thinks like a lawyer. She would have put pressure on him to marry me. It would have been too humiliating. He was at the beginning of a brilliant career, I saw that – and now, in retrospect, even more so. Umberto was ambitious. That trip to America was his big break. At the time, of course, I felt hurt and abandoned. Yet looking back now, I can see that when his agent showed up to tell him about the new US contract, it took him completely by surprise. He had no time to think, he just had to leave.' She shook her head sadly.

'No, it didn't seem right to tell *Maman* and pressurize him with the bombshell that I was pregnant. I would have been a burden to him and he would have hated me for it.'

'Still, Marguerite has risen to the role of grandmother with some relish,' observed Marie-Jeanne.

Catriona smiled at the thought of how loving and supportive her mother had been when she'd needed her the most. 'Once she was reconciled to not knowing who Michael's father was, *Maman*'s independent streak kicked in. "Life isn't always easy," she said, "but you need to pick yourself up and carry on." I remember her drying my tears and telling me: "I've been through this myself, we can bring the child up on our own."'

Marie-Jeanne grinned. 'Your mother is a truly formidable woman.' She paused, taking a thoughtful bite of her pastry. 'So, all these years you've lived with this secret …'

'It's been hard, I admit.'

'You never tried to tell him that he has a son?'

Catriona paused and stared out of the window, watching the sea sparkling in the distance. 'I was tempted once, four years ago. I was established, confident, and I thought my feelings for him had finally died a death. It was only fair that he should know about his son. He was at the top of his career and giving a concert in Paris.'

'I remember you saying that you had been invited to Paris for a weekend. You came back a day later and for the whole of the next week you were in a shocking mood.'

Catriona met her friend's pensive gaze. 'Yes, that was the time. Now it seems such a foolish thing to have done,' she said sadly. 'I went to the concert and afterwards tried to see him backstage, but it was very difficult to make my way through the throng of admirers and hangers-on. Besides, there was security everywhere. So, I left the theatre and – same as I did years ago – I waited for him outside, hidden behind a column. It was winter and I was dressed in furs and a hat, so it made me feel better, knowing I was almost unrecognizable.

'Suddenly he appeared. He was alone. Impulsively, I went up to him as he stood in the doorway. I was going to ask him to sign the programme I'd bought.' Catriona's pulse began to quicken at the memory.

'I called out his name and he turned. I was trembling … He hadn't changed much. He looked at me for a second and, in that moment, I thought I saw a flash of something in those emerald eyes as he stared straight at me. I was mesmerized, lost for words. But then a woman with red hair appeared from the side door and made a beeline for him. I knew instantly it was Silvana.'

'So, she was still on the scene after all those years?'

Catriona nodded without expression.

'And what happened then?' Marie-Jeanne prompted.

'I turned and walked away as fast as my legs could carry me.' Catriona gave a self-derisive smile. 'I'm not sure if he recognized me or not but I realized that I still loved him. Just two weeks later, I read that he'd been blinded by a terrible car accident.'

'*Mon Dieu*, how dreadful!'

Catriona sighed. 'Yes, a tragic end to the story. I felt awful, thinking about what he must be going through, and I wanted to find him. But then …' she shook her head sorrowfully, 'I simply couldn't. I needed to protect the life I'd built for myself with Michael. Besides, that night in Paris, I saw he had Silvana …' Her voice trailed off and she stared down at the table bleakly.

'But you still love him?' persisted Marie-Jeanne gently.

'Yes, I still love him. I always will, I think. When I saw his mother this morning, all those old feelings resurfaced … the passion … the need.'

'And you've never had a man since.' A look of understanding crossed her friend's face.

'No, I'm not interested in dating, as you know. The whole idea of being with someone else doesn't interest me.' Her eyes fell on a little statue of a beautiful naked nymph entwined with flowers in a niche between mirrors. Lit softly by an opaline lamp on the wall above, its provocative sensuality made her look away.

'*Ma pauvre chérie*, my poor darling! It must have been hell those first years.'

Catriona glanced back at her friend. '*Maman* was a real rock, a sacrificing mother in every sense of the word. She left her law firm in Nice in the hands of her partners and we moved again, this time to Aix-en-Provence, where she worked from home, drawing up contracts and writing legal opinions, but never travelling. Michael was born nine months later.' She took a sip of her hot chocolate and smiled a little sadly.

'I know I've told you this before but I was extremely depressed after his birth. *Maman* came to me one day and said she'd heard about a certain Dr Horst Schultz, a specialist in music therapy. Over that next year, he helped me, among other things, come to terms with the fact that I would never become an opera singer. He was a real friend to me – you know how much I valued his friendship – and on his advice I enrolled at the University of Aix to read psychology. He told me it was a part-time course so it could fit in with motherhood. After that I joined his research centre.' She smiled warmly. 'And that is where I met you, of course, my dear friend.'

'In those days, I never quite believed that you'd been married and widowed.'

Catriona gave her a wry look. '*Maman* felt it was the best way of silencing wagging tongues. When we'd moved from Nice she thought it would be sensible to call me Catherine, with the French pronunciation, instead of Catriona, my original name. We dropped the English surname de Vere completely and, from then on, people knew me as Catherine Drouot, an ordinary French widow.'

'That's so weird. All this time I've known you as Catherine when you'd been brought up as Catriona!'

'I know it sounds all so cloak-and-dagger, changing my name and everything, but I think we both felt it was symbolic of my need to start again with a clean slate.' Catriona sighed and added a little hot milk to her chocolate.

'Anyway, *Maman* sold Les Charmilles, the house in Nice, which I really didn't want to go back to – especially seeing it was next to Umberto's. So, you see, moving to Aix-en-Provence was a way of starting a new life.'

'Later, when you told me that Michael was a love child, I wasn't surprised but I had no idea about the rest of it. I can see why you were shocked when Calandra Monteverdi turned up today. Anyway, *chérie*, I feel honoured you've confided in me.'

'You're not only a business partner, Marie-Jeanne, you're also my best friend.'

'And now what are you going to do?'

Catriona sighed. 'I really don't know. I can't just leave everything … my child, *Maman*, the clinic …'

'Will Umberto not relocate? He could stay at his house in Villefranche, or at Les Platanes, and you would be able to treat him.'

'He sold those two houses years ago. He's lived mostly in the United States. It was only after his accident that he returned to the family home on Lake Como.'

'You've followed his movements?'

Catriona blushed. 'Yes,' she murmured. 'Anyhow, there was always something about him in the gossip columns. I didn't need to search very thoroughly. His whirlwind success as a composer ...' she shifted awkwardly in her chair, 'and, of course, the countless woman that came and went in his life.'

Marie-Jeanne's concerned expression softened to sympathy. 'You never let go.'

'Not really. It's taken me ten years to accept that my feelings for him would never come to anything, and then Calandra turned up in my office today ...'

'Taking on Umberto's case would certainly open a Pandora's box,' said Marie-Jeanne thoughtfully.

'Yes, it would test me in so many ways.' Cupping her hands around her hot chocolate, Catriona cast her eyes downwards. 'I can't afford to fall apart, for Michael's sake,' she added.

Marie-Jeanne gave her friend's hand an encouraging squeeze. '*Ma chérie*, let me just say, as a therapist, I can undoubtedly see the benefit of telling Michael about his father. And if there's a chance of him building a relationship with Umberto, that of course would be the ideal,' she reasoned. 'However, as your friend, my instinct is also to urge caution. Both of us know what a minefield this case would be for you.'

'Yet, in all conscience, I do believe that he has a right to know about his son,' responded Catriona. 'Maybe it would help him recover, give him something to live for. Umberto undoubtedly needs help from someone, I'm just not sure if I'm the right person.'

'Calandra seemed quite determined that you are,' Marie-Jeanne mused. 'Maybe you should talk to your mother.'

Catriona shook her head. 'No, *Maman* is so black and white about everything – the lawyer in her, I suppose. She'd insist that I get in touch with him right away and tell him about his son. I'm not ready to do that yet.' She paused, glancing at her friend, a flicker of dread beginning to awaken inside her.

'Michael has grown up thinking his father is dead. His world would be turned upside down if he were to find out the truth. And that's not all … bringing an unstable man into his life is the last thing I want to do.'

*   *   *

Catriona wrote a polite letter to Viscountess Calandra Rolando Monteverdi declining her request, but forwarding helpful information and contacts. A month went by, during which time she tried to forget the diva's visit, but she was restless and irritable, didn't eat much and sleep evaded her. Marguerite had obviously realized that there was something wrong with her daughter and tried many times to quiz her, but Catriona kept her secret close to her heart, as she had done for so many years.

Of late, Catriona had tried to look back on her old feelings for Umberto with a certain scorn. That brief time with him, she reasoned, was nothing more than a fling, made into something more romantic through childish make-believe and foolish hopes. Still, the old emotions she harboured had never died down. Occasionally, a moment of clarity came when the present fell away and those hours of passion she had tasted appeared in their old intensity. It was then that she realized that the past still lived and breathed in her, undimmed.

Sometimes such fleeting moments would occur when her son Michael's face wore a particular expression, especially the concentrated intensity of his gaze when playing the piano. In these flashes he resembled his father so strongly it made Catriona's heart give a painful squeeze. It was uncanny – the boy even had the same red crescent-shaped birthmark on the underside of his wrist. In moments like these she would hurriedly bring her thoughts back to the present – to her home, family and work, which had taken up an increasing part of her life.

Still, her conscience was pricking her and with that a host of emotions had bubbled up to the surface, torturing her. Dreams that had plagued her all those years ago when Umberto had gone away now started recurring … dreams of passion from which she would wake up panting, aching with her need for him, her unsatisfied body begging for relief.

Then one night she woke up feeling oddly stiff, as though she had slept in a cramped position. The darkness seemed impenetrable, like a thick black shroud. She was shivering; it was so cold! Had her covers slipped off the bed? She had better lean over and pull them up again, but her body was numb. Somehow she couldn't move, and it was so dark! She couldn't see anything. It was as if she had been struck blind. BLIND! Oh, my God, she *was* blind! Her heart began to pound … she was icy-cold now and a nasty tingling was crawling up her spine. Was this real? Was it a nightmare? Was she awake or sleeping? She put out a shaking hand, desperately trying to get her bearings. She was blind! Like Umberto!

Struck by panic, she began taking frantic breaths, terrified of being unable to see at all. Then there was a sound that made her stiffen. She listened intently. There it was again: a faint sound, barely audible. Breathing! Someone was there. She wasn't alone. Someone was breathing nearby, but she couldn't see who it was. Perhaps they could help her. 'Who's there?' she cried out, but only the horrible darkness answered her. Then she started to sob.

'*Chérie*, wake up!'

Jolted out of her nightmare, Catriona sat up. Perspiration was running down her face and she was trembling violently as she tried to break free of it, crying out in misery and fear.

The bedside lamp was on and Marguerite was sitting on her bed. 'It's only a nightmare, *ma chérie*,' she said reassuringly.

'Oh, *Maman*, I dreamt I was blind. It was horrible …' she said between convulsive gasps.

'You were crying out in your sleep. *Ma pauvre*, you're under too much stress. Here, drink this.' Marguerite smoothed her hair and handed her a glass of water.

'Thank you.' Catriona took a few sips. 'Had I been asleep for long?' she whispered shakily.

'A few hours.'

'What time is it?'

'Nearly five. Go back to sleep.'

'I won't be able to sleep. I'm sorry I woke you.'

'Don't worry about me, *chérie*. I was awake anyway. Nowadays I don't need much sleep.'

After Marguerite had left the room, Catriona slipped out of bed and crept across the corridor to Michael's room. Easing the door open quietly, she gazed at the sight of her sleeping son, his dark head resting on the pillow, long eyelashes fanned out against his small cheeks. The boy was his father in miniature, she thought, and a wave of love and regret, and longing for what might have been, surged inside her.

She returned to her room to shower and dress, all the time trying to push away the thought of the nightmare that was still haunting her. It was a terrible thing to be blind. Poor Umberto! Questions flooded her mind, as they had when she'd learned of his accident. How was he coping with the loss of his sight? Was he still playing the piano? Did he ever think of her?

For ten years she had tried not to think of him, holding on to the futile hope that time would gently erase her aching love. Yet the memory of him had never diminished. Like a phantom, he was now seeping back into her dreams, returning to plague her in new, disturbing ways, calling to her somehow.

She sat on the edge of the bed, staring into space, one thought revolving in her mind … *I don't know if I'd ever have been strong enough to see you again, Umberto.*

*   *   *

The uneasiness of the dream lingered in Catriona's mind for the whole day, making her unusually distracted. Her thoughts flitted back and forth from Umberto to Michael, who had been asking more questions about his father lately; it bothered Catriona that on more than one occasion she'd been forced to become evasive on the subject. She had tried so hard to be everything her son needed, juggling work with the demands of motherhood; but even with the added support of Marguerite, she knew it couldn't take the place of having a father figure in his life.

It was that day that the second letter arrived from Calandra Rolando Monteverdi. Like the first, a courier had delivered it, but this time it was Marie-Jeanne who brought it to her.

She set a cup of hot chocolate down on Catriona's desk and handed her the envelope. 'This came for you. It's from Italy.' Marie-Jeanne was watching her friend's face keenly as she spoke.

Catriona paled. Heart beating, she held the bright yellow DHL sleeve in her hand and stared at it for a moment before opening it with trembling hands. This time it contained two envelopes – one typed with the name of Antonio Ottaviano & Co. Avvocati, a reputed Italian law firm; the other handwritten, with the familiar Rolando Monteverdi crest. That was the one she wanted to read. It enclosed a single sheet of paper with half a page of almost illegible writing, hastily scrawled.

Dear Dr Drouot,
When you receive this letter, I will be dead. When I came to see you some time ago I was dying of cancer, but I did not think that the end was so close. I write to you today knowing that hours from now I shall no more be of this world. The words you are reading are those of a dying mother who has never loved anybody more than her only son, Umberto. As I told you that day, I do not know the nature of

your past relationship with my son. Umberto was not a saint in his younger days, far from it. Maybe he hurt you … maybe you hurt him. The only truth I am sure of is that at some stage you meant something to each other and that he needs you now. I still maintain that you are the only one who can save him.

With this letter, you will receive another from my solicitor that will explain the terms of my offer. Please don't deny me again. You must be a kind and compassionate person to be in your sort of job, so I beg of you, do not ignore the wishes of a dying woman and may God bless you for saving my child.

With my last breath, Calandra

Catriona's eyes welled up with tears as she read Calandra's words. Silently, she handed the letter to Marie-Jeanne, knowing, even before reading the solicitor's letter, that she was going to comply with the prima donna's final request.

Marie-Jeanne read the letter and handed it back to her friend. 'My goodness, poor woman! What are you going to do?'

'I'm going to go, of course,' Catriona sighed. 'Let's read what her lawyers have to say.'

The second envelope contained a letter outlining Calandra's wishes, the first of which stated that Catriona should treat Umberto in Italy. The terms were more than generous. On the signing of the contract, half a million euros would be deposited in an account of Catriona's choice, in any country she chose, and she would receive the same amount at the end of her three-month stint. During that time she was to take up residence at the Rolando Monteverdi family home on Lake Como, but in a separate dwelling, and Umberto would be her sole personal client. There would be no going back and forth to Nice to attend to other patients. Catriona's mother and son could come and visit her at any time and if they also decided to relocate, she would be provided with larger accommodation. Those were the only requirements of the agreement.

'A generous offer, I must admit,' Marie-Jeanne declared after reading it over Catriona's shoulder and taking up a seat at the other side of her desk.

Catriona put down the letter, looking pensive. 'Of course, the money will go into our company account but will the business survive? It's growing day by day and you know how difficult it is to find good, qualified practitioners in this field.'

'I don't think we'll have too much of a problem. With the sort of money Calandra's offering, if you put a reasonable portion of it into our account we'll be able to afford a suitable replacement for you.'

Catriona glanced up and smiled for the first time. 'I'll put it all into the business, of course I will. And it's very sweet of you not to make waves.'

'Trust me, if it wasn't for the fact that I know you won't rest until you've seen this through to the end, I would have tried to talk you out of it. But you've been so unhappy since Calandra's visit. I could see this coming.'

'So, you think my taking this case is a bad idea?'

Marie-Jeanne seemed to choose her words carefully. 'What I think is that Umberto needs help, and the professional in me would say there's no one better than you to provide it.' Her dark brown eyes scrutinized Catriona. 'But you have a tangled history with this man, and I know what he means to you. Staying detached will be almost impossible, don't you think?'

'Yes, it will be hard. I know it will take every ounce of my self-control,' admitted Catriona as she met Marie-Jeanne's level gaze. 'Because of the personal complications of this job, I thought there was nothing else to do but turn it down. But now, with Calandra writing on her deathbed … and as you say, I'm uniquely qualified for this.' She held her head in her hands and rubbed her temples.

'I do believe that music therapy could help Umberto through the trauma of losing his sight. Not only that, I could get him started with Braille so he can read a score.' Her tired eyes looked into those of her friend, desperate for answers. 'Can I really pass up the opportunity to help the father of my child when I'm best placed to provide the healing he needs? I'm not sure I could sleep at night if I walked away now.'

Not that I'm sleeping much anyhow, she thought ruefully.

Marie-Jeanne's face broke into a smile. 'You see? I told you there was no use trying to talk you out of it. It's a brave decision and I'm proud of you, *chérie*. Now you'll have a chance to tell Umberto about his son and help him at the same time. Still, do be careful,' she warned, her brow furrowed with concern, before her irrepressible self asserted itself again. 'So, what happens next?'

'I suppose I'll have to explain the situation to *Maman*, though I'm not looking forward to opening that can of worms. And telling Michael that I'm going away will be difficult.'

'Yes, I think your mother has a right to know and I'm sure that she won't stand in your way. As for Michael, it'll doubtless be hard for him but you have a strong relationship, and you'll be keeping in touch constantly.'

'It's not the same as having me here with him. Three months is a long time for a boy of his age.' Catriona gave a worried sigh. 'I'll need plenty of time to talk it over with him to get him used to the idea.'

'As for your not being there, he'll have his grandmother,' pointed out Marie-Jeanne. 'It'll give them some quality time together. I'm sure they'll both relish it in their own ways.'

Catriona gave a rueful smile. 'You're right. Michael is very attached to *Maman* and she'll love having him to herself. While I was busy studying and working, *Maman* and I took it in turns to read him bedtime stories and she loved fussing around him.' Her smile brightened. 'She's been wonderful. I don't know what I would have done without her.'

They left the office together but didn't stop at their usual teashop, instead separating at the edge of the Vieille Ville, where Catriona lived. She needed time alone to put her thoughts into some kind of order. First, she must decide how she would break the news of this new assignment to her mother and the fact she would be away for three months. And then would come the harder part, revealing the identity of the man she'd kept quiet about all these years.

It had been raining earlier but, as usual, the showers had not lasted long; at this time of year in this part of the world rain consisted of a mere sprinkling to clear the air unless there was a storm, which happened occasionally.

Catriona climbed one of the steep streets at the back of the town towards Castle Hill. At the top was a public garden, backed by a sombre mass of fig trees, looking out towards the blue horizon of the harbour and La Baie des Anges. Overlooking the Old Town, it was Catriona's favourite place, where she went to think whenever she had a problem.

She sat on one of the little rustic benches facing the view. The early evening light was still bright and, in the distance, the old citadel of Nice, deprived of its ramparts since the eighteenth century, still watched over the busy human hive humming at its feet as far as the line of the Paillon River. Closer, nestling into the hill, lay the maze of narrow streets, old houses and ruined palaces. An atmosphere of yesteryear reigned, with crowds of fishermens' wives crying the centuries-old 'A la bella poutina!' as their menfolk spread their fine mesh nets close to the beach to catch la poutine, the baby sardines and anchovies, a speciality of the Cote d'Azur.

Local food sellers were plying a busy trade, including those young farm girls who had come down for the day from neighbouring villages, selling flowers, cheeses, cured meats and other specialities from all over the Provençal region. From their lips poured forth laughter and song in one of the most striking dialects of the Mediterranean.

After Catriona and her mother had come back from Aix-en-Provence they had decided to live in Old Nice, with its quaint and sober narrow streets. However, she had chosen the area that lay between the new and the old town for her clinic. Here, the vivid splashes of bougainvillea and ivy adorning the houses had the richly varied colouring of the Italian Riviera. Maybe unconsciously she had been trying to stay in touch with Italian culture and, through it, maintain a connection with Umberto, Catriona wondered as she surveyed the toy town lying far below in the unmoving, tranquil air of the declining day.

As the damp grass, earth and leaves yielded up their fragrance, Catriona let her thoughts drift. No one was about, except an old woman who sat on another seat near a statue of Saint Francis. Catriona watched the bent and tired-looking figure and wondered what she was thinking about. At the foot of the statue someone – perhaps the old woman – had laid a bunch of tuberoses.

For a long time, Catriona sat there pondering, thoughts of the past and present and dreams of the future swirling in her head. In flashbacks her mind returned to that veranda of her bedroom at Les Platanes, where she'd sat, looking over the empty garden, the night she had discovered she was carrying Umberto's child.

She still remembered how she had felt. Not for a moment had she considered doing away with the little soul, like her friend Cécile had done with her pregnancy. She would keep the seed that was growing within her. Recalling how she had tilted her face up to stare into the dark velvet canopy above her that night, Catriona remembered the promise she had made to herself: she would be as steadfast as the stars shining so brightly and would face with courage her twilit road, no matter what lay ahead. Her mind had been made up immediately: Umberto's child would be born. Her love for that man, even though it had not been given the chance to flourish, would live on in his progeny.

Catriona had never regretted her decision; Michael was a wonder to her every single day. But still a heavy shadow of sadness enveloped her and at twenty-eight she had never let herself think of another man, let alone date one. Her heart and body lay dormant, shrivelled like winter leaves. Yet since Calandra's visit, all the feelings – the sensations she'd believed were forgotten – had bubbled up to the surface once more. And then today this new letter, another conundrum to face.

Presently, the sun began to set on the jagged mountains behind her and the fleeting magic of the hour was slowly drowned in darkness. Soon, the lighthouse in Nice Harbour and La Baie des Anges would shine and wink. The old woman bestirred herself and hobbled away.

Catriona walked back slowly, thinking of blindness, of suicide, of death; recalling her night of passion with Umberto, her mother's sacrifices and feeling keenly the love she felt for her son which, though vast, would never be enough to make up for the lack of a father.

After a decade, she'd become almost philosophical. That day Umberto had left for America, her world had come crashing down around her. Now she was afraid that he would have the power to hurt her all over again, throwing into chaos the organized, enjoyable, fruitful life she'd made for herself. Once again she would have to lean on Marguerite, and Marie-Jeanne would carry the burden of the clinic on her own.

Was she doing the right thing, running to Umberto's side?

She had read somewhere that love is the essence of all human experience. Was love the main reason for her decision? Certainly, she harboured a glimmer of hope that Umberto could one day be a true father to his son. But what of her own feelings? Deep down, did she still really love Umberto or was she just holding on to the old dream? Was it compassion? To a person as vibrant as Umberto, who loved everything beautiful with a passion, blindness would have come as a terrible blow. Yet the impulse to run to him had nothing to do with that. No, the truth was that she had never stopped loving him. Neither her mind nor her heart had been able to adjust to his leaving, remaining forever trapped in the thrall of a memory, the joys of a night that had elapsed like a dream.

When she reached home it was already past dinner time. Marguerite was sewing in the living room and Michael was upstairs reading in bed, his homework done, piano practice over and his computer turned off. Those were *Maman*'s rules and Catriona had adopted them with her son without question. Marguerite's rulebook had carried Catriona through the ups and downs of her chaotic young life – aside from the upset with Umberto – and she was grateful for it. Today, thanks to the sagacity of her mother, she was a strong, confident and independent woman, with a brilliant career that was envied by many.

Catriona would not go up against her mother without any valid reason. Still, what would she do if, having revealed Umberto's identity to Marguerite, the latter opposed her decision to go? She rushed upstairs to Michael's room. He put down the book he was reading and smiled at his mother.

'*Bonsoir, Maman*, you're home!' He scrambled off the bed to give her a hug. She held him tightly and kissed his cheek, then held his face in both hands as she smoothed his dark hair away from his temple. It now gave her an added pang of awareness to see the way his hair flopped slightly over his forehead in the same way as Umberto's. The big eyes that stared back at her, although brown, had the same intense glitter as his father's green ones. Even the air of maturity beyond his years she fancied had almost certainly come from Umberto.

He jumped back on the bed and she followed him, sitting down on the edge. She made her voice deliberately bright. 'Is that a new book you're reading?' She picked it up. '*Musique au Château du Ciel: Un portrait de Jean-Sébastien Bach* … I'm impressed.' Catriona had herself read this book on the composer's life and had been enthralled, but it was not light reading. She felt a twinge in her heart: he'd never had a father with whom to play football or go fishing. Think how much he could share with Umberto, seeing as both of their chief passions were music and books. Her son's voice came through the haze of her thoughts.

'It's all about Bach's life. *Mademoiselle* Lucette lent it to me.'

'Isn't a little serious for you, darling?'

'Oh no, it's very exciting. Honestly! The man who wrote it … when he was a boy, his parents had a painting of Bach in their house. And he had to hide there. You see, *Maman*, there was a war and he didn't want the enemy to find him.'

'Yes, the Second World War, *chéri*. *Mémé*'s grandfather fought in it.'

'The one with the glass eye?'

'Yes, that one.'

'Well, in my book here, the boy thought the painting stared at him every time he walked past. He was my age, and played Bach, just like me. He's now a famous performer.'

'Yes, I've got a John Eliot Gardiner recording. I'll play it to you, if you like.'

'Okay …' Michael looked up at his mother, his large eyes widening as though a new thought had just popped into his head.

'*Maman*, can I ask you something?' he said suddenly. 'There's a camping trip coming up. They told us about it today at school.'

Catriona smiled. 'Oh yes? That sounds like fun.'

He gave her a quizzical look. 'It's for sons and fathers though, and … well, I don't have a father, so do you think they'd let me go with Emile's *papa*?'

This innocent statement hit Catriona like a hammer. She sat there speechless, staring at nothing in particular. It cut her to the quick that Michael was missing out on simple but fundamental pleasures that he could have shared with Umberto. How much longer could she deny her son the opportunity of knowing his father?

'*Alors, Maman*, you didn't answer me. Is it all right for me to go with Emile and his *papa*?' the boy repeated.

Catriona gave him a pale smile and when she spoke, her voice trembled slightly. '*Oui, oui, mon chéri*, of course you can go, sweetheart. That's very kind of Emile's father to offer to take you. I'll speak to the school.'

He beamed back at her. '*Fantastique! Merci, Maman*. You're the best. I've always wanted to go camping.' He dived under his duvet, then paused, his expression showing that his mind was once more flitting elsewhere. 'I'll be a great composer one day like Bach, *Maman, n'est-ce pas?*'

'Yes, my darling, of course.' She bent over and hugged him. *A great composer like your father*, she thought, her heart weeping. 'And now it's time to go to sleep. It's past nine o'clock and you've got school tomorrow.'

She kissed him and hugged him again, hard against her chest, suddenly realizing how difficult it would be for her to leave him for three months, even if he was allowed to visit during the holidays. All through her studies and her working life she had never left her son for more than a week. Tears threatened to spill down. She had always been demonstrative towards Michael but tonight this show of affection was unusually unrestrained. It had a poignancy that the boy was quick to pick up on. He looked up at his mother, a little frown between his eyebrows. '*Ça va, Maman?* Are you all right, *Maman?*'

'Yes, of course, my darling.'

'Okay, that's good.' He gave a little yawn. 'I love you, *Maman.*'

'I love you too, *petit. Fait de beaux rêves*, sweet dreams.'

Catriona turned off the main light and turned on the green night light, standing a moment more in the doorway to look at her son. She wondered at the beauty and love that were a living part not only of herself but of Umberto, the man she had adored and for whom she still held a candle. Michael was his son.

Once again, she felt a choking sensation as the powerful emotion launched its broadside. To her, Michael was perfection personified, the reason why there was no way on earth – even if she had the power to turn back the clock – that she would ever have chosen to erase the brief, devastating presence of Umberto from her life. At that moment, Catriona knew beyond doubt that she needed to put things right, if not for her or Umberto's sake, at least for Michael's. How could she not go to Italy now?

Studying the small face in the half-shadow of the night light, her eyes luminous with love, Catriona saw a miniature replica of the features she had wanted to forget for so long. She had never been so aware of the resemblance between father and son as she was tonight and, for a heart-stopping instant, she was gripped by a raw and primitive desire for another child by the man she would soon meet again. The sensation left her shaken and confused.

Catriona closed the door and went to her bedroom to remove her work clothes, exchanging them for a pair of jeans and an old sweater before going downstairs to face her mother with the truth.

Marguerite looked up from her sewing when her daughter entered the living room. 'You look tired. There is a nice *Civet de Lapin* waiting for you in the warming oven and Sidonie picked this year's first asparagus from the garden, your favourite.'

'Thank you, *Maman*. I'm not very hungry. I think I might just have a hot chocolate.' She went to the kitchen and made herself a large cup and a thick slice of *pain de campagne* spread with a thin layer of butter and homemade mulberry jam.

When she returned to the living room, the familiar scene looked so warm and peaceful; her mother sewing in her usual comfortable English armchair near the fireplace. In winter, when the howling winds blew over the Mediterranean and violent storms enlivened the usually azure skies, Catriona loved to snuggle up with a book on one of the two Chippendale sofas that ran along either side of the room and listen to the fire roaring in the grate while nature raged outside. Michael liked to watch storms from the safety of this room; the three French windows that opened straight on to the garden always gave a good view of tall beech trees and elegant *pins parasol* swaying in the gusts.

He spent so much time in the living room. Even from the earliest age his eyes were immediately drawn to the shining ebony of the elegant baby grand, watching it glimmer like black fire under the impressive chandelier of Baccarat crystal. Most evenings, though, Marguerite and her daughter preferred the pools of subdued light from the table lamps; sometimes, when Catriona was out at a business dinner, Marguerite would only use the light from a standard lamp near her armchair while the rest of the room remained in shadow, leaving it lit for when Catriona came home. Tonight was one of those nights and the silent room, bathed in mellow lighting, seemed to invite confidences.

Her mother put her sewing down on her lap and glanced at Catriona. 'You're very late. I thought you must be at some official dinner. Bad day?'

Catriona's mouth formed into a very French pout. 'Euuh, not great!'

'Want to talk about it?' Marguerite went on, picking up her sewing again.

I'm going to have to talk about it, Catriona thought with resignation.

'You've been preoccupied all month … so quiet. You're getting thinner, you know. And look at those dark circles under your eyes. Is anything wrong?' Marguerite asked her.

Catriona sat down on the sofa next to her mother's chair and sipped her hot chocolate silently for a long minute.

'I've been offered an assignment,' she said finally, between bites of bread and jam.

'Difficult?' her mother asked, without lifting her head.

'Yes … difficult and unusual.'

Marguerite stopped sewing. 'Worth the trouble?'

There was a pause while Catriona gave her mother a hollow look. She experienced a few moments of apprehension before she blurted out: 'It means I'll have to go and live in Italy for three months.'

Her mother shook her head disapprovingly. 'Ridiculous!'

'They're paying a lot of money.'

'Since when has money been an issue or your aim, *ma chérie*?'

'It's rather more complicated than that.'

Marguerite's forehead wrinkled thoughtfully as she studied her daughter's face.

'Come on, out with it, *chérie*. You'll feel much better,' she said calmly.

Catriona's voice was deep and almost inaudible. 'It's a long story.'

'I suspect it is. I've rarely seen you look so concerned, and the fact you're even considering such madness makes me think that this is a serious matter. What is it, Catriona? You know you can talk to me, don't you?'

'Of course I know that, but I don't want to hurt you.'

Marguerite made an attempt at laughing. 'Hurt me? You could never hurt me, *ma chérie*.'

'This could change our whole lives once again.'

'Why, have you had an offer of marriage?'

'No … no, it's not that … but, you see, it does have to do with what happened years ago.'

Marguerite's eyes flashed. 'You mean that scoundrel has come back into your life?'

Catriona took a few sips of hot chocolate and cleared her throat. 'Well, he's in a bad way and I've been asked to take him on as a client.'

Marguerite now fixed her daughter with an intense look. 'What's going on, Catriona? I have a feeling you're only telling me half the truth. You never told me his name, and I never insisted because you told me that you knew almost nothing about him. A tourist, you said.'

Catriona fidgeted uncomfortably in her chair. 'That wasn't quite true, actually. He's quite a well known figure.'

'Do I know him?' Her mother frowned.

'Well, sort of. You've definitely heard of him … who hasn't?' she gave a derisive laugh.

'And he is …?'

Catriona swallowed. 'Umberto Rolando Monteverdi.'

There was a moment of stunned silence. 'You mean the composer? The one who had the house next door? Whose turbulent life was always in the headlines?'

'Yes.'

Marguerite looked shell-shocked. 'However did you get involved with him?'

'I feel such a fool, *Maman*, but you need to know the whole story now.'

And so, once more, Catriona delved deep into the past, bringing back to the surface all the passion, anger and pain but also the love that had been buried for so many years in her heart. Slowly, she began to relate to her mother her pitiful story, the guilt and remorse welling up inside as tears of hurt and helplessness rolled down her cheeks.

Marguerite sat quietly throughout her daughter's monologue. At first, the old anger at the stranger who had seduced her teenage daughter seemed to have resurfaced, etched on her furrowed brow. Now, only her eyes spoke her sadness in an otherwise expressionless face. 'You still love him, don't you?' she asked when Catriona finally stopped talking.

'I don't know. As a healer, I somehow feel I should go to him, help him get back on his feet.'

'Of course, I can understand that, but the most important point is that you speak to him. No matter what happened in the past, he's the father of your son and you can't deny him the right of knowing it. Now more than ever, when he's in such a bad way.'

Catriona's hackles rose. 'He has no rights as a father. He gave those up the day he turned his back on me without a second's hesitation,' she exploded bitterly, surprising even herself.

Marguerite regarded her daughter with sympathy but she shook her head. '*Non*, Catriona, that is a different matter altogether. He was never given a choice where his rights were concerned. That was your decision. However, nothing will ever change the fact that Michael is his flesh and blood.'

Catriona wiped her wet cheeks with the back of her hand and let out a slow breath. She didn't realize she had buried so much anger. 'Part of me wants to hurt him back, the other part realizes that I need to clarify the situation. Deep in my heart, I know I owe both Michael and Umberto that, even if it's going to create chaos in all our lives.'

Marguerite nodded silently and then sighed. '*Oui*, I suppose so, but three months is a long time. Can't you travel back and forth? Or maybe he could relocate to one of his houses here on the Riviera?'

'He sold all his property in France. Anyhow, the terms of the contract stipulate that I have to be at his villa at Lake Como for three months without a break. You and Michael can come and visit, but I must remain there.' Catriona took out the two letters she had received that morning and gave them to her mother. 'You're a lawyer … the conditions are pretty clear, aren't they?'

Marguerite went through the documents, reading them carefully. 'You're right. You either accept the whole assignment or turn it down. There's no scope for half measures. Not only that but, if you decide midway to leave the job, you have to return the half-million euros you're receiving on signature of the contract. That's draconian, not to say manipulative.' She put the page down and removed her reading glasses. 'In short, *chérie*, you need to be really sure you want to take this on.'

'What should I do?'

'My dear child, only you can make that decision. I will support you in whatever you decide, of course. The letter doesn't say if *il signor* Umberto Monteverdi himself knows about this arrangement. There's no mention of his physical health, only his mental state, and even that is ambiguous. Are you strong enough to take on such a heavy task? If your feelings are involved, will you be able to carry out your professional duty thoroughly and objectively? These are all questions you need to ask yourself before taking such a serious decision.'

Catriona shrugged helplessly and looked away, feeling a moment of weakness. 'Shouldn't I just forget about it, so no one gets hurt?' she murmured.

'I think you know the answer to that question, *ma chérie*, don't you?'

'Why on earth would I want to open the wound again?'

'To lay a ghost to rest for one thing. At a very young and impressionable age you met a man who obviously swept you off your feet. You had a one-night stand that led to a total life change for you, even life crisis, though it's hard to call it that when we have darling Michael as its outcome. It's only natural that the flash-in-the-pan liaison you had with Umberto Monteverdi and its aftermath left you with emotional scars, even though you like to pretend it hasn't affected your life.'

At that, Catriona appeared ready to interject indignantly, but Marguerite silenced her with a knowing look. 'It was ten years ago, *chérie*! You should have got over it long ago, fallen in love with someone else and married him … had other children.'

Catriona said unevenly, her nerves jangling: 'That has nothing to do with my being emotionally scarred. Michael and my work take up all my time.'

Marguerite smiled at her silently until Catriona caved in. 'Yes, all right, I know I've never moved on. And you're right, I've already made up my mind that I can't deny Umberto the right of knowing he has a son. I know that I have to take this case, whatever the consequences.'

Marguerite gave a confirming nod.

Her brown eyes perplexed, Catriona gazed up her mother. 'How do you think Michael will take it?'

'He's very mature for his age. Of course, I don't think we should tell him that the person you will be treating is his father. And he's used to you working very hard. I think if he knows that he can come and visit and spend holidays with you, then it will not disrupt his life too much. *La nuit porte conseil.* Sleep on it, *ma chérie.*'

'I'll have breakfast with Michael and drop him off at school.'

'That's a bad idea if you're going to be disappearing for months. I wouldn't advise a change in his routine,' Marguerite said firmly. 'I think he should go by bus to school as usual.' It was no surprise to Catriona that her mother took up the mantle of control. She did so habitually, but this time it did serve to soothe her tattered nerves.

'As usual, *Maman*, you're right. I'll find time to tell him tomorrow, though. The longer he has to absorb the fact that I'm going away, the better. I need to reassure him that he can come and see me soon and we can talk on the phone whenever he wants, and I don't want it to be done in a rush.'

With a sigh, Catriona stood up, went over to the window and stepped out into the garden.

'You'll catch cold,' she heard her mother say. 'There's a storm forecast for tonight.'

She looked up at a sky hung with stormclouds, its pale moon partly obscured – very like the one on that fateful night with Umberto in Villefranche, she thought to herself as she stepped off the lawn at the back of the house into the grass of the orchard. A chill wind was blowing from the highest peaks of the Alps behind Nice, making a dismal rustle among the fruit trees. She never heard such fatal murmurs nor had she ever felt herself in such a gloomy cast of mind – even after Umberto had left her, even after she had discovered she was carrying his child.

Catriona had never believed in destiny before but everything in her life had begun to take on a fateful complexion. Tonight, she was a prophet of doom, full of melancholy forebodings, which the whispering of the leaves seemed to echo. Her mood bordered upon despair as she felt trapped into embarking on a strange adventure, the outcome of which might well be destructive.

When the storm broke and great drops of rain came cascading down, Catriona returned to the lawn, where she stood under the rain, her face lifted to the sky. She welcomed the feeling of the fresh water drenching her as she watched the fantastic forms of thick clouds continually torn, scattered and reunited by the wind. They looked as if they had been painted by a heavenly brush – shaded dark lower down, lighter above and illuminated dramatically when lightning flashed through them.

As quickly as it came, the storm went. The night sky brightened and then, suddenly, a very pale gleam of yellow light appeared opposite the moon. *How extraordinary*, Catriona marvelled. *It must be a moon bow!* She had read about lunar rainbows, caused by the moon's light refracted off water droplets in much fainter colours than those created by the sun. In local superstition they were considered a good omen, she remembered, amused at her own desire to find meaning in the vagaries of nature.

She was cold now, so she hurried back to the house. Marguerite had gone up to bed but had left her bedroom door ajar to listen out for her daughter. When Catriona went up, her mother called out: '*Ça va, ma chérie?*'

Catriona put her head around the door. '*Oui, beaucoup mieux, Maman, merci*, much better, thank you.'

Marguerite shook her head disapprovingly. 'Look at you, you're wet through! Go and have a hot bath.'

'Yes, I will. But you know the rain did me a lot of good. At least it helped wash away some of my anger.'

'Try not to think of anything tonight and get a good night's sleep, *ma chérie*. The Monteverdis don't have to have an answer straight away, remember. There's nothing in the contract that says that, so take your time.'

'Yes, yes, of course. *Bonne nuit, Maman.*'

'*Bonne nuit, ma chérie.*'

Catriona did not expect to go to sleep. The thought of the night ahead, with Calandra's letter still gnawing away at her, filled her with dread. Her anger had abated but had only been replaced by misery. Stifling a sob of protest as her memories again lit an urgent need in her, she leaned over and turned off the bedside lamp. Since Calandra's visit it had grown worse. It was as though her body had no memory of the intervening years, yearning for Umberto now with the same insatiable hunger with which it had once welcomed him.

She buried her face in the pillows, howling her despair into their softness. He was like a disease that had taken a terrible toll on her, one from which she had never recovered, judging by her inability to form relationships with other men. Her mother was right, she should have moved on by now. She was not short of admirers but although these men were decent and intelligent, the pattern had always been the same: the moment any man showed too much interest in her, a powerful, uncontrollable response was triggered, forcing her to terminate any budding relationship. Invariably, this left her hating herself for her own weakness.

She lay there for hours, her thoughts twisting and turning through the landscapes of the past and whatever unknown terrain was yet to come. Finally exhausted, Catriona drifted off to sleep, slipping into total unconsciousness.

*   *   *

The next morning, Catriona showered and dressed and went down to the kitchen. *I'll make some pancakes for breakfast*, she thought. *Michael loves them and it'll take my mind off things.*

Taking a bowl from the cupboard, she gathered the ingredients on the marble worktop. After wiping a pan with oil, she turned on the radio just as the presenter was saying: 'The world-acclaimed prima donna Calandra Rolando Monteverdi, who had been fighting lung cancer for two years, died last night at the clinic attached to the European Institute of Oncology in Milan. The funeral will be held on Sunday at Duomo de Milano, the Gothic cathedral on the main square of the city. Family and friends are expected to fly from Torno on Lake Como and from every corner of the globe to pay their last respects to the well loved diva. It's believed that almost a thousand people will attend.'

So much for taking my mind off things, Catriona thought as she made a well in the flour and added the milk, eggs and a pinch of salt. Feeling tense, she whisked the mixture more energetically than usual before adding a spoonful of oil. She was just proceeding to pour a small ladleful into the pan when she heard the familiar sound of feet running down the stairs. It always made her smile that her son made enough noise for two people when he entered a room.

'*Bonjour, Maman.*' Michael burst into the kitchen like a breath of fresh air. '*Ça sent bon! Des crêpes pour le petit déjeuner, quel regal!* That smells nice! Pancakes for breakfast, what a treat!' He ran to his mother and kissed her.

'Do you want them plain with sugar and lemon, or would you prefer them with our mulberry jam?'

'With lemon and sugar, please.' And in the same breath, 'Can I go to Jeannot's house after school today? We only have a half day and his *maman* is trying out her new ice-cream machine.'

'What about your homework?'

'We never have much on Thursdays.'

'Wouldn't you prefer me to take you to the cinema? They're showing *The Lorax* at the Pathé Masséna this week.'

'*Non, Maman*. Jeannot's also asked Elise and her brother Jacques. Please, *Maman*, we can go to *The Lorax* another day.'

'Of course, *mon petit*,' she replied, thinking wistfully, *that might not be so soon.*

'*Tu as l'air triste, Maman, ça va*? You look sad, *Maman*, are you all right?'

'I'm fine, *mon chéri*. Just a little tired.'

Michael was a sensitive child, Marguerite was right. She must make sure his life was disturbed as little as possible. Things must continue as normal for him. Catriona laid the plate of pancakes on the table with a big jug of hot chocolate and sat down opposite her son. She found herself almost missing him already as she sipped the steaming liquid, listening to him chattering and loving him more than ever.

Still, her mind was made up: she would call the Italian lawyer today and make her arrangements for the end of the month. The earlier she set off, the quicker this ordeal would be over.

CHAPTER 6

One month later

Catriona stood at the front of the ferry as it moved slowly through the water on its way to Torno. It had been a long but interesting journey: first, by plane to Milan, then by train to Lake Como. The boat itself was quaint, not at all like the multi-storey ferries that docked at Nice and the other harbours on the French Riviera. It had a vaguely fin-de-siècle aura and as soon as the gangplank had lifted and the boat slowly moved away from the shore, the trip began to have an almost unreal feel to it.

Under bright sunlit skies the view of Lake Como was wondrous to behold. A deep sense of serenity overcame her as she stared in rapture at the expanse of blue that lay before her. The lake was the finest of mirrors, never reflecting exactly what was above but converting it to an image so beautifully smudged and broken.

Although Catriona had been tired she found the slow and leisurely ferry ride over the lake exhilarating and almost heart-stopping in its beauty – a lyrical gouache of colour stabbed at intervals by the solemnity of the stately cypress, a tree very much native to Italy. On both sides of the boat the magnificent rocky shores were studded with the gardens of Italian belle-époque villas, crowded with a wealth of rare trees, exotic flowers and broad lawns, with narrow pink or mellow yellow stone staircases that went down to the edge of the lake. As the ferry glided past, her vivid and romantic imagination conjured up bygone scenes of gentlemen in striped blazers, flannels and straw boaters, accompanied on deck by ladies in long dresses, side-buttoned kidskin boots and holding parasols.

Towering over all, and filling half the round of the horizon, reared the mighty Alpine chain with its base wrapped in a robe of imperial purple, flinging its countless crests towards the blue heaven like the defiant arms of the mythic Titans. In the warming rays of the afternoon sun, fragrant blooms were launching their scent on the balmy air while the boat rocked to the liquid ripple of the lake in the infinite silence.

Then suddenly, as if each of her senses was to be assailed in turn, the campaniles pealed out their morning hymn in rich and solemn melodies, each slowly uttered cadence pausing as though listening for the answer from some distant tower.

Thoughts too deep for words began to stir in Catriona. The emotion that caught at her heart, as she listened to the eloquent bells fling their voices upon the air, brought tears to her eyes. She couldn't believe that she was going to see *him* again. As she gazed around her at the almost stifling beauty of her surroundings, anticipation seemed to cling to the stillness of everything. This was Umberto's world. She wondered what sort of a man he had become. Everything she had read about him told her that he was the shadow of his former self, a broken man. Would she be able to help him, she wondered, her self-confidence suddenly shaken.

Half an hour later, the boat approached the shore and Catriona joined a handful of other passengers snaking off the ferry and on to the dock. She had been told that she would be met here, but not by whom. Wheeling her suitcase to a halt on the quayside, she shielded her eyes against the sun and spotted a figure leaning against the railings, smoking. Dressed smartly in a short-sleeve white shirt and dark trousers, he wore sunglasses and was holding a large white sign bearing her name in large black letters.

When Catriona lifted a hand to wave at him he threw down his cigarette and walked over to her. In that time she registered the man's symmetrical face with high cheekbones, an aquiline nose and full lips. He was deeply tanned and his black hair, streaked here and there with silver threads, swept back from a wide forehead. Tall for an Italian, he stood very straight; slender and fit despite his years – which must be nearly sixty, she thought. As he walked with fast and easy strides he looked perfectly serious and professional, although when he took off his sunglasses and shook her hand she saw laughter lines around dark brown eyes.

'*Ben arrivata, signora*, welcome, *signora*,' he said and his face split into a grin she guessed he wore often.

'Pleased to meet you,' said Catriona, feeling immediately at ease.

'I am Mario. I work with the Monteverdi family and will be driving you up to the house. Let me take your case. I hope you had a pleasant trip?'

'Thank you, yes. It's beautiful here,' said Catriona, looking around her at the tall, balconied buildings clustered around the harbour, their dusty orange, pink and white façades a colourful contrast to the dark green hills that reared up behind.

Mario nodded and smiled. '*Sì, bellissmo*,' he answered with, she sensed, a characteristic brevity. He took her case and laptop bag and led her to a silver Lancia parked under a row of plane trees along the quayside.

It was a short journey to the Monteverdi estate, during which time Mario indeed proved himself a restrained conversationalist. He answered her questions politely without giving away very much. She gathered he had been working for the Monteverdi family for more than twenty years and had great respect and admiration for his employer, and for Calandra, whom he clearly missed. '*Era una grande artista e una gran donna in tutti i sensi*, she was a great artist and a great lady in every sense of the word,' Mario told Catriona.

'Calandra was unique,' she agreed. 'She will be sorely missed by a great many people.'

Catriona watched the road wind its way up the hillside, past terracotta-roofed villas tucked away behind cypress trees. She paused, wondering how much Mario would be prepared to divulge about the diva's son, then said hesitantly: 'It must have been difficult for you these past few years … seeing so much happen to the family.'

Mario kept his eyes ahead. 'Change is part of life, we must all deal with that. *Non tutto il male vien per nuocere*, not everything that is bad comes to hurt us,' he added enigmatically.

'You must have known *il signor* Monteverdi since he was a boy.'

'*Sì*,' Mario nodded, turning his head to smile at her. 'Like one of my own sons.'

'It's good he has your support, and there must be others at the house who help him,' she ventured, fishing for information.

He gave a short nod. 'Adelina and I look after him now.'

Catriona searched her memory. The name was familiar. Umberto had talked about her, she was sure. 'Wasn't she *il signor* Monteverdi's nanny when he was a boy?' Then, remembering herself, she added quickly: 'I think Calandra mentioned it when we met.'

'She was his nanny, yes. Now … well,' he shrugged, 'Adelina is Adelina. She cooks and does everything that's needed. Between us, we manage, *signora*.' He glanced at her. '*Mi scusi*, I should call you *Dottoressa*, no?'

Catriona waved his apology away. 'It's fine.'

Mario fell silent for a moment, then said: '*Dottoressa*, it's good that you are here.'

After that, Catriona found him reticent on most subjects to do with Umberto, including whether his cousin Giacomo and Silvana were staying in the house, and although he wasn't exactly forthcoming, Mario seemed like someone she could trust.

They drove along a country lane bordered by a low white fence until Catriona saw an open, wrought-iron gate some way ahead of them. Through it a wide avenue seemed to beckon them in, vaulted by arms of giant live oaks and draped with grey moss. It must be the villa's drive, Catriona thought, her stomach fluttering in nervous anticipation.

As they drove up the avenue, occasional flickers of sunlight penetrated the shady gloom to spot the carpet of green moss and ivy, and other shafts of light gave the impression of white pillars supporting the roof of this leafy tunnel. They passed trails leading off into the different parts of the garden flanking the avenue and Catriona had glimpses of great white statues and enormous urns among the trees. Despite her nerves, she smiled to herself. It was almost like walking down the nave at Saint Peter's in Rome and catching sight of charming little chapels to the right and left. Extraordinary!

Then suddenly they were out of the darkness into the sunshine, and there it was: Villa Monteverdi, standing in all its elegant snow-white splendour against a background of tall, dark-green cypresses, a colourful shrubbery and low bright topiary trees adding lighter touches. The whole scene, as it appeared from the end of the avenue of oaks, formed an arena of myriad colours, among which proudly reposed the magnificent Italian Renaissance-style villa, fronted by an immaculate lawn. They approached from the side of the house and drove slowly past the impressive façade towards a small cluster of conifers.

'*L'Alloggio del Gufo Reale*, the Eagle Owl Lodge is just beyond,' Mario explained, gesturing ahead. 'It's named after the forest behind it, and that's where you'll be staying.'

As the car came alongside a low stone wall at the edge of the trees, Catriona caught sight of a figure perched at the far end of it, watching them. He was a wiry man, fairly good-looking, with a chiselled face and unkempt and greasy black hair that trailed down almost to his shoulders. There was a calculating expression in his cold, piercing-blue eyes as they followed the progress of the car, one that wasn't wholly friendly, and it made Catriona want to turn away when he met her stare through the open window. He took a packet of cigarettes from his pocket and began to whistle a slow tune to himself as the car slowed beside him.

Mario gave him a brief gesture of greeting as the car crawled past, bumping over the uneven path, and the man nodded back, his knowing gaze openly moving over Catriona as the car moved on.

'Who was that?' she asked, seeing in the wing mirror that the man was still watching them and whistling as he lit a cigarette.

'That's Flavio, the boatman.' Mario paused. 'As well as his usual duties, he takes the *signore* swimming in the lake.'

The sight of the boatman had done nothing to quell Catriona's underlying sense of unease. She shivered. 'Has he been working here long?'

Mario shrugged. 'Six years or so.' The car came to a stop. 'This is the lodge, *Dottoressa*.'

Catriona gasped in delight at the beautiful old building that had been obscured by the copse. The main house was impressive but the lodge was a little work of art in itself.

It was a two-storey villa, with a rubbed, dark-pink stucco exterior and a sloping tiled roof, its eaves set far out, throwing afternoon shade over a beautiful old iron front door. Narrow arched windows on the first floor each had their own wrought-iron balcony and looked out on to a garden whose colour scheme reflected different shades of terracotta, whether from the bronzed shrubbery or the trumpet-like day lilies and pink old roses. Catriona climbed out of the car and stood for a moment, eyes closed, inhaling the sublime fragrance of the yellow-and-white scented rose that rambled over the outside of the villa. The place was so exquisite, it had the immediate effect of soothing her qualms.

'It's stunning,' Catriona breathed, almost to herself.

Mario smiled warmly as he pulled Catriona's suitcase from the boot and deposited it on the step. '*Sì, magnifico, eh? Era il rifugio della signora*, the *signora*'s retreat. You are the first to stay here.' He pushed the front door open. 'Let me show you around.'

'*Sì, grazie*,' Catriona beamed, and followed him inside.

The interior was equally beautiful, boasting Italian polished marble floors and vaulted ceilings painted with intricate murals between the exposed whitewashed beams. Lovely colours delighted the eye, from the frescos on the walls to the brocades and silks of the curtains and cushion covers and upholstery on chairs and sofas. For a moment it seemed to Catriona that a transient bloom of feminine loveliness and grace gleamed here, as though in remembrance of Calandra.

Catriona ran her hand down the smooth curtains. 'This is wonderful.'

'All the soft furnishings are made in the Monteverdi silk factory,' Mario informed her.

She was surprised. 'The family owns a silk factory? I had no idea.'

There was a four-sided fireplace in the centre of the living room and a circular staircase of gleaming wood, which led to the upper floor. Soaring windows shaped like gothic arches framed Lake Como, and kept one focused on the breathtaking surroundings. Still, the room that had the most effect on Catriona was the one that Mario described as 'Calandra's haven', tucked on to the end of the lodge on the ground floor. The door was so low that Catriona would have easily missed it, thinking it led to a cupboard, if Mario hadn't pointed it out. Once inside, she marvelled at the spectacular opulence of the room, a real feast for the eye. Not because of the furnishings – it was almost bare apart from the Bechstein piano that took pride of place in the middle of the small room – but because of the side wall that was made entirely of glass.

Catriona heard Mario clear his throat. '*Dottoressa*, I will go now and leave you to explore the rest of the lodge. Adelina will come by shortly to take you to the main house. I've left your case in the bedroom upstairs.'

The butterflies in her stomach started fluttering again. '*Grazie*, Mario. Thank you for everything.'

He nodded and smiled, closing the door behind him.

Catriona let out a long breath and turned back to the room. Somehow it reminded her of that other stark room in Villefranche all those years ago, with only a piano and a roaring fire to witness her and Umberto's passionate lovemaking. A shiver went up her spine and she was glad that she was now alone, her cheeks heating at the memories that seeped into her mind.

She could still picture that night in Villefranche so clearly: the storm, the lightning, the purple and orange dappled shadows of the living room but, most of all, she remembered Umberto's tanned and nearly naked body, muscled and firm-fleshed, leaning against the open French windows that gave on to the terrace. And then the look of male arousal darkening his emerald eyes as he'd said in that deep voice she would never forget: 'Afraid, *cara*?' She felt her body stir at the recollection and as she walked past the piano, she sighed, letting her hand skim the smooth, polished surface.

Catriona moved towards the glass window. Here, in this space, the lushness came from the outside. Adding to the range of vivid red, rose and violet colours that abounded in the garden, there suddenly came into view screens of white flowering bushes – more roses and Mexican orange blossom – and deep patches of bright yellow jasmine. The abundance of floral colours seemed to evoke a theme and, inevitably, she was reminded of music. Everything appeared entirely natural but there was not a branch, a slope, a flowering hedge that had not been planned to produce a well calculated effect … nature's concerto.

Still, in contrast with the rest of the lodge, Calandra's piano room was humble. The other rooms had clearly been refurbished to the diva's own design, each one frescoed with scenes from various ballets and operas so that it had its very own atmosphere. The huge living room had the exotic mood of a harem in an oriental palace as a backdrop for the dancers of *Sheherazade*. The dining area was more sober, taking its inspiration from the Paris salon of the famous courtesan Violetta Valéry from *La Traviata*. Up the staircase, a sliding door led to the second bedroom, where low screens and tables helped to bring to life the Japanese garden in Puccini's *Madam Butterfly*. As for what was evidently Calandra's study, it had the flamboyant red and gold colours of *Carmen*, with more paintings, each representing an act of the dramatic opera.

Catriona followed the beautiful little Renaissance staircase up to a turret where the master suite – bedroom, bathroom and dressing room – jutted over the lake. Large and luxurious, and hung with handwoven silk, of all the rooms in the lodge this was the one that took her breath away. Framed in two of the windows was the wide expanse of Lake Como, the encroaching mountains wading into the deep, still water; the third window overlooked the forest and the outline of the Alps: the perfect scene for Tchaikovsky's *Swan Lake*.

Catriona stared out over the lake. She could just imagine what the room would look like at night with the full moon shining on the water. All the soft furnishings were white, ivory, silver and very pale gold, the furniture of stripped natural oak; only the paintings on the walls held splashes of colour, and even those mostly depicted swans. Standing in the centre of the room, Catriona imagined she had entered an enchanted world.

Against the middle of the back wall stood a magnificent ivory-coloured nineteenth-century Italian king-size bed, raised above the floor on carved and gilt short cabriole legs. Silk curtains were gathered into a crown at its head and it was flanked by matching bedside tables, topped with dainty Murano glass lamps.

The rest of the furniture was in the same hand-painted style as the bed: a *comò*, a chest of drawers; a stunning dressing table with a stool; and a mirrored wardrobe next to French windows that opened on to a small veranda. Flanking the dressing table were two eighteenth-century hand-carved Venetian Rococo armchairs, while a beautiful opaline glass and crystal Maria Theresa chandelier hung from the whitewashed ceiling.

Catriona was climbing back down the stairs when there was a knock at the front door. When she hurried to open it, a woman in her late sixties was standing there, dressed in a black frock with a white collar and matching white apron. She was tall and thin, almost wiry, with a coarse wrinkled face and keen dark eyes; her thick and glistening grey hair was twisted into a high chignon. Her hand was surprisingly strong as she grasped Catriona's in greeting, her smile polite and reserved, though her gaze seemed as though it missed nothing.

'Ah, you must be the new *Dottoressa*. I am Adelina.'

'Catherine Drouot. Pleased to meet you, Adelina.'

'I hope you have found the lodge to your taste?'

'It's beautiful … well beyond what I expected. Thank you.'

She nodded. 'The *signore* is a hospitable and generous man.'

'I can see that.'

The woman gave Catriona a sideways glance. 'No one has been here since the *signore*'s mother passed away. Apparently, she insisted you stay here. You are a very special guest, *Dottoressa*. Come, I'll show you to the main house.'

The light outside had begun to soften as late afternoon slipped towards dusk. Crossing the garden, they entered the main house through an imposing sculpted wooden door within a stone portal. Catriona looked up as they did so, noticing that it was topped by the family's coat of arms, the crowned golden *Gufo Reale* holding a key in one claw, a sword in the other. Then they were inside a magnificent hall with a geometric black-and-white marble tiled floor, a high frescoed ceiling and a curved white marble staircase with a finely chiselled banister. Everything here was eloquent testimony to the wealth of the Monteverdi family.

As Catriona followed Adelina across the hall, she caught a glimpse of heavy Renaissance furniture, richly inlaid with ivory, gold, stone, marble and marquetry. The murals were full of colour and splendour, while the ceiling depicted knights jousting and medieval ladies playing with doves, their winged sleeves sweeping to the ground, surrounded by little cupids darting their arrows of love. Tall arched windows and doors were surmounted by carved friezes set with pieces of jewel-coloured glass and Catriona looked up to see great chandeliers twinkling above her head. The spaciousness and splendour took her breath away – she'd had no idea …

It was not yet quite six o'clock when Adelina left her in the *salone*.

'I will inform *il signor* Monteverdi that you are here. He should be with you shortly.'

Catriona looked around her. It was a beautiful room, though it had a gloom about it, notwithstanding the different coloured marble chips of the highly polished *terrazzo* flooring designed to enhance any natural light. Although magnificent in their richness, the silk damask curtains, green soft furnishings and dark wood furniture were heavy and gave an oppressive feel to the place. It was so unlike the decoration of the lodge which, despite the lavish paintings on the walls, remained light and cheerful. Adding to the rather heavy and depressive atmosphere of the room were the slight traces of dust on the music system and the piles of sheet music next to it. There should have been flowers in the porcelain vases, Catriona couldn't help thinking, and someone at the piano laughing happily, playing with a passionate touch. Yet the instrument's lid was closed and it also appeared dusty and neglected. She frowned. This room was clearly abandoned, now, although it had probably been very different in its heyday before Umberto's accident.

She crossed to examine an oil painting – a family group, it seemed, seated on the lawn in front of the villa. There was an old lady with an ebony stick, a small lace cap on her head. She was flanked by two young men, one of whom she recognized as a much younger Umberto, the other she guessed must be Giacomo. Tall and blonde, almost Viking-like, the latter's physical attributes were the polar opposite of the darker, romantic, almost wild looks of his cousin.

Catriona moved closer. There was also a girl in the painting – in her late teens or early twenties – whom she instantly recognized from the few glimpses she'd had of her a decade ago. But although the girl's flaming red hair and striking looks drew her gaze, it was hijacked a moment later by the charismatic figure seated beside her – Calandra, in her heyday of fame and splendour.

'You like paintings?' asked a voice behind her, and she turned to face the same tall, blond man she'd been studying in the painting: Giacomo Monteverdi. He was clad impeccably in a cream lightweight suit, with an immaculately ironed blue shirt and navy Versace tie that highlighted his startlingly unusual looks. It was like being greeted by a Nordic god, with finely carved features and thick hair the colour of burnished gold, his skin a paler golden tan. It was as though he had just walked out of the pages of *Vogue*. His grey eyes surveyed her curiously and Catriona had to admit that he was as handsome as Umberto, but in a flashier way.

She felt oddly self-conscious as he extended his hand with the words, 'Giacomo Monteverdi.' Before she could introduce herself, he added with a smile that came easily to his perfectly sculpted mouth: 'And you are, I presume, the French specialist who's given up her family and business to treat my dear cousin … *oui*?' Adding, also in perfect French: 'We are very grateful for your dedication.'

Catriona wondered for a moment if she detected a hint of irony in his rather formal words, but his expression took on such a determinedly agreeable air that she dismissed her vague uneasiness. '*Sì, sono Catherine Drouot,*' she answered in perfect Italian. 'I've just arrived at the house. You have a beautiful home.'

Giacomo laughed. 'It is Umberto's beautiful home. I am just the poor cousin, but thank you.' His gaze lingered on her. 'I see you were admiring the family portrait.'

'Yes, I recognize Calandra, of course. She was so striking. Who is the young woman?' she added, knowing the answer full well.

He took a step nearer so that he was standing next to Catriona, almost touching her arm with his. 'Ah, the beautiful siren, Silvana Esposito. You'll meet her soon enough. She's like one of the family.' His gaze flicked between the adjacent pair of women in the painting.

'For Calandra, Silvana was the daughter she never had, I suppose.' Catriona caught but failed to interpret the emotion that flickered across his face, before he added distractedly: 'My aunt always liked this painting, though it was painted at a tragic time.'

Catriona looked at him quizzically. 'But this looks like it was painted some time ago … I mean, wasn't this long before your cousin's accident?'

He glanced at her with a sad smile. 'That was not the first tragedy in our family's history. But enough of such morbid talk, you have only just arrived. You must be tired after such a long journey. Tell me, how long are you intending to stay with us, *Dottoressa*?'

Although she was immediately curious to know what previous tragedy had befallen Umberto and his family, Catriona knew her questions would have to wait. She took a discreet step away from Giacomo. 'The Viscountess requested that I work with *il signor* Monteverdi for three months.'

'Such a long time for you to be away from your loved ones.' He shot her a sympathetic look. 'But we are pleased that you are here, of course. Anything that might help Umberto ...' He then looked back to the painting, appearing wistful.

'It was a terrible thing, him losing his sight, and perhaps he blames himself for that traumatic business in the past. He's always been a volatile character but now he's become so unstable, I worry he might try to harm himself again one day.' Giacomo turned his concerned gaze back to her. 'I'm afraid, *Dottoressa*, you'll have your work cut out for you.'

Catriona smiled politely. 'I'm used to challenging cases.' *Challenging is an understatement*, she thought. She felt a prickling down her spine. The complications seemed to be mounting up. What other traumatic events had Umberto been part of, even before his accident? Suddenly the sombre atmosphere of the grand room seemed strangely suffocating.

She was about to probe Giacomo further when the door of the *salone* opened. Adelina hurried in, looking apologetic.

'I'm very sorry, *Dottoressa*, but the *signore* is indisposed at the moment. He's not able to come down to meet you today,' she said without preamble.

The tension in the room grew. Giacomo frowned speculatively. 'You mean he's having one of his episodes again, Adelina?'

The housekeeper paused. Catriona could see that behind Adelina's attempted casual manner was an anxiety born out of fondness for Umberto. Clearly, his former nanny did not want to present him in too bad a light.

'Yes, I'm afraid so.' She let out a long, taut sigh. 'He shouted at me to go away and has locked himself in his room. He doesn't want to be bothered by anyone, he says.'

'Does this happen often?' Catriona asked, looking at Adelina kindly, trying – and failing – to imagine such behaviour belonging to the charming, lively man she used to know.

'Yes,' answered Giacomo instead. 'Umberto can be somewhat surly and difficult when he's like this. Sometimes he doesn't come out of his room for days. And, shall we say, a few things get broken.'

'It's his … predicament,' Adelina interjected, choosing her words delicately. 'He just needs to get it all out and then he'll be fine,' she declared, smoothing down her apron crisply and casting a dismissive look at Giacomo.

Umberto's cousin ignored her brusque tone. 'As you can see, *dottoressa* Drouot, it's not easy to live with someone whose moods are so unpredictable. I must apologize for my cousin for not seeing you this evening. I have a feeling you may have a long wait for him to reappear.' His grey eyes fixed on her and, for some reason, Catriona fancied there was a strange kind of relief in them. He flashed her a charming smile. 'While you're here, I would be delighted to show you around the lake some time, if you'd like?'

'That's very kind of you,' Catriona replied, hesitating before committing herself to anything. There was something about the way Giacomo Monteverdi looked at her that made her feel it might be unwise to do so. She was on the verge of turning down his offer when she thought, *Why not? This man seems to speak his mind. I might learn a little more about this complicated family.* After all, her son was related to them. 'Thank you very much, that sounds great. I'll let you know when I'm free.'

'Splendid! And now I must apologize too. I have to leave for Torno. I run a tour business there and I have an evening group to show around.' His expression was one of courteous concern. 'It seems as though you will be alone for dinner, *Dottoressa*. But I'm sure Adelina will look after you tonight.'

Once Giacomo had left the *salone*, the housekeeper's demeanour noticeably changed. 'I'm very sorry, *Dottoressa*.

I did try to tell him that you'd arrived but he just refused to see you.'

'It's all right, Adelina. It's getting late anyway. Perhaps it's for the best.' Catriona had steeled herself for this first meeting with Umberto and now that it had been delayed, she gave in to a small amount of relief.

'*Sì, sì, dev' essere stanca*, you must be tired. At least now you can have an early night. As the *signore* won't be joining you for dinner tonight, I will bring a tray to the lodge ... some antipasti with freshly baked bread, and a large cup of my special minestrone.'

'Thank you, that would be lovely.' As they walked out into the hall, Catriona's gaze fell on another grand piano; it too had gathered dust and the lid was down. 'May I ask you a question, Adelina?'

The housekeeper looked at her askance. 'Of course,' she said, though her expression was wary.

'Does the *signore* play music any more?'

Adelina's eyes were dark pools of wistful regret. '*Purtroppo no*. In the past all you'd hear in the house was music ... classical records or Umberto's own playing. Now, when these dark moods seize him, he falls into long periods of silent gloom. Then the whole household tiptoes around, not wanting to upset him.' She paused to open the front door. 'We never know how much further he might sink the next time.'

'I see,' said Catriona, stepping out into the early evening air. The light was now fading fast; the shadows had lengthened with the afternoon and were melting into the darkness of the approaching twilight, robbing the garden of its riot of vibrant colours and replacing them with kinder, softer hues. Nature was preparing for dusk.

Adelina suddenly looked distant, as though she felt she had disclosed too much. 'I'll walk you to the lodge, *Dottoressa*.'

'No, thank you, that's fine. I can find my way back.'

The housekeeper nodded. 'I will go and prepare your tray.'

*   *   *

Leaning against the elegant wrought-iron balustrade of the terrace of her new home overlooking the lake, listening to the gentle lapping of the water directly below her, Catriona was deep in thought. Now more than ever she was full of trepidation. Her heart gave a painful squeeze at the idea of what Umberto had become. Perhaps it wasn't surprising, the professional side of her reasoned. He had already attempted suicide once, and yet it still shocked her to think someone like Umberto could now be so clearly bitter and withdrawn from life.

She surveyed the view of Villa Monteverdi's grounds and the majestic beauty of the surrounding landscape. Umberto's house was magnificent, framed as it was by a host of eucalyptus, camphor and majestic palm trees in a fabulous position bordering the lake. She couldn't imagine anything more gracious and grand than this emerald chalice, set like a jewel in a ring of splendid hills, dominated by the snow-capped Alpine summits to the north. Yet its owner was now denied such a breathtaking feast for the eyes, she mused sadly.

When Catriona had finally agreed to take on this assignment, she had read up on the history of the estate. Apparently, it had been built in the early nineteenth century on a Roman site, and had been turned into a magnificent dynastic edifice in 1897 by Ennio Monteverdi to accommodate his nine children. Catriona was aware of how much lavish care must have been poured into its maintainance over the years as she surveyed the impressive structure.

The three-storeyed villa was square and linked by narrow angular pergolas to four corner towers that gave it a commanding appearance. Three rows of windows with stone frames divided the front elevation and a striking series of rooms in the south basement opened on to the gardens, their outside walls decorated with exquisite ornamentation of pebblework and seashells, mingled with delicately tinted stucco.

The garden at the front sloped gently towards the lake and was dotted with statues and stone benches that sat under ivy-covered trellises. The vegetation seemed almost tropical in its vigour and abundance: camellias, cedars, magnolias, gigantic myrtles, all cohabitating in harmony. Olive and chestnut, mulberry and walnut trees grew side by side. Looking to the left, away from the villa, Catriona could see forest extending up the slope from behind the lodge and beyond, villages with their chapels, ancient ruined castles and cheerful coloured-washed mansions. They hovered on the distant hillsides and stretched away without interruption at the water's edge, amid parks and gardens overhung with large clumps of oleander. After the heat of the day, the fragrance of the abundant flora surrounding her was so heady that she found it almost overwhelming.

Her suitcase lay open on the bed, where she had begun to unpack some of her belongings and put them into drawers. She stared at it with trepidation: it was as if she had left her old life behind and was starting afresh. The feeling was strange and unsettling. Reaching in her bag for her mobile, Catriona quickly tapped in her home number. She spoke briefly to Marguerite to reassure her that all was well, telling her mother that she was very comfortable in her separate cottage, before Michael's voice took over. Catriona smiled at the breezy comments about his day, followed by affectionate questions about her journey. She was reluctant to let the phone call end, comforted to hear the reassuring chatter of her son's voice, punctuated with the odd comment from her mother.

Finally, though, she had to say goodnight and hung up, a little tearful as she did so. Silly to feel homesick already, she berated herself. Then, not for the first time, she experienced a strange torment, thinking that soon she would be meeting Michael's father again, and she struggled to shut away painful memories of a decade ago behind an invisible door in her mind.

Waves of darkness dimmed the sky as day left the earth. Catriona went back down the wooden spiral staircase into the living room, looking for somewhere to set up her laptop and notebooks. Through the open French windows she could see the shadows of the copse in the fading light, the trees stretching their pointed fingers across the grass towards the lodge. As she placed her laptop bag on a table she became aware of a noise outside as though someone was walking alongside the house. She lifted her head, listening more keenly, and thought she heard a whistling sound.

'Hello?' she called out.

The whistling ceased abruptly. She stepped out on to the veranda. It was empty and the silence, which had felt peaceful before, suddenly seemed eerie and made her skin prickle.

'Is someone there?' A bird, startled from a tree, rose up high above her with a harsh cry, making her jump. *I must be more tired than I thought*, she told herself and went back inside, closing the French windows firmly. She took out her laptop and arranged her notebooks next to it.

A loud knock on the door made her gasp. Catriona looked up to see something move away from the edge of the French windows; whether it was the shadow of one of the trees outside or a figure she couldn't be sure.

The knocking came again. Irritated and a little unnerved, Catriona moved cautiously to the front door and pulled it open.

'Ah, *Dottoressa*, your dinner.' Adelina stood there with a tray, on which sat a domed silver plate cover.

Catriona let out a breath. 'Adelina, it's you! Thank you. Please, come in. Was it you outside just now?'

The housekeeper shot her an odd look as she walked past Catriona into the lodge and set the tray down on the living room table. 'No, *Dottoressa*. I've only just come.' She glanced around her, checking to see everything was correct and in its place, then moved straight back to the doorway, seeming reluctant to stay and talk.

'*Buona notte, Dottoressa*. I've put a bottle of fresh water in the fridge and there's a bowl of fruit picked this morning from the orchard. I will bring your breakfast tomorrow morning at nine o'clock.'

'*Buona notte, Adelina, e grazie.*'

'Lock the door behind me, please,' the old woman added as she stepped out of the lodge into the early evening air. '*Il bosco adiacente*, the adjoining forest is vast and well protected by fencing, but vandals could always get in if they set their minds to it. And then, of course, anybody can come in by way of the lake.' She shook her head with a wry smile. '*La signora* Calandra loved this place but I always worried about it being separate from the house.'

Catriona frowned. She wondered if she had in fact seen someone outside. 'Have you had any trouble with break-ins?'

'Well, no, not that I can think of,' answered Adelina. 'Still, *la prudenza non è mai troppa*, you can never be too cautious. *Buona serata.*' And with that the housekeeper hurried away.

Catriona stood on the threshold next to a rosebush and watched Adelina go down the narrow path that led to the big house. There was not a sound, save the last tremolos of birds clamouring before dusk and the whispering of a warm breeze that blew through the trees. As she turned to go back into the lodge, she caught the low-hanging caress of flower petals as they bumped against her cheek and heard a splash simultaneously behind her, which almost made her jump out of her skin. When she looked back, she breathed a sigh of relief and smiled. Just silver fish leaping in the infinite blue water of the lake.

Pull yourself together, girl, she told herself. *This is only the first day.*

*   *   *

Umberto reached for his glass of water and, forgetting where he'd put it, knocked it over. Grasping for it again angrily, he hurled it across the room, hearing it smash against the opposite wall. His head fell back against the armchair and he let out a growl of frustration. Already he had polished off a few glasses of grappa that afternoon and was now sick of his head pounding.

It had been nearly two days since he'd left these four walls. He knew it made no difference that the curtains had been drawn all day, cutting out the sunlight, but it gave him a grim satisfaction that the whole room must be plunged into a sombre gloom – almost the same darkness he had experienced every day for the past four years. A cage of perpetual midnight.

At first, he had been shaken by gusts of rage at his imprisonment, rage that left him weak and depressed and he had longed, like a sick animal, to die. He'd almost succeeded once in a moment of weak despair. Instinctively, his fingers went to the scars on his wrist. It would have been a release from this black hell, but he appreciated that Mario had found him in time.

Still, what had he to live for? He hated himself when he was in this self-pitying mood. The doctors had warned of that danger but his days were endless in their monotony. Sometimes, when Mario brought Umberto his morning espresso, it seemed hardly worth his while to get up and commence the struggle to wash and dress himself. Mario even had to shave him. Over the past four years he had spent so much time working to overcome his new disability, yet no matter how much he learned to master his surroundings, in so many ways he was still like a helpless child. Every so often his rages at this injustice got the better of him and during those times he needed to shut himself away and let his torment exhaust itself.

Umberto sighed. He was sorry he'd shouted at Adelina. However, today he was in no mood to indulge this Dr Drouot, who had just arrived. A tiresome arrangement with which he had complied only because it had been Calandra's last wish. His mother had made him promise on her deathbed that he would try out this new treatment ... so-called music therapy. Presumably, they believed it would work because he was a musician – or used to be, he thought bitterly. Anyway, whatever promises he had made, he wasn't going to make it easy for this *dottoressa*. The woman could work for Calandra's fee as far as he was concerned – and that included waiting until he was ready to see her.

Still, Adelina didn't deserve his foul temper; she was the only person, apart from Mario, who was worth talking to in this house. Who else was there: Silvana? Giacomo? He gave a quiet snort of derision. His cousin was the last person with whom he had anything in common. From the very beginning Giacomo had strongly opposed the idea of a therapist coming to the house. Now he came to think of it, it was that, as much as a desire to honour Calandra's last wishes, which had made Umberto entertain the notion.

Although he and Giacomo had grown up together in the same house, the two had never got on. Calandra had always implied that it was because Arturo, Giacomo's father, had been the younger son, and so Rolando, Umberto's father, had inherited the whole estate.

'He's jealous of you, Umberto, just like Arturo was always jealous of your father,' she had explained. 'You are handsome, charming, rich and gifted, but also kind and warm, and that is why women cannot resist you. Giacomo might also be handsome and intelligent, and perhaps rich in comparison to many, but he's calculating and cold, and women don't like cold-hearted men in their beds. That's why Silvana only has eyes for you,' she told him.

'*Mama*, you only say that because I am your son and you love me,' he'd replied. 'Giacomo's the one who loves Silvana, anyway. And I'm sure one day she'll come round.'

Calandra waved away the thought. '*Quando l'inferno gelerà*, when hell freezes over. Silvana is all woman. You should marry her. She will give you lots of heirs and that is the most important thing, my son.'

'I'm fond of Silvana but we grew up together. I know it wouldn't work. Besides, she's always with some man or other. Hardly waiting around for me.'

'You are too sentimental, my son, and it will not serve you well in life. As your wife, Silvana will never look at another man. She is healthy, beautiful and reared in the old tradition, which is sufficient for a wife.

'You think your mother is blind, *eh*? You think I didn't know what you were up to during those summers? You took her to your bed and gave her a taste of what it's like to be with *you*. She is looking for you in all these other men. She goes with others today because she can't have *you*, trust me.'

'I do trust you, *Mamma*,' he'd sighed. 'The trouble is, I could never trust her.'

'Trust, trust … You are deluding yourself. Tell me you don't want her when you look at her. I don't believe it!'

Umberto gestured in frustration. 'It was the same with Sofia. You wanted me to marry her, even though I didn't love her.'

'You know perfectly well why I wanted you to marry Sofia,' Calandra said coolly.

'No one regrets what happened more than I,' Umberto ran his hand through his hair, wrestling with dark feelings of self-recrimination. 'But marriage isn't just for carrying on the family line, *Mamma*. Don't you care about love and true companionship?'

'If you wish for the foolishness of love, then you must seek it outside the home, but the home is for the founding of a family. You have strong genes, strong enough to build up the Monteverdi clan until it is once again a thriving dynasty, as it was generations ago. Think too about our musical legacy. You have the makings of a great composer. That legacy could go from strength to strength if Silvana was the mother of your children.'

Umberto shook his head vigorously, his temper rising. 'Silvana is out of the question … I wouldn't touch her again if she were the last woman on earth! Just forget this obsession of yours and don't bring up that subject again.'

His mother eyed him haughtily. 'Then you must find yourself a wife, Umberto. You have an estate to run, if nothing else. This place needs heirs, children who will help you run it, and don't forget you've got the silk factory too. Who will support you and take on all the responsibilities an estate and a business like ours needs? You're not getting any younger and, if you want to mould a wife to your liking, you need your health and your wits. I regret now that I haven't given you brothers. I was selfish, only thinking of my career, but you still have time. The family name must be passed on, you can't leave that to Giacomo!'

'To hell with the family name!' he had roared before storming out to get to the opening night of a concert he was giving in Milan.

Calandra had pleaded with Umberto to let Mario drive him but he had refused – he intended to spend the night in Milan with a young beauty whose name he couldn't even remember now. It was a stormy night, with a fierce blizzard coming down from the Alps, and he had been angrily rehashing the conversation with his mother as he drove down the motorway. He was too late to miss the lorry that seemed to come out of nowhere as it overtook him, bumping his car off the road and sending it rolling into a ditch. All he remembered was spinning, twisted metal, shattering glass, then blackness … and waking up to that horrifying blackness, which had not left him since.

Umberto breathed out heavily. Calandra had been right, of course: the Monteverdi name must live on and Giacomo was a lightweight, a waster to whom he could never entrust the fortune of generations. His cousin would squander it all in no time.

No, the role of head of the family still lay with him, he thought broodingly. Still, who would want him now? Silvana, of course, but he didn't want her as the mother of his children. Calandra had been wrong there; all his mother had cared about was for Umberto to provide an heir, and preferably one with impeccable musical genes.

He had to snap out of it. The secret was not to remember what had been – monsters lay in that direction, monsters of shame, regret and pain that appeared with the merest sigh. At that moment shadows of the past loomed up, shrouding him in a darkness far worse than the one behind his eyes. At least he wasn't claustrophobic. How did those people cope if they were suddenly blinded? He shuddered at the thought.

Perhaps one more drink would help. He felt along the table and found the nearly empty bottle, gave it a shake and swore under his breath. Draining the last drop, he pushed it away in disgust.

CHAPTER 7

Catriona surfaced from a deep and refreshing sleep. Despite her jumpiness when Adelina had left her the evening before, such was her exhaustion that she had collapsed into bed early and not stirred all night. She woke to the far-off pealing of bells coming from the church in Torno. The bright Italian sunlight streamed into the bedroom through the tall windows. She stirred and yawned, then awareness of her surroundings settled upon her and, once more, the strangeness of it all returned. Would Umberto appear today? How long should she wait before trying to speak to him? Maybe later, she concluded, part of her still grateful for this short reprieve. It would give her some time at least to become familiar with the place.

She showered and dressed in a simple summer dress of white broderie anglaise. As it was such a beautiful morning she planned to go into the garden to explore the grounds while waiting for a message that Umberto would see her, but as she was coming down the stairs, she heard a knock at the front door. When she opened it, Giacomo's solid build towered over her.

'*Buongiorno, Dottoressa.*'

'Ah! *Buongiorno, signore.*'

He grinned, showing even white teeth. 'No, please call me Giacomo – I am not your client …'

She raised a quizzical eyebrow and smiled back, but remained silent.

'I'm sorry to turn up unannounced, only it seemed like the perfect opportunity. I understand my cousin is still unavailable,' he said casually, 'and as it is a beautiful day, I'm going into town to make sure that Villa Pliniana is open for tourist groups. They're doing extensive renovation work at the villa and it's often off-limits. I wondered if you would care for that drive into Torno? You'd enjoy visiting the villa. It's one of the more important buildings on Lake Como.'

'That sounds good,' Catriona replied. 'And, as you say, I appear to have some spare time this morning.' She wondered whether she shouldn't stay here, awaiting her client's orders but, then again, it might be advantageous to have some information about the family before she had her first meeting with Umberto, she reasoned.

'Splendid! If you're ready we can go immediately, before the traffic hots up.'

'I'll just fetch my bag.'

They walked through the grounds towards the garage, which was situated next to a long stable barn. In the yard a stable boy was forking hay into a wheelbarrow and as they passed, Giacomo called out a greeting to the stocky young man, Dino, who gave a brief wave.

Catriona glanced up at Umberto's cousin. In spite of his charm and good looks there was something about the man striding beside her that wasn't totally at ease; his almost perfect face held eyes that were one minute sincere and the next watchful. Sidonie always said: '*Les yeux sont le miroir de l'âme*' and if that were true, Catriona thought that Giacomo had succeeded in drawing a veil over what truly lay beneath.

Giacomo held the door to his silver Maserati GranSport open for her and she slid into the front seat. As she did so, she noticed his gaze lingering on her with more than an ordinary interest.

'If you don't mind, we'll start at Villa Pliniana, then I can show you around the town, which is very pretty. We might stop and have a coffee or an ice cream somewhere, if you like.'

Catriona gave him a reserved smile. 'That sounds a good plan,' she said.

The drive down to Torno was a feast for the eyes with strange surprises at each turn. The sun was high and hot. Nature burned with a steadfast pulse and a flame of early summer life spread her royal robes over the countryside, woven of light and purple shade. They wound their way past orchards with neatly planted rows of trees laden with fragrant blossom, and down wooded roads packed tightly with stout oaks and linden trees. Dominating the magnificent view lay Lake Como, enclosed by the imposing peaks of its surrounding mountains, which were reflected in its waters.

Giacomo spoke to her of the region in a well informed and easy manner and although Catriona had started off on this expedition in a mood of unease, she could not help thoroughly enjoying the outing.

'Torno,' he told her, 'ranks with Rome, Monza, Milan and Trèves in possessing one of the nails of the Cross. The story goes that a German bishop, carrying a leg bone of one of the Innocents and a nail of the Cross, rested here after returning from the Holy Land in the time of the Crusades. When bad weather prevented him from continuing his journey, he decided that it was a sign from above and deposited his treasures in the Church of Saint Giovanni.'

'I'm always surprised that such treasures haven't been taken or looted at some point over the centuries,' observed Catriona.

'Oh no, they've taken no chances,' Giacomo said with a smile. 'They're kept in a casket locked by seven keys, one of which is held by the parish priest, the others by six of the town's historic families.'

Torno, on its promontory that stretched out into the waters of the lake, was booming with tourists. In the small square, as with the shoreline, the pavements were lined with luxurious hotels, elegant cafés and refined restaurants. Alleyways ascended between curious gated houses painted in warm colours, beyond which were glimpses of the glittering lake. Hanging gardens appeared around every corner, smothered in exuberant vegetation, against which the flowers of the pomegranate flamed out like scarlet stars. Delighted, Catriona found that Torno had a charm wholly different to that of the villages of the French Riviera she was used to.

They passed the small picturesque landlocked harbour, masts pricking the azure sky and dark land encircling a vibrant basin that shone like a mirror. It was dominated by the pretty Parish Church of Santa Tecla with its Italian Gothic façade that gazed out across the lake to the hills swathed with forests on the opposite side. Narrow, winding lanes and stepped, cobbled streets meandered up the hillside from the harbour, losing themselves in greenery. There were hidden courtyards and little squares, and the occasional glimpse of a building much older than its present exterior suggested.

'The villa is not yet open to the public. Restoration began more than ten years ago and it's now undergoing architectural and conservation works,' Giacomo explained. 'It has a long and colourful history, with many myths attached to it. Quite rightly, it's regarded as one of the most valued treasures of Lake Como. I always think it has an aura of legend about it.'

'I must admit, I've never been here before so I'm totally ignorant of Villa Pliniana's history.'

'Well, it's lucky you've got me here, your personal tour guide,' he replied with another of his dazzling smiles.

Giacomo parked the car near the church of San Giovanni with its massive Romanesque bell tower. 'A road is being built so that in the future the villa can be accessed by car, but it isn't yet useable. For now, it can only be reached by a short path that leads through the woods.' As they made their way towards the trees he added: 'Sometimes I wonder if our ancestors didn't build Villa Monteverdi in the image of Villa Pliniana – the two houses are similar in many ways. And notice how the woods here rise at the back, the same as the ones behind your lodge.'

Giacomo glanced at her with a wry smile. 'Don't worry, these aren't haunted like the woods of the Gufi Reali.'

'Haunted?' Catriona shot him a surprised look.

'*Sì*, did you not know?'

For a moment she thought back to the previous evening: the strange feeling that someone had been outside, then Adelina's comments about the woods. A look of unease must have crossed her face because Giacomo laughed. 'There's no need to be afraid, you're perfectly safe at the lodge.'

She managed a faint smile. 'I assure you I'm not afraid. I don't believe in ghosts. They're only the stuff of stories and legends, made up chiefly to alarm ignorant people.'

'That is a dangerous statement, *Dottoressa*. Spirits get upset when they're not acknowledged. From experience, I can assure you they do exist and when you are sceptical, that is the very time they come to haunt you, to prove they are real.'

Catriona raised an eyebrow. 'How does an educated person like yourself believe in such nonsense? The only spirits I believe in are the repercussions of our foolish deeds, coming back to haunt us.'

His gaze sharpened with interest. 'And do *you* speak from experience, *Dottoressa*?'

She had dug that grave for herself, she thought, but caught herself immediately. 'Not especially. I think every person at some time in their life does or says something they regret, and that it often returns to torment them,' she replied evenly as she followed him into the woods.

'Well, there are many tormented souls in the history of Villa Pliniana,' Giacomo went on as they followed the path through the trees. 'Maybe the most enthralling period traces back to the times of the Milanese prince, Enrico Belgioioso, who had a secret love affair with Anna Berthier, Princess of Wagram and consort to the Duke of Plaisance.

'Every night, after the clock struck midnight, the two lovers would wrap themselves in a white sheet and climb down from the balcony overlooking the lake. Their love affair lasted eight years, until the day when Anna unexpectedly abandoned her lover, leaving him all alone in the palace.'

'What happened to Enrico?'

'Literally grief-stricken, he died in Milan in 1858. After that, Villa Pliniana passed to the Belgioioso descendants, who resided there for another century before moving to the castle of Masino in Piedmont. From then on, the villa lay abandoned, haunted by the ghosts of memories and shadows of illustrious visitors who had stayed there in its heyday.'

'It makes a wonderful story to attract tourists.'

Giacomo laughed. 'I see you are determined not to believe in its ghosts. We shall just have to agree to differ, *Dottoressa*. But it is haunted, trust me.'

They walked in silence a short distance, and then they were there. The setting was breathtaking, despite the fact it was clear that building works were going on.

Villa Pliniana's severe and imposing structure stood in a secluded corner of its own cove, the foundations firmly rooted in the depths of the lake. In the shade of an overhanging cliff, the building was framed by cypresses of an astonishing height, which seemed to pierce the sky, and backed by a forest of chestnuts. It looked more like a fortress than a palace. Although the setting was awesome, to Catriona the place felt austere and gloomy.

Giacomo must have read her mind.

'This is, of course, one of the grimmest spots on these usually pleasant shores. You can appreciate that this unfriendly, somewhat mysterious setting would have only increased the terror of its first owner, Count Giovanni Anguissola Governor of Como, when he sought refuge here after taking part in the conspiracy in the sixteenth century that led to the murder of Pier Luigi Farnese, one of Pope Paul III's offspring and ruler of Novara. He was convinced that he was being hunted by murderous hatchet men.'

Catriona shivered, despite herself. 'It is a magnificent building and I'm sure it will be even more striking after it's turned into a luxury hotel.' She smiled and shook her head. 'But I admit, I don't think I could stay here.'

Giacomo nodded. '*Credimi*, believe me, this malaise you feel is the souls of the dead unable to find rest.' And then, almost as an aside to himself, he murmured: 'Another thing it has in common with Villa Monteverdi, if you ask me.'

What was he getting at? Had someone died in the Gufi Reali woods?

Having already asserted her scepticism about ghosts, Catriona had no desire to go down that road again and decided to leave the subject alone for now. 'To each his own beliefs,' she said curtly.

As there were no railings barring the access, they walked up to the main floor. In its centre was a loggia with three arches, supported by Doric columns and overlooking Lake Como's major channel, a darker and wilder scenery of breathtaking grandeur. To the north was a view of the Swiss Alps, descending almost vertically into the water, and to the south the sweep of hill towns fronting the lake formed a colourful necklace in the sunshine.

'This is truly one of the most spectacular parts of the world,' breathed Catriona, overwhelmed by the awesome panorama.

'It's not surprising the villa was visited by so many famous people during its golden era. Byron, Foscolo and Stendhal, composers like Liszt and Rossini stood where you are now.'

Catriona's face lit up. 'Yes, I remember reading somewhere that a remote villa on Lake Como was Rossini's inspiration for his opera *Tancredi*. Do you know, he took only six days to write it? It's funny but I can almost feel how the place, with all its romance and sadness, influenced his music. Eighteenth-century operas were so stiff before Rossini came along, and someone needed to break with convention. Initially, I suppose, it must have been a shock to audiences, but then his *bel canto* style became a feature of all Italian opera of that period.' She glanced at Giacomo, realizing she was getting carried away in her enthusiasm. 'The article must have been referring to Villa Pliniana, don't you think?'

'You must excuse my ignorance. Despite having grown up among a family obsessed by music, I'm afraid my knowledge of composers and their music is a little limited.' He smiled in a self-deprecating way. 'Sadly, I am the least cultured member of the family. Umberto would know your answer.'

He turned his back to the view. 'Shall we continue?'

Although works were still in progress and some of the rooms more difficult to access, Giacomo was able to show Catriona the great North hall, with its beautifully carved ceiling and mythological scenes on the walls.

'Before the house was built, the name Pliniana was already famous on account of an intermittent waterfall behind it,' he explained as they ascended the large spiral sandstone staircase at the centre of the villa. 'Water springs forth at regular intervals, gushing down from the mountain behind the villa in an eighty-metre drop, which was described by the two Plinies and by Leonardo da Vinci. The story goes that it marks the point of convergence between the clear waters of Lake Como and the muddy underground ripples of the rivers of hell.'

Catriona couldn't help but laugh. 'More ghoulish connections?'

Giacomo gave a typically Italian shrug and grinned. 'But of course, *Dottoressa*.'

On their way back to the car he suggested that they had a coffee in town. 'And maybe a *sorbetto napoletano*, the real thing?' He bestowed on her a coaxing smile and Catriona was once more aware of how handsome he was. 'Italian *gelati* are renowned as the best in the world. After all, ice cream came from Italy in the first place, you know?'

She smiled back at him politely. 'Thank you very much. It's been a delightful afternoon but I think your cousin might have woken by now and may be asking where I am. Plus, I do have some notes to prepare.'

Giacomo made a small grimace. 'Oh, I wouldn't worry too much if I were you. I'm sure it'll be a while before you get to see my dear cousin.'

Catriona frowned. 'What makes you say that?'

'Forgive me, *Dottoressa*, perhaps I should mind what I say when I talk about your patient. Of course this is your business, not mine.'

'No, please, tell me,' she encouraged, curious to hear what he had to say.

He paused deliberately. 'I doubt very much that Umberto is taking this therapy business seriously. He only agreed to go along with it to please his dying mother.' He gave a rueful expression. 'Let's just say that I sympathize with the huge task facing you. Don't get me wrong, *Dottoressa*, no one wants Umberto's recovery more than I do, but there will be more episodes like last night's, you can be sure of that. I'm afraid alcohol already had a hold on him long before the accident.'

Catriona's eyes widened in surprise. 'Really?'

'Yes, it was bordering on addiction when he came back from America.' He nodded sadly. 'He had it all – pots of money and the women, too. But even before the accident he seemed to hell-bent upon self-destruction. You see, Umberto is a man with demons. His ambition was his downfall in the end, and the people he cast aside to get what he wanted suffered, too. I suppose the drinking was inevitable. Callous as it may sound, his blindness is only an excuse to indulge his weakness further.'

Catriona was silent for a moment, absorbing this information. She lowered her head as though pretending to study the flowers spread along the grassy verge of the path. Something twisted uncomfortably inside her at the thought that maybe she had just been another of Umberto's conquests. Had she, too, been a mere sacrifice to his ambition? Yet something else stirred in the rational part of her brain. It was strange that Calandra had never mentioned that Umberto was drinking, yet clearly he had been abusive to Adelina and shut himself away. This was a factor she hadn't bargained for, and now her apprehension at seeing him grew stronger.

'These rages,' she said, composing herself, 'do they happen often?'

'Yes, I'm afraid so,' Giacomo nodded earnestly. 'For all his faults, Umberto used to be a charming fellow, everyone will tell you. Now, he's a man full of self-pity and bitterness, railing against the world. Though, of course, he will hide it when he wants to. It's all part of his unstable nature.' He shook his head.

'As his cousin, it makes me sad to think of his decline, but I cannot imagine him ever reforming his ways.'

They had reached the edge of the wood and as the church of San Giovanni came into view, Catriona gazed ahead thoughtfully. Then she said: 'I think you're wrong, *signore*. Umberto has these bouts of desperation because he's not working – he can't or won't compose. If only we could persuade him to get back to his music, he'd find a way back to his life, too. There's nothing like hard work to heal the soul. Often it's the best therapy.'

'You sound like Umberto. He's always preaching the benefits of work to me.' Giacomo gave a whimsical gesture of his hand that was wholly Latin. 'As far as Umberto's concerned, I joined the ranks of the damned and the bohemian a long time ago.'

She glanced at him uncertainly. 'And why is that?'

'Umberto thinks me a playboy because of the job I do. Still, it's the price I pay for remaining here. But I speak six languages and I like escorting these oohing and aahing tourists around wondrous places. Besides, all my expenses are paid for. It's better than being a gigolo,' he added with a low laugh, though as he looked at her his eyes gleamed.

Yes, she could see that being such a handsome man, Giacomo could have easily degenerated into being a rich woman's plaything.

'To return to what I was saying … I appreciate your candour, *signore*—'

'Giacomo, please, I insist.' His gaze remained on her face.

She nodded and smiled, but carried on. 'I would like to enlist your help in bringing *il signor* Umberto back to composing again.'

Giacomo looked away. 'Of course, *Dottoressa*. The only reason I stay here is to help look after my cousin. He is my blood, and family must stick together.'

'That's very good of you.'

'It's what I promised my aunt before she died.' He gave a half-smile. 'So at least one of us will be keeping our word to her.'

She frowned, wondering at his meaning. 'You really think *il signor* Umberto won't comply with my therapy sessions?'

'Well, that, and …' Giacomo stuck his hands in his pockets and gazed ahead as they walked. 'You see, *Dottoressa*, Umberto is a very wealthy man. Of course he's entitled to enjoy his money …' He paused, as though deliberating his next words.

'If you must know, Calandra was about to change her will before she died, leaving me a considerable portion. But after her death Umberto said he would give me an allowance instead. It's a pittance really so, in order to remain at the estate to keep an eye on him, I started up my company. I would gladly give it all up and get on with my life elsewhere if only he were to get better.'

They had arrived at the car and he fished in his pocket for his key.

'I see. So, you've made a sacrifice by staying on at the estate,' said Catriona, pondering the idea.

Giacomo glanced at her. 'My father was his father's brother. As I said, I have a duty to family. I know some would envy him his money and say he supports me just enough to stop tongues wagging,' he said earnestly, 'but I don't concern myself with such gossip.'

'His wealth can't buy him back his sight,' she said quietly. 'Money can be a burden, too. All these women you mention,' she ignored the painful stab in her heart as the words left her mouth. 'Umberto must wonder whether they like him for himself or for his money, especially now that he's blind. No wonder he's bitter sometimes. His fortune is probably a terrible burden.'

Giacomo's handsome, laughing face was suddenly dark, as if a cloud had passed over it. 'Easy enough to get rid of it, if it's such a burden.' His eyes darted to her face. 'I'm sorry, you must think me heartless,' he went on as he opened the car door for Catriona. 'But there are family matters of which you are not aware. I don't know why I'm opening up to you. Maybe it's your calm voice and your incredible poise.' He walked round and took his seat beside her.

'I am a therapist. I've been trained to inspire trust and to listen.' No doubt for that very reason she hadn't missed his oblique reference to 'family matters'. Was this an allusion to whatever tragedy lay in Umberto's past, even before he was blinded?

Giacomo glanced at her shrewdly. 'Don't think I'm complaining, *Dottoressa*. I simply want the best for Umberto. Besides, I need to be around to know how the estate works.' He flashed her a wide grin as he manoeuvred the car past the Church of San Giovanni. 'As the family line is looking unlikely to continue through my cousin, it will probably fall on me to do my duty and marry one day.'

Catriona could no longer keep her questions to herself. 'You don't think *il signor* Umberto will himself marry one day and have children of his own?'

'He doesn't want children now because, as far as Umberto is concerned, what good could a depressive, blind father be to a child?'

Catriona flinched, Giacomo's words cutting through her like a swift fine blade. A vision of Michael's young face, so like his father's, swam into her mind. The idea that Umberto might never accept his own son was too painful to contemplate. She schooled her features into a calm expression.

'A father doesn't need to be sighted to be a good and loving parent,' she said, fighting the strain in her voice. '*Il signor* Umberto's feelings are undoubtedly coloured by his current depression. And that depression can be alleviated.'

Giacomo shook his head. 'No, *Dottoressa*, I assure you, Umberto has never wanted children.' He paused, his eyes following the road. 'It was clear a long time ago that my cousin is not a man you would call the parenting type. The lengths he was prepared to go to avoid such a thing happening … but that's all in the past.'

'What do you mean?'

'Let's just say that sometimes I had to pick up the pieces after he cast his conquests aside. There was one girl … well, he got her pregnant and it ended very badly.'

A confused, sickening feeling came over Catriona. 'Pregnant … a girl?' Her mind raced to catch up with his meaning.

'Yes, a local girl. After he returned from America.'

Catriona's panicked thoughts spun feverishly, tangling in her head. Rapidly, she tried to unpick and make sense of them. 'So, he … he has a child?'

'No, the child was never born.' Giacomo shot her a sideways glance. '*Dottoressa*, are you all right? You look pale. Surely I haven't shocked you?'

'No,' she said, turning so that he couldn't read her expression. 'Not at all.' Yet she did not have it in her to probe further.

They drove in silence. The Maserati slid over the countryside and Catriona kept her eyes firmly glued to the window, gazing

over the shining expanse of lake and fields golden with hay
and young corn. Her conversation with Umberto's cousin had
left her reeling. How much more was there to find out about
this hardened man whom she was about to meet? The man
who cut off his cousin's inheritance ... the womanizer who
had apparently discarded countless women and made a girl
pregnant, just like her. The father of her son, who had never
wanted children.

'This is farming and vineyard country,' Giacomo told her
as they passed rows of vines heavy with green grapes. 'We are
blessed with good soil and plenty of sunshine in this district,' he
explained. 'Farmers generally get two harvests a year.'

'The countryside certainly looks healthy,' Catriona answered
absentmindedly, listening with only half an ear to Giacomo's
patter as he began to tell her about the district. Was this entire
assignment a terrible mistake? Were her efforts to help Umberto
hopelessly misplaced?

The journey back to the villa seemed to take ages. When
Giacomo finally turned off the ignition she almost breathed a sigh
of relief. 'Thank you for an interesting afternoon,' she said, opening
the car door swiftly and placing a foot on the gravelled drive.

'It's been a pleasure. We must find time to do it again. Next
week I have scheduled a visit to Isola Comacina on Lake Como,
a treasure of the early Middle Ages. I think it's one of the most
interesting archaeological sites in Northern Italy. Maybe you
would like to join the tour.' He laughed softly, 'Or we can have
another little tête à tête, where you can turn your analytical
powers on me.'

'Thank you,' she replied politely, feeling the speculative scrutiny
from his extraordinary grey eyes.

'Catherine ...' Giacomo, his smile once again boyish and
friendly, placed a detaining hand lightly on her arm. 'I'm sorry
if I sounded sceptical earlier. Umberto is the best of men, I owe

him a great deal. I assure you that I too want to see him get better and become the great composer he once was.'

'Of course, no apology needed.'

Catriona went back to the lodge. She felt sticky, and reflected that a swim would not only refresh her but also clear her head after Giacomo's disturbing revelations. More than ever now she must detach herself from Umberto and endeavour to view him simply as a potentially difficult client. Yet she had never faced such a challenge in her whole life, and she decided that the first step was to confront him on her own terms.

*   *   *

Catriona stood at the door to Umberto's room. On impulse she had gone in search of Mario, feeling nervous but determined, to ask him to direct her to the right place in the house so that she could speak to *il signor* Umberto briefly. Mario had looked at her askance, clearly deliberating whether or not this was a good idea, given Umberto's present mood, but then he'd relented and led her to the back of the house.

Umberto's bedroom was on the top floor. To get to it, they had passed through another hall, smaller than the vast one at the main entrance but flooded with light from the garden it overlooked. Not particularly wide, it was backed by a conservatory full of potted plants and hanging creepers. A long landing, railed above the arch of the hall below, gave on to a corridor with several doors and passages leading from it, and Catriona realized that the house was even bigger than she had imagined. Eventually, Mario left her outside a dark-panelled door.

She hesitated a moment, her heart suddenly beating violently. After taking a breath, she raised her hand to rap on the door. Her nerves caused her to knock rather timorously at first, so that she feared the man inside the room might not have picked up the sound, particularly if he was suffering from the ill effects of alcohol. Her next knock was peremptory, echoing sharply in the silence of the corridor. Still no movement from within. Then there was a faint sound of movement on the other side of the door. She could hear the scrape of a chair and slow, careful steps as a pair of feet made their way haltingly across the room.

'*Porca miseria*!' he growled out an oath. Then: 'Who is it?' His gruff, deep voice rumbled so close to the door that she gave a start. 'Adelina, is that you? I told you I wasn't to be disturbed.'

'Um … it's Dr Drouot,' Catriona said, her voice strengthening after a first flush of panic. She felt as if she'd disturbed a very grumpy grizzly bear after a winter's hibernation.

He gave a derisive groan. '*Dio mio.* The music therapist, that's all I need.' Catriona guessed from his muffled voice that he was most likely passing a hand across his face as he spoke.

She waited a breath. *Don't rush this,* she told herself. The trained therapist in her was martialling an inner textbook of responses, while the other part of her – the girl that this man, with his deep, bewitching voice had seduced so completely a decade ago – felt her knees threatening to buckle. She glanced down at her hand that had rapped on the door and saw it was shaking slightly. *Great start*, she admonished herself. *Pull yourself together, girl.*

It was time to speak plainly. 'You may think I'm the last thing you need,' she responded with a hint of wryness, instinctively throwing away her therapy rulebook. 'But your mother decided otherwise. When she asked for my help, I said no at first.'

'And then, I suppose, she gave you a king's ransom that you couldn't refuse,' he interjected, irony flooding his tone.

'Not at all,' Catriona hit back calmly. 'I assure you I have adequate funds, and with a busy practice and family responsibilities I wouldn't have dreamed of taking several weeks away in Italy.' She paused, sensing she had his interest now: he would want to know why she had taken this assignment. She could feel a quiver in the air, an alertness from the man on the other side of the door. With this realization came confidence, shoring up that other girlish weakness as her professional faculties returned. *I can do this, I know I can.*

'So, if it wasn't the generous fee, what made you come?'

'Why do you think? I heard the details of your case and realized my particular skills and training were so very apposite to your predicament that I simply couldn't find it in myself to turn your mother down,' she answered. 'And by the way, I'm very sorry for your loss. I can only imagine how that must make you feel on top of everything else.'

There was a silence from the other side of the door, then: 'Yes, well … Maybe.' She detected a less hard edge in his tone. Catriona closed her eyes, remembering that same voice, its softer, more tender cadences of long ago still so fresh in her memory, and she shivered.

Another pause opened up, which Umberto eventually filled. 'Look, I've nothing against you. I have everything against this "predicament", as you so delicately put it.' He gave a mirthless laugh that to Catriona's ears sounded horribly world weary. 'So, just leave me alone, will you?'

'When will you come down?' she asked, refusing to be brushed off without an answer. She was looking for one small step in the right direction, however minuscule.

'I'll come when I bloody well like.'

'I'm not leaving until we agree a time,' Catriona's tone was quietly adamant.

He sighed, sounding suddenly exhausted. 'Tomorrow. I'll see you in the morning, if for no other reason than I've run out of grappa. Without that, I might as well divert myself with you, *Dottoressa*. Satisfied?'

'Perfectly. Thank you for giving me your attention. In that case, I'll see you tomorrow.'

As Catriona turned from the door, her heart was thundering once again. It was no small relief that her first meeting with Umberto had been conducted with a door between them.

She looked up to find her gaze meeting that of Adelina, who was standing just a few feet away at the end of the corridor. How much the housekeeper might have heard of this exchange Catriona didn't know but the older woman gave a small nod, seeming to signify her approval, and Catriona fancied her eyes had softened just a little.

*   *   *

Through his picture-starved eyes, Umberto glared resentfully across the horizon. He had finally managed to pull himself together and venture out into the grounds for some fresh air, where he could clear his head. The sun felt good on his skin. He didn't need his sight to imagine the azure sky scattered with magnolia clouds on this luminous spring morning; the bright green grass, the banks of rhododendrons bathed in rays of lustrous golden sunshine and the lake glittering like a vision still sparkled strongly in his memory, enough to fill his sightless gaze.

If he hadn't been holding a cane, no one would ever have guessed he was blind. He had counted the steps from the house to the beautiful stone balustrade skirting the lakeside where the property ended and where he liked to walk. There were steps down to a jetty, where two yachts that belonged to the family were moored, and there was a small private beach with a pergola covered in sweet-smelling roses where he liked to sit, a spot that overlooked the magnificent vista of Lake Como and the towns bordering its shores. Now, he stopped at the balustrade and felt for its rough surface, leaning one elbow on it.

He liked being outside. Nature in all its grandeur was not wholly inaccessible to him and it spelled freedom – tethered freedom perhaps – but somehow he found the open spaces comforting in his world of shadows. If he could live wholly in the open air, he would.

Inside the house he had to move tentatively, feeling his way around obstacles, which only served to underline his disability. As he walked, Umberto inhaled the delicious air with its scents of jasmine, rose and lemon blossom. Since his blindness, his other senses had become sharper and the fragrances that wafted towards him were sweeter than he remembered. Bees buzzed, birds sang – the sounds of Mother Nature were louder, the emotions they stirred in him more acute. The leaves on the trees whispered gently in the peaceful breeze. They had no choice but to stay rooted where they were. No choice, Umberto thought, they were grounded like him.

Yet Villa Monteverdi was his home and now, more than ever, his sanctuary. Over the years it had not been abandoned, unlike many of the great mansions on Lake Como, but constantly looked after, restored and enriched by each new generation, many of whom had resided there all year round. It was the kind of place that had always housed a proud and determined set of people.

He thought about his family dynasty, how he too had a strong sense of being a Monteverdi. It was hard to imagine any of his ancestors giving up on life had they been in his shoes. He had never been moody, quite the reverse: he had been known to have a cheerful, optimistic disposition. It all changed after the accident when it seemed that his spirits spun alternately downward and upward uncontrollably at any time, without rhyme or reason. After his suicide attempt, the realization that Umberto was going against his very nature had stung his pride and shamed him. Since then he had done his damnedest to battle the dark moods that still overwhelmed him and step up his efforts to master his surroundings.

For exercise Umberto had taught himself to walk the grounds alone – feeling his way around every path and shrub – and to ride a horse without help. Swimming was a different matter: he had always loved ploughing through the waters of the lake but now it was too dangerous for him to go on his own, so Flavio always accompanied him.

Like many of the lakeside houses, Villa Monteverdi also had a private raft moored higher up the lake, between Torno and Blevio, from which the residents and their guests could swim or sunbathe. The boatman, who lived in a room near the boathouse, was available to take people up to the raft in a motorboat at any time of the day or night. Flavio was a good swimmer, and would swim next to Umberto. When it was time to turn back to the raft, he would call out the direction or touch his master's shoulder. Umberto enjoyed swimming, even under these conditions, and this upper end of the lake was secluded, out of sight of holidaymakers.

Still, Umberto's large, healthy body craved something more: something better than this blind crawling about in constant fear of stumbling and injuring himself.

The alarm on his mobile went off: eleven o'clock. It was time for him to go back to the terrace, where he would be having his first meeting with the French therapist, Dr Catherine Drouot. At least she had some spark, that much was clear from her bold, if somewhat officious, appearance at his door yesterday. So, this was the woman his mother had determined to inflict upon him. The diva had got it into her head that the *Dottoressa*'s skills would not only be able to help him deal with his blindness but also regain some sort of joie de vivre so he could compose again. Umberto snorted derisively. This woman had another think coming if she viewed her powers to be so miraculous. Still, she had stood up to him, and he respected that.

After his mother's death he had made some enquiries through his lawyers about Dr Drouot and her clinic and, he had to admit, the report had been positive. She was evidently a specialist in her area with some notable successes to her name. There was not much about her personal life in the file, however, just that she was in her late twenties, was widowed and had a nine-year-old son. Catherine Drouot didn't seem to have any other attachments, apart from the mother with whom she lived. There was no gossip, no hobbies, nothing that would give an insight into her personality. She was pretty much a blank page to the outside world except for the articles and reports of the brilliant achievements she had attained in her field. Somehow this had piqued Umberto's curiosity and made this whole business a more interesting prospect than he had expected.

On his good days, the idea of having a skilled therapist stimulated his rare enthusiasm but on bad ones it irritated him and more than once he had been tempted to call the whole thing off. Yesterday had been one such day. Still, Renato Castaldi, his solicitor and friend, had told him that the *Dottoressa* in question was young and attractive, so maybe this new adventure could be fun – his life was so stale that he had reached the point where he would welcome any kind of diversion to put a bit of spice into it.

He picked up his cane, which he felt too proud to use in public but which was undoubtedly useful, and slowly made his way back to the house. This would be a good day for interviewing the *Dottoressa* because he knew that Giacomo was always showing tourists around Torno on Wednesdays and he preferred for his cousin not to be around during this first meeting.

He was also pleased that Silvana was away. Beautiful, passionate and provocative Silvana, who had offered herself to him so many times, even after he'd lost his sight, that he'd almost been tempted once or twice. True, in the past, before his car accident, he'd sometimes allowed their erotic romps to rekindle but although she would certainly be able to fulfil his sexual needs, he knew that now the experience would leave him nauseated and diminished more than anything else.

Umberto and Silvana had spent almost a whole childhood together, ever since she had come to the Villa Monteverdi when she was six with her widowed mother Carla, a distant relation of Calandra, and her best friend too. Calandra had spotted a talent for singing in the young girl and had taken her on as a pupil. Not long afterwards, Carla had died of cancer and Silvana had stayed on, growing up with the two boys. It was a story as old as time, the eternal triangle: Giacomo loved Silvana, Silvana loved Umberto … and Umberto? Above all, Umberto loved his freedom.

He and Silvana had such a complicated relationship that it tired him out simply thinking about it. Calandra would have liked nothing more than a marriage between her protegée and her son, despite the diva's disappointment that Silvana's talent had never gone beyond technical accomplishment. But although Umberto had found Silvana's sexual allure exciting and the world of music was something they shared – Silvana still sang for him when the mood took him to listen – there was no meeting of minds in a deeper sense, no chemistry other than on the occasions when they had shared a bed, in times gone by.

Besides, from their teenage years onwards, Silvana had always loved trying to wield a power over him, something he would no longer tolerate. Sometimes he wished he could tell her to leave the estate but Calandra had let her have the use of a cottage there and he couldn't very well go against the wish of his dying mother.

Automatically, his mind flicked back to Catherine Drouot. There was something in her voice that stirred an uneasy feeling inside him. Whatever it was, he reminded himself that he needed to keep his wits about him. He had asked Adelina to bring the *Dottoressa* out to him on the terrace. His former governess was a good judge of character; he could trust her and would find out later if her first impressions matched his own.

Chapter 8

'Is that you, Adelina?' The voice came suddenly, breaking in on the silence between Catriona and Umberto's housekeeper as together they approached the side of the villa from the garden.

'I suppose you've brought the *Dottoressa* with you.'

Hearing the composer's deep, powerful voice once more sent a visceral tide of emotion through Catriona even before she saw him, and it was no less powerful than the day before.

'*Sì, signore.*' Adelina moved to one side and Catriona stepped on to the terrace.

Now that it was an immediate reality, the prospect of confronting the man again flooded her with a nervous apprehension that appalled her. Catriona valued her cool detachment above all things. Over the years she had practised and developed it and such instant, instinctive emotional responses were well beyond her permitted scale. She fought to regain complete control; she needed to take charge of this meeting, even if that meant taking the most tentative of steps to gain her client's confidence. She had committed herself to whatever fate had in store for her in the shape of Umberto Rolando Monteverdi and if she were to help him, she would do it as best she could.

Catriona took in very few details in that first moment; all she saw was the unnaturally still, broad-shouldered figure in dark glasses and emerald green sweater sitting in the high-backed cane chair at a table under an umbrella. As she came forward, Umberto turned his head questioningly, evidently trying to judge where she was by the sound of her footsteps. It shook her more than she would have believed possible because in that instant he'd sent a kaleidoscope of images from her past spinning through her mind. Memories so staggering in their clarity of colour, scent and taste that her skin prickled.

A barb of wire seemed to fly into her throat and she flung up a hand as if to stifle that choked feeling. Coming right up to him, she paused in the expectation that he would hold out his hand for her to shake, then, catching the glint of his dark glasses, realized her mistake and reached out and took his hand, somewhat hesitantly, in hers. A shock passed through her as she felt the contact of his long, strong fingers closing firmly round her own. With a tremulous effort to keep her voice steady, she said: '*Buongiorno, signor* Monteverdi, it's good to meet you.'

She thought she detected a sudden stillness in Umberto, as if a film reel had glitched for a moment. Then the hard lines of his face set inscrutably once more and any presumption she might have held that the blind musician would show the slightest vulnerability was quashed immediately.

He dropped her hand somewhat abruptly. 'Let's do away with any small talk, shall we? I don't always find myself in the mood for niceties these days,' he said coolly. 'Take a seat, would you.' He motioned for her to sit at the round teak table, in the chair to his right. 'If there's one thing I cannot bear, it is relentlessly positive chatter. Unfortunately for me, do-gooders seem to think it an imperative when dealing with the disabled.'

Catriona, who had sat down as instructed, took his lead. 'Quite understood,' she said briskly, trying not to quail at his tone.

'And simply mirroring everything I say, *come un tipica strizzacervelli*, like a typical shrink, isn't going to work either, before you start down that track.'

She wished half his face wasn't covered by the dark shield of his glasses. Despite knowing he was now blind, looking into his eyes would have made her feel more confident. 'I can see that. Thank you for telling me. I'll speak my mind, you can rely on that.'

'Hmm … Good!' He sounded somewhat mollified but then the disagreeable downward tilt of his mouth took up residence once again on his handsome face.

'And in case you think you can come rapping at my door whenever you feel like it in order to clock up your hours, you cannot! I will call for you or schedule a session only if and when I feel like it.'

It was clear to Catriona that Umberto was drawing out his battle lines. 'I'm glad you've set the boundaries you're comfortable with—'

'Please don't use typical therapy jargon like "boundaries". Nothing irritates me more. And nothing about my situation is "comfortable". I detest being blind and I won't accept any of that rubbish people love to spout about it being an opportunity life throws at you. I assure you that making lemonade out of lemons is of no interest to me whatsoever.' The same bitter petulance of the day before was still there in Umberto's voice and manner, yet she sensed it was half-hearted now, melting like ice on a warm day.

Now it was Catriona's turn. 'Fine, but let me have my say, please,' she retorted. 'I am here for a purpose: I have a job to do and I would like to dedicate my time and energy to you.' She was pleased to see that he had gone still again and showed no sign of interrupting; she had his undivided attention.

'Like a business arrangement, we will be working together and therefore need a verbal contract that we can agree on right from the start. That way, neither of us becomes frustrated and we build up a sense of trust. I realize you will have good days and bad days. That is quite normal.'

To her surprise, as she finished she saw Umberto's beautiful lips turn upwards in an amused smile.

'I thought you were French. You speak Italian like an Italian,' he said.

She was taken aback by this sudden change in mood, as if the sun had suddenly broken through the cloud on an overcast day. Once she had steadied her suddenly tremulous heart, Catriona realized that although she wasn't being given carte blanche to get started with her assignment, Umberto was offering her a truce. The formal sessions with him could wait, there was plenty of time for that. What mattered now was that his mood had changed to one of acceptance of her – or the appearance of it, at least – and her priority was to build on that connection.

'We were taught some Italian at school and it's such a melodious language that I was inspired to learn it more thoroughly.'

'Ah yes, you are a musician, of course. I suppose every facet of melody has an impact on you.'

Catriona watched breathlessly the dark head tilting slightly, as if he were taking the measure of her voice, judging from it her height and disposition. Memories of ten years ago crowded upon her. For a brief moment she relived the stolen hours of passion, the pulsing strength of his body, the puckering anticipation of hers; and although the memory of his rejection was still surprisingly raw, her heart ached for him and the last drop of her bitterness and resentment drained from her.

Before she could make any response he interrupted the conversation, beckoning Adelina over. 'Adelina, *per favore, ci porti un caffè?*' His head turned an inch towards Catriona. 'Or maybe, as it's a hot day, the *Dottoressa* would prefer something cold to drink?'

'Coffee would be lovely,' Catriona assured him.

The housekeeper's jet-black eyes looked at her sharply. 'Do you like it strong?'

'Yes, very much so, especially Italian coffee. The stronger the better.'

'*Caffè macchiato?*'

Catriona knew that the meaning of *macchiare* in Italian was 'stain'. '*Sì, grazie,*' she answered, knowing that this espresso in a demitasse was merely stained with some hot frothed milk – quite different from a cappuccino, which Italians never order after ten in the morning.

Adelina's face relaxed into a large smile. 'The *Dottoressa* is acquainted with our Italian ways?'

'Nice is only a stone's throw from Italy, so it's natural that I spend quite a lot of time here.'

Adelina gave a look of satisfaction and strode away, murmuring to herself, '*Bene, bene.*'

For a moment Catriona looked around her across the bright landscape, feeling her taut nerves loosening a little. To her it appeared like a freshly painted picture – the beds of snapdragon encircling the pond where the water appeared lustrous in the opulent light … the crimson, saffron and coral colours of the flowers. She tried to imagine how Umberto must experience it in his world: as a captivating harmony of sounds and aromas, where the umbrella pine trees whispered and the cicadas chirped somewhere in the undergrowth, and the sun – fully up now – warmed everything with its pleasant glow, while the fragrance of grass, oranges and lemons lingered enticingly in the air.

'Well, now, I'm glad we have an understanding, *dottoressa* Drouot. I have no intention of being thrown straight on to your therapy couch. So today, you will be my guest and have the day off.'

His tone had a cajoling command and Catriona's heart beat a little faster. 'Anyway, it would be heartless of me to expect you to begin work immediately, *vero?*' The hint of a smile hovered around his mouth.

Catriona, whose usual sound sense seemed evaporate under its beguiling power, did not think to insist on agreeing a time when they would have their first therapy session. Instead, she found herself acquiesing. 'If you prefer, yes,' she said with a smile.

'First, though, I'd like to know a little more about you, *Dottoressa*. Hold out your hand, put it in mine. Here …' She did as instructed, automatically feeling a sense of helpless shock, as if she were a puppet and he controlled the strings. The musician's long deft fingers played over hers, feeling their fine bones, their smooth skin. He deliberately turned her hand and she felt his fingertips travelling over her palm, finding the life lines and the mound below her thumb. *Oh, that exquisite touch!* She hadn't forgotten it, and it stirred feelings in her to the point of excruc, ation.

'Being blind has its difficulties, as you can see, *dottoressa* Drouot. We have to employ such methods in our reading of those with whom we must live and work … so don't mind too much – ah yes, I can feel that you *do* mind.'

The professional in Catriona finally took charge. 'I am well aware that sensations are food for the brain, providing energy and knowledge, and that this is an important factor in a blind person's life. So, whether or not I mind is neither here nor there. A patient's touch has no impact on me. I am your doctor, you are my patient, and the relationship stops there. As long as these explorations are kept to a minimum and are done in good faith, there should be no problem,' she ended coolly.

Umberto released her hand, though he seemed entirely unperturbed by her response. 'You are not smiling any more, *Dottoressa*. Have you always been this feisty? Tell me what you are like,' he commanded. 'How would you describe yourself?'

A momentary spasm of panic took hold of her, but she fought it down and even managed to laugh in a perfectly natural manner. 'Well, I suppose it's never easy to describe oneself,' she replied, as though seriously reflecting on the matter. 'I'm of medium height and build. I have brown hair and brown eyes. I think that's all.'

While she was speaking, Umberto had taken off his dark glasses and the emerald eyes, now fixed as though made of glass, looked directly at her from that deeply tanned face with the proud flare to the nostrils and a strong, aristocratic definition to his mouth and jawline. His gaze reminded her of the beautiful but empty eyes of the porcelain doll she remembered in her grandmother's cupboard in England. Still, with Umberto's eyes, a clever surgeon had somehow been able to restore their keen penetrating quality to make them look as Catriona remembered them: deep-set, their heavy lids adding a sensuousness that now seemed even more evident.

'Umm ...' He seemed to ponder her every aspect. 'Why do I get the impression that you are taller than you admit? Tall and very slim, I would say. You have strong, interesting hands – the hands of a musician, of course. But that's not all. I can tell a whole lot more already,' he declared.

'You must have an expressive mouth, otherwise I wouldn't *hear* you smile. You have a remarkably soothing speaking voice that falls very pleasingly on the ear. In fact, a very unusual tone of voice – low, warm and melodious. Do you sing, *Dottoressa*?'

Catriona swallowed hard, trying to keep her nerve.

'Well, I ... I do sing a little, in a choir.'

Umberto shook his head. '*Peccato*, pity,' he said, seeming to let the subject drop, to the young woman's relief. 'I think there's the making of an opera singer in that voice of yours. But it's probably too late now. A voice must be cultivated and nurtured from a tender age ... *peccato*.'

'I am very content with my profession, thank you. I don't think I'm made for the type of life required of people in the limelight. People like your mother Calandra, whom I admired greatly.'

'You knew my mother?'

'I have all her recordings. I'm a great fan of opera.'

He sighed. 'She was a great lady. Did you meet her?'

Catriona bit her lip and paused. 'Briefly.'

'So, she came to see you in Nice to appoint you for this job?'

'Yes, she did.'

'She must have believed you'd make a difference then. It wasn't like her to go out of her way like that. Especially as she hadn't been well for a while. I used to have a house in Nice myself, a long time ago. A big house …' He stilled, his eyes dropping to the side as though deep in thought, his face darkening.

Catriona held her breath, willing him not to go further down that road. 'Calandra had read about my work with the blind,' she said quickly. 'She knew I was a musician and hoped that you might bear my society better than another sort of therapist. She hoped that I might bring you back to composing, which she felt passionately was your reason for being. And on a practical level she knew that I could teach Braille and that, if you could read music, it would make an enormous difference to your quality of life.'

There was a long silence while Umberto took in her words. Deep in the trees the cicadas went on chirring and the tendrilled leaves of umbrella pines went on whispering. There was a pearliness about the air and the surrounding view; a sky of pale turquoise with a few scattered opalescent clouds that appeared so motionless they looked as though painted. In the distance was more turquoise, reflected in the greenish blue of Lake Como.

Umberto looked remote and a little withdrawn; Catriona noticed the lines around his eyes and a few stray greying hairs among the shock of raven black. She remembered the dust on the piano she had seen the previous day, the sign that he was cut off from what his mother had considered his lifeblood – his music.

Finally, he broke the silence. 'I loved my mother deeply but she could be a meddlesome old witch when she wanted to be,' he said dryly. 'She found it impossible to understand that I really have little inclination for music any more, neither playing nor composing. It's enough simply to learn how to get about the place without my sight.'

Catriona sighed inwardly, martialling her energy, trying hard to fight off a growing despondency.

'You are quiet, *Dottoressa*,' he said, turning his head a fraction towards her. 'Are you wondering if you've done a wise thing in coming here? I understand you have left a son and a mother behind in France.'

At the mention of her son Catriona gave a start. It reminded her, all too suddenly, of what she was hiding. When she spoke, the words sounded a little automatic, such was her distraction. 'As I said before, I have no regrets. I am quite sure I can be of help.'

'Do you think you're going to find it unnerving, *Dottoressa*, to be constantly around a man who goes through life as if it were an unending tunnel of darkness, with no light at the other end? It can be nerve-racking for the sighted to be in the company of someone who could go sprawling on his face if a chair or a table were moved only a few inches from their set positions … If so, speak up. My private plane can always fly you back, if you feel the job will be too much for you.'

For just an instant, Umberto's face had looked hard and menacing.

Catriona forced a confident note into her voice, keen to keep him from lapsing into melancholy reflection. 'I'm perfectly happy with the arrangement, thank you. I'm not leaving until I've had a chance to prove to you that you can still compose. Not only that but also prove that you can appear in public and be the great Umberto Rolando Monteverdi you have been and still are.

'Gifts like yours, *signore*, do not die in a car accident. It wasn't your brain that was smashed, not your hands either. There is absolutely no reason why you cannot pick up your brilliant career where you left off. Have you never heard of the nineteenth-century blind French piano tuner Claude Montal, who taught himself how to tune a piano while studying at the Institut National des Jeunes Aveugles? And what of your compatriot, the tenor Andrea Bocelli? He lost his sight completely when he was twelve after a football accident and subsequently became the biggest-selling singer in the history of classical music. The list is long and the key words are courage, determination, discipline and hard work.'

An intriguing smile tugged at Umberto's lips. 'Thank you for the lecture. You are not afraid to speak your mind, *Dottoressa*. I like that.'

Indeed, she was far from the wide-eyed young music student in awe of the great composer she once had been, the infatuated teenager who'd let him trample all over her love. 'Good, so I'm sure that we'll get along,' she asserted.

Adelina came back on to the terrace bearing a tray with a jug of steaming milk and the *macchiatos* in small cups, which she placed down with her agile, highly veined hands. Catriona was aware that the housekeeper was watching her behind thick black lashes, no doubt summing her up. Adelina had seemed wary of her at first but now appeared to regard her with a new curiosity that was much more approving.

When the housekeeper was gone, after telling Umberto that she was off to the kitchen to fetch something sweet to go with the coffee, he said: 'Adelina came to us when I was a small child. She never knew her parents and was brought up in an orphanage. We became her family and treated her as one of us, although she never took advantage of that status. She's a marvellous cook and although more or less retired, she's insisted on cooking for me since the accident.'

Catriona had the impression that Umberto was trying to tell her something. He hesitated before resuming: 'Adelina might make comments to you that you find … *come dire*, a bit familiar.

You must not take umbrage. She is very protective of me and now that *mia madre* is not with us any more, she feels it is her duty to shelter me from anything you can think of.'

'That must be a little suffocating sometimes.'

'When she becomes too much like a mother hen, I tell her off.'

'She seems devoted to you, though.'

He nodded and his expression softened. 'Yes, she is.'

Adelina reappeared, wheeling a small trolley from which she took two dessert plates and laid them on the table. 'There's something sweet I made for you both,' she declared. The old servant took a spotless napkin, shook it loose and moved to place it in front of Umberto but, with an impressive reflex, he grabbed it in mid-air.

'You see?' he demanded gruffly, dark eyebrows like question marks. He smiled derisively, 'I am treated like a baby.'

Adelina muttered disapprovingly, laying dessert silverware on the table. 'At least when you were a baby, you were easier to deal with. As soon as you could walk, you never let me do anything for you. Always so stubborn, wanting to do it for yourself.' She shook her head. 'Nothing has changed.'

'So, what have you made for us, *eh*?'

'*E' una sorpresa, non sia impaziente*, it's a surprise, don't be impatient. You will like it. It might cheer you out of your grumpiness.'

'Grumpiness? Insufferable woman,' he murmured, though Catriona could tell that he was trying to suppress a grin and was thoroughly enjoying being bossed about by Adelina.

As the housekeeper moved away to the trolley, Umberto smiled indulgently and lowered his voice. 'I know exactly what she's made: *torta sbrisolona*. We normally have it for dessert at lunch or dinner. Actually, it's *her* favourite dessert. She always makes a large one for the house and a small one for herself. It's quite delicious, you'll see.'

With Adelina's appearance Umberto seemed to have perked up considerably. Although she had treated many patients with depression and bipolar disorder, Catriona found this unpredictable flip from gloomy to sunny in the space of a minute almost unnerving. Still, he had been more than honest with her, and she knew now to stay clear if she felt the winds were turning in the wrong direction.

Adelina returned to the table with what looked more like a large almond biscuit than a tart and two tall glasses of cream. '*La torta sbrisolona*,' she announced as she placed the cake on the table and proceeded to divide it into rather large segments.

'Ah, what a surprise,' Umberto exclaimed. 'My favourite and yours, *eh*, Adelina?' For the first time he laughed deep in his throat, those piercing green eyes sparkling to life.

'*Sì, signore*, you know my guilty pleasure,' she replied, looking at him with eyes full of affection, but also tinged with pity. She then placed slices of cake on two plates and placed them in front of Umberto and Catriona. 'Tell me what you think, *Dottoressa*.'

Before Catriona could respond, Umberto picked up his slice and proceeded to break off pieces with his hands. 'Crumble it with your fingers,' he told her, 'and either pour the *zabaglione* on to it or add it to your glass. They are meant to be eaten together. Like this …' There was something touching in the way he showed her how, moving with careful coordination, and Catriona felt her heart constrict and a lump form in her throat.

The cake had a delicious crumbly texture, like a streusel topping. It reminded her of the English blackberry and apple crumble she used to eat every Sunday as a child. She nearly said so but caught herself in time as she added a few pieces to the *zabaglione*. 'Mmm!' she exclaimed as she took a mouthful of crunchy dessert mixture, feeling the pastry dissolve on her tongue. 'This is bliss! *Deliziosa. Grazie*, Adelina.'

The housekeeper's face broke into a large smile that made her look ten years younger. '*Prego, Dottoressa, buon appetito.*'

She appeared delighted and Catriona felt to some measure that she had won Adelina over.

'I knew you'd approve. Adelina's cooking is second to none.' Umberto licked a crumb off his fingers and felt for his spoon. 'You know, sighted people take eating for granted, but the reality is that trying to eat with cutlery isn't easy when one can't see what one is doing … all that fumbling around cutting food, judging the angle of the fork, being able to stab something and raise it to one's mouth.' He gave her a crooked smile. 'They had to teach me to eat, like an infant. Humiliating!' An edge had crept into his voice.

'And just like an infant, I'd fly into sudden rages too. Adelina has been an angel of patience with me … I can't tell you how much broken crockery she has dodged!'

Adelina shrugged and glanced at Catriona with a grin. 'It keeps my old bones from stiffening up, *signore*.'

Catriona laughed, though it was no laughing matter. She'd heard the frustration beneath Umberto's brittle humour and said quietly: 'Don't worry about me, *signor* Umberto, I'm used to sudden rages in my professional capacity, whether from infants or adults …'

'Shall I pour the milk, *signore*?' Adelina asked.

'*No grazie, Adelina, ci penso io*, no thanks, Adelina, leave it to me.'

Umberto felt for the edge of the tray that Adelina had placed between them. His hands scanned the position of its contents by touch, and his long pianist fingers closed neatly around the handle of the jug before pouring a tiny amount of hot frothy milk into each of their cups without spilling a single drop on to the table.

'*Grazie*, Adelina, you can leave us now. I think I can manage on my own.'

Satisfied that they were enjoying the culmination of her efforts, Adelina slipped away.

After the Italian matron had gone, Catriona watched Umberto move her cup towards her across the table. Somehow she founded it unnerving, sitting here miles from home, having coffee with the blind father of her son, a man she had loved with such passion ten years ago and for whom, she realized, she still cared deeply. How long would it be, she wondered, before she had to face Umberto with the truth and tell him that he had been deceived by her for all those years? After all, maybe he didn't care, perhaps he'd never thought of her and had totally forgotten her …

Her wrist shook as she took another mouthful of cake and she had to force herself to some sort of control as she put down her spoon a little too quickly. This was so unprofessional!

'Why is your hand shaking?' he drawled. 'What are you so nervous about, *Dottoressa*?'

Catriona groped for an easy excuse. 'I slept badly last night so I'm still a little tired, I suppose,' she said.

He turned his head sharply. 'Is the bed in the lodge not comfortable?'

'No, no, it's not that,' she answered quickly. 'It's just that it always takes me a few nights to get accustomed to a new place. I'll be fine by tomorrow.' She put her hands in her lap to steady them.

Umberto did not fumble. His lean brown hands made slow, careful movements as he brought morsels of cake from his plate to his mouth.

They ate in silence for a while. When they had finished, he took out a gold cigarette box and a lighter from his pocket.

Catriona jumped up to help him. It was the wrong thing to do, she knew it, but her reaction had been instinctive.

'Please sit down, *Dottoressa*. I am blind, not incapable.'

She watched the confident way in which he sought a cigarette from the jewelled box and took it between his lips, pressing the end of it to the lighter and holding it in position while he inhaled. She marvelled at his adroitness, but then he had always had such certain hands, self-assured and dexterous, and somehow his blindness had increased his sensitivity of touch.

With her gaze full upon him, it seemed incredible that he couldn't actually see the cigarette in his fingers or watch the smoke make blue shapes in the air. If she hadn't known that he was blind, she would never have guessed it. Even his eyes held an expression. Umberto had evidently taught himself to carry on expressing his emotion with his eyes. When speaking, he still rolled them, looking in the direction of the sounds he heard. That, together with his mastery of eating, sitting, standing and walking with such coordinated movements, meant he could easily pass for a sighted person. He had learnt all these skills so well and Catriona marvelled at his ability, knowing that with such discipline and hard work, everything might be possible for this man.

'You don't have to watch me as if I'm going to set fire to myself. Yes, I know you're sitting there like a mother hen, all tensed to spring to the rescue of an errant infant, but I'm really quite capable, *Dottoressa*.'

'I can see that,' she murmured. 'I didn't mean to offend.'

'Practice, and the very definite urge not to be a burden on the sighted, have forced me to become self-sufficient. Like the deaf, my sort can be a pain in the neck.'

Catriona recognized the proud man she had met, and saw too that something of his previous irritation had returned. Still, this attitude didn't chime with a suicide attempt. She wondered what else might have been the cause of that.

'I must make it explicit, *Dottoressa*. No one here avoids the fact that I am blind. No one gets embarrassed if they happen to speak of something that I can't see and share with them.' He puffed on his cigarette and blew a white cloud in the air that touched his eyelids.

'Understood.'

'Those who can see take many things for granted but there are a few compensations for the blind. The imagination can run riot sometimes. For instance, I'm able to place over a blank face any sort of mask that takes my fancy. But with you, *Dottoressa*, I have not yet decided what kind of fascinating face is being denied me.'

He seemed to be staring directly at her as he smoked. Catriona glanced up at him sharply, once more wondering if there was an underlying meaning to his words.

'But I notice that you didn't finish your dessert. Perhaps you didn't like it so much after all?' There was the familiar mischievous tone in his voice that had once made her bones melt, and still charmed her today, but this uncanny way he had of knowing her movements was unnerving. At least it meant that he would be very responsive to the treatment. Yet her previous thought still nagged at her: Umberto had never seemed the suicidal type and his behaviour today only confirmed her first impression, unless of course he was bipolar and prone to erratic mood swings. Artists often were, of course. It wouldn't have been the first time she'd had to deal with that sort of client … Still, he didn't strike her as such.

She smiled, knowing that he would hear it in her voice. 'On the contrary, it's delicious, but I'm not used to eating such a rich dessert mid-morning. How can you tell I hadn't finished it, if you don't mind my asking?'

'Music-makers have keen hearing, and blindness makes mine even sharper,' he replied. 'There is a commonly known expression that says musicians can "hear the grass grow".'

Catriona was on sure footing with this conversation. Her eyes sparkled as she explained what she had learned over the years spent bringing music into the lives of the blind. 'That's so true. It's thought that the massive visual cortex of the brain, though useless for sight, actually carries on functioning in an entirely different way.'

'So, for someone like me it reallocates its attentions and caters to the other senses, I suppose.'

'Exactly. That's why blind people so often have perfect pitch.'

'Blind piano tuners aren't exactly a rarity. Like your Claude Montal, the French piano tuner you mentioned,' Umberto went on, but then suddenly his mouth twisted, some of his previous irritation returning.

'Look, I cannot get excited by all this. I had perfect pitch before, there is nothing blindness has brought except pain and frustration. We're back to this upbeat song and dance about fate dealing you a surprise hand that turns out to be a precious gift. I'm not buying it, *Dottoressa*. I was handed nothing more than a grenade, which blew my life to pieces.'

'A life you'll get back, I know it,' Catriona said fervently. 'Music is like food to a blind person – they need it to live and grow and flourish. You wouldn't believe the transformations I've seen.'

Umberto stubbed out his cigarette and was silent a moment. When he next spoke, the world-weary downward tilt to his mouth had vanished.

'You have spirit, *Dottoressa* … and feeling. It's your therapist's training and something tenacious in your character, *vero*? It was my mother's last wish that you should come over here to treat me, and that was the only reason why I accepted this intrusion into my life. But I'm glad that you came, *Dottoressa*.' He raised his emerald eyes to the sky and took the last gulp of his coffee, and Catriona ached that he saw only the blackness and none of the blueness.

He stretched out his hand to find the small silver bell Adelina had placed on the table when she had brought in the coffee. In doing so, he leaned towards her and his warm breath fanned her cheek, so that Catriona's pulse quickened. Then, finding the bell with his fingers, he rang it and leant back in his chair. She let out a quiet breath. 'I will try to make the sessions as interesting as possible.'

'I have no doubt that you are very skilled at your job.'

'Thank you,' she murmured, aware that suddenly Umberto looked tired and his voice seemed somewhat strained.

'But before we begin these sessions I need to have you know the kind of man I am, *Dottoressa*. Although I will do my best to be as courteous as possible, there are days when I can't even bear my own presence. I keep on thinking of Samson in the Handel opera, of him stumbling on to the stage and beginning to sing that aria. I never had the slightest conception of what it really meant until now. Most of the time I cope with it, but sometimes it all becomes too much. Those times you *must* keep out of my way, you must leave me alone, and if you cannot understand that you might as well pack your bags.'

Catriona gazed at him and felt as if her heart would break. 'Understood,' she murmured.

'I can feel that you are appalled. The truth is often grim,' Umberto said, and he seemed to be looking right at her. 'But it is important that t's are crossed from the very beginning to avoid any confusion, don't you think?'

'Definitely. I couldn't agree more.'

'I hope you will be comfortable in the lodge. The forest behind it has for a long time been a sanctuary for the eagle owl, hence the name Allogio del Gufo Reale. You'll hear them clearly at night, especially when there is a full moon. It used to be a shooting lodge but my mother took it over. She redecorated it and made it her own, an escape from day-to-day life. It's not to everybody's taste, but it reflects her flamboyant and imaginative personality. She used to rehearse there, away from the noise of the main house when it was full of my guests.'

'Actually, I love it,' replied Catriona. 'Your hospitality has been more than generous.'

'You will enjoy Calandra's Bechstein in the small room overlooking the lake. That was my mother's sanctuary.'

'Yes, Mario showed me. It's wonderful, with all that glass inviting such a stunning view.'

'Calandra would be happy to know it was being used. The lodge was one of her favourite places. I'm glad you like it.'

'I'm very touched, thank you.'

He paused. 'You may already know this, but my cousin Giacomo as well as my mother's goddaughter Silvana live on the estate. They'll both be back later on and I thought that it would be good for you to meet them this evening. I hope you will not be too tired to join us for dinner.'

Catriona barely allowed herself to think what it would be like to encounter the redheaded siren after all these years. An image of the beautiful singer flashed into her mind, she was laughing as she left the Nice opera house, arm in arm with Umberto. It was pushed away by the fleeting anxiety that Silvana Esposito might recognize her, but then she remembered how little trouble the soprano had taken to acknowledge her presence, merely pushing past her backstage, and then leaving early, never making it to the party later. No, someone as self-centred as that wouldn't recall a shy eighteen-year-old local girl.

'It will be a pleasure, thank you,' she answered, as brightly as she could. 'In fact, I've already met your cousin Giacomo.'

He frowned. 'You have?'

'Yes, the day I arrived. He was kind enough to take me on a tour around Villa Pliniana yesterday, too.'

An unreadable emotion flickered across Umberto's face before his expression became impassive. 'I'm glad my cousin has been so attentive.'

Catriona remained silent. Something told her that pursuing any conversation about Giacomo now would not be a good idea.

'We take drinks in the small *salone*,' Umberto continued. 'The larger reception rooms are closed as I don't entertain that much nowadays. Adelina will fetch you. The house is big and until you find your way around, she'll be your guide. She seems to have taken to you … that's a good thing.' He gave a wry smile. 'As I'm sure you can guess, she can be a pain when she doesn't like someone.'

'Adelina has your best interests at heart and so no doubt we'll get on like a house on fire.'

Umberto nodded and once more reached for the cigarette box that lay on the table. He picked it up and helped himself to a cigarette before putting the box back on the table in exactly the same place. He then lit the cigarette as easily as he'd done before.

'Do you ride, *Dottoressa*?' he asked after he'd taken two puffs.

'Yes.'

'I hope you brought riding gear with you.'

Catriona laughed outright. 'I wasn't aware I was coming here on holiday.'

'Then we will remedy that as soon as possible. We have stables with some splendid animals here. I sometimes take my exercise that way.'

She wasn't aware that she had marked her astonishment by any movement or sound, but his eyebrow raised.

'Surprised that I can ride?'

'Shouldn't I be?'

'My horse is bomb-proof. I started off by riding in an arena to get the hang of it. As for the trails, the grounds are large, with wide-open spaces, and my horse knows which way to go.'

'It's very brave of you, but quite reckless.'

He shrugged. 'It puts a little excitement in an otherwise colourless life.'

Catriona let her eyes glide over her surroundings. A brilliant explosion of colour was exactly what was present in the beauty of this view. The flowers and the necklace of craggy mountains rising behind the far-off lake, all tinged with blazing spring hues, formed a breathtaking setting she would never forget. Enhanced by the heat, the landscape appeared crude and violent in its colouring: greens, reds, yellows and oranges all flaring in their intensity. The iridescent quality of the atmosphere, the wavering of the heated air, produced a faintness of the shadows in some places and a pronounced density in others, falling upon the ground in myriad tints of lilac, violet and rose ... a Fauvist painting if ever she'd seen one.

'You are admiring the view from here?'

'Yes, I was just thinking that it reminded me of the paintings of Matisse and Van Gogh.'

'At this time of year, the countryside is particularly luxuriant. It's a combination of the heat and the haze that lifts off the lake. This place is beloved by artists from all over the world. Franz Liszt said Lake Como was a "spot blessed by heaven". Unfortunately, now I can only guess its beauty by the scent and feel of it.'

A compelling quality to his voice seemed to vibrate in Catriona's bones.

You must miss it, she thought, and not for the first time that day her heart went out to the man sitting beside her.

Adelina came back to clear the cups and ask if there was anything else they needed. Umberto smiled that charming smile Catriona remembered so well. 'I have kept you long enough, *Dottoressa.*' The smile on the proud, hard, passionate face deepened. 'Adelina will take you back to the lodge and we will see you for the *aperitivo* this evening at eight o'clock in the *salone.* Like in the South of France, we dine late here.' Umberto stood up and held out his hand.

Catriona took it in hers. She could feel the quick beating of her heart as she stood close to Umberto's dark, tall figure. Her eyes were fixed intensely on the Italian features she had tried so hard to blot from her mind. The grip on her fingers tightened and for a moment she wouldn't, couldn't, pull away. She stared at him, mesmerized by the sensual curve of his lips, the strength of his jawline, the thrust of his Roman nose, the black eyebrows above the glassy glint of his emerald eyes. Although the light had gone out of those eyes, they fixed on her now, staring blindly but with a glimmer of curious awareness. A tremor passed through her ... or was it through him?

'Have a pleasant afternoon, *Dottoressa*. I've enjoyed talking to you. Most interesting,' he murmured as he released her fingers. 'It has been a tradition in this house to dress for dinner and, although my eyes cannot appreciate the gesture, some pretence of civilized behaviour must be observed.'

As she wandered off with Adelina, Catriona still felt the imprint of warmth his hand had left on hers. Though tempted to look back, she walked on as birdcalls, echoing from the trees around the house, seemed to hold a mocking note. It was as if they sensed the dangerous stirrings of intensity inside her, the same excitement that had once trapped her so long ago. She wished she didn't feel it; she was still attracted to the man who once hurt her so badly, and the knowledge was terrifying.

CHAPTER 9

The lake lay bluer than the sky with rays of light dancing delicately across the water. Catriona jogged at a steady pace, relishing the freedom of letting her thoughts meander and the chance to work off her pent-up energy. Instead of lunch she'd just snacked on fruit and, after a distracted few hours trying to catch up on work, she'd given up and pulled on her running vest and shorts, hoping some exercise might drive away the restless thoughts of Umberto that kept invading her mind.

She'd hesitated before deciding on her route. She wasn't keen on going for a run in the grounds in case she encountered Umberto, Giacomo or even Silvana Esposito. It was intimidating enough that she'd be meeting the stunning soprano at dinner that evening and Catriona had no desire to risk bumping into her now on the estate. She wondered about the relationship between Silvana and Umberto. Had they been lovers? Were they still? The idea made her insides clench uncomfortably and she pushed the thought away.

Seeing Giacomo again didn't exactly fill her with enthusiasm either. He had been both welcoming and friendly yesterday – a charming companion, in fact – but beneath his handsome smile she detected something that made her distinctly uneasy, a watchfulness that was more than simply an overfamiliar interest in her.

As for Umberto … his unpredictable moods were unnerving – one minute a mass of dark tension, coiling like a tightly wound spring, the next, charming and cheerful. Not to mention the fact that after all these years he still had the power to get under her skin.

No, she needed to be alone and a run was just what she needed to ease the tension. Tonight was not going to be easy and she had to clear her head before facing the full, complicated force of the Monteverdi clan.

When she had gone for a swim the previous afternoon after being dropped at the lodge by Giacomo, she had noticed at the end of the quay bordering the lake a small gate which, she assumed, led out of the estate into the countryside. She'd been right, and now she sighed with pleasure at the majestic beauty of the landscape that confronted her as she ran. Early this morning, delicate gauze-like mist had veiled the dark green forests and mountains, floating up to rest in silver wreaths of cloud upon the peaks. Now the heat of the afternoon sun made them appear in sharp colourful relief against the brilliant azure sky, as if they had been gilded in certain places with the paintbrush of a skilled artist.

The full-leaved trees of early summer swayed in the warm air with the hum of bees, the expanses of grass white and yellow with daisies and buttercups. She ran past waving fields of wheat and barley, past the bright green foliage of the forest. Then, once she had completed a good distance, Catriona looped around and gradually made her way back towards the house. This time she spotted a right-hand path that turned off the main drive where she'd started her run. It then circled back on itself, up past the family church and presumably into the mountains. It was the kind of path that might be taken by anybody who didn't want to be seen from the house.

She slowed to a walk, deciding to cool down by walking the rest of the way and taking a detour to see where the path led.

On passing the church she saw a small track that skirted a stream and, beyond it, a stile. The mountain rose steeply above her. As she walked along, the stream became partly hidden by trees but through them she could glimpse the rushing foam of the water as it made its way over glistening rocks. She guessed there would be waterfalls above; there seemed hardly a cleft in these hills that did not spout water, whether a thin white trickle or a raging torrent.

Catriona was suddenly met by a screen of trees backed by a tall wall of rock. A different entrance to the Gufi Reali forest or, more likely, the forest boundary, she thought. If she took the path that led into it she would probably find herself back at the lodge.

As she went deeper into the woods she glimpsed, between the trees, tiny falls tumbling over mossy boulders and swirling in miniature whirlpools. Up above, a deep, ominous roar became more and more persistent.

All at once Catriona came upon a waterfall. Moving cautiously round the base of a massive boulder, she found herself standing on a projecting bank, facing a torrent of green water that fell into a tempestuous frothing pool far below her. Fascinated, yet alarmed by its sheer drop, she stepped closer to view the whipped-up turmoil below, glimpsing it through arching branches of the trees clinging to the side of the gorge. Feeling the wet ground beneath her feet, she drew back again, trembling.

Suddenly she heard a voice close by and swung round to find herself face-to-face with an old man in a faded blue shirt and trousers, wearing a beaten-up straw trilby and leaning on a long bamboo stick. He beckoned her away from the bank.

'I couldn't make you hear, *signorina*. I was trying to tell you not to go too near.'

They both stepped away from the gorge.

'People don't often come here alone,' he told her, his eyes regarding her apprehensively.

Catriona gave him a bright, questioning smile. 'Don't the residents of the villa and their guests come here for walks or picnics? It's all very grand and beautiful.'

The man shook his head vigorously.

'*No, non dalla casa grande*, not from the big house, no. Not since that young woman died.'

Catriona drew in a sharp breath. Hadn't Giacomo alluded to a 'tragedy'? He'd certainly made it sound as though someone had died in the Gufi Reali forest.

'It was here …' she murmured to herself. 'Tell me, was this young woman anything to do with the Monteverdi family?'

The old man shifted his weight and gestured with his stick back towards the villa. 'There are strange things going on at that house. Odd people, the family … been here for generations. Terrible business it was … and they say she was driven to it. *È meglio non ricordare ciò che è da dimenticare, ed è meglio non dimenticare ciò che vale la pena ricordare*, it is better not to remember what is best forgotten, and better not to forget what is worth remembering,' he rambled, fixing her with a significant look.

Catriona faltered, not quite knowing how to respond. 'I'm sorry, I don't know what you mean.'

From the hills came the plaintive duets of lambs and ewes, and dogs barking.

'Bringing the flock down, I was,' he muttered. 'Scattered they'll be if I don't go.' He touched his hat in farewell and the next moment Catriona was alone again.

Carefully, she picked her way down the track again until she came to the path where she had started. As she made her way back towards the gate to the quayside she wondered who the young woman might have been. Undoubtedly there was a mystery surrounding Umberto's family and its past. A past that had more to it than appeared in the report she'd been given before she'd taken on this assignment. Was the shepherd's revelation the first piece in the puzzle of the Monteverdis?

Reaching the gate, she looked up as a figure caught her eye. Ambling up the path from the quayside was the lean figure of Flavio, winding a coil of rope around his hand and forearm, a cigarette hanging between his lips.

Catriona hesitated, but it was far too late to divert her steps and find another way just to avoid the unnerving boatman. Telling herself not to be so silly, she took a steadying breath and kept going.

He squinted through the smoke as he saw her and gave a cocky smirk, flicking the cigarette away as he pushed the gate open for her.

'*Prego, signorina.*' His piercing gaze followed her as she passed, not bothering to hide his interest. 'You like to exercise, *eh*?'

It was all Catriona could do not to openly grimace at the way he was looking at her, his smile now flashing crooked white teeth.

'Yes, I've just been for a run,' she managed to respond, slipping through the gate and putting as much distance between them as possible. She shot him a cool smile. '*Grazie.*' And with that, head down, she hurried past the quay, feeling his eyes on her back, watching her every step of the way.

*   *   *

Catriona reached the terrace of the lodge and, after stretching out her tired limbs, she stared out over the brilliance of the landscape that only this morning had been the backdrop to her first meeting with Umberto. Everywhere was a wild mass of dynamic shapes and colours: bushes of oleander sagging beneath the weight of their clusters; paths bordered with trailing plants; and a profusion of flowering shrubs and trees – camellias, magnolias, myrtles, pomegranates with trunks gnarled like plaited ropes, orange and lemon trees, steely blue cacti erect as swords, and enormous fleshy-leaved aloes.

The run might have taken the edge off her restlessness but her head was still full of Umberto. Even the landscape seemed to live and breathe reminders of him, the sheer ferocity of its colour and form automatically bringing an image of his face, unbidden, into her mind. She half closed her eyes and a tremor ran all the way through her. Oh God, she had tried so hard to forget Umberto Monteverdi's Latin face, the firm yet full lips, the lean jaw and broad, straight shoulders, not to mention his long, expressive fingers. Most of all, she had tried not to remember those glittering emerald eyes, lit from within, and in passion incandescent.

God help her, she had burned in those eyes that indelible night in Villefranche. The recollection of it swept over Catriona, making odd little nerves tighten like silk threads deep in her abdomen so that she gripped the iron balustrade and took deep breaths of air in order to steady her swimming senses. As if separated from her mind, her body was instinctively reacting to those memories as if primitively yearning to be possessed by him again.

She was surprised at the effect Umberto had had on her. Despite the years, it seemed that her feelings for the composer hadn't altered; he still had the power to make her heart beat faster, make her feel weak at the knees.

Sunset and a gentle afterglow swooned. Catriona glanced at her watch: it was six-thirty. Lilac, fading rose and gold were drifting from the east into the west. The day was growing old … Michael must have returned from school by now. She just had time to ring Marguerite before showering and dressing for dinner.

A quarter of an hour later she was upstairs undressing in her bathroom, which was as luxurious as the rest of the lodge, with antique pearl ice mosaics and white iridescent glass tiles that had been all the craze in Europe for some time. Catriona showered, then dried her hair before deciding what to wear. Among other details about the area and the household, she had already been informed by Calandra's lawyers that the family dressed for dinner before Umberto had mentioned it, so she had packed an ample collection of outfits to suit various occasions. It hadn't been a problem – Catriona's penchant for beautiful and fashionable clothes was still as strong as ever and before leaving France she'd enjoyed having an excuse for a great shopping spree at the designer boutiques of Cannes and Nice.

It was a difficult decision to make, as she wasn't sure what the members of the household would wear. She wondered if other guests might be there, though she doubted that.

As her fingers trailed through the evening dresses in her wardrobe she could hear Umberto's enigmatic whispering words: '*I have not yet decided what kind of fascinating face is being denied me.*' She wished she knew what had gone on in his mind when they had been speaking that morning. Did he sense a familiarity about her that had softened his initial hostility? Was it her fanciful imagining that a frisson of awareness had taken hold of him as he'd held her hand as they parted?

Finally, Catriona decided on a gown of soft, mint-green silk georgette, intricately embellished at the shoulders and waist with tiny beads and crystals. The dress was flatteringly cinched with a grosgrain band and had a sheer back and a narrow low-cut V-neck to the front, allowing tantalizing glimpses of skin. Keeping her accessories to a minimum, she chose a Dior Indian silver cuff and a set of dainty white gold and diamond earrings in the shape of crescents that swept delicately up her earlobes.

She wore her hair away from her face and clipped at the nape, emphasizing her neat classic features and perfect skin, and added discreet touches of light make-up to her eyes, lips and cheeks. She slipped into a pair of elegant silver stiletto Jimmy Choo sandals that gave full value to slender ankles. It was not lost on her that unconsciously she had dressed for Umberto as though he could still see her … as though, like ten years before, he might gaze at her approvingly and want to take her in his arms.

Oh, Umberto, Umberto, she thought despairingly as she glanced at herself in the long wardrobe mirror, *why did I have to fall for you all those years ago and complicate my life in this way?* Yet there was comfort in knowing that maybe soon she need hide nothing from him, she must just bide her time. Still, besides what her body was telling her, was this really true love? Had it ever been? Wasn't it merely an instinctive reaction to a man whose masculinity was so powerful that it was irresistible? The man to whom she'd surrendered her virginity?

Just before eight, Adelina called on Catriona to take her to the main house.

'*Ah, com'è bella!*' exclaimed the housekeeper when Catriona met her at the front door. 'The *signore* was in a much better mood today. I think you will be good for him ... an experienced *dottoressa* with a good reputation. I'm sure you can help him.'

Catriona smiled, relieved at how quickly Adelina's manner had warmed to her since that morning. 'I will certainly do my best to help the *signore*. He's a great virtuoso ... it would be a huge loss to the music world if he stopped composing.'

They crossed the garden that was now steeped in shadows. Welcoming the evening, fragrant blooms waved their small sensors on the night, filling the air with their sweet-smelling scent. The countryside had exchanged its day garment for a dim habit weaved of dusk and falling dew. The view of the garden dwindled in the semi-darkness, while the flowers, the trees, and the birds singing a twilight hymn became cloaked in mysterious shadows.

As they entered the *salone* Giacomo was already standing there beneath the painting.

'*Dottoressa*, delightful to see you again.' He smiled and moved towards her, his bright eyes taking in her appearance with open approval. 'May I say how ravishing you look this evening. Brains and beauty too ...'

Catriona smiled awkwardly at this obvious flattery. 'Thank you, *signore*.'

Any further conversation was interrupted as the door opened and Umberto appeared on the threshold. Once more, she noticed he was without a cane.

'Ah, Giacomo, I thought I heard your voice. You have already met the *Dottoressa, vero*? Glad to see you're punctual for dinner tonight.' There was a wry note to Umberto's voice and Catriona thought he sounded as if he were addressing a wayward scamp, even though their childhood days were well behind them. Like Giacomo, he was dressed in a black dinner suit, but he looked so much more elegant and *à l'aise* in these surroundings. 'Am I the last? Is Silvana here too?'

'Just behind you, *caro*.'

The woman who had followed him into the room was just as ravishing as she had been a decade before. For the first time Catriona had the opportunity to regard her properly. Now in her mid thirties, she looked as stylish and confident as ever – and as hard as nails. She wore a most provocative lustrous red satin gown with waist-defining cut-outs, which displayed parts of her bare tanned skin, and with a long vertical slit at the front that showed off long, beautifully shaped legs. As she moved towards Catriona, her lustrous red hair that fell abundantly around her shoulders caught the light streaming from the chandelier, giving it burnished glints. Her face was like a cameo: a wide and provocative-looking slant to a pair of grey eyes fringed with thick lashes; her beautiful mouth a sensuous curve accentuated by vermillion lipstick.

Silvana smiled as she held out a perfectly manicured hand to Catriona, who gave an inner sigh of relief that the soprano didn't seem to have recognized her. 'How very nice to meet you, *Dottoressa*. I hope you'll be very happy here during your stay,' she said in a light voice that nonetheless had a rich purr to it. 'I am Silvana Esposito, an intimate friend of the family.'

Then, without waiting for Catriona's answer, she made her way first to Giacomo, pecking him on the cheek, and then to Umberto, her kiss missing his cheek and lingering rather longer than was necessary at the corner of his mouth. Catriona stiffened but kept her smile dutifully fixed on Silvana's face while she watched for Umberto's reaction. There was none: he remained completely still and unreadable.

Silvana gave a bright smile at no one in particular, saying: 'Shall I serve everyone a drink?'

'Yes, go ahead and do the honours tonight,' Umberto answered as he moved to an armchair and sat down. Only then did he ask: 'What will you have to drink, *Dottoressa*?' It occurred to Catriona that once ensconced in his chair, it wouldn't be obvious to the assembled company that he wasn't sure where she was standing as he didn't need to turn his head in a particular direction.

The redhead turned to Catriona. 'Negroni? Americano or just Campari for you?'

'Silvana's Negroni is unmatched. I recommend it,' Giacomo said.

'I think I would prefer an *analcolico*, non-alcoholic drink, *per favore*.'

'Oh, come on,' Giacomo exclaimed, 'this is occasion for celebration.'

Silvana arched a brow. 'What d'you mean? What are we celebrating?'

'My cousin here is playing the piano again. I heard you, Umberto, and it sounded pretty good, considering you haven't been practising.'

Catriona saw Umberto wince, his grip tightening on the arms of his chair. 'You've got it wrong, Giacomo. What you heard, cousin, was a recording of Beethoven's *Pathétique*,' he said coldly. 'Perhaps I should be flattered that you confused Daniel Barenboim's playing with mine.'

The vibrant Silvana laughed. 'Poor Giacomo. You've never had an ear for music. I don't know how you've survived in this household.' Then, turning to Catriona, she explained: 'Calandra insisted we all take music lessons when we were children, but Giacomo always used to find an excuse to play truant. Do you remember, *caro*? The day you ran away into the woods and got lost. It took almost a whole day to find you.'

Giacomo shrugged and, going to the bar, poured himself a Campari and orange. Catriona wasn't fooled: there was something in his studied nonchalance that spoke of a man who hated being humiliated. It must be murder for him living with Umberto and Silvana if he was a regular butt of their jokes.

The atmosphere was strained. There was nothing tangible, nothing she could pinpoint, but she could almost feel the air crackling with electricity.

'Here, try this,' Silvana said, handing her a glass. 'It's my *aperitivo analcolico alla frutta*,' she smiled. 'Not a drop of alcohol, I promise.' Then, turning to Umberto: 'A Negroski for you as usual, *amore*?'

'Yes, please, but go easy on the vodka,' he said, reaching into his pocket for his cigarettes and lighter. At this, Giacomo caught Catriona's eye, as if to bring to her attention the fact that Umberto had so recently indulged in an alcoholic binge. There was nothing at all about the man, however, that made her think him an alcoholic. He had achieved too much in the four years since the accident: skills that required intense focus and perseverence – learning to move about confidently, even to ride a horse – and none of that suggested a man who couldn't control his liquor.

Having mixed the drink and poured herself a Campari and orange, Silvana gave Umberto his glass and perched on the arm of his chair.

'Allow me, *caro*.' She took the cigarette from between Umberto's lips and placed it in an ashtray on the side table next to his chair.

There was something intimate in the gesture Catriona felt with a sinking of her spirits. She saw Giacomo shake his head, his steel-grey eyes narrowing.

Umberto, oblivious, took a swig of his drink and took his cigarette from the ashtray. 'Perfect,' he said with a satisfied smile and laid his head against the back of the chair. 'Now, I want to hear something of the *Dottoressa*, who is being very meek and mild, but whom I expect is watching us with a keen professional eye. I wonder, Dr Drouot, what you must make of us?'

Catriona, who had just been wondering at the mental affinity between Umberto and Silvana, was nonplussed momentarily. She certainly couldn't voice what was on her mind: that Umberto's dark aloofness and Silvana's ardent flamboyance were surely an illustration of how opposites attract. Were they lovers? If so – and once more her heart gave a sickening lurch at the thought – she sensed Giacomo, who was trying his hardest to appear insouciant and debonair, wasn't at all happy about it.

While she groped for an answer, Umberto flicked his ash and, missing the ashtray, it fell like a star on the wooden parquet floor. He was distracted, his mind playing with the little drama of his own making. 'Well, never mind. It's not usual for a therapist to share her intimate deductions and impressions, I imagine.'

At this moment, the deep note of the gong announcing dinner broke into the silent room.

'Saved by the gong,' Giacomo said, winking at Catriona.

'Ah, dinner is served, *Dottoressa* … such a pity.' Umberto stubbed out his cigarette before Silvana, from her perch on the arm of his chair, could take it off him proprietarily. He rose to his feet. '*Non importa*, never mind, you have just arrived and we have plenty of time to get properly acquainted.'

The double sliding doors to the dining room had been opened and a uniformed waiter announced dinner.

'Silvana, as my mother is, alas, no longer with us, you will sit opposite me at the head of the table. Our guest, *dottoressa* Drouot, will honour me by taking her place on my right and Giacomo, as usual, on my left.'

The dining room was austere, despite the four elegant waterfall crystal chandeliers diffusing their bright light on to the high, frescoed walls and the fact that the much lighter ceiling was painted with representations of the four elements: water, fire, earth and air. An imposing fireplace, standing between two tall, narrow, elegant windows, was of red Nakoda marble. The dining chairs and curtains were all upholstered in heavy Bordeaux damask silk, and the length of the table was impressive, explaining Silvana's peeved expression at being banished to the other end of the room.

On the opposite side to the fireplace, Catriona's attention was drawn to a central cupboard flanked by quadrant cabinets of burnished and polished sculpted wood decorated with marquetry. A drawer with beautiful bronze handles surmounted each panel, as did the top, which was made of variegated black-and-cream coloured marble.

'I see you are admiring our credenza, *Dottoressa*,' Giacomo remarked.

'Indeed. It's a beautiful piece of furniture. It looks very much like a modern-day sideboard, but heavier and much larger.'

Umberto took his place at the head of the table. 'Its name comes from the idea of belief or trust. In the sixteenth century, food was displayed in this kind of cabinet and tried before it was served in order to make sure that it hadn't been poisoned or contaminated. Hence the word *credenziere* – the person who looks after the larder,' he explained. 'It's said that my great-grandfather won this particular one in a gambling venture from a long-established aristocratic family, who had acquired it after the 1547 fire that destroyed many rooms of the Doge's Palace in Venice.'

'It's a beautiful piece.'

'Is this the first time you've visited Lake Como, *Dottoressa*?' Silvana asked as the waiter filled their glasses with a chilled and sparkling white wine.

'Yes, I've travelled through most of Italy but never to this part. It's lovely.'

'I have turned down many a concert in order to live here. So many lucrative requests for performances … I'm a singer, you know, once Calandra's protégée, but I couldn't bear to be taking jets all over the globe when my heart lies in this place.' Catriona knew that Silvana had never risen to the heights of stardom; she also sensed that the soprano wanted her to know that she wasn't just a hanger-on, that she could have had a glittering career.

'Turning down a sheikh's birthday party or the opening of a shopping centre when you could be lounging about here,' Umberto remarked with a twisted smile. 'Noble of you.' A comment that earned a tight-lipped scowl from Silvana.

The waiter came round with the first course: an appetizing fresh fig, mascarpone and pesto torte, accompanied by Italian bread sticks cut diagonally into thin slices that had been lightly toasted.

'I heard Adelina's been cooking up a storm,' Giacomo remarked. 'Is this in honour of *dottoressa* Drouot?'

Umberto raised an amused eyebrow. 'I think it was love at first sight … well, almost. She's very taken by you,' he said, turning to Catriona.

'She seems very loyal to you, *signore*, and so I suppose it's normal that she should feel hospitable towards your guest.'

'No, I can assure you that's not the case with Adelina. She gave me a lecture about you this afternoon.'

Silvana pursed her lips. 'Ugh, I really detest the way she takes liberties with you, *amore*. Especially now that Calandra is gone she behaves as if she can do anything she wants. This evening, as

I passed her in the hall, you wouldn't believe the disapproving look she gave me. And she actually had the affrontery to comment on what I'm wearing.'

Giacomo gave the young woman a sidelong glance and added: 'I'm not surprised.'

Umberto turned his head sharply. 'She's known you since you were in pigtails, Silvana. Sometimes she just forgets we're grown up now. It's no big deal, get over it.'

Silvana gave a shrug but continued to fume silently from her end of the table.

Sensing the conversation might degenerate into something unpleasant, Catriona smiled. 'This is really delicious. The centre is so soft and mellow.'

'Adelina makes her own mascarpone,' said Umberto. 'She used to make all our cheese when she was in charge of the house … so much better than what you find in the *supermercato*.'

'She still makes a lot of it,' Giacomo added. 'I've seen her. She's changed the shed in the garden of her cottage into a small kitchen. She sells it on the quiet.'

'There's nothing wrong in that,' Umberto told him coolly. 'She's just trying to make a few extra bucks.'

Silvana's expression was pettish. 'I think those cheeses are a health hazard, *caro*. It was all right when she was doing it in the house but her shed is most unhygienic. You wait, one day someone from the Health Department will come sniffing around and cause you a lot of grief.'

Umberto shrugged. 'Don't make a drama out of everything, Silvana.'

Catriona could tell he was annoyed and he pointedly turned to her, his body language dismissing the stunning soprano whose face was now pouting sulkily. He raised his glass. 'Let's drink to *dottoressa* Drouot's health,' he said. 'May her stay at Villa Monteverdi be a happy one.'

Catriona felt a pink hue rush to her cheeks as the others repeated the words after him and lifted their glasses to their lips. She noticed, however, that Silvana didn't actually take a sip.

Though she was reluctant to drink much alcohol that evening, she decided it would be rude not to partake at all. She placed her glass down amid the silence. 'This wine is wonderful.'

'The Monteverdi wines are among the very best in Italy,' Umberto announced proudly. 'The Franciacorta is akin to champagne but much subtler than its French brother.'

'It's delicious,' Catriona said. 'It has an unusual taste and no acidity at all.'

'The grapes grown in our vineyards are said to have the sun of the slopes in them, and also a touch of the snow from the peaks of the Alps.'

'I'm surprised there is such delicious wine grown in this part of the world. I was under the impression there were no vineyards to speak of around Lake Como.'

'That is partially true,' he answered and Catriona could see that he was becoming more talkative now that the conversation had moved on to a safe subject. 'The grapes come from the Franciacorta region and we are very much an exception to the rule. The story of our small private vineyard began at the end of the nineteenth century when Ennio Monteverdi took his barren wife Magdalena to see a healer who lived on the hills between the southern shore of Lake Iseo and the city of Brescia. They were both teetotallers but the healer produced a bottle of Franciacorta wine, without telling them what it was. A month later, Magdalena was with child.

'Beside himself with joy, my ancestor went back to the healer to thank him and buy some more of his potion. Finally, the man told him that the secret of his powerful medicine was a potent wine. "You see," he said, "wine is like rain. When it falls on the dirt or mud, it makes it fouler but when it hits the good soil, it rouses it to beauty and to bloom."

'From that day on, Ennio and Magdalena drank wine with all their meals and Magdalena gave birth to nine healthy children. Ennio decided then to import soil from the Franciacorta region. A hectare was put down to vines, the grapes of which he turned into wine. The tradition continued and today our small vineyard yields between five hundred and one thousand bottles a year, but we only produce it for our own consumption, and for friends. Plus, at Christmas each member of our staff is offered a case of Monteverdi Franciacorta wine.'

'What a lovely story. And I can quite understand your pride in the wine. It's really delicious,' Catriona said.

'Our generation of Monteverdis haven't exactly managed to sire the same multitude on the good old Franciacorta,' said Giacomo, whose open, humorous expression belied any snideness that might be carried in his remark. Catriona thought back to his assertion that Umberto didn't want children and she squirmed inside.

She glanced towards the top of the table, where Silvana sat silently, looking from one cousin to the other. So far, the redhead had seemed unafraid of speaking provocatively to Umberto, and Catriona wondered if there was more to Giacomo's comment than she understood. Umberto merely turned a flintlike stare in his cousin's direction, which caused Giacomo to give a nervous laugh.

Catriona was glad, locked in their little family drama, none of the trio noticed the colour that had risen in her cheeks. The conversation made her stomach squeeze anxiously. How difficult this was all going to be! How could she possibly tell him about Michael? Besides, how could she ever find the courage when her own heart beat so thunderously whenever Umberto was near?

The waiter came back into the room and cleared the table before bringing in the main course and a bottle of Châteauneuf-du-Pape.

'Are you familiar with *osso buco alla milanese*?' Umberto asked, finally breaking the silence, and Catriona was grateful he had set the conversation back on neutral territory.

'Yes, it's one of my favourite dishes. I adore saffron.' She had always loved this dish: veal shanks braised with vegetables in a delicious sauce of white wine and stock, served with *gremolata* and saffron rice. 'I always order it whenever it's on the menu, even back home.'

Giacomo, who had been eating quietly, looked up and directed his attention to Catriona. 'Tell us a little about the work you do. That is, if you and Umberto are comfortable with your discussing it?'

'So long as you don't talk about me while I'm sitting here,' Umberto said coldly. Catriona was struck how he seemed to switch quite suddenly from polite host to morose misanthrope in the blink of an eye. It didn't make for a relaxed meal, and she found herself looking for signs of his mood swinging, as though she was watching some kind of emotional weathervane.

Silvana eyed the two men and Catriona could have sworn that, for the most part, she enjoyed the tensions and undercurrents that bubbled uneasily below the surface. The redhead laughed unkindly. 'I'm not sure Giacomo will grasp the sense of it. He's never understood the power of music. Hard to when you're tone deaf, isn't that right, *tesoro*?' Her cat-like eyes teased mercilessly while Giacomo tried his hardest to maintain a smiling countenance.

'Maybe … but being as close to Umberto as a brother, and wanting of course the best for him, I am honestly interested to hear how this works.'

'I warned you, Giacomo, don't talk about me as if I'm not here,' Umberto snapped, his face dangerously dark. 'You've enough of your own concerns. I ask you not to trouble yourself with mine.'

For a few moments no one said anything as they ate, then Umberto finally broke the silence, allowing the conversation to resume. 'Now, let's hear what the *Dottoressa* has to say. It'll be a relief after your bickering,' he added in a low voice.

Silvana, realizing the comment was largely aimed at her, coloured slightly but said nothing, while Giacomo still managed to preserve his benign expression, much to Catriona's amazement.

She took a breath and began to explain. 'In my work I tend to concentrate the focus on a piece of music that matches the mood of the client. It might be a child with autism or an elderly person with dementia. All sorts can benefit, although music therapy does have exceptional results with certain conditions.'

'Like a loud march when they're angry, that kind of thing?' Giacomo asked.

'Yes, it could be. Something to give the emotion free rein, allow the person to express it. Then you might draw on more poignant pieces. The ones that pierce the heart can work on bringing out other feelings, such as grief. When I work with a client, I draw on a kind of musical mood board which uses pieces that are especially personal to the individual. Often we improvise – play creatively with the music.'

'What if they don't have any musical knowledge, or if they're totally unmusical?' Giacomo asked. 'I can't believe it would work then.'

Umberto turned his head slightly in the direction of Catriona. 'My cousin has always been a philistine where music is concerned so you must not take him seriously.'

'It has nothing to do with my being a philistine, Umberto. As a composer, you have always lived and breathed improvisation. What about those lesser mortals who are not particularly interested in music, or even dislike it?'

Silvana took a sip of her wine. 'Nonsense, Giacomo! How could anyone dislike music?'

Catriona smiled. 'Actually, he's made a good point. And the answer is that in all cases, I try and find the best fit,' she explained.

'Everyone is different. An autistic boy will need repetition and something almost monotonously rhythmic – Carl Orff did some excellent work in this area. Then again, with an Alzheimer's patient, it's all about unlocking memory, and music – especially songs and pieces they enjoyed when young – is the very last thing that goes. With dementia, even when there's such damage to the brain that there seems to be nothing left, music finds its way in. It's a wonderful thing.'

Umberto continued to eat and drink but Catriona sensed that he had been listening to her explanation with quiet absorption. Silvana gave a glance in his direction before resuming the conversation, as if a little wary that she might tread on sensitive ground, although at the same time Catriona got the impression that the soprano was looking for drama … for Umberto's attention.

'What about depression? Trauma?' the redhead asked, her glittering eyes slyly watching Umberto's hand tighten on the stem of his wine glass as she posed the question. 'In those cases, I imagine you'd need a specialist's help.' Although Silvana hadn't explicitly said it, Catriona knew she meant 'proper' specialist. 'Medical help, drugs, that sort of thing, surely? Not just music.'

Although Silvana was polite on the surface, the scorn underlying her question was perfectly apparent. Catriona fought to keep her tone even. 'Sometimes, yes. But a good therapist knows when what they have in their toolbox isn't going to fix things. Most of us make it our business to know exactly where to refer our clients if the need arises.'

'I still don't quite understand how it works,' said Giacomo. 'For instance, I have no trouble being told that the key to overcoming depression can be physical exercise … endorphins and all that.' He smiled sceptically. 'But music … well, really?'

Umberto leaned forward in his chair, his hand curled into a fist on the table, and Catriona felt tension radiating off him. 'You cannot help but show your scorn of the one thing our family holds sacred, can you, Giacomo?' he sneered. 'Don't bother to answer him, *Dottoressa*. He needs to show more respect to our guest.'

Without thinking, Catriona placed her hand over Umberto's and felt him shudder at her touch. She felt the sweet ache of longing in her bones but managed to control the slight quiver in her voice. 'Please, *signore*,' she said in a calm tone, very similar to the one she used with her patients, 'I am not in the least offended. I meet this sort of attitude every day in my job and it is quite understandable from people who are not familiar with the concept. Let me explain …'

'Thank you for being so tolerant, *Dottoressa*. I wouldn't take any notice …'

Realizing her hand was still touching his, Catriona gently removed it. 'No, I think it is important that more people begin to understand the valuable power of music in our lives.'

'Please go ahead. I'm not stopping you.' Umberto reached for his wine glass and gulped down the contents in one go.

Catriona fought to express herself clearly, determined not to let any emotional undercurrents get in the way of her professional cool. 'As I've said, on a simple level a person who is suffering from a broken heart will find that sad music is a more cathartic way of releasing the pain than, for example, the shoulder of a best friend. You feel understood on a deep level, and *that* understanding provides a release which can allow you to move on. It's as simple as that. Music has innate healing qualities and,' she glanced at Giacomo, 'like exercise might release endorphins, it really does affect the brain. More than that, it helps take you into a creative space, one accessed by your right brain, where you can connect with the unconscious. That's where the healing can really start to happen.'

'Sounds pretty … alternative … to me.' Silvana's little pauses spoke volumes and her words hung in the air.

Umberto banged the table with his hand. 'Enough, Silvana!' he growled. 'Once again, I apologize, *Dottoressa*. You shouldn't have to put up with this kind of insolence.'

They fell silent as the waiter came in to clear the dishes and brought in a large platter of Italian cheeses. Silvana sulked at the top of the table, her mouth a moue of displeasure.

'Do you like cheese, *Dottoressa*?' Umberto asked, his voice now even once more.

Catriona laughed lightly, relieved at the change of subject. 'How could I be French and not have a special weakness for cheese?'

'Ah, but this is Italian cheese and only from our region … *molto superiore!*'

'I love cheese. It doesn't matter where it comes from. I'm afraid it's one of my guilty pleasures.'

'*Guido, per favore, appoggia il tagliere qui in mezzo, tra me e la dottoressa Drouot*, Guido, please, place the cheeseboard here between *dottoressa* Drouot and me. Try the Branzi first. It's made from whole cow's milk and comes from the Alta Brembana province. You'll find its flavour delicate and slightly salty.'

Silvana shook her head irritably and rolled her eyes. 'Umberto, can't you let *dottoressa* Drouot choose her own? I'm sure she knows about Italian cheeses. This is not the first time she's travelled to Italy.'

Umberto stiffened and his black brows drew together. His jaw clenched tight, the muscles twitching along the base of his cheeks. 'I don't need you to tell me how to behave at *my* table, Silvana.' He spoke impatiently. 'If I fancy telling the *Dottoressa* about the cheeses here, then I will do so,' he ended roughly.

His features had hardened as he leaned back in his chair, one hand on the edge of the table, his fingertips tapping a staccato rhythm. Catriona could see that his nerves were unbearably strung; she knew that he was feeling his disability deeply.

One way or another, the whole conversation tonight had been turning around his blindness and she wished she could make his darkness a little brighter.

Catriona sampled the cheese and found it delicious eaten with Adelina's homemade ciabatta. After that, the waiter brought in a *torta sbrisolona*, a huge crumbling tart, but by now dinner had become a decidedly subdued affair.

After Umberto's outburst the atmosphere became more strained than it had been all evening. Silvana looked glum, her mouth turning down at the corners, and she made no more effort at conversation. Catriona sensed that Giacomo was rejoicing in the tiff that had just occurred between the young woman and his cousin.

Why did Catriona get the impression that Umberto was punishing Silvana, and not only for what she had said? There was nothing tangible, nothing she could pinpoint, nothing she could grasp at and say 'these two are having an affair', but she had no doubt that there was – or at least there had been – something going on between them and that Umberto was trying to get back at the beautiful redhead.

As soon as they'd had coffee, Catriona made an excuse to go back to the lodge. While her observations about the Monteverdis were still fresh in her mind, she wanted to make some notes that would be useful for her first session with Umberto, whenever his unpredictable mood decided that might be.

Giacomo immediately jumped up from his chair. 'I'll walk you back. It's a dark and misty night and the area around the lodge when there's no moon is quite eerie.'

'Please don't trouble yourself. I can find my way easily.'

Silvana smiled enigmatically. 'He's referring to the owls that live in the forest. They are particularly noisy on nights like this.'

'I'm not bothered. Actually, I find an owl's hooting quite romantic.'

The redhead arched a perfect eyebrow. 'Really? How interesting! In this country, we believe that owls are the only creatures that can live with ghosts so, if an owl is found nesting in an abandoned house, the place must be haunted. And the forest since the tragedy has been infested with them.'

Catriona's mind flashed back to the shepherd at the waterfall. Before she could stop herself, she blurted out: 'Haunted? Why—'

But Umberto cut her off before Silvana could reply. 'Stop this immediately, Silvana. *Dottoressa* Drouot is an educated woman, who I'm sure does not give credence to such superstitions,' he said drily, though his body language was a great deal tenser.

Silvana looked at him peevishly. 'Come on, Umberto, you must admit that since … well, since that unfortunate incident, the owl population in the Gufi Reali forest has increased at an alarming rate, and whether you …'

Umberto banged the table with his fist. '*Basta*, Silvana, enough!' There was an abrupt silence. '*Non tollero questi discorsi in casa mia*, I will not tolerate such talk in my house.' His fist was clenched so tightly that his tanned skin was almost white across the knuckles and Catriona could read anger in the set of his shoulders. He reached out and twice rang the bell on the table next to him. Adelina appeared almost instantly.

'*Adelina, per favore accompagna la dottoressa Drouot al suo alloggio,* Adelina, please accompany *dottoressa* Drouot back to the lodge.'

'*Sì, certo, appena la Dottoressa è pronta*, yes, of course, as soon as the *Dottoressa* is ready.'

Catriona stood up. 'I'm ready, thank you, but really, I can find my way back without any help,' she said. Then, turning to Umberto and knowing that it would be wiser to comply, she added: 'But if it will reassure you to have Adelina accompany me, then no problem at all, and thank you for your concern.'

Umberto rose from the table and held out his hand. She took it in hers. 'Good night,' he said in a voice that sounded suddenly weary. 'I hope you have a restful night and we'll speak in the morning. Adelina will bring over your breakfast at nine o'clock and then we will have a meeting in my office.'

Catriona could feel the heat of his hand seeping into her own and once more her blood began to race, her skin to tingle, but she managed to reply quite naturally. 'Perfect. Thank you for a delicious dinner and your hospitality.'

After saying goodnight to Giacomo and Silvana and, as Adelina was closing the door behind them, she just had time to hear Giacomo say: 'Well, well, well, cousin, this is a real volte-face you've made ... so, you *are* going along with this after all, *eh*?'

Catriona didn't catch Umberto's reply but she felt baffled and ill at ease. It had been a strange evening, to say the least; an uneasy atmosphere had hung over the group from beginning to end, something indefinable. It was as if each of them had been playing a part in some Kafkaesque play.

Outside, night swallowed the earth. The sky was a black void with no moon or stars, and barely a sound could be heard. A pleasant breeze was blowing from the lake, but not strong enough to whisper in the trees. All was still. It was as if the trees and flowers had gone to bed and sent slightly more ominous versions of themselves to take their places. Only now, filling her lungs with fresh air, did Catriona realize how stifling the atmosphere had been in the house. Adelina shone her torch in front of them and went silently and quickly through the dark shadows of the garden with its ghostly ranks of trees as though anxious to avoid any lurking dangers. An uneasy awareness of the solitude of this spot came over Catriona. At this hour, on a moonless night, this was decidedly a lonesome place and she was grateful for the housekeeper's company.

To distract herself from the obscure, distorted shapes thrown up around them by the light of Adelina's torch, Catriona probed her companion with an innocuous question. One she knew the answer to already.

'Were Calandra and *il signor* Umberto close?' she asked as they made their way alongside the dark mass of the copse, where the path curved round towards the lodge.

'*Sì, sì*, of course. *La signora* Calandra was a strong woman and a good mother. They understood each other very well.'

'It must have been hard for her when her son became blind.'

Adelina sighed heavily. 'Yes, and even harder when she found out she herself was ill and would not be here to look after the *signore*. But she tried her best to help him before she left this world.'

Now at the turn of a corner, as they reached the edge of a big clump of trees and bushes, bats flew over them, swooping to and fro almost soundlessly in the cool air, shadows blown about by the breeze like phantoms of the night, their small forms fluttering away into the dark sky. The silence was eerie, almost sinister. Adelina shone the torch along the stone wall and quickened her pace.

'It was *la signora* Calandra who hired *il signor* Agostini, the horse trainer,' she continued. '*Il signor* Umberto loves horses, has done since he was a boy. His mother knew that if he could learn to ride again, it would give him motivation, something to make him get a grip on life again, *capisce?*'

'Yes, of course. She was a clever woman,' said Catriona, feeling sad once more for Umberto.

'The *signore* asked me to give you some riding clothes,' Adelina told her. 'You'll find them in the bottom of your wardrobe. So perhaps soon you'll see how much the *signore* changes when he's with his horses.'

An owl hooted just as they were reaching the lodge. Adelina made the sign of the cross, mumbling: '*Santa Maria, Madre di Dio, proteggici dal male stasera esempre,* Holy Mary, Mother of

God, protect us tonight and always from evil spirits.' She opened the door and Catriona stepped into the front room of the lodge, which glowed with the light of a freshly lit fire.

Adelina switched on the light and said to her in a hushed tone: 'I have closed all your shutters, *Dottoressa*. There is no moon tonight, which is not good in this forest. It is as black as coal outside and, on nights like this, ghosts walk the land.' Her eyes darted around the room as if checking for some unknown presence.

Adelina obviously belonged to that generation of rural folk whose beliefs were still dictated by superstition. Catriona suppressed a sigh and wondered whether some people would ever emerge into the twenty-first century, even though part of her acknowledged that the atmosphere in the dark wood was particularly spooky that night. She was used to Sidonie's stories and, as a teenager, her gullible young mind had been disposed to such romantic notions, but those were far-off days …

'I understand,' she said courteously, not wanting to distance herself in any way from the Italian servant, whom she knew had Umberto's best interests at heart. She sensed the housekeeper would be a vigilant ally if she ever needed one, so she hesitated for a moment, adding: 'Why is it that you think the forest is haunted? I've heard that a young woman died somewhere around here. Is that true?'

Adelina looked grave. '*Sì, il bosco* is not a safe place tonight … the poor tormented soul of *la signorina* Sofia is looking for a place to rest, and it will not find peace as long as the truth is hidden. Who knows what vengeance she might be looking for …'

'The truth … what do you mean? How did she die?' Now Catriona's sense of unease deepened. She waited, but Adelina seemed to realize that she had said too much.

'It's not my place to speak any more about it,' she said warily. 'I'm sure that the *signore* will tell you about his family himself, if he wishes.'

Catriona smiled. 'It's very kind of you to worry about me, Adelina, and you can be sure I won't go near a window tonight.'

Adelina's black eyes warmed as they looked up at the young woman. She seemed relieved that Catriona had not pushed the matter further.

'*Buona notte, Dottoressa*. Mario has put more logs for the fire in the basket. Please, lock the door behind me and keep the shutters closed.'

'Don't worry, Adelina. I'll be fine, really.'

Left alone, Catriona remained pensive, a prey to all manner of perplexities. She shivered and moved close to the fireplace; the temperature seemed to have dropped substantially. The flames were flickering; spiralling columns of orange, yellow and blue light making distorted patterns, fragments of vitality. She peered into them as she thought about her first meeting with Umberto and what tomorrow might hold.

It had come as a shock to realize that the years had not erased her feelings for the composer but, strangely enough, time had altered them from the fluttering infatuation of an eighteen-year-old to a much deeper mixture of sentiments to which she could not yet put a name but which, nevertheless, troubled her deeply. No less because it seemed that Umberto was unlikely to welcome with open arms the news that he had a son, if what Giacomo said was true. Then this evening, meeting Giacomo and Silvana, the two people supposedly closest to Umberto but towards whom, at times, she had sensed he was almost hostile.

Who was Sofia, whose restless soul apparently roamed the forest? Was this death related to the tragedy Silvana had been referring to at dinner? Still, Adelina had spoken of 'the truth' being hidden and of vengeance, too. Had this woman Sofia perhaps been murdered in the forest? A pang of unexpected fear made Catriona stiffen for a moment before she pulled herself together.

She threw another log into the flames. Sparks flew up the chimney and the fire danced, wrapping greedy tongues of red and yellow around the logs. Dreams floated in her mind: dreams of Umberto making love to her that night in Villefranche in front of a blazing fire, the memories still so vivid that a surge of craving flooded her, igniting feelings she had thought had died so many years ago.

She sat for a long time in the armchair next to the fireplace watching the wood burn, wondering if she had done the right thing in accepting this assignment – and whether she was going to get hurt by the same man for a second time. What kind of tangled web had she caught herself in?

Then, finally shaking off the remnants of her foolish fantasy, she stood up, went to her table and began typing up her notes for tomorrow, knowing she was still in Umberto's thrall and that he had taken on an added compulsion for her now.

*   *   *

Umberto clenched his jaw and leaned back in his armchair. Dinner had tried his patience to the limit. He hated being spoken about as though he was some kind of pitiful case study. At times it had taken every ounce of effort he possessed not to upend the table and tell them all to go to hell.

Sofia … he hadn't thought about her for a long time, though the guilt was never far away, gnawing at the back of his mind like a malevolent whisper, never completely gone. Why did Silvana have to bring up that tragedy tonight? And all that business about the owls; he didn't like that one bit – it smelt of mischief, and God only knew what mischievous dirt Silvana would be prepared to dredge up for her own devious purposes.

She had been so charming to the newcomer but he knew her well: Silvana was the type of woman who purrs and then scratches. Umberto had no doubt that the redhead would be threatened by the new doctor, merely because Catherine Drouot would be having time with him alone and Silvana had always wanted to keep him for herself.

How she'd tried in the past! But he had resisted … even now he resisted, although sometimes the needs of his body begged him to give in to Silvana as he had years ago. His nights had been empty of a woman's touch for a long time, but he would never relent to her again.

Umberto ran a hand through his hair and closed his eyes. His thoughts turned to the young doctor. There was something intriguing about Catherine Drouot. She could certainly hold her own against Giacomo and Silvana, he mused, with their clumsy challenges and downright rudeness. He was sceptical himself about her treatment approach, but she was a guest in his house and Calandra's wishes would be respected. Besides, she spoke very intelligently and he was more impressed by her than he'd expected to be. He knew she had been frustrated by the conversation this evening – he could hear it in her voice though she had tried valiantly to hide it – and yet she'd kept her cool.

Not for the first time, he tried to picture her face. Usually he was quick to conjure up the features of a person and his interest ceased after that. Yet with Catherine Drouot it was different, and his curiosity continued to stir his imagination.

Adelina had confirmed that she was beautiful. 'Two huge eyes, almost too big for her face,' she'd said.

'Funny, I once knew a girl like that,' he'd replied. Something had echoed in his mind, the ghost of a memory, but like so many troublesome thoughts of the past, he'd pushed it away.

He hadn't thought to ask Adelina what colour the *Dottoressa*'s eyes were … a warm shade of brown, he imagined. He knew that Catherine had deep, chestnut-coloured, shiny hair. She certainly sounded like she had dark hair, with that rich, slightly husky voice. He found himself wondering what her hair would be like to touch, to run his fingers through …

His thoughts strayed back to her voice – a singer's voice. Perhaps one day he would find out if she could sing … a fascinating notion. Yes, he would see what the *Dottoressa* had planned for him …

He must have dozed. Half awake, half asleep, he became aware of a presence in his room.

'*Mi scusi, signore*! I knocked, but no one answered. You are not yet in bed?'

Umberto shook himself awake. 'Ah, Mario. What time is it?'

'After midnight.'

'Already? I must have fallen asleep. What are *you* doing here at this hour?'

'I was helping Adelina make cheese out in the shed. As I was going home, I saw that your curtains were not yet drawn. You usually draw them before going to bed.'

Umberto gave a low, bitter laugh. 'Open or closed, it doesn't make much of a difference nowadays,' he muttered, as though talking to himself.

Mario's voice came closer. 'You seem tired tonight, *signore*. Shall I help you into bed?'

'*Grazie*, Mario, but that won't be necessary.'

From the very first day he'd been told that he was blind, Umberto had refused to be an invalid or be treated as such. He had promised himself that he would attend to his basic needs as soon as he could learn how, and would only ask for help when absolutely necessary. It made him free to come and go as he wished. Still, he wasn't free; he was at times as dependent on others as a suckling baby, and that was what he found so humiliating and what pained him the most.

'As you wish, *signore*.' The servant moved towards the door.

'Actually,' he called after Mario, 'first thing in the morning, will you tell Dino to saddle up Vulcan, please? I'll be going out before breakfast.'

'Forgive me, *signore*, but will *la signorina* Silvana be riding? I could have him saddle Fortuna for her.'

'I will not be riding with *la signorina* Silvana tomorrow.'

Umberto sensed Mario backing away. 'Very well, *signore*. *Buona notte.*'

'Goodnight, Mario, and thank you for your concern.'

The door closed and the servant's steps receded.

Umberto rose. He passed his hand over his face as he made his way to the bathroom. His fingers scraped against the stubble already starting to grow on his chin despite his shave earlier that evening before dinner. Damn! The blue shadow would be even darker in the morning. The last thing he wanted was for Catherine Drouot to think of him as unkempt. He didn't need any help with putting on his riding gear but shaving was a different matter … He thought of ringing Mario on his mobile and because he was not concentrating, he bumped against a stool. Kicking it out of his way, he swore, '*Al diavolo!*' and hit the wall with his fist. He was condemned to a lifetime of this.

CHAPTER 10

Catriona woke up with a headache and the distinct impression that someone was hammering her senses. She glanced around the room, not quite remembering where she was, then after a moment, with a groan she realized that someone was indeed hammering – but on the front door, not her head. Stumbling out of bed, she searched for something to wear and found her silk kimono hanging in the wardrobe. Wrapping it loosely around herself, she went to the door, opened it an inch and peered through the crack.

'*Buongiorno, Dottoressa.*' Astride the most beautiful Arab horse was Umberto, grinning from ear to ear, his eyes covered by dark glasses. Gone was the tension of the evening before, although a certain suppressed energy seemed to remain in his bearing as he held the reins and patted the side of his black stallion. 'Forgive me if I've drawn you out of bed at this early hour, but I thought a gallop in the countryside before the heat gets up would be a good start to the day.'

Catriona took in the fit of the brown breeches that he wore with a careless elegance, the shirt tucked into them crisp and white. His hair was as black as the horse beneath him. His shoulders seemed broader than usual, but his body was perfectly suited for riding: long, lean and graceful in a way that had nothing to do with femininity. For want of a better word, Umberto was a beautiful man. The lines and planes of his classic bone structure drew her gaze as always but, this morning, his strong jawline seemed even more prominent. He looked so naturally at ease on horseback that Catriona once again had to remind herself that he was blind. She couldn't help but smile.

'*Buongiorno, signore*, I must admit this is a bit of a surprise.' She paused, groping for a reason not to go along with his plans. 'I didn't realize that we would be riding first thing this morning. Adelina did tell me there were clothes in a drawer for me, but I hardly thought …'

'Ah, *Dottoressa*, I'm sure it won't take long to get ready.'

Catriona, feeling suddenly helpless, her excuses sounding hollow when matched with the sunny confidence Umberto was displaying, nearly gave in. Yet she needed to push back.

'*Signore*, I don't want to seem ungrateful but I really should start work with you today or we won't make any progress …'

He nodded. 'Quite understood, *Dottoressa*. But my view is that our session will be much more effective after a bit of fresh air and exercise, not to mention a good breakfast.'

She smiled a little uncertainly, still harbouring the fear that she might well lose the reins of her assignment altogether if he had his way.

He grinned roguishly, adding: 'Your patient must keep his spirits up, *non è così*, isn't that so?'

Although Umberto's eyes were hidden behind his dark glasses, Catriona remembered how they had shone with mischief once before when he had persuaded her to swim naked in the sea at Villefranche. Suddenly a blinding light shone inside her head. She saw the past unrolling like a film … Umberto naked … She had never forgotten his sensuous words, '*I will make each atom in your body sing until they all meet in a magnificent chorus …*' That swim had been her undoing. It had changed something – a ferocity had been revealed between them, a hunger, a piercing need.

She made herself fight the sweet weakness that was sweeping over her when he added: 'Riding is one of the rare times when I feel free from constraints and restrictions in my life.' He gave a hollow laugh. 'Are you going to deprive me of that, *Dottoressa*?'

Oh, he was clever! With a single phrase he had quashed her misgivings. Yet there was also something new about him this morning; he did not appear the same man she had sat next to at dinner the previous night. The playful charm of the old Umberto seemed to show through in the tone of his voice and the upward curve of his mouth. Still, even if she were to give in to him, she needed him to know that she was in charge. She was being paid an enormous sum to do this job and and unless she kept to her part of the bargain, Catriona would feel a fraud.

'*Signore*, perish the thought that I should deprive you of your enjoyment but you are paying me a great deal of money to draw on my skills and expertise and I won't be able to remain here if you don't allow me to get on with my job.'

'I'm not hearing your smile, *Dottoressa*,' Umberto said, assuming a contrite tone of voice, before adding softly: 'Indulge me this one time and I promise you that there will be no more infringements, I will comply with your rules.'

Catriona let out a quiet breath. 'Very well, it's a deal, *signore*. Give me twenty minutes to get ready.'

'I'll be back in twenty minutes with your mount. Do you prefer a gentle or more spirited animal?'

She smiled. 'I haven't ridden for a long time. I'm sure whatever you choose will be fine, so long as I can keep up with your beautiful stallion. He looks as if he definitely belongs in the spirited category.'

'Splendid! *A presto*, see you later.'

Catriona went upstairs to get ready. It had been years since she'd had the time to ride and she felt rising in her chest a sense of excitement, the like of which she had almost forgotten existed.

In the bathroom she stared at her reflection in the long mirror with numb amazement, seeing her skin burning with colour, her eyes hectic and darker than she had ever seen them. Slowly, she studied herself as if seeing herself for the first time, and then turned away, her hands clenched at her sides, as though she could not face whatever lay buried in the depths of her own gaze.

She stepped into the shower and turned the water down to cold – she needed something to whip out the longing and need she was feeling for Umberto to hold her, to possess her as he had done that one time. All night she had been tortured by memories that refused this time to be banished and conquered; sensations that now resurfaced with a vengeance.

Looking in the drawer at the bottom of the large wardrobe in her room, she discovered a leather box, inside which was a set of riding clothes, as promised. As she pulled on a pair of exquisitely tailored cream jodhpurs by Vestrum, the best in Italian equestrian designerwear, which fitted her long and shapely legs like a glove, Catriona found herself making firm resolutions. She needed to keep herself and her unruly hormones under control if this assignment were to succeed.

Umberto must never guess how she felt … she must be doubly careful how she approached him. Even though he couldn't pick up on the cues of body language and facial expression everyone else took for granted, he was nonetheless scarily perceptive and seemed to possess a disturbing ability to hear not only what a person said, but also what they *didn't* say.

She pulled on a pair of glossy black Secchiari riding boots, which fitted perfectly, and was just slipping into the riding jacket when there was a knock at the door. She glanced at the alarm clock on her bedside table: it had been exactly twenty minutes. Umberto was a punctual man. She grabbed her riding hat and two peppermints from a tin she kept on her night table and went out to meet him.

The stocky figure of Dino the stablehand hovered near the door. '*Il signor* Umberto is waiting for you at the stables,' he informed her. 'He said to walk you round.'

It was a beautiful mellow morning, with the sun shining and not a cloud in the sky. Spring rayed all the earth with asphodel, crocus and anemones, spreading her emerald kirtle with silver, azure and crimson; and the splendid scented air weaved a veil of fragrance over the grounds.

Umberto was standing outside the stables, leaning against one of the doors with his back to her. He seemed to hear her approach even before she had reached him because he turned round. The world stood still for a second as Catriona experienced that feeling of déjà vu. Hadn't he been standing exactly in that same way at the French windows the night of the storm?

He'd taken off his dark glasses and now smiled, looking towards her as if he could see her and holding out his hand, gesturing her forwards. 'We have many horses, *Dottoressa*, so I thought it would be better for you to choose the one you feel the most comfortable with.'

Catriona moved to his side, letting his hand go to her elbow to guide her forwards. She saw him pause and lean in a fraction as though catching her scent. A tremor passed through her body as he touched her and she watched his brow furrow in concentration. For a moment she thought she saw a flash of recognition on his face, but then he guided her ahead of him. 'That's thoughtful, *signore*, thank you,' she murmured.

Catriona entered the stable barn that housed eleven horses. It was spotless. No doubt Dino had been up early to muck out and feed and water the animals. Delightedly, she breathed in the familiar scent of leather, hay and horses that reminded her of her childhood in Norfolk, where her father had kept the most wonderful stable of thoroughbred hunters. For a moment she felt a sharp stab of longing for those happy, carefree days.

Umberto's horses were mostly Arabian with their recognizable dished profile, prominent eyes, large nostrils and small teacup muzzle. There were also two Hanoverians, which she recognized by their strong athletic build and height. Although known to be quite even-tempered, they were much too high for her, standing, she guessed, at approximately sixteen hands. With their floating trot and their round, rhythmic canter, they were more like dressage animals, and that had never caught her fancy. Two heavy horses munching on fresh hay stood docilely in the next stalls.

As Catriona walked past each box, she was aware that behind her Dino was murmuring to his master, giving a running commentary on the state of the animals as they moved from box to box. Finally, she stopped in front of the last stall, where a beautiful palomino mare with a shining gold coat and white mane and tail gazed curiously out of the box at the newcomer. Catriona turned to Umberto. 'She's beautiful ... the best of the lot, isn't she?' she whispered.

Her host tilted his head to one side as if contemplating her comment. 'Strange that you should choose this mare,' he murmured. 'She was Calandra's horse, one of my last acquisitions. I bought her seven years ago when I was in the States. A good choice, *Dottoressa* – I agree, Wandering Gypsy is a handsome mare. She's very bright and responsive. And with the right person she's quite tame, although she doesn't take to everyone. She's managed to throw off many of my skilled stable staff but, with Calandra, she was docile as a lamb. You're welcome to try her ... you'll know immediately if she's right for you.'

Catriona knew that, when training a horse, if you fed them at random, you would only end up with a confused horse. They'd try all sorts – like sniffing, licking or nipping – not understanding which deed actually merited a treat. So, she said tentatively: 'May I give her a peppermint?'

'Calandra used to give her brown sugar lumps just before mounting her. We might still have some here at the stables.'

'*Sì, signore*,' Dino told him before Umberto had had a chance to ask. He went to a cupboard in the tack room, took out a box of La Perruche brown sugar lumps, and gave it to Catriona.

The young woman put a handful in the palm of her hand and spread it out in front of Wandering Gypsy, who immediately gobbled them down, two at a time. When she had finished, the mare nickered quietly and moved closer to Catriona.

'She's saying hello,' Dino said. 'She likes you, *Dottoressa*.'

Catriona petted Wandering Gypsy on her withers, the ridge just between her shoulder blades. She had been taught that horses at play nuzzle each other there, making it a good place for humans to rub to make the horse think they are one of them – far less scary than sticking your hand in their face and making them flinch.

'Would you like to ride her, then?' Umberto asked.

'I'd love that, please.'

'Dino will saddle her in no time.'

Dino fetched a bridle from a hook on the opposite wall and was about to put it on the horse when Catriona laid a hand on his arm. 'May I do that, if you don't mind?' she said with a smile. Stroking the animal soothingly on the neck, Catriona waited until Wandering Gypsy lowered her head before she slipped the bit into the mare's mouth. She then positioned the bridle over the horse's ears, fastened the buckles and thanked Dino, who returned her smile approvingly and went to fetch the saddle.

Umberto and Catriona walked out of the stables and into the sunshine.

'You have a big stable here,' she remarked. 'Do you breed horses?'

'No, but they have always been in my blood. At one time when I was much younger, I did a lot of show jumping and competitions. Calandra was a keen rider and I was put on a horse almost before I could walk.'

'So, you've always ridden?'

'Yes, but much less in the past ten years or so. I never had time …' He stilled, staring fixedly ahead as though lost in some distracting thread of the past. A moment later, his eyes shifted slightly. 'Horses represent freedom.' Catriona felt a slump in his spirits quite suddenly. She understood how it must feel, and that when on a horse he wouldn't feel blind in the same way. She remembered how she herself used to close her eyes when riding because it was all about feeling your horse and really engaging. Her riding teacher used to tell her it was like dancing a tango – feeling the interaction of energy and harnessing it.

Umberto shrugged. 'Calandra knew what horse riding meant to me so she engaged Piero Agostini, an amazing trainer who specializes in working with the blind. He gradually let me ride his horses, got me back in the saddle and took it at my pace. Over time I found my feel for them again … But here is your mount, *Dottoressa*.' And with that, he broke off and turned towards the footsteps of Dino, who had just appeared with Wandering Gypsy all saddled up.

'She's a real beauty. I think I'm going to enjoy riding her.'

Dino came forward with more sugar lumps.

'Yes, good idea. Thank you, Dino,' Catriona said as she took them from him and, placing them on her palm, presented them to Wandering Gypsy. She was rewarded with a sigh. The mare raised her head and pricked her ears in Catriona's direction, her eyes bright and alert.

'She's telling you that she likes you,' Dino told Catriona with a broad grin. 'You'll have no problem mounting her.'

Umberto gave a gruff noise of approval. 'If that's Dino's verdict, you can rest assured she's all yours for as long as you're here.'

Catriona let out a soft laugh. 'Great! Thank you.' Her fingers made contact with the horse's soft nose, and hot air blew at her face. She stepped forward, running a hand up the mare's head and along her neck. 'She's lovely.'

As if she had understood and was part of the conversation Wandering Gypsy whinnied and began to sniff and nuzzle Catriona.

Another stable boy appeared with the same handsome black stallion she had seen Umberto riding earlier. He too talked to his horse in soothing tones, and then mounted him with a grace and agility Catriona could scarcely believe.

Dino gave the young woman a leg-up and she swung herself on Wandering Gypsy's back, who pranced on the spot, anxious to enjoy her morning jaunt.

'It's a beautiful stallion you have there.'

'Yes, Vulcan is a young horse but he and I have a special relationship. We were trained together by Piero. He knows this property almost as well as I do and when I'm on his back, I know I can trust him with my life.'

'It must be very reassuring to feel you can ride without fear.'

Yet Umberto didn't seem to be listening any more. He patted the horse's flank and whispered into his ear: '*Vai verso il sole*, head towards the sun.'

It was just nine o'clock when they set off. Catriona leaned forward, hugging the mare's neck. Her lips curved into a smile and a wave of exhilaration ran through her.

As if sensing that he carried precious cargo, the stallion walked along the access paths at a gentle pace. The track was soft and covered with a reddish sand formed of powdered gneiss and glistening with fragments of mace. They were surrounded by eucalyptus, mimosa, pine, broom – and nowhere else had Catriona seen such beautiful arbutuses.

The lake that she could see through the foliage glistened in the morning sun. In the background, the endless dips and rises of the hillocks were a constant source of enchantment for her, and at every point masses of azaleas of every hue and colour, and roses of every kind tumbled over balustrades of villas or fell from the stems of bushes in a crimson cascade; Madonna lilies, giant geranium bushes – everywhere a wealth and a glory of colour.

Catriona watched Umberto riding beside her and then closed her eyes, trying to imagine how it would feel to be blind as they cantered in silence past groves of peach, plum and pear trees, laden with heavy blossoms that gave off an intoxicating scent. A mixture of emotions swept over her. Excitement … elation … tenderness … and a feeling of profound admiration for this man whose courage was tested every minute of every day.

Soon they had left the orchards and Umberto called out to her: '*Andiamo*, let's go!' as he encouraged Vulcan lightly. The stallion responded instantly to his master's soft command and picked up his pace. A rhythmic gallop began through the grass, the horses neatly swerving around the evergreens. They were flying straight into the wind, steel-shod hooves pounding out a drum-roll of elation, muscles bunching and lengthening, ears flattened.

It was not long before they came to an expanse of ground nestled in a valley, closely cultivated with mulberry trees and overlooking the lake. Umberto reined in Vulcan till they proceeded at a leisurely walk. Until now, neither he nor Catriona had felt the urge to speak. She knew that Wandering Gypsy was enjoying herself from the way her body relaxed. The ride had been so exhilarating that Catriona didn't want this morning to end; she'd almost forgotten that Umberto was blind and that she was here with him in a professional capacity.

Vulcan came to a standstill near a cluster of trees, apparently content to nibble on the sweet grass. Umberto raised his face to the sky and then took a deep breath. 'I can tell by the position of the sun and its warmth that it's still fairly early, not yet nine-thirty. We'll amble slowly down into the valley. There's breakfast waiting for us there.'

The sky seen from this height was breathtaking, with many varieties of gas-blue, pink and orange coloured air threading down from the mountains. How exquisite the countryside looked on this crystalline morning. Elated, Catriona drank in the distant view: far upon the glistening mountainsides clumps of soaring birch trees stood with a nimbus of light around them, delicate and lovely; the flocks of mountain sheep looked like pearls scattered over the swelling shoulders of green. No wandering breeze ruffled the atmosphere and, like so much of this place, silence and stillness appeared to halt the hours. And in this timeless moment – this perfect moment which she felt belonged to them – it seemed to Catriona that she was transported back in time. A warm sensation doused her from head to toe. Her girlish infatuation with the composer, that emerging star of a decade ago, was resurfacing and, not for the first time since her arrival, she felt that she was in danger of it erupting into something more, something far stronger …

Umberto adjusted the reins in his hands. '*Facciamo una gara*, let's have a race. We'll gallop down to the pergola. Can you see it? Down there, on the edge of the lake beside those cypresses.'

Race? Before Catriona could protest at the notion of competing downhill at a gallop with a blind rider, Umberto had launched Vulcan along a narrow track leading down to the valley on an alarmingly steep slope. His powerful legs clamped Vulcan's sides and he settled into the horse's stride, letting reflexes ingrained by years on horseback take over. His mount ran like unleashed hell.

He's going to break his neck, Catriona thought in alarm before following him in the mad descent.

The valley was reached in no time and soon they were galloping along a wide path on each side of which were planted a sea of mulberry trees with corrugated browny-orange trunks, short and wide, above which their many branches formed a full, spreading crown. Wings of the silvery blue waters of Lake Como flashed through gaps between the thin, satiny, light-green leaves. Catriona relaxed a little; Umberto was an experienced rider and there was no doubt that Vulcan knew his way. Horse and rider were in total harmony, moving as one, and she was reminded of her teacher's words at riding school: *'Do what your horse does, and do in your body what you want your horse to do in his.'*

The ride was glorious. The grass bordering the path was carpeted with summer wild flowers: poppies, buttercups and cornflowers, and every bend promised a new, more spectacular vista. Now, as the riders approached the lake and the pergola covered in creepers, it was as if the world was suddenly under magnification: the sky bluer, the grass as lush as a prairie, the looming mountains taller and more majestic, and the air purer, moist and fragrant with the scent of pine needles and wild grape vines.

Finally, they came to a halt in front of one of the clumps of giant cypresses that stood like sentinels on each side of the pergola, as though guarding the entrance to a secret refuge.

'*Allora, Dottoressa*, what is your verdict, *eh*?'

'I'm impressed,' she admitted, still breathless from the gallop.

Umberto let out a deep, booming laugh. His mood was certainly transformed, so different from the irritable, spiky personality of previous days.

Mario appeared at the entrance to the pergola.

'Ah, Mario! *Buongiorno … e' pronta la colazione*?'

'*E' pronta e la aspetta*, *signore*, breakfast is ready and waiting for you, Sir,' he replied, beaming.

The pergola was not large. It had round columns built with *pianelle*, curved bricks made in Italy since the time of the Romans, when the columns were plastered to resemble stone. It stood at the edge of the water with a breathtaking view of Lake Como and the surrounding countryside with its terraces and gardens, meadows and woods. Unmilled wood had been used for the horizontal beams and joists, supporting the climbing pink-and-white rose and grapevine across the top, creating a living piece of art in the dappled shade. Flagstones bordered with rosy-toned gravel provided a firm surface for the lovely chipped stone table and a pair of rustic chairs, creating a sweet-fragranced and cool outdoor dining room.

Although most Italians traditionally started their day gulping down a cup of *caffè latte* or *espresso*, with perhaps a couple of *biscotti*, a copious breakfast awaited them, laid out on a trolley.

'What a feast!' Catriona exclaimed, surveying dishes piled up with *cornetti* – cornet-shaped pastries filled with cream, chocolate or apricot jam; platters of paper-thin slices of various cured prosciutto, cheeses and salamis; and a bowl of *macedonia*, a colourful fruit salad made with jewelled cubes of seasonal fruit from the region.

Removing his dark glasses, Umberto turned on her his sightless emerald eyes and smiled that boyish smile that had charmed his public in the past, but which today had something more poignant and touching about it. 'I thought after our long trek I owed you at least a reasonable breakfast at the end of it.'

'I really enjoyed our ride. Wandering Gypsy is a wonderful mare.'

'As I told you earlier, she does not take to everyone. You must be a good rider.'

Catriona watched as he dismounted easily, passing his reins to Mario, who was waiting next to him. She noticed that Mario gave a very subtle steering gesture to Umberto as he turned, and she thought back to the way the composer used to stride so confidently everywhere, even when he'd carried her that night after she'd fallen over in Saint Paul de Vence. Now, Umberto made his way slowly towards his chair.

'Let's eat. I don't know what got into Vulcan today, he was more spirited than usual. He gave me a hard time, I had to keep a firm hold on the reins.'

'You seemed very much at ease. It certainly didn't show.'

'When I lost my sight, I was taught to surrender my sense of control and go with the flow of the horse. Maybe today I was a little stiffer than usual and my resistance upset him. Anyhow, the ride gave me as much if not more pleasure than usual. It's good to have a challenge.'

Catriona, gazing at the amazing panorama that stretched beyond the leafy colonnades of the pergola, reflected how he must have challenges enough without needing to add to them. Once again, she was impressed by the sheer determination of her blind host.

The lake from this point looked more like a majestic river, its shores lined with villas and gardens, while above them vineyards, olive groves and woods clothed the slopes of the green mountains. Across the lake she could make out the renowned Villa d'Este, originally built by Cardinal Gallio, but now a hotel.

Umberto guided himself to his seat by the railing next to one of the columns. They settled down at the table and Mario poured out the steaming coffee and offered Catriona the pastries.

'*Grazie.*' She smiled at Mario and helped herself to a chocolate-filled *cornetto*.

'Let's start with some champagne,' Umberto suggested. 'It will be refreshing after our race.'

'*Signore*, might I remind you that we will be beginning work immediately after breakfast.'

'Come, *Dottoressa*, we all need a little opium for the senses, otherwise the things we have to face would be damn hard to endure.'

'That may be true, but I never drink when I'm on duty.'

Umberto made an irritated gesture with his hand. 'Duty … duty … I would prefer if you didn't describe our sessions that way, *Dottoressa* …' and then, '*Basta*, I prefer to do away with all this formality. You will call me Umberto and I will call you by your name, Catherine. Or maybe the Italian version, *Caterina*.'

He stared blankly at her face and his voice dropped as he added absently. 'I am very fond of the name Caterina. I once knew someone, a long time ago, who was called that. Strangely enough, there's something in your spirit that reminds me of her.'

Catriona's heart gave a violent jolt. Her cheeks burned but she managed to keep her voice steady. 'If you wish. Although I would prefer it if you would use my real name.'

'Very well, I'll try. Anyway, you must call me Umberto.'

'Agreed.'

She tore her eyes away from those coveted lips. Staring that way when he couldn't see felt like an intrusion, an invasion of his privacy, like she was some sort of voyeur. She needed to get a grip on herself.

If she relaxed, let down her guard, she was bound to give herself away … and then where would they be? Still, would that be such a bad development? Eventually she would have to tell him about Michael, his son. Still, it was too early for that … and what was all that about Caterina? Maybe he already knew. Maybe Calandra had done some research …

'What are you thinking?' Umberto probed, struggling to hide his growing impatience as the silence stretched. 'I don't like not being able to see your face.'

'So far you have been able to read me without seeing me,' Catriona retorted, chewing on her lower lip. Ever since her arrival, Umberto had been able to guess what she was thinking almost before she knew herself.

'I could never read people before the accident. Now that I'm blind, I must rely on other senses to get by. I can usually gauge a person's sincerity. You're difficult because you don't say very much and I can't really rely on your voice to give away your emotion. You are quite secretive, Caterina – I mean, Catherine.' He corrected himself, but not before her stomach gave another reflexive lurch. Umberto reached for the glass that Mario had filled with champagne.

'Shall we drink to the success of … umm, let us call it our new partnership? Where you have your sessions but I dictate whatever happens in the free time between them. Let's try it that way for two weeks. We'll start this afternoon, straight after lunch. What do you say?'

'You're a good negotiator,' she conceded, her expression abstracted as she bit into the chocolate-filled pastry. 'But the thing about pacts with the Devil is that they sound terrific until you read the small print and then you realize you've signed your soul away.'

Umberto frowned. 'The Devil, *eh*? Surely that's typecasting?'

'I will indulge you because, contrary to what you might think, I am not narrow-minded and set in my ways. I'm quite prepared to try different approaches to my healing methods and always happy to admit it when new ideas work.' Although she said the words, Catriona was troubled. She knew Umberto's suggestion was overstepping the boundaries that she, as a therapist, always tried hard to maintain. She'd always been a stickler for professionalism but now she felt helpless. Persuading herself it would be worthwhile to go with the flow was wrong and she knew it.

She was at sea, in a tumult of emotions and longing, and sitting here with a client sipping champagne was hardly professional. But then the situation was in no way normal. Agreeing to come to Italy to take on this case had been dancing with the Devil from the start.

His sudden grin bathed her with sunshine. 'At last we agree, *eh*?'

Her misgivings had lost their battle.

Catriona lifted her glass and took a sip. 'Two weeks … I will give this experiment two weeks. If it works, no one will be more pleased than I, but if it doesn't, then we revert to my way or I leave.'

'It's a deal.' He raised his glass. 'So, let's drink to our new partnership.'

Exhausted by their fencing session, they ate their breakfast in silence for a while.

A magnolia tree laden with blossoms scented the air while a choir of birds – thrushes, blackbirds and finches – provided a concert for their ears. Now and again, the liquid note of a black cap, so often mistaken for the nightingale, infiltrated the happy chorus and Catriona thought how lucky she was to be sitting in this Eden of a garden without being obliged to be herded round it by a guide in the company of tourists, like so many of the other lakeside villas.

She had accepted Umberto's deal knowing the pitfalls and dangers it entailed. She'd play his game. Gone was the innocent girl she had been at eighteen. Today, she was a young woman who, although not bitter, was nevertheless free of illusion or false belief, armed with the knowledge of what a man could do to one's life – what *this* man had done to *her* life.

Yet the enchantment remained. Umberto could still weave his spell over her; she could feel it now in the air around them, imprisoning her in its magic. Although his eyes were lifeless, he still had a potent sexuality that overwhelmed her. Sitting opposite him now, Catriona knew that if he suddenly took her in his arms, she would find it almost impossible not to surrender to him and to her own need. *Just one finger, one touch, one sweet moment …* she thought, letting the past gush from the recesses of her mind. Her future lay before her, clear and untarnished, and it was for her to make the most of the present.

They talked of this and that, and of the various places they had visited in the world, more in accord than they had been since her arrival. Surprisingly, she discovered that he wasn't like most men, who invariably wished to talk about themselves. He asked her about her work and how she came to be especially interested in using music with the blind.

'It happened quite early on, soon after I qualified,' she told him, pleased that he had brought up the subject. 'At that time I was working, gaining valuable experience in one of the best clinics in France. There was a boy who was brought to me. He had contracted meningitis when he was three. Not only had he become blind but he had developed seizures and had extremes of mood. He was difficult … impulsive.'

Umberto was a good listener, becoming involved with the story. 'So, what was it about that boy that so interested you?'

'He was the first musical savant I had come across. As I worked with him, I realized that music was the only way to communicate with him effectively. On a bad day, I would play or sing to calm him down. Anyway, it wasn't long before I discovered what an extraordinary gift he had. Some people have a photographic memory, his was phonographic. I could play a Beethoven sonata or a Debussy prelude and, having never heard the piece before, he could sit down and play it back to me perfectly.'

'So, after that you jumped to conclusions and thought that the blindness was a key to this kind of musical genius, did you?' asked Umberto, suddenly sceptical, guarded.

She answered his question calmly. 'I didn't just jump to conclusions, as you put it. I simply took on more and more blind clients and learned all about them and how to work with them. Later, I helped one group form a chamber orchestra. Then one thing led to another, I suppose. And two years ago, I gained my Braille qualification.'

He nodded. 'Louis Braille was a countryman of yours, of course. I remember visiting his childhood home in Coupvray as a boy, when Calandra took me on one of her European tours. I seem to recall that Braille refined the system of raised dots and dashes the army had been using on the battlefield. Clever – that way soldiers hadn't needed to speak or use torches at night, which might have given themselves away to the enemy.'

'That's right,' said Catriona, enjoying that their conversation was back on an easy footing again. 'But what was so very fortunate was that Braille was a keen musician and made every effort to create a form of notation flexible enough for any instrument.'

'So, Calandra thought you'd be able to teach me, I suppose?'

'I think she understood that as a musician and therapist with various strings to my bow, I'd be able to help you. So, yes, that probably was in her thinking. She didn't make the trip to France to see me without good reason.'

'Well, I'm sure she had my best interests at heart,' Umberto said quietly. Then, in a more clipped manner: 'But I have no intention of learning Braille, *Dottoressa*. And there's an end to it.'

Catriona noticed that he had called her 'Doctor' rather than using her name. Once more she saw how difficult this tightrope would be. One minute they would be chatting easily, the next, the subject of his musicianship would be touched on and he'd close up like a clam. She decided quickly to change the subject and bring things on to more neutral ground.

'Tell me about Lake Como's silk industry. We passed a mulberry grove on our way, didn't we?'

'Now that is a subject close to my heart,' Umberto said, smiling. 'You know we have a factory?' She nodded. 'Well, you'll find we have two types of mulberry trees growing on the estate. The white mulberry we use for the rearing of silk worms, but you'll notice we also have red mulberry trees dotted around the garden. Because their sap is bitter, few insects are drawn to them but they're useful nonetheless,' he told her.

'While the leaves of the white nourish the silkworms, the fruit of the red are delicious, and what would we do without Adelina's excellent jam? The wood has its value too. When we have storms, sometimes we lose some of our trees and we get a good price for the wood from local joiners. What we don't sell, we burn in our fireplaces in winter. One day, I'll take you to visit our silk factory and the nursery where our silk worms are reared.'

'I'd love that,' said Catriona, adding, 'There was a red mulberry tree in the garden of our neighbour when I was a child. Some of its branches hung over the wall and I loved the berries.' That same tree had belonged to him for a brief time, she suddenly realized; it had been in his garden. She coloured, disconcerted, and panicked for a moment, fearful she might have somehow given herself away. It was so hard trying to keep her past secret in these conversations that flowed so easily. What other details might she drop in carelessly? One slip and he might begin to guess the truth about her. And if she let him know her identity that way, only confusion, pain and anger would be her reward.

Umberto continued, unaware of her turmoil: 'Yes, and they're beautiful too, aren't they? That's why they are used to ornament our streets and why so many of us have them in our gardens.'

'I've never come across the white mulberry.'

'It's actually much more widespread than the red, especially in the wild, where the latter is almost extinct. There is a legend that explains this in its own way. Do you know it? The one of Pyramus and Thisbe?'

Catriona smiled inwardly as she was reminded of the legend he had told her above La Baie des Anges, and remembered that Umberto had been brought up on a diet of mythology by Adelina.

'No, I don't.'

'Well, like many Greek legends, it's not a happy story.' He gave a twisted smile. 'But as happy stories tend to bring on a bad mood, I'm inclined to tell it to you.'

'Why not? I've always been interested in mythology.'

'Ah, another thing we have in common, Caterina, *vero*?'

Catriona forced herself to laugh, although the use of the name disconcerted her all over again. Yes, she was beginning to think that they did have much in common, but she quickly reminded herself not to relax into such an observation, and that she really couldn't trust this man.

'So, are you going to tell me the legend or will I have to go and look it up myself? You've aroused my interest now.'

'*Va bene, gliela racconto.*'

Umberto shifted in his seat. They had finished eating and he signalled to Mario to fill up his champagne glass. Then he lit a cigarette in the efficient way Catriona had witnessed the day before.

'In the city of Babylon there lived two lovers, Pyramus and Thisbe. They were neighbours, but were forbidden to marry because of their families' rivalry. But where there's a will, there's a way, and the lovers found a means of communicating through a crevice in the wall between their properties.

'Finally, they decided to run away and get married, come what may. They chose to meet by a white mulberry tree near the tomb of King Ninus, which lay outside the city gates.' He paused to draw on his cigarette before continuing.

'Heavily veiled, Thisbe managed to escape her home unnoticed and made her way stealthily to the mulberry grove near the tomb of Ninus. The place was deserted and she lifted her veil to look around for Pyramus. Instead of her lover, she found a lioness, its mouth bloodied from a recent kill. Thisbe fled, inadvertently dropping her veil. The lioness sniffed at the veil with curiosity, tore and tossed it with her blood-stained jaws and then crept away.

'When Pyramus arrived, he did not find his beloved Thisbe. Instead, there were tracks on the ground made by a wild beast and near them, a woman's veil, torn and blood-stained. He instantly recognized it as Thisbe's. Mad with sorrow and guilt because he had not been there to defend her, he drew his sword and fell upon it at the foot of the white mulberry tree, soaking its roots with his blood.

'Meanwhile, by now convinced the wild animal had gone, Thisbe crept back to their meeting place. She found Pyramus there with his sword in his heart, her veil still clasped in his hand. The dying Pyramus opened his eyes and fixed them upon her and she gazed back at her lover, heartbroken. With the same sword she stabbed herself, and the lovers perished together.

'The parents found them after a weary search, and the lovers were buried together in the same tomb. But the berries of the mulberry tree turned red that day, and that is how the red variety was born.'

'It's like a Greek version of *Romeo and Juliet.*'

The ghost of a smile hovered on his well formed lips. 'Do you think that all love stories end in a tragic way?' he asked lightly. The air between them seemed to pulsate with something enigmatic and once more his expression became still, as though he was watching her reaction despite his sightless eyes.

Catriona was spared the necessity of answering as they suddenly heard the stallion and mare whinnying softly.

Umberto's brows drew together. 'Who's there? Someone's coming!'

Catriona looked up quickly and saw in the distance a horse bearing a woman cantering towards the pergola, followed by a second ridden by a young groom.

'Silvana,' she exclaimed.

Silvana it was, in khaki-coloured jodhpurs and a loose white silk shirt. She wasn't wearing a riding hat and, in the dapple of sun and shadow, her abundant hair resembled a flaming halo as it glittered and danced in the breeze, the red intensified by the golden rays falling through the roof of leaves. She was riding a beautiful, sensitive chestnut that delicately sniffed the air and, as it slowed, picked its fastidious way along the rotted leaves and tiny ferns of the track.

Oh, what a picture, Catriona thought.

Umberto seemed irritated. 'What's she doing around here? She never comes this way.'

Catriona wondered what Silvana would think, seeing the two of them seated opposite each other, their attitude one of cheerful intimacy in such an idyllic spot, drinking champagne at ten o'clock in the morning instead of working on sessions for which she had been handsomely paid.

Silvana's large grey eyes, fixed and unsmiling, searched Catriona's face, revealing a hidden fire that seemed to smoulder in the deep and intense places of her mind. '*Dottoressa* Drouot and Umberto? I thought you'd be inside somewhere. What are you doing here?'

Umberto leaned back in his chair and retorted coolly: 'We're having, as you can see, a champagne breakfast.'

Silvana was neither amused nor pleased, her vivid red mouth refusing to relax into a smile. She looked down at Catriona from the top of her ominous throne. 'Champagne? And at this hour? I was under the impression that this was a working day for you, *Dottoressa*.' Silvana's rich voice could never be other than lovely, but it could hold a most menacing ring.

Catriona flushed crimson and her hands clenched. *I must not lose my temper*, she thought grimly. Silvana's claws were finally coming out and it was obvious that the singer was doing her best to provoke some kind of reaction.

Umberto gave her an insouciant smile. 'We have already had our first session and we were just celebrating our first step to success.' He turned towards Catriona as if silently messaging her not to contradict him.

Silvana dismounted and with an imperious gesture she motioned to Mario to pull up a chair for her. Then, tossing back her long straight hair in a manner only just short of insolence, she sat at the table.

'I still don't really understand. Explain, will you, *caro*?' This time she shot her question at Umberto, and in the same ominous tones.

'There's nothing to explain, Silvana. We were celebrating the success of our first excellent session.' He spoke the lie decisively.

Silvana turned her sharp grey gaze upon Catriona. 'Well, I'm glad to hear it went well. Although I'm sure that when Calandra employed your services, she did not expect you to spend your time being wined and dined by your patient.'

Umberto's head jerked sharply. 'How dare you talk to *dottoressa* Drouot in this manner,' he bellowed, dark red colour lying across his cheekbones. 'I shouldn't have to remind you that she is a guest in our house.' Once again his mood had turned, like a dark storm after a quiet sunlit morning. Catriona didn't like to imagine what it boded for her *real* first therapy session with him that afternoon.

Silvana's eyes flicked back to him and she gave a casual shrug of the shoulders, though her gaze was now wary. 'I am only trying to make sure that no one takes advantage of you, Umberto,' she retorted.

A flash of anger hardened Catriona's expression. In spite of her resolve to remain calm, thereby denying the other woman the satisfaction of seeing that her words had hit home, her precarious self-control snapped.

'*La signora* Calandra employed me to achieve results. At no time did she did stipulate how I should carry out my work and, without being rude, I don't see that this business has anything to do with you, *signora*. And now, if you'll excuse me …' Pushing back her chair, she left the table and walked swiftly out of the pergola.

As she walked back to where the horses were tethered she heard Umberto snap: 'She's damn right! None of this has anything to do with you. You have a vicious tongue, Silvana, and you'd do well to leave the *Dottoressa* alone, or you'll have me to answer to.'

*   *   *

Leaving Umberto at the stable block, Catriona wandered back towards the lodge. Here, to the south of the main house, behind the garage and stables, the grounds were shaped more like a small meadow, ringed by a few trees. The wild flowers were a riot of colour on the fading green: purple thistles, blue cornflowers, red poppies and tall asters with their yellow centres. There was no design to them, unlike the garden displays in Nice, just a free-for-all choreographed by the breeze.

Walking along the path, Catriona's gaze was caught by an old cottage that she hadn't spotted before. It crouched low into the grassy embankment, as though trying to hide, but the misshapen slate roof was too large to go unnoticed. Next to it stood a stone outhouse the size of a large potting shed. She could see the coarse, unevenly sized grey stones that made up the walls and the domed roof and fancied it looked rather like a beehive. As she got closer, the occasional flash of colour – some blues, others greens or browns – emerged from the grey stones that looked like eyes trying to steal a glimpse of the world.

To the left of the cottage lay an expanse of tall wild asphodels, their wistful off-white flowers quivering in the breeze. At the edge of them, Catriona recognized the wiry figure of Adelina moving slowly between the plants, picking leaves and humming to herself as she dropped them into the basket hanging from her arm.

On impulse, Catriona turned off on to the small track that led to the cottage. As she drew nearer, she waved and called out: 'Adelina, *ciao!*'

Adelina looked up and her weathered face broke into a broad smile. '*Buongiorno, Dottoressa!*' As Catriona came forward, the housekeeper took in her appearance. 'I see you have been riding with the *signore. E' bravo, eh?*'

Catriona smiled back. 'He's certainly impressive on a horse.'

Adelina glanced down into her basket, stirring the leaves with her wrinkled fingers, then beckoned to Catriona. '*Andiamo dentro*, come inside with me. I've made some fresh *burrata* cheese and I need to wrap it in these leaves. It keeps it fresh. When the asphodel leaves dry out, then you know the cheese is no longer good.'

In tacit agreement, Catriona followed her through the garden. 'So, you live here?' she asked, gazing at the cottage, which looked like a picture from a children's book. It was dwarfed by two huge trees that grew on either side of it, one with red and orange leaves, a maple brought over from Japan when the house was built, Adelina explained, going on to tell her that the tree was hollow and inside lived a family of squirrels; occasionally, a woodpecker or an owl would visit too. To the right lay a tiny pond with lilypads and a few ducks, and perhaps a frog or two. The grass was yellow in places, scorched by the blazing sun.

No wonder Adelina seemed so wiry and fit for her age, mused Catriona. There was a sizeable vegetable plot, with the grass trimmed short between long rectangular beds. Among the carrots and onions, leeks and green beans, the old housekeeper also grew herbs. The air was scented by their aromatic leaves: the thyme tiny and bright green, the rosemary with its dark green needles. Then there was a mass of sprawling oregano with its sweet pungent smell, mint in a large clay pot reaching for the sun, chives growing like grass, their round purple flowers on tall stems, and basil waving gaily in the summer breeze. Next to that was a row of garlic, which kept the aphids at bay, Adelina told her. Combined, what music they made: each Italian dish they graced would become an orchestra of flavour.

'*Sì*, I've been here ever since I started work for the family, thirty years or more.'

They entered the shed and were met with the earthy aroma of stone walls, tangy cheese and wine, which was stored in stoppered carafes on shelves, all overlaid with the scent of rosemary from the bunches hanging from the rafters. Inside it was cool, though the shuttered windows were open, allowing a subdued light to spill into the small space. Catriona looked around her and saw that to one side was a marble preparation table draining into a large white sink, a heavy brass tap above it. The whole preparation area was spotlessly clean. The place was not at all unhygienic-looking, as Silvana had remarked the night before: simply rustic and utterly charming.

Adelina ushered her to sit at one of the stools next to the wooden table. 'I have some homemade lemonade in the fridge. Would you like some?'

Not used to drinking champagne during the day, Catriona still felt a little light-headed from her breakfast with Umberto. 'Yes, that sounds lovely, thank you. I must admit I'm quite thirsty now.' As she perched on one of the stools, her eyes ran over the shelves of kitchen utensils – spoons and perforated ladles – and the pots and pans of stainless steel, glass and enamel. There was also a large cheese tub, piles of butter muslin, cheesecloth and cheese mats, stacked together with moulds of all shapes and sizes.

'So, this is where you make all your own cheese?'

'*Sì*, ever since I came to this house.'

Catriona's attention was drawn to what Adelina explained was the cheese press, a straight-sided drum three feet high and two feet in diameter, in the middle of the back wall. Gleaming brass fittings held its vertical wooden staves tightly in place. A round wooden plug topped the drum, which was attached to a long wooden lever fixed to the wall with a weight on the end that was used to bear down on the drum's contents. Adelina pointed to the short wooden arm pressing down on the plug of the drum beneath the lever.

'It's vital to get the lever and the arm dead centre, otherwise the weight of the lever is not even and you will get a lopsided cheese,' she explained, placing her basket down on the large kitchen table.

'It looks like it's quite an art,' Catriona observed.

'The key thing is the distance from the wall to the centre of the plug. You see, it is about thirty centimetres,' the older woman continued. 'The weight on the lever is five kilos, if it is fixed at that distance. If we move the weight to the next notch out, the lever pressure will be doubled to ten kilos.'

Catriona nodded with genuine admiration, seeing that Adelina took pride in the meticulous skill she practised here. The housekeeper explained how, during this final draining period, the shape of the final cheese was determined.

'Today, I'm making *burrata*, the fresh cheese made with the *ritagli*, scraps of leftover mozzarella,' Adelina announced, putting on her apron. 'I wrap the pouches of cheese in the leaves of asphodel while they're still green, tie the pouches in a topknot and moisten them with a little whey. Tomorrow, I will make *cingherlino*, a mixture of cows' and goats' milk, seasoned with olive oil and pepper. It's *il signor* Umberto's favourite.' She beamed. 'Even when he's not hungry, he cannot resist it.' She went to one of the fridges in the corner of the room and took out a jug of pale lemonade, pouring some into a small glass.

Catriona thanked her and took a large gulp of the refreshing cold drink. She was intrigued. 'Where did you learn to make cheese?'

Adelina fetched a large bowl of soft white cheese from the other fridge. 'I grew up in an orphanage. The woman who ran the place was very kind to me and taught me how to cook. When I grew older, I used to go to her house and see her family. Her brother became like a father to me. He used to work in one of the *parmigiano* factories and I learned the skill from him.' She began sorting through the leaves in her basket and laying them out on the wooden table. 'So, you saw today how *il signor* Umberto is much happier when he rides a horse, *vero*?'

A vision of Umberto's muscular figure on horseback swam into Catriona's mind. His mood had been noticeably elevated, it was true. 'Yes, it's obvious that he gets a kind of release from riding. It certainly affects his mood in a very positive way.' She then remembered his equally marked return to a stormy temper with Silvana and frowned slightly.

Adelina's dark, alert eyes missed nothing. 'It was not all good though?'

'Well, Silvana arrived and …'

The housekeeper frowned. 'She caused trouble?'

Catriona gave a wry smile. 'She certainly doesn't seem to approve of my presence here.'

Adelina shook her head and muttered. '*Madre di Dio,* no, I expect she doesn't.' Her work-roughened hands moved impatiently over the leaves, sorting through the largest ones and setting them aside. She glanced at Catriona. 'But then it is not for me to comment.'

Judging the most effective way to draw out more information from her, Catriona said casually: 'I would have thought Silvana would welcome any chance of help for *il signor* Umberto, as she's so close to him.'

'But if you help him, then he would not depend on her so much, would he?' Adelina gave her a wry look. '*La signorina* Silvana is something of a companion and sings to him when he's in one of his better moods – rides with him too – but to think that *la signora* Calandra thought she could be the one to make him happy …' She shook her head disapprovingly.

'So, you don't think *he* has feelings for Silvana?' Catriona asked tentatively.

Adelina looked up sharply. 'Feelings? Only those of every hot-blooded man when a woman throws herself at him! As the saints are my witness, that girl is no good for the *signore*, never has been.' This appeared to be a subject that vexed her, making her speak more freely now.

'I mean no disrespect to *la signora* Calandra, but she was *sentimentale*. Silvana was poor and the daughter of her best friend. It was natural, I suppose, for her to want a marriage between her son and her protégée. After all, it would have been very convenient.' She gave an amused snort. 'Imagine all those musical babies they could have had ... *la signora* Calandra would have loved that. *Sarebbe stata al settimo cielo*, she would have been in seventh heaven.'

At the housekeeper's words Catriona felt a sharp pang and her eyes dropped to hide her expression. The idea of Umberto and Silvana having children was disturbing, to say the least. In fact, Catriona was distinctly unsettled by the dazzling, talented ex-lover of Umberto's. Silvana was as alluring as ever. How far did their 'companionship' go, she wondered. Did Umberto still succumb to her charms, as Adelina had seemed to suggest? Perhaps the power of Calandra's dying wish would hold enough sway to nudge Umberto towards marriage with his mother's protégée.

Once more Catriona realized that she had become entangled in a painful web that could leave her even more damaged than before. She raised her head to see Adelina looking at her curiously. The housekeeper took the cheese from the bowl and began tearing it into fistfuls, shaping one into a large ball while watching her.

'You and *il signor* Umberto are getting on well, I think. He likes you. I hope you are not finding him too ... difficult. *E' un uomo orgoglioso, sa??* He is a very proud man, you know?'

Catriona nodded. It was now her turn to be probed. 'Yes, I can see how important his independence is to him. Teaching himself how to move around without a cane is remarkable enough, but being able to ride like that ... well, it's incredible,' she said truthfully.

'For him it is a matter of survival,' said Adelina. Her brows knitted together thoughtfully. 'I remember, not long after he became blind, the *signore* began to practise feeding himself; he would drop his food and fly into a rage and all the plates and tablecloth would end up thrown to the floor. Later, he would apologize to me. One day, he clasped my hand and he thanked me …' The housekeeper's expression suddenly looked anguished at the memory.

'He held my hand so tight, it told me without words how much misery and frustration he felt that he was so helpless, that a Monteverdi man could be in this position.' She swallowed her obvious emotion. 'I have never forgotten that. Now he is determined not to let this blindness conquer him, even though sometimes I know that he finds it unbearable.'

Catriona's heart squeezed painfully. Umberto's bravery took her breath away and she wished she could persuade him to turn such tenacity towards his music. 'He is lucky to have someone like you, Adelina,' she said softly.

The housekeeper sighed and gave a half-smile. 'I've known him since he was a small boy,' she said. 'Who else will look after him now? He can't do everything, even if he thinks he can. Mario will tell you.'

'Yes, Mario seems very protective of him, too.'

'He's a good man. What I cannot do, Mario does. It is a shame Mario cannot swim too …' Adelina stopped, as though checking herself.

'Why is that?' Catriona asked. She noticed the look of consternation that had crossed the other woman's face.

Adelina seemed to choose her words carefully. 'Mario would be a better person to take the *signore* swimming in the lake.'

'*Il signor* Umberto swims in the lake? Who takes him?'

'Flavio.'

Catriona remembered the creepy-looking boatman and his piercing gaze. It almost made her shudder. She hadn't liked the look of him one bit and, judging by her expression, Adelina was not enthused either. 'How does Flavio help him swim?'

'They take the boat out and Flavio gets in the water to guide him. He swims next to him to make sure he doesn't go too far.

It's true the *signore* is strong and fit and needs keeping an eye on.'

'*Il signor* Umberto must trust him a great deal to place himself in his hands,' Catriona said, watching the other woman's reaction.

There was almost a look of fear in Adelina's dark eyes. 'The *signore* does not listen when I tell him that I do not trust Flavio with such a job.'

'You don't? Why is that?' she asked cautiously.

Adelina wouldn't meet Catriona's eyes as she wiped her hands on her apron. 'I have my reasons. Mario tries to keep an eye on things, to make sure *il signor* Umberto is safe, but he cannot watch him all the time.' She glanced at Catriona's empty glass. 'I'm glad you enjoyed the lemonade, *Dottoressa*.'

It was clear that Adelina had signalled an end to the conversation.

'Yes, it was delicious, thank you,' said Catriona, getting up from her stool. 'I ought to go. I'm meeting with *il signor* Umberto again this afternoon and I need to get out of these riding clothes.'

'*Sì, Dottoressa*,' said the housekeeper, with an awkward smile. 'Now you know where I am, you must come back again and tell me how you are getting on.' She paused, then added: '*Sa*, even before the accident the *signore* missed out on real living.'

'What do you mean?'

Adelina's eyes suddenly glittered with sadness. 'He had stardom and money, but no time to enjoy them. Today, he has all the time in the world, but now he's imprisoned in darkness, there's little he can do to enjoy life. I hope you are successful in bringing back his music.'

Catriona gave her a reassuring smile. 'I promise I will do everything in my power to help him.'

Deep in thought, she left Adelina's cottage. She had found out more about Umberto than she had expected. Now it was time to see what insights she could gain herself about how his troubled mind worked.

CHAPTER 11

After a quick shower and a change of clothes back at the lodge, Catriona helped herself to a light lunch from a tray Adelina had brought over. Still slightly replete from her breakfast under the pergola, she couldn't manage more than a tiny piece of Adelina's salty homemade cheese, a couple of artichoke hearts from a colourful plate of antipasti, and some tomato, lettuce and basil salad. The carafe of wine went untouched – she needed a clear head for work.

Her decision not to have a glass was evidently a sensible one because the moment Adelina ushered her into the spacious, sparsely furnished ground-floor room of the main house, Catriona knew she was going to need her wits about her.

The room was painted white, with gilded cornicing and a parquet floor. A piano stood in the middle, facing two tall French windows that led to a patio, while on the opposite wall, two other windows opened on to the garden. A sofa and four easy chairs formed a seating area in one corner. Umberto was seated on one of the chairs, looking steeled for the worst. Catriona's gaze took in the tray on the coffee table where, along with water and a few glasses, she also registered a bottle of Hennessy XO extra old cognac. It was hardly appropriate for a fruitful session and she would have preferred to see just the jug of water but *one step at a time*, she reflected patiently.

Umberto greeted her coolly and motioned for her to sit on the sofa. Catriona was ready for this – she had met such behaviour so many times before at the start of a course of therapy. Ignoring his sulky expression, she exclaimed: 'What a lovely room! So light and airy.' She glanced up at the high, vaulted ceiling. 'And the fresco is wonderful.' Above her, Apollo was sitting on the omphalos, the navel of the world, holding his lyre.

Umberto gave a tight smile, which vanished almost as soon as it appeared. 'The room used to give me inspiration. Of course, the brightness of it offers me nothing now and I cannot see the fresco. It's a place I tend to avoid.'

Catriona could have met his words with an awkward silence but she understood what Umberto was up to. Before, he had used flirtation and other means of distraction to keep her from her purpose, now he was employing the tactics of a moody child. Neither was going to work on her this afternoon. She was determined to take the direct approach, explain the fundaments of her work and, if he didn't wish to join the conversation, she would continue to expound them anyway.

'You talk of avoidance and that's probably as good a place to start as any,' she said. 'You are too clever not to know intellectually that avoiding an issue isn't going to make it go away. Wounds simply start to fester under the surface. I'm going to explain a few things now about how the therapy works. Please let me know if I make unwanted presumptions about what it is you might be feeling and experiencing. Are you happy if I proceed? If you want me to stop at any time just let me know. Raise your hand, if you like.'

Umberto nodded brusquely. His body was turned away from her, revealing so tellingly how reluctant he was to be there.

She began, her voice soft and even. 'One of the hardest things for my patients, if they have come through an accident or trauma, is that negative images often come into their mind unbidden, whether they like it or not. This will happen very often in cases of depression, too. Sometimes even suicidal images, what we call a "flash forward", may be involved. In these cases, I often use guided imagery with music therapy, a pairing that can be extremely effective.'

'Not another therapy! An additional string to your bow … Is there no end to your skills, *Dottoressa*?' Umberto blurted out rudely.

But Catriona refused to take the bait, knowing a verbal skirmish was exactly what Umberto wanted in order to deflect her from her course. 'Let me continue. When these involuntary images pop up unbidden, we begin to divert them. The patient learns to evoke new positive images. It's a strange mix of both focusing on the trauma and distracting oneself from it.'

She watched Umberto closely. He had almost imperceptibly turned his body towards her, the better to listen. Was she beginning to get through? But it seemed he certainly wasn't ready to submit yet.

'I can think of only two things that distract me,' he declared, leaning further back in his chair, 'and they do so remarkably effectively. Alcohol and the diverting company of *una donna ricettiva*, a receptive woman.'

His voice had dropped and for a moment she was almost undone by the provocative huskiness of his tone. Trying to ignore his sparring, she continued determinedly. 'Sticking plasters, *signore*, and I think you know that,' she said gently but firmly. 'The trauma, the images, the nightmares will keep coming, bubbling up from deep inside. And the only way to instigate healing – and it is something a patient does all by himself – is to go down deep into the unconscious and heal whatever is going on there. Using music, meditation scripts and visualized images will help take a person to that place. Creativity has its seat in the right brain, and this is the best way to tap into the unconscious.'

Umberto had no sardonic response this time, but stared straight ahead, his features impassive. The only movement he made was to feel for the ashtray on the table and move it an inch towards him. Seeing that he was in no hurry to speak again, Catriona stood up, poured herself a glass of water from the tray and walked over to a large display cabinet set along one wall. Books, musical scores and rows of CDs lined the shelves, many of which she saw were the works Umberto had composed and the recordings of various of his concerts. She felt at ease in the silence of the room, happy to let her words settle, knowing she had explained enough for now.

Through the French windows it was as though the great flourish of trees and flowers in the garden poured into the room with the sunshine. Wisteria, trailing vines and banksias fell in thick masses over the sides of the patio walls. These were flanked by different-sized urns, jars and pots overflowing with bright flowering plants: wave petunias, violets, pansies and various coloured calibrachoa superbells.

Behind her, she heard him pour himself a brandy and light a cigarette.

Catriona realized that she would have to develop a plan, one that would coax Umberto into not only engaging but also believing in the power of the method. She had learnt over the years what an extraordinarily complex organ the brain is, and also how much patience the therapist and her subject invariably needed; the healing process was never fast, and could take years. It was too early to assess how long it would take for Umberto to recover from his devastating experience. She knew that the best thing was to let matters progress at their own speed, like a flower's petals unfurling. If her attempts to help were met with defensive barriers, so be it. She hadn't met a client yet whose resistance held out forever.

Catriona moved to one of the windows overlooking the garden. She stood on the threshold and let her gaze wander over the fabulous scenery. Meanwhile, Umberto continued to stare into oblivion, occasionally drawing on his cigarette or taking a gulp of brandy. His recalcitrant mood was a challenge she would simply wait out. Inauspicious, yes; impossible, no.

She returned to sit on the sofa and stole a glance at him. Since their ride and breakfast at the pergola he had showered and looked fresh, his jet-black hair still wet and combed back. She expelled a silent sigh as her gaze slid down the long, lean length of him, a weakness invading her limbs as a deeper shuddery sigh left her with parted lips. He looked incredible in a pale-blue, short-sleeved shirt that he had left half-way unbuttoned, revealing his broad, tanned chest with its fine covering of dark hair. A pair of jeans moulded themselves to the hard contours of his thighs. He was the epitome of male beauty, sitting there, close enough for her to touch.

Only she wasn't going to – she still had a grain of good sense left. This was strictly a professional encounter and, even if it wasn't, past experience had taught her that when any form of physical contact with Umberto took place, things got dangerously out of hand.

He couldn't see, so there was no need to hide the hungry look in her eyes. And he couldn't read minds – she hoped. Catriona tried to drag her gaze away and inject the necessary degree of detached coolness into her voice as she attempted to draw him out of his muteness.

'It's a beautiful piano you have here. A Steinway! This is the third piano I've come across at Villa Monteverdi since I've been here, and this is the best of the three.'

'We had it tuned before you arrived.' He stubbed out his cigarette. 'After Calandra died, I hadn't bothered to keep the pianos in good order. What's the point when they're not being used?'

Catriona studied his face: this was at least a positive sign. 'I'd love to hear you play.'

It was a simple request, honest and sincere, but Umberto's reaction was as sudden and explosive as a grenade going off.

'Never!' He rejected the suggestion with such violence that Catriona flinched.

'I'm sorry,' she said, instantly contrite. 'I didn't realize that your aversion was so strong or I would have waited.'

'I can't bear the thought of performing. Can you imagine ... being led to the piano, fumbling until one found one's bearings on the keyboard?' He gave an exclamation of sheer disgust. 'No. I'd rather never play again than make such an exhibition of myself.'

'I think you could get over it. It's all about adapting. But if you dig your heels in, it's not going to get any better.' Catriona paused. 'Maybe it's easier for the blind children I work with. Being younger, they're more adaptable, I suppose. But you've already dealt so well with the physical part of it. Seeing you move around and handle day-to-day life ... you manage perfectly.'

He waved a hand in the air as if to dismiss this statement. 'But then they all stand over me, spoonfeeding down my throat the must-dos and must-nots as if I'm some sort of infant.' His frown deepened. 'I don't have to do a damn thing I don't want to.'

'Of course you don't. However, you will find that playing an instrument will not only relax you, but will help your body to access and then discharge deeply locked-in material. The key stimulus is sound,' Catriona explained. 'Not just heard through the ears, but felt as vibrations through the whole body. That's why I asked you to play.'

He was not wearing his dark glasses and he turned his sightless but still beautiful emerald eyes towards her. 'I will do it simply to please you, is that what you think?'

'Definitely not to please me. This has to come from you.'

'Good. At least we agree on one thing.' He rose from his chair and walked slowly over to the Steinway. 'And now, having had to endure your lectures, maybe you'll allow me to suggest something.'

His tone was suddenly smoother, yet pointed. 'I wish to hear *you* play. According to your CV you are a very accomplished musician. This is so-called music therapy after all. Let's see what you can do to plumb the depths of my psyche, shall we?'

Catriona read the challenge in his voice that bore an edge of hostility. She took a breath, telling herself that this was a perfectly normal part of her work. After all, she would often play, helping her clients in a session of improvisation. If that's what Umberto wanted, then that was fine.

'Very well, I'll just choose a piece from here.' After flicking through the sheet music and scores on the piano, she drew out a music book bound in red leather that was protruding from the bottom of the pile. She drew a sharp silent breath when she saw what it was: 'Songe d'une Nuit d'Amour', the piece he had played that night they made love in Villefranche. Something, a force outside of her, a thing almost supernatural, made her place the pages on the piano stand.

Catriona didn't need the sheets of music to play – she knew the piece off by heart. She had played it so many times: from memory at first, then following the CD once it had been released and, finally, from the published sheet music. For months it had been on every classical radio station all over the world and she had listened to it again and again, torturing herself with the memories that flooded back to her. Her mother had eventually confiscated the sheets of music, but it was too late – she had memorized every note. 'Songe d'une Nuit d'Amour' had already filled Catriona's heart and mind.

She sat on the stool, rested her fingers on the keys for a moment and then began to play. All the sadness and pent-up longing of the past decade communicated itself in the chords, sonorous and plangent. She played, lost in those poignant echoes of the past. Her breathing quickened and she felt tears gather, ready to fall. They didn't get the chance, though. Suddenly Umberto was beside her and, with a violent sweep of his arm, knocked the pile of music from the piano, the leatherbound score crashing to the ground, sheet music floating in their wake.

'Damn you and your damned therapy!' he growled, and already one muscular arm shot out to sweep yet more items from the piano in his fury. A vase smashed to pieces as it fell in the litter of papers on the floor. Catriona didn't know whether to be alarmed or admiring of such an obviously virile display of anger.

Umberto stood tensed like a coil, his breath coming heavy and his knuckles white as he gripped the side of the piano. 'Now, just get out. Leave me alone, will you.'

Without a word, Catriona left the room, closing the door behind her quietly.

*　　　*　　　*

Dinner that evening was a strained proceeding and Catriona couldn't wait for it to end. Umberto had been taciturn throughout, largely disengaged. She threw him a furtive glance, still kicking herself for her risky move in playing that particular piece to him at their session. It had clearly backfired. His green eyes barely moved as the stilted conversation carried on around him and she would have given anything to know the thoughts that were occupying his mind.

However, Umberto's distant mood hadn't prevented Silvana from making bids for his attention and, when her efforts failed to succeed, she had indulged in a session of sniping at Giacomo. There was something positively toxic in the dance in which the three inhabitants of this great mansion were locked. It was clear that Giacomo was infatuated with the redheaded beauty – how deep his feelings ran, Catriona wasn't sure – but her good-looking admirer's every comment was treated with such ridicule and spite by the disdainful soprano that Catriona wondered what sort of man could be so masochistic as to allow the object of his affections to treat him this way. She found it uncomfortable to witness.

'So, Giacomo, I heard you were seen coming out of the casino at three this morning,' Silvana declared, her eyes slanting maliciously. 'What was it this time? Baccarat? Poker? I'm sure you wouldn't be such a *zotico*, peasant, as to indulge in the slot machines.'

'I had some clients I had to entertain,' he said shortly.

'What *I* heard is that you were with that layabout Flavio and a couple of dodgy Mafiosi types. Perhaps the kind of client one should try harder to avoid, mmm?'

Her comment finally roused Umberto from his brooding. 'This is none of your business, Silvana,' he interjected curtly, clearly now intent on shutting down the conversation. 'I'm sure the *Dottoressa* doesn't want her evening spoiled by the pair of you bickering.'

'I was only concerned for Giacomo,' said Silvana defiantly.

'Like hell you were,' muttered Giacomo under his breath. He looked the worse for wear, his eyes red and watery, although Catriona sensed that it wasn't just the result of a hangover after a night on the town. There was something else behind this nervy distraction – one didn't have to be a psychologist to see the man was agitated. He was taking great slugs of wine and asking repeatedly to have his glass refilled.

'Anyway, I'm sick and tired of all this gossip. Nothing good ever comes of it,' Umberto said decisively. Reaching out, he grasped the brass bell on the table and rang it. He then asked the servant to clear the table and bring the coffee.

Catriona was longing for the meal to end. Surely she could make her excuses and return to the lodge at that point? It had been torture watching Giacomo and Silvana locked in their unhealthy squabbling, almost as uncomfortable as watching Silvana's desperate efforts to gain Umberto's attention, all of which were ignored or cut off brusquely.

Catriona almost felt sorry for the soprano, who was dressed in a revealing backless dark-green silk dress, showing off an elegant bronzed back of such graceful curves they could have been sculpted by Rodin. But to what avail? It wasn't as though the composer could see her. Silvana only had her words to woo him and she wasn't making a successful job of that. All she'd managed to do so far was rile him, as she had that morning when she had barged, uninvited, into their breakfast by the lake and had proceeded to insult Catriona.

Yet it might be different when they were alone. Was Silvana more than Umberto's companion, as Adelina had half suggested? Perhaps, mused Catriona unhappily, when the soprano sang tender love songs to him, she bewitched his senses. Catriona pictured the alluring redhead singing to him – like one of the sirens who tried to entice Ulysses – before offering the composer her body. After all, at the therapy session that afternoon, Umberto had made a cutting reference to his seduction of women, one of his 'distractions'. For a man, no doubt Silvana made highly 'diverting company', as he had put it. She could imagine their limbs entangled, their passion heightened to an erotic pitch by the rich and emotive words of some tragic aria.

The thought made her head ache. How ironic. Earlier, she had explained to Umberto all about unwanted images bubbling up unbidden; she might as well have been describing what was happening to herself. She was the one who needed therapy, she reflected wryly. What torture this was!

Umberto broke into her uneasy reverie, and Catriona was relieved to be distracted from it. 'I suggest we have our coffee in the *salone*.' He pushed his chair back so abruptly it nearly toppled over. Silvana leapt to his side and took his arm. 'Leave me be,' he growled. 'I may be blind but I'm not incapable.'

She flushed a little and gave a false-sounding tinkling laugh. 'Of course not. I never said you were, *caro*,' she said soothingly.

'Although I must say, I had expected you to be better tempered after your sessions with the *Dottoressa* today. If anything, they seem to have made you more troubled.'

Umberto's head turned sharply. 'Will you stop your infernal sniping, Silvana? Just find something else to think about. I am *not* your project.'

'It's a shame that you haven't had any invitations to sing,' offered Giacomo, his bloodshot gaze moving up and down the petulant-looking redhead as he took another gulp of wine. 'It might do you good to get out of here for a bit.'

'I've turned down plenty of requests, *se è per questo*,' Silvana snapped back. 'My agent was on the phone today, if you must know. But my first duty lies here. Calandra wouldn't have wanted me to waltz off, putting myself first.'

'You have a few weeks while the *Dottoressa* is in residence,' Giacomo said with a small shrug. It was obvious that he knew full well the reaction his words would cause, and appeared to enjoy watching Silvana bristle. 'It seems to me the ideal time to have a break. Why don't you and I catch some sun somewhere? The Amalfi coast, maybe?'

Silvana shot him a withering look. 'I think the wine must have gone to your head, Giacomo,' she responded scornfully.

Now it was the turn of Umberto's cousin to shove back his chair. Staggering to his feet, he made his unsteady way to Catriona, wine glass in hand. 'Let me escort you, Catherine,' he said with a fair attempt at gallantry, in spite of his inebriation. His use of her first name added extra fire to the coals of Silvana's ire and Catriona caught him throwing a smirk at the redhead.

Meanwhile, Umberto, who was standing at the *credenza* giving instructions to his servant, had broken off, a scowl darkening his handsome face. 'She can find her own way perfectly well. Keep your hands to yourself, Giacomo. The *Dottoressa* is not one of your tour ladies, who can be flirted with for tips.'

Catriona almost flinched at the harshness of these words. How Giacomo could bear to stand by and take such casual rudeness she could not imagine. It made her wonder all the more whether the younger cousin's professions of familial care and support for the blind composer should be taken at face value. Both Umberto and Silvana seemed to treat Giacomo so dismissively that these dinners must be sheer purgatory for the poor man, who had been nothing but charming and welcoming to Catriona, if a little over-attentive at times.

They moved into the other room and Silvana poured coffee for them all.

'So, *Dottoressa*, you must have been a musician in a previous life,' she said, eyeing Catriona shrewdly. 'At least one would hope so, given your current profession,' she drawled, her sardonic tone only thinly veiled.

Catriona gave a polite smile, her gaze sliding away as she took the cup Silvana offered her. She glanced over at Umberto as he walked directly to an armchair, negotiating the space with assured ease. *In a previous life … Yes, it seemed like a lifetime ago*, she thought sadly. 'I play the piano and I used to sing a little.'

'Oh, really?' The redhead arched a sceptical eyebrow, as though whatever Catriona's musical ability might be, it was undoubtedly paltry compared with her own. Rudely, she turned her back on her now. 'Shall I sing for you tonight, Umberto? What are you in the mood for? It always makes you feel better when I sing, doesn't it, *tesoro*?'

Umberto had seemed engrossed in his own thoughts until the moment Silvana questioned Catriona about her singing. Then he had raised his head, suddenly attentive. He paused now, as though turning some decision over in his mind.

'Since you ask, I think I'm in the mood for a soulful bit of Schumann. Something from *Dichterliebe*. Maybe the *Dottoressa* would oblige us all with one of the *Lieder*? The score's there in the cabinet.'

Silvana's head whipped round in shocked reaction while Catriona stood at a loss for words, a delicate flush rising in her cheeks. 'Goodness! I haven't sung in a while. I'm familiar with the songs but they're awfully sad. Why doesn't Silvana sing us something lively?'

Umberto's piercing green gaze turned in her direction, a curious expression lighting them. 'Because I don't want Silvana to sing, I want you to. Humour me, will you?' Like granite, there was something inflexible in his tone and he seemed impervious to the emotions seething in the room: Silvana's jealous hurt, Catriona's nervous disinclination to cause any trouble.

Giacomo was the only one who appeared to be enjoying himself, looking from one to the other of the women with something approaching the glee of a man attending his first prizefight.

'This is good,' he said, almost to himself. 'Yes, come on, *Dottoressa*. *Accontenti Sua Altezza*, do indulge His Highness.' Catriona felt there was an underlying statement hanging in the air – *that's what you're being paid to do.*

She took a steadying breath and decided not to demur further. After all, she was being paid a handsome sum to instill in her client a new joy for music, to inspire him to compose again. How could she refuse to sing for him?

'Very well, I should be honoured. I only hope you aren't appalled by my humble efforts. I haven't sung these Schumann *Lieder* for ages.'

Umberto gave a gratified half-smile, his first of the evening, and sat back in his chair relaxed, his long, muscular legs outstretched. He lit a cigarette.

'Excellent! You're being far too modest, *Dottoressa*. I'm sure we will enjoy hearing you sing. We're rather starved of musical entertainment these days. Silvana obliges us often, but it will be a pleasure to hear a new voice.' If his eyes had been able to see, he would have noticed a furious glint in the soprano's grey irises. Instead, his gaze was fixed where Catriona was standing.

'Did you know that Robert Schumann said: "I should like to sing myself to death like a nightingale"?' He gave a short, mirthless laugh. 'He never did manage to kill himself, although he was sent to an asylum for the insane after he threw himself in the Rhine.'

Catriona, uneasy at the macabre turn the conversation was taking, moved to the cabinet and scanned the volumes on the top shelf. She found what she was looking for and took the songbook over to the piano. *It's lucky I'm used to accompanying myself*, she said to herself. It was a tall order to have to perform without any practice, let alone to the man she found so unsettling that his very nearness made her go to pieces. Thankfully, she knew the *Lieder* well, having immersed herself in the poignant love songs ten years before, when her longing for Umberto had left her so helplessly forlorn. Schumann had written them when he had been separated from his beloved Clara, whose father refused to give the pair his blessing. The songs had spoken to her very soul.

Her heart was racing suddenly. It was as though she was a nervous teenager back on that stage at the Saint Cecilia competition, singing only for Umberto. She hoped she wouldn't break down with emotion now on singing the *Lieder* again after all this time. Although the painful wound of losing Umberto had healed over, her longing to be in his arms, hearing his voice tenderly whispering words of love, was as sharp as ever.

She sat on the stool and flicked through the pages at random until she settled on her favourite song. Every one of Heinrich Heine's poems seemed doomed to strike a blade into her heart, but this was the one that always stirred her the most. She took a shaky breath then started, her soprano voice clear and true. Her rich natural vibrato extracted every ounce of meaning from the poetry so that the air quivered with tides of emotion, as if she sought to pluck the heartstrings of every one of her listeners. She communicated every nuance of expression and meaning with such an instinctive understanding that she lost herself in the music:

Ich grolle nicht, und wenn das Herz auch bricht,
Ewig verlor'nes Lieb! Ich grolle nicht.
I blame thee not, although my heart is breaking,
Oh, love forever lost! I blame thee not.

The words told a truth of such poignancy that the song could almost have been written for her. '*For I saw you in my dreams, and saw the night within your heart.*' Every phrase built in volume and intensity, Catriona's voice soaring easily as it climbed the scale to a powerful crescendo. It wasn't like an aria, where an entire opera house would be filled with sound, this song had a throbbing intensity that was quite different: inward-looking, almost brooding. None of her listeners moved, they didn't seem even to breathe until the last note died into nothingness, the air still once more.

Catriona lowered the lid of the piano, her hands trembling a little. Giacomo clapped her efforts with a '*Brava!*' and she turned to smile her appreciation. When she did so, she saw that Silvana looked dumbfounded, her jaw frozen into a forced grimace of congratulation, obviously having expected the doctor to fumble through the song like a hopeless schoolgirl.

Suddenly embarrassed, Catriona finally dared look at Umberto. She felt as though he had seen her naked; she had poured so much that was honest and profound into the song that she couldn't believe her interpretation hadn't voiced all her secrets out loud to him.

She found him frozen like some adamantine statue, whether as a result of boredom or shock she couldn't tell. His voice, though, when it came, was thick with an emotion she found difficult to read.

'Thank you. I think that will do for tonight, I for one am tired.' He stood up abruptly and rang the bell on his side table. 'I'll ask Adelina to accompany you back to the lodge.'

*   *   *

Still dazed, Umberto rested one forearm on the edge of the mantelpiece, flexing his fingers in and out of a fist in a restless gesture, his mind whirling. He had recognized her as soon as she had started to sing. Catriona de Vere: that was the name she had gone by in those far-off days.

Ever since the woman who had introduced herself as Catherine Drouot had arrived, something about her had fascinated him but, in truth, he hadn't fully accepted it. Even her scent had stirred something in the depths of his memory that he didn't want to face. Now he knew why. In the back of his mind she had always reminded him of his Caterina.

His Caterina … what was he thinking?

Umberto sighed and dropped into his chair by the fireplace. The twigs snapped and popped in the hearth. He closed his eyes and pretended he could see the flames dancing against the walls of his bedroom. He could remember how the fire had looked as the reflection of it had played on Caterina's young body all those years ago, how it had caressed her flawless skin. It had seemed that she was wrapped in light – a shimmering creature, more fragile than the finest crystal, her daintiness inspiring awe, every line of her lovely self so wondrously perfect. She had looked so pure and innocent, so very beautiful, it had stolen his breath away. He had stood almost frozen, afraid that if he had dared move or speak or touch her, that enchanted moment would shatter and never again would he know such unspeakable delight. And then she had come forward with need and desire shining in her eyes and offered herself to him. At that moment, the earth had turned upside down and he had lost his head.

He smiled grimly and took a large mouthful of brandy. Ah, the incomparable flavour, the warmth, the spicy tang of a good cognac. It took his mind off the darkness around him for a few seconds. But tonight, nothing could drive away thoughts of the woman who had just sent him reeling. In ten years, her speaking voice had matured further into a more assured and measured version of her teenage self. Perhaps that's why he hadn't immediately recognized it. And of course she hadn't been speaking in her native tongue. Yet he could never forget that sublime singing voice. This evening, it had made the hairs on the back of his neck stand up.

He still remembered her extraordinary performance at the competition in Nice. She would have made a wonderful opera singer. He wondered why she had given that up. At the time she had been so sure of where she was going and what she wanted to be – having won the contest, it seemed a great pity she hadn't pursued her dream.

Of course, she'd been very young; people changed, their circumstances changed … She had fallen in love, it seemed, married, had a child – she had almost certainly been faced with choices and, as he well knew, a career in the limelight did not always make for stability and happiness.

Now, chance had put her back on his path. It was strange, the way fate played games with people's lives. Ten years ago, she had been the young pupil in awe of him, the rising star; today, she was in the driving seat. Umberto shook his head. It irritated him that his pride stung at the irony of the young Caterina now calling the shots. In fact, he found everything about this situation unsettling.

Of course, *she* knew who he was. His annoyance grew as he thought about her subterfuge. But then again it was Calandra who had obviously approached her, so he couldn't blame Caterina for the twists and turns of destiny, he supposed. Professionally, she would need to keep her personal identity from him, he could see that. Still, why had she taken the job? From what he understood, it had meant more or less turning her life upside down. Was it for the money? Of course, a great deal of money was at stake. Still, the reports he'd received were that her clinic was doing well. He remembered that Caterina was half English. Naturally, with the small fortune she would be receiving for this assignment, she could double the size of her business, maybe open a clinic in England.

Was that truly the reason she was here? Somehow he doubted it. Everything about her presence at Villa Monteverdi now intrigued him. Umberto took another gulp of cognac, listening to the sound of the wind increasing outside. Now, more than ever, he wished for his sight back so that he could look at Caterina de Vere once more.

Umberto's perception had become so much sharper since he had lost his eyesight – his touch, smell and taste were now hypersensitive – and that evening, even though she was a sight denied to him, Caterina had excited his senses. He'd suddenly recognized the perfume she had worn all those years back, Aqua Allegoria Mandarine Basilic, and within seconds, the memory of that fragrance, mingling with the scent of her arousal that night at Villa Rossini, had hit him like a sledgehammer, making his body grow as hot as the flames now licking at the logs beside him.

He had often thought of that night in Villefranche and of Caterina, especially when he had returned to France after four years of relentless work in the States to give a concert in Nice. He'd tried to find her again and had ended up at Le Beaumont Club restaurant in Saint Paul de Vence, where Batiste, the head waiter, had given him the photograph that had been taken of the two of them over dinner.

He had been back to the Conservatoire, but no one could tell him what had become of her. He had even gone up to Les Charmilles one afternoon and, finding the house was closed, had asked the gardener about the occupants. He had informed Umberto that they had moved away when the *mademoiselle* had married.

He remembered feeling surprised by the strong pang of disappointment he felt, envy almost, before putting her out of his mind. He'd told her to forget about him, hadn't he? Consign their night of passion to a cherished memory. And so she had, it seemed – within a year marrying some other man and having his child. His chest tightened. All those years ago, had Caterina actually meant more to him than just a random sexual romp?

The second time he'd returned to France was for a concert in Paris, two weeks before the accident. Umberto had drunk more than he should before the performance, and after it too, and his thoughts had been hazy. He'd had a fight with his agent, who had wanted him to go through more television interviews, more tours. The composer's downward spiral had already started months before. He'd had enough of the limelight and tramping around the world. It turned out the opportunity he'd seized hadn't given Umberto the life he'd expected. All he wanted at that point was to be left alone to compose, just for himself, and not because of some projected career plan.

That night a woman had been standing outside the opera house and had called out his name. As she stood in the shadows she had seemed familiar, but he'd thought at the time that the effects of the alcohol had made him imagine it. Only later had it suddenly dawned upon him that Caterina was the lady in furs and jewels who had approached him. She must still remember, he'd thought, but yet again the whirlwind of fame and his schedule had taken up all his time and he had postponed his intention of looking her up. Then the accident had happened, rendering him a human wreck.

Holding his cognac, Umberto rested the glass on the arm of his chair and closed his eyes. His mind clung to the notion that Caterina still remembered their night of passion. It was said that one never forgot the first time. What had her husband been like? She was a widow now. Had there been other men, too? He probably had no right to know such personal matters. Still, once she had been his …

Umberto dismissed such foolish thoughts. It did no good to think of her in this way. Perhaps he hadn't been served well by his sight in those days. Had he been blind then, he might have listened more closely to his heart. He sighed. There was more than one way to be blind, it seemed.

What might have happened if that night had ended differently? If he'd stayed in Nice? Umberto had immediately guessed Caterina's infatuation for him, and he had been flattered, but she had seemed inaccessible and, because of her young age, he had tried very hard to put brakes on his desire all through that evening. It had taken so much of his willpower – after all, he had been young too. But old enough to know better. Caterina had been like the bud of a flower not yet exposed to the light, closed and mysterious. Then when she had so candidly offered herself to him and they had made love, the little bud had opened and bloomed out of all recognition, lavishly spreading its intoxicating fragrance, and something in his heart was forever changed.

Now Umberto realized with a shock that in every woman he had dated or slept with after her, it had been Caterina he'd been looking for. Meeting her again all these years later, nothing had changed. He'd been so busy resisting 'the *Dottoressa*'s' attempts to get inside his head, he had failed to see what was happening to him. Each time he was in Caterina's presence, he'd experienced a troublesome state of excitement, one he sought to conquer by baiting her, if only to distract himself. She merely had to stand near to him and his pulse accelerated.

Umberto hadn't had a woman since his accident and tonight the ache was overwhelming. It shocked and alarmed him a little because it was a different ache, a different need to the one he felt during the lonely days and nights spent in darkness. It was a desire prompted by Caterina's presence under his roof, conjuring up confusing emotions that tortured him, body and soul. It seemed that he wanted her more than ever, with a scorching passion that he couldn't remember having felt before, even on that night at Villa Rossini.

The woman she was now was as intoxicating as the teenager she had been then. Her voice, her smell, her touch still had the power to move him as no other woman had. Umberto's heart squeezed and he shook his head, a helpless laugh escaping him – fate was cruel sometimes.

The door of the French windows began to bang intermittently in the wind. Umberto opened his eyes and set his glass down on the table. Standing up, he automatically calculated the steps from his chair across the room to the glass doors and felt for the fastenings. As he was securing them, he smiled to himself.

Tomorrow, he would find out the real reason why Caterina de Vere had come back into his life … and if, and when, she was planning to admit who she really was.

CHAPTER 12

The next morning, Catriona entered the piano room feeling a flutter of trepidation. Would Umberto be angry, silent or blithely upbeat again, as he'd been out riding yesterday?

The night before, after she had sung *Ich Grolle Nicht*, she had been unable to read his mood; partly, she admitted, because her own feelings had spun out of control when she had been taken over by the song. Now, for the first time in years, she felt at sea: her whole career thus far had been spent learning about the brain. She had worked with clients who had every kind of neurological disorder or peculiarity, but here she was, unable to work out what was going on in the mind of the man she was meant to be treating. And she called herself a therapist! Catriona braced herself and, for the hundredth time since arriving at Lake Como, berated herself for her weakness, promising that this time she would put her professional training to good use.

The white room was bathed in sunshine. Outside, the opera of dappled light filtering through the trees at this hour had become all the more powerful – it was as if the golden rays were being conducted by an invisible baton that brought them together into a song that called forth everything beautiful.

This time, Catriona's client was standing at the French windows with his back to her as if looking out beyond the patio with its wisteria and trailing vines to the brilliant azure of the sky and the still waters of the lake. What was he thinking? She had thought about how should she begin the session but now her head was empty except for the sound of her beating heart, which seemed to thunder in her mind, fracturing her thoughts.

Then Umberto turned and she sensed a veiled aggression in his stance. He didn't look guarded or withdrawn so much as watchful, quizzical. Her first instinctive thought was that somehow he had found out about Michael and her real identity. Then she discounted the idea, concluding it was only her guilt at being here incognito that was feeding her paranoia.

'Ah, *Dottoressa*. I'll call you that for now as it's our formal therapy session. Plus, I know you'll be going on about professional boundaries again if I'm not careful.' His tone was ironic, not particularly warm. 'So, what have you got in store for me this morning? Should I lie on the couch?'

'Certainly not!' Catriona gave a nervous laugh. 'But let's sit down and we can talk. Later, I propose we move to the piano.' At her words she saw something flash in his green eyes only to be replaced immediately by shuttered calm. Undaunted, she continued: 'It's time we start working with music so that you can experience what it has to offer.'

They sat down, he on the sofa this time, she on the chair next to it. Gone was the brandy on the tray; now there was simply the jug of water and two glasses, everything conforming to what was proper. So why did she feel that he was toying with her in some way?

Catriona cleared her throat; Umberto folded his arms. His smile was perfectly benign yet she could have sworn there was an edge of hostility there.

She began, taking refuge in the safe barricades offered by her professional identity, keeping the territory neutral and safe for now: 'Have you ever heard of the Mozart Effect?'

'I don't believe I have. Perhaps you'd like to explain. You have an hour, and I'm all ears.' Again, there was a derisive chill to his words.

She tried not to wriggle uncomfortably and kept her tone even. 'Dr Alfred Tomatis, a Frenchman, wrote a book called *Pourquoi Mozart*, claiming that Mozart's music had particular vibrational properties that promoted healing and development of the brain.'

'*Pourquoi pas* Beethoven or Bach for that matter? I can't see why Mozart should get all the glory.'

So that's how it's going to be, thought Catriona. There was something not just playful but scoffing in his tone. But at least he was conversing; with many of her clients, she was met with a frozen wall of incommunicative silence.

'Well, I think it comes down to those particular qualities of Mozart's music,' she answered. 'The thinking is that neither the tidal wave of emotion you get with Beethoven nor the tapestry of sound of the mathematical genius of Bach quite does the job.'

'Not too fast, not too slow. Just right? Like Baby Bear's porridge.' His voice still leaked irony, although on the surface it was perfectly good humoured. Humouring her, more like. It felt to Catriona that he was patronizing her and she fought to maintain her sangfroid.

'I suppose you could say that. Apparently, there are monks in Brittany who play Mozart to their cows to give more milk. And in Japan, they're using it to make yeast grow thicker so they get the best *sake*.'

He arched a dark brow. 'And you believe this? Come on, *Dottoressa*. I do hope you're not going to take such a narrow-track approach with me.'

'Actually, no. I've never been able to believe in a one-size-fits-all sort of therapy so you're spared.' She gave a slightly awkward smile and then wondered if he could sense her discomfort.

'Often the loss of sight is like being grief-stricken after losing the thing or person most dear in the world. There is shock, denial, mourning, depression. In the past I've treated patients who go about their everyday lives feeling frozen, like a walking zombie. Then a piece of music will catch them by surprise, melting the ice around their heart, and that opens the door into feeling emotion once more.'

Her voice had a commanding intensity and in the seconds of silence that followed, it was if the planes of Umberto's face had shifted, softened. Then the sardonic mask reasserted itself.

'Frozen sounds good to me. Anaesthetized is preferable, I would have thought. Alcohol only goes so far.'

'Oh, but you cannot hope to get better like that,' blurted Catriona, frustrated.

A humourless laugh escaped him. 'So, you'd rather I was throwing plates at the wall and shouting the place down?'

'Strong emotions I can work with. If I can use music to "contain" certain feelings for a period of time so that they can be explored, examined and worked through, we really are on the road to recovery.'

He gave an irritated sigh. 'Sounds rather like the dentist's chair to me.'

Catriona smiled wryly. 'I can see the analogy, though I don't much like it. You see, a person can be mute, roaring, violent … unable to put into words the emotion they're feeling or what it is that is most disturbing them, and music therapy can still work its power. That's the beauty of it. It's non-verbal and has a very particular way of getting to the unconscious to tackle the issues that haven't even shaped themselves into words yet.'

'*Mi creda, Dottoressa*, believe me, *Dottoressa*, you would not want to see me roaring and violent.' Umberto gave a twisted smile. 'I'll save that for the sanctity of my room, if you don't mind.'

'I understand, and that's fine,' said Catriona. 'So, I've devised a different plan for you.' She pressed on boldly: 'When I was a little girl, I got fed up with a particularly strict piano teacher.

Everything was so regimented … "Do this, do that, lift your wrists, curl your fingers, straighten your back". After a year of it I'd had enough. I swore I would never touch the instrument again.'

Umberto turned his head a fraction. 'So, why did you?'

'My mother found a new teacher. He was so clever, he told me I was only allowed to play the piano for ten minutes a day. I should practise, but no more than that. It was a marvellous piece of reverse psychology. The moment I sat down to play, I became so involved that I couldn't bear to stop after ten minutes … After that, problem sorted.'

'So, how does this relate to me?' said Umberto, amused detachment seeping into his question.

'You will play, but for no more than ten minutes at a time. And you can play anything. I suggest nursery rhymes – "Frère Jacques" or "Fra' Martino" as you call it in Italy, something as simple as that. Bit by bit, you will be drawn back into the love of playing, of composition. That is my hypothesis.'

'Ah, and you think me so perverse that I'll do it just to prove you wrong, do you?' he laughed. 'And then it'll be too late and magically it will work.'

At this, Catriona couldn't contain herself. The sheer waste of talent, of years that he could have spent composing, had upset her more than she realized.

'You mustn't give up. It grieves me to watch so much talent being thrown away and I'm here to help you make that first step that will bring you and your genius back to the public who adore you. Do you realize the gap you've left in the music world by moving into the shadows?'

Umberto made a dismissive noise and got to his feet, searching in his pocket for his cigarettes. Finding the packet empty, he glowered and made his way over to the French windows. Without a word, he stepped on to the terrace, bracing his hands on the balustrade.

Catriona knew he needed time to absorb what she had said. On impulse, she got up and walked over to the glass-fronted, walnut cabinet and scanned the various leather-bound volumes until she spied something tucked away at the end of the second shelf. Pulling it out, she found it to be a folder of handwritten music. Her eyes skimmed over the pages with their occasional scribbles in the margins and orchestral notations. It was clear that they were Umberto's own compositions. Her breath caught in her throat: this was the scheme for a piano concerto. Hadn't Calandra mentioned that Umberto had started to compose a new one?

Crossing to the Steinway, she propped the papers up on the music stand and very softly began to pick out the notes with one finger. The melody line was exquisite, plaintive and sad, yet with a sureness to each note that bespoke a complete mastery on the part of the composer. Entranced, she played it through, adding more of the harmony each time so that it gained richness and depth. Suddenly the French windows crashed open. '*Che diavolo crede di fare?* What d'you think you're doing?' Umberto was standing in the doorway to the terrace, his expression thunderous.

Catriona jumped and swivelled on the stool, her amber eyes shining with excitement as she smiled up at him.

'Umberto, when did you compose this? This concerto is absolutely beautiful!'

His voice was low when he spoke but she could hear the undertones of anger that he was trying to control. 'You will please put that away, *subito*, at once and don't ever mention it again.'

'But Umberto, it's beautiful. You can play this, I know you can. You've written it, every note of this music is locked inside you.' She needed to get through to him somehow. 'Sight is not an absolute requisite for a pianist. Once you've regained confidence and learned the art of being blind, which you seem to have already mastered, it would be perfectly possible to make a distinguished career again and this looks as though it's as brilliant as anything you've composed before, if not better!'

'Put it back!' Umberto said forcefully. 'I never want to hear that concerto again.' His chest was heaving. 'I have no wish to finish it.'

Realizing she had gone too far, Catriona went back to the cabinet in silence, returning the folder to its original place while Umberto's face was averted from her, dark and brooding.

Finally, his anger spent, he turned his sightless but still beautiful emerald eyes towards her. There was a new tension in him that was nothing to do with his previous anger as he crossed his arms over his broad chest. His change of mood was as capricious and extreme as ever.

'Why are you here, Caterina?'

The shock and unexpectedness of the question completely disconcerted her. *He knows. He must know. But how?* Oh, that voice and the way he said her name … it rolled over her like silk. How did he make it sound so sensual, a breeze blowing over naked skin?

'We've already gone through all that.' She made a brave attempt to answer evenly, trying not to pay too much attention to the butterflies fluttering in her stomach.

'Are you going to answer me or ignore me?'

'I'm not ignoring you, but we need to move forward.'

'I need to know what you look like.'

'I really don't think that's important.'

'How do you expect me to confide in you if I don't even know how you look?'

Catriona exhaled a shaky breath. He was toying with her again and she realized helplessly that she was no longer the one in control. 'There's nothing to get excited about. I'm very plain. Tall, slim, with long brown hair and brown eyes.'

'I bet they look black when you're angry,' Umberto said, warming to his theme though unable to see how unnerved Catriona was by his uncannily perceptive image of her, almost as if he knew the person he was describing. 'And you have a rather reserved face,' he continued. 'You wear very little make-up and a discreet scent, which probably means that you don't want to attract men.'

Where had he learnt that bit of psychology? She didn't know what to answer.

'Exactly! I have a very ordinary face and I'm a very ordinary person really.'

He gave her another of his twisted smiles. 'I've heard that you are actually very beautiful and not at all ordinary.'

She walked over to her chair and stood there perplexed, wondering what should be her next move.

There was a hint of lazy humour in his voice now. 'Adelina described you to me. She said you had an elegant, interesting beauty, like one of those gazelles that I used to hunt up in the hills.' He inclined his head to one side and added: 'But she also said that she could read in the depth of your eyes a certain sadness. So, what do you have to say about that, *dottoressa* Drouot?'

'This is not about me.'

'I like to know the people I am dealing with. Tell me about your life.'

'You've had my CV. My life holds nothing of interest to you.'

'That's not quite true. Tell me, was your husband your first love, Caterina? You were widowed young, yet the report that was sent to me says that you have no attachments except for your mother and son. Are you staying faithful to his memory? That's quite unusual for a beautiful woman, don't you think?' A harsh quality had permeated his tone.

Catriona faced up to him squarely. 'All you need to know is that I am very competent at my job and that's why I was recommended to you.'

Umberto took a few measured steps back into the room and sat down on the sofa again. He tilted his head towards her as she remained standing next to her chair, almost unable to move. 'What was his name? Was he French?'

'His name was Hugue and yes, he was French.'

'Was he handsome? Did his body make you go wild with desire?'

Her eyes widened in alarm at this sudden audacity but she kept calm. 'I don't see what all this has to do with you or this job.'

'Are you the secretive type, Caterina?'

'This conversation is going nowhere.'

'What are you afraid of, *eh*?'

'I'm not afraid.'

'Prove it. Sit next to me and let me feel if the mask I've imagined fits your face.'

He seemed to be enjoying the somewhat playful antagonism volleying between them. She could see that he was working himself into a dangerous mood.

'Don't be ridiculous. You're the one who's afraid.' She regretted this unprofessional response as soon as it was out of her mouth.

He let out a derisive laugh. 'Me? You're mad.'

'Am I?' Catriona challenged. Anger warred with intuition and won. 'You're afraid that your talent has left you, along with your sight. You're afraid of looking foolish, of people talking about you, pitying you, instead of being thankful for your remaining blessings. You could have died in that accident but you are alive and healthy and armed with a brilliant gift, and you're wasting every second you don't do something about this. You think that by—'

As fast as lightning and as if he had the full use of his eyes, Umberto grabbed her wrist with steel fingers, twisting her hard and pulling her towards him. Catriona let out a cry as she was propelled forward, landing almost on top of him.

'How dare you!' she gasped, trying to thrust him away, her hands pushing at his broad chest and inadvertently touching his bare skin through the opening of his shirt. *Oh, the warm smoothness of that skin* … And despite herself, she was reminded of their night of love so long ago.

Catriona wriggled, attempting to pull herself out of his grasp, but he was holding her tight and she found herself sitting on his lap, the proof of his desire pushing against her thigh.

'You're afraid of me,' he whispered in her ear, his hot breath fanning her cheek. 'You're afraid of my touch, afraid of what it will awaken in you.'

Oh yes, she was afraid of his touch, afraid of remembering. Afraid now that he knew who she really was … 'Just because I don't want you pawing me doesn't mean I'm afraid of you,' she managed to say through clenched teeth, still fighting to disentangle herself from his embrace.

'Stop fighting me, Caterina. Relax, I won't hurt you. Just let me pass my fingers over your face to make sure that the picture I have of you in my mind is real,' he said in a quiet voice, which reminded her of the balmy breeze that fills the air just before a hurricane rips reality in half.

She should have objected or at least mouthed a word of protest, but Catriona realized to her horror that she was even more vulnerable to her emotions now than she had been ten years ago. She could feel his need for her growing out of control and the sudden flip in her stomach told her that nothing much had changed: he could still turn her on, still make her melt with desire. Part of her was desperate for him to make love to her again, even though she knew that it would be complete madness.

She stopped fighting him, now held too tightly in the vice of her own seething hormones to try any longer.

Oh God, get a grip! What is the matter with me? Why does this man have so much power over me?

Umberto's hand moved up to gently caress the heat of her cheek and she shivered.

'Your skin is like satin.' Brushing the tips of his fingers along her jaw, he settled two of them on her mouth, tracing her lips, learning the shape and curve of them, teasing the crease until they parted.

A voice at the back of her mind reprimanded her, but she could think of nothing but the feel of his hard body under hers and the touch of his fingers on her lips.

'*Ti voglio così tanto …*' he murmured raggedly against her neck.

She wanted him too, ached with wanting him, and knew she had done so ever since she'd set eyes on him again – *had she ever stopped wanting him*? A sob of desperation welled but came out only as a breathy moan as she felt a rush of liquid heat settle between her thighs. Denying those feelings any longer was pointless. Now was now, tomorrow could take care of itself.

She flicked her tongue along his fingers and he gave a tortured sound in his throat. 'Caterina,' he breathed as he crushed his mouth against hers in a kiss of total need and possession, burning hotter with each stroke of his tongue, moving sensually over her teeth, before dipping into the darkness within. He tasted rich and real, of masculine heat, peppermint and warm brandy – *had he been drinking*? – and she let herself go with the sensation, the ecstasy of him filling her mouth.

The length of Catriona's body was curved against Umberto's, making her fully aware of his arousal, the warm strength of his desire and, as his hands moved caressingly up and down the length of her spine, she could feel her body moulding even closer against his. She melted into his arms, his lips warm and firm against hers; this was no gentle, exploratory kiss, but an explosive one, releasing the passion that had been instantly there between them, simmering beneath the surface until now. It was as if ten years hadn't really elapsed since they had last been in each other's arms, as if fate had only been biding its time until this moment, waiting for them to find each other again.

One of his hands found her breast and she gasped as his fingers grazed her nipple, searing through the light fabric. His touch was a brand on her, exploring, pushing, urgent and hot. Need radiated inside her like wildfire, the flames spreading wider until every part of her was alight. She couldn't stop this even if she wanted to … and at this moment she didn't want to, she wanted all the pleasure Umberto had shown her at Villefranche, wanted again that singeing warmth of desire … once … just once more …

But she stopped!

'Caterina …?' Umberto asked dazedly as she pulled abruptly away, trembling, trying to control the flames of passion licking at her body. He frowned, at a loss to understand the reason for her sudden action. *'Cosa c' è, mio tesoro*? What is it, my treasure? I'm not trying to rush you.' He shook his head, one hand moving up to caress her face, his frown returning as she flinched from that touch.

Catriona wrenched away from him completely and stood up, breathing heavily. Her eyes darkened until they looked like smouldering coal. 'This is not only unethical, it's … it's wrong,' she managed to say in a tremulous voice.

'It felt right to me. What is so wrong in two people finding pleasure in each other's company?'

She could feel the colour still flooding her cheeks and the intense dryness in her mouth that made the notion of speaking seem like a chore. Her head felt as heavy as lead and the ache between her thighs was torture, but she forced herself to keep her chin lifted because she wasn't going to cower away and pretend that nothing had happened. Somehow she needed to claw back the upper hand, to be once more in control of a situation that she was in danger of losing for good.

'This had nothing to do with finding pleasure in each other's company,' she said, feverishly tucking her blouse back into her skirt.

Umberto gave a short laugh. 'You're now going to tell me that you didn't enjoy any of it, I suppose?'

She wished her voice didn't sound so infuriatingly husky as she replied: 'That's not the point.'

His lips curved into a mischievous smile. 'I thought it was exactly the point. Anyway, your sessions are meant to relieve my stress, my so-called depression. Well, this is a – let's say – different interpretation of "therapy". Nothing is more soothing, more calming and relaxing than a little of what you French call *pelotage*, petting … When I started to touch you, you seemed turned on, so I did exactly what you wanted me to do.'

'You're outrageous,' she breathed. 'I must go now. I'm not sure I can continue with this assignment under these circumstances. We will resume our conversation later, *signore*.'

At her words a muscle twitched in Umberto's cheek and he appeared to be fighting to control a strong emotion. His face was flushed, his jaw clenched with exasperation, and she could see that he was desperately trying to hold himself in iron reserve. His lean body seemed to embody all that was primitive and, underneath it all, Catriona sensed his simmering mood, the desire to impale her like a moth on a pin and watch her flutter helplessly while finding out her innermost secrets.

Her mind and her senses still in chaos, she glanced at him once more before picking up her bag and rushing out of the room. How could she possibly stay at Villa Monteverdi after this? The sands of time were running out. Soon, she would have to confront Umberto with the truth.

*   *   *

Umberto heard the click of the door close behind Catriona as she left the room. He was stunned at how much his passion for her had returned like a wild tornado. Desire still throbbed at his groin as he imagined the sweetness of her hand stroking him there. In his mind's eye she was guiding him into her soft, moist warmth as she had done all those years ago and he recalled the way her body had moved in the light of the glowing flames as he caressed every part of her, tracing each contour with his fingers.

He knew her skin was smooth and soft; he knew the way she moaned with pleasure when parting her thighs, eager for his touch, for his hot mouth, for his possession; it still filled his head and his senses. He could almost smell ... taste her sweet feminine juice. Actually, in a room crammed with hundreds of bodies he could have picked out her subtle womanly fragrance. He was sure it had nothing to do with some sensory compensation he had developed, it had all come back to him vividly when their lips touched a few minutes ago.

There was no doubt of her identity now.

Umberto grimaced. He had to face the fact that he had started off on the wrong foot. He shouldn't have been so impatient, pulling her on to him as he had done. That might be the way to act with most of the women he had encountered in his jaded life, but not Caterina, she was made of gentler stuff. His throat tightened as emotions swelled in his chest.

He rose to his feet and, with that firm tread that would deceive anyone who didn't know he was blind, went to the table by the French windows to find some more cigarettes. He leaned his shoulder against the glass door, his brows drawn together as he took one from the golden box and lit it, taking a deep lungful of the smoke and expelling it through taut nostrils.

She got what she deserved. She wanted you as much as you wanted her, a defensive voice inside him whispered, but self-justification didn't make him feel any better ... nothing would, except an apology.

Umberto squirmed at the idea. He hadn't apologized to a female since he was fourteen years old – Silvana had spotted him watching her through the leaves of a willow tree as she bathed naked in the lake. Quick as a flash, she had run and caught up with him. He still winced inside when he remembered the humiliation she had put him through, insisting even after he had said he was sorry that he drop his shorts and show her the bulge that had stretched the fabric taut across his thighs. She had then touched him right on the tip, exclaiming: '*Santo cielo, e' così grosso…* Good heavens, yours is so big!' and to his shame his milky fluid had exploded in a strong, uncontrollable jet all over her hand.

He had apologized profusely again and Silvana had brushed off the incident with a shrug. The next day, she asked him if he wanted to go for a swim, naked, in the lake. That had been the beginning of a summer of forbidden games when she had taught him how to please a woman's body with a finesse way beyond his years. By that time her virginity had long gone, lost in inept romps in the hay with a couple of stable boys who had not lived up to her expectations. That summer, when the incident with Umberto had occurred at the lake, she'd been looking for greener pastures. Silvana had been very matter-of-fact about the whole thing. No challenges, no games – an eager participant, full stop. This state of affairs went on for three more summers and then on and off until music competitions and recitals absorbed all his time.

Once Umberto's career had taken off and after he'd returned from the States, Silvana had often been at his side, sharing in the social whirl and the partying; they'd enjoyed their casual games in bed once more, but only when it suited him. He would never let her have the upper hand ever again. Silvana's physical allure and oozing sex appeal, while undeniable, now seemed merely a symbol of his past life, of empty glamour and success.

Silvana's whole persona was dazzling, of course. Still, as the memory of Caterina's beauty sprung to life in his mind, he had to admit the Frenchwoman was in a different league – so much more subtle and mysterious. Almost subdued by comparison with Silvana's more blatant charms, somehow it was far more exciting once Caterina's passion had been unleashed because it was such a surprise. He guessed Silvana's sixth sense had somehow recognized that.

Only now did he fully acknowledge that he had found the young Caterina hard to forget after their night in Villefranche; the memory of her had haunted him for a long time afterwards. Maybe that had been partly why he'd never committed to Silvana, or any other woman for that matter. Umberto frowned. If Silvana were to find out the truth about Caterina's identity and their liaison a decade ago, she would undoubtedly make trouble. He drew deeply on his cigarette, enjoying the aroma of the mild, woody tobacco, and found himself missing the simple sight of the smoke spiralling away from him in the air. He breathed out thickly. His conscience was weighing heavily on him.

He rang for Adelina, who arrived promptly.

'You haven't eaten so I brought you something for lunch,' she told him. 'Bread and cheese with Parma ham.'

He waved a hand in the air. 'I'm not hungry, *grazie*. Maybe later. Have you seen *dottoressa* Drouot?'

A quiet, disapproving noise accompanied the clatter of the tray as she placed it on the coffee table. 'The last time I saw her was twenty minutes ago. She was going towards the lodge.'

'Do you think you could pick me a small bouquet of flowers? Violet hyacinths and white orchids, I think.' In his previous years of courting, Umberto had often used flowers to relay his message to women and he knew the right flowers for an apology.

'You have upset the *Dottoressa*, *eh*? That is not good.' Adelina was talking to him in the way she used to when he was a little boy and had done something wrong.

Umberto shrugged. 'Women are so complicated.'

'This one is different …'

'D'you think?'

'*Sì, sì … è una persona sensibile*, she is a sensitive person, not at all the type you usually brought home.'

'*Per l'amor del cielo*! I didn't "bring her home", as you put it, Adelina. She's here in a professional capacity. Besides, you've never approved of any of the women I've known before, except for Sofia.'

Adelina sighed. '*Sofia era un angelo e per questo Dio l'ha rivoluta con se' così presto*, Sofia was an angel and for that reason, God called her back so early.'

'It seems callous to even say it now, after what happened, but I would hardly call her an angel.'

Adelina nodded. 'Maybe angelic is not the right word,' she conceded. 'But she was wholesome, very close to the earth, and she *did* love you, God rest her soul.'

'At the end of our relationship I felt only manipulated, then trapped. Sofia got pregnant on purpose, she admitted as much. And it was at precisely the moment I was seeking to disentangle myself from her. What could be worse?'

'I admit it was underhanded, but she was a young girl from a poor background, who didn't know any better. She reckoned on your mother making things right for her.'

Umberto ran a hand through his hair. At the time he'd felt used but recalling the whole tragedy now, he didn't know what to think. 'Calandra insisted I do the proper thing and ask her to marry me. But I didn't love her, so how could I?'

'*La signora* Calandra was a woman of principle, but I know she wasn't pleased at the match.'

'Of course she wasn't. She deplored what she called my promiscuous life.' He smiled ruefully. '"*Your life is dictated by that thing you have between your legs, not the one you have between your ears*" was one of her favourite phrases.'

Adelina chuckled. 'I used to tell her that a man must sow his wild oats while he is young. If not, how is he expected to stay

faithful to one woman all his life? And she used to answer crossly
that *women* are expected to stay faithful so why not men? And I
admit my reasoning didn't stand up.'

Umberto felt for the ashtray on the table and stubbed out his
cigarette. 'I would have given the child my name and it would have
lacked for nothing, but I couldn't share a lifetime with Sofia. You
must admit we didn't have much in common. She would have
made a wonderful wife to one of the local farmers but not to a
composer and performer – she didn't even like classical music.
We were worlds apart.'

'*Lo so. C'ero anch'io*, I know, I was there. You were very young,
of course. Too young to be saddled with a wife and child, and you
had your career to think about. But you were wrong to have taken
her to your bed in the first place, even if you were not the first.'

A shadow passed over Umberto's face. 'When she died … that
was a terrible thing she did.'

The housekeeper crossed to the sofa, automatically plumping
up the cushions and smoothing them back into place. The patting
sounds paused. 'Sofia had a love of nature, animals and of life
itself. *Gesù Santo*, suicide, would never have crossed her mind,
even in the worst circumstances.'

'I know you never believed she could have done it. But who
could possibly have wanted her dead? In the end, it was the only
conclusion that made any sense at all.' Umberto didn't need his
sight to sense from Adelina's silence that she was still buying
none of it.

At the time, an investigation had been launched, of course.
Umberto would have been the prime suspect in a murder inquiry
but, as he'd had a cast-iron alibi, the local *polizia* very soon closed
the case. Sofia wouldn't have been the first girl who had got herself
in trouble and looked for a way out through suicide.

Afterwards, Umberto had been advised by Calandra to stay
away from the villa on Lake Como for a while until the whole thing

had blown over. People have short memories, she assured him. However, what had happened to Sofia had not been forgotten. It only added to the regrets that haunted Umberto. Part of him had always thought that his blindness was a punishment.

'I wonder if things might have been different if I hadn't gone to the States all those years ago?' he muttered, half to himself.

Adelina had picked up another cushion but paused. 'What do you mean?'

Umberto shook his head. 'It's nothing.'

The housekeeper resumed her smoothing of the cushions and he could almost feel her speculative gaze on him.

'Don't try anything stupid with the *Dottoressa*,' she said suddenly and, not for the first time, Umberto noted Adelina's uncanny perception at work. 'I can tell that you like her.'

He breathed a sigh of resignation – nothing got past Adelina. 'It's more complicated than you know.'

'It's always complicated with you, Umberto,' she answered, the fond chiding obvious in her voice.

He couldn't help his mouth curling in amusement. 'So, what are we having for dinner?'

'*Pavese* soup and *vitello tonnato* with boiled new potatoes and a green salad.'

'That sounds splendid. I'll have dinner at the lodge tonight with *dottoressa* Drouot. Please could you bring us a tray with some good wine, some of your homemade cheese and bread and a selection of *frutta* from the orchard.'

Adelina gave him a sideways look. 'I'd be careful where I tread with the *Dottoressa*, if I were you. This woman is not a pushover, there's more to her than we understand.'

'Some things are inevitable,' he murmured.

'Just let her help you – and keep your appetite under control,' Adelina grumbled. 'I'll go and pick your bouquet but remember, a bouquet works only once. We cannot direct the wind, but we can adjust our sails. Do not play with fire this time – the flames may scorch you with scars that will never heal.'

Umberto laughed deep in his throat. A mischievous light glowed in his almost blank eyes. 'You forget that I'm an old hand at that game. It's the people who don't know how to play with fire who get burned.'

'*L'arroganza è un ostacolo sull'autostrada della saggezza*, arrogance is a roadblock on the highway of wisdom, my father always said,' Adelina mumbled glumly.

The old housekeeper took herself off, leaving Umberto pensive. He was thinking of his whirlwind night of passion with Caterina years before ... surely it had left its mark? The kiss and the brief, heated fondling they had just shared proved that at least she still desired him. For a moment she had surrendered totally to him and they had been transported back to that far-off night. But it was too early to expect more, he had been too impatient.

Adelina was soon back with the small bouquet. 'She's playing the piano at the lodge,' she told him. 'She plays beautifully. Maybe she will encourage you to go back to the concert halls again.'

'Don't be ridiculous,' he snapped. 'All that's finished for me ...'

'*La signora* Calandra would ...'

'Leave my mother where she is, may her soul rest in peace,' he barked angrily. 'You may have wiped my bottom when I was a baby but that doesn't give you the right to interfere in my life today.'

Adelina didn't answer but he heard her sigh as she left the room and he immediately felt guilty for having lost his temper. She was used to his mood swings, especially since the accident, but that was no excuse for being hurtful.

Umberto went to the coffee table and poured himself a large cognac, downing it in one, then sat down to eat what Adelina had brought for him. He didn't feel remotely hungry, but he had known the housekeeper long enough to work out that if he did justice to her food, it was one sure way of pleasing her. It helped assuage his guilt for causing her grief. *I don't know how she puts up with me*, he thought to himself ruefully.

He spent some time smoking, still deliberating whether or not to go down to the lodge to apologize. He hated the idea, but he hated even more the thought of Caterina packing her bags and leaving.

Swallow your pride and do the right thing, he told himself. Fate had put her on his path and it wasn't often one was given a second bite at the apple. Then the knowledge that nothing could ever come of this hit him. What could he offer Caterina now but his anger, his bitterness and his pain? Umberto hit the wall with his fist. Still, a part of him held on to the fact that no other woman had ever affected him like this. And there had been many women before.

He poured himself another finger of cognac and then, armed with his bouquet and cane, made his way out of the French windows and along the narrow path that led from his music room to the lodge.

*   *   *

It was mid-afternoon. The birds were almost silent, the cuckoos had ceased their singing although wood pigeons were still cooing; the crickets were chirping away. The only sound Umberto could hear clearly was the loud hammering of his heart in his chest.

He had almost reached the door when he heard Catriona gasp: 'Umberto?' She had probably seen him from an open window. He liked the way his name rolled off her tongue: a soft melody, a caress.

He heard her footsteps come to the door and then she opened it.

'I thought you might like these,' he said, holding out the bouquet. He smiled awkwardly, 'A peace offering.'

'I love flowers, thank you.' She took the bunch from him. Her hands were wet and cold. 'I've just had a quick swim in the lake … ' she sounded tentative 'but please come in, I'll make us a cup of coffee.'

Umberto cleared his throat. 'Actually, I came to apologize … I was out of line, it won't happen again.'

There was a slight pause and then she answered, '*Va bene, non pensiamoci piú*, it's fine, let's forget it.'

Had he just heard a tremor in her voice?

He followed Catriona into the kitchen. He knew the lodge like the back of his hand, having spent so much time there with his mother, especially since her illness. She drew a chair out for him and he sat at the kitchen table while she turned on the kettle.

'I need to get out of this wet bathing suit,' she told him. 'I won't be long.'

'Yes, yes, of course. I'll wait here.'

She was in a bathing suit … she was going to shower … Naked, she would be naked … Caterina naked … Caterina moaning with pleasure as he stroked her in the water … Images of the swimming session they'd had at Villefrache crowded his mind, the memories flooding back. A spasm of desire passed through his body, stirring him to a hardness that he tried to ignore. He was glad she had left the room. The pulse at his temple throbbed. He reached in his pocket, pulled out his cigarettes and lit one with trembling hands, inhaling deeply. Maybe he should leave now before the inevitable happened. The idea of being in close proximity to Caterina without being able to touch her was hell. He stood up and paced to the window. Clenching his fist, he groaned. What a fool he was to torment himself in this way …

'Umberto?' His name sounded with the musical allure of a flute. When he didn't answer, she came up to him and placed a hand on his shoulder. 'Are you all right?' she asked, concern lacing the clear notes of her voice.

'I'm fine.' He turned in her direction, smiling, and together they walked back to the kitchen table. Umberto felt for the chair and took a seat at one end.

She poured them each a cup of coffee and then filled a vase with water from the tap and arranged the flowers he'd brought her. 'These flowers are beautiful, thank you.'

'You're very welcome. Did you enjoy your swim?'

Catriona pulled out a chair and sat down at the table next to him. 'Yes, it was wonderful. It's the second time I've swum in the lake. The water seemed a little warmer this afternoon, it's lovely having no currents to worry about.'

'Calandra used to swim from the lodge, too. The little creek at the bottom of the steps is very protected.'

'This lodge is really idyllic, so peaceful and picturesque.'

'Calandra loved it. We spent some happy times together here.'

They sipped their coffee.

'I only met your mother when she came to the clinic. I've always been a fan.'

'Did you see her perform on stage?'

'Unfortunately not, but I collected many of her CDs.'

'She died before her time but the doctors promised me she would not suffer. A small consolation.' He gulped down his coffee, sensing her eyes on him.

'Shall we go next door?' she suggested. 'We could sit on the terrace outside the piano room. It's a lovely afternoon and it seems a pity to waste it indoors.'

Oh, he could see her coming a mile off. She was taking him to the piano room. The next thing, she would be asking him to play, Umberto thought, but he decided to enter into the game: he could always refuse.

She tried to take his arm to help him but he shook his head. 'I know the way, thanks.'

'I used the piano this afternoon.'

Wham! There … she had come out with it earlier than expected. 'It's a wonderful piano.'

'In that case, I'm glad I had it tuned.'

A brief silence fell between them. Umberto's jaw clenched slightly. At some point soon, she would be coaxing him to play for her. He had to nip it in the bud or before he knew it, she would be asking him to play in public.

'Look, we both know what you're trying to do. Like I said, I came here to apologize, and I don't want another battle or I'll only be bringing you another bunch of flowers. Just leave it for now. Please.'

'It was our talking of Calandra,' she answered cautiously. 'I think it reminded me how much she wanted you to play … to compose … again.'

'I've told you, I will not put myself out there again. I can just imagine the gossipmongers. "Umberto Monteverdi, he used to be a great player, a composer with such promise. What a waste, such a shame."' He ran a hand through his hair.

'You know, in a way it would almost have been better for me if I'd been killed in that car. There's something proud and splendid about going out on the crest of a wave of glory at the height of one's career, don't you think?' He gave a cynical laugh.

'But that's so wrong! You know the reason I love working with blind children? If a child has been cut off from the visual world, they'll usually make up for it with a very rich world of touch and sound,' Catriona explained earnestly.

'And you know why Calandra came to me? Because I had worked with blind children whose talents were off the scale. If one sense is removed, the brain compensates in remarkable, wonderful ways. Look at Beethoven.'

'He went deaf,' Umberto snorted. 'That doesn't count.'

'He was deprived of one of his senses, so it does. But haven't you ever thought how the orchestral works written after he went deaf are more gifted than those he wrote before?'

Umberto had to concede she had a point and gave a small nod.

'Well, anyway, that's what I think Calandra knew instinctively. It's not just that composing will save you, it's that the compositions will be so much richer for the very fact that you're blind. She was ambitious for you, she saw limitless possibilities.'

'Of course my mother was ambitious for me, Italian mothers always think the best of their sons.' His voice was warmly resonant. 'She was naturally biased so I'm not sure her view counts.'

'Have you heard of Maria Theresia von Paradis?'

'Mozart's friend? Famous for a musical memory almost as good as his, I seem to recall. Dedicated a piano concerto to her,' Umberto answered, feeling somewhat amazed at his own memory.

'Exactly. Well, she had been blind since childhood, which must have been responsible for some of her prodigious musical talent.'

'I don't know how you can prove that, Caterina. I know it suits your argument.'

'No, it's not that. You see, something rather strange happened to her. In her late teens, she got back a little vision while being treated by the famous doctor, Franz Mesmer. But what she found was that afterwards, she experienced a sharp decline in her ability to memorize and play music.'

'What happened afterwards? Did she ever recover her gift?' Umberto was rather enjoying the narrative, even though he felt himself being led into the sticky web of Catriona's persuasion.

'Luckily, Mesmer left Paris, ceased treating her, and her sight faded again. Instead of feeling bereft, she was delighted. You see, her talent returned and her brilliant career was back on track.'

Umberto frowned. 'I do find it annoyingly glib of you to keep harping on with that blindness-is-a-gift notion.'

'Well, you're so very resistant. All I'm asking is that you play something … anything … for a few short minutes. Yet at every turn, self-pity and arrogance prevent you doing anything to help yourself.'

Utter silence fell on the patio for a split second. Umberto felt himself pale as he turned his sightless gaze upon her.

'*What* did you say?'

'Just what you thought I said,' she replied resolutely. 'And as you can probably tell from my voice, I'm not smiling.'

'No,' he said slowly, 'you're not smiling. One doesn't when one tells someone the disagreeable truth, I suppose. Though it's somewhat unorthodox for the therapist to be telling her client he's arrogant and self-pitying, isn't it? But perhaps,' Umberto smiled wryly, 'your eyes are charcoal black.'

'Charcoal black?' she repeated, perplexed.

'I guessed your eyes would turn charcoal black when you were angry. I thought,' his smile deepened ruefully, 'just now, you sounded as though your eyes were that colour.'

She was silent. Had he scored the right note or was she really angry?

'You're very quiet.' Umberto frowned impatiently. 'Have you decided to be offended now or something?'

'N-no.'

'Then, what's the matter?'

Catriona sighed. 'I didn't mean … I shouldn't have said …'

'You meant exactly what you said,' he told her drily. 'And you were perfectly right to say it. I *am* arrogant. I suppose I've always rather fancied myself that way. And unless there's someone there to check me fairly brutally at times, I suppose I might become self-pitying. Arrogant people do when the tide turns against them.'

'Well, I'm here to help and, hopefully, not in too brutal a way,' Catriona said, falteringly. 'I've always admired your music and I honestly think I can help you if you would just give yourself and my methods a chance.'

Damn her! She'd got to him. Umberto took a deep breath, forcing himself to relax, but instead was gripped by frustration:

he had left himself open. She had slipped through his defences with her quiet, warm and sympathetic voice; probably studying him now, looking for telltale signs of capitulation. Well, as far as he was concerned, she could watch until the cows came home because capitulating was not in his vocabulary. Attack! Now *that* was a word he understood well.

Caterina was still playing this game of doctor and patient as though she'd never met him before. Did she guess that he knew her real identity? Intoxicated even more by the way she was getting under his skin, he felt an urge to push at her subterfuge, wanting to break through her professional poise.

'Enough about me. Let me listen to *you* play again. You were very impressive the last time.'

Her answer came back to him hesitantly. 'I have always found great pleasure and release when playing.'

Umberto moved to Calandra's glass cabinet of music books and took out a red leatherbound score, similar to the one she had taken from the pile in the music room at the villa.

'I must apologize for my extreme reaction before,' he said as he opened the book on the first page. 'That piece you started to play to me before is one of the first pieces I composed: "Songe d'une Nuit d'Amour". It's very dear to my heart. Here ...' He placed it on the piano stand. It had been hard to listen to her impassioned playing of it at their first session when he didn't know who she was, but now he wanted to hear Caterina's fingers across those notes again, feel her every reaction to the music.

'Yes ...' she murmured. 'Of course ... I just hope I can play it with the skill and artistry it deserves.'

He wanted her to remember that night. Being in the same room and sensing the electric charge that quivered in the air between them was more than he could bear. Her voice, her scent, the vibes she emitted, were all driving him to the edge, threatening to make him explode. He wanted to touch her, to run his hand along her breasts and thighs, and make her as crazy as she was making him.

Of course Umberto had no right to want her, to make her his again. He should stop pining. He should stop trying … but not yet! Not until he had come just a little closer to her fire, had warmed himself just a bit longer, driven out some of the chill that had crept like an enemy into his soul since the accident. Yes, he wanted her to remember.

He cleared his throat. 'There's nothing difficult in this piece, as you've already seen. From a musical point of view, it's rather simple,' he said as he went to sit in an armchair facing the piano. 'What made it a favourite with the public is the emotion that runs through it, building in a crescendo of passion that erupts at the end in a volcano of fire.'

He heard her sit on the stool, lift the lid of the piano and run her fingers over the keyboard. 'Dear Lord,' she whispered before the first notes of the piece filled the room.

Umberto leaned his head against the back of the chair. His eyelids closed over his emerald irises and he listened. The intensity of her empassioned execution made everything in him still, except his heart, which stirred alarmingly. This was indeed a dangerous game they were playing. Forcing Caterina to remember meant opening up a wound he never knew existed, one that had been bleeding inside him all this time. This confusing thought sent anger surging through him. Anger over lost opportunities and wasted lives, thoughts of what might have been. He had no control over this terrible longing.

He tried to stem the unwanted tide of memories but already his body was reacting to them, reminding him – if he needed a reminder – of how fully he had swollen and stiffened to her touch. Each note was a new torment, a sweet thirst that craved quenching with Caterina's kiss, spicy as orange tea, hot as the flames licking his tortured frame. And as the emotion built up inside him, his pulse quickened. His sightless eyes burned with tears that welled up behind them, tears he was no longer able to hold back, now rolling down his cheeks in an uncontrollable stream.

*   *   *

As Catriona's hands moved over the keyboard of the Bechstein, the expressive melody weaving and tangling in the air and building in intensity, she now knew beyond all doubt that Umberto remembered. Emotion welled up in her even more keenly than before. Not only did he remember, but he was trying to tell her that he did so … that he pined for that night of passion they had shared. Of course, she shouldn't read into it more than it really was. Day upon day in darkness, what else did he have to keep him company except for his memories? Doubtless, she was one of many.

Catriona's gaze turned towards Umberto as the end of the piece was nearing. Noticing the tears that bathed the composer's face, she faltered, then stopped. Spontaneously, she rushed to him and knelt beside his chair, her hand going to his eyes and wiping the wetness from his cheeks. She tried to talk, but couldn't. What could she say? Comfort was nothing more than a whisper, stuck painfully in her throat.

Eventually, she breathed, 'No, Umberto, please,' in a strangled voice, knowing she must stop this recklessness … knew it all the way to her bones. The trouble was, her bones weren't cooperating much, neither was the rest of her. This chemistry between them was insane.

This is all wrong. Totally unprofessional, a recipe for disaster. Catriona knew it could only poison their work when, sooner or later, one of them would sour the relationship.

He took her hands and kissed them again and again, softly whispering her name among a flow of tender words. They were shaking like trees in a brisk wind. Umberto reached up and touched his fingers to her lips.

'How long have you known it was me?' she said shakily, trying not to lean her face into his hand.

'Not long. Since you sang to me.'

She sighed. 'Umberto, this wasn't what I—'

He brushed his fingers over her mouth again, gently silencing her. 'Hush, not now … That night was magic,' he added in a choked voice. '*Non ti ricordi*, don't you remember?'

'*Sì, sì*, of course I remember, but it can't happen again,' she answered in a trembling voice, carefully drawing away out of his reach as if to prove her point.

'*Perché? Non ti era piaciuto?* Why, didn't you enjoy it?'

She tried to keep her voice even. This denial was taking so much of her self-control. 'Of course I enjoyed it. It was the most beautiful experience I've ever had.'

'Then why? Is there another man in your life?'

'There's no one in my life, but we have to accept the fact that giving in to this … this …' *Damn, she couldn't find the right word* – 'would be wrong.'

He smiled wistfully. '*Passione* is the word you can't bring yourself say, this fire that's raging between us.'

'Passion or not, I am a doctor and you are my patient.'

'All the more reason for a collaboration. We can help each other in a way far beyond psychology and music. Curing the body helps cure the soul.'

A tremor of apprehension ran over Catriona. She sighed. This was impossible, she'd already gone too far. 'Please, Umberto, don't make this any harder than it is.'

He gave a hoarse laugh deep in his throat. 'Frankly, *amore*, I couldn't if I tried.'

She caught his double entendre in a flash … the stretch of the jeans across his groin made quite plain the way he was feeling.

The mischievous curve of his lips made her smile and she could feel herself faltering.

'We're having an attack of nostalgia, that's all,' she told him. 'If we ignore it, it will pass.'

One side of Umberto's mouth crooked upwards. 'Perhaps *you* can ignore it. As for me, trying to ignore this,' he gestured towards his flies, 'is like trying to ignore a Frecciarossa train hurtling towards you.'

He leaned forward, his breath fanning her hair. The scent of him attacked her senses, pulsed through her veins and drowned out everything, especially common sense.

'Caterina?' he whispered.

She closed her eyes. 'Umm?' A wave of uncontrollable desire spread through her, making her dizzy. Warmth was flooding her loins as the secret place between her thighs throbbed and ached, calling for his touch … begging for release.

He trailed a finger down the side of her neck and drew lazy circles around her collarbone, sending tiny shivers through her, making her forget why she was here … that she was on assignment … that she was *never* going to get involved again, especially not with *him*.

'You arouse the animal in me,' he growled close to her ear, the deep vibrations coursing straight down her body. She felt the last of her self-control slipping away …

He lowered his head and touched his lips to hers, slightly off-kilter, but quickly made the correction and kissed her hard, instantly communicating the desire that was flooding him.

His kiss was a flame that swept through her, making ashes of her inhibitions. With a sensuous slowness, his lips drew away from hers.

'Straddle me,' he ordered.

'But … Umberto …'

'Straddle me,' he repeated.

Her hand moved towards his flies. 'Let me do this for you,' she whispered. 'You'll feel better afterwards.'

'No, not now. First, let me touch you … let me feel you. I want to hear you moan … I want to hear you scream with pleasure. Remember how it felt, *amore mio*? I know you remember. I can feel your desire quivering in the atmosphere around me. I can smell its sweet fragrance …'

His voice was low, hoarse and provocative. If he continued to speak to her in this way, she would climax before he'd even touched her.

With trembling hands, Catriona lifted her skirt, each part of her brimming with anticipation, then wrenched away her briefs and straddled him. Her wetness met with his caressing fingers.

It was as if a dam had burst, sweeping aside layer upon layer of hurt and resentment in a torrent of pure, cleansing emotion. All those long empty years of lying alone in her bed, wondering if she'd ever know the kind of soaring pleasure she'd once found with him, dispersed in the heat of his touch, like thistledown on a summer breeze.

She gasped at their contact. 'Yes … oh yes.' Her whole body was coming alive. There was no shame about the desperation and passion that he must have heard in her cry. He had outmanoeuvred her with his sensual words, and now she wasn't able to get away from him. She wanted it … she wanted him – all of him.

Feverishly, her hands went down, wanting to feel the power of him. She unzipped his flies in one go and he growled low and rough as she slipped one hand into his jeans, his muscles contracting sharply beneath her touch. *Dear God!* He wasn't wearing anything underneath and he was hard … he was hot, his skin like satin. Still straddling him, she freed him from his jeans and, encircling him with her palm, she placed his velvet tip against that part of her that had been faithful to him all those years. They moved together, stroking and rubbing in a rhythmic cadence.

'Caterina,' he rasped, his voice strained, his hand cupping her bottom, urging her to come nearer to him. 'Let me in, *mia strega* … I want all of you …' He lifted himself and took her lips with his mouth, plundering them voraciously as she spread her legs a little wider, moving her swollen core against the shaft of his virility while he brushed his hand up and down the inside of her thighs.

Umberto's kiss was feral and all-consuming. Catriona could sense the hunger in him as his eloquent tongue caressed hers … tasting her, wanting her – wanting everything except to end that kiss, he left her no doubt about it.

'Mmm …' she moaned, entwining her hands around his neck, clinging to him fiercely, giving herself totally to his kiss. Nothing else mattered but the feel of his biceps flexing beneath her hands, his muscled thighs that rubbed against her, the salty-sweet intimacy of him inside her mouth, their hunger bridging all differences, all difficulties.

'Move your legs up on to my shoulders,' he commanded, breaking his kiss and moving his hand down between her legs. 'Give in to me, *amore mio*. Let me push you over the edge of pleasure,' he murmured huskily, now stroking her slick folds, drawing more wetness up.

Dizzy with pleasure, revelling in the ecstasy of what his magic fingers were doing to her, Catriona was beyond arguing. She rid herself of her blouse and placed her legs on his shoulders, supporting herself with her hands on his knees and watched as he leaned back in the chair, the pride of his masculinity rearing its arrogant head, taunting her.

Instinctively spreading her thighs wider, she pressed against him, wanting the whole of him where it mattered most. His deft fingers continued to tease the tiny throbbing nub before he sank gently into her hot, silky flesh, filling her slowly, allowing her body time to stretch again after so many years of abstinence, to accommodate him. Then he began to move inside her at an enchanting pace, his hardness pushing her into a maddening frenzy. His thrusts grew more and more urgent and Catriona moved with him in a whirling, sensual dance as each sinew, each nerve in her body, sang to the tune of their lovemaking.

Umberto's pumping movements became uncontrolled but she met his heavenly onslaught with equal fever and lifted herself once more to his loving, seeking her own pleasure as she gave him all that she knew how to give. Throwing her head back, she gasped for air. It felt so damned good as she squeezed her muscles around him, tight, urgent, inflaming … drawing him deeper and deeper with the relentless pressure building inside her. She could feel him growing stronger, harder, his thrusts coming quicker and quicker. *Delicious … so delicious*, she never wanted it to end.

Umberto cried out something harsh, guttural and triumphant as he emptied himself into Catriona's shuddering body. His burning essence flooded her and she pitched over the edge, calling his name as waves of pleasure rippled violently through her again and again, with such strength that the convulsions they produced seemed never-ending.

Finally, she collapsed against his panting chest. Umberto held her to him, his hands splayed across her sweat-slicked back. She could hear his heart pounding heavily against her ear. She didn't want to move; she just wanted to revel in the moment.

'Caterina,' he whispered finally.

'Umm …'

'The fire never went out for either of us, did it?'

Chapter 13

Catriona woke slowly, her body aching slightly as she moved, but it was a pleasurable ache. Through half-closed eyes she saw that the room was bathed in a gold and pinkish hue. The sky outside the window was on fire. For a moment she wasn't sure of the time: was this dawn or was it sunset? What was she doing lying naked on her bed *and* ... what was this strange languorous feeling of wellbeing that seemed to envelop her entirely?

She then opened her eyes wide and turned quickly to look at the man lying with blatant nonchalance on the bed beside her. Umberto! Staring in amazement at his naked body, all the memories of the past few hours came rushing back. They must have both dozed off for hours.

Her gaze took in the beautiful frame of her lover. His broad shoulders, his muscular arms and deeply tanned chest shadowed by dark hair, which curled in a V before it arrowed down to his flat stomach and beyond. Even in repose, his manhood was sizeable. Untamed, dark and unnervingly sexy, this man might have been a model in the pages of a magazine. Her response on seeing Umberto's magnificent body completely nude again was startling: immediately her pulse rate accelerated, shifting her up a gear from sleep-dazed neutral to very wide awake in record time.

For a few minutes more, Catriona's gaze lingered upon the handsome features of the man who had just made love to her.

Umberto's face was relaxed, almost boyish, completely vulnerable. Tentatively, she reached out to touch his cheek, not wanting to disturb his sleep but just needing the physical reassurance of feeling him. But then she pulled back.

After their first whirlwind of passion they had showered and then made love again. Umberto had been gentle, treating her body almost reverentially as though performing a sacred ritual, taking his time with each kiss and caress, savouring the pleasure of stroking and fondling every part of her slowly and tenderly. He had been a masterful lover, unselfish and caring, raising her to new heights time and time again. All the while she'd had the feeling of being cocooned in the warm emotions they evoked in one another.

Catriona was still incredulous at her own abandonment to passion, at the way she had let Umberto take not only physical possession of her but also let him fill every recess of her mind, which now kept recalling the tenderness of his touch, the gentleness. She had wanted to lose herself in his arms, not only to assuage her aching body, but to gain solace for her lonely soul. It confirmed to her that it hadn't been the touch of *any* man she had craved during all those years of abstinence, it was Umberto's touch. She had missed *him*. Today, the way he'd caressed her had finally vanquished the emptiness that had flooded her during those long barren years; he had made her feel cherished, wanted, loved … like a woman. Her heart was beating again.

Heart? … Love?

Annoyed with herself suddenly, she tried to shake herself from this languid dreaming. What had her heart got to do with it? It was her body and its uncharacteristic, uncontrollable desires that was longing for him. It was one thing to know Umberto Monteverdi desired her, quite another to start fantasizing that he might love her. She had let him wreck her life once. Back then, she'd had an excuse: she was young and innocent. Today, she had no such defence. Men like him didn't change their spots – they had affairs, not relationships. They had mistresses, not wives, and she and her heart had better never forget it!

Still, all the logic in the world couldn't blot out how he had made her feel in those wonderful moments – far more warm, responsive and female than she had ever felt in her life.

Catriona shivered, admitting to herself that if Umberto ever chose to touch her again, she would find it so hard to resist – the mere thought of it made her knees go weak. After all, why should she resist? He was the father of her son. Maybe, having driven him out of her system, she could get on with a normal life. Suddenly the very thought of her tidy office, of her colleagues with whom she loved to discuss her work, of her patients – every one of whom she steered towards a happier life through the music that mattered so much to each of them – all this, together with her relationship with Michael that made each day a thing of wonder, came flooding into her mind. How she longed for the organized and fulfilling life she had in Nice.

Then she turned to look at the chiselled face of the man beside her, its lines and planes softened in sleep, and her heart fluttered with longing again. This time the physical longing was eclipsed by an equally strong emotion: a heartfelt desire to fill the gap he had left in her existence, a yearning to have him in her life.

He is the father of my son.

A tremor ran through her as the thought returned. He was also a man who didn't want children, had never wanted children. Knowing that, how could she risk letting Umberto into Michael's life? She had spent years creating a comfortable existence for them both through hard professional graft and tender care to provide a safe and loving home. How could she endanger all that? But then again, Michael had been denied a father for the whole of his life. Didn't a son deserve to know his father, and a father his own offspring?

Her mind switched back to thoughts of her work at the clinic and the practice of which she was so proud. Anger flamed instantly: how could she have stepped over the line like this? She could be struck off for what she had done with Umberto, a patient with whom she had an almost sacred contract. A man with depression, who before now had tried to take his life. How could she have behaved with such a lack of sense? Not just flouting the rules but doing so in the clear knowledge that the consequences could be serious for her client. Surely what he needed was a steady helping hand as he focused on making the most of his life again?

Instead, Umberto had persuaded her, though admittedly she hadn't needed much coaxing, that he would feel better, more positive, with her in his arms. Was that really so? Might it not turn out that he sailed on a high, only to be cast down into the depths of despair when life became difficult and complicated again?

The whole situation was a mess.

The enormity of these disturbing thoughts brought her quickly out of bed. Taking care not to wake Umberto, she pulled on a robe and quietly made her way on to the veranda overlooking the lake.

The sun rained its dying golden beams over the countryside. Like fire dancing on every tree, it painted with light a wonder on the edge of the night. The whole dark sweep of Lake Como flamed under the aureate sky of twilight, igniting the waters with sparks.

Lilac, evanescing rose and gold were drifting from east to west. A fresh breeze had started up from the lake and on the glassy swell she could see the reflection of small white clouds passing one by one, the blue sky shaken out in a few undulations and the round, flashing sun riding the smooth waves like a diamond.

With shaft upon shaft of fading light, the wand of dusk was weaving its shadows over the lake, the forest heights, the far-off mountains and the houses along the shore. Birdsong that had been shrill during the afternoon had now fallen silent in a soft cascade, while the chirping choir of cicadas had intensified into a clamorous concerto.

'Well, well, well … how intimate and so very provocative!'

On the veranda Catriona started, turned and stiffened. She stared through the doorway at Silvana, who was standing beside the bed in a black-and-red bikini, gazing down at Umberto's tanned body sprawled dormant on the white sheet.

Umberto stirred and opened his eyes.

'I'd almost forgotten what I'd been missing,' added Silvana, her hand resting in mock surprise on her breast.

The sound of her voice penetrated Umberto's drowsiness and he sat bolt upright, his hand feeling for the sheet and tugging it over himself.

'Silvana!' he growled. 'What are you doing here?'

'I came over to ask the *Dottoressa* if she wanted to come down to the lake with me for a swim.' She glanced over at Catriona, now standing in the doorway of the French windows, and gave a trill of laughter. 'I must admit you don't waste any time,' she commented drily. 'So much for music therapy sessions!'

'How dare you walk into someone else's house without being invited!'

'The door was open, how could I have known?' She turned towards Catriona, who had stepped into the room, and fastened her arrogant gaze on her. 'He's good, isn't he? I was his first, you know. I taught him what women like to have done to them, so you have me to thank, *Dottoressa*.'

She spat the last word with such scorn that Catriona recoiled, her own guilt so fresh and raw in her mind that Silvana's contempt hit home. She was at a loss for words, floored by the awfulness of the situation. Suddenly everything that had seemed so right, so romantic, had been cast in a dubious light and trashed.

Silvana glanced back at Umberto with a lewd smile. 'You know, his tongue is just as agile as his …'

She hadn't time to continue. In a single fluid movement Umberto had grabbed the bedsheet and stood up, securing it round his waist as he sprang at Silvana, finding her arm and gripping it.

'Get out of here!' he roared as he tried to push her towards the door, his other hand flat against her side.

Struggling to hold her ground and managing at the same time to plaster herself against him, she looked up at his furious face. 'Remember our games?' Her left hand stroked his chest, moving swiftly downwards, making for the sheet around his waist. 'Let me remind you.' Her voice was suddenly a hoarse purr, though her eyes held a dangerous glint.

Catriona saw Umberto's face darken in an angry flush. His blindness in that moment, she could tell, was fuelling the rage that was already threatening to explode. He grabbed her wrist in a vice-like hold.

'Don't make me use force on you,' he uttered between clenched teeth. 'Don't make me hurt you. I'm stronger than you are.'

'I like it when you're angry. That's when you're at your best …' Silvana struggled to free her hand but pushed herself closer still, her face now inches away from his. 'Deep down, you're a sadist and you've always said I'm a masochist,' she murmured. 'The perfect combination.'

She was panting now, her face and body glistening with perspiration. Catriona stood mesmerized and horrified, realizing that Silvana was turned on by the fight, so much so that she had forgotten her rival's presence. Catriona summoned all the calm authority she could muster.

'Go, both of you,' she said quietly. Silvana stopped and looked dazedly at her, while Umberto's head also turned towards her. As he stilled, he gave Silvana the opportunity to wrench herself from his grip.

'I'm going,' she said in a trembling voice, stumbling back and rubbing her wrist. Her face was taut, her eyes like knives.

'You may think you've won, *Dottoressa*, but you haven't. You should be ashamed of yourself,' she added with contempt as she stood on the threshold, glaring at her rival. She smiled nastily.

'I wonder how people will react when they realize what sort of therapy methods the renowned *dottoressa* Drouot uses on her clients. How she takes advantage of the weakness of her patients. I'm sure the media will be more than interested to learn about the goings-on between the master of Villa Monteverdi and the high-and-mighty *Dottoressa*!'

Catriona felt the blood drain from her face. For a moment she held Silvana's gaze but then it was she who looked away. Umberto's anger, inflaming once more, wasn't enough to quell the sense of shame curling its insidious way through her.

'*Fuori di qui puttana*, get out of here, you whore!' Umberto bellowed as he slammed the door in Silvana's face and then leaned against it. Running a hand through his hair, he turned his face towards Catriona.

'Are you okay?' he asked, his chest still heaving.

Catriona's voice was shaky with anger and humiliation. 'Yes, I'm fine, but I don't think I can stay here any more.'

Umberto paled. 'What d'you mean? You can't be serious.'

'I've never been more serious,' she told him simply.

'Don't do this to me, Caterina,' he said, moving quickly to her side. He tried to take her in his arms but she pushed him away gently.

'This was a mistake from the very beginning. I shouldn't have taken this job.'

'Do you regret what happened between us this afternoon?'

She bit her lip. *How could she regret the paradise he had taken her to when she was already missing his touch?* 'No,' she murmured. 'But this would never work.'

He pulled her against him and this time she didn't resist … couldn't resist. He was so beautiful, so intoxicatingly beautiful. The sight of him, the feel of him, the smell of him …

'No … what are you doing?' she exclaimed, shaking her head, scared at how easily she was giving in to him again. 'I can't stay here. Look at the chaos I've created.'

'You can't let that woman come between us, you can't give up on me. I promise we can make it work.' His voice was low and strained, laced with frustration. 'I can be a good patient.'

He played with her hair, twisting it around his hands, threading it through his fingers, creating sensations that flooded through her. Though he held her firmly, there was an edge of desperation in his movements and she felt her resolve weakening.

'I'm not giving up on you, but you must see that this is an untenable situation,' she persisted. 'I will send Marie-Jeanne, my partner, in place of me. She is as good a therapist as I am, if not better.'

His jaw clenched. '*You* are my therapy, don't you get it? You've given sun to my dark days.'

He lifted her face to his, exploring her features with reverential fingers, stroking each contour as if sculpting her out of clay. Then he began to spread butterfly kisses over them.

'Caterina, please don't do this to me,' he begged in a strangled voice. 'I will do anything you ask,' he murmured against her skin. 'I'll play the piano, I'll even try and compose again. Remember, you were the muse of the greatest piece I ever wrote.'

Catriona managed to disentangle herself from him. 'Your other lover has explained the situation very satisfactorily and—'

'Silvana is *not* my lover!' he growled. 'We had a thing going when we were both younger, but you can hardly hold that against me!'

'Come off it, Umberto. She's still as keen on you as ever. Don't tell me you haven't fanned the flames in those times you've been with her since then.'

Umberto shrugged. 'Not for years, and it never meant a thing, she knew that. There's only one of us in this family who hangs on her every word, and it isn't me.'

She took another step back. 'Poor Giacomo. What a desperate triangle the three of you form, it's not good for anyone.'

Umberto sighed and moved to the bed, where he sat on the edge, forearms resting on his knees. He paused in mute acknowledgement. 'Silvana won't give him the time of day. There's a type of woman who always wants what she can't have.'

'Is that why you resist her, so she'll continue to throw herself at you?'

Was that jealousy rearing its ugly horns? Catriona pushed the thought away.

Umberto jerked his head back as though struck. '*Dio mio*, Caterina! What must I do to prove to you that there is nothing between me and Silvana? I admit she was the first girl with whom I had sex. She seduced me when we were teenagers. She had this total confidence and boldness, having slept her way around Torno.' He paused, then continued, his voice suddenly gentler.

'You wonder why we persist in this hopeless trio at Villa Monteverdi? She was close to my mother, she had nobody else. Silvana is a vain, self-serving creature, but I suppose she's a part of what's left of the estate, of my home … a link with my childhood.' He sighed.

'Over the years my mother tried to persuade me to marry Silvana. No doubt she put the idea in the girl's head, which hasn't helped. But the idea is preposterous. I feel nothing of that sort towards her. Whatever happened between us fizzled out long ago, when I came back from New York. After I met you.'

'Fine, let's forget the sex angle,' Catriona conceded, folding her arms. 'What about my reputation as a doctor? Didn't you hear her? She was threatening me.'

'No one would take Silvana's accusations seriously,' Umberto tried to reassure her. 'Anyway, I know her. She wouldn't take things that far, she's too afraid of being cast out of the estate.'

Catriona shook her head determinedly. 'I think you'd better go and I'll start packing.'

'Marry me,' Umberto said. The words dropped into the still room like a heavy stone into a pool.

Catriona's heart missed a beat as the ripples cast by this utterance spread outwards and filled the space. Her emotions were rocketing around her chest as if threatening to break through the barrier of her ribcage. Her arms fell to her sides. 'What did you say?' she murmured faintly, unable to believe what she had just heard.

He shrugged and repeated his proposal calmly as if they were discussing the weather or the menu for dinner and, by the look on his face, Catriona could see that he was serious.

'No,' she replied simply.

'Why?'

'Because we have no future, only a past.'

'We can make a future. Surely that's possible, *cara*?'

'No.' Pulling her robe tightly around her, she turned away, unable to look at the crestfallen expression on his face. 'I'm afraid that isn't possible.'

A cynical smile curved one side of his mouth. 'Why, because I'm blind?'

'No, because marriage is not a game and I don't take it lightly.'

'Neither do I.'

'We hardly know each other.'

'Really? I think we know each other pretty well.' His expression was amused now.

She began pacing back and forth. 'The fact that we've had good sex doesn't mean that we know each other.'

'Is that all this was to you, Caterina … just good sex?'

'Marriage should be based on love, compatibility, and so many other things,' she said.

'We have a lot in common if you come to think of it.'

'Not really,' she replied, trying to smother the needling voice at the back of her mind, telling her that they actually had a son in common.

'Is it because you want to stay faithful to your husband's memory?'

She came to a standstill. *Oh no, he wasn't going to bring her 'husband' into the conversation.* She would have to lie to him. More secrets, more deception, more lies … Her conscience was already nagging her. She could hear Sidonie's voice admonishing her when she was a little girl and caught in a lie: '*Attention, les mensonges ont de courtes jambes*, careful, lies have short legs.'

'Were you in love with him, Caterina?'

'Why else would I have married him?' Panicked, she was now on the defensive.

'Maybe to forget someone else? That night in Villefranche you felt something for me, I know you did.'

Now she was getting angry. 'Yes, I did. But then I was a naïve little eighteen-year-old with stars in her eyes, who had never been kissed and had just given you her virginity,' she threw back at him.

His jaw clenched. 'I never forgot that night, Caterina. It meant a lot to me, too.'

'Is that why you left me the next day without a second look?' There were tears in her eyes, fuelled by a tide of anger. He had been honest with her at the time, almost brutally so, but she still remembered the searing pain. 'I didn't know anything could hurt that much, it was like being dropped from a great height. You don't bounce back after a fall like that – you're left lying there, smashed into a thousand pieces.'

His face softened with contrition. 'I was young and selfish … arrogant. The lust for fame had gone to my head, I admit. But I couldn't get you out of my head. I tried ringing your house … I even sent a note, care of your music teacher, which you never answered. By the time I came back to look for you a year later, I was told you had married and moved away. I couldn't believe it, you were still so young.' He gave a hopeless shrug. 'After that, I had to accept you were gone.'

Stunned by this revelation, Catriona lost the thread of her thoughts so she remained silent. Then she ventured: 'You didn't recognize me that night?'

'When you approached me in Paris?'

'You knew who I was?'

'Not immediately. You were in the shadows, the collar of your fur coat pulled up. The next thing I knew, you'd vanished.'

'We were interrupted,' she answered hoarsely. 'Don't you remember?'

'Yes, I know, *cara*, I know.' He nodded, then sighed. 'I promised myself to look you up and then this accident happened and …' His voice sounded strained and she saw that his face suddenly looked worn.

She fell silent once more and Umberto raked a hand through his hair. When he spoke again, his inflection was infiltrated by a note of wistfulness.

'I recognized your voice the moment you started to sing. That timbre, that absolutely natural vibrato. I'd have known it anywhere. Possibly the greatest sadness in all this is that you never made singing your career. Did I put you off your stride? I would hate to think that …' He paused, then continued without waiting for her response.

'Anyway, for the first time since the accident a little joy, a little hope entered my heart. I felt the senses I had thought dead revive, and then today … this was not just sex, *amore mio*. We made love … beautiful, passionate love.'

Catriona closed her eyes. He was exposing his vulnerability to her. 'Don't do this to me, Umberto … it's unfair.'

'Don't deny it. We loved each other, our bodies trembled and rejoiced in each other. This wasn't simply something carnal, we were not just animals copulating for pleasure. Trust me, I know what I'm talking about, I know the difference. *Ti amo.* No woman has been able to awake in me the emotion and tenderness that I have felt holding you in my arms. You gave yourself to me with the same generosity and absolute passion I remember.' He stood, his head tilted a fraction, questioningly.

'Surely you still have some sentiment for me. If not, how could you have surrendered so entirely to my lovemaking? What you feel is love, Caterina. Don't lie to yourself, don't fight what this is.'

He came closer and she raised a hand to ward him off but Umberto was quick as a flash, despite his blindness. He grasped her arms and jerked her towards him, lowering his head to hers, his strong embrace easily overcoming her frantic efforts to keep him at bay. Still fighting him desperately, Catriona's teeth closed on his lips, until she could taste his blood in her mouth, but still he would not let her go.

Roughly, he pulled her closer still, hip to hip. She felt his body harden against hers as, with grim persistence, his mouth possessed and ravaged hers, his tongue making its own exploration ... until weakness and her own inherent need of him turned panic into passion. It was as if shards of white light splintered through her, numbing her brain and momentarily blinding her.

What was happening? *This had to stop. Now!*

'Please, I ...' To Catriona's horror her voice came out in a hoarse moan, revealing exactly how little control she had over her body. She wasn't fighting him, she couldn't fight him; she was begging him to possess her again.

As if sensing her partial submission, his lips softened and now his probing tongue was smoothly sensuous. His hands moved to stroke her neck, tracing the contours of her ears, and slid them down further over her shoulders to her breasts, stopping to stroke the tips of her nipples under the silky material of her robe, instantly hardening them. Then drifting smoothly to her waist, his fingers brushed away the folds of her dressing gown to explore the soft skin of her stomach that lay beneath, before finally pushing the robe from her shoulders.

The garment fell and she gasped. Her blood leapt and surged, turning to molten lava as she felt his burning hardness against her. Umberto's hands had been gentle in their exploration but now she felt their strength as he pressed her flesh more firmly.

'Damn you!' Her words were an angry croak directed as much to herself as to him.

'Stop fighting me, Caterina. You know you don't want to.'

She turned her head away from him, though her body stayed pressed against his. 'Leave me alone,' she panted, trying to blot out her ache for him.

'I couldn't even if I wished to. I'm burning for you, I want to fill you ... flood you with my liquid fire,' he murmured in her ear, nibbling at the lobe, his tongue driving her to distraction.

Now his hands spread over her spine and moved further down, moulding the curves of her thighs and bottom ... warm, gentle and erotic. Her skin tingled like champagne. With unquestionable expertise he was reducing her to a state of total surrender and Catriona's senses stirred in latent desperation.

'No ... this is madness,' she said in a half whisper.

'Love that is not madness is not love.' Umberto leaned into her and Catriona's vocabulary disintegrated. His hands drifted up again to her breasts, his fingers sensuously teasing the taut peaks, and she forgot to breathe.

Love.

Her brain registered it in confusion. Even now she couldn't trust herself to let go, but her wilful senses rebelled. Intoxicated by his words, they wouldn't obey her silent command. In an instant she flared with need, her lips parting to allow him to plunder her mouth in a way that sent frissons of pleasure winging through her entire system.

A moan escaped Catriona's lips, her hands grasping him, not so much in exploration but in an urge to keep him touching her, to keep the pleasure flowing.

Umberto's tongue thrust into her mouth still deeper as he lifted her up with one arm, then he put her down on the cool, white sheet and dark heat consumed her, blotting out everything but him.

Leaving her lips, his mouth found the tiny beating vein in her neck. Hoarsely, he whispered her name, 'Caterina … Caterina … *mio bellissimo angelo*,' his hands gliding with featherlike caresses all over her hankering flesh, mesmerizing her while her body trembled against his. His head swept down to her breast, taking one nipple and then the other in his warm, wet mouth. She was lost.

Closing her eyes, Catriona was panting heavily, stroking his night-black hair as he suckled her. Umberto's hand strayed down once more to the curve of her hip, exploring her inner thighs and settling over the soft triangle of hair between them, his palm now moving up and down, stroking her rhythmically until her arousal began to build and, in needy desperation, she spread her legs wide on each side of him. Cupping the round cheeks of her backside, he lifted her towards his own desire, the tip of him brushing against the swollen moist folds of her sex. He was moving her up and down his hardness, just missing the hard little bud aching for release. She tried wriggling to direct him to the right place but he held her firmly in his embrace and the urgency of her need kept climbing and climbing.

Her heart pounded. She was acutely aware of the strength of his arms and the steely hardness of muscle beneath his smooth, velvet skin.

'You're so hot … so wet for me, *amore mio*,' he whispered against her mouth, his tongue teasing first her upper lip and then the lower one. 'Patience, *tesoro mio*. Soon, I will sink myself into your soft honeyed core where the stars of paradise will meet us and the angels will sing for us both.'

It was shameful how the combination of Umberto's low, throaty voice, his unabashed sensuality and inflaming touch drove everything out of Catriona's head except the longing for more erotic murmurings, more stroking, more kisses, and the urgent need to feel his power as he possessed her entirely. As the throbbing between her legs increased, the sound of her laboured breathing and the banging of her heart against her ribs made it impossible to think.

What was he waiting for? His tongue flitted along her skin as the velvet tip of him kept stroking her relentlessly. It would only take a matter of moments before she exploded. Catriona's mind begged for release as the last of her self-control slipped away and she twisted her body with a cry. He entered her then with one forceful thrust, his hands wrapping her legs tightly around him, pressing himself into her, rocking her back and forth in a passionate, primitive mating unlike any she had ever conceived of. It was so much more overwhelming because, so far, their lovemaking had been slower and more subtle, Umberto being a true connoisseur of sensual pleasure.

Still, it felt good, oh so good! Spiralling out of control, her release came hard. Umberto continued to move inside her. Faster and faster, deeper and deeper … With every thrust, he made her climax roll through her repeatedly. Tears of pleasure ran down her face. She sobbed his name lovingly, wanting him never to end the ecstasy in which she was wallowing.

Finally, he arched away from her, his head thrown back as he joined her, crying out his need for her with a guttural sound that echoed in the room, making her shudder. Submerging her feminine core in a sumptuous flood of his liquid fire, Umberto brought them both to a violent mutual convulsion of groaning ecstasy, which left them panting and weak with sweet exhaustion.

Sighing with contentment, Umberto collapsed next to her. He automatically gathered her close, his strong arms wrapped tightly around her, one hand stroking her hair. Catriona lay there, her cheek against his chest, listening to his thudding heartbeat while slowly regaining a semblance of normality, not sure whose pleasure had thrilled her most, his or her own. All she knew was that she had never felt so fulfilled. She didn't want to move, she wanted to stay right where she was, secure in her lover's embrace.

In the haze of passion that still surrounded them, Catriona heard the faint hoot of an owl in one of the trees outside and wondered at Silvana's superstitious words that first night at dinner. An image of the redhead flickered through her mind. What would be the consequence of this delirious moment of self-indulgence? Still, she felt too languorous to worry about that now.

'That was lovemaking, *amore mio*,' he whispered tenderly. 'Say you'll be *la signora* Monteverdi.'

His words brought her back down to earth. Her reply came in an almost imperceptible voice: 'Let me think about it.'

The torrid lovemaking they had just enjoyed seeped into her bones, bringing with it a yawn of mental and physical exhaustion.

'Sleep, *mio bellissimo angelo*,' Umberto murmured, his hands hypnotically soothing as they stroked softly up and down her arm. 'Sleep …'

The last thing she remembered was the cool pillows beneath her cheek and the silky sheet being drawn up over her limp body.

*   *   *

Outside, the night enveloped the earth in its velvet cloak. Umberto loved these early summer nights, when the moon looked down from her blue mansion and flocks of stars trailed in the sky over the twinkling lake. He knew them well, not needing his sight to recall their beauty and romance. Tonight, he could smell it in the air. One of those wanton nights when nature was in a provocative mood, it made one lonesome, with an urge to share its magic … a night for lovers. His unseeing eyes narrowed.

He stood very still against the balustrade of the veranda outside his bedroom, listening to the sounds of nocturnal life – the sighing of the breeze, the faint rustlings in the undergrowth – surrounded by the dreadful black loneliness that this idyllic summer night could not penetrate. The pain he felt was almost physical, as if the blood was draining from his heart. He gave a twisted smile. At least night evened the odds: in darkness, no one could see.

The cheerful sound of the cuckoo clock chimed out its twelve strokes. Already midnight. In Caterina's arms the hours had slipped away, unnoticed. A cold hand gripped his heart as the old rage surfaced within him.

What on earth had possessed him to make a fool of himself and ask Caterina to marry him? He must have been out of his mind. She was a successful doctor with her own thriving business and a son … a life. Why would she give up all that? As a husband, he would always be at a disadvantage, unable to do things with her, unable to protect her. What kind of a husband would this blindness make him? Bitter, moody, angry … what could *he* offer now?

'*Niente!*' he said aloud, the word carrying an awful emptiness.

He'd had his chance ten years ago. Caterina had been standing on the threshold of life – young, eager, intelligent, trustful – and all he had done was take her innocence away. Then, like a fool, he had walked away. Too preoccupied with his own future, his own career, he hadn't recognized at the time what had been staring him in the face.

You don't deserve her and you never will.

Umberto went in and turned on his CD player. Debussy's 'Clair de Lune', originally known as 'Promenade Sentimentale'. The poignant notes seemed to describe the way he felt tonight.

He seated himself in his armchair, hugging his bottle of cognac – his best friend on those lonely nights – and, not bothering with the glass, took a swig before resting his head against the back of the chair and closing his eyes.

He didn't fear darkness, he didn't fear danger, but the idea of being helpless and confined was loathsome to Umberto – and however much he acted as if he could see, he was imprisoned. Every day, he fought this darkness, struggling to hold on to his independence. This for a man who had enjoyed climbing mountains like those girding the lake … and skiing, swimming, riding and driving fast cars. He'd never again do any of the thousand things he once took for granted.

Driving fast cars … his thoughts drifted once more. He hadn't been driving fast on the day of the accident, nor had he been drinking, but his memory afterwards was hazy. Umberto had never understood the spin – there had not been any sign of a shower, and the frost had thawed the day before. For the hundredth time, his mind replayed those blurred final seconds. Seeing the trees coming at him, he had wrenched the wheel round as he hit the brakes, expecting to veer to the side. But somehow the car hadn't responded and had spun completely out of control.

It had been an accident, he reminded himself grimly – an unfortunate act of fate. If he thought anything else, he'd go mad. At the time, the police investigation into the failure of the steering mechanism had been inconclusive.

And then he had shut himself away, initially throwing himself into writing his concerto with his mother's help. That was when he still thought there was a good chance his sight might return. But months later, when he found out his hopes had been futile, Umberto became a proper recluse: his only desire then was to get away from his friends with their facile sympathy or their cheerful optimism that medical science or a divine miracle might turn things around for him.

He punched the side of the table with his fist, grazing and bruising his knuckles in the process, wishing he could put his hands on something he could smash into a thousand pieces. Bad idea ... it only alleviated his rage for brief moments and then the frustration came flooding back. Keeping him awake at night, the feeling rarely faded with the heralding of day. He was used to it now; it was his familiar protean sprite, his companion in light and in darkness.

'Caterina,' he breathed, leaning forward and dropping his face into his hands.

Umberto's thoughts were consumed by her. He burned to feel her bare flesh beneath him once more. To fill his palms with her breasts and feel them harden under his touch, to bury himself once more in the soft moisture of her feminine core. He wanted to tip her over the mountain of pleasure and hear the moaning of her ecstasy as she climaxed.

Had he gone too far? He'd only meant to touch her. Still, she had been so willing, so responsive ... Yes, she'd experienced the same passion he had; she'd relished it equally.

Other questions crept into Umberto's thoughts. Had it been as incredible with her husband? Had it been like that with other men?

Caterina had been created for lovemaking. It didn't make sense that she could have remained celibate since she was widowed, she enjoyed sex too much ... revelled in it. How could Umberto believe that no man but he had discovered that about her? He felt his blood boil at the thought of other men touching her, possessing her, pleasuring her. Jealousy jabbed at him and he groaned like a wounded animal. It hurt too much: Caterina was his, his alone. He had given that beautiful young body of hers its first shudder of pleasure. It was his name she had cried out when she felt the first notes of ecstasy.

What they'd had was nothing to do with primitive mating, not just sex. Raw, naked emotion that went beyond even the most intense erotic exploration, it had been the instinctive union of two souls. Umberto's only mistake today was in asking Caterina to share his bleak life by becoming his wife. He drank again and let the liquor burn down his throat into his chest.

If only Silvana hadn't come in with her accusations and threats. Perhaps then Caterina wouldn't have wanted to leave and he wouldn't have panicked, wouldn't have dared make such a ridiculous offer.

He must do something about Silvana. He knew the woman too well. She wouldn't rest until she'd driven Caterina out of his life. He remembered the way she had been with Sofia. Sometimes he wondered if it hadn't been Silvana's machinations that had driven the poor girl to suicide … But poisonous as Silvana could be, he couldn't justify levelling that sort of accusation at her. Besides, nothing could alleviate the weight of his own culpability in Sofia's death. He had hurt her badly and now she was dead.

Umberto cursed violently and took another swig of the cognac bottle as his demons took hold, sinking their claws deeper into his mind. There wasn't enough brandy in all the world to drive them away but he could dull their bitter voices at least.

In the stillness of that long night Umberto's thoughts tossed and turned, guilt gnawing at him. He was an egotistical fool. Caterina had suffered deeply from his insensitive selfishness and callousness. Would she ever forgive him? The weight of his self-reproach clung close to his tortured spirit as the cloud did the sky, cleaving to him as the wind did to the wave. How many more women had he scarred?

The alcohol and exhaustion finally overcame him and for a while Umberto drifted into a deep sleep that would transport him to a world where vision was not an obstacle, and where he could become a normal healthy human being again.

*   *   *

Although Catriona slept through the night, she did so uneasily, haunted by dreams of wedding dresses and red roses. When she awoke, it took her a few moments to open her eyes. Then, as the events of the previous evening came into focus, she sat up, her hands pushing through her hair.

She shook her head in perplexity. What was she to do? Should she pack and leave as soon as arrangements could be made for her return journey? It seemed the only reasonable decision – but was it?

So much had happened between her and Umberto in the course of just one afternoon. Their bodies had rediscovered each other as if they had never been apart. Then they'd talked and made love over and over again until they were exhausted. She realized that during these past ten years, it was as if she had been torn in two. In Umberto's arms, she had become whole again. If they parted now, Catriona knew that her life would never be the same. She could never let another man touch her in the intimate way she had surrendered to Umberto – was that what people called love?

Still, there were obstacles. Silvana for one, no matter what he'd said. Then there was Umberto himself. As much as she knew his body, almost as well as she knew her own, she was still building a picture of how his mind worked. He was full of contradictions and his blindness had taken a toll on the stability of his character and the man he really was deep down.

The idea of committing to being his wife was daunting. She loved him and they had a son together but was it enough? Even if they could be reunited as a family, would her love be enough to carry them through the long years ahead into old age? Umberto was already a difficult man to live with. How would it work if Catriona tried to treat his problems professionally, from within the boundaries of their personal relationship? That would be a minefield, but one she was willing to risk if she thought she could help him. She didn't imagine he would accept Marie-Jeanne as his new therapist. But one thing was certain, if Umberto couldn't come to terms with the overwhelming reality of his blindness, it could turn him into a tyrant. And she couldn't subject Michael to that.

Catriona sighed. She must stop torturing herself. Anyhow, she doubted very much that Umberto's proposal had been serious. It was a spur-of-the-moment thing; merely an excuse to stop her leaving.

Glancing at the clock on her bedside table, she saw that it was almost nine-thirty. She would go for a walk before it got too hot, she decided. It would help clear her head and dispel the recurring, handsome image of Umberto Monteverdi. No need for hasty decisions, she told herself as she scrambled out of bed.

Catriona felt hot and sticky so she quickly showered then went downstairs and into the kitchen for a glass of water. Her breakfast tray was there, laid out with juice, pastries, a bowl of large ripe peaches and a big cafetière of coffee that was still piping hot. Adelina must have come by not too long ago.

Catriona smiled. She didn't think much of the inhabitants of Villa Monteverdi – they were an odd lot – but Adelina was entirely different. Her loyal devotion to Umberto was clear and, if Catriona decided to stay on, maybe she should engage Adelina's help in understanding the maestro better. Feeling only marginally hungry, she grabbed one of the pastries to eat while she walked, plus her mobile from the table, and went out into the sunshine.

She sighed with pleasure: she was free. Wandering past the garage and stables, past the meadow where Adelina's cottage and stone shed nestled next to the tall white asphodels, Catriona moved further south, away from the main villa, and skirted the forest. As she walked, her eyes roamed the ever-changing landscape: cypress trees stood with laurels, and beside them banks of tall mullein stalks with their bright yellow flowers rose into the air. The aroma of camelias, magnolias and rhododendrons mingled with lily of the valley while, bubbling over in an ecstasy of song, the gentle sound of larks floated on the air. Apart from the birdsong and the buzzing of bees, a great hush cloaked the surroundings. It was as if everything in nature was listening, in an expectant mood, and the world was lost for a moment in its own unfolding, dazed by its own happiness, wondering, like her, what this day would bring.

Following a path into the chestnut trees on her left, assuming it would eventually lead back to the Gufi Reali woods, Catriona's mind flitted from one thought to the next before being startled out of her reverie by the ringing of her mobile.

'Hello?'

'Hi there, it's Marie-Jeanne. I'm sorry to disturb you. Is this a bad time?'

'No, not at all. I'm out having a walk.' Distracted, she glanced ahead to where the path forked and kept walking. 'What's up?'

'Nothing I can't deal with. Don't worry, everything's fine. It's just that we've been inundated with applications for the assistant job, and I was wondering if you wanted me to send over a shortlist, or whether you'd be happy for me to decide.'

Catriona let out a quiet breath. 'Don't do anything yet. Things are complicated here and I might be coming back much sooner than we'd thought.'

'Oh dear. Why? What's been happening?' Marie-Jeanne asked, alarmed.

Finding a large boulder covered in moss, Catriona perched on top of it. It seemed a reasonably secluded spot for a long and personal conversation. Butterflies hovered from shrub to shrub and the air was full of dancing insects.

The reception was excellent and a call from Marie-Jeanne was exactly what she needed to clear the cobwebs that were preventing her from reasoning clearly. Catriona gave an embarrassed laugh. 'Oh dear, how do I say this …? I've been a bit impulsive and haven't exactly kept my hormones under control.'

'Oh no! You haven't?'

'Yes, I have.'

'Umberto?'

'Yes, Umberto.'

'Oh, *chérie*, you must be in quite a state. No wonder you're off walking on your own.' Like a balm, Marie-Jeanne's down-to-earth, no-nonsense voice soothed Catriona's frazzled nerves. 'All I can say is your feelings for the man must be very strong. There's no way I can see you stepping outside your professional code of conduct with a client otherwise.' She sighed. 'But then it's not exactly a usual client-patient relationship, let's face it.'

'I know … and it's only got more complicated, if that's even possible.'

'What do you mean? Presumably you've told Umberto who you really are?'

'I didn't need to – he knew the moment I sang.'

'You sang to him? Ah, I must admit that is kind of romantic. What are you going to do now? Have you told him about Michael?'

'Not yet, and that's killing me. But there's more … he's asked me to marry him, which is inconceivable, of course.'

'I'm not sure why it should be. Not if you feel the same way. Though obviously, you'll have to cut yourself loose from him as his therapist …' Marie-Jeanne waited for Catriona to say something.

Then, when she didn't: 'What worries me more is that you don't sound very happy. There's something else, isn't there?'

'Yes, there's another complication.'

'As if it's not already difficult enough!'

'Her name is Silvana and she's his ex-girlfriend. Childhood sweetheart, in a way. She caught us together and has threatened to report me.'

Marie-Jeanne let out an exclamatory breath. 'If she's that jealous then maybe she's not as "ex" as Umberto's been making out?' Her tone was more circumspect this time.

'That was my worry, too. But I think he's telling the truth and the affair was over a long time ago.'

'So, what's she doing at his house? This doesn't sound right.' Marie-Jeanne's voice held an ironic note of disbelief.

'Silvana's a protégée of his mother's – kind of a ward – who grew up at the villa and has a cottage in the grounds. She's there at dinner every evening, as is Umberto's cousin, who is in love with her. It really is the most toxic web you could ever imagine.'

'It certainly sounds like it! No wonder you can't get your head around what's going on with Umberto, for heaven's sake.' Marie-Jeanne's voice was serious, caring. 'The important thing though is how you feel about him.'

'I honestly don't know. I'm sure you'll think I'm off my head if I tell you that I love him. I did, I think, all those years back. It might have been infatuation, but with time … and seeing him looking so like Michael …' Catriona shrugged and tears welled up in her eyes.

'You just said that you found the idea of marrying the man inconceivable.'

Catriona wiped her tears with the back of her hand. 'I know. I'm afraid to commit to a man who has been, as far as I can gather, a serial womanizer without the least intention of ever wanting a child.'

'Ah, that does make things difficult, I guess,' Marie-Jeanne said with a gentle laugh, making her feel a little better. 'Look, you set out for Italy knowing you needed to broach the subject of Michael. I don't think that has changed, has it?'

'No, it hasn't. I think Michael has a right to know who his father is, even if building a relationship with him isn't ultimately possible.'

'Not only that,' Marie-Claire added, 'but I imagine you're still of the opinion that Umberto should know he has a son.'

'Yes,' Catriona said faintly. 'Although I'm damned if I don't tell him and quite possibly damned if I do. From a psychological angle, he's already coping with a lot of mental turmoil. I may be dealing him a card that's such a shock it could well tip him over the edge.'

'I'm sure he's made of stronger stuff than that. Umberto wouldn't have got so far in his career if he hadn't a tremendous amount of fight in him.'

'That's true. I admire his courage ... he's got heaps of that ... you should see the way he manages. Sometimes I have difficulty believing he's blind.'

'There you go then. He'll be fine.' Marie-Jeanne's voice was soothing, but then her rejoinder cut to the quick: 'Although he may well be angry when you tell him. The years he's missed being a father ...'

'Although if he really doesn't ever want to be a father ...'

'Well, there's only one way to find out how he's going to react – and that's to tell him.'

'I will ... just not yet. When the time is right.'

'And what if the time never feels right? Lies have that way of winding themselves about you until you feel completely trapped by them. I wouldn't leave it too long, if I were you.'

'I won't. Then again, I can't help but question if I'm doing the right thing bringing Michael anywhere near the Monteverdi family. It's a real house of shadows and secrets and, while Silvana lives here, I really don't feel comfortable – safe even. I have a feeling she's determined to marry Umberto and won't be accommodating to anyone who gets in her way. Do I really want to bring Michael into all that?'

'I think this so-called house of secrets could do with a thorough sweep out, and you're just the one to blow the cobwebs away.' Marie-Jeanne gave a chuckle, chiding her friend gently. 'You read too many romantic novels.'

'No, really. A girl died on the estate years ago. Everybody is being weird and mysterious about it, and a general atmosphere of unease hangs over the house. It's no wonder Umberto's depressed.'

'Hmm. My conclusion after this conversation is that you have two choices: one, you pack your bags and run a mile from all these problems, but you'll probably always wonder if you missed out on the love of your life. Or two, you stay and get engaged to Umberto, after which anything Silvana says to discredit you probably won't have the power to hurt you. Either way, you should return your fee, which will put you in a stronger position morally. The clinic's bank account won't exactly be healthy, but we'll survive.'

'I'd already decided to do that. Taking money from the Monteverdis felt utterly untenable.'

'Good. So, how about you spend time with Umberto anyway and try to help him in a semi-professional capacity?'

Not for the first time Catriona felt a warm glow towards her friend and colleague for her big-heartedness.

'Give yourself three months,' Marie-Jeanne continued. 'Tell Umberto about Michael sooner rather than later. Then it'll all come out in the wash one way or the other.'

'You make it sound so easy. But then again you haven't got hormones like mine to contend with!' Catriona gave a tired laugh. 'I try to do the right thing, then he just has to come close and I'm all over the place.'

At that, her friend's voice on the other end of the line sounded wistful. 'I feel rather jealous. I've forgotten what it feels like to be in the first throes of a love affair.'

'Sometimes it feels like the purest agony,' Catriona admitted with a sigh.

'Well, let's hope it's worth it. The important thing is that you get yourself together and that your son grows up knowing he has a father who's alive and, hopefully, with whom he'll be able to interact. Don't lose sight of that in your surge of hormones.'

'What about my mother and Michael? I really don't think it would be a good idea to announce my engagement at this stage.

Maman might understand, but it would completely unbalance Michael.'

'I agree. You could tell Marguerite, but wait until later to tell Michael. Maybe it would be best if you brought Umberto to Nice so that your son feels secure at home when you speak to him, then break it all to him at once. Children are remarkably adaptable, you know. All they long for is parents who wish the best for them and give them a loving home.'

'Bless you, Marie-Jeanne. You're such a dear friend. What would I do without you?'

Laughter tinkled down the line. 'You'd drown!'

'You can say that again. I might be good at analyzing other people's problems but when it comes to my own, I'm lost.'

'I think we're all made that way. Anyhow, I'm happy that I've been able to help. Let me know what you decide.'

Catriona chuckled, feeling a great weight had lifted from her shoulders and as light as the blue butterfly that had just flitted by gracefully. 'After speaking to you, my mind's made up. I'm staying, of course, and giving Umberto and myself a chance.'

Marie-Jeanne's voice came back full of teasing affection: 'Ah, to think there might be wedding bells in the near future …'

Catriona laughed. 'Hey, wait a minute! One step at a time. But thank you, I feel so much better now.'

'Good. So, I'll sift through this mountain of CVs and make a choice, yes?'

'Yes, please.'

'Great. *Au revoir, ma chèrie, bonne chance et à bientôt.*'

'Yes, speak soon.'

Catriona put her mobile back in her pocket and glanced at her watch. The heat was beginning to rise. Time had marched on; she must have been out longer than she realized. She needed to get back and find Umberto. Maybe he'd changed his mind by now and wasn't so eager to tie his life to hers. If that was the case

… Her heart gave a tiny squeeze – she'd cross that bridge when she came to it.

A cuckoo chimed his relentless song, making Catriona lift her head to the clear blue sky. Hot air throbbed over her face. High above, a dove was brooding in her nest and from a neighbouring oak her mate took up his call, repeating the note of love. Suddenly the countryside was singing in all its glory, matching the summer in Catriona's heart.

She turned to retrace her steps but was now uncertain of the right direction. When she had come across the boulder, she had been on the phone and had not paid much attention to landmarks. *This must be the way* … no, it was wrong. Catriona began, inevitably, to walk in circles, exasperated and a little nervous but half-amused by her predicament. Just when she believed she was at last making headway, she found herself back in the same spot where the mossy boulder protruded from the undergrowth.

A twig cracked loudly behind her. Turning, she thought she saw a flash of something moving between the trees.

'Hello? Is anybody there?'

Catriona stilled, listening and watching the shadows among the trees, but there was nothing except the sunlight glinting down through the canopy of leaves above, their gentle rustle mingling with the intermittent warbling of bird calls. Annoyed with herself for being so skittish merely because she'd lost her way, Catriona began walking back along the same track.

Suddenly she heard the pounding of hooves and saw Silvana cantering towards her along one of the shadowy paths. Not in riding gear and without her hat, she was beautiful, almost surreal with her silky flame-red hair piled up on her head like a glowing crown. Everything about the woman spoke of elegance – and of hours spent in front of the mirror.

'Still here, *Dottoressa*?' she sneered, pulling on the reins and bringing her horse to a halt in front of Catriona. She glared down at her from the saddle, her steel eyes gleaming like grey diamonds in the sunlight.

Catriona looked up at her coolly. 'Obviously.'

'How long before you leave?'

'As long as it takes.'

Silvana's brows curved upwards in distaste. 'It won't do you any good, you know, clinging on here.'

'I have a job to do and I intend to do it.'

At Catriona's determined tone Silvana's eyes widened a fraction. 'A job? I think you've done enough harm already! It's scandalous, the way you've been carrying on with your *patient*,' she said, biting sarcasm in the final word. With a humourless laugh, she added: 'Was it really worth risking your professional standing, your good name, for a sweaty fling with a blindman?' Catriona stiffened, her hand curling into a fist by her side, but her chin stayed lifted while Silvana went on: 'Anyway, what exactly will you be doing?'

What indeed, Catriona thought. She cleared her throat and met her rival's steady stare. 'Not that it's any of your business, but I'll be helping Umberto gain confidence in playing again … in composing as well. I plan to teach him the rudiments of reading a score with Braille and help him make the move back into the professional world he's been missing. He needs to go to concerts, at the very least, before he feels ready to perform in public again.'

Silvana nodded. 'Oh!' It was amazing how much she managed to convey with that tiny syllable. 'Of course, what you're trying to do for Umberto is commendable … really commendable.'

The amazon's eyes narrowed to slits, and with her high cheekbones and minute nose, she looked like a beautiful cat. She paused a moment, tilting her head to one side, her full lips pushed out into a pout.

'I suppose offering your body was just part of his therapy … loosen him up so that he's amenable to the other parts of your programme. How very avant garde!'

'That is between him and me. As I said before, it's none of your business. Any further discussion would be demeaning to us both, don't you think?' Catriona attempted a tone of asperity but felt distinctly the underdog in this exchange, especially as Silvana had the benefit of height, glaring down from her mount.

'I'm just trying to protect Umberto. In his vulnerable state who knows what types might take advantage of him?' Silvana read the fury in Catriona's face and the redhead's horse skittered uneasily.

'Money apart, I just hope you're doing this for the right reasons because if you're hoping that by hanging around you can make him interested in you, you're wasting your time. Umberto's days are empty, his only release is sex. He's just using you instead of his hand to alleviate the tension.'

'You're disgusting,' Catriona exclaimed.

Silvana gave a throaty chuckle. 'Just being honest, *Dottoressa*. You see, I understand Umberto, I'm well aware of his needs. We've been through a lot together, he and I. Oh, I know he's had affairs with women all over the world, but he always comes back to me.' Her lips curled at the corners and her eyes flashed dangerously. '*Always.*'

Catriona shrugged. 'It has nothing to do with me what he has or hasn't done. All that matters now is that he gets better.'

Silvana's strained laugh joined the shrill monotonous creaking sound of crickets that with noon had started chirping in the trees. 'Oh, come *on* … "nothing to do with me"?' she chorused, mimicking Catriona's words. 'Well, after yesterday, I think you know, *dottoressa* Drouot … I think you know perfectly well what it has to do with you.'

There was hate in her, Catriona felt – the kind born out of the pangs of frustrated love, eating at her heart like a cancer. She couldn't help but reflect that it made Silvana a dangerous adversary, especially when she had the benefit of being armed with a piece of information that could undo her rival.

'Will you kindly point me in the right direction so I can get back to the house,' Catriona asked with as much dignity as she could muster, though anxious to get away from Silvana's threatening stare. 'I lost my way earlier,' she explained, 'and have been walking in a circle.'

'Try not to lose your way in life, *cara*,' the other woman scoffed. 'When losing your way in the countryside, you will always find someone to show you the way. But losing one's way in life is, as you say in French, *une autre paire de manches*, another kettle of fish. Only a fool would fall in love with Umberto Monteverdi but something tells me, *dottoressa* Drouot, you're no fool.'

Having delivered this vitriolic message, Silvana flicked the reins of her restless mare and overtook Catriona on the path.

'Follow my horse, I'll lead you back to the villa.'

Chapter 14

When Catriona returned to the lodge she found Adelina waiting for her, sitting on the steps, her head in her hands. The old woman seemed deeply distressed and immediately rushed towards her, wringing her hands.

'*Meno male che e' venuti!*, thank God you've arrived! Where were you, *Dottoressa?* We've been looking for you all morning.'

'I went for a walk and got a bit lost.' Seeing how agitated Adelina was, concern leapt into Catriona's throat. 'What's up, Adelina? Has something happened to *il signor* Umberto?'

'*Sì, sì* … he's been locked in his room since this morning and won't let anyone in. Normally, he shouts and then at least I know he's all right. But this morning …' she spread her hands emphatically, '*niente*, nothing.'

'Don't worry, take me to him.' She placed a reassuring hand on Adelina's arm. 'It'll be all right, trust me.'

'*Speriamo*, let's hope, *Dottoressa*.'

The house was completely quiet when they got there. They ascended the stairs opposite the conservatory and Catriona was reminded of the last time she had been up there, trying to coax Umberto from his room. So much had happened between them since then.

Although she was loath to show her concern to Adelina, Catriona was worried. There was a tightness at her temples and a hollow feeling in the pit of her stomach. The day before had been full of heightened emotions and in cases like Umberto's, where patients were prone to extreme changes of mood, this could be extremely dangerous. He might well have been drinking again. How unprofessional and irresponsible she'd been … if something had happened to him, she would never forgive herself.

'This way, *prego*,' Adelina said laconically, leading her down the corridor to where the dark-panelled door was firmly closed at the far end.

The housekeeper knocked. There was no answer. She knocked again.

'*Signor Umberto, la Dottoressa è qui per vederla*, the doctor is here to see you.'

Adelina's words were met with silence.

By this time Mario had joined them, armed with a sledgehammer. He turned to Catriona, looking for direction. She needed to think quickly. She was beginning to have a bad feeling: Umberto might be lying there, unconscious.

'*Signor Umberto, per favore apra la porta.*' This time it was Catriona who called out.

Adelina was wringing her hands again and sobbing, praying, imploring God and all the saints for mercy.

'Break the door,' Catriona commanded. She glanced at Mario. 'Unless, of course, you know of a different way.'

Mario shook his head. 'We had to break the door last time,' he told her.

Catriona nodded. '*Allora fallo*, go ahead then.'

He didn't need her to say it twice. Standing perpendicular to the door, Mario swung the sledgehammer back with both hands and struck at the lock. It broke after a couple of tries and they hurried into the room.

A heavy smell of alcohol filled the air. A vase of flowers had been smashed to the ground, together with a whole load of books and two large, framed, black-and-white photographs. Umberto's armchair was overturned and a round, heavy Renaissance table lay on its side against one of the tall windows. It must have taken the strength of Samson to heave it so far.

Umberto lay face down on the floor in a pool of brandy, a smashed empty liquor bottle next to him and another half-drunk on the table next to his upturned armchair. He was breathing torturously, his naked chest glazed with sweat, hair in damp curls plastered against his forehead.

Catriona rushed to kneel beside him, ignoring the sharp sting as a piece of glass sliced through the fabric of her thin trousers and into her knee. She quickly glanced over him, calling his name and trying to get a response, but he lay unconscious. The knuckles of one hand were badly grazed and bruised as if he had knocked his fist into a hard object, the fingers of the other twitched. She took his pulse and heaved a sigh of relief.

'His pulse is a little faint but he seems all right. He must have tripped or passed out.'

She examined him further to make sure nothing was broken and noticed that his face was badly bruised around his right temple where he must have banged his head. There was a little swelling and coagulated blood and Catriona feared he was probably concussed and needed immediate attention.

She turned to Mario. 'Please lift the *signore* on to the bed,' she instructed, then turning to Adelina: 'You need to call a doctor. Drinking can hide the usual signs of concussion and his head injury might be more serious than it looks. Although I think the worst is past, he'll need some attention. Maybe a sedative after he comes to. Go … I'll stay with him.'

'*Lo chiamo subito*, don't worry, I will call the *dottore*,' Mario said, taking out his mobile phone and proceeding to ring the family doctor.

Catriona watched Umberto's chest movements. He was breathing heavily, which was normal with alcohol intoxication, but he needed looking after. His skin had a deathly pallor under the tan. She was shocked by his appearance: the purple-shadowed eyes in their deep sockets, the lines of strain carved on his taut features, a full day's growth of stubble darkening his jaw. Catriona could smell the liquor on his breath and that, plus the empty bottles, told her that he must have been drinking non-stop since he'd left her in bed at the lodge the previous night.

What unbearable pain had brought him to such a state, driving him to drink himself unconscious? What had so subdued his proud, arrogant spirit? It was as if he had been driven to the end of his tether. She was appalled that it might be partly of her making. Did he regret his proposal to her of last night? Such emotional upheaval as she had caused in the past twenty-four hours was bound to take its toll on a man already battling dark torments … torments that went far deeper than his blindness. This was certainly not the outcome Calandra had expected from an experienced psychologist and therapist when she had chosen Catriona for this assignment.

Her heart squeezed, torn by what? Guilt? Compassion? Tenderness? Love? A combination of all four, she thought, but it was mainly guilt that sat heavily in the pit of her stomach.

Catriona longed to put her arms around Umberto and hold him close, erase the lines of weariness and strain from his face, exorcising the demons that drove him. She wanted to tell him that she wanted to give their relationship a go.

Adelina had calmed down and was now fretting about Catriona. '*Dottoressa*, you have had nothing to eat since yesterday's lunch,' she protested. 'This morning, when I took away your supper tray, it was untouched and I noticed you'd hardly touched your breakfast either.' She eyed her closely. 'Do you not like our food?'

Catriona blushed, embarrassed. When had Adelina brought round her supper? Had she been aware that Umberto was upstairs in her bedroom and realized what they were up to? Had she heard the scene with Silvana?

'It's nothing to do with your cooking, Adelina, quite the reverse. I'm, *er* … not used to eating more than twice a day.'

The old servant nodded and gave her a sidelong look. '*Adelina non è nata ieri*, Adelina wasn't born yesterday,' she mumbled as she began to tidy up the room, picking up the pieces of broken glass scattered around the floor.

Mario left the room and returned swiftly, clutching a washbasin, sponge and pitcher of steaming water, and proceeded to give Umberto a careful wash.

Catriona approached the still figure on the bed and took the cloth from the servant's hand. 'Let me do that,' she murmured.

Without conscious volition, the back of her hand caressed her lover's cheek and stroked a lock of dark, wet hair away from his brow. His skin felt damp and sweaty. She dipped the cloth into the water and gently wiped off the moisture that formed tiny pearls at his hairline.

Umberto suddenly groaned and flinched at her touch. His lashes flickered open to reveal those bewitching emerald eyes. 'What the hell's going on?' she heard him whisper and then, 'My head …' he groaned, his hands reaching across his eyes. Then he extended an arm to push Catriona away.

Although he couldn't see her, he had obviously realized that it wasn't Mario who was performing the usual task of cleaning him up after one of his episodes. He turned his face away as though trying to shut out her presence. 'I've had too much to drink, you shouldn't be here.'

But Catriona was not to be deflected. 'Maybe not, but I am.'

She could see that he was struggling to pull himself together and resume the iron control that was so much a part of him;

an effort that brought more beads of sweat to his forehead and down to the corded muscles of his throat. It was not only his abused body he was fighting to marshal, Catriona knew that he was working equally hard to clear the mist from his brain brought on by the alcohol he had consumed and compounded by his concussion.

As she began to unbutton his trousers, Adelina approached the bed. 'Mario and I will do this, *Dottoressa*. The *signore* is used to us. Maybe you should go and relax and I will bring you some lunch and let you know when the doctor is here.'

Catriona hesitated.

'Go away,' Umberto murmured hoarsely. 'Please, just go …'

Without a word, she stood up. This was not the time to argue, not the time to be stubborn. Of course he was humiliated, he obviously didn't want her to see him in this state. She moved away slowly. Then, allowing herself a last glance at Umberto, she left the room.

*   *   *

Catriona returned to the lodge and changed out of her trousers, cleaning up her knee and finding a plaster. It was understandable that Umberto hadn't wanted her there after he'd collapsed amid the chaos of his smashed-up room, she told herself. Yet it was hard to ignore her pang of disappointment at having been turned away so emphatically.

More than anything, she realized how remiss she had been not to plan a therapeutic programme more concertedly, pushing to have Umberto work at the sessions with her. She needed to select appropriate pieces of music that would demand his engagement and use every possible instigation to encourage him to listen. Playing on his proud and arrogant nature, she would find pieces played by musicians he loathed – that would be sure to irritate him. Every emotion was valid; she would even use anger to draw him in. Her therapy plan needed to be modulated carefully to direct Umberto away from his depressive obsessions and deliver him back to his first passion, his music.

As she made her way back to the villa, hoping to meet Enzo Camilleri, Umberto's doctor, to discuss her client's state, she met Adelina, who told her that the *Dottore* had already been and gone.

'I wanted to call you, but the *signore* asked me not to.'

Catriona frowned. 'How is he? What did the doctor say?'

'The *signore* is much better now. He's sleeping. He was violently sick before *il dottor* Enzo arrived. The *Dottore* gave him a mild sedative but said the *signore* had been badly concussed by that knock to the head.' She raised her eyes to the heavens with an exasperated expression.

'And that the amount he'd drunk would have made it worse. He recommended the *signore* should make an appointment with his eye specialist as soon as possible. Just to check the impact of that knock hasn't further damaged his eyes in some way.'

They turned back towards the lodge and Catriona fell into step with Adelina, her eyes wide. 'So, he needs to make an immediate appointment?'

Adelina nodded, though she looked doubtful. '*Sì, sì*, but the *signore* said he has no intention of going through a whole load of tests like last time – what was the point? His eyes couldn't get any worse.'

'I'll talk to him.'

'No, please, *Dottoressa*, don't do that. He'll know that I've told you and he will be very upset. I will try to convince him slowly, but the *signore* is very stubborn and you can't rush him. Believe me, I know him better than anyone else – I'm the one who brought him up. He's as wilful now as he has always been.'

'Can I go and see him at least?'

'Maybe this evening. He is sleeping now and *il dottor* Enzo said that after a good night's sleep, he should be fine. But, of course, he must stay away from the bottle.'

'That should be easy enough. Don't buy any more and remove any bottles of spirits in the house.'

Adelina shook her head and made a helpless gesture with her hands more telling than words. 'You would think! *Basta volere,* where there's a will, there's a way.' She gave an indulgent smile as though she was talking about a naughty boy. 'When the doctor asked him how much he'd had to drink, the *signore* said, "*Gli anni e bicchieri di vino non si contano mai*," age and glasses of wine should never be counted.'

Catriona laughed. It was just like Umberto to say a thing like that. 'At least he was feeling better enough to be mischievous, but he must understand that we only want what's best for him.'

The old servant sighed. '*Speriamo*, hopefully, he will come to his senses.'

'I'm sure he'll listen to you. He's very fond of you and respects you.'

Adelina sighed again. '*La confidenza toglie riverenza*, familiarity breeds contempt, *Dottoressa*. He doesn't always listen to me, particularly when he's had one of his episodes, when he's been drinking. The only person who had some power over him is not with us any more.'

'You mean his mother?'

'*Sì*, even though I was the one who brought him up, *la signora* and her son were very close.'

Catriona looked pensive. 'Yes, and I can see that he has a difficult relationship with both Silvana and Giacomo.'

Adelina cocked her head to one side, her dark eyes studying Catriona as though deliberating how much more she should say at this point. '*Sì, il signor* Umberto has only contempt for them.

Anyhow, neither have his best interests at heart.' At Catriona's questioning look, the housekeeper dropped her voice.

'Each in their own way wants to put their hands on his fortune: she by marrying him, Giacomo by hoping his cousin will die soon, leaving him with all this wealth.' Adelina threw her a glance full of insinuation, giving a large sweep of her arm, alluding to the property and all it contained.

Catriona frowned. 'What d'you mean?'

'*Il signor* Giacomo is the only heir to *il signor* Umberto's estate. The day, *Dio non voglia*, God forbid, something happens to the *signore*, his cousin gets it all.' Adelina cast a nervous glance around her as though to search out some unseen eavesdropper and grasped Catriona's arm.

The Italian woman flushed darkly, her features tight with anxiety, almost fear. 'There's something going on around here that I don't like, *Dottoressa*.'

Catriona looked back at the other woman, trying to follow her meaning. 'What are you talking about, Adelina?'

'*Flavio*,' she hissed under her breath. 'He's always somewhere he's not supposed to be, sly as a fox skulking out of the henhouse … And *il signor* Giacomo, always whispering with him when they think no one's watching. They're in cahoots over something, as the saints are my witness, I know it.'

'Perhaps Flavio and Giacomo have estate business to talk about?'

'Estate business?' Adelina waved her hand dismissively and they continued walking. 'Some other business maybe,' she muttered. 'They say that *il signor* Giacomo is mixed up with some bad characters. I wouldn't be surprised if that weasel Flavio is involved somehow. He's no good, that one. I don't trust him.' Her dark, shining eyes became almost fearful as they turned back to Catriona. 'I am always on my guard, looking out for the *signore*, and so is Mario,' she added intently.

Catriona met the housekeeper's steady gaze but made no comment as they continued to the door of the lodge. Adelina had been in service with the Monteverdi family for decades and her loyalty to Umberto was fierce, as was her protectiveness, but was there any foundation to her suspicions? As she pictured the sly Flavio, with his leering eyes that looked her up and down, her unease returned.

*   *   *

Although it was already early evening, the warmth of the sun still lingered as Catriona started back to the house to see Umberto. The sky was all broad stripes of lilac, green, rose and amber – everything wrapped in a glory of colour. Such a beautiful sight! She was aware of the wild pulse of nature in this garden, where stone nymphs and satyrs flirted in the twilight. Another beautiful and balmy evening, full of the breath of the myrtle, Catriona thought as she made her way through the shadows, held by the magic of the lake and the broken song of a bird.

She had expected to find Umberto resting in his room but instead came upon him much sooner. He was alone, lounging on a comfortable reclining chair in the garden in front of the terrace. Her heart beating, she stopped next to an oleander bush at the edge of the lawn to absorb the picture of him. Umberto was leaning back in the chair with his legs stretched before him, his beautiful, unseeing emerald eyes staring straight at her while he mechanically drew circles on his thigh with one hand. His shirt was unbuttoned to his chest, as usual, and a pair of worn jeans clung to his supple, narrow hips. The curls of his raven-black hair fell over one side of the bandage that was wrapped around his forehead. A small frown tugged at his mouth. Altogether too handsome, and suddenly looking so vulnerable, Catriona thought to herself.

She remained motionless for a long moment, watching him from afar, shocked by the pallor in his burnished face and his drawn expression. He looked like an unhappy convalescent teenager. Then she walked slowly towards him as the sun slowly sank towards the horizon and the first cold of evening stabbed the warm atmosphere with the precision of a knife.

Umberto sat up immediately, plagued by a strange agitation. 'Is someone there?' he asked in a low voice, as if anxious that from the world of darkness in which he was plunged would be born some new misfortune.

'It's only me.'

He drew an audible breath. 'Ah, *Dottoressa*, good evening.'

Catriona winced a little at the formality of his greeting. 'How are you feeling? You still look very pale. How's your head?'

A sarcastic smile tugged at his mouth.

'I don't need a nursemaid, thank you.'

Catriona didn't respond at first. Instead she pulled up a chair and sat down in silence. Then she said quietly: 'You made that perfectly clear when you ordered me out of your room. I would have thought that after last night …'

'What about last night? I had a little too much to drink. So what? It happens. You should know that about me by now, *Dottoressa*,' he added irritably.

Her immediate instinct was to recoil in on herself but then her psychiatry training asserted itself. *He's just being defensive, feeling vulnerable.*

'I'm not the young girl you met ten years ago, Umberto,' she said, quietly but firmly. 'I'm not going to play a game with you, where I go along with some pretence that last night didn't mean something.'

He rubbed his jaw and settled his gaze in the direction of her voice. 'What it meant was that I ended up with a sore head and, if that wasn't bad enough, people decided they couldn't just leave me in peace.'

He was hurting, that much was obvious. If she wasn't careful, she could provoke another wrathful incident.

'Umberto, stop this.'

'Stop what?'

'You know perfectly well,' she said quietly. 'You asked me to become your wife.'

Catriona leaned across and laid her hand on his thigh. 'Umberto, what is all this about?'

He reached out, found her shoulder and ran his fingers down her bare arm, before his features became tense. 'You are beautiful, talented … desirable,' he burst out. 'What on earth was I thinking? You could have any man.' He shook his head in resentment as he pointed down at his trousers. 'Just look at me – the mere scent of you sends my whole body into chaos. I'm as hard as a rock.'

'Umberto, please …' she began.

'Don't say anything for a minute, let me finish,' he went on intently. 'Today, I sent you away because I was ashamed … and afraid.' He clenched his jaw as though the admission pained him.

'Ashamed of having given in to self-pity and drunk myself to oblivion last night, and afraid that you wouldn't want anything to do with a pathetic blind drunk.' He put a hand over his eyes. 'I've never wanted to marry anyone, Caterina, I've always been too selfish … always putting myself first.' He raised his head, his glittering green eyes staring, searching the air for her face.

'You, on the other hand … You married … were able to have a life and a child.' His voice was raw. 'I didn't wreck things for you, did I?'

Catriona ached to tell him that he hadn't ruined her life. Instead, he had given her the most blessed gift in Michael. *Should I tell him? Should I show that he has so much to live for? A son, who looks so much like his father … who plays the piano like an angel … who is loving and special in every way.* But with Umberto's next words the moment was gone.

'I don't know if I'd ever want a child now.' His words fell like
a heavy stone, crushing Catriona's imaginings of a thrilled and
whooping Michael being spun around in his father's arms. 'How
could I? It's enough that I have to fend for myself. I can't imagine
you ever wanting to stick with a blind, fumbling depressive ogre
of a man. You'd get bored after a while, Caterina, realizing what
you were missing. You'd find someone else eventually ...'

'After what happened between us ... not only yesterday, but all
those years ago, do you really think I could *look* at another man,
let alone want one? You must have a poor opinion of me,' she told
him, her voice like a whisper of the wind in the trees.

'Still, you married ... you gave that man a child and, if the
reports given to Calandra were right, it couldn't have been long
after we'd met.' All of a sudden his voice was seething with a barely
contained rage. 'How can I believe that you'd stay with me, no
matter how convinced you seem to be about it now?'

His reproach wounded her but she kept silent, waiting for his
next outburst.

But he was spent now. Whatever jealous monster had provoked
this outburst, it had had its fill of him. Umberto closed his eyes
and laid his head on the back of his chair. 'Caterina, what are we
going to do?' he said in a weary voice.

The sunset stained the wide waters of Lake Como every
shade of red and orange and gold so that the sky and the lake
looked as if they were on fire. In the distance, Catriona took
in the view that began at the crest of the mountain then swept
down between bush-covered slopes to the small townships on
the edge of the shore.

The fitful pealing of church bells floated on the pinion of that
summer night. The melody echoed around the far-flung bridges,
the ancient ruined castles, winging over the forests and upland
behind the town of Torno – a most melodious, medieval chime,
a silver sobbing by the still and bright patinated lake.

Catriona watched the sundown work its magic on the countryside. 'We are going to get engaged,' she said calmly.

Without a word, Umberto took her hand and kissed it slowly and tenderly. She knew that they were coming to a crucial crossroads in both of their lives. They would either grow together or grow apart and, in both cases, the outcome would have an important impact on Michael. At the end of the day he had paid the price for their heedless passion and, this time round, she needed to make sure she didn't ruin all three of their lives.

*   *   *

Following their conversation, Umberto and Catriona were curiously at peace with themselves and each other. They had spoken for a little longer and afterwards, as if by some tacit understanding, Umberto went to the piano room. He had promised that if Catriona were to stay on, and if they were to have time off to explore the region – not to mention exploring each other, body and soul – then he would need to honour the original agreement that he play the piano every day for a short while, starting only with the simplest of nursery pieces.

He sat down on the stool and raised the piano lid. Resting his fingers lightly on the keys, he felt a strange stirring within him – not quite fear but something close to it. He brought himself back from the brink of this familiar dark unease and centred himself, remembering Catriona's instruction to keep it simple – so simple that failure wasn't an option. She had told him to try to picture something positive and hold it in his mind as he was playing, a place where he always felt safe and happy and, if negative images bubbled up to the surface, he shouldn't struggle to push them down but give them free rein. The music would lead Umberto safely to a deeper part of his psyche, where the healing would take place. In time, Catriona had assured him, the traumatic pictures that had been flashing into his head, often in a terrifying loop, would cease to have the same power over him.

Umberto wiped his palms, which had become sticky with perspiration, on his trousers. He hit a single note, letting the sound echo around the room for a few moments, then breathed out heavily. *Here goes.* Instead of a nursery rhyme he chose the simplest tunes from Schumann's *Scenes from Childhood*, which Calandra used to play for him when he was small, and which he'd known how to play by heart from the age of seven.

'Blind Man's Buff' seemed as appropriate a place to start as any, he thought wryly, and as his fingers ran up and down the keys, the pianist found a dark humour in the skittering notes that so cleverly mimicked the running feet of children fleeing from the blundering, blindfolded child in pursuit. From this piece he moved to 'Knight of the Hobby Horse', a thumpy little melody that held all the determination Umberto needed right now in its few bars. He ended with 'Child Falling Asleep'.

It was with this third piece that Umberto seemed to move almost into a trance-like space. He played it over and over again and, little by little, found himself improvising on Schumann's melody. As he did so, his fingers moving autonomously as if by some supernatural magic, questions seemed to rise up inside him as though from his very soul. *Will I ever be able to compose again? What can I do to make amends for Sofia? How can I ease the pain in my heart for everything I've lost ... my mother, my sight? How can I keep her, my Caterina, my life?*

His heart was full and although the pain did not diminish, he also sensed that what was happening here and now in this room was the best medicine.

Umberto knew exactly how the room would look at this hour, with the night peeping in through the dusky windows and, here and there, clusters of green leaves and sweet-smelling roses shining in the lamplight as they peered in curiously from the garden. How many summer nights had he spent sitting at his favourite instrument, transported into another world – the world of his fantasies and dreams? A curious blend of emotions chased one another like billows through Umberto's heart: love and pain, predominantly, but also joy, hope and excitement because she had said yes.

Since Caterina had arrived, so much had happened. He felt suddenly uplifted by the surging tide of a new life, in the same way that a boat, after a long period of inactivity upon the sandy shore, is abruptly swept away and tossed upward by the waves. A surprising sense of elation filled him as he listened eagerly for a voice to guide his inspiration.

At first there was silence and darkness. Then certain vague sounds strove to rise to the surface. Still, he could not grasp their tones, form or colours, but somewhere from the depths of his soul, Umberto could hear the emerging modulations of musical phrases. He seemed to see the row of ivory keys flashing in the darkness as they rippled like a gleaming, silken ribbon under his fingers.

All at once, a shaft of light penetrated the darkness within and Umberto's improvisation took him to a whole new place. Uplifted by fresh waves of emotion, he surrendered himself to the tide that swept forward in full, resonant and tumultuous chords.

Though at first hesitating and vague, each note evoked by Umberto's fingers gave voice in low, soft tones to the countless memories of his past life and surroundings. Everything was there: the moaning of the wind, the whispering of the forest, the ripples of the lake. Most of all, there was that indefinite murmur of an inner feeling, the sense of something lost in the remote distance of one's subconscious that he struggled to illuminate. It formed a sort of background for the deep and inscrutable agitation that was swelling his heart, leaping up in his soul at the bidding of inspiration's mysterious whisper – a feeling one couldn't easily define. Was it sadness? Why was it then so sweet? Was it joy? If so, why was it so profoundly, inexplicably sad?

Umberto's imagination strove to gain control over this flood of chaotic images, at first without success. The powerful influences of his impetuous and passionate nature, even though confused and almost desperate, had taken full possession of him. From time to time their raw energy intensified, fuelling his strength as he tried to tame this influx of emotions and combine them into a melodious and perfect deluge of harmony.

Still he was struggling, curbed by this unusual depth of feeling that was submerging him and dragging him in its tide. He stopped and started again repeatedly, in stubborn desperation. Every time the notes tried to surge to their full height, they suddenly fell back into a plaintive murmur, like a wave breaking into foam and spray, and nothing was heard but their sad lingering sound that hung like unanswered questions in the air, echoing through the silence of the music room.

Then, all of a sudden, he had a vision of Caterina, his muse, his love, coming towards him, wrapped in a clinging primrose nightdress. *Mio Dio,* she was even more beautiful than he remembered. Her smile was so wide that her whole face lit up and she moved with sensuous grace as she came towards him, looking at him with those beautiful, pleading, honey-coloured eyes, gazing insistently, deeply into his as if spellbound. Knowing that she could no more take her eyes off him than he could tear his from her sent a surge of power through him.

Mesmerizing memories came rushing forward: magic moments, smouldering fires, insatiable passion ... He was inhaling the sweet fragrance of her hair, his mouth lingering for only a moment before lightly kissing her pink, full, parted lips ... her face, her delicate, swanlike neck. A soft moan, a sigh, escaped her lips and he could feel her heartbeat pounding under his fingertips with wanton desire.

Now that Umberto's muse had come alive with a beating heart and was speaking to his bursting soul in the language of love and music, he played this piece again. From the very first resonant chords, there was such brilliance, animation and genuine feeling in the music that it stunned him. It flowed out of him naturally, completely in tune with his spirit, and instantly he recognized that old feeling of wonder mingled with delight that had so often transported him into another world. For a moment he forgot that he was blind and let himself be lifted up to the heavens, where his innocent angel was waiting to enfold him in her warm and loving embrace.

After the last notes had died away, Umberto remained seated, still as a statue with his hands on the keyboard. He was overwhelmed by a new sense of happiness and the potent impression left by the transcendent experience. A storm had risen out of the depths of his brain and carried him aloft with such a powerful and exhilarating force that, even now, he felt he was still flying. Umberto played the piece a few times more, changing a chord here, enhancing a note there, but overall he was satisfied. Still, he wouldn't tell anyone about this: he would finesse his composition until it was perfect and then give it to Caterina on their wedding day.

The clock struck midnight. Umberto's hands finally stilled over the keys. He should be going to bed – if not, he would be unfit for their trip tomorrow. Before Caterina had left him on the terrace, he'd insisted on taking her to the Isle of Comacina to see the festival of San Giovanni, which meant starting first thing in the morning. She would love the spectacle, and he ... well, the timing was right. Tonight, the composer had rediscovered something in himself that he thought long dead, and the euphoric feeling was still warm within; that was something worth celebrating. Besides, he needed to push himself out of his voluntary solitude – the festival would provide the perfect opportunity.

It was just as Umberto was reaching out for the piano lid that he received the first bright flash of light across his eyes. A stab of excruciating pain followed and he almost blacked out for a few seconds. His hands fell on to the keyboard, the discordant notes ringing out in the room as he waited for the pain to subside long enough for him to stand.

Slowly, he crossed the room to the door, concentrating on the number of steps. Cursing under his breath at the lack of his usual spacial awareness, Umberto was determined not to call for Mario. Everyone would only make a fuss around him. No, he could do this himself. He took a step out into the hallway, then inched his way towards the staircase, running his hand along the wall until he found the banister.

Umberto was almost at the top of the stairs leading to his bedroom when a second bright light burned behind his eyes and almost threw him off balance. He stumbled over the remainder of the steps but somehow managed to make his way into the room and on to his bed. Fumbling in the drawer of his bedside table, he found the painkillers *il dottor* Enzo had prescribed for him that morning. Swallowing a couple, he rested his head against the pillows and fell into a deep sleep, still fully dressed.

*   *   *

After their long conversation, Catriona had left the house satisfied that Umberto had sounded quite reasonable and level headed. They had agreed to spend the night separately so that he would be on top form the next day to take her on a trip to Isola Comacina, where they would spend the weekend. At first, Catriona had wanted to postpone the visit.

'You know what *il dottor* Enzo said,' she'd pointed out. 'The best treatment for a head injury like yours is plenty of rest and not overdoing things. With that bruise, I don't think it would be sensible to go off on a trip just yet. We'll have plenty of time for excursions.' But Umberto had been insistent and asked her not to fuss.

'You worry too much, *cara*. I'm feeling much better and I know what's best for me. Sitting around here isn't the answer. This trip will make a nice change and it'll get me out of the house. I haven't been to a public place since the accident and it's about time I left this cocoon, don't you think?'

'In any other circumstances I would have agreed with you, but after …'

'Let me be the judge of this, Caterina,' he replied, a note of frustration edging his voice. 'The visit to the island is a must. It is the only island on Lake Como and the views of the lake and its surroundings are magnificent.'

'What's the great rush?' She frowned. It was obvious he was restless but this all felt too soon.

Umberto sighed. 'Tomorrow is the festival of San Giovanni. The festival has been celebrated for three hundred years, on the anniversary of the destruction of the island in the twelfth century. There's a great show of splendid illuminations over the lake, with myriad boats processing along its shores. The day after, a Mass is said among the remaining stones of the Basilica of Sant' Eufemia. It's a very emotional celebration.' He gave her a slow, reassuring smile. 'I am feeling really well this afternoon after my sleep and, as I said, it will be an opportunity for me to reappear in public after so many years.'

Catriona hesitated – it sounded rather wonderful, she had to admit, though the stunning views would be wasted on Umberto. 'It won't be much fun for you.'

He laughed. 'Why not? Because I'm blind? I've visited the island many times. It's not very large but there's a wonderful restaurant there and the history and legends surrounding it are fascinating. It's an occasion not to be missed,' Umberto had assured her and although she would have preferred him to take a few more days to recover, Catriona had given in.

Returning to the lodge, she steeled herself to ring her mother, whom she couldn't be sure would react positively to the news of her newly ignited relationship with Umberto, let alone of their engagement. Before she did so, though, Catriona called Marie-Jeanne to discuss the events of the day and how best to broach the whole subject with Marguerite.

The call was just what she needed. Marie-Jeanne's sensible tone did much to settle her friend's nerves. 'Just tell her straight,' she advised. 'It's your life, remember. You've done enough stepping around, trying to please everybody else. This is what you want, isn't it?'

'Yes, it is,' admitted Catriona. 'And yet it's still so much of an emotional roller coaster. Umberto is on cloud nine one minute and in the depths of despair the next. He drank himself into a stupor last night and ended up with concussion.'

She then realized how bad this would sound to her friend and prepared herself for a strong warning: *are you sure you want to tie your future to someone as unstable as that?* But instead, Marie-Jeanne took a different line.

'It's only natural. He's an artist, after all, which makes him that much more sensitive. Added to which, remember he's an Italian – and a noble, highly strung stallion type at that. His passion and highly tuned emotions are probably what attracted you to him so strongly in the first place.' But Marie-Jeanne's words didn't come without a warning.

'However, your feelings for Umberto do appear to be developing so quickly that I fear for you.' Her friend's voice softened in concern. 'I hardly recognize you, *chérie*. You've hurtled headlong into this love affair like a young girl with her first crush. You must get a grip if you don't want to get hurt.'

'I know but I feel like I'm at sea, having left my good sense behind. It's like the other me, the sensible working mother, is a different person entirely. I barely recognize myself either!'

'At the risk of sounding trite, you need to understand that Umberto today is like a man whose soul has withered in the desert. To him, you are like a cool, gently flowing stream: life-giving, healing. You're his lifeline now but you can't be sure how he will react the day he's back on his feet.'

Catriona knew that Marie-Jeanne was right. It also raised the question: how could you possibly help or heal other minds if your own wasn't under control?

Still, everything had changed since that first meeting with Calandra and even more so since she had seen Umberto again. Coming here to Lake Como had made Catriona recognize that she'd always believed deep down that Michael was not the product of a one-night stand so much as the seed of a burgeoning true love cut short by unfavourable circumstances. This, she tried to explain to Marie-Jeanne, was a journey that had merely been interrupted and then picked up once again. Catriona felt instinctively, not through any sense of logic, that she was treading the path meant for her.

'Well then, I wish you luck, *mon brave*,' Marie-Jeanne chuckled. 'I'm far too down-to-earth to believe in fate, but I have a great weakness for happy endings.' On a more serious note, she concluded: 'But do guard yourself in all this, *chérie*. I sense you are vulnerable now that Umberto has opened you up to all these feelings. If it all gets too much for you, get on the first plane home.'

Feeling so much better after speaking with Marie-Jeanne, Catriona rang her mother, who, as she had feared, proved much more difficult to handle.

After Catriona had finished asking about Michael – whether he'd been eating properly and getting enough sleep in the hot weather – Marguerite immediately moved the conversation on to what was obviously most on her mind.

'I don't suppose you've managed to tell him the truth yet.'

Catriona marvelled at how her mother could, at times, sound exactly like the courtroom prosecutor she was.

'I will in my own time,' she replied hotly, any calmness Marie-Jeanne had left her with vanishing immediately. 'It has to be handled carefully.'

'Well, the point is that Umberto has a son and you can't deny him the right of knowing that.'

'Okay, okay! On that we're agreed, *Maman*. It's no use hectoring me about it.'

How was it that Marguerite could make her feel so exasperated with just one comment? Catriona needed no more reminding. Now, Michael had a real chance of knowing his father. At least he *had* a father who was still alive – Catriona remembered how she had treasured hers for the short time he'd been in her life. She wasn't going to be responsible for taking that away from her son. 'Anyway, there's something else I need to tell you about …'

As Catriona had guessed, Marguerite was strongly opposed to the engagement. Being a lawyer, she pointed out how it could ruin Catriona's career if, at some stage, someone with a grudge were to report her for forming a relationship with a client.

'And you need to send back that money sitting in the clinic's bank account immediately.'

'Yes, I know. I'm about to deal with that.' By now, Catriona was getting annoyed, partly because this had hit a raw nerve. The promised hefty fee was earning interest, which didn't feel right at all. Of course, she needed to speak to Umberto and send the money back as soon as possible. She let out a frustrated sigh. 'I just wish you could be happy for me, *Maman*, and not constantly seeking out all the potential problems. I'm not one of your legal cases.'

'I'm sorry, *chérie*, you're still my daughter and with everything you've been through, well … I just can't help trying to give you guidance if I can. Of course, all I've ever wanted is for you to be happy.'

After that, Marguerite took a softer tone and called Michael so that Catriona could speak to him. Hearing the excited chatter and little details of his day soothed her instantly so that by the time she hung up, her temper was quite restored. *After all*, she told herself, *Maman is only trying to protect me. It's only natural when you love someone and you've spent half a lifetime caring for them.*

At least they were agreed about one thing: Michael's happiness and security were of paramount importance, and nothing should risk threatening that.

For the remainder of the evening, Catriona kept herself purposely busy on her laptop, excitement about the following day's romantic excursion with Umberto mingling with a sense of trepidation that was to stay with her until morning.

CHAPTER 15

'*Buongiorno, carissima*,' Umberto called out as he approached the lodge.

Catriona was ready and waiting for him in the doorway. As always when she saw him, her heart leapt and the irresistible need for him flooded her; for a few moments, she had a strong urge to pull him inside and delay their trip for an hour until she managed to bring her unruly hormones under control.

He had taken the bandage from his head and a dark bruise was now visible at his temple. Despite this, the freshly shaved Umberto looked healthy with is raven hair, golden tanned skin and strong, broad shoulders. Catriona stared at the persuasive contours of his forearms with their smattering of tiny hairs burnished by the sun.

Umberto was wearing beige chinos with a white shirt, and he'd thrown his jacket over one shoulder, holding it hooked casually with one finger. Sunglasses were perched high on the crown of his head and the intense emerald of his eyes was dazzling. He seemed happy and light hearted; so solid, so good looking, so alive.

Although Catriona knew he wouldn't be able to see her, she'd taken particular care to look her best for him. She wore a softly structured and sleeveless summer mini dress in bright yellow with ruffles at the shoulders and hem. The nipped-in waist and sculpting seam details enhanced the flattering shape of her silhouette. Yellow was a colour that suited her, bringing out her golden complexion and the chestnut tones in her hair and hazel eyes.

Warmth and charisma rolled from Umberto in waves, threatening to engulf her in their tidal force. With one arm, he pulled her to him, pressing her against him as he kissed her near the ear. He wore a tantalizing new aftershave and she felt the warmth of his minted breath on her cheek. 'I dreamt of you all night, *cara*,' he whispered and bit her earlobe.

Catriona shuddered. 'Isn't it a little early to begin all this, Umberto?' Her tone was half amused, half reproachful.

He gave her a slow, roguish smile. 'Haven't you missed me?'

'Of course I have, but there's a time and a place for everything.'

He shrugged and his lips curled into a very Italian sort of pout. 'These things cannot be controlled.'

Catriona shook her head and couldn't help but laugh.

The sun was already hot. Blossom trees scented the air with citrus; blue haze was already quivering over the mountains, and the lake lay like a shield of burnished metal far below. The drowsy tinkling of cowbells from the higher pastures and the monotonous rattle of the *cicale* were the only sounds that broke the intense stillness.

The steps leading down from the lodge to the lake seemed to follow the elegant meanderings of a Bach fugue. Here, as with the rest of Villa Monteverdi, a profusion of greenery and flowers provided astonishing glimpses over the sun-spangled lake for any visitor coming to the house by boat.

Catriona gave Umberto her hand to lead him down the stairs to the pier, but he pushed it away gently. 'We're still on Monteverdi ground here. I know this place like the back of my hand. After the accident, I spent months calculating paces around the grounds so that I could move about easily, like someone who wasn't blind. It kept me sane during that first year.'

Concerto was a forty-foot cruiser yacht with a strikingly graceful white exterior of fluid curves and a spectacular structural covering. Having noticed with a smile the name of the boat, Catriona's expression changed when she saw that Flavio the boatman was standing not far away with his back to them, hosing down the Monteverdi yacht in preparation for their excursion. Although she was excited at the idea of spending the day visiting the fabulous island and being wined and dined by Umberto, the disquieting presence of Flavio suddenly made her uneasy once more.

She was surprised, though relieved, that it was Mario who helped them on to the boat. The older man gave her a nod of greeting and a quick smile.

'I thought Flavio was the boatman,' she murmured to Umberto as he felt for her hand and they moved along to the bow end.

Umberto shrugged. 'Adelina insisted that it should be Mario who accompanies us. She favours him far more, and these days invents all sorts of excuses to keep him on the estate. As for Flavio, Adelina thinks that he doesn't want to be here. She says that he's never forgiven his grandmother, Rosita, for taking him away from the Casino Campione on the Italian Swiss border, where he was a waiter, so he could replace our boatman Guido when he retired eight years ago. Anyway, luckily, Mario sails as well.' He smiled, flashing white teeth. 'People who live around the lake are in and out of boats all the time.'

'I wonder why Flavio was so reluctant to leave his other job?'

Umberto raised an eyebrow, wryly. 'Because he thought that the status of this one was a very poor exchange for the excitement of casino life. Although he receives a much higher salary here, he's always maintained that the casino's tips were sometimes magnificent. As he vulgarly put it, there were rich pickings to be had whenever one of the women in beautiful clothes eyed him up with interest. He still goes back there to work on his holidays and at weekends.'

'I must say, I've found him rather cocky and arrogant when I've seen him around.'

Umberto frowned slightly, his hand tightening on hers. 'You should have told me, *cara*. Has he been bothering you? I can see to it that he doesn't come near you if—'

'No … no, please, Umberto don't make a fuss. I don't much like him, that's all …' She paused for a moment as she remembered something Mario had told her. 'Doesn't Flavio accompany you when you go for your swims?' The more she thought of it, the more she realized she was not at all sure she liked the idea.

'Yes, he's an excellent swimmer. He won some sort of medal when he was twelve. That's why Giacomo recommended he be in charge of me when I swim off the raft. It keeps me fit, plus Flavio's been around boats all his life so it made sense to make him our boatman, too. He's very useful to have around.' He cocked his head to one side as though sensing Catriona was unsettled. 'What is it, *cara*?'

'I don't know … there's something shifty about him that makes me feel uncomfortable.'

Umberto huffed in amusement. 'You're becoming like Adelina – she doesn't seem to care for him much either. She doesn't like that he's so friendly with Giacomo. When she's out shopping in town, she's often seen them having a drink at the bar on the harbour. I don't find it that surprising. They're almost the same age, single and they've both been working in the tourist industry.' He grinned. 'I suppose even my slippery cousin must have someone to drink grappa with.'

Catriona studied his face, remembering Adelina's fearful suspicions about Flavio and Giacomo, though she'd been rather vague.

'Adelina just has your best interests at heart, Umberto. You know that.'

'She also has a very vivid imagination and often sees cloak-and-dagger stories where there are none. Come, let me show you inside.'

Catriona said no more. God knows, Umberto's whole life had been turned upside down without her peopling his already dark world with shadows he could not even see. Without anything more concrete from Adelina, there was no point warning him to be careful. Perhaps Flavio was simply no more than an obnoxious, creepy employee and the housekeeper's loyalty had made her over-protective.

She followed Umberto into the spacious saloon. The sizeable interior was made of a combination of golden-brown wood, cream leather, silk blinds with dark green and cream stripes, and chrome fittings. Although it was only able to accommodate one couple and one crew member, the cabins were spacious. They comprised a lounge with bar, a dining area and an open galley, a single bedroom with shower en suite and a double bedroom with full en-suite bathroom in elegant Carrara marble. *Very cosy*, Catriona thought to herself, her heart giving a small pinch as she imagined the queue of women who must have experienced Umberto's passion on the beautiful king-size bed with its magnificent, embroidered silk covers.

'We'll spend the night here,' Umberto told her as he entered the room behind her, encircling her waist with his arms. He buried his face in her hair. 'You smell nice, *amore mio*. Guerlain's Aqua Allegoria Mandarine Basilic, am I right?'

'Yes,' she breathed, his desire transmitting itself to her so that her knees threatened to give way. She leaned in against him. 'How do you know?'

'I've always liked it on you. I asked you what you were wearing that night in Saint Paul de Vence and you told me. I've never forgotten it.' He sighed. 'All those years wasted, all that time in relationships with other women that led nowhere because they weren't you.'

Sensing he might slip into gloomy retrospection, Cariona reacted swiftly. 'Don't dwell on the past. Circumstances were against us, that's all. You can't beat yourself up forever because of that.

Come, let's go upstairs. Let's not waste any more time – I thought you were taking me to visit Isola Comacina,' she said, trying to jolly him out of this sudden dark mood. 'We'd better get moving.'

He kissed her tenderly, this time on the forehead, and there were no erotic undertones to this gesture. '*Mia bella colomba, gentile e innocente, un angelo custode si e'preso cura di me il giorno in cui ti ha messa sulla mia strada*, my beautiful, kind and innocent dove. A guardian angel was looking after me the day he put you in my path.'

*   *   *

The Monteverdi yacht bore them along the shore of bright, luxuriant Tremezzina. The landscape had a breathless, majestic beauty. Apart from being fruitful and fertile, the district was so lush, the colours so vivid, that an artist could never paint anything so serene and lovely, Catriona remarked to Umberto.

'It is the Garden of Lombardy,' he told her.

Around the smiling bay, olive groves and green laurels, delightful gardens and orderly vineyards, myriad splendid villas, patrician houses and magnificent *palazzi* glittered in the sunshine, like jewels planted in the dazzling countryside.

Umberto wanted Catriona to get a closer look at the scenery so the yacht drifted slowly along the stretch of clear, limpid lakeshore by Renaissance-styled villas buried behind hedges of roses or smothered by magnolias and oleanders, trees of verbena and heliotrope, groves of myrtle and golden orange. There were great masses of crimson creepers festooning rocks and walls, or climbing over grey olives or down the dark green sides of majestic cypresses, where they seemed to flow like streaming red rivers. The yacht rounded little headlands crowned with cactus and aloe, while long weeping-willow branches trailed in the wavelets.

A big white steamer passed them on its voyage to Bellagio, the deck crammed with tourists laughing, chattering and taking pictures. All around the lake, small boats sped about their business, and from here the Como waterfront looked like a child's toy harbour with its brightly coloured boats, striped awnings over cafés and shops, and the women in their cheerful summery frocks promenading under the chestnut trees.

They stood leaning against the railing and as the island came into view, Umberto drew closer to Catriona and encircled her waist with his arm. 'Tourists these days are always out with their binoculars, trying to catch a glimpse of various celebrities who've made their homes on the western shore,' he explained, moving his head slowly from side to side as if scanning the lake.

'Local people say Hollywood riff-raff are taking over, but I like to think of it as just the latest in a long history of artists who've taken up residence here. For instance, if we were sailing these waters in 1837, we'd be desperate to catch sight of Franz Liszt, whose *Hungarian Rhapsodies* – not to mention romantic good looks – drove his fans wild. Liszt was the biggest heartthrob of the nineteenth century. Whenever he appeared in public, his female admirers fought for one of his velvet gloves or a silk handkerchief, which they would invariably tear to shreds in their frenzy.' He grinned.

'Liszt … Hollywood stars … *plus ça change*. Locals always complain that celebrities lower the tone and raise the property prices around Bellagio and it was no different in Liszt's time.'

'I'd certainly rather have you than the glamorous Liszt,' Catriona said, the playful smile obvious in her voice. 'Though he did sound rather dashing.'

Umberto laughed and turned his face towards her. 'Then it's lucky for me that time travel isn't yet possible.'

'Didn't Bellini have a villa here too?' she asked.

'Further down the shore, near Moltrasio: the Villa Passalacqua, a beautiful place. It's now a hotel named after that aria from *Norma*: Casta Diva.'

'Ah yes! I know it's been over played but I can never hear enough of Callas singing it.'

'Back in the 1820s, Bellini's favourite diva was Giuditta Pasta, who had her own villa just across the lake from his. Legend has it that he could hear her voice echoing over the water and it helped him compose. She was his muse, as you are mine, *mia bellisima promessa sposa*.'

Whether it was the sudden breeze off the water or her own sense suddenly of the enormity of the task before her, Catriona gave a little shiver. 'I certainly hope that turns out to be the case,' she murmured, thinking of the clear reluctance Umberto had shown to visit the piano room.

She wondered how his playing had gone, or even if he had done any before slamming the piano lid back down. Umberto could be the composer of his day, of this she was sure. How tragic that he had lost the inclination for it. She understood why, but it was all so frustrating. She didn't believe in muses; she believed in hard work and application. Maybe it would come in good time; nonetheless, she felt that their future happiness depended on his being able to perform and compose again.

Umberto tightened his clasp around her. 'You're not cold, are you?' came his tender murmur.

'No, I suppose it was just a sense of ghosts from ages past,' she told him lightly. 'So many people, so many artists have made their homes here, the vast majority consigned to dust. Only a few stories remain and they're fascinating.'

Umberto appeared thoughtful as his vacant green eyes directed their gaze towards her. 'Did your mother read you stories when you were a child?'

'No, it was Sidonie our cook and housekeeper who used to tell me them as I sat in the kitchen with her while she baked cakes.'

'Another thing we have in common …' He paused, then turned his face back to the lake, the breeze ruffling his hair, making him seem very boyish suddenly. 'As a child, I used to be afraid of ghosts. I hated the dark but Calandra wanted me to get used to it so Adelina used to sit with me and tell me stories until I went to sleep. Sometimes I wonder why Calandra was so insistent that I should get used to the dark. Maybe her mother's intuition told her what would happen to me one day.'

'For someone who fears the dark, I don't think you do so badly.'

'*Per mia fortuna*, I got over that phobia a long time ago.'

They broke off from their conversation as they were drawing closer now to Isola Comacina, which sat in the middle of the lake like some fabulous ship in a spot where, Umberto told her, the waters were always smooth and unruffled. Between the shore and the island lay a narrow reach of water, serenely sheltered, a silken mirror glowing with reflected colour.

'It's the Conca dell' Olio, the Bay of Oil,' he explained. 'And it owes its name to the oily smoothness of its surface, which is rarely ruffled by the winds, thanks to the protective land around it.'

Indeed, nestling under the olive-fringed shore of the lake and upon the silver surface, each vision was a miracle: dreamy distant peaks, the nearer forests and precipices, inviting grottoes and ravines with castellated crags, and villages whose church campaniles rang with sweet-singing bells. All around, the delicious scents of the rarest pot-pourri gave up the best treasure trove of all.

'It is said that at sunset and sunrise some lucky people have seen angels' robes and wings whirling in the sky. If you believe in an unseen world then, legend has it, things that are invariably dim and obscure are made clear to human eyes here.'

'The atmosphere is really magical,' she said, 'and the views ...' Catriona wished she could share them with Umberto and her heart ached.

As if he sensed it and wanted no part of her pity, Umberto turned away from her and spoke to Mario: 'We must be approaching the island by now. You can moor her at the jetty.

We'll go to Ossuccio to watch the fireworks tonight.' Umberto put his hand in his pocket and took out a couple of hundred-euro banknotes.

'Here,' he said, handing them to the older man, 'it'll be a long day, and that should cover everything else.'

Umberto patted Mario on the side of the arm, murmuring something out of earshot.

Mario glanced at Catriona and beamed back at him. '*Grazie, signore*, as usual, you are very generous.'

Once the boat had moored, Umberto reached out to Catriona. 'Give me your hand. People haven't seen me out and about since the accident and I'm not about to use a cane.'

Yet, off the boat, she marvelled at the speed at which he moved as they made their way towards the steps that took them to the top of the island. She squeezed his hand. 'Turn to the right now. Slow down,' she said. 'There's a group of tourists just coming off one of the steamers.'

He slowed down. 'I expect another hundred paces until we get to the stone stairs.'

'A little less than that, but you are doing very well.'

She clasped his warm fingers and felt them close over hers, urging her towards him. Neither spoke as they made their way up the stairs leading to the island. His footsteps were measured and even, and Catriona guessed he was counting his way.

If you hadn't known he was blind behind his black glasses, Umberto looked like any other sighted person.

Locanda Dell'Isola Comacina was the only restaurant on the island and they reached it through a private sloping walkway that led directly to the patio where Benvenuto Puricelli, the *oste*, host of the establishment, greeted them warmly. He was a cheerful, wiry, middle-aged man, who obviously knew Umberto well.

'Ah, *Maestro, bentornato*, welcome back!' he cried, almost embracing the composer as they reached the top of the stairs.

'I am the happiest man today because you have returned to my restaurant. I was very sad to hear about the accident but you look so well. I've reserved your usual table, *signore*.' He then turned and smiled at Catriona, giving a slight bow. '*Signorina, benvenuta sull' Isola Comacina*.'

The restaurateur showed them to a prime spot on the terrace in the shade of overhanging hackberry trees, overlooking the languid waters of the lake. Umberto beamed at his host, clearly delighted at the hearty reception he'd received. 'I've missed the place, Benvenuto. It's good to be here.'

Catriona looked around her. The terrace was enormous, studded with tables covered in checked cloths, some of which had colourful umbrellas to shade them.

Inside, the bar's walls were graced with photographs of Benvenuto and the celebrities who had dined at La Locanda, and the indoor dining room had a rustic decor that reminded her of a Swiss chalet. Catriona could imagine the huge fireplace – the largest she had ever seen – piled with massive blazing logs in the winter. Copper frying pans were hung around it and beside it stood a milk machine, which was used to separate cream and make cheese. The whole room offered an alternative ambience to the sun-drenched terrace with its breathtaking vistas.

Once they were seated, a waiter came over to ask if they wanted an *aperitivo* and gave them a couple of stylish-looking menus.

'What would you like to drink?'

'I think I might join you in a Negroni,' Catriona told Umberto with a smile in her voice.

'*Spendido!* I will order the wine.'

'What is their speciality here?'

'La Locanda has served the same menu every day since 1947 – but what a menu, *cara*!'

The drinks arrived promptly and they sipped their Negronis silently for a while. Umberto seemed lost in thought, while Catriona was feasting her eyes, taking in the breathtaking scenery of the lake and its surroundings and watching the cosmopolitan clientele.

Suddenly Umberto took Catriona's hand as he slid a jewellery box from the inner pocket of his jacket. 'It is an accepted custom in Italy for a *fidanzata* to be given a betrothal bracelet of gold,' he said with a half-smile, opening the box and displaying a bracelet of diamond flowers with leaves of small emeralds. They had the charming frailty of real flowers, the lovely stones mounted tremblant on a fine gold chain, quivering as his long, elegant pianist's fingers touched them.

'Oh, Umberto, this is for me?' she gasped, admiring the dainty and elegant piece. 'Thank you, but you shouldn't have.' Inwardly, she quailed. *Oh no*, she thought, *I really don't want him to start lavishing me with presents. There is still that half a million sitting in the clinic's bank account.*

Umberto took her wrist, where her pulse beat so madly, and snapped the chain around it. The little green stones glimmered among the sparkling ones. He grinned. 'I've always held the rather cynical view that the Italian girl prefers to be given a bracelet because it has more gold in it than a ring. Luckily, you have different sensibilities.'

Catriona laughed, despite her discomfort. It made her feel better that he joked about the gift. This betrothal was still so new and she felt conflicted, mired as she was in her own secrets and deceit.

'You are so generous. This was really unnecessary.' She gently pulled away her wrist to admire the bracelet.

He grabbed her hand again and laughed. '*Aspetta! Lasciami finire*, wait, let me finish …' He pushed his hand this time into the side pocket of his jacket and withdrew from it another small box. 'However,' he continued, 'as you are French, I am going to give you a ring that belonged to my mother. Her family goes all the way back to the crusading knights and this has been handed down the years to many different brides. I think it will fit. Touching your fingers yesterday, I reckoned they must be almost the same size as Calandra's.'

Catriona couldn't move her hand from the living steel of his grasp, then she felt the gold grip of the ring as he slipped it on the third finger of her left hand.

She gazed incredulously at it. The band was of gold, set with star-shaped diamonds surrounding a large emerald that sparkled like a tropical dawn. Deep in the heart of it was a lighter green flame, glowing and alive, and the gem sent out shafts of fiery colour as the sunlight found it and added its rays to the glory of the stone. Catriona was suddenly reminded of Umberto's beautiful eyes.

'This is too much, Umberto …'

He grinned, his amusement apparent. '*Aspetta*, you are one impatient woman, you know. Let me finish this speech. I was rehearsing it all night.'

Catriona stopped fidgeting. 'I'm sorry,' she whispered, and Umberto drew a deep breath.

'Caterina, *mia bella strega*, my beautiful witch, will you have a man, free, handsome, rich?' At that, he grinned roguishly again. 'Who loves you to distraction and, although rather past the first flush of boyhood, is not without a bit of vigour left in him.'

'Oh, Umberto,' she whispered, adoring all the mischievousness of his proposal, her heart filling with emotion and her eyes moistening.

She gazed at the ring. The stone shimmered and a tear broke on her lashes and rolled down her face. Events were moving too fast for her; it was as if a big wave was sweeping her off the safe shore and carrying her away into the unknown deep waters of the ocean.

Unaware of the extent of her emotion, Umberto continued: 'Will you do me the great honour of becoming my wife? I promise to be a good husband and will spend the rest of my life proving how much I adore you.'

Catriona didn't trust herself to speak. She *couldn't* speak. Emotion clogged her throat as she counted her heartbeats in the silence that hung between them.

'Umberto,' she breathed unsteadily, 'are you sure that what you feel for me is not just a physical thing?' she asked in a trembling voice, wanting him to declare himself properly. 'You said once that I aroused the … the animal in you.'

'You do,' he growled. 'Animal, protector, companion, lover. I will be all of those, if you let me. I lust for you, yes, but I love you at the same time. That's how it should be between a man and a woman, *no*? That's love, *amore mio*. Be honest now, don't I arouse the tigress in you?'

'Yes,' Catriona said, her eyes shining.

'Yes, I arouse the tigress in you, or yes, you will marry me?'

'Both,' she murmured.

Umberto lifted her hand to his lips and kissed it reverently. '*Grazie, mio tenero amore*, my tender love. You've made me a very happy man. My only regret is that we've wasted so much time!'

The waiter arrived with grilled lake salmon trout, served with a trickle of virgin olive oil, a twist of lemon and salt and pepper, and he filleted it at the table.

'So simple and yet so delicious,' Catriona said as she tasted the flavoursome and flaky pink flesh.

'Simplicity is always better, *eh*?'

'Yes, definitely.'

'That is your English blood talking. The French, and certainly the Italians, are much more … *come si dice*, how do you say it? … fancy in what they wear, what they eat, how they decorate their houses. La Locanda is an exception.' He smiled and added thoughtfully: 'Our children will have a mixture of Italian, French and English blood running in their veins. A good mix, don't you think?'

His words came like a bolt out of the blue. Shocked, Catriona found no words to reply. She had been so persuaded that he had no intention of ever having children … and now this. Then her heart pinched with guilt. Was this the right time to tell him he already had a wonderful and beautiful son? No, she needed to prepare him. Or if she were honest, she needed to prepare herself for such a serious confession. This was not the moment and, yet, when would it feel right to tell him?

'You do not want more children?' he asked, breaking the silence, and Catriona wondered if he had sensed her discomfiture.

'I love children,' she told him hesitantly, 'but isn't it a little early to be talking about having them?' She gave a small, nervous laugh.

'No better time than the present.'

Suddenly he lifted his hand to his head and an expression of excruciating pain twisted his features.

'What's wrong, Umberto?'

'Nothing, nothing,' he said, reaching into his pocket for a silver box, from which he took two small pills.

'Do you have a headache?'

'A slight migraine. It will pass in no time with these painkillers.' He popped them into his mouth and washed them down with some water.

'You never mentioned to me that you had migraines.'

He made an attempt at a mischievous smile full of innuendo. 'There are many things, *amore mio*, that I haven't mentioned to you.'

'Come on, Umberto, I'm serious.'

'So am I, *carissima* … Look, don't fuss, Caterina. I hate that. I saw *il dottor* Enzo yesterday and he wasn't worried.'

'But it's important, Umberto. These migraines could be caused by your eyes. As soon as we get back, I think you should see him again.'

Before he could berate her further for fussing, the waiter arrived with their next course, interrupting their conversation by announcing the speciality chicken dish he placed before them. For the rest of the meal they moved on to other subjects. As long as Catriona didn't talk about his reluctance to compose again, Umberto was only too ready to discuss music with her. It was, after all, the passion that stirred the both of them.

They hardly noticed the time passing but at some point, as the afternoon shadows had started to lengthen a little, the waiter appeared with their dessert plates. Scooping fluffy vanilla gelato straight out of an ice-cream maker, he laid it on top of the slices of orange on their plates before covering it with *Crema di San Giovanni* and sluicing some banana syrup over the top.

'You know,' Umberto said thoughtfully, after Catriona had exclaimed at the deliciousness of the sweet confection. 'Ever since you sang that song from *Dichterliebe*, I haven't been able to get Schumann's *Lieder* out of my head. His love for Clara pours out of every note ... When I heard the depth of your own emotion as you sang, you cannot begin to imagine how much that moved me.' His green eyes glittered intensely, just like the emerald on her finger, as they stared almost directly at her face.

Catriona didn't speak; her heart felt suddenly too full. She sensed he had more to say, something important to him.

'Then I started thinking of the love Clara Schumann later had for Brahms, her husband's young protégé who wrote her such impassioned letters.'

'The three of them did make the most extraordinary love triangle,' mused Catriona.

'Yes, and you know what I ended up thinking? What a waste it all was. When Brahms and Clara were finally free to love each other – after Schumann had died – Brahms bottled out. Clara waited, but he didn't come to her.'

'Maybe he could only feel passion when there was some impediment.'

'Quite possibly.' Umberto's fingers stroked the stem of his wine glass. 'But I was thinking of them the other evening and … I don't want to be like that. I don't want to miss out on the one love I've waited for my entire life.' He leaned forward.

'I had you once and you slipped out of my fingers. Life is too short, *amore* … we've wasted so much time. I know it feels like things have moved so quickly … becoming engaged and everything. Well, I've seen how fickle life can be and I'm not playing games any more. I don't want to hide in the shadows, I want to tell the world right now.'

Catriona felt all at once enchanted by this burst of passionate enthusiasm and yet wary, too. She was here in the role of therapist and now, more than ever before, she felt how invidious her position was.

'Wait, Umberto, please wait. I need to talk to you about something that has been on my mind almost since I arrived and now that we are engaged, it is of the utmost importance that we set this right.'

Umberto frowned. 'You worry me, *cara*. Your voice seems so serious … *come dire* … severe.'

She looked at him directly, even though he couldn't see her face. 'Well, this is a serious matter and I do hope that you won't disagree with me.'

'How could I ever do anything to upset you, Caterina?'

'I would like to return my fee. The whole of it.' There, she had said it. She couldn't believe she hadn't broached the subject long before.

Umberto sat very still. Only Catriona's expert and concerned eye could have detected the crease furrowing his brow, the tense lines tightening his mouth, the proud set of his head.

'From now on, what's mine is yours, isn't that how it is between a man and his wife?' he said in a low, wary tone.

'But we're not married yet. Besides, this isn't *my* money so I'd be returning it on behalf of the clinic,' she answered carefully.

'It feels wrong to have it still in that account. I could be struck off for what's happened between us.'

'I've told you that will not happen. I will not let it. We will announce our engagement and you won't be my therapist in any official capacity any longer. Everything will be above board.'

Although there was something in his voice that warned her that he was on a dangerously short fuse, Catriona gathered her nerve and pressed on. 'But as you say, it has all happened so quickly. If I returned the fee now and we allowed a little more time before we made it public it, would create some breathing space … make things easier to explain.'

'*Allora*, Caterina, do you want to marry me?'

Her eyes widened at the bluntness of his question. 'Yes, of course.' She could see he was not moving at all.

'But you want breathing space, *vero*?'

He was misinterpreting her entirely. Deliberately, she threw down the gauntlet. 'Yes. There's nothing wrong in that, is there?'

Umberto's expression darkened. 'I think there's more to your prevarication than you're admitting. You don't want me to announce our engagement for some other reason perhaps?' There was a fierce set to his jaw now. 'You promised yourself to a man before quickly enough, it seems to me. Is this about him? Maybe you've not forgotten him yet.'

'That's not true at all,' she blurted out, knowing he had it all wrong. 'Umberto, that's ridiculous …'

He rose from his chair, as ominous-looking as a thundercloud. 'You are mine, I am yours. Surely that is the only thing that matters? What do we care if the whole world knows about us?'

Catriona stood too, glancing around the room. 'Please, Umberto, sit down. Let's talk about this reasonably.' As she spoke, she inched towards him, closing the gap between them. 'I was only thinking of how this looks, professionally speaking.'

'You think too much,' he growled.

Before she realized what was happening, Umberto had pulled her towards him, his arms clamping around her waist so suddenly that she lost her balance and fell against him. His kiss was merciless in its demands. In sheer outrage, she tried to pull back, but his hand was tangled in her hair so that she was powerless to move. In spite of herself, her pulse accelerated madly as she felt the hardness of his lean body pressing against her own and the plundering of his tongue.

He released her as roughly as he had seized her, making no effort to mask his ragged breathing. Catriona's eyes flew open. If they had been alone, his possessive touch would have excited her beyond reason. But they were not. Shocked into reality, she saw that the other diners, sitting at their tables, were watching.

'People are staring,' she murmured, putting a hand on the table to steady herself.

'So what?' Umberto replied with indifference. 'I've just asked you to marry me and you've accepted. We're in love. If you think I'm going to let the world dictate my behaviour, you're mistaken – especially when it comes to kissing you.'

Catriona was gripped by the creeping awareness that whether she liked it or not their relationship was now up for public consumption. Tongues would wag, gossip columnists would have a field day.

I'm meant to be his therapist. This will look awful. Then the realization came to her in a rush. *Oh no, Michael doesn't even know yet! What if he finds out before I've had a chance to prepare him?*

Without another thought, and although he couldn't see the other diners, Umberto put on his most charming smile and directed it to the wide terrace. '*Signore e signori, vi prego di scusare questo atto spontaneo,* ladies and gentlemen, please excuse this spontaneous act. This young lady has just done me the great honour of agreeing to be my wife, and this made me so happy that I couldn't resist taking her in my arms … and you all know what happens when a man takes such a beautiful lady in his arms, *eh*?'

A roar of laughter and deafening applause erupted from the terrace. Some people whistled, others shouted, '*Congratulazioni!*' Catriona flushed with embarrassment and alarm. Tomorrow, this incident would be all over the Italian press and maybe even abroad. Surely someone had taken a photograph? With camera phones, nothing could be easier. The famous composer was back in the public eye, she thought to herself, and a tiny part of her wondered whether he had been seeking the publicity even though he'd been so reluctant to meet his public again before now.

Catriona had no time to berate him for his behaviour, nor would she have wanted to create a scene – there had been too much of that already. A handful of people were already at their table wanting to congratulate them personally and welcome the maestro back into society after his long absence. It was as if Umberto had never been away; he talked and smiled and laughed, and she watched him captivating his audience without playing a note.

'*Andiamo*,' he said, when the last of his admirers had finally left them. 'It must be late. What time is it?' Although he had a talking watch, Umberto rarely used it.

'It's almost six.'

He missed the tension in her voice, still glowing from this interaction with his fans. 'We'd better get back if we're going to have time to change for the fireworks tonight.'

'That's fine with me.'

By the time they returned to the yacht, there was a gentleness to the sun, like a blessing, and Catriona felt her annoyance dissipate a little in its honeyed warmth. She went below deck to the bathroom to shower, while Umberto went next door for Mario to give him a shave.

As she was finishing soaping herself, she felt him come in behind her. He took the soap from her.

'Let me do that …' he whispered.

'Umberto, let me be … please.'

She pushed past him and stepped out of the shower.

'Ah! Your eyes are charcoal black, *vero*?' he replied with a smile in his voice as he started to soap himself.

'Probably.'

'You are cross, Caterina?' he asked, his tone slightly sheepish.

'You didn't think of me when you made that scene at the restaurant.'

'*Cara*, I am an impetuous man … passionate, jealous. I know it's crazy to be jealous of a man who's no longer alive, but I find it hard to control myself when you're around.'

'Then you'll have to learn how,' she said vehemently. In her annoyance, her mind skirted over the fact that his jealousy was unfounded for another reason altogether – a reason she'd still not been able to reveal to him.

'We're not in the jungle here. You're not Tarzan and I'm not Jane. Anyway, it wasn't just that. You gave no thought to the fact that I might not feel comfortable for our relationship to be on everybody's lips, spread over the news before even Michael knows about it!'

He stepped out of the shower and wrapped himself in his towelling robe.

'I'm sorry, you're right. Will you forgive me? I got carried away. After all, what is life without impulse, without passion, without fire, *eh*?'

'I'm all for passion and fire, but this was in the wrong place and at the wrong time.'

He put his arms around her. She pushed him away gently.

'I'm dressing now, Umberto,' she told him calmly, although she could see he was aroused.

'It would seem I can't come near you without wanting to make love to you. I don't know how to fight it, Caterina, but fight it I will.'

'Good,' she murmured, although her body had responded treacherously to his arousal with a slow ache between her legs that she was refusing fulfilment.

Umberto proceeded to dress himself slowly and once again Catriona admired the way he managed his blindness without help. *He's quite something*, she thought, her heart melting.

She stepped into a floor-skimming dress crafted from two layers of delicate fuchsia silk organza, the fluid skirt flowing from a bodice with a plunging V-neckline and cut-out back. The stunning hue of the dress was the focus of the outfit, Catriona having teamed the gown with neutral stiletto sandals that gave the impression she was walking barefoot. She let her hair fall loose over her shoulders in cascading chestnut waves. Although the bracelet Umberto had offered her at La Locanda did not quite suit the colour of the dress, she kept it on – it matched the ring and she didn't need any other jewellery.

As usual, she dabbed some gloss on her lips and put a little mascara on her naturally thick, long eyelashes. Checking herself in the mirror, she was pleased with her reflection, longing wistfully that Umberto could see her tonight as she'd dressed entirely for him.

He was now in a formal dinner suit with a white jacket. His bow tie still hung, untied, around his neck. As his fingers moved up to feel for the edges of it, Catriona went to him. 'Let me do this for you, Umberto,' she murmured, suddenly faint with longing.

'Am I forgiven then?' His voice was hoarse and she knew he had been hurt by her earlier rebuff.

'I suppose you are,' she said softly. Then fixing him with serious eyes, she went on to say: 'I love you, Umberto – you and no other man. You know, don't you, that part of why I felt so embarrassed and uncomfortable was because I am still your therapist. Paid by you. Surely you understand that my position – certainly in the eyes of the world – is utterly untenable? I have to return my fee as soon as we get back.' Her quiet tone brooked no argument.

'Of course I want to help you get better but not in a paid role.' She reached up to him and quickly kissed his cheek.

He nodded. 'I understand it now, *amore mio*, even though I would like you to have the money. But I can see how you feel. In the meantime, Caterina, I will let you get away with that chaste little kiss only because we are going out,' he said, lifting her face to his.

'But tonight, after the fireworks on the island, *amore mio*, you will not escape me and we will have fireworks in bed.' His mouth lowered towards hers so that he murmured against her lips: 'I have had hours to plan my exploration of your body … and what a journey that will be.'

'Who wants to escape?' she whispered. 'I'm all yours, body and soul. You know that, don't you?'

'*Sì, tenero amore mio*, yes, my tender love.'

As they reached the door, he asked: 'What are you wearing?'

'A long, pink dress in silk organza with a V-neck and a cut-out back. The only jewellery I'm wearing is the beautiful bracelet and ring you gave me.'

'Have you let that long, shiny hair fall over your shoulders?'

'Yes.'

'Will you let me touch your neckline?' he asked softly.

'Yes,' she murmured, and taking his hand, she placed it on the opening at the front of her dress.

Skirting the deep V that showed off her cleavage, Umberto's fingers lightly traced the curve of her breasts, sensually grazing them with a featherlike caress, making her shiver. His voice was low and gravelly. 'You like it when I do that, *vero*?'

Catriona shut her eyes. This was heaven and hell … his touch felt so good but the need for him was excruciating. She almost wished they weren't going out – she wanted him to take her now! 'Yes,' she murmured. 'Yes, Umberto, I like it when you do that.'

He gave her a smile that didn't need words to explain the pleasure he felt at her admission of desire for him. 'And your eyes are the colour of burnt honey now. Such an unusual colour … That's the way they become when you're aroused, did you know that? I noticed it that night at Villefranche when you were swimming and I caressed you. That colour and the expression in your eyes when we made love were extraordinary.' His hand moved away from her breast to her neck, her jaw, his fingers then gently following her brow and around her cheekbone as though framing her gaze, which remained locked on his face.

'I just had to look into them to know how you felt when I touched you. The pleasure, the ecstasy, the need for more as you approached your climax, it was all there for me to read. No woman has ever stirred me the way you did that night, just by looking into my eyes.'

Catriona turned and caught her reflection in the mirror. Umberto was right: her eyes were the colour of the lavender honey of Provence.

Her breath caught in her throat. 'Yes, Umberto,' she whispered, stirred by the image of her own arousal. 'Yes, you're right …' she repeated slowly, almost mesmerized by what she saw, something she had been unaware of until now. Still, how could she have known? She had never made love with anyone but Umberto.

CHAPTER 16

The sun had just gone down as they were taking their seats at a table on the terrace at the Grand Hotel Ossuccio, a majestic five-star hotel whose soaring windows overlooked Lake Como. There, they had a splendid view of the Isola Comacina; below them, hundreds of lights were twinkling in boats, abandoned on to the stream of the lake, or on the balconies of the pretty pastel houses along the shoreline. Catriona's eyes shone. 'The view is breathtaking. It's as if the lake is on fire.'

'Even in my darkest times, I've always tried to come here,' said Umberto. 'My memory of the lights across the water serves me well enough. The villagers fill empty mollusc shells with wax or lamp oil and cast them out on to the waters of the lake. Traditional fare for the pilgrimage was always polenta and snails so someone had the bright idea to use the discarded shells.'

'It's beautiful,' breathed Catriona wonderingly. 'It's like something out of Dante, souls crossing to the other side.'

'That's always been my thought. In fact, the *lumaghitt* is all about remembering souls who sought salvation on the opposite shore when fire engulfed the island in the twelfth century. That time it was Barbarossa's doing, but L'Isola Comacina has always been hotly fought over. It's the perfect strategic position for a fort.'

'I can imagine,' said Catriona. 'I thought maybe the light festival was a pagan one. We're near the summer solstice, aren't we?'

Umberto nodded. 'Actually, you're right. I think a pagan festival would have predated this Christian one and, like many of the dates and celebrations in the Christian calendar, they conveniently overlaid previous ones. Then it became imploring the help of San Giovanni Battista with a solemn procession by boat to his church on the island. Apparently, the original procession was made by locals who implored the saint to rid them of some particularly violent June hailstorms that were destroying their harvest. He granted them a miracle. The storms ceased so the pilgrimage continued every year.'

The moon had come up and was casting her silver track across the still lake. With the hundreds of floating lights turning the water into rivers of shimmering gold and diamonds, the incomparable panorama had an enchantment of times gone by that made Catriona feel as though she had been transported to another world.

They dined on polenta and snails, keeping with tradition, and a bottle of Cristal Brut Nature champagne.

'A symphony of purity and elegance,' Umberto told her as the waiter poured the sparkling elixir into their glasses. His hand felt across the table for the glass. 'It reminds me of you.'

Catriona looked at him, puzzled. 'Of me?'

'*Sì, amore.* It has the silky texture and fruity aromas of your skin, the freshness and purity of your innocence, and the powerful potency that you exert on my senses.'

She smiled, happiness warming her insides. 'You do say the most poetic things.'

'I am only showing the instincts of a normal male around a very beautiful woman.'

At ten-thirty on the dot the first rocket was sent into the air and, suddenly, sonic booms filled the sky with a magnificent show of fireworks sparking off the island. Showers of colourful fire rained down from heaven, disappearing behind the horizon, their bright blooms eclipsing the stars on a velvet navy canvas.

Rumbles of rainbows exploded overhead, keeping the awaiting crowds in suspense, as the next rocket rose high into the night. The lake was crowded with motorboats and ferries as the gathered throng remembered the burning and destruction of Comacina Island centuries ago.

'Michael would have loved to see this,' Catriona couldn't help saying, imagining her son's eyes lighting up at the sight of the fireworks.

'Tell me about him, *cara*,' said Umberto, who had moved close to her so that their arms were touching. 'He'll be a part of my life very soon. I am a lucky man. Not only do I have the most gorgeous woman to call my own, but a boy I can call my son.'

At the word 'son' Catriona gave a little start, which Umberto felt and was quick to interpret. 'Don't worry, Caterina,' he said, feeling for her hand and giving it a reassuring squeeze. 'Maybe that was insensitive of me. I can never replace his actual father but I would like to be a loving stepfather and mentor to the boy. I want to honour him as I do you.'

'No, that wasn't what I was thinking. Of course you and Michael should be close,' she almost cried out, the familiar guilt crowding in. 'There's nothing more I'd like than that the two of you should have a strong relationship.'

Umberto put his arm around her shoulders. 'So, tell me about him. I want to know everything.'

'Well,' Catriona said haltingly, 'he's very musical ... loves to sit at the piano, composing his own tunes. He's not an introvert though, he likes an audience.' She laughed, thinking of the imperious little maestro.

'My mother and I are always being called upon to listen and applaud energetically at the end of his performances. The number of times poor Sidonie, too, has had to sit down in the music room, her hands covered in flour. Whatever any of us is doing has to take second place,' she laughed.

He chuckled along with her. 'That sounds like me at that age.'

Catriona didn't know how to reply to that. This was, in some ways, the perfect opening for her confession, and yet somehow she couldn't take it … and then the moment was gone. A shower of noisy rockets exploded above them with a deafening volley of sharp crackles and all further conversation was impossible.

As she watched the fireworks burst, the thought crossed Catriona's mind that the two of them were each experiencing the celebration in different ways. She was entranced by the colours flowing up above her and illuminating the sky, while for Umberto it had to be all about the noise: no other part of the experience was open to him. Still, he didn't seem to mind the loss of colour and light. Catriona turned her head a fraction to gaze at him and was happy to witness a wide smile of enjoyment lighting up his face at every explosion of sound.

'Fire in the sky, fire on the lake and fire in our hearts and bodies,' Umberto murmured, his voice husky with emotion as the flamboyant spectacle ended. 'The night promises to be long and if we don't go soon, our bed may be a cradle of flames. Come, *amore mio*, let's go back to the boat.'

Catriona was mesmerized by his low baritone voice, feeling his breath caressing her cheek with every word. When he spoke to her like this, it never failed to make a flush heat her skin. Tonight, more than ever, there was passion and a need for Umberto simmering within her – that lingering deep desire that he stirred in her, whether he was close or she was just thinking of him.

They walked hand in hand towards the boat under a twice-sized pearly moon that smiled down in silent delight, like a flower among the keen white summer stars shivering in the inky canopy above. The minute globes seemed so near that it appeared as though a long arm could reach out and pluck them. A soft breeze kissed the lake, singing through the trees bordering the water, a deep-voiced song of rushing cadences. The fragrant air was fresh and biting and it somewhat sobered up Catriona. She took a deep breath.

This love I feel is consuming me … I can't control it. Where will it lead? Despite the outward signs, she knew that Umberto was not cured of his depression. He was still volatile. *He might make love to you today, but what about tomorrow when the weight of his disability takes over once again and the bouts of anger and bitterness return to haunt him?* Would he become jealous of every man he decided was a threat because he thought himself less of a man?

It was normal that Umberto would feel diminished by his blindness. His manhood was humiliated by it and his only way of fighting back was sex … the one thing he knew he was still capable of and at which he excelled.

Yet the more they made love, the more vulnerable she felt and the more the quicksand of her love was drawing her deeper into its abyss. Still, despite Marie-Jeanne's cautious warnings and her mother's misgivings, Catriona had no doubt she loved Umberto. The truth was she had never stopped loving him and the risks of being with him were worth it, if it meant they had a chance of happiness together.

'You are very quiet, *amore mio*. Did you not enjoy your evening?'

'I had a wonderful time, Umberto, thank you.'

'And so, what is taking you away from me, *eh*?'

'Nothing. On the contrary, I was thinking of you, and of all the ways I would like to please you tonight.' Catriona took in his handsome profile in the moonlight. Awareness of her desire for him bloomed suddenly, hot and strong. She smiled up at him although he couldn't see her. 'I want to make love to you, Umberto. I want to show you how I feel about you.'

He lifted her hand to his lips and kissed her palm and then each finger, one by one. '*Mia piccola strega sexy*, my sexy little witch.' His voice had thickened. 'There's nothing I want more, *amore*, than to be inside you. I could spend hours between your legs, teasing, sucking, tasting you … Just the thought of it makes me hard as granite.'

As if he had actually touched her, Catriona's nipples tightened under the thin fuchsia silk of her bodice and her limbs were flooded with a hunger only Umberto knew how to awaken. No wonder women were crazy about him; he had such a seductive way of talking.

They had reached the yacht.

'Where's Mario?' she asked, looking around and seeing that the boat was deserted.

'I've given him the night off and told him to enjoy the festivities. He'll be back in the morning, in time to give us breakfast and take us to the island for Mass and the boat show.' Laughter reverberated in his throat.

'The night is ours,' he said hoarsely as he gathered her to him, taking her lips against his hot mouth, his tongue searching and sliding against her own, drawing the breath from her body until she thought she would die with pleasure. His hand on the small of her back, he pressed her against him so intimately that she could feel the hard length of him through the thin fabric of her dress.

A host of sensations rushed through her with wild excitement. The warm male smell of his skin, the heavy pounding of his heart against her breast, the strength of his hands as they moulded her hips to his, and his arms tightening around her so that she could not escape his powerful body, so clearly aroused.

'Oh, Umberto, Umberto. I want you so much …' she muttered almost incoherently, breaking their kiss, dazed by the mounting dull ache she could feel in her groin. 'I can't wait to touch you, to feel you. I want to make love to you. Tell me how to please you – I'll do anything.'

Umberto lifted his head slowly. 'Anything?' he breathed, as if shocked by what she had just said.

'Anything,' she murmured resolutely.

'Come, let's go inside.'

Once in the bedroom, Umberto pulled Catriona against him. 'Did you really mean it when you said you would do anything to please me?'

She let her eyes wander over every detail of his face, a face she knew almost as well as her own. 'Yes, I really meant it,' she said softly, caressing his cheek tenderly. 'Yes.'

'Strip for me.'

Catriona was puzzled; she wasn't sure she had understood. 'Strip for you?'

'Yes, I want you to perform a striptease for me.'

'But, Umberto—'

'"But, Umberto, you can't see" you are going to say, *eh*?' he cut in.

She didn't answer, afraid to offend him.

He trailed his fingers slowly across her chin and down her neck. 'I never forgot that night we spent in France together … and the other day when we made love I realized that I remembered every intimate part of you as though we had never separated. I don't need to be able to see to know the way your eyes burn when you're excited, the way your breasts swell when they want to be caressed, the way your body moves when I stroke you. Just tell me what you're doing while you strip. The rest I'll see in my imagination.'

Catriona felt her heartbeat quicken and a certain elation seize her. 'I've never done it before, but I'll drive you wild with a striptease you'll never forget,' she whispered against his mouth, entering into the spirit of the game.

For a moment he looked taken aback and she guessed he had expected her to argue, or at least prevaricate.

'I know I'm asking a lot,' he said huskily, taking her into his arms and drawing her unresisting body closer to the potent magnet of his. He buried his face in her warm neck, his lips scorching a trail over her ear and the curve of her cheek. Then he was doing it again, kissing her long and hard, with depth and sensuality, with a power and a promise that left her reeling.

'I have one condition,' she breathed when Umberto finally released her.

'That is?'

'Don't try to touch me while I'm performing.' She knew that if he touched her, she would melt and that would be the end of it.

'I promise. I won't touch you, but I will tell you how I feel. The anticipation of touching you afterwards will make it all the more exciting. *Caterina, amore mio, voglio fare l'amore con te tutta la notte*, I want to make love with you all night long.' And Catriona heard the note of hunger in his thickened voice.

Faint with longing herself, she watched as he undressed and threw off the last piece of clothing: the black briefs covering his manhood. As he did so, she felt a fierce thrill of womanly pride that he could be so ready for her before she had even started her performance.

She stacked a few pillows up against the headboard of the bed for him and stepped away. 'Do you want music?' he asked huskily, the air between them thick with sensual awareness.

'You have some here?'

He gestured behind her. 'They're all in there.'

Catriona turned to see a sideboard with a built-in CD player and disks stacked in an alcove in the cabin's wall. Music might help her feel less inhibited, she thought as she moved across to it, wondering if there would be anything to fit the mood. Immediately, her eye caught one of the CDs towards the end of the row. *Perfect.*

'Lean back on the bed and let the show commence,' she commanded as she slipped the CD into the player.

Still, Catriona realized that her confident tone only went part-way towards helping her do this; she needed to remove all her inhibitions and visualize herself taking on a different personality.

She imagined she was a sexy actress in an exotic, avant-garde cabaret and Umberto was a client she wanted to seduce.

A bottle of cognac and two glasses lay on the side table. She had never even tasted cognac and, although she'd had a few glasses of champagne with dinner, it seemed a good idea to indulge in a small shot before her performance to work up to it and help lessen the trace of nervousness in her voice.

As Umberto took his place on the bed she poured some of the amber liquid into two glasses.

'*Salute*,' she said, giving him a glass. Reclining against the pillows, he looked like the sculpture of a Roman god in repose, his magnificent tanned lean body contrasting with the pure white of the silk sheet, his hand covering his sex.

'What a splendid idea,' he said. Taking the glass from her, he lifted it. '*Salute, amore mio.*'

For her own benefit she dimmed the lights and placed a chair in the middle of the room – *one can't have a striptease without a chair*, she thought. Some years ago she had seen a striptease performed at a nightclub in Cannes and the performer had executed all sorts of sexy poses around it. Then she pressed the play button on the CD, went to stand at the far end of the room and took a deep breath.

Very quietly the strains of Ravel's *Boléro* began, the snare drum beating out an insistent tattoo, the flute beginning its swirling, provocative melody over the top. Catriona saw Umberto's eyebrows raise in surprised recognition and then he smiled.

Suddenly more confident, Catriona began. 'I've turned down the lights and there's a chair in the middle of the room, quite close to the bed. I'm walking towards you, looking you straight in the eye, my lips slightly parted, strutting as though I'm on a catwalk, moving one foot in front of the other, a hand on one hip.' Her pulse kicked into a faster rhythm as she focused on his face, which was turned towards her expectantly.

'My head is held high, my shoulders back, the deep V of my dress flaunting my cleavage. My whole body is offering itself to you, telling you to look at it and to want me.'

Umberto was completely still on the bed as though watching a film. 'Yes, I can see you, *bellissima*, with your long hair tumbling down your shoulders. Moving in a cloud of fuchsia silk, you're swaying your hips sexily as you come towards me.' His gaze remained steady. 'Your eyes are fixing on me … alluring, but not quite yet that burnt honey colour … and your lips, yes, they are parted, waiting for my kiss.'

Catriona's eyes travelled down his muscular body, a rush of aching heat pooling between her thighs as she took in the rigid length of him.

'I've reached the chair now and I'm wriggling out of my dress slowly, gyrating a little, rolling my hips. I'm moving my hands up and down the sides of my body and caressing my hips and stomach just the way I'd like you to caress me, Umberto … Now, turning away from you,' she announced as she proceeded to turn around. 'I push my dress over each shoulder and wriggle it down over my body … then bend slightly forward and hook my thumbs into it as I roll it down over my hips. Letting it fall to the ground, I kick it aside.'

Umberto let out a low growl of approval. 'My hands want to caress your hips and stomach. I love the soft silky touch of your skin … This is killing me, Caterina. I want to be inside you already.'

She licked her bottom lip and swallowed. 'I've tossed my hair back and I'm licking my lips, caressing my breasts as I imagine your hands on me. Pressing myself against the hard back of the chair, I'm now stroking the rest of my body, imagining your strong and powerful hands are on me.' Her voice became breathy. '*Mmm* … it feels good, Umberto. But it's not you, it's not the same.'

The game was catching up with her and she could almost feel his hands on her. The music continued to swell against the constant beating rhythm.

Umberto leaned forward. 'Let me touch you now, *amore mio*. You're excited, I can hear it in your voice. You want me to touch you … you're missing my hands on you, *vero*?'

'Don't move,' she said in a hoarse voice. 'Remember your promise not to touch. Touching will come later.'

She waited until Umberto leaned back again with a tense but resigned expression on his face as he took a sip from his glass. He was coiled like a spring and she felt almost giddy with delight at the power she wielded over him.

'You can now see my bright pink lacy bra with its low cut that makes my breasts stand out. They're aroused and hard, their rigid peaks pushing against the silky material, begging to be licked by you. My thong is also bright pink and see-through. It covers the part of me that's yearning for you.'

'Take it off and lift your leg,' he said, his voice thick, a glazed expression on his face. 'I want to bury my face in your softness.'

'All in good time,' she whispered, her voice sultry and provocative.

'I want you very badly, Caterina.'

She kicked off her heels quite noisily so he could hear her.

'You've taken off your shoes.'

'Yes, and now I've put one foot on the chair and I'm going to take off my stockings … I'm stroking my leg up and down, imagining your hands are caressing me and, slowly, I'm starting to roll down the stocking,' she said, and then tossed the garment to Umberto.

It landed on his chest, catching him by surprise. He groaned and lifted it to his face. 'You smell good, *amore mio* … so good,' he whispered as he inhaled the musky fragrance.

His hand had slipped from his groin and Catriona could see that he was almost painfully aroused. She averted her gaze to calm her own arousal and the ache that was increasing between her thighs.

'And now, I'm gradually rolling down the stocking on my other leg. Both my legs are bare and all I'm wearing are my bra and my thong.'

'Yes, I remember … I can see your beautiful long legs and your thighs.' He licked his lips, the expression on his face taut. His eyes were shining, almost focused directly on her … she had never seen him so excited. 'Caterina, you are driving me crazy. Let me touch you … just once.' He moved to get up.

'We're almost there,' she said, her voice low and breathy. 'And I'm almost ready for you. I've slipped into my high-heeled shoes again. Look, I'm unclasping my bra. It's just covering my breasts so you can't really see them. I've turned around, showing you my bare back. I'm taking off my bra now and my head is thrown back, my hands roaming over my bare breasts …'

'Give me your bra,' he rasped.

The tenor saxophone took up the sultry, unrelenting melody. 'I've turned around, but I'm still covering my breasts with my hands and gyrating while I stroke them in the way I want you to stroke me later.'

'Take your hands away. Uncover them for me … please,' he choked. 'I want to see them, I want to touch them.'

'And now as I face you, I uncover them for you to see how swollen and aroused they are.'

'*Sei bella, bella, bella … ti voglio*, I want you … I want to be inside you now, Caterina.'

'Soon, very soon. There's only one piece of clothing covering me now,' she uttered, her voice catching in her throat.

'Yes, yes. Take it off quickly … quickly, and come to me.'

Umberto's breathing was now almost a pant, his chest rising and falling rapidly. The proof of his virility, aroused as she had never seen it before, was straining like a tethered beast, begging to be soothed and released from its tension. She had difficulty in restraining herself from reaching out and touching it.

'I'm still wearing my high heels,' she said in a trembling voice, the view of his excitement stimulating hers. 'I am showing you my back as I gently pull down the last piece of my underwear.'

He cursed softly beneath his breath. 'Yes, the one I've been waiting for. Give it to me. I want to bury my face in your fragrance ... inhale all of you. You're torturing me.'

Catriona kicked off her shoes once more. 'I'm facing you now and still covering my private parts with my hand. Moving them away so that you can see all of me. I'm caressing my body as I come to you, trembling with desire ... throbbing with need for you ... totally ready for you to take me now.'

She straddled him, placing the heat of him between her legs and against the silky soft dampness of her desire, savouring the delicious shock as her flesh touched his.

Umberto let out a primitive groan and Catriona felt his shudder of response like an electric shock piercing every limb. He closed his eyes, his body surrendering as she fondled him, brushing his velvet tip against her swollen moist core.

'Does it feel as good for you as it does for me?' she asked in a husky low tone.

'*Sì ... Fammi entrare in te*, let me inside you,' he said as he drew her down, moulding the long indentation of her spine, smoothing the curve of her hips. His arms went around her with a strength she gloried in, moulding her body to his so that she could not escape even if she wanted to.

Raising her head, her chestnut hair tumbling over his shoulder to the pillow, she welcomed his fierce, possessive kiss and the thrust of his tongue, opening to him with all the generosity of her nature in a hungry response, her nails digging into his back. All the while the music in the background crescendoed, the drum beating steadily, whirling higher and higher, louder and louder, like an exotic, imperial onslaught on the senses that mirrored their own rhythmic passion.

Oblivious to everything but the pulsing movements of his body and her own needs, Catriona buried her face in Umberto's shoulder, her nostrils filling with the musky scent of his skin and its tantalizing warmth. She ran her fingers through the rough hair that went from the hollow of his throat to his navel. And because he had found and was caressing the secret places of her body – those places that only he had known – she let her hands return to his groin, and to the velvet core of his desire, brushing her fingers lightly over the tip, which broke the last shreds of his control.

He groaned her name deep in his throat and then they rolled over and moved wildly and savagely in ecstasy, she luxuriating in the feel of him, pleasure inundating every part of her.

Catriona's yearning for Umberto brought her so close to the edge of her release that when he entered her, she cried out, lost in the white heat of her body's rhythms, filled with him, completely herself yet at the same time completely united with him, as it had always been. Together, they rode higher and higher until they reached the crystal clarity of that pinnacle and, at nearly the same point, *Boléro* burst into a majestic shower of fireworks at its finale. They fell from its dizzying height to lie spent in each other's arms, their minds left to wonder dazedly in an awestruck silence, chests still heaving with the effort of their spent passion.

Sleep took the lovers almost immediately, their bodies tangled and intertwined as though they needed to remain as one.

*   *   *

When Catriona woke up, dawn filtered through the porthole showing that the place on the bed next to her was empty. Her body still warm and languorous, she pulled on her dressing gown and went on deck. Umberto stood there in a navy silk robe, smoking and looking as if he were staring out across the lake.

She came up behind and wrapped her arms around him, resting her cheek against his back. He had showered, his hair was still wet and he smelled of tobacco, aftershave and mint.

The landscape was hushed and of a fiery intensity. Dawn's vibrant gold light leapt and sparkled over the horizon of Lake Como, bathing the land in summer radiance, gradually burning the heel of night as it spilled its red flames on the countryside. Everything that had been grey was suddenly bright. The dawning sun flushed the rippling waters, which had sparkled like silver under the moon. The golden glow dressed the shoreline and gradually each rock, each villa, each *palazzo* was veiled with rainbow light. Above, the morning star was a diamond accent from heaven.

'*Buongiorno, mia piccola strega passionale,*' Umberto said, turning and pulling her into his embrace.

Catriona lifted herself on tiptoes and kissed him on the lips. 'You're up early.'

'Dawn comes with a musical silence, the soul hearing the melody that the ears cannot,' Umberto replied. 'It's the best time of day on the lake. Everything seems so quiet to sighted people but, since I lost my sight, I can hear so many hushed noises I wasn't aware of before.' He smiled and turned his face upwards in the gentle morning air.

'You see, *amore mio*, Como softly whispers to me. I can hear the plop of a jumping fish, the flutter of a bird's wing as he dives into the water to catch his prey, and the soft murmur of the lake lapping the shore. It's all music. Sometimes it's the melody of the lake's rippling surface as the breeze dances above it, or the sound of the swell as it crashes a symphony over the rocks.' He sighed. 'It somehow makes me grateful that I can still hear, smell and feel.'

'You love the lake, don't you?' she said, placing an arm around his waist and snuggling closer to him, her head resting in the deep hollow under his shoulder blade. 'You talk about it with such poetry.'

'It's been a great source of inspiration for me, as it has for so many artists. There's an overwhelming sense of romance here. Look around you. In each corner of the lake and its elegant shores you'll find the remains of a beguiling, belle-époque world where the ghosts of opera divas and composers, writers, painters and a few exiled kings and queens float across the lake's royal-blue waters.'

'It could still be a source of inspiration for you,' she put forward tentatively.

She immediately felt his body stiffen.

'*Cara*, in life, you must never go back. Things are never the same and the disillusionment if you do can have much deeper consequences than you could ever imagine,' he said gravely.

Catriona said nothing. In due course she would find the words or the way to coax his genius back into composing. She stood a while in the quiet, tranquil morning, huddled against Umberto's warm body, watching a fountain of melted golds and reds mark haphazard designs on the jagged points of the tall mountains and draw thin lines on the horizon. Neither muffled murmur nor echo of a dream disturbed the silence of nature's still soundless slumber. Time froze.

Overhead, gulls and terns drifted and soared, allowing the breeze to carry them without flapping their wings. A family of eider ducks were playing and diving close to the shore, tipping their bodies forward and looking for food.

As the sun burst into the sky, inundating the countryside with its blazing light, Catriona spotted Mario hurrying down the quay towards the yacht. As he walked on to the gangplank, whistling to himself, she noticed he was carrying two bags of fruit and some bread. For a moment she felt self-conscious, standing there in her dressing gown, and pulled it tighter under her neck as though the gesture would make her feel more presentable; wishing she'd had the foresight to pull on some clothes before coming out on deck. Then she reminded herself that she and Umberto had just got engaged. Besides, wouldn't both Adelina and Mario have guessed by now what was going on? Glancing at Mario, she could see that this was undoubtedly true: he seemed totally unfazed by her appearance.

'*Buongiorno, signore, Dottoressa,*' he said with his usual open smile. 'Although we have plenty of fruit for breakfast in the fridge, I found some local orange blossom honey and ripe cherries. It's the beginning of the season so sometimes the cherries are tart, but these are really juicy.'

'*Buongiorno, Mario. Ottimo*, well done.' Umberto grinned approvingly. 'What time is it?'

'Eight o'clock, *signore.*'

'Very well. We have plenty of time to dress and enjoy a leisurely breakfast before we need to be on our way to Comacina for Mass.'

'I love honey,' Catriona said as they were going back to the bedroom. 'We had a beehive in my grandparents' garden in England and I used to eat pots of it.'

Umberto grinned. 'That explains a lot.'

'What do you mean?'

He laughed deep in his throat and pulled her to him as he closed the door behind them. 'It explains this, *amore mio.*' He took her lips with his mouth and her body reacted to its warmth immediately, pressing against him instinctively.

He grinned again. 'See what I mean?' He kissed the tip of her nose lightly.

'Come on, out with it, Umberto, I'm getting annoyed.'

'Ah … the eyes are turning charcoal black?'

'What's the great joke about me eating pots of honey?'

'Your sex drive, *amore.*' He raised both eyebrows. 'There are a number of explanations for the term "honeymoon" that tie it to the use of honey by newlyweds as an aphrodisiac. These stories could possibly be a modern creation, but there's a history of the association of honey and sex in antiquity. Honey was a common offering to the ancient Egyptian fertility god, Min, and was recommended by the Greek physician Hippocrates to boost libido.'

Catriona hammered his chest lightly with her fists in mock indignation. 'That's unfair! It's only you that brings out this wanton, uninhibited creature in me. I've never wanted or desired any other man but you, Umberto. You awaken all sorts of appetites I never even knew existed.'

His hand intercepted one of her wrists and held it a moment. 'Although you were able to have a child by another man,' he remarked, the playful tone all at once leaving his voice, 'that child couldn't have made itself, and if my deductions are right, it must have been very shortly after we met.'

Catriona was taken by surprise but somehow the lie made its way from her lips. 'That was ... that was on the rebound after you left me. He was an old friend of the family's ... a sort of father figure, I suppose.' She was grateful that he couldn't see the blush flooding her face as she stammered the words. She had read somewhere that one lie was enough to question all truths. How would she be able to extricate herself from this web? She was only making things worse by giving extended shape to her deception.

Umberto nodded without answering and proceeded to dress silently, his face closed. Catriona could see that he was angry but she was scared that if she tried to placate him, he might start to ask more questions, ones that she would find even more difficult to answer, and so she went into the bathroom to shower.

When she came out, Umberto was already dressed in grey trousers and a navy blazer with a crisp white shirt and a burgundy Hermès tie that was knotted perfectly. A matching silk handkerchief spilled elegantly out of the top pocket of his jacket.

As she began to dress, Umberto came towards her. 'The idea that you belonged to another man maddens me,' he said a little sheepishly. 'I know I have no right to feel jealous but when I imagine you abandoning yourself, as you have with me, I just can't control my anger. I'm sorry.'

'Umberto,' she said, knotting her arms around his neck. 'It was never like that. I promise that I've never craved or even been attracted to any other man but you. You, and only you, make my blood burn with a fire that nothing can quench but your possession of me. That very first time I met you, all those years ago, I threw to the wind all the principles I was taught, forgetting any rules of morality, and nothing has changed. I have a reputation for being cool, composed and unemotional but when I'm around you, I barely recognize myself. You're such a wonderful lover that I can't help becoming overheated and wanton.'

He gave a sigh and pulled her against him, running his hands up her back. 'It isn't anything I do,' he said softly. 'It's us. Something we create together. What happens between you and me is like a miracle, and I can assure you that I haven't felt it with any other woman.'

'Just standing like this against you makes me want you to do all sorts of things to me,' she whispered huskily.

Umberto chuckled. 'Wanton is good … but only with me.' He pulled her towards him and began to plant butterfly kisses all over her face.

Catriona reluctantly pushed him away. 'Go and have breakfast. Otherwise I'll never be ready.'

'You're right, we don't want to be late for Mass. Shall I bring you a cup of coffee?'

'No, thank you. I won't be long if you just let me dress.'

'*Ai vostri ordini, signora, me ne vado subito*, at your orders, Madam, I am leaving immediately.'

*   *   *

Half an hour later, they arrived on Isola Comacina. The waters of the Zocca dell'Olio were alive with *Lucie*, the local boats, bearing boatmen in historical costumes. The brightly dressed craft had glided in a traditional procession from the parish church in Ossuccio around the shores of Comacina, transporting eager crowds to the festival and fair. A large barge decked with flags, resounding with chants and music, was at the head of the floating procession, carrying a group of priests in richly ornate vestments.

'They are carrying the *Abundi*,' Umberto explained. 'The relics of the saints that Sant'Abbondio brought to the island. Every year, the priests take them to the ruins of the ancient Basilica of Sant' Eufemia. The Mass dedicated to Saint John the Baptist is sacred to the people from the villages all around.'

'It's amazing how people still believe in the power of relics to this day,' Catriona remarked. 'A bone, a piece of cloth … what many would regard simply as hocus-pocus. The symbolic importance of it is undeniable, of course.'

'Yes, the villagers are simple folk. They delight in these sorts of ceremonies and every bit of arcane tradition attached to them. The priests are only too aware that festivals – however full of "hocus-pocus" as you call it – keep religion alive for their parishioners.'

'Yes, that makes complete sense.'

'It's sad that parts of the festival have fallen away over the years. Up until the middle of the nineteenth century, they put on a kind of mystery play, enacting the life and martyrdom of San Giovanni. The Fiera di San Giovanni, the fair that has taken its place, is all we have left to mark the tradition. But you'll love that. Everyone picnics under the olives and plane trees later on.'

It was noon and the sun was high in the sky by the time Mass was over. Catriona had felt acutely the sacredness of the old Romanesque basilica and the few remaining stones of its ruins. The place had seemed to conjure a spiritual ecstasy in many of the congregation and she, too, had felt herself carried along on a wave of emotional fervour. Beside her, Umberto had been impassive but she had sensed something like an electric current running through his veins as he allowed the sound to wash through him.

The promontory, which the afternoon before had been a peaceful enough place in which to dream away an hour, was now thronged with the faithful, and the sound of chanting and sacred hymns floated over the lake to the mountains beyond.

By now the crowds were dispersing to have their picnics in the shade of Comacina's great trees. The sun had turned its cheerful smiling face to the west and the blue sky burned with blinding rays, which beat down upon their path as Umberto and Catriona made their way down the hill to the boat. The air had such a shining clarity that Catriona wanted to drink it in, and not a ripple of wind stirred the dry grasses along the verge.

'Mario has prepared a picnic lunch for us,' Umberto explained as they picked their way down the hillside, Catriona guiding his steps, her arm linked in his. 'These fairs become rather rowdy with the great amount of wine consumed. You'll hear chants of quite a different nature ripple across the lake later on. I thought it might be nicer if we cross over to the small village of Fiumelatte by boat and picnic there under the trees.'

'Sounds lovely.' Catriona gave a sigh of contentment. She was not going to let anything disturb their almost perfect day. For the moment Umberto was the picture of serene happiness, and the feeling was infectious.

'The village got its name from a stream called Fiume di Latte, the river of milk, which emerges from a cave and rushes down in a cascade of milky whiteness to the lake near Varenna. It starts quite suddenly in March and increases until the summer heat dies down, then gradually decreases until the end of November when it actually ceases to flow.'

'I remember Giacomo telling me about these streams that appear and disappear mysteriously.'

Umberto nodded. 'It's strange that the two Plinies, who so carefully described every natural phenomenon they came across, never alluded to Fiume di Latte. They discoursed at length on the mysterious spring at Villa Pliniana, but there's no mention of this.'

On either side, Catriona took in the soft bright slopes curving downwards; the trees stood along the bottom, bunchy and motionless, thick with leaves. They looked as if woven in a tapestry, their dark green plumage captured for eternity. Far below, the lake loomed ahead of them, translucent and still catching the sun pouring its light over the blue water and the land.

'I can smell the spicy scent of the gorse,' Umberto remarked as they passed bushes that grew beside the path with their spiky yellow flowers and thorny leaves. 'The scent of clover is so strong in the air at this time of year. Although nothing beats the tang of resin from the fir trees – that really touches my heart, for some reason. Together, they seem to encapsulate the steady deep fragrance of Italy.'

Not for the first time, Catriona marvelled at how much Umberto was able to offer her, his very blindness opening her own senses to more wonders than she had ever been aware of before. She was his help and guide, yet didn't he have an equal amount to give?

Mario was waiting for them by the boat. They motored to the small village of Fiumelatte, which rose about two hundred metres above the shore, and then he accompanied them to the village, carrying the picnic basket.

The gardens they passed when they reached the tiny village were beautiful, punctuated with tall cypress trees, Roman-style statues and fountains. They glowed with vivid-coloured, sweet-smelling flowers that grew thickly up to windowsills and climbed over fences and walls.

Still, the views across the lake and on all sides surpassed them all: with spires, towers and domes of churches soaring up, silvery and grey, above the green elms; while *palazzi* and country villas were scattered across vineyards and large expanses of dense forest. At the head of the lake, the blue waters melted away and seemed to blend themselves with the hazy blue mountains, whose higher peaks were still lightly capped with snow.

They sat in the shady coolness of a chestnut tree a little distance from the milk-white foaming cascade that thundered down a steep and rocky channel into the water below. Mario left them with the wicker picnic basket and a large plaid blanket, which he spread out before heading back to the boat.

'All this looks intriguing,' Catriona said, surveying the packaged contents of the basket, which looked as if it could easily feed six hungry people.

'Let's start with the wine.'

Catriona glanced at him sceptically. 'Perhaps we should stick with water.'

Umberto heard the warning in her voice and laughed. 'Believe me, Caterina, it's only spirits that are my downfall. Wine I can drink like pomegranate juice.' His hands ran over the contents of the basket until there was a clinking sound. 'Besides, it looks as though Mario has only packed a couple of bottles, so we can choose between them if you prefer.'

He handed Catriona the two bottles that were on offer and she read out the labels.

Umberto smiled with satisfaction. 'Ah, a Sangiovese Chianti from Montalcino. Let's have that. After we spoke about Mozart's music supposedly having an effect on the natural world, I ordered this wine. It's from a little vineyard in Tuscany.'

'How wonderful! The wine has been grown to Mozart?' said Catriona, her eyes sparkling.

'Yes. The owner, one Giancarlo Cignozzi, does indeed play Mozart to his vines. He was considered a bit of a lunatic at first, but then he showed how the vines that grew nearer the speakers produced grapes with a higher sugar content.'

'That's wonderful,' said Catriona, who had the deepest faith in the ineffable power of music and would never have considered the man crazy. 'It never seemed strange to me that plants might perceive sounds and specific frequencies. Thank you for tracking the wine down. How exciting to have the chance to actually try it.'

'Well, Giancarlo's now got a scientist from Florence University to conduct a study and it seems not only do the plants become more robust when serenaded, but insects and birds leave the vines alone, so he doesn't need to use pesticides.'

'I suppose the vibrations must put them off.'

She proceeded to open the bottle and pour the limpid ruby-red wine into their glasses. As she did so, Catriona realized how far from her original task she had strayed over the past days. She had been distracted – albeit in the most delightful way – but she knew instinctively that Umberto must engage with his music again or he would only grow morose and bitter. In the same way those grapes grew strong and sweet, so, she believed, would Umberto if only he could be persuaded to compose again.

Catriona took a sip of the wine. It was glorious, a symphony in itself. She decided to change the subject otherwise she would be tempted to speak about what was troubling her and it would only spoil the mood. 'Is there a legend for Fiumelatte? You always seem to have a fund of myths surrounding places on the lake.'

His mouth quirked at the edges. 'Well, of course there is.'

'And?'

'A poetic legend claims that the Madonna was supposed to have washed the clothes of the Baby Jesus in the cascading waters of Fiumelatte.'

Catriona laughed. 'You've made that one up.'

'Not at all. It's one of the attractions of Varenna for that reason.'

She began to unwrap the food, which was nicely packed in brown paper bags and tied with string.

'What a spread!' she exclaimed when she had taken everything out of the basket.

'What has Mario prepared for our *scampagnata,* outing?'

'A loaf of *foccacia*, and one of *schiacciata* flatbreads, I think it is. They've used tomatoes ... and here's another with pancetta. Now this,' she said, peeling away a wrapping, 'looks like a rocket and Taleggio cheese tart. Ooh, and here we have a frittata with zucchini. Then there's an enormous plate of Italian cured meats and another of vegetables in olive oil and vinegar. There's also a whole load of cheese and a stunning array of fresh fruit ... Ah, and a box of chocolates too! This is a feast – we'll never be able to walk down again if we're not careful.'

Umberto laughed, seeming thoroughly satisfied with this enthusiastic response. They started off with the cheese tart and some antipasti. For a while they both tucked into the food, feeling no immediate need to talk, then Umberto spoke.

'I think we should get married as soon as possible,' he said suddenly. 'Tomorrow, if you like. I know you've been worrying about giving back the fee, and maybe that's the best way to quieten wagging tongues.'

Catriona looked startled. 'You know that's quite impossible, Umberto. I need to speak to my family ... prepare my son.'

'Your mother and Michael are very welcome to come over. There's plenty of space for guests at the villa.'

Her mind quickly sought another means of deflecting him. 'What about Giacomo and Silvana. Have you told them that we're engaged?'

'No, not yet. There's time enough when we get back.' He speared a piece of salami with his fork with perfect coordination.

'Besides, I wouldn't be surprised if word had already reached them while we've been away.'

Catriona shifted uneasily; she could just imagine Silvana's reaction to the news that Umberto had finally slipped through her clutches. And what of Giacomo? Was he only interested in getting his hands on the estate, as Adelina had intimated? If that were true, he wouldn't welcome Catriona as Umberto's new wife either.

'But first things first,' Umberto continued. 'You must bring your family here to visit as soon as possible.'

Something in his tone alerted her that they were moving on to shaky ground, and that he didn't want to be put off with reasons for taking things slowly. If only there wasn't this unfinished business between them. She felt herself shy away from telling the truth like a nervous colt, and another excuse came out quickly: 'My son's going on holiday with some friends. I can't change his plans.'

'For the whole summer?'

Catriona felt herself blush. 'Yes … no,' she admitted in a stifled voice, the enormity of her deception rising before her like a cloud.

'Yes or no? What are you hiding from me?'

'*Tell him everything now,*' her shattered conscience urged. Still, she feared his reaction, his judgement of her … that he would never look at her in the same way again. And so, cowardly, she kept silent and sunk more deeply into the quicksand of her lie.

'Nothing. But it wouldn't be practical to bring him over here.'

'I haven't lost my natural judgement, even if I've lost my sight,' he told her. 'And my guess is that you *are* hiding something from me.'

'He's only a child. Springing this on him so suddenly might be devastating for him.'

'He will have to know at some stage.'

'Yes, of course … but that can come a little later. Let me do this in my own way and my own time, Umberto. I've only been here a few days and already you've turned my life upside down.'

'That's a good thing, isn't it, *cara*?' he asked hesitantly, a worried expression on his face.

'You must admit it's been a shock to the system. I feel like my body and mind have been through a tsunami.'

'Do you regret it?'

'Of course I don't, but it has disorientated me. I feel the rational self I knew, that I could depend on, is no longer in charge.'

'Why do I still feel that you are being elusive … or maybe evasive is a better word?' Umberto rubbed his jaw. '*Sì, evasiva*. You dance around most questions about yourself and I'm beginning to think there's a big dark secret hiding behind those beautiful eyes I still remember.'

'I'm just being realistic and I'm trying to be reasonable here.' Yet Catriona was squirming with discomfort.

'You're right, *cara*,' Umberto conceded with a conciliatory half-smile. 'Perhaps we shouldn't get married straight away. Let's extend our engagement for a few months and if, at the end of that period, you'd like to break it off, I won't hold you to it. If all goes well, then we'll have a big wedding. Does that put your mind at rest?'

Catriona almost breathed a sigh of relief. 'Yes, it does, thank you.'

'I'd like to meet your son in the meantime. Have him come over for a week or two as soon as he's free this summer and I will give orders here to everyone not to breathe a word of our engagement until you're ready. What do you think?'

Catriona dithered, unable to commit. On the one hand, if she brought Michael over and the relationship between herself and Umberto didn't work out then it would destabilize the boy. He was an astute child, bound to notice what was going on between his mother and this strange man. On the other, it would be good if a warm bond could be established between Michael and his father, paving the way for the time when the truth of his parentage would not be such a shock to him. She had to discuss it with her mother, for a start; Marguerite must be involved.

'I need time to think it over,' she said finally.

'I hope you decide on it sooner rather than later, *amore*.' He gave her a rueful smile, nodding his head knowingly. 'You know what they say, tomorrow is often the busiest day in the week.'

Catriona opened her mouth to make a sharp retort then closed it again as she discerned the note of sadness in his voice and the almost lost expression on his face. 'Yes, Umberto, of course. But I can't rush it. This is a delicate matter and any hasty decision could have unfortunate consequences.'

He turned away and, feeling for the bottle, picked it up and filled his glass. 'Let's have some more wine and enjoy our picnic.'

They ate in silence for a while with the voice of the leaping water singing in the background. Catriona, no longer bearing the same untroubled countenance of earlier, sat lost in her thoughts.

It was only when a lighter flared and smoke filled the warm air that she fell out of her meditation and jumped a little, giving a barely perceptible gasp.

'You have gone away from me again, Caterina. What's troubling you, *eh*?'

'Nothing, I'm just a little tired. The sun and the fresh air probably.'

Umberto drew on his cigarette. 'Have you ever had the odd feeling that people are keeping something from you, like a child who senses the adults are withholding some of the harsher realities of life?' Catriona remained silent, unwilling to go over this again. 'The report the lawyers submitted to Calandra said that your son is nine.' He stopped for a moment, then added: 'You must have had him very quickly after you married. In fact, not so long after … after that night.'

Catriona swallowed. 'Yes. He was conceived on our honeymoon.'

She felt Umberto stiffen.

'How old was he when his father died?'

'Very young.'

'How old?' he persisted.

'One and half.'

'What did your husband die of?'

'A sudden heart attack.'

'How old was he? Was he sick?'

Anger shot through Catriona, not so much at Umberto for being so persistent in his interrogation, but with herself for the tangle of lies she had created. If she had only stopped to think, she would have realized the injustice of taking it out on him, but instead she lashed out: 'You have no right to fire these questions at me!'

Umberto's voice was harsh. 'You are going to be my wife. Have I no right to know about your past life? I wouldn't hesitate to answer *your* questions honestly.'

Catriona wanted to tell him how much she did value trust like that in a relationship – how honesty was the most important thing to her – but she couldn't take that stance now when she was prepared to lie about his son.

'You know the important part of my past life. Isn't that enough?'

'I want to know everything about you … from the day you were born,' he said, more gently now, stretching out his hand to find hers.

Catriona gave him her hand. 'Fine. But now isn't the moment.'

'When then?'

'I promise that before we marry, I will tell you my life story from A to Z.' She forced a self-derisory laugh. 'But I can tell you, I've had a pretty uneventful life.'

'Not that uneventful. You are a respected authority in your field.'

'That's true, but it didn't come easily. I worked very hard to get where I am.'

'You could have become a great opera singer, like my mother.'

Why did he have to remind her of that unfulfilled dream of her youth? Catriona sighed and tried not to sound wistful as she said: 'That wasn't meant to be. It was all too complicated. Anyhow, I would never have reached the top.'

A sudden gust of wind ruffled the trees and swept over the picnic rug, interrupting their conversation. A couple of the paper food bags were blown away and a few clouds, rolling their rainy pillows, appeared in what was no longer an azure sky. Then a deadly calm fell on the countryside. The bees and butterflies that had filled the air abruptly vanished and the sky was quiet except for the panicked gulls and swifts, which were flying low in swooping curves and spirals, looking for shelter in the now frigid atmosphere.

Catriona looked up. All this had happened in a matter of seconds and now large banks of grey cloud were creeping across the sky from behind the mountains, descending on to the lake and towns, hiding the sun. Thunder cracked in the distance, rolling round the mountain tops; the lake far below them gleamed like dull pewter.

'I think there's going to be a storm,' she noted.

'Yes, you're right. We should get going before it breaks, although I can tell by the thunder that it's still far off. I'll ring Mario to come and collect the picnic.'

Catriona glanced at her watch: five o'clock already. The hours had slipped away, unnoticed. She should have been happy – she'd spent two magical days with Umberto – but she was perturbed by their last conversation. This situation couldn't continue. The answer was, of course, to bite the bullet and come clean but first she would talk to her mother about bringing Michael over to Villa Monteverdi and she would take it from there. Yet, for some reason, this decision filled her with fear and, although she had never been superstitious, Catriona looked up at the darkening sky and saw the storm as a bad omen.

Those troubled thoughts continued to fill her mind as soon after Mario appeared and the threesome made their way slowly down to the village of Fiumelatte and back to the boat.

Because of the storm, the journey back to Villa Monteverdi took much longer than the day before – more than three hours – and Catriona was more than thankful when they finally arrived. Umberto hadn't asked her any more questions and they had travelled almost in silence as if a gaping chasm had opened between them, threatening to swallow her up at the slightest wrong move. It made her heart feel heavy, like an insufferable weight in her chest.

The first thing she did when she returned to the lodge was to ring Marguerite and tell her everything that had happened since their last conversation. It was a relief to hear her mother's voice which, as always, comprised a good helping of lawyer's logic combined with an unstinting maternal warmth. Unsurprisingly, she was adamant that Catriona should immediately tell Umberto that he had a son.

'We've been over this,' she told her, a hint of reprimand in her voice. 'I can't understand why you haven't told him yet.'

'I keep thinking about it, but then the moment is never right,' Catriona said with a defeated sigh.

'The moment will never feel right. *Alors tu devras tout simplement franchir le pas*, so you'll just have to take the plunge. Come out with it,' she urged. 'It will only get more difficult the longer you wait.'

After that, Marguerite suggested that Catriona should come over to France to prepare Michael for the all-important encounter before initiating a face-to-face meeting between father and son.

In her heart Catriona had always known this was the right way to proceed, so why hadn't she initiated the correct course of action herself in the first place?

Her mother picked up on her frustration and her tone became gentler. 'Look, *chérie*, you mustn't be too hard on yourself.

You've done everything for the right reasons, to protect those you love. He'll realize that, you'll see.'

'And what if he doesn't, *Maman*?' Catriona almost wailed. 'I can't bear to lose him!'

'If he's the right man for you, he'll come round. From what you tell me, he has a big heart and he's a courageous fellow who is not going to be defeated by this. *Courage, mon enfant!*'

Before hanging up, Catriona warned Marguerite that the French press might well get wind of her and Umberto's engagement. She asked her mother to keep an eye on the newspapers to try and shield Michael from learning the truth from any other source. She would come back to Nice to tell him herself as soon as she could.

After they'd finished speaking, Marguerite went to find Michael so that Catriona could say goodnight. For the first time since she'd left, he sounded like he was missing her dreadfully. 'When are you coming home, *Maman*? Will you be away much longer?'

'Soon, *chéri*, I promise.'

'It's not the same without you,' he said, his voice sounding suddenly strained and so young that it almost broke her heart. As they said goodnight, it was all she could do to keep her own voice steady. She had never been away from him this long and the tug at her heart made her feel even more confused and divided.

In spite of her various fears and qualms about Michael and the web of lies she had spun in her cowardice, Catriona did know one thing. There was nothing in the least ambivalent about her feelings towards Umberto. The love she had given him with the reckless, unquestioning naïvety of an eighteen-year-old had survived the passing of time. She had loved him in the sunlight of innocence and, now a grown woman, she loved him as passionately as ever.

It was this knowledge that kept her glimmer of hope alive: that one day Umberto and Michael would know each other as father and son … and that love would be the saviour of them all.

CHAPTER 17

Umberto woke early. All was quiet in his room and there was no movement in the house yet. He had left the window open during the night, despite the storm, and through it now came the freshness of early morning. He lay for several minutes in bed, listening to the twitter of a solitary bird in the garden and to the feelings stirring within his own heart.

His mind ambled back to the discussion at Fiumelatte with Caterina, and his thoughts wandered around it, repeatedly returning to Michael. He could have sworn on his life that she was keeping something important from him. It was clear to him now … no more than nine months had elapsed between the night they made love and the boy's birth. When had she had time to meet her husband, get married and conceive? Unless, of course, he'd been a very premature baby, which was improbable.

Umberto struck his forehead with his fist. How was it possible that he'd never thought of this?

The child was *his*, of course.

Caterina had married this older man, this friend of the family, to avoid a scandal. It was true – it had to be – and it had never crossed his mind. What a fool he'd been!

That simple realization fell like a pebble on the glassy surface of a stream. One moment it was placid, serenely reflecting the sunlight and the blue sky, then a toss of a pebble and it was shaken to its very depths.

Now he awoke like one newly born. As he recalled, one by one, the words of their conversation, he heard with fresh insight the accents of Caterina's altered voice. She *had* been hiding something from him. Although he couldn't see her face, he was sensitive to the intonations of her voice.

He needed to talk to her. Needed to confront her with what he was now sure must be the truth.

This had changed everything.

Instantly, he rose, showered and dressed. He rang for Adelina and asked her to prepare breakfast on the terrace and then made his way across the garden to the lodge.

*   *   *

Catriona went out on to the terrace with a cup of hot chocolate and gazed out across the lake, breathing in the fresh morning air. She had slept through the night without interruption and although she'd woken early, she felt rested and full of energy. Her first thought had been for Umberto. '*La nuit porte conseil*, sleep on it,' her mother had said to her once and, indeed, this morning there was no doubt in her mind that today she would tell Umberto about his son. Maybe the status of being a father would give him a new focus in life that would help him to forget his condition, perhaps even inspire him to take up composing again.

Umberto's headaches also troubled her so, while the sun's first rays pierced the horizon, she had gone straight to her computer, spending time on the internet looking up ocular migraines. Now that she'd resolved to speak to Umberto, she made a mental note to first persuade him to see his eye specialist. Then she would broach the subject of Michael.

The storm had subsided and already the day was glowing bright with an unfathomably clear sky. The sun was just swimming up above the mountain peaks and the vault over her head was a joyous, fire-heated gold. The lake shimmered glassy bright, more light than water; the wind had stilled and the waves that had rippled its surface had sunk into long, low undulations. At this early hour, Lake Como was already throbbing with life. In the distance, she could see the foam from the wake of a couple of motor yachts cruising over the water, a tall sailing bark with her flat foreladder of sails delicately moving across the light, and a far-off steamer on the horizon. On the edge of the shore more boats had left the quayside. A great hawk hovered over the black rocks to her right, stooped to catch a fish and was gone, disappearing yonder into the clouds.

A fresh, awesome beauty and stillness prevailed as Catriona stood above the world, surrounded by a sculpted wonderland of the steep lakeshores. She pondered how she should announce to Umberto that he was a father. This would also reveal her guilt in keeping this secret from him for ten years – and also how she had deceived him over the past few days.

She showered and chose a breezy dress of pale pistachio cotton, with a nipped-in waist and a halter neck that elegantly framed her shoulders She hoped the oufit would somehow boost her confidence. After donning a pair of dainty golden sandals, she grabbed her bag, and was just coming down the staircase when the front door flew open and there was Umberto standing on the threshold.

Catriona rushed to him and kissed him on the lips, her pulse racing nervously. '*Buongiorno*, I was just coming to see you at the villa.'

He pulled her into his embrace and returned the kiss, taking her whole mouth heatedly. '*Buongiorno, amore.*' He let his palms run over the bare satin skin of her shoulders. '*Sei così bella*, you're so beautiful,' he said in a deep, hoarse voice, close to her ear, the sound of it rumbling right down to her very core. Umberto let his hand slip to the small of her back and crushed her against him. 'You just need to touch me for my body to go wild.' He buried his face in her long, lush hair and inhaled her scent.

Catriona closed her eyes as she felt the hard strength of his arousal and the deep stirring inside her, drenched with her own need.

Still, he pulled away. His restless body language seemed to hold more than mere sexual tension.

'Later, *amore mio*, I will love you as I have never done before. But first, we must have breakfast. We have much to talk about … much to sort out, *sì*?'

There was a sense of urgency in his voice, a note of pent-up excitement that she had never heard before, and she wondered …

'I've ordered breakfast on the terrace of the villa,' he continued, taking her arm gently and almost marching her out of the lodge.

'That sounds lovely. I've only had a cup of hot chocolate this morning. Did you sleep well?'

'Yes.'

'And the headache?'

He made an irritated gesture with his hand. 'Forget about the headache. Do you never have any headaches?'

'Yes, sometimes, but I haven't had concussion. A knock on the head can be dangerous, and if the headaches recur, I think you should have a scan.'

'*Basta*, enough, Caterina. I don't want to talk about headaches. That subject is closed. *Capito*? Understood? There are other issues we need to discuss today … now, *subito*!' He was agitated and a red flush had crept to his cheeks.

'Yes, of course,' she acquiesced, feeling nervous all of a sudden, knowing deep down that the urgent subject he wanted to broach was Michael. He'd had all night to work things out.

They had arrived on the terrace. The table was tastefully laid with a much more modern version of breakfast than the typical Italian *colazione* consisting of cappuccino and *biscotti*. Mouth-watering pastries, a luscious, jewel-like *macedonia* in a crystal bowl, muesli, yoghurts, bread and an array of homemade jams, and colourful jugs of both orange and pomegranate juice were a joy to the eye.

'Just looking at your table makes me hungry,' Catriona remarked with a tense little laugh, though she actually felt too nervous to eat.

'Yes. Calandra was very strict on presentation and she's the one who trained Mario. Will you have a cappuccino or something else?'

'A cappuccino would be perfect, thanks.'

Umberto turned to Adelina, who had just appeared on the terrace. '*Un cappuccino e un doppio espresso, Adelina, per favore.*'

Catriona noticed that the housekeeper was watching Umberto with an expression of wary concern, but then Adelina's dark eyes turned to Catriona, her face softening. 'Welcome back, *Dottoressa*. I hope you had a good trip to Isola Comacina?'

'Yes, thank you, Adelina.' Catriona smiled up at the grey-haired woman. 'Yes, it was … wonderful.' Her eyes darted over to Umberto, searching his impassive features.

Adelina nodded, evidently pleased, though she too gave Umberto a speculative glance before bustling out to fetch their coffees.

'Shall I give you some fruit salad? It looks delicious,' Catriona asked him.

'Not yet, thank you.' He appeared calm but distracted, and a small indentation had appeared between his brows.

Catriona helped herself to a tiny amount of fruit, all the while worrying about what was simmering beneath the surface in Umberto's mind and wondering if she should bring up the subject of Michael first.

Adelina came in with the coffees and placed them on the table.

'*Grazie*, Adelina. We don't want to be disturbed,' Umberto told her. 'If I need you, I will ring.'

Before she hurried away, the housekeeper paused only long enough to cast Catriona a speaking look and, at that moment, some kind of understanding passed between the two women. Both of them seemed to feel the same sense of trepidation at Umberto's air of nervous excitement.

When the housekeeper had left the terrace, he leaned back in his chair and took out his cigarettes. He lit one and inhaled deeply, paused as if choosing his words, and then went straight to the point.

'Tell me about Michael.'

Blood rushed to Catriona's ears and she could hear her heart beat as if in slow motion, though she knew it was racing. She also knew what was coming next. It didn't matter that he'd guessed – she was going to tell him anyhow – but she would have preferred for it to have been her initiative instead of it looking as if he was forcing her admission. She was aware he wasn't going to let it go and she was somehow relieved that the truth was about to come out in the open. Still, this was going to be difficult.

'Michael is my son,' she began cautiously, the words 'and yours too' dying in her parched throat.

'I think you know there's a lot more I am asking, *cara*.'

Catriona wiped her palms against her dress before looking up at him. He couldn't see her but those green irises were fixing her so severely it was as if they could see right through her. Acutely aware of the pronounced pallor beneath his golden-olive skin, she felt sorrow, pity, remorse. Her heart fluttered like a frantic bird in her breast.

Oh God, I can't do it, I can't. He'll hate me forever. How could I bear that?

She swallowed, trying to ease the constriction in her throat, and then blurted out: 'Michael is also your son.'

Umberto slammed the table with his fist. 'I knew it!' Then, shaking his head, he added in a low, bewildered tone: 'Why, Caterina? How could you do something like this to me? How could you leave me for so long in complete ignorance?'

She wished he would yell at her. Yelling would be better than hearing the pain come through his confused, calm voice.

And as silence echoed all around them, Catriona knew more than ever her mistake in denying Umberto the joy of being a father. She could only raise her head and look into those unseeing eyes as she remembered their one night of passion so long ago … the misplaced teenage dream that had given her one of life's greatest gifts with one hand and taken away the love of her life with the other, most cruelly.

'Do you know what Michael means?' It wasn't the immediate answer to his question but it was the best she had. 'It means "gift from God" and, ever since I found out I was pregnant, that has been my only thought. A wonderful gift, the fruit of one night of love, which I never forgot and to which I've remained faithful all these years, Umberto. Until I met you again.'

He was still oddly quiet, then he said: 'Why didn't you tell me?'

'Pride, perhaps? The fear that your glamorous life would mean you would only end up discarding me and Michael as an inconvenience.'

'You thought I would reject you?' His tone was stunned. 'You thought I would be that sort of father … that sort of man?'

She shook her head, a flush of shame heating her skin, but she needed to make him understand. Every other day there had been a new story about his latest flame. No doubt the press would have relished the story of him fathering a child. Should she have exposed Michael to the repercussions of that in later life, taunted by old newspaper accounts?

'You were a great composer who had risen to the top. The newspapers were always full of news of your affairs.'

'And that gave you the right to keep me from my son?'

Catriona did her best not to rise to his accusations. 'It took away any sense of trust I had in you. I'm … I'm sorry.' All her fears about his reaction to the truth were coming true. She pressed her lips together to stop them from trembling.

Umberto scowled at her across the table. 'You're sorry?' he repeated scathingly as if the enormity of what he had just discovered had only just hit him. 'Don't you dare say that to me. You cannot begin to know the meaning of the word. *Maledizione*, God damn it, Caterina!' he snapped. 'Have you no idea what this feels like? What it is to discover that for all these years there's been a life, a part of me, that I didn't know existed? You've been here over a week. We've talked, made love … and all this time you said nothing. Not a single word.'

'I wanted to tell you, I came to Italy to tell you, but I was afraid of how you would react.' She was aware that this was a lame excuse but tears were quivering at the edges of her eyes and she knew she had no true defence for those days of deception.

Though his gaze was fixed, there was thunder in his expression. 'You had no intention of telling me, as you have no real intention of marrying me, a blind useless man only fit to make you writhe with pleasure when he takes you to his bed, but not suitable for anything else.'

This reference to her unrestrained wildness in bed struck her as hard as if he had slapped her across the face. Catriona felt something harden within her.

'Tell me, Umberto, what is it exactly that you feel?' she demanded suddenly, pitilessly, the woman who had suffered all those years taking over from the one blinded by passion.

'Love? You don't know Michael. All that's happened is that nature took its time-honoured course – the man taking his pleasure and the woman left picking up the pieces.' She glanced down at her hands and was puzzled to find them shaking, despite the fact that now she felt peculiarly calm.

'Or is it the fact that my son happens to have Monteverdi blood in his veins, the glorious Monteverdi genes in his make-up?' She stopped, despite the part of her that was desperate to continue, halted by fear that the bitterness that had been smothered over the years would now demand its own voice.

'You speak as though I'd been offered a choice and rejected it,' he rasped dazedly. 'Ugh! And I'm supposed to be the blind person?' He gave a sardonic laugh. 'You gave me no choice – for nine long years you denied me all knowledge of our child, and you see yourself as the victim?'

'How could I have risked telling you?' Catriona asked urgently. 'I was the tiniest interlude in your otherwise hectic, exciting life. You were building a career, performing in a different town every other day, with no time to spare or think of anything other than the star you were trying to reach … You left Nice the morning after we slept together. You were off to America! I may have been young but I knew how it must be for you, living in the limelight. We would have been a millstone around your neck, jeopardizing your future.'

'Don't you think that was for me to decide?' he bit out savagely. 'You were carrying *my* child, yet you took it upon yourself to keep it from me, leaving me in total ignorance.'

How could Catriona have done things any differently? Should she have thrown herself on the mercy of a man she barely knew … a man she had trusted but who had let her down? In time, the successful Umberto might have married someone else and sought custody of Michael. Who knew what might have happened?

'I didn't think you'd want to know. There were so many stories about you in the media. I made the only decision I was able to make in the circumstances.'

'That decision wasn't just yours to make. You set yourself up in judgement over me.'

'I was only eighteen, for heaven's sake, with no experience of life.' She eyed Umberto, anticipating what must have been going through his mind. '*Maman* didn't know who Michael's father was. If I'd told her, no doubt she would have prescribed a different course … but I didn't.'

'Even at eighteen, didn't it even cross your mind that he was mine every bit as much as he was yours?'

'I didn't know what to do,' she almost wept. 'You were half-way across the world and I couldn't see how it would help either of us to have you come back and find out that one mistake, one night that should never have happened, had made you a father.' She swallowed hard.

'Besides, we agreed that we wouldn't hold each other to anything, even though I had longed for more. I figured that was how grown-up men and women behaved. This was just for one night and then we were both supposed to move on …' Her voice tailed off piteously, then came back stronger, harsher.

'And the next morning, you proved that. Telling me to get on with my life, and leaving without so much as a backward glance.'

The expression on his face grew blacker than ever, as though he would like to strike her. 'Don't play the innocent with me any more. I'm not buying it,' he spat. 'You're full of excuses, but all I can see is that you cheated me out of having my son and you cheated Michael out of knowing his father. You should have tried to find me immediately. Don't deny it, you had no intention of telling me the truth. You've had plenty of opportunities to do so and yet you still tried to keep it from me. You were never voluntarily going to let me know that I have a son, were you? You've only told me about Michael because you had to … because you couldn't see any way out of it.'

'I was coming to you this morning to tell you about him – and that, Umberto, is the honest truth, I promise you.'

'Of course you were. After our conversation yesterday, you realized I was beginning to guess and you didn't have any other option: the game was up.' Umberto's voice was a gravelly rasp.

'Well now, Caterina, you've dropped the bombshell. I am father to a son who will one day be my heir … and now *you* will have to accept the consequences.'

Catriona felt the colour drain from her face. 'What consequences?'

'What did you think would happen once I knew I'd fathered a son?' he snarled. Umberto put his forefingers between his brows and frowned. 'From this moment on, I intend to be a father to Michael. That means my being there when we break the news to him, including the whole truth about my paternity. Then you will enter into a legalized relationship with me so that I have free access to him. You will have to marry me, Caterina. No maybes, no buts, no more excuses.'

Catriona paused, at first unable to answer. Then her voice came out in a tremble. 'I will marry you, Umberto, but not because you say so and not because of Michael but because I've loved you from the first minute I laid eyes on you and I've never wanted or loved another man but you.'

'Well, we both know that's not strictly true,' Umberto rasped, shaking now with barely contained anger. 'You speak of honesty but you have no idea, do you?' Catriona tried to say something but he cut her off, slamming his hand down on to the table so that his coffee cup spilled over. 'Just leave me. Don't say another word or we'll both say things we might regret.'

He slumped back in his chair and winced. Catriona only now noticed that his forehead was damp with perspiration and he was evidently in pain.

Umberto gritted his teeth. 'Just go, damn it! I can't talk to you right now.'

With a smothered sob, she left the table. Her legs felt as if they would buckle under her as she rushed from the terrace and blindly made her way across the garden in the direction of the lodge. She wanted nothing more than to hide there in a dark corner forever, nursing her wounded heart.

✳   ✳   ✳

Back in the house, Umberto sat in the music room waiting for his headache to subside. He couldn't help but relive the exchange he'd had with Catriona, word by crushing word, and the enormity of what he'd learned and what he had been deprived of almost sent him spiralling downwards into the familiar blackness again.

He'd missed his son taking his first wobbly step … saying 'Papà' for the first time … his first day at school – bright, shining face and smart new uniform. And he hadn't been there to nurture his boy's talent or teach him how to play the piano. That was possibly the greatest agony of all.

He had heard Caterina's explanation and her apology, and understood now why she had done what she'd done, but that didn't change the feeling of loss that swept over him – and the anger too – when he thought of how he had missed the first nine years of his son's life: some of the closest years a father might ever have with his son. He still felt confused by Caterina; he thought he was getting to know her intimately, but then everything seemed to shift and change until now he seemed to have competing thoughts of her inside his head.

There was the honest, pure, loving and compassionate Caterina, whom he loved more than life itself, and then there was her other self, veiled in secrets, who had not only kept his son from him but had continued to deceive him these past days while also making love to him.

While he had forgiven her, thinking about her deception now still pierced his heart like a barb. That she should have kept her pregnancy from him after their one night together was understandable, but that she should persist in her deceit after her arrival in Italy was inexcusable to say the least.

We would have been a millstone around your neck, jeopardizing your future … You told me to get on with my life, leaving without a backward glance. Her words reverberated in his head, making him wince. That must have been how it appeared to her: that he had dropped her callously after she'd abandoned herself to him, giving him her innocence.

A shaft of warm sunlight lay across the room, stretching over the piano like a iridescent gossamer veil. Umberto, who had been pacing the room back and forth in anguish, filled with pent-up frustration and doubt, paused and ran his hand over the tension that was building at the back of his neck. He looked thoughtful for a moment, then his steps finally led him to his piano, the place he had always sought in the past when emotion had been too hard to handle. His refuge … his solace. It felt almost reflexive to do so; he was so used to playing the piano at times when he needed to think, when feelings of joy or anger smothered him. So often before, playing had exerted a tranquilizing influence on his mood. Only once Umberto had become blind had the desire to play suddenly left him; after that, even music hadn't the power to alleviate his black moods. At first, he had tried to seek refuge in the sad melodies that filled his soul, but it had felt bitterly pointless when the sanctuary he'd been hoping for had eluded him.

During these last years, amid the dreary whispers of the lake, the chirpy murmurs of the garden, the peaceful everyday life of Villa Monteverdi, Umberto had lived on the edge of the universe, hearing about the events in the world only from the lips of others. Nothing had moved him. There had been no incentive to get on with life. No inspiration. He had felt like a dead soul in a live body.

Still, today was different. This time the pain he felt was live and keen, pulsing and outwardly directed, not introverted and stagnant or driving him into the shadows. He was still at the centre of a vast dark world, but now there was so much to look forward to: love, fatherhood, a new life … a new leaf. There was promise, there was hope, if only he could get beyond his bitter grief at Caterina's betrayal.

Then suddenly, this sensitive expectancy pushed its way forward and blossomed in Umberto's mood. In a flash he felt that the energy was about to stretch forth its invisible arms and arouse by its touch all the sentiments that lay dormant in his heart, waiting only to be summoned. His muse was growing tendrils in his soul in an even stronger, fiercer and more forceful way than she had done a few nights ago. Sounds that had been elusive before began to reach him – the voice of his heart, the voice of his soul, the voice of his muse. It was as if a storm was thundering in the sky, echoing through space, and Umberto's music in the next moment evoked the whistling of the wind floating over the lake and through the forest and mountains, until it reached the garden and from there into the room, reviving vague dreams of the past.

With enough adrenaline flowing through his veins to raise a shipwrecked tanker, Umberto lifted the piano lid. He struck a single note. It resounded in the room, full and pure, then slowly died away. He struck another and another, and each time the note was swallowed by the dark silence in the room.

He let himself slide on to the stool, his lifeless eyes staring down at the keyboard, remembering the ivory and ebony notes. Something wavered to and fro in the darkness towards the composer with wistful and enticing eagerness. It called and beckoned, awakening answers slumbering within him since Umberto had guessed that Michael was his son. A strange and powerful elation pulsed through him. Then, like a man in a dream, he began to play and, with absolute trust in his muse, he drew from the depths of his soul the notes that shaped themselves into the most poignant melody he had ever produced.

Playing with a fervour that echoed his early days as a composer, the cool, sweet air of Lake Como at dawn spread behind the villa and came through the open window to bid him good day like a caress, blowing away his anger, frustration and doubts as he now faced the whole truth instead of just part of it.

Yes, Caterina had kept the knowledge of his son from him but, maybe, he had driven her to such an action by taking advantage of her innocence then leaving her without a backward glance. And yes, since she had come back into his life she had continued the deception, but wasn't he in some ways just as guilty? He hadn't tried to be tender with her, hadn't given her the reassurance she needed to know that he had changed, that it was safe to gift him the truth. Yes, they had made love. Yes, it had been wonderful. Still, all the time, his feelings had been cloaked in a sort of hard and bitter carapace ... Umberto had been holding back the true love for her that overwhelmed him at times, expressing his lust instead of the depth of his sentiment, in case she discovered his vulnerability and hurt him. She was the one in control and, until now, he would rather have died than let her guess the power she held over him.

Years ago, he had been blinded but this past week he had been doubly blind. The time for pretence was over, he told himself, as a rush of hope filled his heart.

Now, as Umberto played and mysterious springs leapt to the surface from a well deep within his soul, the past came rolling back and he examined the situation from a different point of view. What would have happened if Caterina had sought him out when she had learned that she was carrying his child? She was right: he'd been riding the waves of stardom, the sky was the limit – a woman in every town and the world at his feet. An unwanted pregnancy and marriage to a teenager he hardly knew would have frustrated all his hopes. And he remembered just how urgent had been his desire to become the world's greatest concert pianist and composer.

Still, he also recalled how disappointed he had been when told that Caterina had married and moved away. He had even resented it … had felt a stab of jealousy. *How could she have married another man?* Another man – this Hugue – had held *his* baby, the one he should have had in his arms. The pain was intense and yet …

Somehow he'd always known Caterina was the only woman for him. He scooped in a deep breath, then let it out slowly. Umberto's flesh stirred as he recalled that one night of passion ten years before … how she'd offered herself to him, the way she had opened her soft, sweet lips and taken him into the heat of her mouth … and then, later, the passion with which she had welcomed him into the warmth of her sensual body.

Every other woman always paled in comparison. Caterina had then, and every time since, brought him to such peaks his entire being sang when he thought of them. They belonged together.

By this time Umberto was totally immersed in his music. He felt power in his forearms and magic in his fingers as he leapt into the next complicated piece in his composition, a movement that required the kind of technical brilliance he had never managed to apply before. He was completely involved in the music, feeling the passionate harmonies in every fibre of his being as the pure, exquisitely chosen notes floated in the golden air of morning. Minute upon minute ticked by as his new composition slowly took shape, transforming as if by enchantment from a chrysalis into a beautiful butterfly; changing from the echo of a dream into a wholesome reality. He was scarcely aware of the passage of time. Something that had been drawn far too tight for far too long had gradually relaxed inside him; he had come home after a long exile.

The clock in the room struck eleven … *Already!* He needed to wash and dress quickly if he were to be on time for his appointment with *il dottor* Antonio Mastroianni, the eye surgeon. Much as he had brushed off Adelina's and Catriona's concerns, the persistant headaches, accompanied by flashes of light, that had occurred since his fall had worried Umberto and he'd finally rung the hospital to arrange for a consultation with the great surgeon.

Later, he would go and find Caterina at the lodge and his heart swelled in his chest at the thought of their reunion. It would come out all right in the end – he had a sense of that now.

CHAPTER 18

On the terrace of the lodge, Catriona stared out over the glittering lake, watching the odd boat skudding across the water and birds hovering and swooping in the sky. It had been agonizing sitting there, wondering if every sound might be Umberto, hoping that he might have softened, might need her arms around him as much as she did his.

A knock at the door made her look up sharply.

'Yes, who is it?'

The door swung open and the figure of Adelina appeared, carrying a pile of fresh towels and linen. Catriona tried to hide her disappointment that it wasn't Umberto; nonetheless, she was glad to see the housekeeper. Painting a bright smile on her face, she went inside to greet her.

'*Buongiorno*, Adelina. Thank you, but I already have plenty of clean towels.' One look at the housekeeper, however, told Catriona that this visit had little to do with laundry.

Adelina placed her bundle on the kitchen table and regarded Catriona with shrewd dark eyes. 'For someone so recently engaged, *Dottoressa*, you do not look so happy.'

Catriona gave an awkward smile. She should have known that nothing ever escaped Adelina. 'So, you've spoken to Umberto?'

'*Sì*, last night when he returned.' The housekeeper grasped Catriona's hand in both of her own, suddenly unable to contain her delight. '*Congratulazioni! Tanti auguri e figli maschi!* May you have many sons together!' The creases around her eyes deepened as she smiled warmly. 'Have you set a date for the wedding?'

Catriona glanced down, running a fingernail along the table distractedly. 'Well, no, not yet … it's complicated.'

Adelina's threw up her hands. '*Ay!* Always complications! It's simple – you love him, he loves you. Now, you get married.' She shook out one of the towels and refolded it. 'You're meant for each other. I heard the *signore* playing again earlier. He's like a new man. Such music!'

Catriona looked up. 'Umberto was playing this morning?' A flutter of hope quivered in her chest. *Just playing or composing?*

'*Sì,* he was working out new melodies, playing bits again and again. You have restored him to us, *Dottoressa.* For that, I cannot thank you enough.' Adelina fixed her with a more knowing look. 'But now I see this is only half the story. The *signore* also told me that the two of you had found each other again after so many years, isn't that right?'

Catriona nodded. 'Yes, we knew each other long ago. It was chance that brought me here.'

Adelina waved a finger emphatically. 'This is destiny at work,' she pronounced.

Catriona smiled. 'Perhaps.'

'But something is still eating at the *signore,*' the housekeeper added, studying Catriona's face as if to find the answer there.

Catriona looked away. Much as she would have liked to confide in Adelina, she was still too bruised from Umberto's reaction to her confession about Michael. She didn't think she could go through it all again and risk Adelina's damning judgement as well.

'You have argued about something, *vero?*'

Catriona looked up. 'Yes. It's not something I can put right easily.' Then she added quietly: 'He's very angry with me.'

Adelina seemed to meditate on her words. 'As the saints are my witness, I do not pry, but I know a love match when I see it. Listen to me, child, that man is stubborn. His temper can be terrible, too. But trust me, whatever it is that has come between you, he will see the truth of what's important in his own time. You know what they say: *Non puoi insegnare niente a un uomo. Puoi solo aiutarlo a scoprire ciò che ha dentro di sé*, you cannot teach a man anything, you can only help find it within himself,' she asserted firmly.

The words sent a small ripple of comfort through Catriona but it was not only the rift between her and Umberto that pained her now – there was still their son in the middle of it all. She smiled at the housekeeper. 'Thank you, Adelina. I appreciate your kindness.'

The old woman nodded, her mouth curving at the side. 'Come by and see me later, if you want to. You like almond *biscotti*?'

'Well, yes, I love them, but I don't think I could eat anything.'

'That's what happens when you're in love, *Dottoressa*. Your stomach feels as if it has shrunk to the size of a nut. But wait till you try my *cantucci*!' With that, she picked up her stack of towels and headed for the door. 'You never look like you eat enough,' she added with a gently chiding look as she let herself out.

When Adelina had gone, Catriona found the atmosphere of the lodge suddenly oppressive. Grabbing her mobile in case Umberto should call, she headed for the door. She needed to walk, to be out in the open.

Half of her wanted to fly back to Nice straight away and anchor herself to the solid and comforting parts of her life there: her clinic, Michael, her mother. It was only when she was outside, breathing the fragrant scent of pine, gorse and lavender in the clean fresh air, that reality returned sharply.

She could never go back to how things were before.

Umberto knew Michael was his; the whole landscape of their lives had changed. Her work now was to make sure it all went smoothly for her son, that he didn't become some sort of pawn, shuttled back and forth between warring parents.

Surely that would never happen! But then the vision of Umberto's livid face floated into her mind's eye and her certitude wavered. The coward in Catriona half-wished that this morning's dialogue between them had never happened, that things could be as before: so passionate and tender. Then the better part of her stepped in, berating herself for the very idea. No, it was best that the truth had come out. She'd hated the deceit and could not have endured her tangle of lies any longer. It had eaten her up like a cancer and now she had been justly punished for it.

Catriona dried her eyes with the back of her hand and straightened her spine. From now on, her every action would be done in total honesty, with the good of her family and Umberto in mind. That way, she could help make reparation for the hurt she had caused by a wrong decision made a decade ago when she had been too young and inexperienced in life to have known any better.

Catriona was so lost in her thoughts as she walked back to the lodge, past the garage and stable block, that she didn't notice the wiry figure of Flavio standing next to his neon green motorbike until she was almost upon him. He had a cloth in his hand and was eyeing her thoughtfully, eyes narrowed. His sharp face leered with a snidely suggestive smile and, when he spoke, his tone held an insinuating inflexion.

'Is life treating you bad, *Dottoressa*?' He glanced up at the sky. 'Why such a long face on a day like this?'

'No, I'm fine,' said Catriona, not caring that she was being short to the point of rudeness. There was something wholly unsavoury about Umberto's boatman and she had no desire to be drawn into conversation with him.

'Things are good one day, trouble the next, that's how it is,' he said. 'If there's anything you need …' His eyes seemed to cut through her like a saw through plywood.

She couldn't bear his insolent stare a moment longer and with a brusque, 'No, thank you,' walked swiftly past him, feeling his eyes burning into her back.

It was almost one o'clock when Catriona walked through the door of the lodge. To her dismay, she found Silvana waiting for her in the kitchen, a cigarette in one hand and a glass of white wine in the other. Catriona took a steadying breath, praying her eyes didn't look red – the last thing she wanted was for her distress to be pounced on by the singer, who would only delight in making her feel so much worse.

There was something theatrical about Silvana's pose, her long, slim, beautiful legs crossed over each other. She was lovelier than ever, or maybe that was the effect of the sunlight on the sleek, red hair that framed her face and contrasted so beautifully with her creamy complexion.

'Silvana,' Catriona exclaimed with a smile that she hoped looked amiable enough, belying the apprehension she felt. She was sure this visit had not been prompted by friendliness.

Silvana considered her like someone eyeing a snake. 'Yes, Silvana … surprised?'

'A little, I must admit. I'm afraid I'm not really in the mood for guests. I've got a headache.'

'I doubt you've been getting much sleep if the word on the grapevine is true. Nothing stays secret for long in Como.'

'Ah, so you've come to hear it from me,' said Catriona, choosing to get straight to the point. Maybe that way she'd be rid of the woman more quickly. 'It is true that Umberto and I have become engaged.'

A slow, dark flush suffused Silvana's face and her grey eyes spat rage. 'Engaged, yes,' she repeated in shrill voice. 'Is this a joke or something?'

'Not at all. We are quite serious.'

'You silly little bitch! No doubt you think you've been very clever.' Silvana's mouth curled contemptuously. 'Is it greed or pity that motivates you, *eh*? Both probably. I know how easy it can be to twist a man around your finger. They can be such fools when their heart is between their legs.'

'Umberto is far from being a fool.'

Silvana gave her a chill smile. 'You think Umberto will be grateful because you're prepared to marry him even though he's blind? Well, he won't once the euphoria of lust has passed. He won't thank you for complicating his existence, you know. He is an artist, a free spirit. He can't bear to be handcuffed. In no time he'll be done with you, as he has with so many women before.'

Catriona was prepared to give as good as she got. 'Are you speaking from experience?' she asked coolly.

Silvana's eyes narrowed ominously. 'You don't understand. I'm not some starry-eyed fan impressed by his fame,' she said disdainfully. 'We are emancipated. We understand each other in a way that you wouldn't even begin to comprehend. You see, we are very similar, he and I. We have so much in common … our passion for music, as well as for the estate here, where we both grew up and learned about life and love together. Not to mention the pleasure we found in each other's bodies, something that has never left us. How can you compete with something that runs so deep?' she declared haughtily.

Although anger tightened her spine, Catriona gazed directly at the sneering redhead. 'It's over, Silvana. You're playing the same track, caught in an unhealthy groove, again and again,' she said earnestly. 'You should do yourself a favour and go somewhere else … find someone else, someone who will actually love you.'

Silvana's rage moved up a notch, her eyes gleaming with the malevolent desire to thwart her rival. 'Oh yes, you're so high and mighty, *Dottoressa*,' she scoffed. 'You think you're untouchable now you've got him cornered. I saw the way you hungered after him right from the start. It was embarrassing to watch. He might be blind but other people aren't. *Sei come una cagna in calore*, you're like an alley cat sniffing around for the nearest mate.'

Catriona said nothing, choosing to ignore the other woman's vitriolic torrent of insults.

'Just remember that sex for Umberto is a natural need, like breathing. His interest in you won't last.' Silvana eyed Catriona thoughtfully, as if deciding which barb could do the most damage. 'You see, *Dottoressa*, when two people are as compatible as Umberto and I, then it is earth-shattering … like an earthquake, you know.' She drew on her cigarette. 'But I suppose you don't. This sort of thing doesn't happen to just anyone.'

Catriona gritted her teeth and managed to stay calm. 'I really don't think we should be having this conversation. Maybe you should leave before you become more offensive.'

But Silvana was not listening, too busy pouring out her bile. 'We never kept ourselves exclusively for one another. If either of us felt like a change, we just went and found someone else. Like Umberto has been doing with you. You …'

'What are you doing here?' The interruption came from the doorway.

At the sound of Umberto's voice, both women turned sharply.

'I would have thought it was obvious. I'm trying to save you, as I always have,' Silvana declared shakily as a look of wariness crossed her face and she swallowed hard.

'*Per l'amor di Dio*, Silvana, what kind of trouble are you hoping to stir up now, *eh*? You shouldn't be here, you know that.'

Silvana's voice rose shrilly. 'It's not only your eyes that are blind, your heart is too! Have you forgotten what we mean to one another?'

'We don't mean anything to each other and we meant nothing, even years ago. Don't try to make out our youthful fumblings were any more than that,' he snapped back.

Silvana turned to Catriona. 'You see? That's how he always acts. He did it years ago to Sofia. He got her pregnant and then refused to marry her,' she spat, her beautiful features now contorted in spiteful fury.

'If it hadn't been for Calandra insisting he did the right thing by her, he would have thrown her aside like dirt. She killed herself. Everybody said it was an accident but she killed herself in desperation.'

Umberto took a step towards Silvana, where she sat at the table, his hand now gripping the back of a chair. 'Now, do you get out of here with your dignity or do I have to throw you out without it?' he snarled.

Silvana laughed mockingly. 'Oh yes, that would make a pretty scene, wouldn't it? Don't worry, *caro*, I'm going,' she said contemptuously, getting to her feet in a graceful movement and walking to the doorway. 'You don't need to show me out.'

Then, just before she slammed the door after her, the redhead fired her parting shot: 'Just don't come crying to me when this all goes wrong. She's not going to tolerate a miserable, drunk, blind man for very long. Especially one whose fame is becoming a thing of the past.'

Incensed, Umberto lunged forward, knocking the chair across the floor with a startling explosion of strength. Catriona, who had rushed to his side, stayed his hand. 'Ignore it, don't go after her,' she said quietly. 'It has nothing to do with us and everything to do with her own disappointment. Let her be.'

At that moment, she was too stunned by what had just taken place to process Silvana's troubling words about Sofia and tried to push them to the back of her mind. Her gaze travelled over Umberto, whose every muscle was tensed as he struggled to contain his rage. Then his expression changed as though a host of tormenting thoughts threatened to engulf him. He stood beside her, a tall, powerful man with his shoulders slumped in bitter weariness, defeated by emotions she couldn't define.

Catriona slid her hand over his arm, trying to pull him back from the brink. 'Come, let's sit down outside and have a glass of wine.'

'The darkness swallows me, Caterina ... it never lifts. I can't continue this way.'

The stark, cold pain in his voice caught at her heartstrings and she stroked his back soothingly, aware of the strength and the muscle beneath ... so strong and yet so immensely vulnerable.

'I must have been very wicked in my life to be punished in this way. I'm certainly atoning for my sins now.'

'Come on, Umberto. That's nonsense and you know it,' she said as she took two glasses out of the cupboard and poured some wine from the bottle Silvana had already opened.

'No, it's true. I've always taken, Caterina. Always taken. Being born a Monteverdi placed too many advantages in my lap at too early an age. I wanted to toss the world in my hand like a shining ball – and I did, and then I lost everything. Perhaps it's only what I deserved.' He drew a deep, harsh breath. 'When I look back – when I think of my own arrogance! Sofia would have been alive now if she had never known me.'

Catriona didn't interrupt him; he needed to talk and she needed to hear the truth about Sofia from him.

'I wanted the laughter and exuberance of that simple farm girl but, once again, I was not prepared to give in return. Let her amuse me! She was just one of a long string of girls, of course ... *Dio*! How utterly heartless I was.' He put his hand over his eyes. 'She took her life in the pool below the little waterfall, up there in the hills. What Silvana said was true, *amore mio*: Sofia was carrying my child.'

Catriona was silent for a moment. The uncomfortable truth that Umberto had got a girl pregnant was no longer news to her, but that such tragic circumstances had touched his life even before he'd been blinded filled her with a confusing mix of sadness, shock and sympathy.

'Here, I've poured us some wine,' she said soothingly. 'It's still lovely and cool. Let's sit in the sun for a while.'

They moved outside and sat down at the wrought-iron table, each of them taking a large gulp of wine to settle the stress that had played such havoc on their nerves that morning.

Eventually, Catriona spoke. 'Thank you for telling me about Sofia. Poor girl,' she almost whispered. 'But I think you've been punished enough. It's time to let the guilt of it go, if you can. Otherwise you'll always be drowning in a tide of self-chastisement and grief over what's already done. Leave it now.' Then she added: 'What are you going to do with Silvana?'

'She's no longer welcome here,' he growled. 'I only suffered her presence because my mother was fond of her. But that's it, she's gone far enough. I'll give her an allowance, I suppose, after I've told her to pack her bags. Calandra would have wanted her looked after financially at the very least.' Umberto gave a tired sigh, turning his head slightly.

'But I don't want to talk about her. We have other, more important things to discuss while we're in the mood for getting things off our chests. There must be no secrets between us.'

Catriona gave a brief nod and when she spoke again her voice was quiet but steadfast. 'Look, I want to say sorry. I want to explain about what happened after I got pregnant. You never gave me the chance, but it's important. There are things you still don't know.'

Umberto frowned. 'I just couldn't bear to think of you running straight off to find yourself another man, taking his name as your own and passing off my child as his,' he said, the heat rising in him irrevocably like a slow tide. 'Is it any wonder I was angry at the thought?'

'It wasn't like that,' she murmured. 'Umberto, listen …'

But he was still caught up in the strength of his feeling. 'I couldn't see how you could bring yourself to lie next to a man you didn't love, belonging to him body and soul …' He tried to steady his breathing, but failed to calm himself.

'Or was it me you were thinking of when he touched you, *eh?* You never answered my question when I asked you whether this Hugue of yours drove your body wild with desire. So Caterina, tell me, how did it feel? Did you tremble in his arms the way you did in mine? Did you cry out his name or mine when you came? Did you dig your nails into his shoulders, urging him on, as you did in mine?'

He was standing now, towering over her, gripping her by the shoulders and shaking her as if trying to exorcise the hurt that was tearing him apart.

She absorbed the impact of his sarcastic fury. Tears welled up in her eyes and no voice came out when she tried to speak.

Umberto pulled her up against him and into the cradle of his arms. 'Tell me … tell me how it felt. How did he caress you? Did he kiss you like this?'

His mouth slammed on hers in the most savage kiss he had ever given her and she surrendered utterly to his lust and anger and yearning. His hands moved over her with sensuous brutality, knowingly and expertly shaping her, squeezing her breasts with a desperate passion. He was hurting her and yet she was engulfed in a scorching tide of helpless longing, wanting him to feel that it had always been just him, only him.

Finally, he pulled back and let go of her. He was panting and tears of frustration were rolling down his cheeks. 'How could you belong to another man when you respond so passionately to me? Even when I want to hurt you, you surrender without hesitation, with blind trust …' he murmured in a choked voice.

Catriona pulled him back to her and tenderly kissed his lips, caressing his face, wiping away his tears.

'*Amore mio*,' she murmured, for the first time using his words of endearment as she sprinkled butterfly kisses on his face. 'There has never been anybody else but you, my dearest love, my *only* love. Hugue was an invention of my mother's to silence wagging tongues. I left Nice a *jeune fille* and came back a respectable widow with a young child. This mythical husband was her idea, and it was wrong. Only now I fully know what pain and confusion such lies can create.'

He pushed her away gently, an expression of mixed incredulity and relief lighting his features. '*Ripetilo, per favore*, tell me again. What did you say?'

'I said that Hugue never existed. My mother invented him so people wouldn't gossip about me. And, more than that, she didn't want Michael to suffer for being the product of a one-night stand.'

'So, Michael never knew a father?'

'When he asked, I told him Hugue had died in an accident when I was still pregnant.'

'What about photographs?'

'As far as he is concerned, we keep no photographs in the house of our life before his birth.'

'Lies and more lies,' he murmured. 'The only things more shocking than the truth are the lies people tell to cover it up.'

'Yes, I know,' Catriona said hopelessly. 'My mother was trying to protect me and I was trying to protect Michael. One thing led to another and a large web of deception was woven.'

He shook his head without answering.

'I'm very sorry, Umberto,' she whispered. 'I know how much I've hurt you.'

He gave a little sad smile. 'Do you?' And she flinched at the distress she read on his face.

They stood silently facing each other for a long moment, their bodies almost touching, dazed by what had passed between them. Outside, the world continued blithely, the sun soaking the garden and the trees with its opulence of light and the countryside singing with summer glory. Everywhere, nature was glittering with joy, without a thought of fear, without a single sigh. A moment later, a sudden cheerful pealing of far-off church bells, mellowed by the distance and the chirping of cicadas in the trees, found an echo in Catriona and Umberto's heart: *one must love and be happy*, they seemed to be chanting.

'Maybe we should let go of the past?' Umberto suggested quietly.

'I want that too.'

He pulled her against him. There was severity in his expression. 'Never, *never* lie to me again.'

A flush travelled all over her flawless skin. 'It was despite myself.'

He dismissed that with a wave of his hand. 'Promise me, say it. *I'll never lie to you again, Umberto.*'

'You say it too,' she whispered.

'I have never lied to you, *cara*, never.'

'Do you forgive me?'

'*Non posso vivere senza di te.* I can't live without you.'

'But do you forgive me.'

'*Sì*, I forgive you, though the hurt will take some time to subside. But you still haven't promised …'

Catriona touched his face with a trembling hand. 'I promise never to lie to you again, Umberto. Let's try to be kind to each other.'

'*Sempre*, always!' he murmured, and his handsome head dipped once more and he began to kiss her in earnest. So deeply, so ravenously that after a while Catriona expected they would both topple to the ground, captives of that hungry passion.

It was beautiful … it was agonizing … it was a language both of them spoke perfectly.

'We'll leave for Nice as soon as we can. I want to be with you when you tell Michael about me. Is that all right, *cara*?'

Catriona nodded, smiling up at him. 'Of course, *amore*.'

*   *   *

After the events of the morning, Umberto told Catriona that he wanted to take her out, away from the confines of the estate. It seemed the perfect opportunity for him to show her around the family's silk factory; besides, their tattered nerves needed a break.

Umberto was filled with a new purpose and vigour since their various truths had been aired and he wasted no time in giving Silvana her marching orders. He'd sought out the singer the moment he left the lodge, informing her that his lawyers would draw up a more than generous financial settlement only if she would consent to leave him and Catriona alone.

Catriona agreed with Umberto that it would avoid any awkwardness or further scenes if the pair of them weren't around when the vituperative redhead left, and so Mario had been instructed to drive Silvana to a hotel near the airport. From there, the singer would catch a flight to the Gulf the next day, or so she said. She had apparently told Umberto that she had an invitation to sing for Bahrain's royal family but Catriona thought it was more likely that Silvana was simply trying to save face and there was no such concert booking.

Once Umberto had left the lodge, Catriona rang her mother. Marguerite was delighted that her daughter had finally told Umberto the truth and agreed that they should come over to France to break the news to Michael about his father. Her mother's reaction put Catriona's mind at rest and as Michael was still on holiday with friends, she decided she and Umberto would definitely travel to Nice the following week.

The silk factory was only eight kilometres away from Torno so they left after a quick late lunch, with Catriona at the wheel. A luminous mist clung to the lake like a halo hovering over a Renaissance saint as they followed the curving line of the natural shore. Here, the old houses clung right to the water's edge, the curving tiles of their roofs encrusted with coloured lichens, their peeling stucco walls reflecting pastel tints – pink, green, mauve and blue – in the deep, calm water. Stone steps led directly down to the lake from each cottage and there were boats moored to the iron rings in their ancient stone walls.

As they passed the little towns Umberto would occasionally point out something of interest – where Liszt had written his 'Dante Symphony' in Villa Melzi's garden, or where Mussolini and his mistress, Claretta Petacci, had been captured in Dongo, while attempting to flee to Switzerland – but mostly he wanted to hear from Catriona every last detail about Michael, right from the moment he was born.

'What does he look like? Describe him to me.'

'Funnily enough, Michael had blond curls when he was younger. He looked like a little angel when he smiled. He has your dark hair now. Apparently, he has my mouth and nose but the shape of his eyes reminds me of yours, though his are jet black.'

'You won't believe this, but I didn't start off with dark hair. I was fair until I turned five.'

'Just like Michael! He's tall and athletic for his age, too. Good at tennis and swimming.'

'What about music?'

'He does have your wonderful gift.'

'Yours too, *cara*. Does he sing as well as you do?'

'He does have perfect pitch. It all comes so naturally to him. He loves the piano, of course, and plays the violin too. He adores the Conservatoire. His teachers say he has great promise.'

'And friends?'

'He's always been popular. He's kind ... shies away from quarrels.'

Umberto laughed. 'So, in that he is not like his *padre*, *eh*? I was always fighting at school – it was as if quarrels found me. My poor mother was called to see the head at least twice a month.'

'I don't think he takes after me either. I was always impetuous and impulsive. Mind you, that was probably a reaction against the strait-laced way my mother brought me up.'

Umberto gave her one of his mischievous smiles. 'If you hadn't been rebellious, you would never have run off with a near-stranger to Villefranche when you were only eighteen. And then Michael wouldn't have been born. Fate has its way of working out, with a little help from that rebellious streak of yours, *vero*?'

The Monteverdi silk factory was on the outskirts of Como, in the small town of Cernobbio. The town's shores were dotted with grand villas dating from as far back as the sixteenth century, the water glinting between sharp Swiss peaks on one side and rolling Lombard hills on the other. Ferries and anglers skittered across the lake's surface like bugs on the hunt as Umberto and Catriona drove along the side of the lake. Umberto pointed out small seaplanes up ahead, buzzing in and out of the Aero Club at the water's edge in next-door Como. Then they left the shore as he directed Catriona through the town to Piazza Santo Stefano, where they drew to a halt in front of a pair of imposing black, wrought-iron gates on which the family logo was set.

As they waited to gain entry to the factory, Catriona looked around her, hands resting lightly on the steering wheel. Everybody was out on this sparkling summer day and the streets were humming with the energy of Italian life. Crowds bustled around the nearby market, exuberant youngsters chased pigeons and darted around on bicycles, while in the pavement cafés teenage rakes chatted up chic young women to the sound of serenading accordion players in the piazza.

Then they were driving through the gates and Umberto told Catriona where to park. A young man greeted them at the entrance.

'Ah, Giorgio, *buongiorno*,' Umberto greeted him warmly. 'Are you taking us around today?'

'*Sì, la signora* Adelina rang me this morning to inform me that you were visiting with a guest.'

'Splendid!' Umberto introduced Catriona, adding: 'Our plant manager, Giorgio, has been with us for three years and, in that time, he's doubled production.'

She shook hands with the young man as a slow flush of embarrassment and pleasure spread over his cheeks. 'It's kind of you to make the time to show us around,' she said.

They started with a tour of the grounds. 'We have a large mulberry plantation as well as the manufacturing buildings,' Umberto told her.

The trees were planted in parallel lines across the fields. They looked quite different to those in the mulberry groves Catriona had seen on the estate the morning she'd gone riding with Umberto. These were tall and straight with thin, oval leaves and looked more ornamental than functional.

'We cultivate the Cattaneo mulberry,' Giorgio told her. 'It's native to Italy and the best for silk.'

'Why is that?'

'The leaves are full of nutrients that help develop the silk glands of the worm. The trees grow quickly, too. Give a nice big yield.' He slapped the trunk of one of them with proprietorial fondness, as if he were a rider tapping the flank of his prize horse.

'As soon as the hatching season begins, tender young leaves are gathered to provide food for the worms. We spread them out on frames in the rearing house once they've laid their eggs on them. Later, once the silk glands of these little *piccoletti* are nice and fat, we transfer them to another room, where the frames contain dry branches. That's where they start their cocoons. When they reach the chrysalis stage, all worms except those needed for breeding are killed, usually by suffocation.'

'Oh, that's horrid,' Catriona exclaimed.

Giorgio shrugged. 'That is nature's law, *Dottoressa*. If the chrysalis isn't killed, it develops into a moth which breaks through the cocoon and, immediately after, starts mating.'

Umberto felt for her hand and gave it a reassuring squeeze. 'It is said that during his brief life, the silk moth lives on love and water. Isn't that beautiful?' His mouth curved in a wry smile.

As they walked to the filature building, Umberto put his arm around Catriona's waist and held her close. 'You can choose the type of silk you want for your wedding dress,' he murmured softly. 'We could use single thread for the very sheerest silk so that it falls like a diaphanous sheath of flowing water. I only wish I could see you wearing it.'

She leaned into him. 'You'll feel it, though, and that's almost the loveliest thing about silk.'

By now they had moved on to the spinning room where large skeins of silk were being wound on to bobbins. Ahead of them was a small party of tourists, Americans by the sound of it, and Catriona looked up to see that the person leading them was Giacomo. As soon as he saw Umberto and Catriona, he seemed to pause an instant, not coming over immediately as Catriona had thought he would. When he walked across the room to pay his respects finally, she was a little taken aback by the *froideur* that had crept into Giacomo's demeanour. It was so unlike him to hold himself aloof that she couldn't help but feel slighted. She couldn't tell if Umberto, who greeted his cousin in his usual offhand manner, had noticed anything.

'You haven't visited the factory for years, cousin,' Giacomo drawled.

Umberto's eyebrow quirked up. 'I didn't know that the Monteverdi silk factory was part of your tour.'

'It seems to go down well with tourists.'

'I suppose you get a kick-back if they buy the silk,' Umberto said coolly. 'I expect your ladies like it well enough.'

Giacomo chose to ignore any barbed insinuations carried in his cousin's comments and turned to Catriona with a stiff smile. 'I hear congratulations are in order, *Dottoressa*. I hope you'll be happy with my sometimes less-than-genial cousin.'

'News reached you, I see,' said Umberto, though he didn't look surprised.

'The whole estate is talking about it. Rather sudden, isn't it? Or is it a case of *amore a prima vista,* love at first sight, *eh*?' Catriona noticed the smile never once reached Giacomo's eyes, which bore a distinctly stony look. He had lost every ounce of his debonair warmth, for which she had been grateful on her first couple of days at the estate. The sudden change in him was making her a little apprehensive, she realized. *This man bears us ill will, I can feel it. How can I bring Michael here with these undercurrents disturbing our peace?*

'It's no secret that Caterina and I are old friends,' Umberto answered smoothly. 'We met years ago in Nice.'

Giacomo's darkly speculative gaze swept over Catriona. 'Strange. I don't remember either of you mentioning it before,' he said with an acid smile. This was followed by an awkward pause, which Umberto clearly didn't feel the need to fill, so Giacomo went on: 'Well, let me congratulate you again, cousin. A thriving silk factory, a huge estate, and a beautiful fiancée too! You're a sly devil. We all thought you'd remain the reclusive bachelor for ever.' With that, he took Catriona's hand and raised it to his lips.

'I must say you do surprise me, *Dottoressa*. Still, one probably cannot hope to read the mind of a psychologist. Still waters undoubtedly run deep.'

'I think your party is waiting for you,' Umberto said dryly. 'You'd better join them before you say something you might regret.'

Giacomo laughed softly, patting Umberto's shoulder. '*Stammi bene*, you take care, cousin.'

Umberto and Catriona continued their tour but the atmosphere had been tainted somewhat by Giacomo's remarks. Catriona couldn't help but feel his final salutation carried something of a threat but she did her best to shake off the feeling.

They walked through the remainder of the high-ceilinged rooms quickly, past vats of pungent dye and where spinning skeins of neon-coloured silk rolled on to spools – hundreds of spinning ovals – the threads thin and bright and somehow strong enough to withstand this torture. Patterns formed at the edge of the cloth as if they'd been made out of thin air. The noise of acres of looms, bars slamming back and forth, was incredible and Catriona, her head starting to ache, wondered how Umberto's workers could withstand this racket for eight hours a day.

A few minutes later, they were out in the open and saying their goodbyes to Giorgio. As they drove out of the factory, their car passed Flavio on his motorcycle on his way in through the gates.

'There's Flavio!' Catriona exclaimed. 'What's *he* doing here?'

Umberto frowned. 'Flavio? Are you sure?'

'Yes.' She looked back over her shoulder once more before steering the car into the traffic of the piazza. 'He's pretty obvious on that luminous green motorbike.'

She felt Umberto stiffen next to her.

'Is something wrong?'

'He shouldn't be here. There's plenty to do at the villa.'

Catriona bit back the comment that the boatman never seemed to have enough to do. Whenever she had seen him about the estate, he was invariably lounging against a wall or gatepost smoking. There was always something so insulting in the gaze he gave her, and even the tune he whistled seemed calculated to cause unease.

'I've said it before, I know, but I don't like him at all. In fact, he gives me the creeps,' said Catriona. 'Whenever I see him, he doesn't seem to be engaged in doing anything much at all. As you said before, Adelina doesn't care for him, and I'm sure Mario doesn't either.' She hesitated, not wanting to put any dampener on their feeling of warm togetherness, but her dislike of Flavio had become a nagging unease.

'I know I'm probably speaking out of turn and shouldn't meddle in matters of the estate, but I do wonder if you should perhaps think of letting him go.'

Umberto seemed pensive. 'Caterina, as you will in just a few months be doyenne of the estate, of course you must have a say in whatever is going on, including whom we employ. That's what a good marriage is all about, *cara.*' He sighed.

'It's at times like this that my blindness is such a curse. If Flavio's taking advantage of my disability, lazing about when he should be working, then of course he must go. He may be a useful swimming partner but I can find someone else.' He shrugged. 'I'll speak to Mario and Adelina before I do anything, then sort this out tomorrow, I promise.'

On their return to the villa, Catriona said she needed to phone Marie-Jeanne about clinic business and probably catch up on some emails. Umberto told her he would have a light supper sent down to the lodge for her and, in the meantime, he would spend a quiet hour or two in the music room. Catriona resisted asking him whether he had started composing again but something in his manner, a suppressed and urgent excitement, betrayed him. She had worked with composers and artists before so she knew the signs – that distracted way they had about them. It was almost as though he was longing to be alone so that he could step into a world woven by his musical imagination.

Her face lit up and, as if he could see her expression and read her mind, Umberto smiled quizzically and reached for her, drawing her close.

'You are my muse, you know that?' he said softly. 'I know you're longing to ask, so I'll tell you. Yes, I have started playing again and some ideas have come to me. There, it is said! There's no need to nag at me now – your magic is working, *Dottoressa.*'

Catriona buried her face in his chest and smiled.

*   *   *

Umberto sat at the Steinway for a time without playing a note, letting the sounds of late afternoon wash over him: the blackbirds singing as if they were calling in the long shadows of dusk, and the cruisers on the lake sounding their horns every now and then.

The afternoon spent with Catriona had rejuvenated him. The golden thread of love and understanding that had spun itself between them had given him hope for a new beginning.

In the past, his whole existence had pivoted on whether or not he might regain his sight and, if he had ever harboured a fragile sort of optimism, teetering on a knife edge, it had long ago been sent hurtling into the abyss.

Initially, after Umberto's accident, the eye specialist had been hopeful that his blindness would be only temporary. X-rays showed that the force of the impact during the accident had caused two tiny shards of bone to bury themselves in his skull. For weeks, he had gone back and forth to the hospital while he underwent a series of tests. During those early days Umberto was full of hope and spent endless hours composing, with Calandra looking after him. That was when the unfinished concerto had been born.

When, finally, the specialist announced that the nerves in the optic tract had almost certainly been severed, Umberto was devastated. Feeling chained to an eternity of darkness, now that the flame of hope had been snuffed out, he hadn't wanted to live in this hell. Eventually, suicide had seemed the only way out.

He remembered very little of that day. Only sinking back into the warm water of the bath, feeling the reassuring pain in his flesh, his consciousness seeping from him bit by bit as the ultimate oblivion beckoned … then Mario hauling him out, something binding his wrists … his exhausted despair at having failed to leave this black world.

After that, the numbness remained and depression hung like a shadow over Umberto so that he couldn't compose, and didn't even want to sit at the piano to play. Until … until Caterina had strolled back into his life, bringing him the most valuable present a man could hope for: a son.

What he hadn't shared with Catriona was the latest prognosis. His eye specialist, *il dottor* Mastroianni, had said that his recent fall might well have dislodged one or both of the shards – hence the headaches – and that the optic nerve seemed not to have been severed after all. However, the fragments were still lodged in a tricky place and to operate would be dangerous. Yet the doctor was confident that now the fragments had moved, with time they would shift again to some other less problematic site, from where he should be able to remove them.

Oh, that flame of hope was reviving … Umberto might then be able to see again. Yet his hopes had been dashed once before and the experience had been agonizing. That afternoon, every time he had thought of telling Caterina about his session with Mastroianni, he had balked at the idea. He knew she would be thrilled by this new development and might dream of a whole different future for them together that might come to nothing but dust and ashes. Then he'd have her disappointment to deal with as well as his own.

At least Umberto would no longer contemplate suicide. Beethoven had felt the same when deafness increasingly took away his ability to hear his beloved music. He would rest his head on the piano so he could feel the vibration of the soundless notes. The thought made Umberto brighten a little. At least in his blindness he could hear the sweet notes of a symphony or listen to Caterina's pure, sultry voice. He would hear her singing and rejoice in the sound. Yes, he had all he needed, all the colours were there for him in a never-ending tapestry of precious sound.

Caterina still was, and would always be, his muse. She had lit the spark of his inspiration, and now he'd made the first breach in the wall that had encompassed his world for the past few years. The first resounding waves had already made their way through the barricade and the equilibrium of Umberto's soul was shaken by its onslaught. There was a strange fascination in this new ardent anticipation, something akin to the indomitable power of a challenge.

Inspired by the new feelings that had taken possession of his whole being, feelings to whose healing influence he was yielding, Umberto sat down and began to play. The notes of his composition poured from him like a torrent of the clearest water, a glittering stream running pell-mell over the stones. Every now and then he would pause to play a phrase over again. It was as if a piece of driftwood that had temporarily obstructed his path was pushed free before the waters of the brook went headlong on their way again. Composing was the purest ecstasy and his gratitude at having the treasured gift of inspiration restored to him was boundless.

Umberto had just finished recording the new material he'd been shaping into a first movement – gone were the days, of course, when he could simply jot it down with a pencil on blank score paper – when he was interrupted by Mario bringing him his dinner on a tray, as had been the custom in the old days when Umberto was working.

'Flavio is asking whether you want to go swimming tonight. He says that the lake is calm and warm, and the weather is due to get colder in the next few days. He was being quite pushy about it

… saying you'd not been doing your exercises for a while, talking about you making the best of this balmy night.'

There was an irritated edge to Mario's voice that made Umberto look up. 'Everything all right, Mario?'

'*Signore*?' There was a note of wariness in the other man's voice.

'You don't think much of him, do you? Flavio, I mean.' Umberto trusted Mario's opinion. Unlike Adelina, he was a very private person and did not give his opinion freely, nor did he get into disagreements easily.

There was a pause. 'The boy is work-shy, that's for sure, *signore*,' Mario muttered. 'I just don't know why he's so keen tonight. He's usually moaning about having to do anything at all. It's not like him. I'll tell him you're busy if you prefer?'

Umberto knew that tonight was not the right time to speak to Mario properly about Flavio. Tomorrow, he would catch him when they had more time. Yet he had to admit, Flavio had never before sent word asking him if he wanted to go for a swim. Maybe the boatman was sucking up to him, wanting a pay rise perhaps. Anyway, he might as well take advantage of the man's enthusiasm – he could do with the exercise after sitting so long at the piano. Umberto had always made sure he kept fit, even after the accident. It gave him something else to focus on.

'No, it's okay. Tell Flavio I'll come and find him once I've finished here,' Umberto replied. 'Don't wait up, Mario. He can help me to bed if you want to get off.'

There was a pause, then, 'Very well, *signore*.'

Later, Umberto was just closing the piano lid, listening to the sounds of the villa settling down for the night, when Adelina stuck her head round the door.

'You haven't touched your dinner,' she scolded.

'You know how it is when I'm composing, Adelina.'

The old woman chuckled. 'Yes, I heard you playing. Your mother would be so happy if she were here. The *Dottoressa* is good for you. *La signora* knew it and that's why she asked for her help. She was a wise woman, *che Dio l'abbia in gloria*, may God rest her soul. Goodnight, *signore.*'

Umberto smiled at the warmth in her voice. 'Goodnight, Adelina. *Grazie.*'

He waited until he heard her leave with Mario and lock the front door. Now the house was empty and silent, a silence broken only by the chiming clock and the occasional hoot of an owl.

Umberto made his way slowly to his room and changed into the thin, short-sleeved wetsuit top and shorts that he usually wore for late-night swims. He then went down the stairs to the side entrance to the villa, where the path went directly down to the boathouse.

The gentlest breath of wind met him as he walked out into the night. He inhaled the fresh air deeply, listening to the sound of the white pines, those great whisperers and musicians sounding their Aeolian harp of needles, which only he seemed to be able to hear. Was there a moon tonight? He liked it when Caterina described the scenery to him … he liked to see the world through her eyes; somehow things seemed kinder, more poetic. Caterina … she was probably asleep at this hour. Was she dreaming of him? he wondered.

Flavio was right, the air was warm; it had a closeness to it that invariably heralded a storm. He thought he could just make out the rumbling of thunder in the distance, trembling over the mountains, and he could smell the dark, still waters thirty feet below the balustrade that steadied his progress as he made his way down to the jetty.

As he approached the boathouse, he could hear Flavio whistling as he tinkered with one of the boats. Umberto supposed he should have a word with the man, ask him to come to his study the next day. After he'd questioned Mario and Adelina to gain some concrete examples of the employee's insubordination. Yes, that would be the best way to proceed. But for now, he would have his swim.

Umberto called down to him. '*Buona sera*, Flavio. Not too late for our swim, I hope?'

'It is a warm night, *signore*. I was waiting for you. Mario said you would be coming but if you hadn't, I would have gone fishing. *Si appoggi a me, signore,* take my arm.' Flavio guided him into the rowing boat. The grip of his hand was muscular and, for some reason, the very strength of it made Umberto wonder, with a ripple of nerves, what would happen should his guide be unable to perform his duty out there in the water. He was so dependent on Flavio and he didn't altogether like the feeling. Still, needs must, and swimming was the best way to keep up his fitness. *There must be many a blind man who has let himself run to seed*, he reflected ruefully.

As Flavio rowed them strongly but quietly up the lake, it seemed to Umberto that he was taking them further than usual. The steady splash of the oars and the boatman's infernal whistling seemed to go on for ever before finally the boat thudded into the side of a wooden raft.

'*Eccoci, signore!* Here we are.'

Something wasn't quite right. Umberto knew the lake well; he had swum in it all his life. He sensed this wasn't the raft belonging to his villa. They were in deeper waters, he felt sure. As he was helped from the boat on to the raft, he noticed that the texture of the mooring rope was different and there was a piece of wet coconut matting on the planking that had not been there before. His senses had not deceived him: for some reason Flavio had rowed to a different destination of his own choosing. Strange … the man didn't usually take any initiative.

'Not our usual raft, Flavio?'

Flavio, who was busy tying the boat to a mooring ring, didn't answer, merely whistling through his teeth. '*Venga!* The water is cool – good and cool, *signore*.'

They slid into the water almost in unison and swam away from the raft, stroke for stroke, Flavio using their customary routine of touching Umberto's bare shoulder from time to time. In the sultry heat of the night the lake, fed by underground rivers, was wonderfully cool. He should feel free, Umberto reflected, and find the even rhythm of their steady strokes relaxing but, for some reason, he could feel tension in the air, possibly an effect of the distant thunderstorm that rumbled among the mountains like a menacing omen.

'It is good, *signore*, very good, is it not?'

Was it his imagination or were they going out even further? The water seemed to be growing progressively colder, making Umberto glad of his wetsuit. Still, the strange thing was that usually he could swim two miles without feeling the slightest bit tired and yet now he found himself beginning to pant a little. He was obviously not in as good condition as he had thought, Umberto reflected wryly.

By now, Flavio should be bringing him round in a loop back to the shallower waters near the shore but the water felt ever colder. This wasn't right.

'Flavio!' he called sharply, listening, waiting for the light touch on his shoulder.

There was no sound except the grumbling of the thunder and his own breathing.

'Flavio! Damn it, man. Where are you?' His voice sounded strained to his own ears and, when his words were met by silence, he tried to remain calm.

In the following minutes while Umberto trod water, continuing to shout out, praying some boat would pass by, he still maintained the forlorn hope that the boatman would answer, would call laughingly from a yard away or touch him to guide him back to the raft. But he knew something was off: Umberto had sensed it from the moment Flavio had helped him into the rowing boat.

There had been nothing of his companion's usual relaxed talk; even his whistling sounded tense, now he came to think of it.

Damn it! Damn the man! Perhaps he'd got wind of the fact that Umberto was about to issue him with his marching orders. Maybe this was some form of payback? But surely Flavio wouldn't go so far as to harm him? Did he plan to abandon him here? If this was a prank, it was one hell of a dangerous one.

Umberto tried to breathe steadily and not let panic take over. If he got cramp now in this icy water, it would be all over in a few seconds. How ironic, he thought to himself, that it might end like this, when he'd found Caterina and started to compose some of the best work he'd ever achieved. Maybe this is how fate punishes you after all. Just when the prize is within reach, it's snatched from your hands.

'Flavio,' he called again. Then more loudly: 'Hey, is there anybody out there?'

There was no answer, only the quiet lapping of the water.

Just then, his wrist hit something and he realized with relief that it must be the edge of the raft. He gripped the sides of it with his hands. His arms felt so tired now they were shaking as he attempted to haul his body out of the water. *Maledizione!* He felt as weak as an infant.

And then, just as Umberto was poised to pull himself on to the deck, something hit the side of his head like a jackhammer, throwing him back into the water. Umberto went under, spluttering, the lake water filling his mouth and nose. He came up gagging and coughing, reaching blindly for the side of the raft. Disoriented, he cast his arms out on all sides until he found the edge of the raft again, then clung on with one hand. Next, a stab of pain cut through him, so acute he cried out. Something – a man's boot – had come down hard on his fingers.

Sudden savage anger filled Umberto and he shouted Flavio's name in fury, along with a string of curses.

'No point in shouting, *signore*. No one can hear you.' The voice – was it really Flavio's? – had a cool, pitiless quality to it that made it barely recognizable. 'You may as well give up.'

'What is this?' Umberto gasped between gulping breaths. 'What do you want, Flavio?'

'Me, *signore*?' The boatman gave a nasty laugh. '*Soldi*, money, of course. Your cousin has promised me my fair share once you're out of the way.'

'Giacomo …?'

'*Sì*, your cousin.' Flavio annunciated the words with mocking clarity. 'Like he said, if we don't sort you out, the pretty *Dottoressa* will soon be in charge, mistress of the Monteverdi estate. You see, that bothers Giacomo. He reckons she's not just a pretty face. In no time she'll nose out our little side businesses. No more messing with cases of wine and rolls of silk to sell on to our contacts in Bellagio. No more extra cash, no estate for Giacomo. So, you won't get away this time.'

'*This time?*' Umberto said through gritted teeth, the pain burning through the hand that was being crushed beneath Flavio's heel.

'The car accident … Giacomo's idea,' said Flavio. 'And what a mess that was. Trying to tamper with your steering when Mario and Adelina were noseying around the whole time wasn't easy. And the lousy *bastardo* tried to get out of paying me, *lo lo spilorcio*, the skinflint …' he spat derisively and trod down harder on Umberto's fingers. 'He'd better pay up this time.'

Umberto winced but refused to give the treacherous *bastardo* the satisfaction of hearing him shout out in agony. 'I didn't know he hated me this much …'

'He needs cash, I need cash. Nothing more than that. You *ricco sfondato*, stinking rich types are all the same, *eh*? Keep it all to yourselves, then get someone else to do your dirty work. It makes me sick.' Flavio spat on the deck again.

'That girl you got pregnant is better off dead … *Stupida puttana*, going with stuck-up *ricconi* nobs.' He snorted. '*Che idiota*, what an idiot! We did her a favour.'

'Sofia … You mean … you and Giacomo?' Umberto gasped in disbelief. 'Why on God's earth? What did she ever do to you?'

'*Heh*, you still don't get it. Well, too late.' The boatman's voice became leering. 'But that *Dottoressa's* a fine-looking *sottana*, bit of skirt, I must say. No wonder you can't keep your trousers on around her. I wouldn't kick her out of bed myself if the occasion presented itself. Which maybe it will when you're not around to keep her happy, *eh*?'

'Shut your filthy mouth!' Umberto tried to launch himself upwards but the boatman kicked him in the shoulder, making him roar with pain and fury.

'That won't work. It's me in charge now, *signore*,' Flavio hissed. Then he swore an obscenity and at that moment the pressure lightened on Umberto's agonized fingers. He could hear the sound of the man's boot scraping the planks as though he might have been drawing his foot back to aim another vicious kick at him. As he did so, with a reflexive speed born of desperate instinct, Umberto pulled himself up and lashed out with his arm, given new strength by his savage fury. His hand connected with the other man's ankle and the force of the strike brought Flavio down. The boatman gave a loud grunt as he hit the deck, winded, his feet having slipped from under him on the wet planks. Umberto grabbed wildly and managed to get a hold of some part of Flavio's limbs, he wasn't sure which. Another yank and the boatman was in the water, spluttering and gasping for air.

Umberto felt a moment of sheer primitive joy to be fighting one-on-one at last as his hands grappled with Flavio. He found it almost impossible to get the upper hand, though: the other man was like a slippery eel, wriggling out of his grasp.

Then Umberto had hold of him for an instant and they were wrestling in the water, torso to torso. Umberto seized his chance. Remembering a martial arts move he'd learned as a youth, he found an artery in Flavio's neck and pressed. The pent-up storm in his own nature was released; it matched the savagery of the hot night, the cracks of thunder.

They surfaced together and the sudden downpour of rain deluged both their faces, bouncing up in cool steel rods from the surface of the lake. For a moment, Umberto's grip on the other man's neck relaxed, giving the boatman the upper hand again.

Now Flavio was dragging Umberto to the side of the raft where, with sickening thuds, he banged the composer's head against the wood again and again. Umberto tasted blood and lake water engulfed his throat as he took desperate gasps, trying to cry out, struggling to breathe. Then he felt himself slipping away into numbness, his lungs filling, and he gave into it, losing the struggle, his arms limp. He barely registered a sudden clamour of voices, one of which sounded like Mario's, before he finally passed out.

CHAPTER 19

'*D*ottoressa Drouot,' A tall man in a surgical gown walked towards Catriona as she paced back and forth in the waiting room. 'Please come into my office.'

'Ah, *dottor* Mastroianni. How did it go? Please, how's Umberto?' She followed him into a brightly lit room with tall cabinets on either side.

'The operation was a complete success,' he said as he offered her a seat and took his place behind his desk.

Catriona moistened her dry lips and breathed a sigh of relief. 'Thank God,' she whispered. 'I thought … I thought …' Her eyes brimmed over with tears.

'Oh, he's a lot tougher than that, *Dottoressa*,' the surgeon said with a kindly smile. '*Il signor* Monteverdi wouldn't let a couple of knocks and a lungful of water finish him off. He'll have a long, full life ahead of him, don't you worry.'

'I'm so relieved,' she whispered. 'I thought I'd lost him.'

'Not only have you not lost him but there may actually be good news. That's what I wanted to talk to you about. *Dietro ogni nuvola si nasconde un raggio di sole*, behind every cloud, there is a ray of sunshine, as we say in Italy.

'The head trauma he received – not only when he fell in his room, but also at the lake – caused two bone fragments that had embedded themselves in his skull during the car accident to move.

Our new X-ray showed that the optic nerve hadn't been severed after all. The shards had been pressing on the nerve to the extent it had totally lost function. So, if he hadn't been assaulted and hadn't hurt his head …'

She gasped: the truth seemed almost inconceivable.

'That's right. Your *fidanzato* has a fifty-fifty chance of being able to see again. It may take two or three weeks before we know for sure. He'll need lots of rest. I'll prescribe some painkillers as it'll take a while for the headaches to subside. Until everything settles down, he needs to convalesce *in tranquillità.*'

Catriona could barely contain her joy. That Umberto was alive was precious news in itself, but that he had a chance of regaining his sight seemed like a miracle. Her eyes, still wet from her tears, sparkled with emotion. 'I will make sure of that. When can I see him?'

'He'll be in the recovery room until nine, maybe later. Why don't you go home and relax? There's quite a wait yet.'

The surgeon stood up and Catriona grasped his hand in both hers. '*Grazie,*' she whispered, then added with a teary smile, 'What an inadequate word!'

Mastroianni grinned. 'Ah, I nearly forgot. Before you go, *Dottoressa*, put out your hand.'

Puzzled, Catriona did as he asked.

He pulled a small bottle from the pocket of his gown containing two minuscule diamond-shaped fragments. He smiled. 'I believe this is a souvenir you'll want to give to him.'

She stared at the contents of the bottle then closed her hand around it. These tiny shards had entered Umberto's skull and deprived him of his sight. Now she held them in the palm of her hand. Incredible!

When Catriona came out of the surgeon's office, a red-eyed Adelina and a pale-faced Mario were waiting outside, looking shell-shocked. Adelina had spent the dark hours of the night fearfully waiting with Catriona for news of Umberto's condition, while Mario had just got back from the police station, where he'd been giving a statement.

'How is he, *Dottoressa*?' they said almost as one.

'It's all good news. He'll be as good as new in a few weeks, once he's had a proper rest.'

Adelina dabbed at the corners of her eyes and blew her nose. 'He'll lack for nothing, *Dottoressa*. Rest, my good food … He'll be better in no time.'

Catriona smiled at her warmly. 'No one takes as good care of him as you, Adelina. He's lucky to have you.' The housekeeper shook her head. 'No, it is Mario *il signor* Umberto is lucky to have.' She turned to her friend and gripped his arm, her dark eyes swimming with new tears. 'You are his saviour again, Mario, *Dio ti benedica per sempre*, God bless you for ever.'

Catriona then looked at Mario, who had been standing there solemnly. 'What can I say?' Now it was her turn to wipe fresh tears away. 'Mario, thank you for saving him … *dal profondo del mio cuore*, from the bottom of my heart.'

'If only we'd got there quicker,' he said, looking drained and hollow-eyed. 'I knew something wasn't right. I should have told the *signore*, shared my suspicions, then he wouldn't have gone swimming … I won't forget the sight of that *bastardo* trying to bash his brains out.'

'*Oh povero bambino mio*,' Adelina broke out into full sobbing. '*Perché proprio lui? E' un uomo così buono e generoso*. Why him? He is such a good and generous man.'

'Don't cry, Adelina.' Catriona put an arm around the old housekeeper's shoulders. 'He'll be okay, I promise. The surgeon says there's every hope he'll be able to see again, so wipe your eyes. We should be celebrating.'

At that, Adelina's dark eyes shone through her tears and she declared in a whisper: 'Oh, *San* Raphael be praised!'

Mario, as always, a man of few words, broke into a broad grin but his eyes too were glistening.

A little later, as the three of them were making their way to the hospital car park, Catriona fired questions at Mario, eager to find out his side of the story. She'd already learned from Adelina the horrifying news that Giacomo had been behind Flavio's attempt on Umberto's life. She was stunned. How could she have misjudged Umberto's cousin so completely?

She frowned quizzically. 'Why did you rush out to the lake when you did, Mario? How could you possibly have known?'

'I saw *il signor* Giacomo in the grounds. Hiding in the shadows, on his phone. I crept over and listened. I guessed it was Flavio on the other end. Talking about the swim … the whole dirty business. It wasn't hard to guess what was going on.'

'How did you get to Umberto in time?'

'I grabbed Dino, the groom's boy, and that new gardener living in the apartment over the stables, and the three of us ran down to the lake. We could see they weren't out at the usual raft so we took the motorboat. Only just found them in time,' he said. 'I rang the police as soon as we had a sight of them.'

'Presumably they've got Flavio safely in custody?'

Mario nodded, scowling as though entertaining his own ideas about the kind of justice the boatman deserved.

'And what about Giacomo?' Catriona suddenly felt sick at the thought that Umberto's cousin might still be at large.

Mario's expression brightened a little. 'One of the policemen, Lorenzo, is a good friend of mine. I spoke to him earlier. Apparently, Flavio sang like a canary. *Il signor* Giacomo won't be able to talk himself out of this one when they get him.'

'So, they haven't arrested him yet?'

Mario shook his head. 'He took off as soon as he realized his plan had failed.'

Adelina's eyes sparked with malevolent fury at the thought of Giacomo's part in it all. 'To think, the *signore*'s own flesh and blood. *Maledetto*! May God bring down all his curses on that Judas!'

*   *   *

A week went by, during which Umberto stayed in hospital and Catriona went to visit him every day. News of the attempted murder was all over the European press and she regularly had to duck a gaggle of paparazzi hanging around the villa gates or in the hospital car park. As it had swiftly turned into a media circus, Catriona was relieved to know her mother and Marie-Jeanne were such level-headed types. They'd taken the news in their cool-headed stride, and this helped her stay calm.

A warrant was out for Giacomo's arrest and for nine days Catriona heard nothing. Then, as she was parking at the hospital one morning, she was about to switch off the car radio when her hand froze. '*The Swiss police have confirmed that the driver of the car was Giacomo Monteverdi, a person of interest in the attempted murder of his composer cousin, Umberto Monteverdi. Heavy rain had made the road slippery on the Saint Gotthard Pass and all the indications are that Monteverdi was taking a steep turn too fast. A police spokesperson confirms that the driver was killed instantly.*'

*   *   *

Lavender and pink rays of daybreak filtered through Catriona's bedroom window, falling across the bed where she lay in Umberto's arms. A slow stealing of light had begun along the horizon as night died. In the distance the mountains met the vault of heaven with a bold black line, an orange flame above it blazing fierce and bright. Catriona slowly disentangled herself from her lover and propped herself up against the pillows, feasting her eyes on the beauty of this harmonious hour of wakening birds.

An owl chanted its plain, hooting song from the forest, bidding goodbye to the night; fit music for that still morning half-light. In the early chill, a team of ducks glided quietly by, feathering the cloudless sky.

The light was still muted as the rising sun trampled down the lingering shadows of the west, its ruby-tinted warmth drying the dewy tears of dawn that clung to the flowers, grass and trees. A single shaft, like the pinion of a wing, was lifting itself upward towards the zenith. In a moment another shaft began to rise by its side, and then another and another until the whole half-arch of the heavens above the lake resembled two spread wings of almost biblical sublime beauty. Catriona sighed, her heart filling with wonder and tranquility.

Umberto stirred. He stretched out an arm, his hand reaching for her, wanting to make sure she really was there.

'I'm here,' she murmured as she dipped her head and kissed him on the lips. 'I was admiring the dawn … the best hour of the day.'

He opened his beautiful emerald eyes and they played over her face. There was a difference in his gaze – something that hadn't been there before. Her breath caught in her throat.

Umberto blinked. Closed his eyes and then opened them again. *He was trying to focus.*

'Umberto?' She hardly dared hope.

'Shush, *amore mio*, don't move. Let me look at you,' he said as he stared up at her with an intensity that held her mesmerized.

Was it possible? Had the miracle happened?

He passed his hand over his face, his expression anxious, disbelieving. '*Dio mio!*' he whispered.

'What is it, Umberto?' Catriona's heart was beating wildly, her eyes blurring with tears of hope.

'I think … I think I can see.' His eyes widened and he stretched out his hand to run a finger down her cheek. For a few moments, neither of them spoke, then he murmured, 'You are even more beautiful than I remember … *angelo mio*. You're a little hazy, but I can see … *Non sto sognando*, I'm not dreaming!'

'Oh, Umberto!' A radiant smile broke on her face and, touching his hand with her own, Catriona kissed his finger tenderly.

Raising himself on his elbow, Umberto moved his hand wonderingly down her jawline to her neck, tracing her collarbone and the top of her naked shoulder. His eyes darted around the room and back to Catriona's face.

'No, I'm not dreaming,' he declared with positive conviction now, his voice agitated, the emerald irises glistening with tears. 'My sight … it's back. *Sia ringraziato Dio*, God be praised!' He fell back on to the pillow and ran both hands through his hair. Then he grinned up at her. 'You've brought me luck, Caterina.'

She beamed back at him. 'You need to rest now and we'll talk to *il dottor* Mastroianni later, when he's likely to be in his office.'

Umberto glanced at the clock. 'We just have time for a little romp,' he said with a mischievous twinkle in those bright-green eyes that were now gazing at her adoringly.

Catriona laughed. 'No romping until the doctor has checked you out properly!'

'Do you really think I can wait that long?' he chuckled, and she felt his desire press hard against her as he pushed her down gently on to the mattress. 'I need to see you beneath me.' He caressed her naked breast. 'I hadn't forgotten how these looked … firm, full, soft, and so receptive.'

An enticing warmth spread through her body. Her lips parted to receive his tongue and she melted underneath him, opening up to greet him with all the love and passion that flooded through her.

Through the bedroom window came a delicate breeze, laden with the sweet scent of roses and grass. Around Villa Monteverdi everything lay quiet and still. The only movement was the slow drift of tiny level clouds in the sky above, then gliding across it came a pair of wild ducks, who flew into the water with a splash and swam away, side by side, towards a group of willows.

In the distant villages the bells began to ring the morning Angelus and from the surrounding farms, the cows began to clamber down leisurely towards the meadows, their bells a gentle tinkling accompaniment to the deeper, resonant sound of the church bells.

The sun soared into the sky, leaping and sparkling as it bathed the world with its dazzling light, its brightness giving gladness to the fields, the mountains, the lake and the countryside, and colour to the flowers, trees and the towns nestling along Como's shores. The glorious morning seemed to blaze with a brighter intensity than ever before – at least for the two occupants of Villa Monteverdi's lodge who, for a little while longer, lost themselves in each other's arms.

*   *   *

As their trip to Nice drew closer, Catriona's fears as to how Michael would react when he met Umberto continued to dominate her thoughts. How would he take the news of his parentage, or that she and Umberto had become engaged?

Unconsciously, she paced up and down the room in her mind, examining this conundrum from all angles. Should she tell Michael the truth beforehand, or was she going to let him walk into the situation without warning? One look at him and Umberto would immediately identify with his son, but what about Michael? Would he recognize Umberto as the father he had never known? Would he feel that it was his fault that his mother had been rejected? He was such an intelligent and sensitive child.

During the days before they left for Nice, Catriona, Umberto and Marguerite had many discussions via video calls and agreed on a plan whereby Michael would first be introduced to Umberto, the great composer whom his mother had helped get back on his feet and who had come to France to convalesce, and then they would take it from there.

'Just have a little trust, *cara*,' Umberto told her soothingly. 'Everything will turn out all right, I know it will. We're all standing together in this, wanting the best for Michael, and it will go fine, you'll see.' He held her close, kissing her temple tenderly, hushing her fears for now.

Once in Nice, Umberto stayed at the palatial Negresco, the oldest hotel in the city, overlooking one of the most beautiful bays on the French Riviera. Its façade on the Promenade des Anglais rose white and imperious to its pink roof and dome which, Umberto told Catriona with a twinkle in his eye, had been inspired by the breast of the architect's mistress. 'You see, *mia bella musa*, all through the centuries women have inspired men to create beautiful things.'

Although Marguerite had prepared Michael for Umberto's visit and the child had been beside himself with excitement for days at the idea of being introduced to the famous composer, Catriona waited a couple of days – to both Umberto's and Michael's frustration – before inviting Umberto over for tea.

The house was resounding with Debussy's *Clair de Lune* when Marguerite and Catriona opened the front door to him. From the archway in the hall there was a clear view of the salon, where the piano stood. The room was bathed in sunshine, the smooth ebony surface of the baby grand gleaming in the light. Michael was sitting at the keys, playing one of Umberto's favourite pieces of music, especially chosen by Catriona for the occasion.

Umberto stopped dead at the threshold of the room with a sudden indrawn breath as his eyes took in the most perfect vignette he could imagine. He stood there silently, watching the black-haired boy, whose slim fingers flew over the keys, his whole body absorbed in what he was doing, the sunlight shining on hair that had the same satin patina as his own.

Catriona saw the man she loved tremble and then slowly walk towards the piano as if drawn to his son by a magnet. She remembered how moved she'd been every time she'd watched the final act of *Madam Butterfly*: the father returning to claim his child. She could only guess at the emotion Umberto felt, but she knew that he was overwhelmed.

Michael continued until the end of the piece and then, looking up for the first time, he realized someone else was there. He blushed and stood up.

'I didn't hear you come in …'

'That's fine, *mon chéri*. This is *il signor* Umberto Monteverdi.'

Michael turned to Umberto and stretched out his hand. '*Je suis Michael Drouot*,' he said in a most serious voice, looking up into his father's eyes with a shy smile.

Umberto smiled and cleared his voice. 'You play very well, Michael, though your fingering could be improved in that last part. You played it a little too slowly,' he said, and Catriona caught the note of emotion in his throat that was almost strangling him. 'Would you mind if I sat beside you? I'll show you, if you like,' he added.

Michael gave a nod and his face bore a star-struck intensity that made Catriona and Marguerite meet each other's eyes and smile.

Umberto seated himself on the bench next to his son and repeated the passage while Michael watched intently, then played the passage again.

'That's much better but you need to practise it to reach perfection.'

Michael played the passage again, more confidently this time.

'That's the idea, my boy, very good indeed. If you continue like this, you will be a great pianist one day.'

Michael's eyes shone with delight and pride. 'Like you?'

'Oh, much better than me, much better. But to be the best you need to work very hard.'

'Oh, I love playing! I could play all day but *Maman* and *Mémé* make me go to school and do homework. It's not fair.' He glanced at Catriona and Marguerite sheepishly.

Umberto laughed deep in his throat and patted Michael on the head. 'School and homework are also very important. You need to strike a good balance, that's the only way to do it.'

Marguerite caught Catriona's eye and gestured with her head towards the kitchen. 'Carry on at the piano, you two. We'll go and prepare the tea.'

At one point a little later, Catriona tiptoed out of the kitchen, where she and Marguerite were laying everything they needed on a tea tray, to check on father and son. As she approached the salon door she heard the happy hum of voices and the occasional bellow of laughter from Umberto, but just hearing them wasn't enough – she wanted to commit to memory the sight of the two of them, so precious, as they played the piano together. They'd moved on to duets now and Umberto was making Michael howl with laughter, showing him a rambunctious version of 'Chopsticks'. She was astonished at the carefree happiness she read in their faces; even Michael was lit up in a way she hadn't seen before.

Later, as they were consuming enormous quantities of lemon cake, Michael – who had by now lost every trace of shyness – asked incessant questions of Umberto, who seemed amused by his son's boldness. Every now and then the eager boy was interrupted by Marguerite, who gently chastized him for talking with his mouth full, but Catriona barely said a word, so brimming with happiness that she didn't want to break the flow of father and son chatter.

'*Maman* said you're staying in Nice,' Michael said as Umberto was finally making a move to tear himself away. 'How long for? Will you be here for my birthday?'

'Yes, I'll be here for a few months.' Umberto's mouth curved into a smile. 'I would very much like to see you on the big day.'

Michael thought for a moment, his bright eyes keen as a robin's. 'Could you maybe … give me lessons?' For a moment Catriona could see he was holding his breath, hardly daring to hope, before he rattled on: 'My teacher at the Conservatoire says I should find someone to teach me after school so I can get on quicker. Someone really good …' He let his words tail off and honoured Umberto with a dazzling smile. Had Umberto recognized the cajoling charm that his son had inherited from him? Catriona wondered.

Umberto gave a spontaneous laugh deep in his throat. 'I think that's a brilliant idea, Michael. You're just as ingenious as your mother. She must be very proud of you.'

'So, you'll do it?' Michael asked, adding impishly: 'Every day?'

'*Assolutamente sì*, it's a deal.'

Michael, his face split with the widest grin, turned to Marguerite.

'*Mémé, Monsieur* Monteverdi will be coming for tea every day! We need to make sure we have enough cake *pour le goûter*.'

'Ah, so we'll all get very fat, *cheri*!' she laughed.

*   *   *

Every day for the next two weeks, as promised, Umberto came to give Michael his lesson. Afterwards they would have tea and sometimes a swim in the pool. One evening, he stayed for dinner and then played for them afterwards and Michael was allowed to stay up and listen.

One afternoon, nearing the end of Umberto's stay in Nice, father and son were playing chess together in the salon when Catriona caught a snatch of their conversation from the hallway as she walked past the door to fetch some biscuits.

'*Maman's* different now.'

'Really? How so?'

'She doesn't go to the office as much, and she's laughing a lot.'

'Didn't she laugh a lot before?'

'Yes, but sometimes she was sad.' With the directness children invariably display, he went on to add: 'She likes you being here. I like it too.'

'Well, that's good, because I like being here too … so we're all happy.'

That was the moment when Catriona decided Michael was ready to be told the truth about his father. That evening as she tucked him into bed she told him she didn't want to read a story just yet, but to talk to him about something instead – something nice – and to show him some pictures. Sitting on the edge of his bed, she stared at her son's features that were becoming more and more like those of the man she loved. Marguerite had taken a few photographs of Michael and his father playing the piano together and it was these she was holding in an envelope.

Catriona cleared her throat. 'I've never really spoken to you about your father.' She gazed steadfastly at her son, watching as his sleepy face became suddenly alert. 'I'm sorry about that as you must have so many questions.'

Michael's eyes lowered and he spoke without looking at her. 'You only said that you loved him very much and that you missed him.'

'And that is the truth.'

'How can that be? When you love someone, you talk about them. And there aren't even photos of him. Bernard's *papa* died and they've still got photos of him in their house.

You've got pictures of *Papi*, even though he died when you were a little girl.'

'Well, *mon chéri*, I never told you the whole truth. I wanted to wait until you were ready …' His eyes were fixed on hers now. 'You see, Michael, your father didn't die.'

Wide-eyed, Michael he tried to process the news. 'So … what …?' he murmured, unable to frame the words.

Catriona ran the back of her fingers gently over his smooth cheek. 'Your father and I met one time a long time ago. We never met again and that's why we couldn't get married. No one except me knew who he was.'

'Not even *Mémé*?'

'Not even *Mémé*.'

'Why?'

'Because he was a great man, and I didn't want to get in the way of his career.'

'So, did he know about it?'

'No. I didn't tell him until a few weeks ago, which I now know was very wrong of me. So, you mustn't think that he abandoned me, or didn't bother with you during all these years. He couldn't because he didn't know you existed.'

'And now?'

'Here, let me show you.' Catriona snuggled up next to Michael on the bed and drew him close so that his head could lie in the crook of her arm. She took out the photographs that Marguerite had brought in that afternoon and passed them to him.

The child looked at them with a half-smile that again reminded her so much of Umberto.

'*C'est lui*, it's him.' He stated it plainly and gave a little nod of satisfaction almost as if he knew it already. 'We look very much alike, *n'est-ce pas, Maman*?'

'*Oui, mon chéri*, like two peas in a pod … You couldn't be anyone else's son.'

Michael gave a little chuckle. 'You know, *Maman*, I kept telling myself that it couldn't be.'

'Well, you get on so well together, I'm not surprised you felt it. You clicked immediately.'

'*Oui*, but it wasn't that.'

'What was it, then?'

'He has a red mark on his wrist, exactly like mine.'

'Yes, you're right. You've both got that same birthmark. I should have guessed you might notice that.'

'So, will I get to be called Michael Monteverdi instead of Michael Drouot?'

'Of course, *mon chéri*. Umberto has been sorting all that out on the mornings he hasn't spent with you.'

At that moment the bell rang.

'Go and see who's at the front door,' she told him.

Michael rushed to the door as though he had guessed who this late visitor might be. Then Catriona heard him cry out: '*Papa, Papa …*'

'*Figlio! Mio caro figlio! Finalmente …*'

And then she burst into tears of joy and relief.

Epilogue

Backstage, Umberto walked back and forth, smoothed his hair and took a deep breath. Flexing his cold fingers, he blew on them, then peered through the small hidden window overlooking the stage below. Faces, a sea of them, floated around that big black ship of a piano. People in eveningwear were taking off their coats, looking at programmes, greeting each other, settling down. A couple seemed to be arguing about seats.

Umberto turned and stared for a few seconds at the closed door, the final barrier between himself and the stage, that treacherous territory he had tracked so many times before. Each time the terrain was different; each time was the first time and now, more than ever, he felt like a novice performer. Even when he had faced the public for the first time, he hadn't been overcome with such stage fright.

Still, a delicious dread rushed through him; his nostrils flared and he inhaled deeply. Then, opening the door, the maestro set off for the stage, taking the stairs down to it two at a time.

For a split second Umberto's self-control faltered but he recovered immediately. *Steady*, he told himself, *I will play that concerto tonight for her and for my son, and I'll make them proud of me.*

*   *   *

The Opéra de Nice was thrumming with low voices and the impatient rustling of programmes as Catriona leaned back in her seat in the box closest to the stage, watching with the keenest anticipation all that went on around her. She looked not only elegant and glamorous but radiant in the gown she had chosen for the event. Dressing with particular care, she had put on each item as if conducting some sort of rite, knowing she wanted to be beautiful for Umberto. The look of pride and adoration in his eyes when she had appeared in the family drawing room had given her the reassurance she needed; she knew that some of the world's most beautiful and desirable women would be at the concert tonight to hail the great composer's return.

The gown Catriona wore had the signature of Elodie, a young designer who had taken the Paris and London fashion weeks by storm. Crafted from swathes of almost weightless emerald plissé silk tulle, it fell to an elegant floor-sweeping hem. The bodice was cut with an alluring V-neck and back split, with a nude silk lining that created the illusion of bare skin. Rows of opulent beads and crystals along the back meant Catriona could forego wearing a necklace, so she had accessorized the dress only with the gold and emerald bracelet and engagement ring Umberto had given her on Comacina Island. The gown's elegance lay in its simple lines and sheer fluidity – 'a breath of spring,' Umberto had whispered when she'd entered the room.

Marguerite, Michael, Adelina and Mario sat in the box with Catriona. They had all come to support Umberto and give him confidence, and there was something about the little group's fierce loyalty – as if their hands really were connected in a tight-knit circle of love – that made Catriona feel warm and secure. With their united presence showing Umberto they believed in him, nothing could possibly go wrong.

The wedding-cake tiers of the auditorium, decorated ornately in white, gold leaf and lush wine-coloured velvet, buzzed with a public that had come from all corners of the globe. Journalists, television crew, agents, film directors and numerous heads of cultural establishments held their breath as they awaited the return of the great composer, who had once taken the world by storm. The excitement in the atmosphere was palpable.

The last stragglers were coming into the auditorium quickly now, hurried into their seats by the attendants, bending their heads over small change as they paid for their programmes; too late for the cloakroom, they were folding their coats and putting them under their seats.

Suddenly Umberto appeared, striding onstage like a keen thoroughbred approaching the starting gate. The audience thundered its applause. He smiled in the same self-possessed way Catriona had seen him do in the past, his left hand lightly touching the edge of the keyboard with complete assurance while he bent forward to acknowledge the cheers. Still, she also knew that as he clutched the polished black wood he was taking a deep breath, his head lowered, trying to force air into his constricted lungs.

And it was as if she were back again, on that night ten years ago, watching him for the first time, her heart reaching out to him as it was tonight. Yet there was a small difference: then he had been unattainable, tonight she was his and he was hers. Catriona looked up and caught his glance, reading in it the meaning of his impassioned gaze. No one but she saw the kiss he blew towards her as the lights went down.

Michael clasped his mother's hand. 'Do you think he's afraid?' he whispered.

'Just a little,' she murmured. '*C'est le trac*, the jitters.'

Nevertheless, with an outward air of quiet cool, Umberto Rolando Monteverdi sat at the piano. He even paused to glance around him and, rearing his head back, sounded the first chords even before the clapping had ceased. Some would call it arrogance, most would call it magic, but Umberto had told Catriona that he called it survival. 'You have to appear confident for your audience to trust you,' she remembered him saying to her once.

Gradually the noise died away until there was complete silence, the music flowing out over the auditorium, spinning like magic from Umberto's hands. He played as though he was feeling the piece inside himself as an entity and, while he played, that intimacy was evident to Catriona – as it was, she was sure, to everyone in the opera house, even those who had come to the event out of curiosity, to be able to say they had attended the comeback of the great composer.

As the first movement progressed, concentration and intensity increased in the auditorium, the audience drawing close to Umberto in spirit, like moths to a flame. He swept through the second movement with momentum, unerringly spanning the terrifying skips at its end, and in the third movement slowing to grandeur and a final statement that was fervent, yet majestic.

'*Il est merveilleux, mon papa, n'est-ce pas, Maman?*' Michael whispered, his eyes shining.

'*Oui, chéri.*'

The huge auditorium was hushed and still as the wistful melody threaded its way towards the concerto's final crescendo. Catriona, motionless in her seat, felt as if every bone in her body had turned to water. It was so beautiful, so moving, so passionately performed, that it was almost as if she were hearing it for the first time. The romantic lyricism of Umberto's work, the vein of melancholy that made the melody so haunting, touched her more than anything she had heard him play, because he told her the piece had been inspired by his dormant love for her. It was clear that when he had begun to compose the piece following his accident, Umberto had been searching, yearning for a love that would fulfil him and, by the end, the notes clearly reflected the joy and passionate gratitude that now sweetened his life.

After the last quiet low B sounded, applause erupted. The audience rumbled like the first tremor of an earthquake. Then the throng rose to its feet, roaring at full force. Catriona rose abruptly to join the ovation, brushing a tear from her cheek.

Umberto seemed startled as he stood up. He hesitated, gasping for air, and rested one hand on the keyboard's lid, his head lowered. Then, acknowledging the cheers graciously, he smiled and finally bowed.

A woman rushed forward from the front row and held out a single red rose to him. Umberto took it and bent to kiss her hand, bowing as he did so while the audience screamed: 'Encore! Encore! Encore!'

Umberto smiled and glided through his encores as Catriona's heart swelled with love and admiration. He'd never played so well, never been so good.

The sheer scale of ovation when he was finally able to leave the stage surprised even Catriona. Tears were rolling down her cheeks as the lights in the auditorium went up. Next to Marguerite, Adelina had also been weeping silently with emotion.

In his excitement, Michael was talking non-stop, praising his father. '*Un jour je serai un grand compositeur comme Papa, n'est-ce-pas, Maman?* One day I'll be a great composer like *Papa*. Isn't that so, *Maman*?'

'*Oui, oui, bien sûr, mon chéri,*' Catriona said, hugging him to her. Then her only thought was to be next to Umberto, to hold him and tell him how brilliant he'd been and how proud of him she was. Then once again he was back on stage, standing motionless with that air of authority and almost nonchalant grace peculiar to him. The maestro turned to the audience, commanding instant silence.

'I am here today thanks to the love of a woman who, selflessly leaving her life behind, came to me when I was down, gave me hope and patiently helped me climb back up from a very dark place and into the light.' He pointed to where Catriona was sitting. '*La dottoressa* Caterina Drouot, my fiancée, whom I first met a whole decade ago. We are to be married at my home on Lake Como in the spring.'

Applause filled the hall and Catriona felt herself flush, tears spilling over once more. A few minutes later, outside the auditorium, an enormous line of well-wishers twined around the staircase and out to the lobby, voices buzzing. Friends, flesh-pressers and admirers wanting to touch their hero were standing in their hordes, many of them presenting their programmes for Umberto's signature.

As Catriona and Michael made their way towards Umberto, a concert manager from Germany was in the midst of congratulating the composer and presenting his card. A moment later, an American journalist had interrupted, asking for an interview – 'a brief one, sir. Just a few minutes' – before being supplanted by a woman in a fox fur jacket, who kissed him on the lips, sighing: 'You gave me such pleasure, such pleasure! I still have goosebumps.'

That's the second woman this evening to make a pass at him, Catriona thought, her heart giving a tiny squeeze. Then her eyes met Umberto's and he winked at her, a mischievous light gleaming in those beautiful emerald irises.

Catriona listened to the chant of inadequate words that went on for almost another hour as more and more fans pressed forward. She was reminded of the night she had attended Umberto's concert in this same opera house and had been unable to meet him in his dressing room because of the long queues. She was glad that she had sent Michael back to the house with Adelina and Marguerite.

Finally, it was just the two of them in Umberto's dressing room, where he collapsed on to the small sofa. 'Phew! At last it's just us. That was quite something.' He pulled her down to sit beside him, hugging her close. 'That was the greatest night of my career. Any successes I might have had in the past pale into insignificance beside what has happened this evening – and do you know why?'

Catriona looked up at him adoringly. 'Why?'

'Because you and Michael were watching me and I didn't want to let you down.' He drew her even closer. 'Sorry to have kept you all this time. You did well to send Michael home, I'd forgotten how crazy this can be. You must be tired.'

'Me? Oh no, not at all, but you must be exhausted.'

'As a matter of fact, I've never felt less tired.'

'You're amazing!'

He smiled down at her tenderly. 'It's you who is amazing. You are my backbone, *amore mio*, do you know that?'

She laughed. 'But I wasn't the one who just played a long and arduous programme after years of not performing.'

'Was that me?' Umberto teased, kissing her on the temple and brushing her cheek with his lips.

'And,' she continued, smiling, 'you greeted your public graciously, and tirelessly gave them your time afterwards.'

'Did I?' he said, sliding one hand behind her waist and up along her back.

'And yet,' she added with a smile, 'you still seem to have a great deal of energy left.'

'*Certamente,*' he agreed, his eyes glazing over as he pressed himself against her. 'A great deal of energy and appetite.' He pulled her to him and kissed her passionately on the mouth. '*Stasera, ti desidero più che mai, amore mio,* tonight, I want you more than ever, my love.'

Catriona reluctantly broke their kiss and stood up, a little breathless. 'That will have to wait. Unfortunately, we still have to face the inevitable reception in your honour.'

He sighed. 'Ah yes, I'd forgotten about that.'

Standing up, he reached for her again, encircling her with his arms. 'We'll put in an appearance but we won't stay long because I have a surprise for you.'

Catriona looked puzzled. 'A surprise for me?'

'*Sì, amore mio.*'

'What is it?'

He laughed deep in his throat, caressing her with his penetrating emerald eyes, which reflected from their depths such love and desire that it took her breath away.

'If I told you, it wouldn't be a surprise, would it?'

*   *   *

The Maserati drove through a set of tall, wrought-iron gates. 'You can open your eyes now,' Umberto announced as he stopped the car and turned off the ignition.

Catriona did as she was told, gazing out of the car window. 'Villa Rossini,' she gasped as she recognized the house in Villefranche that had filled her dreams for so many years. The house that had seen the birth of their love.

Umberto was devouring her with his eyes, the expression on his face glowing at her joy.

'But I thought Calandra had sold it.'

'And I bought it two weeks ago.'

'Oh, Umberto!' she exclaimed, then kissed him. 'How clever of you! I've dreamt of this house so often.'

'It's yours now, Caterina.'

'Mine?'

'*Sì, il mio tenero amore*, yes, my tender love. The least I can do is to offer you the place where you showed me such generosity and trust … where you gave the most precious gift a woman can give a man.'

'My love … my darling.' Catriona reached across, locking her arms around his neck and kissing him passionately on the lips.

'Wait,' he whispered, gently disentangling himself. 'Let me carry you into the house.'

Catriona gazed up at him. 'It's such a beautiful night, let's go for a walk first,' she said. 'I'd forgotten how beautiful this place is.'

His eyes wandered down her front. 'Shouldn't you take off that glamorous dress first?'

'I know what will happen if we go into the house and get out of our clothes.'

He burst out laughing. 'I promise to keep my hands off you until after our walk.'

Catriona reached out her hand to cup his face and kissed him again tenderly. 'The question is, will *I* be able to keep my hands off *you*?'

'We'll be restrained, knowing that we have the whole night ahead of us, *eh*?' he chuckled. 'But let me kiss you once more to keep me going until then.'

He drew her against him, his mouth claiming hers then moving from her hot lips to her jaw and her throat, then the soft curve of her breasts. 'I've wanted to do this all evening,' he said, his tongue darting into her cleavage, his hands restlessly running up and down her breasts, making her skin heat instantly.

Although his touch was wildly arousing, Catriona knew that if she didn't stop him now, she was lost.

'Anticipation, remember?' she reminded him as she gently pushed him away with a soft mischievous laugh.

He pulled her back against him. '*Sì, sì*, but you are so irresistible, *mia piccola strega seducente*, my seductive little witch,' he groaned as his tongue found one taut peak and nipped at it, drawing an involuntary moan from her.

Still, Catriona found the strength to push him away slowly. He gave her a crooked smile as his eyes bored into her. 'I'll take my revenge later. I will drive you crazy as you're doing to me now. I'll make you beg for your release …'

She felt her loins flood and throb at his words, conscious that Umberto had known the effect they would have on her, and smiled inwardly because she loved the intimate awareness they had of each other's bodies. Nevertheless, she ignored it and, giving him an impish smile, she let herself out of the car.

Ten minutes later, they were walking along the beach.

Beautiful by day, the scenery at Villa Rossini was more impressive by night, with the moonlight silvering the tall backdrop of mountains until they looked like vast fortresses of marble, their dark pines standing in silent ranks, the tops spread against the dark-purple western sky. The sand on the beach gleamed white as winter snow. Moonbeams twisted and flashed upon the water, making it glitter like a sheet of jewels as though dancing with life. All was quiet, with only the occasional thundering crash of a comber, swinging up the rocks, its shattered crest flung high in the air like a cloud of steam with a long, drawn-out hiss as it receded. The air was pure and balmy and filled with the fragrance of salt, seaweed and iodine.

They walked hand in hand in silence right to the end of the private beach and then stood a while on the shore, Umberto with his arm around Catriona's shoulders, watching the clear wavelets as they rose, curved, curled and broke at their feet, rhythmical and harmonious, in a symphony of blue and white.

'You played wonderfully tonight. The audience were beside themselves. You're back in the saddle, my love. I'm so proud of you,' she told him as she snuggled against him.

He stared down at her, searching her face, his emerald eyes flooded with love and desire. 'Do you really want me to go back to public life?' he asked in earnest.

'Why wouldn't I, and how could you not? Your fans adore you and you thrive on that adoration.'

'*No, amore mio*, I thrive on your love and approval. Without that, I would lose my way.'

'You looked so happy tonight, as if you had come home.'

'I was happy because you and Michael were there. I wanted you both to be proud of me.'

'Michael couldn't contain himself. He was so proud of his *papa*.'

He squeezed her hand as they walked. 'I want a family life. I want to be with you and Michael always. I've missed such precious moments, wasted so much time.'

'We're together now. Forget the past, think only of the future.'

'*Certo, sto pensando al futuro*, I am thinking of the future. I will continue to compose because that's what I love most, but I won't play in public – I'll leave that to the young up-and-coming generation of musicians. Who knows? Maybe those future stars will immortalize my work. That's the dream of every composer. I'll open a school for promising young musicians and every year there'll be a competition with scholarship prizes to give a place to five talented boys and girls.'

'That's a wonderful idea,' she said as they started back along the beach.

Villa Rossini came into sight and minutes later, they walked up the stone steps on to the terrace. Through the open French windows she could see burning embers crackling in the grate. Next to the fire a thick rug had been laid, as it had been ten years ago.

Above them in the purple vault, the starry flocks trailed their way across the vast heaven and the moon looked upon them from her deep-blue mansion, her smile loaded with innuendo. One glittering star had made its way on golden chariot wheels over to the bay. Catriona recognized it. It was the star that shone brightly over Les Platanes and to whom she had entrusted her secret passion as a young girl.

'Venus,' Umberto said, reading her thoughts and then, dropping his head a fraction, he lifted her face towards his and looked deep into her eyes. 'Venus, the brightest star of all. You were the brightest among all the stars at the concert tonight … my Venus.'

The playful sea breeze lifted her hair suddenly, blowing it across her face. Umberto pushed the rebellious strands away and, in the silence that followed, they gazed at each other with all the things they were leaving unsaid. He kissed her again and as it deepened, she clung to him tightly, her fingers threaded through his hair. Finally, he lifted his head, his green irises glittering as bright as the stars in the sky.

'*Andiamo, mio angelo*,' he whispered in a hoarse voice. 'Let's go and give Michael a sister, what do you think?'

Catriona smiled. 'Or a brother.'

'*Maschio o femmina non importa, perché sarà comunque il frutto del nostro amore*, it doesn't matter if it's a boy or a girl, as long as it's the fruit of our love.'

That night, like vibrant instruments playing a duet of desire, they flew on a rising cadenza of love, need and want until, at last, they exploded together into the finale. Satiated and languorous, they fell asleep in each other's arms, their steadfast hearts beating in unison, in time with the far-off rhythm of the sea.

About the author:

Q AND A
WITH HANNAH FIELDING

Romantic Rhapsody

Why did you choose the theme of music for *Concerto*?

I love music. I used to play the piano and had ballet lessons for eight years. My mother played the piano beautifully and many members of the family played an instrument of one kind or another so I was exposed to music from an early age.

I am always listening to music, whatever the genre. My favourite treat is going to watch a ballet or an opera in London; and during my travels in Europe, I've been lucky enough to see performances in opera houses in Vienna, Paris and Warsaw, to name but a few. I grew up in Alexandria, Egypt, and in those days the country's culture was particularly rich in music. We had wonderful foreign ballet companies, like the Bolshoi and the Kirov, which visited and my parents made a point of always taking me and my sister to these shows. Those nights when we were allowed to dress up and go to the Mohamed Ali Theatre in Alexandria were magical. It was always regarded as a special event – the theatre-goers dressed up in their most beautiful attire so it was a real fairyland for a child of six. All through my teens I cherished those moments that, to this day, have remained very dear to me.

I have three thousand songs and various types of music on my iPod. I always play music while writing and often choose a style traditional to the country where my romance story is set. It carries me to that place and somehow teaches me about the people native to that land. I learned a lot about flamenco when I was writing my *Andaluçian Nights Trilogy*, and I have always enjoyed Greek music as I had a lot of Greek friends when I was growing up in Egypt. For *Concerto*, I listened to Debussy's *Clair de Lune* and *Deux Arabesques*, which to me conveyed the romance and poignancy of the story. There is a despair in the notes of *Clair de Lune* that touched my heart deeply and conjured up the essence of the love scenes I wrote. Also, Beethoven's *Moonlight Sonata* was one of my mother's favourites and I heard it played so often throughout my childhood.

I find music soothing, relaxing, exhilarating, mood changing and therapeutic – that is why I decided that Catriona, my heroine, should be a music therapist. Music therapy has proved useful to people who have a disability or injury because music touches our soul in various ways and affects each person differently. It is a powerful tool of communication: one needs no words to convey emotion. All these aspects, together with my nostalgic memories, made me decide to write a book in which music formed the core and the hero was a pianist composer.

How would you say *Concerto* is different to your previous books?

Like my other books, *Concerto* is first and foremost a romance but with this book I have touched on an issue prominent in our modern society – that of the single mother. I wanted to convey the strength of women who find themselves in that situation: their courage, sacrifice and hard work. My books have never had a child as part of the main equation before and so the nature of Catriona's dilemma is very different to those faced by my previous heroines. And, of course, *Concerto* features the poignant story of a reunion between a father and son.

Also, for the past few years I have been around blind people. People who were energetic, independent and free before they lost their sight and suddenly found themselves in the difficult position of having to rely on others for everything. I watched their anger, their depression and despair, their fight to remain independent as they once more taught themselves all the basic needs of living in order to keep their sense of dignity and, finally, I witnessed their courage and acceptance as they tried to make the most of a horrible situation.

Portrait of a Hero

What inspires you when writing your heroes?

Dreaming up the hero is, for me, one of the most enjoyable parts of writing a new book. Before he takes shape in my mind, I know some fundamentals about him: he is ruggedly handsome, strong, intelligent and confident. I need to bring into being a hero who makes one's pulse race and knees weak, someone who is so attractive that readers will wish him into life. Yet part of that appeal is he is also – and this is absolutely essential – humanly flawed.

What is the timeless appeal of a literary hero like Fitzwilliam Darcy in Jane Austen's *Pride and Prejudice*? The answer: he is the archetypal romantic hero. Rewind to the first half of the nineteenth century. Europe is going through great changes: the industrial revolution is transforming forever how people live and work, the Age of Enlightenment is introducing new ways of thinking. The result is that the traditional hero, the man who conformed to and upheld social order, was pushed aside by a new, far more exciting and attractive man: the romantic hero. Brooding, introspective, rebellious, passionate, powerful.

My own leading men are inspired by the romantic heroes I have 'met' in literary worlds. These are determined individuals, who have made their own way in life. They are successful businessmen but they are not conventional. Although these heroes project auras of strength, resilience and power, as the heroines discover, they are men who have rich inner worlds of thought and emotion. Romantic heroes are typically mysterious and isolated in some way, and my heroes likewise carry heavy burdens in the form of secrets that torment them.

Most of all, these men are passionate. They are men who feel very deeply and for whom the emotional landscape can be beautiful but also dark and treacherous. For them what matters most is love: only that can light the landscape and chase away the shadows. In Umberto Monteverdi from *Concerto*, all these qualities are combined and magnified intensely by his tragic blindness and thwarted musical gift.

I cannot imagine writing my heroes differently, penning a hero who is a conformist, for example, who is all about action, not thought, and who does not feel much of anything. *Quelle horreur!*

Machismo: a positive or a negative quality?

Ever since I discovered romantic novels at the tender age of eight, I have devoured them and, in those early days, did so without much discernment!

As time has gone by, I have noticed a gradual but clear change in the characteristics of the heroes and heroines I read about. With the heroine, much of it is to do with an increased sense of sexual empowerment. With the hero, it centres around the idea of machismo.

The term machismo (from the Spanish *macho*) is widely known – most romantic heroes, after all, exude this quality. But the word has different connotations, both positive and negative.

Certainly, dictionary definitions of the term lead to confusion, allowing room for both interpretations from the largely negative 'male behaviour that is strong and forceful, and shows very traditional ideas about how men and women should behave' (*Cambridge Dictionaries Online*) to 'strong or aggressive masculine pride' (*Oxford English Dictionary*), which does at least leave room for machismo to be a positive trait.

The interpretation of machismo is a question I have cause to ponder every time I begin writing a new novel. There is no doubt that it has come to suggest male chauvinism, domination, aggression and even violence (epitomized by characters like Stanley Kowalski in *A Streetcar Named Desire*). Frequently, the term is used synonymously with male chauvinism.

If machismo were purely about aggression, violence and domination, then why is romance, in which macho men abound, the bestselling book genre? Because, I'd argue, machismo is only negative when used in the extreme. In fact, machismo has plenty of positive connotations as well.

Academics point to a fellow term from Spanish: *caballerismo*. A *caballero* is a gentleman, and *caballerismo* relates to honour and chivalry. Machismo can embody this *caballerismo*. Macho men can be honourable, loyal, responsible and fiercely courageous.

Certainly, this is an apt description of all my heroes. Strong and virile, they are men to take charge. Above all, they have machismo in the Oxford sense: 'strong masculine pride'. My stories are often set in the mid-twentieth century and in a location where male pride is indomitable. Given the role of my heroes in their stories and the situations that arise, they all embody this pride. They are macho but does that mean they are 'aggressive' and 'traditional'? Sometimes. Still, for me, this machismo must be rooted in a very positive sense of pride that is admirable for the heroine.

So, there you have it, machismo is a multi-layered trait. The secret, I suppose, is to strike the right balance – admittedly, something with which I sometimes struggle, having grown up in a very conservative country.

Do you enjoy writing from the hero's point of view?

It is natural for a female romance author to write from the heroine's perspective because this creates such a close relationship between the author and the heroine and, in turn, the reader and the heroine. Put simply, we want to see the romance unfold through the female gaze and to be able to imagine ourselves in the heroine's place.

But aren't we also similarly fascinated by the hero's point of view, by how he experiences the developing love story?

One of my favourite books is *Jane Eyre*. I have loved Charlotte Brontë's novel since I first read it in my teenage years. It is easy to feel close to Jane because she tells us the story from her point of view ('Reader, I married him.') But I have always been intrigued by Mr Rochester, the enigmatic master of Thornfield Hall. What goes on in Edward's mind? How does he feel when he looks at Jane?

This fascination with the male perspective informs my writing and, with each novel I write, I find I linger a little longer in the hero's point of view. I want to know what shaped him into this strong, proud man; what vulnerabilities lie behind his mysterious façade; how his developing desire for the heroine plays out in his thoughts and feelings. Most of all, I think, I am seeking to make him *real* to myself and to the reader: he's not some unattainable, perfect god but just a man, as flawed as the heroine, who is capable of loving deeply and who, simultaneously, needs to be loved.

Find out more at www.hannahfielding.net